About the Author

Award-winning author Anne Easter Smith's books "…grab you, sweep you along with the story, and make you fall in love with the characters…" (Historical Novels Review) and Kirkus Reviews called her best-selling debut *A Rose for the Crown* "Remarkably assured... a delightful, confident novel... a strong new voice in the field of historical romance." *The King's Grace* won the 2009 Romantic Times Best Historical Biography award, and *Queen By Right* was nominated in the same category in 2011. Romance Reviews Today gave *Royal Mistress* "A perfect 10! Entertaining, informative, and impeccably researched. I highly recommend this wonderful book." Anne is a native of England who has resided in US for fifty years. She lives in Newburyport MA with her husband, and when not writing can be found directing or acting in community theater.

Visit Anne at:
www.anneeastersmith.com for blogs and Book Group Discussion topics
Facebook: https://www.facebook.com/anneeastersmith/
Twitter: @anneastersmith
Instagram: anneeastersmith

BOOKS ABOUT THE THE WARS OF THE ROSES
BY ANNE EASTER SMITH:

A Rose for the Crown

Daughter of York

The King's Grace

Queen By Right

Royal Mistress

THIS SON OF YORK

Anne Easter Smith

BELLASTORIA PRESS

Bellastoria Press
P.O. Box 60341
Longmeadow, MA 01106
bellastoriapress.com

Cover Design by Sanford Farrier
Cover Illustration by Frances Quinn
Inside Boar Illustration by Kirsten Moorhead

First Edition

ISBN-13: 978-1942209638

DEDICATION

For Scott,
whose patience with my passion for Richard
enabled this book.

Plantagenet Family Tree

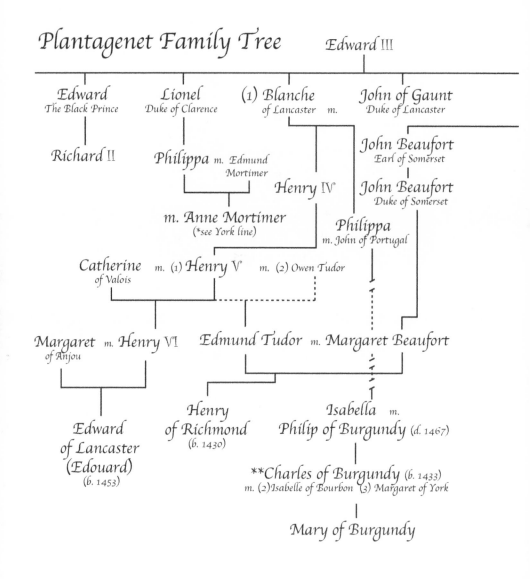

Edward III

Edward
The Black Prince

Lionel
Duke of Clarence

(1) Blanche
of Lancaster m.

John of Gaunt
Duke of Lancaster

Richard II

Philippa m. Edmund
Mortimer

John Beaufort
Earl of Somerset

Henry IV

John Beaufort
Duke of Somerset

m. Anne Mortimer
(*see York line)

Philippa
m. John of Portugal

Catherine   m. (1) Henry V   m. (2) Owen Tudor
of Valois

Margaret m. Henry VI   Edmund Tudor m. Margaret Beaufort
of Anjou

Edward
of Lancaster
(Edouard)
(b. 1453)

Henry
of Richmond
(b. 1430)

Isabella   m.
Philip of Burgundy *(d. 1467)*

**Charles of Burgundy *(b. 1433)*
m. (2)Isabelle of Bourbon (3) Margaret of York

Mary of Burgundy

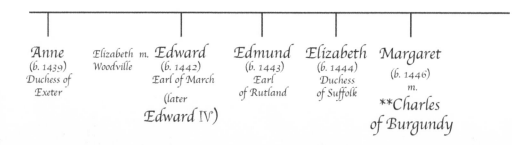

Anne
(b. 1439)
Duchess of
Exeter

Elizabeth m.
Woodville

Edward
(b. 1442)
Earl of March
(later
Edward IV)

Edmund
(b. 1443)
Earl
of Rutland

Elizabeth
(b. 1444)
Duchess
of Suffolk

Margaret
(b. 1446)
m.
**Charles
of Burgundy

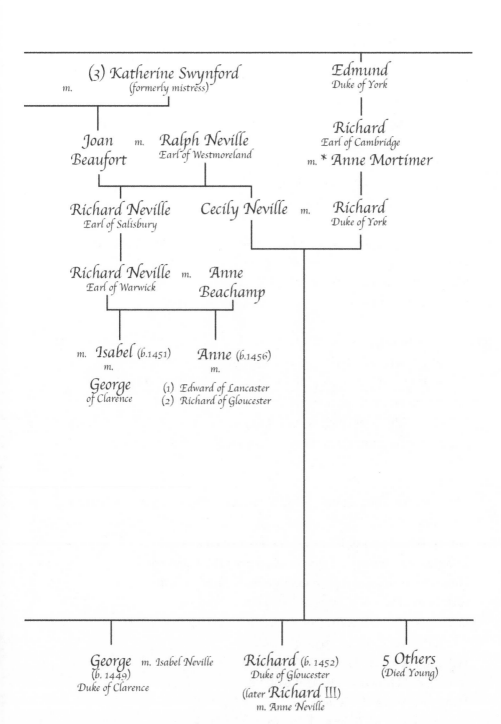

(3) Katherine Swynford
(formerly mistress)

m.

Edmund
Duke of York

Joan
Beaufort

m.

Ralph Neville
Earl of Westmoreland

Richard
Earl of Cambridge

m. * Anne Mortimer

Richard Neville
Earl of Salisbury

Cecily Neville

m.

Richard
Duke of York

Richard Neville
Earl of Warwick

m.

Anne
Beachamp

m. Isabel *(b.1451)*

m.

George
of Clarence

Anne *(b.1456)*

m.

(1) Edward of Lancaster
(2) Richard of Gloucester

George
(b. 1449)
Duke of Clarence

m. Isabel Neville

Richard *(b. 1452)*
Duke of Gloucester

(later Richard III)
m. Anne Neville

5 Others
(Died Young)

Dramatis Personae

York family
Richard Plantagenet, duke of York
Cecily Neville, duchess of York, *his wife*
Edward (Ned), earl of March, later Edward IV, *their oldest son*
Edmund, earl of Rutland, *their son*
Margaret (Meg), *their daughter*
George, duke of Clarence, *their son*
Richard, duke of Gloucester, *their youngest son*
Edward of Middleham (Ned), *Richard III and Anne's son*
Young Edward, *Edward IV's heir*
Young Richard, *Edward IV's younger son*

Lancaster family *(descended from John of Gaunt and Blanche of Lancaster)*
Henry VI, *only child of Henry V*
Margaret of Anjou, *his wife*
Edouard of Lancaster, prince of Wales, *his only child*

Neville Family
Richard Neville, earl of Salisbury, *Cecily of York's brother*
Richard, earl of Warwick ("The Kingmaker"), *Salisbury's oldest son*
Anne Beauchamp, countess of Warwick, *Warwick's wife*
Isabel Neville, later duchess of Clarence, *Warwick's daughter and heir*
Anne Neville, later duchess of Gloucester, *Warwick's daughter*

The court
Margaret Beaufort, countess of Derby, *descended from John of Gaunt and Katherine Swynford*
Henry Tudor, earl of Richmond, *Margaret's son*
Thomas Stanley, earl of Derby, *Margaret's third husband*
Henry Stafford, duke of Buckingham, *Richard's cousin*
Elizabeth Woodville, *Edward IV's queen*
Jacquetta Woodville, duchess of Bedford, *Elizabeth's mother*
Anthony Woodville, *Elizabeth's brother*
William Hastings, *Edward IV's councilor/chamberlain*
John (Jack) Howard, later duke of Norfolk, *councilor*
Margaret Howard, *his wife*
Thomas Howard, later earl of Surrey, *Howard's son*

DRAMATIS PERSONAE

Francis, Lord Lovell, *Richard's friend*
Sir Robert Percy of Scotton, *Richard's friend*
Sir Richard Ratcliffe, *Richard's friend and councilor*
William Catesby, *lawyer and Richard's councilor*
John Kendall, *Richard's secretary*
John Parr, *Richard's squire*

Miscellaneous (*fictional character)

*Kate Haute, *Richard's mistress*
Katherine, *Richard and Kate's daughter (later countess of Pembroke)*
John, *Richard and Kate's son (known as John of Gloucester)*
Dickon, *Richard and Kate's son (known as Richard of Eastwell)*
Anne of Caux, *the York family nursemaid*
*Constance LeMaitre, *Cecily's attendant and physician*
*Piers Taggett, *Richard of York's falconer*
Gresilde Boyvile, *Cecily of York's attendant*
*John Lacey, *master of the Middleham henchmen*
*Geoffrey Bywood, *Kate Haute's brother*

Now is the winter of our discontent
Made glorious summer by this son of York…
　　　　　　—Richard the Third, *William Shakespeare*

The night before a battle affected men in various ways. Some spent it drinking and carousing with the camp followers; some spent it hiding in the woods and nervously emptying their bowels; others passed the time playing dice; others in prayer; and still more, like Richard, in contemplating the insignificance of their earthly lives. "No matter what the priests tell you about each of us being important to God," Richard had once said to his wife, "How can one life mean any more than another among so many throughout the history of mankind? As an anointed king, I must be more important than the beggar in the street, but in truth, I know I am not. When we die and molder in our graves, who will remember us then, one any more than another?"

"God will," Anne had said simply, "you must believe He will. And because you are a king, your grave will be marked by a fine tomb announcing to the world who you were." She had laughed then. "If I am lucky, I will lie with you and be remembered, too." *Dearest Anne,* he thought guiltily as he lay on his elaborate camp bed, *I must see to it that you are remembered.*

The night was warm, and his tent was open to any welcome breeze that might waft by. In the past on the eve of battle, Richard had recited his prayers, had a cup of wine with fellow commanders, and slept well. Tonight, he knew, was different. Tomorrow he must fight for his crown as well as his life. He could not quite believe it had come down to this moment. He had acted honorably all his days, he thought, done his duty to his family, England and, lately reluctantly, to God.

A remark of the earl of Warwick's occurred to him: "Scheming is a virtue if kings are to survive." *Is that what I have done—schemed? Nay, it is not,* he reassured himself, *it is not.* The other part of his mentor's homily had warned: "To be a great leader, you must learn the skills to be flexible in wooing allies to your side." It was a skill that had come easily to Edward, but Richard's reticence to trust had not charmed those he should have sought as allies. Was that where he had gone wrong? Instead of winning with words, friendship, and diplomacy, he had tried to buy men's trust with land and offices. How many of his men understood him, he wondered.

Richard gave up examining his flaws, failures, and missteps, knowing he must concentrate on the morrow. He tried to close his eyes to the pricks of light from the hundreds of campfires and his ears to the drunken shouts, laughter and singing of the soldiers, the stamping and snickering of a thousand horses, and the clinking of the armorers and smiths making last-minute adjustments or repairs to harnesses. Everyone faced death in his own way, and Richard had no illusions that this might not be his time. He had a fifty-fifty chance, because in the end it would come down to him or Henry. Only one of them would wear the crown after battle, because the other would be dead—either in the field or later by the axe.

Part of him wished the two of them could fight it out alone and let all others return to their homes. He had no doubt he would run the Tudor through. Richard had trained hard since boyhood and fought in many battles to become the experienced soldier he was now; Henry of Richmond, wrongly claiming the crown, would be seeing battle for the first time, and, as Richard had heard, had not enjoyed the rigors of knightly training while languishing at Brittany's court. Another part of him relished the thought of a glorious military victory and of extinguishing Lancastrian hopes forever.

He was suddenly jolted back to the other time he and Edward believed Lancaster had been vanquished, and, as was their wont, his thoughts returned to King Henry's demise. Son of the great victor of Agincourt and Edward's predecessor, Lancastrian Henry VI had played a part in Richard's life since he'd been in swaddling bands, Richard mused. He sat up, pushing black thoughts back into hell, and reached for his book of hours—the very one given him as a gift by Henry when Richard was but a lad. *How I wish I had listened to your advice, Your Grace, and never agreed to wear a crown.* He groaned. *Sweet Jesu, how has it come to this,* he asked himself yet again. Paging idly through the prayer book, the gold and silver of the illuminations glinting in the candlelight, he indulged in pondering his life and began to wish he could return to the days when the worst of his troubles was being called the runt of York's litter.

Part One

Dickon
York's Youngest

Leicester, August 25, 2012

I arrive at the car park just as the 360-degree excavator is ripping into Trench One, and the first piece of the tarmac is removed. The machine will very shortly be going right over the painted letter 'R', close to where my instinct told me Richard's remains lay when I first came here. I still believe it. Nothing has changed my mind....

I can't take my eyes off the excavator and have to pinch myself as I watch....

The scoop arm drops down and begins to lift out giant clods of earth, debris and rubble, swinging them on to the spoil heaps. I check my watch. It's 2:15 p.m....

Suddenly Mathew Morris's hand shoots into the air. The excavator stops and Morris jumps into the trench. He looks up at me.

There's a bone.

—Philippa Langley, The King's Grave

CHAPTER ONE
SUMMER 1459

Runt.

When was the first time Richard became aware the unsavory word was being used to describe him? Possibly as early as age seven, and it was then he began to understand he would have to fight for his place in his illustrious family and indeed the world. Far too young, in truth.

It did not help to dispel the cruel moniker often given to a last-born that Richard, nicknamed Dickon to avoid confusion with his father, the duke of York, had a short, skeletal stature and had succumbed to frequent childhood illnesses. However, not long after Richard's birth, when King Henry had happened by Fotheringhay, principal residence of the house of York, the king had raised the infant Richard high and proclaimed him, "A perfect prince!

"He shall be king some day," the king had declared. Duchess Cecily's smile had frozen on her beautiful face as attendants gasped their horror. Not that the statement was untrue, but no one present could possibly have guessed Richard's destiny. He was the fourth son of a duke—of royal blood, it needs to be said—but he was no king's heir. Certainly there was mounting conflict between Henry's house of Lancaster and the house of York as to which had the better claim to the Plantagenet crown, but war between these cousins was far from anyone's mind. No, poor befuddled Henry had simply and sadly mistaken this child for his own, as yet, unborn son—although the queen was indeed pregnant. The king had had lapses of sanity of late, it was true, but he appeared perfectly well, and thus the

York courtiers could be excused for believing the king's words, which they thought tantamount to treason. But how could a king speak treason against himself? Or, more intriguing, was the king's gaffe an omen? Being superstitious, many of them crossed themselves.

But Cecily knew better; she recognized the blank stare with which Henry gazed on her son and knew the king's fragile mind had drifted. She realized he had no inkling of his lapse, and she felt sorry for him. Despite their quarrels, she and Henry had always liked each other—Cecily's feelings more of concern, to tell the truth—and now to silence the murmurings around the room, she swiftly came to the king's rescue.

"Your Grace, this is my son Richard," she had declared brightly. "Let me take him from you before he pulls off that pearl button. We cannot have him swallowing such a treasure! I see he already has good taste," and she chuckled. "Your son will be born soon, I hear," she had run on smoothly. "Such happy news!" Turning to her steward she asked that he escort the king to his chamber. "I can see you are weary, Your Grace. I pray you allow Sir Henry to make you comfortable." And with her gracious and quick-witted intervention, the duchess dispelled what had been an embarrassing but prophetic slip of Henry's tongue. Looking down at her child, gurgling in his cradle, she could not possibly have dreamed what Fortune had in store for him.

Dickon was told this story years later by his nurse, Anne of Caux, when he was old enough to understand it, and it became their little joke whenever Dickon broke a nursery rule. She would click her tongue and reprimand him: "Not such a perfect prince now, are you?"

However, Nurse Anne was his champion whenever he came running to her for sympathy during his first half dozen years of trying to learn his place. His brother George, three years older, and his playmates had used the delicate child for target practice during "who-can-kick-the-ball-and-hit-Dickon first" game they had invented, as Dickon scampered around the inner bailey avoiding the inflated pig's bladder. George would leave Dickon far behind while the bigger boys streaked on longer legs through boggy fens around Fotheringhay to hunt for tadpoles and frogs on fine spring mornings. George callously dubbed the lad "babykins" when Dickon ran to hide from the taunting or cried when George wrestled him easily to the ground. How he hated that name.

Then one day, a day four-year-old Dickon would never forget, George lost his temper with his young brother over a missing toy knight. Nurse Anne was out of the room when George, his face white with rage, plucked a pillow from the bed and, holding Dickon down, pushed it over the terrified little boy's face.

"Where is it, you thief? You stole my soldier. Give it to me or else!" he hissed.

"I can't breathe!" Dickon's muffled voice was desperate. "Please George, I can't breathe." He flailed his little arms and kicked at George while trying to take in air. Panic set in and he saw lights behind his eyes and heard his own heart thumping unnaturally. When he thought his lungs would burst through his chest, George came to his senses. He released the now-limp Dickon and threw the pillow back on the bed.

"Serves you right, you little monster," he muttered and then threatened his sobbing brother further: "Stop blubbering. You say one word to anyone about this, and I'll do worse to you." Then as though nothing had happened, he went back to his miniature army. Dickon, crawled beneath the bed and curled up into a ball. Puzzled, Nurse Anne found him there later, fast asleep. George lied and feigned ignorance.

Thus, certainly, Dickon was no stranger to tears by the time he left the nursery, but he learned to hide them and his hurt in the sanctuary of his favorite place at the castle, the kennels. There, the dogs yelped a welcome and, some of them twice his size, slathered him in sloppy kisses. In the kennels, "runt" was reserved for the dogs, and Dickon was accorded the respect due a duke's son from their handlers. It was no wonder he preferred their company to his brother's bullying playmates.

He remembered at age five when, following a tussle in the nursery with George, Nurse Anne had soothed his wounded pride one day as she rubbed salve into an ugly blue-green bruise on his arm. "You must sometimes endure pain to grow strong, *mon petit*," she told him then in her soft Norman tongue. "You have *la peine* of being the youngest. Often it is the hardest place in the family, *tu comprends?*"

He had understood only too well: he would never match up to his three brothers. There was extrovert Edward, then fifteen and by now a warrior of a prince standing more than six feet; gentler Edmund, Edward's junior by only a year but equally strapping; and eight-year-old George, a head taller than his youngest sibling and already well aware of his good looks and charm. Even more aggravating to Dickon, because she was a girl, his sister Margaret had inherited the Neville height. Was it any wonder Dickon spent his time at Mass praying that he would grow big and tall, too? As the fourth boy with no particular charm or good looks, what chance did he have to be noticed by his powerful father and beautiful mother? He thought his mother loved him well enough, but with seven living children with whom to share her love, he felt sure his portion was the smallest—and yet he yearned to be her favorite. As for his noble father: aye, he would tousle Dickon's mop of darkening hair and occasionally bring him a gift, but he rarely visited the nursery and, it seemed to Dickon, would heap praise on George for no good reason while believing his brother's tattle-telling. Pleasing his father was all young Dickon craved.

Ned and Edmund had protected Dickon for those first few years, but now they were gone, and, as was the custom for noblemen's sons, they were living with their own households in far away Ludlow on the Welsh borders, learning to be leaders of men. Dickon hardly remembered anything about them except for a large presence when they had visited the nursery. And he was certain they now did not give him a thought.

Why, there were those dark days when the little boy wished he had not been born at all!

Now, at thirteen, ten and seven, Margaret, George and Richard were the only siblings left at home. They played, squabbled and attended to their lessons, sheltered in the confines of massive Fotheringhay Castle and unaware of the dangerous times in the lawless land they lived in. Ruled by a weak king, his ruthless wife and ambitious advisors, England was but a shadow of the kingdom left by Henry the Fifth not forty years before. Even more humiliating, Harry's feeble son had since lost all the Norman lands his hero father had given his life to reclaim. A hundred years of war with France had all but crippled England, leaving its people disgruntled and beggared. It was no wonder the woods were as crowded with outlaws as the birds perched in the branches above them.

Cocooned as he was at Fotheringhay, Dickon had always felt safe and loved when he was wrapped in his elegant mother's arms at the end of the day as she recited their nightly prayers. Cecily taught him to talk to God, and soon the boy found himself taking comfort from Him in those trying times when George teased him. When he was old enough to be told stories from the Bible, the angels of Dickon's imagination took on his mother's face and cloud of golden hair. The duchess of York would not admit that this small boy tugged at her heart, not only for his resemblance to his father, but for his innocent piety. At least one of her children understood the magic of a heavenly Father. She was aware of his childish adoration of her, but it did not occur to her to demonstrate her love. These were Plantagenet children, and strong backbones, morals, and a sense of duty were needed to perpetuate the dynasty, not coddling and indulgence. Proud Cis did not dare allow herself to show favor, although her husband often teased her about her special attachment to Edmund. "Pish!" she would retort.

But even those precious times Dickon spent with her were few and far between. Cecily insisted on being with her husband as often as she could, leaving the youngest siblings in Nurse Anne's capable, plump hands, which had caressed or disciplined all of the Yorks' twelve offspring.

"God bless your father, your brothers and sisters, dear Nurse Anne, and all Christian souls," Cecily of York whispered to the thin little boy on her lap on one of those rare nights.

"And God bless you, Maman," Dickon replied softly as he buried his dark-blond head into her long neck and hoped jealous George could not hear. "God bless you most of all." He often added a prayer that God would give him another brother or sister, so George could no longer call him runt.

A pity Cecily did not see the bully in the older boy. It was hard to look beyond the unruly fair curls, brilliant blue eyes, angelic smile and ready charm George reserved for those from whom he required attention. Cecily did not know the George who only felt strong and important when he was crowing his triumph after a wrestling match, or who would sulk unattractively when Nurse Anne chastised him for tormenting his smaller sibling. No one so far, except Dickon, had witnessed how swiftly rage could overtake him. It was a trait both he and Dickon inherited from their father, it was observed later in their lives.

Had Edward and Edmund been present to witness George's unkind behavior, they might have influenced George to pick on someone his own size. Cecily's older daughters Anne and Elizabeth were married and long gone. Only the last of her living daughters, Margaret, or Meg, who often bemoaned the fact that she towered above her older sisters, remained. "I have a neck like a giraffe," she would complain. When George was born,

Meg was fascinated by her baby brother, and a deep bond had formed between the two. When Dickon arrived, after Cecily had lost two other babes, Meg was out of the nursery, and George was old enough to feel an intense jealousy for the newcomer. And it had festered.

Who would have blamed Dickon for resenting his treatment at the hands of George—especially after the suffocating incident, but instead an observer would have been startled by the devotion of the young brother. Dickon trailed George closely like a wayward thread on the hem of a gown, and when George deigned to allow Dickon into a game or to practice at the butts with him, the small boy's wheatish complexion would glow almost rosy with pleasure, and he momentarily forgot his hurt.

On an idyllic English summer day, when the bells in the new tower of Fotheringhay's church rang across the meadow to remind those going about their daily business in the castle and the village that it was time to pray, Dickon's small universe changed forever.

Two riders in the York livery of murrey and blue cantered over the drawbridge of the double moat and into the castle yard. A flurry of grooms and servants ran to assist them, and as Dickon watched from his lofty window perch in the keep, the messengers disappeared below him into the great hall.

"Messengers, Meggie," he called across the solar to his sister, her nose in a book. "Two of them, and they are in a hurry."

George scrambled up from a game of fox and geese he was playing with his page, and jerked his head towards Dickon. "Let us go and see what their business is." Exultant to be included, Dickon hurried to keep up as George was already through the door. They ran down the steep spiral staircase with the sure-footedness of familiarity and stopped where they could peer through a squint into the hall. They watched as the messengers were greeted by Richard of York's steward, left in charge of Fotheringhay while his master moved around the country ensuring the strength of his other great castles in this time of anarchy and unrest in England.

"Their graces, the duke and duchess, are two days from Ludlow," Roger Ree, the duke's usher, announced. "They charge you to ready the household within the week to join them, and that the duke's children be given a sufficient, armed guard. The queen is on the move south, and my lord of York fears Fotheringhay is vulnerable to attack."

"That's Queen Margaret," George hissed in Dickon's ear. "The She-wolf, Mother calls her. She rules the king and thus the country. She is Father's enemy."

The smaller boy shivered. He did not like the word *enemy*; it conjured the evil-eyed, black-clad, misshapen monsters of his nightmares. But at seven, he was beginning to understand that his father and King Henry were not on the same side, despite the king's famous visit some years ago. The man did not sound like a monster to the boy. Hadn't his mother used the words "gentle and amiable" when Dickon had asked if the "Perfect Prince" story were true? Dickon could not imagine why his beloved father and the king would be enemies. And so now he shrugged off his fear.

However, the conflict between his father and the king confused the child, not surprising given the complexity of the Plantagenet succession. As far back as he could remember and understand what he was told, his mother and father had instilled in all their children the sanctity of loyalty to one's sovereign. "Except in the case of evil or incompetent governance should a man turn against his king," Richard of York had insisted. "When you are older, boys, you will swear fealty to King Henry. 'Tis an oath you will never want to break. Loyalty, above all virtues, should be your watchword. Certes, loyalty to your family should never waver, and do not forget that Cousin Henry is both our kin and our king."

So how can anyone in our family be an enemy, the boy wondered, but as none of his siblings had questioned their father's lesson, the youngest had not dared speak up.

Now considering George's whispered comment, young Dickon recalled a spring day at Fotheringhay when he had watched a contingent of mounted knights, their chainmail and sword hilts glinting, ride across the drawbridge and disappear into the fenlands. "They are going to join your father, Dickon," Cecily had explained, her smile belying her anxiety, "because he has been betrayed by the queen, and she has forced him to march against his king. Henry is now our enemy, and 'tis a sad day for our house." York had met the king's army at St. Alban's a few days later and, against his better judgment, he had fought and defeated Henry. Only those who knew Richard of York's conflicted loyalty understood why he had not pressed on to London right then to assert his claim to the throne. It was an ill-judged decision and led the Yorkists to retreat to their stronghold in Ludlow.

The boy refocused his attention on the conversation in the great hall, and tugging on George's sleeve, Dickon asked: "What is happening?"

"Ssh! I am trying to hear, you idiot," George snapped, edging his brother aside. "It would seem we must go to Ludlow."

Dickon brightened. "That's where Ned and Edmund are, is it not?"

George nodded. "We have to go in haste, they are saying. Come, let us find Meg."

The day before they set out for Ludlow, the three noble children were sent out into the fresh air by an impatient Nurse Anne as she readied their baggage for the journey. As they walked in the inner bailey, the duke's master of the hunt approached.

John Hood bowed. "My lords, Lady Margaret, I have a surprise for you, if you will follow me to the kennels." He grinned at Dickon and winked. "Aye, young master, Damosel had a fine litter while you were kept inside last week with your grippe." He put out his hand for the boy to grasp. "Would you like to see the pups?"

Dickon didn't hesitate. He took the huntsman's hand, unaware as yet of the jealous nature of his handsome big brother. He had no idea that George had resented him from the first day their mother had brought the squirming bundle into the nursery and introduced him as their baby brother, Richard. George wanted no rival for his mother's affection, and, what was more galling, the puling brat had been given their noble father's name. As far as he could surmise, George, the only child born during the duke of York's governorship of Ireland, had been given the inauspicious name of one of Cecily's many brothers. Meg had once upbraided her favorite brother about his petty jealousy. "Dickon will never eclipse you in stature, charm or good looks, George, and you will surely exceed him in any honors bestowed by the crown because you are older, so do not waste your time in making him feel any smaller than he is, poor child."

Dickon skipped along with John Hood to the kennel compound, a high wooden fence enclosing a sturdy two-level shed and an outside run. Dickon often spent time in the company of the young pages of the hunt, supervised by the huntsman and learning the dozens of dogs' names, the breeds and their function, and the language of the hunt. It had all fascinated the small boy from the time he could walk, and thus it was no wonder that Hood would seek out Dickon to give him the good news about a litter from the prized wolfhound Damosel.

Among the hounds, lymers, lurchers, spaniels and terriers, Dickon felt more at ease than with George and the other nobles' sons who lived within the castle walls. Often excluded from that group, Dickon turned to the children of the lower classes who peopled the great castle—potters, bowyers, smiths, chandlers, carpenters, armorers, joiners, washerwomen, and stablehands. He played their games of hot cockles, spit the cherrystone, and follow-my-leader. He enjoyed the exuberance of these boys and girls and ran in and out of their simple huts nestled along the castle wall, not realizing yet the deep divide between lord and vassal. The warmth inside those cold abodes came from the close-knit families and cheerful acceptance of their lot in life. Simple folk with strong values, they gave Dickon an early yet unrecognized lesson in the divide between rich and poor. There was time enough for him to learn how to be a great lord, Anne of Caux thought, and she was glad those yeomen, whom Dickon knew by name, had warmed to the little boy who didn't put on airs. This youthful ability to mingle with commoners taught him to listen and to care for others, qualities that would accompany him throughout his life.

But the yeomen's respectful affection for Dickon was nothing compared to that which he found at the kennels.

As the little group entered the compound, Dickon was greeted by sharp, affectionate yelps, slavering tongues and thumping tails. The boy laughed happily. "Down Driver, Maulkin, and Merry-boy!" he called to three lurchers, and much to his siblings' amazement, the dogs obeyed.

Bending to go through the opening of the shelter, the huntsman straightened up inside and beckoned for the children to follow. There, lying prone on the straw, Damosel was giving suck to seven chubby, sightless bundles, hungrily kneading their mother's teats. The children giggled delightedly, watching as one by one the satiated pups dropped off a pap and slipped to the ground. Soon all were tripping over each other, unable to do much more than squeal and snuffle in the straw.

The huntsman crouched down and stroked the bitch's shaggy head, and as she raised weary eyes to him, she managed to wag her tail. Reaching into the squirming bunch of pups, he plucked one from their midst, watching as it tried to wriggle free and mewl in protest. "This is the pick of the litter, Master Dickon," he said. "And he is a parting gift for all your hard work in the kennels. When you return, which shall be soon I am certain, he will be yours. What say you?"

George roughly pushed Dickon aside. "I should have the pick of the litter," he declared. "I am older and entitled to the best dog."

John Hood was taken aback, but bowed low. "To be sure, my lord, you have the right by birth, but, by your leave, your brother has earned it."

George was about to chastise the man, when Dickon took the puppy and promptly offered it to George. "It is true, Master Hood, George should have the pick. I don't mind; there are six more. I pray you, brother, take him."

"Well played, Dickon," Meg murmured from the shadows. "Crisis averted."

Grinning at his brother, George took the wiggling pup and nuzzled its velvet nose. "My thanks, Dickon," he said. "He's a fine fellow. I think I shall call him Captain."

Another pup had escaped from the pack and, even though it could not see, was bravely exploring a corner of the pen when the kennel master swooped it up and handed it to Dickon. "This one has pluck," he observed, "he'll suit you, young lord." The boy might lack for strength, the man thought, but he does not lack for backbone.

Dickon held the dog aloft as it struggled and mewed to be put down. "What do you think, pup, shall you and I suit?" An indignant yip made the boy smile and release the animal onto the straw, where it promptly resumed its explorations. "Aye, I believe Master Hood is right, you are a brave one." He admired the adventurous spirit of the pup as it wandered from its mother, and he turned to the huntsman, his blue-gray eyes shining his thanks. "I shall call him Traveller. May he come to Ludlow with me?"

Master Hood shook his head. "They are too young to leave their dam, my young lord."

Dickon was indignant. "But I know how to feed a pup with milk on a cloth. You taught me how. And I can carry him inside my jacket so he stays warm."

"And he'll widdle on you all day long," George pointed out. "Certes, we must leave them, Dickon, you milksop."

"Do not call me that," Dickon protested, balling his fists, " or…. or…"

"Or what, babykins?" George taunted, discarding his puppy. "Try and reach my chin?"

Meg intervened, taking George's arm and pulling him out of the kennel. "Leave him alone," she hissed. "He gave you the prime pup. Don't start a fight."

As usual Meg mollified him, and George sighed. "I know, I know, I should be more patient, but he is just *so* annoying."

John Hood patted Dickon's head and assured him Traveller would still be there on his return. "Why don't you keep watch here with Will tonight, if Mistress Anne will allow. Damosel will be happy to have you for company, and you can get to know your pup better."

Still smarting from George's slight, Dickon nodded politely, thinking for the thousandth time of one day getting even with his bully of a brother.

For the next two days as the attendants of the York children readied their young charges to travel, Dickon frequented the kennel to play with Traveller, who began to recognize its master's young voice and scramble towards Richard, its hairy tail waving its pleasure. Dickon fondled the velvet ears, examined the leonine paws and rubbed his cheek against the irresistible softness of the coat, communing with his new friend. Here was a living creature that looked on him as a gentle giant, someone in control, and it gave the boy confidence.

He was determined to take the dog to Ludlow, and use the milk-soaked cloth drip along the way. He had already found a suitable corked vessel to fill with milk from the dairy and would hide it in his chest of clothes. He had not yet thought how he would extract the bottle once the luggage was piled high on a cart—nor that the milk would spoil.

As soon as the cock crowed on the appointed day of departure, Nurse Anne roused Dickon and helped him to dress. "I trust you will be a good boy and not cause any trouble on the road, *mon petit*," she counseled him. "I am to sit up with the driver, but not to forget I have *les yeux* in the back side of my head."

Dickon was wide-eyed in his innocence. Had Nurse Anne guessed his secret? "Trouble? What sort of trouble?"

The faithful old nursemaid chuckled, put her arms about the fidgeting Dickon and held him close. For nearly twenty years she had nurtured the duke and duchess's many children. She had sat with the duchess while they listened to the feeble cries of two of the babes who did not live to see their second sunrise, and had taken little Brigid from her mother's arms when Cecily refused to believe the infant was dead; she had cried when her first charge, Anne, had been sent away to be married so young; and she had been as proud as any mother at the blossoming of the heir, Edward, into a giant of a young man, yet had thought nothing of upbraiding him for his wandering eye. Whether she was getting soft in her dotage, she did not know, but she had never felt as protective of a child as she did this youngest of the Yorks.

An hour later, Dickon, holding his cloak tightly around him, climbed nimbly into the carriage behind his siblings and huddled on a seat in the corner. The vehicle was nothing more than a brightly painted cart with a wooden roof holding leather curtains that could be rolled up and down according to the weather, but it proudly flew the pennants of the house of York, the white roses mingling with the falcon and fetterlock.

The little cavalcade was already halfway through the outer bailey when an angry shout came from the carriage.

"Stop, I say! Stop!" It was George's voice. What now? Anne thought crossly. Only a nursemaid can truly know her charges, and, sadly for her, this boy, with his shallow, self-centered nature, had lost his charm.

As she turned to see that a squabble between George and Dickon had turned into a fully fledged fight, she smacked the driver's hand to make him stop. Meg was attempting to pull the boys apart while the armed escort reined in their mounts and stared openmouthed. The captain of the guard was clearly amused, but Roger Ree rode up to the carriage and demanded an end to the fracas.

George glared at his father's emissary and pointed at Richard. "It is his fault, Master Ree," he cried, imperiously. "Dickon has smuggled his dog aboard. Look! 'Tis not permitted. Master Hood said they were too young to leave."

"Is this true, Lord Richard?" Ree lowered his brow at the shamefaced Dickon. Before the boy could reply, George delved under his brother's cloak and held aloft the wriggling Traveller.

Humiliated, tears ran down Dickon's cheeks. He could hardly believe it. George had betrayed him. Dickon was mortified as the escort laughed at the scene; oh, how he hated being mocked. And, at this moment he detested his brother.

The chuckling Ree turned his mount towards Fotheringhay's open gate and deposited the dog into the groom's hands for return to the kennel. Even Meg's comforting arm offered no ease for this deeply hurt and confused little boy. He was struggling with a valuable lesson: if he could not trust his family, whom could he trust?

It was Richard's first experience of betrayal—and at the hands of his own brother. Was it as early as this that the seed of the boy's later hatred of George was sown?

CHAPTER TWO
SEPTEMBER 1459

Hampered by the cumbersome carts, the journey to Ludlow took the Fotheringhay party a week through mostly friendly Neville country. Had Queen Margaret of Anjou been aware of the movements of these important children, she might have sent a troop to intercept them. It was always valuable to have a hostage or two to barter with—as Warwick had hoped to have with the captive king after Northampton, until he clumsily lost his prize at St. Alban's. Happily, however, fortune smiled on the youthful travelers until they reached their destination on the edge of the Welsh Marches—the borderlands between England and Wales.

"Ned favors you, you know, George," Meg had said idly as they passed by a village named Market Bosworth during one of the boring stretches of the Midlands' rolling road, the carriage's curtains tied up on all sides.

"And you are Father's favorite," George had shot back resentfully. "He never notices me."

"Or me," Dickon joined in. "I'm not sure Maman does either. I think she loves Edmund the best. I don't remember much about Ned and Edmund, but I'm sure they wouldn't favor me."

"Don't say that, Dickon," Meg said, kindly. "I'm sure someone loves you best."

George laughed. "Aye, every peasant at the castle—and don't forget the dogs."

All of a sudden, Anne swiveled around on her perch. She could not bear to listen to one more of George's taunts. "It is better to have the honest love of the common folk than the *loyaulte faux des nobles*," she pontificated, "the false love, *vous comprennez? Et bien*, do not ever forget it."

The children were speechless. Like all sensible indentured servants of her time, Anne was not prone to voicing her opinions. Of common Norman stock, she was grateful for her position in the powerful York household, and thus she limited her platitudes to issues surrounding her charges' safety and good health. She knew she had overstepped her bounds, but when she quickly turned back, the carter patted her hand.

Dutiful Dickon mulled over what she had said and kept it in his heart.

A thrill of pride warmed Dickon as he looked up at the sturdy walls around Ludlow, the town strategically perched on a hill above the River Teme. The castle within was another residence owned by his family, and he was beginning to realize what a great landowner his father was. Rumbling under the Broad Gate and up the cobbled street to the Market Square, its market cross standing sentinel, his several disappointments vanished as he anticipated the reunion with his older brothers.

Dickon stared up at the two giants grinning down at him. Could these be the same brothers he vaguely remembered as rough-and-tumble boys? He sidled close to George, who shook him off, puffed out his chest and extended his hand to Edward and Edmund. "Ned, Edmund, 'tis good to see you again," George drawled, blocking Richard from their line of sight.

Edward stepped forward to grasp George's wrist in an affectionate greeting. Dickon noticed with dismay he was eye level with Ambergris, his oldest brother's wolfhound, who lapped Dickon's face in greeting. *Pray God Ned doesn't call me runt*, he thought, finding the dog's ears. *In truth, I pray he doesn't notice me at all.* A shadow fell on him as Edmund approached. With the ease of an athlete, the fourteen-year-old Edmund sank down on his haunches to a level with his youngest sibling. "Remember me, Dickon?" he asked gently. He had observed the boy's reticence and was anxious to reassure him. "It seems you have grown since I last saw you. How old are you now?"

A grateful grin lit the small boy's face, and Edmund noticed the striking likeness to their father. "I'm nearly seven, and I know how to let

an arrow fly now," Dickon said proudly, his fear banished. "Piers Taggett
showed me."

"A good man, Piers," Edmund replied.

During those long September days, Dickon, George and Margaret were
wide-eyed observers upon the high ramparts above their apartments on
the western wall of Ludlow's impressive fortifications as they puzzled
over the hurly-burly below them in the inner bailey. Meg was able to glean
from Edmund some news of the many meetings held in the ducal audience
chamber, while he enjoyed getting to know his quick-witted sister.

"Edmund says our father is summoning more men to support his
petition for the king to recognize his rank as royal duke and to acknowledge
his loyalty," she explained to her younger brothers. "He says Father does
not want to fight, but he has to protect his rightful claim to the throne. 'Tis
complicated, in truth."

Dickon was staring out at the Welsh hills and idly fingering a tiny
dagger at his waist given to him by Ned. He did not understand all this
talk of petitions and rightful claims; he just wanted this wonderful time
with his family to go on forever. He had told his mother all about Traveller,
whom he sorely missed. He had not noticed her secret smile when he
owned up to trying to smuggle him out of Fotheringhay; she delighted
in his boyish attempt at guile and his honesty in owning it. Dickon had
not, however, revealed George's betrayal, which lay buried and festering
somewhere inside.

"So, he did not tell you that George informed on him?" York asked
Cecily later when she regaled her husband with the story. "Aye, Roger
Ree told me the whole tale. Not betraying George—that's the part I will
remember, Cis, not the act of rebellion. Our son learns quickly, and he
learns well. He has promise."

The tension in the castle was mounting daily as messengers cantered in
from the town and out again with alarming regularity. The children were
forbidden to leave the castle's inner yard, the women were discouraged
from riding out to hawk, and lookouts were stationed night and day on
the ramparts. Cartloads of armor and armaments trundled over the Teme
and up the cobbled streets of Ludlow Town along with mounted soldiers
and yeomen on foot carrying pikes, halberds and makeshift weapons.

That York was mustering a force must surely have reached the king, who was heard to be advancing from Coventry, with his queen's army north at Chester.

When George was not tied to the schoolroom with Dickon, he escaped to join his older brothers at the butts, supervising the forging of their new suits of armor, or exercising their horses in the yard.

It was during these tedious afternoons, when he had been left alone to study his Latin or complete a mathematical problem, that Dickon discovered men were not the only creatures who supervised life in the castle. He was learning the importance of organization and that life in a castle did not happen without order. And Dickon liked order. He followed his mother and Meg to the kitchen one day and watched as Cecily instructed her daughter how to inventory what was in the pantry, to assess how many mouths there were to feed and with what, and when the pantler showed the duchess his accounting, she made Meg add it all up to make sure it was correct. Candles needed to be counted, laundry supervised, and complaints heard from staff. Dickon was astonished that his mother had so much to do, and that the servants, who were all male but for a few, listened to and obeyed a woman.

"Do you like being a girl?" he had asked Meg once and had been struck by her vehemence when she replied. "No, I do *not*. You are always ruled by a man your whole life: first your father, then your husband. And some men are perfectly stupid, and it could be I will be made to marry a fool."

"Why?"

"You and your questions, Dickon. Families like ours need to make contracts with other noble families so we carry on the noble names." Margaret shrugged, irritated by a subject she loathed. "We cannot marry beneath us, you see."

Dickon's eyes were wide. "Beneath us? What does that mean?"

"It means you cannot mix the peasantry with the nobility or the natural order will be undone, Mother told me."

"Will I be made to marry someone even if I don't want to?" Dickon's worried frown made Margaret laugh.

"Boys are different. But yes, you will have to do your duty and marry well. Our two sisters were married when they were younger than I," Meg told him. "It was arranged by Father and Mother. Lizzie cried when she had to go to marry Suffolk, and he didn't know her either. It's just the way of the world." And she had hurried off, unsure she knew the answers to the rest of the boy's interminable questions. But Dickon was impressed with how much Meg knew. Why, she was much cleverer than George, he decided, and she was a girl.

His admiration of Meg, his mother and women rose considerably not only on that day but upon straying into his mother's physician and confidante's sanctuary on another. It was not usual for a woman to become a doctor, but Constance LeMaitre had grown up a physician's daughter in Rouen, where Cecily had first offered her a place in the York household and where she had lived for almost thirty years. A progressive man, Doctor LeMaitre had sent his bright young daughter to Salerno to attend medical school and she had come to Cecily's attention when the Yorks had spent time in Normandy.

"Why are you not married, Constance?" Dickon wanted to know. "You are pretty and very clever."

Constance laughed. "You must learn not to ask such difficult questions, Master Dickon. I have no need of a husband, because your mother lets me do what I love to do best—and she pays me," she explained. She put her finger to her lips. "Don't tell anyone, but I would dearly like to know what love is—like the love your mother and father show each other. 'Tis very precious and very rare." She sighed. "But I am more useful as a doctor than as a wife, I fear. So I love my work instead of a husband."

Dickon blinked a few times, for in truth he had not understood some of this conversation, but he enjoyed the feeling of being a confidante, and it warmed him that Constance trusted him. Perhaps she could be his friend, he mused; he sorely needed one. Or, and he suddenly asked:

"Do you want to marry me, Constance? Are you allowed to choose?"

Constance's laugh rang merrily around the infirmary. She curtsied. "Merci beaucoup, milord, but I cannot marry you, because I am not born noble like you."

Dickon nodded sagely. "You are beneath me. Now I think I understand." He beckoned to her to bend down to him and whispered, "We may not marry, but I would tell you that I love you."

"Then let this be our secret, Dickon," Constance said earnestly, and kissed him tenderly on the cheek.

Embarrassed, Dickon stared up at the dried lizards, newts and frogs hanging above him. "What did you want to show me, Doctor?" he said hurriedly. Soon he was enthralled by the bottles, jars, vials, liquids bubbling over a flame, scales, dried herbs, colorful powders, collections of dead insects and small bones, and the overpowering scents the preparations gave off. He watched, fascinated, as Constance ground substances in her mortar and added liquids that changed color in oddly shaped glass tubes.

Dickon left the dispensary not only warmed by her special attention, but in awe of Constance's knowledge, and again he marveled at a woman's capabilities. He came to the conclusion moreover, that it was not merely his mother's rank that made her so capable. Constance was every bit as clever. He told himself there and then it would be the last time he would underestimate any female—even good old Nurse Anne.

It was a wise decision, because in his life, Dickon was to face a few formidable women and even fall in love with one who was quite beneath him.

One glorious afternoon, when Dickon had slipped away from Anne's care and was on his favorite perch high above the Teme on the south side of the castle, he was surprised to see his mother, accompanied by Piers Taggett and three others, ride over the Dinham Bridge and up the grassy banks of Whitcliff Hill. Dickon had yet to understand that whatever his mother wanted, his father was loathe to deny. An avid hawker, Cecily had obviously prevailed upon the duke to relax his no-riding rule for her. Dickon was learning fast that the world was not strictly run by men.

Today, Dickon's focus was on the falconer, Piers, who carried the duchess's hawk expertly on his wrist. Dickon had known Piers all his life, and he would demand the solid Piers tell him the story over and over again of how he came to be the York's falconer. As Dickon grew into a thoughtful little boy, he probed deeper into Piers's boyhood and why he had attacked Duchess Cecily in a forest one day and made off with her horse and betrothal ring.

"My father was killed fighting under the Salisbury banner when I was two," Piers had told him, "and as soon as I was old enough, I had to work hard to help put food on the table for my mother and sisters. Your mother's horse and ring would have fed my family for a year. Times were hard," he had explained. Piers did not like to tell a duke's son that times were still hard for the yeomanry, and that many of them, like him at that earlier time, had been forced into the woods as outlaws. "Your mother was alone and I was desperate," Piers had confessed.

The more Dickon heard the story, the more he thought about it, contemplating the criminal act of the man who seemed the most trustworthy of all their servants. "And you would have hanged had it not been for my Mother, you say. How clever she is! She understood that you were only trying to stop your family from starving, in truth. But why did you not go to your lord, my uncle Salisbury, and ask for food?"

Piers had laughed. "A peasant does not have the right, young master."

"It doesn't seem fair that you should be punished for something that was not your fault."

This statement astonished the falconer. The boy had grasped the heart of the matter, but the conversation had made Piers uneasy.

"I would do anything for her grace, your mother," he assured the young lord, hoping the boy would not relay the dangerous conversation to anyone else. "She took a chance on a poor country boy. In truth, I should not be talking to you like this—you a duke's son. We all have our place."

"Place?"

"I am a servant, young master. Some would call me a peasant. You are a lord, and you make the rules—the laws."

Dickon was learning his own place, although he had not felt different playing with the boys at Fotheringhay. What made one boy noble and another a peasant? It was not a philosophical question a boy of seven might usually pose, but Dickon was unusual. His lack of physical prowess had made him rely on his mind, which was expanding daily.

"Then perhaps the laws should be changed," Dickon said almost to himself.

Piers winked at him. "Only the king can change the laws, Dickon. Are you going to be king?"

Dickon grinned then, his pensive mood relieved by Piers's good-natured jesting. "Nay, Master Falconer, I have no wish to be a king. Besides, King Henry has a son who will be king after him, Mother says. That is the way of the world," he said, borrowing Margaret's grown-up phrase and making Piers chuckle. "I shall never be king."

Still unaccustomed to his surroundings and never tiring of exploring the castle ramparts so high on Ludlow's strategic hill, Dickon turned and ran along the wall walk to the Northwest Tower looking towards the darkly wooded Welsh hills. A glint of metal in the distance caught his eye—lots of metal, he saw now. Then he was aware of a peculiar thrumming. Unused to hearing the sound of men on the march, he tried to imagine what it might be. As the noise grew louder, and he could now see the snake of men, he knew. "It must be the king," he gulped and raced along the precarious walkway to the closest watchman, who called: "I see 'em, young lord."

Grabbing his shawm, the sentry puffed out his cheeks and pushed his breath through the long, wooden instrument, deafening Dickon with its sharp wail of alarm.

Fascinated but fearful, Dickon watched the army of mounted men and foot soldiers slide like a moving carpet of gleaming silver over the landscape. Then wasting no more time, he scampered down the stairs to tell George that an army was at the gates. He should have waited to recognize the standard in the green and yellow colors of his uncle, the earl of Salisbury. The castle was not under attack after all. Even so, the boy would not soon forget his first sight of an army on the move. What he had also not waited long enough to see was that this army, which had recently seen battle, was a bedraggled and wounded horde of men straggling through Ludlow's streets towards the castle.

When he joined his family in the courtyard, Dickon stared horrified as his uncle Richard Neville, earl of Salisbury, and his immediate entourage were helped from their mounts, blood and muck streaking their tabards and their beards. The colorful trappings on their horses were cut to tatters and dark blood caked the animals' sides; one man's head was wrapped in bandages, most of his jaw missing; dozens of foot soldiers supported others hobbling through the gateway on broken limbs or carried on makeshift litters; and the sounds of human suffering chilled Dickon to the marrow. He wanted to be sick, but he was a son of York and forced down his bile.

Many of the wounded had dropped where they stood once inside the safety of the curtain wall. Cecily picked up her skirts and began to move from one man to another offering prayers and words of encouragement. The common soldiers stared in awe at the beautiful duchess, clad in crimson damask and silk, who tore strips off her petticoat to wipe a bloodied brow here or staunch a wound there. Dickon stood in George's shadow and observed his mother with pride.

Not long after her mistress jumped into the fray, Constance arrived with her bag of supplies and went from one victim to the other, ascertaining their condition and giving instructions to rush the badly wounded into her makeshift infirmary in the lodgings adjacent to the kitchen house. After years of caring for routine ailments of the household, she finally felt useful and was dispensing orders to the duke's servants with the confidence of a battlefield commander. Then Dickon saw Meg run forward with a ewer of water and hold the vessel to the parched lips of as many as called for it. The women seemed fearless, and he could not stand idly by. As soon as he saw Meg's pitcher was dry, Dickon picked up a pail and hurried to the well hard by the kitchen to fetch her more water. It felt good to him to be of use.

"There's a good boy," Richard of York called, seeing his youngest heaving the bucket back to Meg. "These men have given their blood for our house. Help as many as you can. George!" he cried, striding towards the great-hall steps with Salisbury and his oldest sons, looking to his brother-in-law for a full report. "Make yourself useful, like your young brother."

Dickon waited his turn to fill his wooden bucket and then tentatively moved towards a figure lying awkwardly on his side. A battered tin cup lay abandoned on the ground, and picking it up, Dickon dipped it in the water, hoping to slake the billman's thirst. He gently shifted the man onto his back and then jumped back in horror. The boy—for certes, he was no more than Meg's age—had only half a face. His lips clung to where his mouth once met his cheeks, exposing his teeth and gums in a bloody, gaping hole. His remaining eye was fixed on Dickon, and he cried out something unintelligible so desperately that Dickon, overcoming his disgust, knelt down beside him and took the lad's out-stretched hand. It was then he saw the young soldier's other arm was missing below the elbow and a wad of blood-blackened linen had helped to stem the flow of blood. Constance had told him how every living creature only had so much blood running through its veins, and when it ran out unheeded as this poor lad's had, even Dickon, young as he was, understood the lad must be dying.

He searched the melee for Constance or any adult who might better save the boy than he, but, seeing everyone was already occupied, he reluctantly turned back and resorted to prayer. *"Pater noster, qui es in coelis,"* he recited, trying to comfort the billman with the familiar words that always helped him when he felt sad and alone. "Hallowed be thy name...." All at once he faltered as he felt a lifelessness in the fingers he held, and he knew instinctively the man's soul had flown. *"Requiescat in pace,"* he whispered, crossing himself and carefully released the cold hand. Staring at the inert form, he suddenly imagined himself lying on a bloody field, his own life seeping into the soil, and he wept—as much for himself as for the unknown yeoman.

Playing at soldier with George, Dickon had often feigned dying, but witnessing real death this day would forever change the boy's understanding of the seriousness of war.

Sobbing in Nurse Anne's arms later, he wondered whether he wanted to be a knight at all. He doubted his courage to face awful maiming and death. He could not erase the image of the billman's gray face and glassy eye, which would haunt his dreams.

"And I did not even know his name," he moaned, as Anne rocked the trembling boy in her arms.

Much later, Dickon's curiosity—and a good dose of Anne's wisdom and chamomile infusion—took him down to the hall to join his mother, where her brother had been enthralling his audience by reporting on the battle with the queen's army near Market Drayton. Dickon's eyes were still red from crying, but Cecily was too engrossed in Salisbury's tale to notice.

"Praise God, we routed them," Salisbury told York. "I will take credit for two ruses—one that feigned flight—which not only won the day but allowed us to make our way here without pursuit. As well, many of the queen's men joined our side. It seems there are Englishmen who believe in your cause, Your Grace," he told the surprised York. "'Tis a brave man who risks treason to join you."

York nodded, his gray eyes thoughtful. "How many slain?"

The company gasped when they were told: "Our side lost a thousand good men, and our adversaries lost twice as many, but after the rout, when many of my soldiers followed the fleeing enemy and cut them down, 'twas hard to tell."

Dickon shrank back. One death from battle wounds had been terrible enough, his young imagination could hardly contemplate thousands.

"Do you want to hear my ruse?" Salisbury said, and Dickon was startled to hear his uncle laugh. *How can there be anything to laugh at?* he wanted to ask. However, he listened as Salisbury told a preposterous story about paying a priest to man a canon all night, who let fly a ball or two to pretend his army was still there. Dickon stared around at the amused courtiers and tried to comprehend how grown-ups could bemoan thousands of deaths in one breath and make a joke in the next. Still numbed and close to tears, he forced himself to join in the laughter, but whether his was from amusement, grief or relief, Dickon did not know.

CHAPTER THREE
OCTOBER 1459

By the time Salisbury's son, Richard, earl of Warwick, arrived from Calais to swell the Yorkist ranks, Dickon had grown accustomed to the sight of so many knights and foot soldiers milling around the castle yards. The adults were far too intent on plotting strategy, sending messengers back and forth to the king with new pledges of fealty, strengthening defenses, and seeing to the wounded to worry about the daily routine of the youngest members of the household, although George and Dickon were expected to adhere to their studies. Meg, at thirteen, was made to shadow her energetic mother around the castle, helping dispense medicine, food, and prayer—in that order—to the wounded, keeping York's steward informed of dining and housing requirements for the castle's growing occupancy, and supervising the duties of the duchess's ladies and tiring women.

It was unusual for a nobleman not to have contracted any of his three older children in marriage by now. York's long absences from home, in an effort to rid the king of the influence of power-hungry dilettantes along with other worries, had left no time to plan any of his children's futures. Dickon and George should already have been learning the chivalric arts from a relative or other patron, and Richard and Cecily had preferred to set up the older two boys with their own households at Ludlow under the supervision of a guardian until they came of age.

With strict instructions to keep within Nurse Anne's earshot, George and Dickon roamed the ramparts, watched the knights at practice, learned the art of wood whittling from idle soldiers, fished from the stew pond, or had their turn with the bow at the archery butts. George was a fine shot, Ned remarked one day when he had tired of the endless parleys of his father, uncle, and cousin of Warwick and had wandered out to coach his young siblings: "But do not discount young Dickon; for all his lack of height and heft, his skill will match yours soon, George." George had accepted Ned's compliment gracefully and even nodded an acknowledgment at Dickon for his; it was no hardship when he knew he could always best Dickon at wrestling.

There was something about having so many of their family about them that invigorated the duke and duchess and made this Yorkist stronghold a castle of confidence, despite the threat of attainder hanging over each lord. No one could have imagined the main protagonists being accused of treason for refusing to attend a Great Council in June, for they were some of the most powerful men in England. The truth was the queen had made sure the Yorkists had not been invited. Her influence and that of her closest adherents was creating a weakling of the king. It was to York's credit that he still believed in Henry's goodwill and reluctance to fight. And so he persisted in petitioning his sovereign to refute the allegations made by the queen that he, York, was a traitor. Yet, still he was refused an audience as the royal army moved ever closer to Ludlow.

York had taken this opportunity of having all his sons together to instill in them the ideals of chivalry that so governed his own behavior. He had explained patiently to Dickon what the awful word "attainder" inferred. "It means being branded as a traitor. It takes away all your lordly rights. A good man never wants it uttered about himself," he said at the end of another evening of a father-to-sons' lecture (at least that was what Ned had disrespectfully dubbed them). "It is a hated word in our family and one I have spent my life trying to live down."

Dickon's eyes widened. "Why, Father? What did you do wrong?"

"'Twas not I, boy, but your grandfather, also named Richard, God rest his traitorous soul." He pulled Dickon close to his chair, gripping the lad's arm a little too tightly. "I shall tell you now, Dickon, as I have told your brothers before you, but we shall not mention it again." His sharp eyes roved from one son to another for their assent. "My father was accused of plotting to kill King Harry— of Agincourt fame, you remember." He paused, seeing Dickon nod vigorously. "He was tried, attainted and executed when I was only four. His head was stuck on a pike for all to see." Finally letting go of Dickon's arm, he uttered ominously, "such an ignominious way to die."

Dickon's look of horror aroused York's paternal concern, and he pulled the boy into an embrace. "My father was a traitor, you understand, and now there are those who whisper I am following in his footsteps. Never fear," he added hastily, "'tis not true."

"Is that what the king thinks, too?" Dickon asked. "Why don't you tell him you are not like your father?"

York smiled. "So full of questions, young one. I know this is confusing, Dickon, but trust I have my reasons for standing up to my king and I intend no treason. King Henry has allowed dishonorable men to govern his subjects. The kingdom is suffering, and I have a duty to my country as well as to my king to set things right." He sighed and held the boy at arm's length.

"Whatever happens in life, Dickon, never forget your loyalty to family, king and country. Loyalty must always come first, no matter how hard. 'Tis your God-given duty. And now it is especially hard for me. I have never been disloyal to the king, I swear, but the king has been disloyal to his subjects for a long time. I only want to make him see how that is weakening England. The counselors, and the queen, think I seek the crown. But by Christ's nails," he cried suddenly, raising his fist as though addressing those same accusers, "I do not." Then seeing his sons' startled expressions at his outburst, he softened his voice again. "As a royal prince, 'tis my duty to my country to keep trying to make the king see reason and dismiss the rats around him. Do you understand—all of you?"

"We do, my lord Father," Ned solemnly answered for them all, moved by his father's vehemence. "And we support you to a man." He smiled at Dickon, who was too engrossed in his thoughts to notice the gesture.

"Is betraying someone the same as being disloyal, Father?" Dickon blurted, thinking now of his brother George.

"Absolutely, my lad. You have the measure of it," York answered, pleased. "I hope it never happens to you, Dickon, but in everyone's life there comes a time when you may make a choice for the right reason but another will see it differently and accuse you of disloyalty." He drew the boy once again into his arms and murmured, "Keep all of this close, my son, and remember, whatever happens, your father is not a traitor."

But Dickon's worried eyes were fixed on George.

And so this loyal house of England, this peaceful house of York, reluctantly prepared for war.

Thirty-year-old Richard, earl of Warwick, walked among his troops dispensing a good word here, a laugh there and making sure his sergeants were keeping his army fit and ready for a fight. Soldiers polished their weapons; bowers replenished the invaluable long-bowmen's sheaths with new arrows; farriers checked horses' hoofs for damaged shoes; smiths forged news ones; grooms curried the nobles' destriers; and Dickon found himself captivated by these fighting men and their daily routine. As well, his recent experience had made him less squeamish at the sight of blood.

"What happens if a horse loses a shoe in battle?"

"Suppose your bowstring breaks?"

"I pray you, can I try and make an arrow?"

"What's the difference between a horse's noseband and a cavesson?"

The men obliged this multitude of questions with good-humored answers and lessons, impressed the boy had sought them out and wanted to learn. Warwick did not discourage his young cousin from dogging his footsteps when he went on his rounds, and in fact admired Dickon's quiet, respectful way with the grizzled soldiers from his Calais garrison.

"When you are older, perhaps we can arrange for you to come to Middleham and learn your knightly skills with my master-at-arms. What say you, young Dickon?" Warwick asked.

"I should like that very much," the boy replied eagerly. "When will that be?"

"In a year or so, I expect."

"Will George come, too?"

Warwick shrugged. Perceptive, he had already determined during his few days in their company that George and Richard ought to be separated, and the sooner the better. He was surprised his uncle and aunt had not disciplined George about bullying his brother, but being a man of his time Warwick recognized that leaders of men were not made from soft childhoods. He turned to one of his Calais commanders and veteran of the

French wars, Andrew Trollope, and asked: "Don't you think this lad might make a soldier one day?"

Dickon looked from one man to the other. He liked the burly Trollope with the ostrich feather in his cap, his ruddy cheeks, white whiskers and merry brown eyes.

"Aye," the knight nodded, smiling at the expectant face staring up at him. "I warrant the master-at-arms will knock the boy out of you right enough. You'll need to build some muscle and put on some flesh before you wield a sword, though."

"I should like to learn to fight like you," Dickon said. Still not far from his thoughts, however, he quickly added, "but I don't want to be a billman. It's too dangerous. I want to be a knight on a horse."

Warwick grunted, growing tired of the boy. "Certes, you will be a knight."

"Will you ask Father soon, my lord?"

Warwick nodded absentmindedly as he walked back over the bridge from the outer bailey towards the great hall in the western curtain wall. Trollope bent down and told Dickon, "Fighting is not so bad, when you are properly trained, young 'un." He winked. "I'll remind his lordship, never fear."

"You will?" Dickon wasn't sure if he could trust this man yet. "Do you promise?"

Trollope chuckled and drew a cross over his heart. "And hope to die," he agreed. "Now run along." Dickon thanked him solemnly, feeling reassured, and ran off to tell his friend Piers Taggett.

Trollope straightened and his smile faded as his eyes followed Warwick's walk across the bailey. Aye, he was under the earl's captaincy of Calais and would be expected to obey the earl, but Trollope had taken an oath to obey King Henry long before the upstart Warwick had set foot in the Calais garrison. He harrumphed. Loyalty was a matter of convenience to this old soldier, but he decided it was too early to see which way the wind might blow in the matter of York versus Lancaster.

The harvest feast of Michaelmas was celebrated in Ludlow with its usual fanfare, despite the influx of so many soldiers billeted in and around the castle. York told the parish priest to preach a gospel of peace and harmony, letting his tenants know that the Yorkist force in their midst was merely insurance against any attack by the unpredictable queen, but that he, York, was in negotiation with the king.

The Michaelmas festivities in the castle were extended to fete Dickon's seventh birthday, and the duke and duchess stood by watching their youngest in the place of honor shyly accept the servants' good wishes. York whispered, "You may say he is the quietest of our brood, but he is certainly not lacking in courage. And the questions! The never-ending questions."

Cecily nodded, chuckling. As well as carrying his name, Cecily loved the way her youngest son resembled his father, not least in the way their prominent, determined chins would jut forward while contemplating a problem. "Aye, he has spirit, but I worry for his future. What are the prospects of a fourth son?" she said.

The duke smiled indulgently at his beloved wife and stroked his tuft of a beard. "Perhaps he will surprise you, my love. He is a good listener, and I have noticed how he bristles at any injustice." He chuckled as he remembered an example. "I chastised a boy for bringing me the wrong bow at the butts yesterday, and Dickon stood between us and reminded me that it was Tom Archer from whom I had requested the bow and surely the boy was only obeying his master. That took courage: I could have boxed his ears for gainsaying me, but I was too impressed to reprimand him."

Dickon sat proudly as York proposed the toast to his "right beloved son," and every one of the most important members of the Yorkist party rose and raised their cups. It was not for Edward, nor for Edmund, not even for George, but for him—for Richard Plantagenet, and he thrilled to it. The hairs stood up on the back of his neck as the rafters rang with the sound of his name, and for the first time in his life, Dickon now understood what it meant to be the duke of York's son. He looked around at his family all smiling at him, and he swore solemnly to himself then that he would never betray any of them.

York liked his boys with him when he made forays across the Teme to ride up Whitcliff. It amused Salisbury how all four of his nephews would vie for their father's attention. Privately, he thought York was both an indulgent father and inattentive. Ned was already a man, for Christ's sake, and yet no mention of a bride had yet been made. He watched while Ned raced his brothers to the top of the hill. Here was surely every nobleman's dream of a son: more than six feet tall, strong, athletic, handsome, and charismatic, Edward was always the center of attention even at seventeen. But there was an indolence that crept occasionally into Ned's behavior, and Salisbury had noticed how the young man could not resist a pretty girl. "You should keep an eye on his philandering," the earl had advised his sister in an intimate moment recently, but Cecily had dismissed the remark with a "Pish! He's just a healthy boy."

Dickon watched his two brothers enviously. George was growing into manhood, his voice changing and his lankiness filling out into athleticism. He also handled his horse superbly. Was it any wonder Dickon despaired of ever equalling his brothers in their father's eyes. He sat sadly on his horse, unnoticed as always—or so he thought.

The early October evening was drawing in before the duke's party cantered into the castle yard and relinquished their mounts to the grooms' willing hands.

"Your Grace," Roger Ree cried, exiting the keep where he had been watching for York. An over-exuberant Ambergris, waiting for his master, flung his huge body at Ned. "The king has sent his answer to your last petition, and 'tis not good news. The messenger awaits in the great hall."

All York's good humor following the invigorating gallop down to Ludford Bridge vanished in a scowl. Impatiently, he shouted to Ned, "Keep that dog of yours under control," as he walked over the drawbridge followed by Salisbury, Warwick and the others. "Let us hear the king's response."

Dickon hurried to catch up with George and Edmund. "What does this mean?" He was almost afraid to ask. "Will Father have to go to war?"

"How should I know?" George snapped, hiding his own anxiety.

But Edmund seeing the fear in his little brother's eyes, reassured him, "The king is a merciful man, Dickon, and he knows Father is his loyal subject. Perhaps it will not come to war."

It became obvious to Dickon, however, that his father doubted the king's mercy now. For the next two days, the castle and town were abuzz with the news that the royal army was approaching. From the top of the keep Dickon and George watched the completion of the extensive barricade York had ordered built on the opposite side of the river. Darkness was falling when they turned to descend the stairs, and they could see the hundreds of men lighting their camp fires and munching on their meagre rations.

Dickon shivered in the cool evening air, and George, guessing his brother was afraid and not merely cold, put his arm around him. "I hope there is a fire in the hall," he said, cheerfully, "we'll be warm there." Unused to the kind gesture and certain he would be called "babykins" if he accepted the offered corner of George's cloak, Dickon hesitated. It was enough to irritate George, who snapped, "Suit yourself," and walked off.

George's mercurial temper was roused again the very next day when he argued with Meg over a chess move she had made. Dickon, with Ambergris at his feet, looked up from his whittling of what he hoped would be a fair facsimile of Traveller, and was glad it was Meggie for once who was the victim of George's outburst. "You cheated!" George accused her, leaping to his feet. "I was looking out of the window, and you moved your bishop before you moved that pawn." Dickon cast his eyes back to his carving and waited: he knew one did not accuse Margaret of York of cheating.

"Take back that slander this instant," Meg demanded, standing up to emphasize her height. "You are a poor loser, George Plantagenet, and you always have been. I do not have to cheat to beat you, you stupid boy. I could do it blindfolded!"

George never had a good answer to Meg's sharp retorts, and he did not have one now. Instead he upended the entire board, and the brightly colored figures flew in all directions, startling Ambergris, who began to bark. Meg's attendant Beatrice got to her feet "tut-tutting" and commanded George to pick everything up and apologize. George simply stormed off, pushing his sister aside.

"Holy Mother of God," Meg swore. "I do not like George sometimes."

"Sometimes?" Dickon muttered to his block of wood, but he put it down and went to help Beatrice pick up the chess pieces. As he righted the board, he glanced past Meg to the window and gasped.

"S...soldiers!" he stammered. "Look! They are coming over the hill."

Beatrice shrieked and got up from her knees so quickly she knocked her high hennin askew. "Dear Lord have mercy, it must be the royal army. Quick Dickon run and alert your mother. Meg come with me."

Dickon obeyed as fast as he could, dashing through the castle passages that ran inside the curtain wall to the solar in the Northwest Tower. But his mother wasn't there. "She went up on the ramparts with Edmund," Cecily's chief attendant, Gresilde, told the boy, her face pale when she heard Dickon's news. "She must have seen them, too."

Not waiting for further instructions, Dickon scampered up the circular stairs to the roof of the tower. There he saw his mother and brother staring horrified at the thousands of troops massing across the Whitcliff hill, the royal pennants and banners as thick as any forest.

The shrill alarm from a shawm was real this time, and soon the air was filled with pealing bells, loud trumpets, and most frightening of all for those inside a castle, the grinding sound of the portcullis being lowered and the drawbridge raised against attack. Dickon ran to his mother's side, terrified. Edmund swept him up in his arms, and Dickon was surprised to see fear in his brother's eyes, too. It made him feel better that he was not alone.

"Come boys, we must prepare for our royal visitors," their mother said airily, as though the king was here merely to dine with them. Despite himself—and the threatening horde at the gates—Edmund managed a smile.

Dickon stared at his mother's retreating figure in astonishment. *Prepare for the visitors? Is she serious? Doesn't she know fear?* he wondered. If the duchess was not afraid, then perhaps he could pretend he wasn't either.

"You will fight the king?" Dickon whispered, daring to question his father, who had come to wish his boys goodnight. "What about the attainting thing?"

"Dickon!" George hissed, making York smile wanly.

"'Tis his right to ask, George. It is in God's hands now, Richard. But I must save England," he said and drew the boy to him. "It would be Englishman against Englishman," he told them both, "and nobody wants that. So I suspect the king will relent. Pray for me and your brothers. Pray very hard, and perhaps the king will see reason and go away."

But Dickon could not let it rest. "If you do fight the king and win, Father, who will be king then? Will it be you?"

Was this the right time to wend his way through the Yorkist claim to the throne, Richard wondered. Nay, he would wait to explain the vagaries of the Plantagenet family tree that had led King Henry VI to sit on the throne. Some day, he would have to explain how, when the fourth Henry, called Bolingbroke, deposed his cousin Richard II at the end of the previous century, he had skipped over one of his uncles, Lionel, second son of Edward III, whose sole progeny, and thus insignificant, was a daughter. But Richard of York was descended from that daughter as well as from Edward III's fourth son, Edmund of York. No one had questioned—or challenged—the Lancastrian line to the throne until now, and it was only because of this Henry's inability to govern that York was asserting his claim. All this passed through York's mind as quickly as he chose instead to say: "Edouard, prince of Wales is heir to the throne as you well know, Dickon, should the king die...." he paused, "...let us leave it at that for now. God give you both a good night. We can talk more on the morrow."

"But...but, do you want to be king, Father?" The question was innocently asked but that night it exasperated York.

"Have I not told you a thousand times *nay*, I do not desire to wear the crown. Now, enough of your questions, my lad. Say your prayers and go to sleep. The men are waiting."

He kissed both boys and left the room to return to the great hall. He had sent many of the troops to camp at the foot of the hill across the river from the king's huge force. He had also ordered several volleys from cannons on the walls to be fired during the day to warn the royal army to come no closer. Now as twilight closed out the day, it was time to prepare for battle.

Dickon dutifully said his prayers and climbed into the soft tester bed. His father may have answered his questions of kingship, but there had been another hanging on the boy's lips that he had not dared voice: "What happens if *you* die, Father?"

How could he sleep, worried so about such a calamity?

No one noticed the small, pale face peering down at the departing knights from the minstrels' gallery. As soon as the tapers had been extinguished but for one night light, Dickon had slipped out of bed and run along the passageway to the gallery above the great hall. He had arrived in time to see his parents' loving farewell directly below him, shielded from the others by the massive aumbry. It was not the first time he had witnessed his parents' affection for each other, but he was troubled by his mother's tears. Was she afraid after all? He had never seen her cry before, and he curled up against the balustrade wondering: Would his father die? Would

Ned and Edmund? And he began imagining them lying on the bloodied ground with half their faces ripped away, and he could not stop trembling.

Servants quietly extinguished the torches in the hall below, leaving only the flickering firelight to cast eerie shapes upon the walls. Dickon, in his fear, fancied he saw his father's and brothers' shadows walking there and hurriedly crossed himself in his dark hiding place, wishing he were back in bed. There was now no ambient light from the hall in the passageway, where grotesques or ghosts might be lurking that were far more real to the boy than the king and his army menacing the town across the Teme. He begged his favorite St. Anthony to protect him.

No help came for the devout little boy huddled half asleep and cold in the little minstrel gallery as an hour dragged by. Then suddenly Dickon was jolted awake by the flinging open of the massive door to the hall, and the boy heard his father's urgent, angry voice. "Light! Give us light, I say!" Sleepy servants jumped up from their makeshift beds by the fire to obey the duke. The other lords, now fully harnessed, clanked in behind him. By now Dickon was wide awake. Had there been a battle and had he slept through it? But nay, none of the men looked bloody or even dirty.

"That whoreson traitor Trollope!" York cried. "If I ever find him, I'll string him up by his bollocks…"

Warwick sneered. "Nay, my lord, that will be *my* pleasure. Trollope is … *was* under my command."

Captain Trollope? The nice man with the twinkly eyes? What had he done?

Dickon returned his attention to his father's fury—or was it fear—and his mother's clumsy attempts to calm the duke as she tried to unbuckle his sword. "What happened, my lord?" she asked her husband, but before York could answer, Warwick's commanding voice bellowed.

"Those sons of bitches! My own men of Calais. Pah! Traitors and cowards all! May they be damned in hellfire!"

Dickon, whose heart was thumping, heard his father announce that Trollope had deserted the Yorkists and in the cover of dark had gone over to the king's side, taking all of the Calais troops with him and more besides. "In the end, the turncoats claimed they could not bear arms against their king."

Traitor? That word again! Dickon knew all about that word, remembering the story of his grandfather. But Trollope had promised to speak up for him with his father. *He crossed his heart and promised,* he remembered, feeling again the desolation of betrayal; trust would be harder to bestow after this. His heart constricted, and he felt cold.

Then Ned surprised Dickon. Magnificent in his breastplate and mail that made him look like a warrior god, he too cried: "God damn them! Traitors, all!" Dickon was transfixed as the hall resounded with the echoed words from others. "Traitors! Traitors!"

So many traitors, Dickon thought, gazing sadly at his father. So much disloyalty. As he listened to his father bark orders and make arrangements, he resolved never to be a leader. The gravity of the decisions the duke of York was having to make for everyone in the room—nay, the whole army—may not have been understood by the youngster, but he took note of his father's anguished face and felt the tension mounting in the men below. They had to trust their leader, didn't they? He trusted in Father, but would these Yorkists? Would they stay loyal in the face of danger? He knew he would because he could not yet imagine turning his back on his family—right or wrong—but could they? He watched and shivered.

"Dickon! What are you doing there, *mon garçon?*" Constance's voice came from behind and startled the boy. He put his finger to his lips and, peering over the railing, she was astonished to see the hall filled with the same soldiers she had seen leave an hour before. Meg's coughing had drawn her to the children's quarters where she had noticed Dickon was missing, and hearing voices in the direction of the great hall, she guessed he must be there. She drew her bedrobe more tightly around her and looked down on her beloved mistress, who was obviously distressed.

"Captain Trollope is a traitor, Constance," Dickon whispered, turning a distraught face up to hers. "He has betrayed Father. And I liked him very much. But now he has gone to join the king and taken a lot of men with him."

"*Sacre Vierge!*" Constance mouthed, understanding the disaster at once. The Yorkist army would be hopelessly outnumbered and could not possibly hold the town against the king's forces. She knew she ought to take Dickon to his bed, but instead she knelt down next to him and covered his shoulders with her shawl. "You should not be here, you know," she admonished the boy, but she enveloped him warmly and let him stay to listen. It was his fate, too, she knew.

As the leaders huddled making a plan, Cecily went to sit on the steps of the dais, and Constance saw her eyelids droop and her body sag with exhaustion and worry. Aching to support her mistress but loath to leave Dickon, she coaxed him to go with her down to the hall, where they slipped in and joined Cecily. The duchess was too tired and unnerved to chastise either Constance or the boy for being there.

"Take my hand, Mother," Dickon whispered, looking up into Cecily's tear-stained face. "Constance and I are here to comfort you." Cecily's wan smile cheered him as she took his hand, drew him close and gave him a squeeze. *Mother is trembling,* Dickon thought, an odd protective feeling surprising him.

Richard of York suddenly lifted his head from the small group gathered in close conference around a table and pounded the top of it with his fist, making Dickon jump. "So we are agreed. Our cause is lost if we fight with such diminished numbers, and if we surrender we will surely be executed to a man and our names attainted." He looked around slowly before deciding. "I say we should allow our troops to slip away as best they may—or join the king, like Trollope, and seek a pardon. Tell me we are agreed."

"Aye." The response was reluctant—more obedient than committed.

Dickon was aghast. Flight? Hadn't he been told that was for cowards? Surely his father meant something else, or else York would be called traitor *and* coward. He had his answer soon enough when an indignant Edward shouted: "Flee, Father? Every knight disdains such cowardice. 'Twas not how I was trained to behave."

All eyes swiveled to York.

"How dare you!" he roared at his son. "Retreat now offers us our only chance of reorganizing. We go now or our cause is lost." Dickon watched in awe as Ned tried to stare his father down in the silence that followed, glad he was not in Ned's shoes. The defiance lasted a few seconds before Ned respectfully bowed his head. Lucky for Edward, York's anger never lasted long—it could be fearsome but mercifully short, as all his sons knew. In a more moderate tone, the duke now addressed his brother-in-law. "My lord of Salisbury, you will return with Warwick to Calais and take Edward with you. Rutland will come with me. If we are split, perhaps we will confuse the queen. I fear most of us will be attainted anyway, but let us bide our time until the moment is ripe to return."

Dickon's heart sank. Edmund was to flee, too. Where would he and his siblings go? In his desolation he jumped up and cried: "What about us? What about George and Meggie and me?"

No one had noticed the boy slip in with Constance and thus all heads turned to look at him now. Cecily and Constance both grasped an arm and tried to pull him back down between them. At any other time he would have realized the rashness of his act, but he was desperate, and so he wrenched his arms free and stood his ground. "George and I can fight too, my lord. I am skilled with the bow, and George has his own shortsword ..." his voice faltered when he saw Ned's warning frown.

Richard of York, however, was filled with pride. He went to Dickon, led him by the shoulders and presented him to the commanders, who were clearly taken with the boy's audacity. Had it been any other time, they would probably have been amused, but as all of their lives hung in the balance, they simply stared, and Salisbury shook his head at York's parental indulgence.

"Can we be serious, Your Grace," he said. "We do not have much time."

"He is my son, my lord, and has a right to know." York held fast to Dickon and thrilled his son by whispering, "Well done, lad."

Emboldened by his little brother's courage, Edmund now spoke up. "I crave your pardon, Your Grace, but Dickon is right. What plans have you made for my mother, and my brothers and sister? Will they go with us to Ireland?"

Dickon nodded vigorously. That is what he wanted with all his heart. *Take me with you, Father,* he wanted to shout.

"My thanks to you, Edmund, but I do not need reminding of my duty to my wife." York now turned to Cecily. "On the advice of your brother and some of my other counselors, my lady, I shall ask that you remain in the safety of the castle and put yourself at the mercy of the king."

Edmund's face turned white with anger. "Upon the mercy of the *queen,* you mean, Father!" he shouted, as all eyes turned back to him. "That woman hates us; I would not put it past her to murder mother and Meggie, George and Dickon in cold blood! I shall not go with you. I shall stay and defend them with my life."

At that, Edward jumped to his feet. "And I shall stay with Edmund, my lord."

Dickon ran to Cecily. "I, too, shall defend you from the queen…" he declared, faltering as the words "murder in cold blood" suddenly conjured visions of a woman in a crown, blood dripping from her hands, thrusting a dagger into his heart. He flung himself into his mother's arms.

"Take him back to bed," Cecily instructed her physician. The child should not be listening to this disturbing talk, and besides she needed to voice her defense of Richard's plan. Constance wrested Dickon gently from his mother and escorted him back upstairs. Dickon did not complain and allowed his dear Constance to tuck him into bed, where George stirred briefly but turned over and slept again. Dickon wished with all his might that he could too, but his sleep was fitful.

It was still dark and two hours before dawn, giving the Yorkist troops plenty of time to gather their belongings and steal away into the night. Below in the hall, the company made reverences to Cecily as they quietly exited, until none but her family was left.

Constance reappeared on the scene just in time to see Cecily take both her soldier sons in her outstretched arms and give them a mother's blessing. As her boys closed the heavy door behind them, Cecily felt her confidante's strong, capable arms encircle her and she let herself cry on Constance's shoulder.

"What should I do without you," Cecily wept.

Constance patted the trembling hands. "You shall never know, Your Grace, for I shall always be here with you."

Upstairs, Dickon pulled the covers over his head to block the muffled sound of horses on the cobbled courtyard, their hooves bound with rags, as they carried away his father, two brothers and their army in flight.

CHAPTER FOUR
1459–1460

Years later when Dickon thought back on those few hours at Ludlow on the thirteenth day of October, his memories had blurred into a nightmare of dead bodies; yards of bloody entrails through which terrified horses slithered; screaming women slammed against walls as men thrust up brutally between their legs; houses on fire; pandemonium in the streets; and menacing soldiers brandishing pikes, clubs and daggers in the faces of the little group of women led by his dogged mother, who walked proudly with her young sons through the castle grounds to the market square, seeking the mercy of the king. How terrifying that, other than a few trusty servants, the duchess's little party had no men left to defend them. Every second Dickon had expected to be separated forcibly from her, beaten, or stabbed, and he clung to her hand with every ounce of strength he had.

It was an angry army that awoke to find it had been hoodwinked that morning. Queen Margaret was livid her arch enemy had escaped and so allowed her troops to tear apart the barricade, swarm across the trench and over the bridge into Ludlow, where they ransacked the town. The screams, alarm bells and clashing steel penetrated the fitful sleep of the inmates in the castle, and soon pandemonium broke out behind the thick walls as those servants who remained and their noble charges hurried to dress and ready themselves for surrender.

"We shall not fight," Cecily cried from the top step of the great hall, her weeping over. Proud Cis had emerged from her chamber earlier with a purpose. "I pray you put your trust in Our Sovereign King Henry. I am commanding that any man who is able to walk leave by the postern gate immediately. My ladies, my children and I shall walk out to meet the king and save the castle," the duchess declared as though it were a routine, everyday task. When Duchess Cecily set her mind on something, it was pointless to object—although many in the room had fearful misgivings.

Constance had no qualms about leaving her mistress in charge as she slipped away to the infirmary to tend to the wounded, while the men of the household staff paid their respects to the duchess and began to leave through the postern gate. Only faithful Piers Taggett, his eyes never wavering from his mistress and savior, stayed by her side. Even had the duke not ordered him to stay with Cecily, Piers would have remained.

"I hope my plan works," she said to her ladies.

"No one would dare to touch you, Your Grace," Beatrice spoke up from behind, her hand entwined in Meg's. "You look magnificent."

"The more regal I look, the more respect I shall get," she said, more hopefully than she felt as she adjusted her spire-high hennin with its azure blue veil. Cecily was a head taller than many of her companions, and she intended to exploit her height and wardrobe to inspire awe in her daring enterprise.

Cecily had told Nurse Anne to clothe her charges in somber clothes as their mother hoped the troops they must surely face would only focus on her and not her young, vulnerable sons.

"Father's gone now, hasn't he? And Ned and Edmund?" Dickon asked as they waited for the duchess in their chamber. Nurse Anne nodded.

"What do you mean 'gone'?" George demanded, but stopped as Cecily entered. Even Dickon was lost for words when she appeared in the doorway, resplendent in her purple mantle over dark blue gown, her magnificent sapphire necklace sparkling at her throat.

Quietly she told the dumbfounded George of the flight. Kneeling between the boys, she took a hand in each of hers and smiled encouragingly. "Are you ready to embark on an adventure?"

George was dubious. "An ad...adventure, Mam? What kind of adventure?"

"We shall go to the king and prevail upon his mercy. He will not harm us, I am sure of it."

"'Tis the best plan, George," Dickon assured his incredulous brother. "I heard it all last night when I couldn't sleep..."

"And you didn't wake me?" George cried, pummeling Dickon. "How dare you?"

"Enough!" Cecily pulled the boys apart. "This is not the time to fight. I know this is a shock, George, but you must listen to me carefully. If I have my two strong boys with me, I think I can be as brave as any warrior as we go to find the king. Do you think you can be brave with me?" she asked.

Dickon's heart was thumping. What was his mother thinking? Surely not to walk through the town to the king's pavilion pitched high on Whitcliff Hill? How could he tell her that all the shouting and screaming he could hear from the chamber window and the smoke rising over the castle walls frightened him. He was ashamed of his fear until he looked across at George and saw the terror on his brother's face as well. He forced his legs to stop trembling and nodded at his mother. "I can try," he whispered.

George drew himself up and in a steady voice said, "Me, too."

"Then let us join the others in the great hall. Come, boys."

Once there, Cecily marshaled her women, Meg among them, and straightened a headdress here, tweaked a cloak there. Looking around, she suddenly demanded: "Where is Doctor LeMaitre? Dear God, do not tell me she has already gone to tend the wounded?"

Beatrice nodded. "She left early, Your Grace."

Cecily called to Piers. "Master Taggett, be so kind as to go and find Doctor LeMaitre. Quickly!" Piers nodded and went in search of the physician. Satisfied, Cecily took her boys' hands and with deliberation began her journey to face she knew not what.

If ever there were a time to attribute great courage to Cecily of York, it was now.

It was less than half a mile to the market square, but when Dickon chose to remember their slow march that day, it was dreamlike. Much of it became buried under more vivid memories, like recognizing Constance's screams from behind the castle keep and his mother's cry of anguish when the doctor was heard no more.

"God rest her soul," Cecily had whispered, the words informing Dickon their dear friend must be dead. He whimpered. True, he had witnessed death first-hand with the young billman, but he had not known the lad. He knew and loved Constance and had understood then he would never see her again. She would never sit by his bedside cooling his fevered head with a sweet-smelling cloth; never tell him tales of her time at the university in Salerno or of her childhood in Paris; nor help him catch butterflies; nor show him how to recognize poisonous herbs; nor make a poultice for the boils that often plagued him. He had swallowed a sob. Dickon grieved for her until his childhood memories faded over the years.

Dickon would also never forget how filthy soldiers fingered his hair, stuck out their tongues in his face, reached out and pulled at Cecily's gown making disgusting sucking sounds. "Whore! Bitch!" they called, but proud Cecily walked on, eyes fixed on the castle gate, ignoring the taunts and insults.

Somewhere along the perilous path out of the castle grounds, Dickon had sensed a mysterious shield around his mother, George, and him. The soldiers had suddenly looked almost afraid and stepped away. He peeked up at his mother and, seeing a strange glow on her face, knew she had felt it, too. Was an angel guarding them? Nay, it must have been his imagination he would later tell himself, but at the time it lessened his fear.

Cecily had finally reached the sanctuary of the Market Cross and stood firm, surrounded by bloodthirsty enemy soldiers, before King Henry himself arrived on his huge warhorse, parting his troops and confronting Cecily. Dickon remembered holding his breath. Had his father been right? Would the king show mercy? Or were they all going to die? It had been a huge gamble based on York's trust in King Henry's honor and the chivalric code they all lived by.

Meeting King Henry for the first time was another vivid memory Dickon carried from that day. Hoping no one would notice him, Dickon had dared to look up into the face of his sovereign. Doesn't every child imagine his king to look like a warrior or a god? This king looked like a plain man with a kind face. Why, didn't everyone know that kings should lead their armies, brandishing a weapon, and boasting of victory— someone like King Arthur or even his father? But Dickon had thought this reedy, delicate man looked as though he would have preferred to be anywhere else, even at home in bed. Dickon felt profoundly disappointed. He had heard his father and uncle describe the man as weak, lily-livered, and easily led, but not until that moment had Dickon believed it.

But then the king's eye had fallen on Dickon's tear-stained face and his mouth had hardened, and at once Dickon feared for his life. It was in that moment Henry suddenly seemed to awaken to his kingship and, holding himself erect on his horse, he addressed his men: "Turn around!" he thundered. "Disband and return to camp!" It had felt like a miracle to the small boy watching in terror.

Cecily was on her knees, which had finally given way after her brave stand. Henry moved his horse closer, and Dickon stepped forward to protect his mother and glared up at Henry. Henry's mouth softened into a kind smile, and it was then Dickon knew they were no longer in danger.

"I shall not harm you or your children, Duchess Cecily, you have my word." The king had stretched out his hand to the courageous woman. "Rise and let us take you all to the safety of my pavilion." He called to Cecily's brother-in-law, "Buckingham, take charge of Her Grace and her children. We shall confer at the camp."

King Henry wheeled his courser around and, with his escort, left the square. They were soon followed by Buckingham's party, and the little procession, believing their ordeal was over, made its way down the hill, past burning houses, dead and distraught townsfolk, and gawping, drunken soldiers.

But one last tragedy was to play out for the York family that morning.

An anguished cry from the city gate halted the escort's progress over the Teme to the royal pavilion. Recognizing the voice, Dickon swiveled around from his seat in front of a knight and watched in horror as Piers Taggett, his friend and champion, staggered down the hill to reach them, a crimson river streaming from a bloodied stump where his arm should have been. Dickon had stared for a second, gruesomely fascinated, but then without warning had leaned over the knight's leg and vomited onto the bridge. Ashamed, he lifted his face again only to see his mother catch the faithful falconer before he fell, his back shot full of arrows and giving him the grotesque appearance of a human hedgehog. Cecily had cradled Piers in her arms, tears running unchecked down her cheeks and onto his dear, now-ashen face, while Dickon's escort urged on his horse to spare the boy more misery.

Even though there had been no battle in the full sense of the word, it had been Dickon's first taste of war, and he would never forget what he experienced at Ludlow. Apart from the horrors perpetrated by the unruly royal troops, Piers and Constance had been taken from him in the space of an hour; he had not known when he would see his father and brothers

again; and, looming in the frightened mind of a young boy was the
question: where would he be on the morrow? He would forget the small
details, like how he had asked the hardened soldier holding him, "May we
go home to Fotheringhay now?" and the knight's response of, "You'll go
somewhere, young 'un, but His Grace the King will decide where," or that
he had wet the bed that night.

King Henry had decided that Dickon's Aunt Anne of Buckingham's
residence of Maxstoke would be the place where the attainted duke of
York's family should reside. It would be a long time before Dickon saw
Fotheringhay or knew peace again.

That first night in the Buckinghams' country residence, Dickon's nightmares
began. The horror of Ludlow was revisited in scene upon terrifying scene
of leering faces, bloody entrails, screaming horses, hands that mauled his
mother, and the vivid image of Piers Taggett lurching towards him waving
his gory, shredded stub of an arm and crying out to the boy to save him.
Then the ashen face of the devoted servant dissolved into the jeering face
of Andrew Trollope who came towards him, shouting, "I have come to get
you, Dickon of York... You traitor!" Dickon screamed so loudly, he woke
himself up. George leaped from the bed and cried out for help. At once
the room was filled with people Dickon loved; Nurse Anne was first to
comfort him, but in a second, she gave up her place to Cecily, who gathered
the boy in her arms, stroked his damp hair and shushed him. Meg sat on
his other side and took his hand. That role used to be Constance's, and
Dickon was once more reminded he would never see her sweet face again
and renewed his sobbing.

With all this attention, who could blame George for being resentful.
George didn't have dreams, he had proudly told Meg one day. "They are
for girls," he had declared. Now, George watched sullenly in the shadows
as Dickon was fawned over.

"Babykins," he muttered.

"Mam! I don't want to go! Don't let them take me, please." Dickon
protested one blustery day in March after six months in Buckingham's
custody. "I want to stay with you."

The hand that caressed his head abruptly stopped. "You are a son of York, Richard," Cecily said, upsetting him even more by using his proper name. "Behave like one!" Inside she was praying she wouldn't lose her nerve, pull him close and cry herself. As though fate had not dealt the poor woman enough blows in the past six months, she was to lose her boys as well. Edward had entreated the Archbishop of Canterbury to take his brothers under the cleric's wing at Lambeth and continue their education. All very charitable, but uncharitably Cecily railed silently at Ned. Couldn't he have foreseen the pain it would inflict on her in this miserable captivity with her estranged sister.

"I will go gladly." George's voice interrupted her thoughts and she turned to him, surprised. "If Ned believes this is the best for us, then we would be ungrateful not to accept." He gave his mother an angelic smile. "Besides," he added, "this place is tiresome, and Dickon and I would dearly like to see London." Dickon opened his mouth to protest, but George's scowl stayed him.

"Nicely said, George." Cecily nodded her approval; she could always count on George to be tractable. His benevolent parent somehow never saw the darker side of his nature, or how his smile would turn into a sulk as soon as his mother's attention wavered from him, which it did now as she turned to Dickon. "Run and find Nurse Anne and have her ready your belongings. And use your kerchief not your sleeve to wipe your nose, Dickon. His Grace the Archbishop will think you have been brought up in the gutter."

Archbishop? Were they to be shut up with monks? His youthful imagination conjured a damp abbey or monastery, where the archbishop would surely keep them in cheerless cells, make them wear hair shirts and only let them out to pray and learn their lessons. Dickon had seen the meagre quarters of the Yorks' chaplain and had spent nights staying in abbeys along the road to Ludlow. He knew how clerics lived, and he was determined to resist Ned's edict one way or another.

"How could Ned do this to us?" Dickon was incredulous as he and George made their way to their chamber. "I like it here. We have a tutor; we are doing our lessons. I thought you liked it too."

George shrugged. "I like it well enough."

"Then I don't understand. Why did you tell Mother you will be glad to leave?"

"Because that is what Mother wanted to hear, you boil-brain. 'Tis easier to be charming, Dickon. The sooner you learn that, the more you will get to do what you want. Besides, I do want to go to London."

Dickon stopped his brother. "To an old priest's dreary abbey? Have you eaten toadstools that have caused madness? Well, you can go, but I am *not* going," and he marched ahead. "I'll run away," he shouted. "That will show them!"

"And anger our father?" George called after him. "He will be coming home soon, you know."

Dickon turned. "How do you know?"

"You read the ballad. All of England is waiting for him to return— remember?

'Send home, most gracious Lord Jesu most benign,
Send home thy true blood unto his proper vein,
Richard, duke of York ...'" George recited.

Dickon nodded, but, although he desperately wanted to do something daring like run away, he was reluctant to disappoint his father. Oddly, he had fewer qualms about disappointing his mother. The chance never came, alas, for the boys learned they were to leave on the morrow, and Cecily, wanting to spend every last hour with her sons, did not let them out of her sight.

And so, once more Dickon found himself hoisted in front of a Stafford knight and bidding a forced farewell to a home he had come to know. Part of him thrilled to see London, but the child in him longed for familiar surroundings with the people he loved and, most of all, where he felt safe.

The rain was unrelenting that summer and even now was running down the tiny leaded panes of the Lambeth Palace windows in depressing rivulets. Despite the weather, however, the sun had shone on the house of York when Edward of March, Richard of Warwick and Richard of Salisbury— dubbed the lords of Calais—had landed in June and marched with their army to a welcoming London.

When will we ever leave this dreary place, Dickon wondered that day, oblivious of the priceless tapestries hanging on the burnished, walnut-paneled walls around him, the richly colored Turkey carpet covering the table, and the finely carved furniture. Dickon had been wrong about the penury. It seemed the archbishop lived in greater luxury than all but the wealthiest of nobles despite protestations by the country's premier churchman to show charity to the poor. The archbishop was a kind man, and the boys had not been as confined as they had feared. It also appeased Dickon's resentment of his oldest brother's decision to send them there that Edward came to see them often and brought them sweetmeats and news from across the river in Westminster.

"*Ignavi coram morte quidem animam trahunt, audaces autumn illam no saltem advertunt,*" droned the dry tutor, Timothy Birdsall, his rheumy eyes peering at his well-worn copy of Caesar's De Bello Gallico. "My lord Richard, I pray you translate."

Dickon sighed. He abhorred Latin almost as much as he loved archery, and he chewed the end of his quill trying to find anything that gave him a clue about the sentence. He suddenly noticed George was kicking him under the table, and looked up. George mouthed across at him: "*Cowards fear...*"

"My lord, you are not to help him," Birdsall admonished. "Try again, Dickon," and he repeated the sentence.

"Cowards are fearful of death, but the brave never take notice of it," a voice from the doorway broke in, and the two boys gave a shout of joy. "Ned!" they chorused, and ran to greet their grinning brother.

The tutor tut-tutted and closed his text with a snap. He knew when he was beaten; no one of his stature would dare point out to one of the lords of Calais that the lesson was not finished.

"Your translation is correct, my lord," Birdsall simpered as he eased past the six-foot-three-inch earl of March and disappeared along the passage. "The boys would do well to heed it."

Edward laughed heartily. "My brave brothers have no need, Master Tutor. We Yorks do not even know what cowardice means. We are as brave as Julius Caesar, are we not boys?"

"Aye, Ned!" George cried, gripping Ned's outstretched hand. Dickon hung back, his eyes full of admiration for his magnificent brother, who appeared to have a small cut above his eye. Ever since Master Birdsall had begun using the conqueror's Gallic wars' exploits as his text, Dickon had conjured an image of the great Caesar, and he looked exactly like Ned— but in a toga.

This was not the first time Edward had come to visit since his arrival from Calais, and the citizens of London spoke warmly of the solicitous young earl. Family matters to him, they thought, just as it does to us common folk. Indeed, Edward had assured his mother he would keep an eye on the boys, and he was true to his promise. However, the unrest in England had prompted the archbishop to confine his charges to Lambeth and had only once taken them by boat to show them Westminster Hall and the great abbey, directly across the river from his palace. They still had not set foot in the city of London, two miles down the Thames on its northern bank. Dickon wished there were not such a sharp bend in the river that prevented even a glimpse of St. Paul's far-off spire when they went fishing along the south bank.

"I wonder how brave Caesar was when he faced death at the hands of his friends?" George mused. "It must have been worse to die at their hands than at his enemies."

Ned laughed. "What a morbid thought, brother. But aye, the final thrust from Brutus must have come as a shock. You will learn that no good can come from being a tyrant." He leaned in close. "But let us not contemplate such a degrading death today, because I have good news for you." The boys listened eagerly. "Your uncle, cousin, and I recently won an important victory outside Northampton. Did you hear of it?"

The boys shook their heads. "No one tells us anything," George complained. "'Tis as though we are on the other side of the world, not just the other side of the Thames. My lord archbishop still tethers us close, more's the pity."

"Is the battle where you hurt your eye, Ned?" astute Dickon asked. "What happened?"

And for the next half an hour—which was exactly the time it had taken for the Yorkists to win—Ned regaled the boys with those battle details he thought suitable for such young ears, including a nick from a shortsword when he had inadvisedly pushed up his visor to see more clearly. "A lesson learned, boys. For 'tis better to have limited vision through a visor than end up with no vision at all."

Dickon had listened transfixed, as he could not imagine facing those hideous soldiers of his dreams. He had to ask: "Were you frightened, Ned?"

"Certes, I was, little one," came the answer, "but once you have been trained to fight, as I have, you know what to do to stay alive."

"When will Father come?" Dickon ventured. "And what is the news from Mother?"

Ned sat back on his chair and patted his knee. Dickon slid onto it although he feared George would taunt him as soon as Ned left. George was easy to read, even for one as young as Dickon.

"We—your uncle Salisbury, our cousin Warwick and I—are laying the path for Father's return. Did I remember to tell you that at the end of the battle, we captured the king in his tent and brought him back here to London?" He grinned. "Aye, I do not lie. The king is in our custody—he is our hostage now. We have sent word to our lord Father, and we hope this means he will leave Ireland soon."

"We met the king, didn't we, George. In his pavilion at Ludlow. I hope you have been kind to him, for he was kind to us," Dickon told Edward.

"Pah!" George was unimpressed. "How can you say he was kind? He sent us to that dull Maxstoke, didn't he?"

"Mother said that was the *queen*, not the king," Dickon retorted. He was impatient to find out more. "Where is the king? Is he in prison, Ned? I hope you haven't put him in chains."

Edward laughed. "Certes, he is not in chains. He is being well watched in the royal apartments in Westminster. He can live the way he is accustomed to, but he cannot leave, 'tis all. As our hostage, he may prove a useful bargaining tool."

Dickon shook his head. "Bargaining tool? What's that?"

George enlightened him, eager to shine in front of Ned. "If the queen would attack London, our uncle Salisbury could threaten to kill the king unless she retreats." He laughed. "Not even Margaret of Anjou would dare put the king in jeopardy. Am I right, Ned?"

Ned chuckled. "You are in so many words, George."

"Kill the king?" Dickon was horrified. "In cold blood? Would you really do that? But he is such a nice man," and then remembered, "and he is the Lord's anointed."

"George has painted the blackest picture, never fear. 'Twill not come to that," Ned assured the earnest young boy. "Besides, I have better news. Mother and Meg are released and coming to London. You will see them at the end of the month, I promise," Edward said, reminding himself to carry out his mother's wishes to procure a house for them all. "We shall be together again."

Dickon could not suppress a whoop of joy, while George muttered under his breath: "Praise be to God. No more Latin."

Dickon had lost count of how many beds he had slept in since leaving Fotheringhay almost a year before. But he didn't care; Mother and Meggie were coming that very day to the handsome Falstoff mansion that Ned had rented south of the Thames in Southwark. Dickon and George had been graced with their big brother's presence every day since they moved into the comfortable, spacious house, with their own servants to attend them.

What was more astonishing to the boy, who often wondered if anyone ever noticed him, was that Edward did not treat Dickon with any less consideration than he did George. In those days before the arrival of his mother and sister, Dickon affirmed a lifelong devotion to his oldest brother. No one could speak a bad word of Ned without Dickon coming fiercely to his defense. Certainly he did not understand the innuendo whispered about the handsome, virile young earl of March that he could not keep his pestle in control when any passing-fair girl crossed his path. Dickon wasn't sure why Edward needed a pestle, and, as he had never seen Ned with one, he was certain the whisperers were wrong about him owning one, and he would tell them so in all earnestness. There was no one to explain to a nearly eight-year-old why this brotherly defense caused such amusement. George, at eleven, was not about to reveal his own ignorance and instead laughed at Dickon along with the rest.

"Do you have a pestle, Ned?" Dickon asked one day, and Edward had looked puzzled.

"What an odd question. Why would I need one? 'Tis a handheld tool with a rounded end used to pound herbs and spices in a smooth-sided bowl…"

Indignant, Dickon frowned. "I know what it is, Ned. I have just never seen you use one. Why do people say you cannot keep yours under control?"

Ned stared at the serious but pleasant young face, its slate-gray eyes too dark to read, and then he grinned, and then he laughed, a throaty, genuine sound quite unlike their father's extraordinary neigh. Ned and Dickon had been alone that day angling on the riverbank, with George a hundred yards away casting his line with a lad he had met from Southwark village.

"My dear Dickon," Edward said, wiping his eyes. "This is the best laugh I have had for a month. Nay, do not look so chagrined. You were right to ask, and as I am acting as your father for the foreseeable future, perhaps I should explain the joys—and tribulations—of being a man."

And so with the gleaming, whitewashed walls of the Tower standing sentinel across the river, a universally awkward conversation took place that left Dickon more than adequately educated but frightened enough to decide he would just as soon avoid the opposite sex altogether. Ned had a twinge of guilt that perhaps the boy was a little young for the facts of life—a notion his Father verified in no uncertain terms when the topic came up a few months later—but at the time, Ned's confidence had led him to believe the instruction had been for the best.

Dickon had had his nose pressed against the upstairs solar window of Falstoff Place most of the morning waiting, while George pretended nonchalance and played chess with one of the gentleman attendants. But the pawns went flying as soon as Dickon squealed, "They are come, George. Mother and Meggie are here!" and he was right behind his brother, running down the staircase through the great hall and out onto the front steps of the cobbled courtyard.

Edward was already there watching as a groom opened the door to the cumbersome carriage. A huge wolfhound, glad to be set free from such a confined space, bounded out, pulling Meg on his leash behind him.

"Down, Ambergris!" Edward called crossing the courtyard in three long strides to take hold of his ecstatic hound. "And who is this beautiful young woman you have brought with you?" Meg raised an eyebrow and said archly, "You cannot flatter me as easily as you do other women, Ned. Come, give me a kiss." She did not protest, however, when her brother picked her up as though she were still a child and bussed her cheek.

"Pray help me out of here!" Cecily called to her son, her tall, still-lithe frame filling the doorway of the carriage, "I swear every bone in my body is broken." Edward let Margaret go and lifted his mother like so much goose down, setting her gently on the ground. Cecily gazed up at her oldest son, his gold-red hair curling nonchalantly to his shoulders and his handsome features all smiles. *Sweet Mother of God, I sent him away a boy at Ludlow and he has returned a man*, she thought. Ruefully, she acknowledged that the first battle would always do that to a youth. Edward had tasted blood at Northampton and had acquitted himself well.

"God's greeting to you, Mother," Ned said, kissing her hand, "we are all delighted to see you and to welcome you to your new home away from home."

"Do not remind me. I should be at Baynard's," she grumbled. Among the confiscations of York property after Richard's attainder, the loss of her favorite Baynard's Castle by the river was one of the bitterest for Cecily. Looking at the new house, she was not displeased, but before she could compliment Ned on his choice, she was almost knocked over by her two younger sons.

"My dearest boys," Cecily cried, bending down and embracing them both, "how we have missed you. Look how you have grown!"

"We missed you, too," George told her, "but Ned has come to see us every day, has he not, Dickon?"

Dickon nodded happily. How glad he was his family was together again. "And he takes us fishing, and," he told Cecily in whispered confidence, "he took us to a bear-baiting. I didn't much care for it."

"I should think not!" Cecily was appalled. "Edward, you and I need to have a conversation." When Edward looked sheepish, Dickon flushed scarlet. Had he betrayed Ned? He gave his big brother a sidelong glance, but Ned was already smiling at his mother and offering her his arm.

"Come, Mother, let me show you your new home." Cecily took his arm gladly, and when she reached out her hand to Dickon the boy's joy was complete. He had been singled out by his mother for once, and he reveled in the gesture. He stole a glance at George to see if George might realize how it felt to be left out for a change, but Dickon's small victory was lost on George, who was wrapped in his much-missed sister's warm embrace.

Disappointed but not daunted, Dickon held tight to his Mother's hand and tucked the precious moment into his heart.

The atmosphere at Falstoff's Place in those first two weeks of September was as charged as in an audience awaiting the first lines of a play, and the boys and their sister were left to their own devices as messengers and other visitors from London, Westminster and farther afield came and went in rapid succession. Ned had set up the York headquarters at the house, and even my lord of Warwick had crossed the bridge to confer with him.

Dickon was a little afraid of his cousin, but the earl was always quick to tousle the boy's hair and ask if his archery was improving.

"Am I still to go to Cousin Richard's household for military training?" Dickon dared to ask his mother once. "Father talked about it. And even the earl himself talked about it at Ludlow to me and to Captain Troll…"

He shut his mouth quickly before naming the faithless commander. He still could not understand how the man could have betrayed his father or his impressive cousin of Warwick. He, Dickon, would be proud to fight for this superior knight—after his father and Ned, to be sure.

Dickon's knightly training was low on Cecily's list of priorities, and she brushed the question off with a "wait until your Father comes home" response. But she was curious about the boy's enthusiasm. "Are you sure you are ready to be a soldier, Dickon. What about your nightmares?"

"Oh, those," Dickon scoffed. "I don't have those anymore. I'm nearly eight now! I just want to learn from the best knight, and our cousin of Warwick is the best, isn't he?"

Since the arrival of the lords of Calais in England only three months before and the capture of the king at Northampton, Richard, earl of Warwick, was gaining a reputation far greater than his father's—and dare one say, even that of his uncle of York's. The Neville descendants of Ralph of Westmorland and Joan Beaufort, which included Dickon's mother, had been endowed with taller than average stature, intelligence and ambition. However, of them all, only the thirty-two-year-old Warwick had that same combination coupled with an uncanny understanding of politics, an imperious presence in the field, and a contrasting generosity towards his inferiors that enabled him to become one of English history's most revered figures. He had already eclipsed his important uncle and father in the hearts and minds of the people.

"If you have to learn from someone, then my nephew would certainly be my choice." Cecily smiled at her youngest. "But you know, Ned is fast catching up to him." It was clear to her that eighteen-year-old Edward had earned Warwick's respect during the past months in Calais and now in England, and the two men had become fast friends.

Quiet and observant, Dickon, too, had noticed the friendship grow between the cousins in those early days of September 1460 and wished he had a friend he could trust. It had to be said that he had not stayed in one place long enough to make a real friend, and it must have seemed to Dickon that as soon as he counted on someone—like Piers Taggett or Constance—they were taken from him. There was always Nurse Anne, but she was more like an old aunt than a friend. It could have been George— and indeed they had their good times, but after the Traveller incident, Dickon had decided that his brother was simply untrustworthy.

Nevertheless, the two boys had only each other for playmates during those autumnal days in Southwark, and, on yet another rainy day, they were competing with hoop-rolling in the great hall when a man arrived wearing the York murrey and blue and demanded to be taken to her grace, the duchess. Ambergris bounded after him as the steward admonished the boys to stop their sport and marched the messenger up the staircase.

"Stay, Ambergris!" Meg commanded, and astonishingly the huge hound skidded to a halt on the rushes and sat down obediently in front of her. The three siblings gathered around the dog at the bottom of the stairs wondering at the urgency of this particular messenger's mission. When they heard their mother's cry of excitement, they guessed at once.

"Father has come!" Meg exclaimed. "It must be." And she lifted her voluminous skirts and started up the stairs. Dickon and George grasped each other's shoulders and were jumping up and down making Ambergris bark when Cecily appeared at the head of the staircase.

The lines of worry and the pain of the past year's separation had fled her now radiant face as she looked down on her children. Dickon had always known his mother was the most beautiful woman in the world, but now she seemed to glow. "Your father is at Chester, my dears, praise be to God," Cecily called to them. "Aye, 'tis worthy of jumping for joy." She laughed like a girl, her cheeks flushing. Dickon was too young to recognize love, but her radiance moved him.

After seeing his mother safely onto the road west to meet her husband, Ned sat his siblings down one evening and prepared them for their father's homecoming. He explained what had led up to the retreat at Ludlow, and why it was now time for their father to assert his position with the king once and for all. It took a patient Ned to draw up a chart of the Plantagenet family tree and show how, in fact, York's claim to the throne of England was stronger than the Lancastrian Henry's.

"So Father should be king?" Meg had asked after studying the makeshift chart. "But Henry is God's anointed, and as Father swore fealty to him, he cannot wear the crown. Is that not so, Ned?"

"Aye, Meg, and we Yorks do not break our vows. As he has said, he has no ambition to wear the crown." *More's the pity,* Edward secretly thought. "Indeed, all these years, Father has attempted and failed to remove the bad counselors governing England because our saintly king is too weak to deny them. Each time he has tried to take his place as Henry's chief counselor, the others have poisoned the king against him with the help of Queen Margaret, who has more aggression in her little finger than her husband in his entire body. 'Tis she who rules Henry and thus the council, and she fears Father's claim to the throne."

"Why does Father not simply tell Parliament that he is the rightful king?" George demanded. "Then *we* would be heirs to the crown—not that lily-livered Edouard of Lancaster."

The boy was always thinking of himself, Edward had noticed during his visits; it was one of George's least charming traits. It was Dickon who was growing into the more reliable younger brother.

"As I said only a few minutes ago, George, Father will not break his oath to the king," Ned insisted, attempting to curb George's ambitions. "Besides which, we all wish to prove to the English people that despite our attainders, we are still loyal subjects of the crown. We are *not* traitors. We have been wronged yet wish to do right. If we were the villains Queen Margaret would have everyone believe we are, why then, after our victory at Northampton, did we not simply kill the king and take the throne? Instead, Henry is still our liege lord, and now, from a position of strength, Father can return to give the king obeisance and persuade him to be rid of the likes of Exeter and Somerset for the good of England."

Dickon had been trying hard to follow all of this. Yearning for Ned's approval and not wanting to be thought ignorant, he braved: "Why will the king believe Father this time?"

"A clever question, little man. If you remember, we hold the king hostage. If Father was so ambitious for the crown, why is the king not dead?"

Dickon nodded slowly. "So, it is his loyalty that makes our father the greater man."

Ned's approving hand had come down hard on Dickon's back, almost knocking the boy off his stool. "You have the measure of it, Dickon. Ambition is a fine thing, but it cannot override duty. We, as princes of the royal blood, have a duty to England first, the king, then family, and our own ambition last. 'Twas what Father taught Edmund and me, but as he is not here to teach you, I will. 'Tis what we must all abide by."

These words would nag Dickon during his brother's lifetime of disavowing them, especially when it came to Edward's personal desires.

After more than a week, Meg was almost more impatient to have Cecily return than her beloved father as she found playing mother to her brothers had almost, she told her attendant Beatrice, driven her to uncork a flagon or two. Nurse Anne was getting too old to run after two boys, one of whom, she believed, should have been sent away for his knightly training long before now. And as far as she was concerned, the lads had suffered from the lack of discipline the customary military training would have provided.

"Boys at this age have no other objective than to hit each other; climb trees; throw stones at the poor crows; roll around on the grass, soiling their nice clothes; filch food from under the cook's nose; and utter war whoops just as one is carrying something fragile," Nurse Anne grumbled to Beatrice. "I dropped a water pitcher last week when one of them jumped out at me as I was leaving the pantry."

The two servants were thus relieved to see the earl of March arrive on his chestnut palfrey that tenth day of October and order his brothers to deck themselves out in their finery. No one had noticed that it was almost a year to the day since Richard of York had fled from Ludlow.

"We are going to join our father's procession into London," he told the boys. "I am sorry, Meg, but ..."

"But what, pray?" Meg countered, irritated. "You will not ride from here without me."

Edward chuckled. "I pity your poor husband, sister. However, I have not made provision for a horse for you, so I am afraid..."

"I shall ride pillion behind George," Meg interrupted, "and you can take Dickon up with you. He's small enough to sit in front, and there's an end to it," and she ran off to change into something more festive, leaving Ned with his mouth agape.

It would be a glorious homecoming, Ned told them en route to the Newgate, as Parliament was sitting at Westminster, the king was virtually a prisoner in the royal apartments above, and their father would at last receive the honor and respect due him.

The sun had finally returned for the York siblings as they rode over London Bridge and through the city to be on hand when their father and his retinue of five hundred men entered the gates, and to Dickon seated in front of his magnificent brother, all seemed right with their world.

CHAPTER FIVE
AUTUMN 1460

Londoners loved a procession. They had heard the duke of York was to enter the city that day and so were gathering to watch along the wide Shambles and under the wall of the Franciscan Friary. It was always wise for a leader to show his face in the capital and pay homage, even though Parliament and the king sat at Westminster a little more than a mile away. The citizens had welcomed the lords of Calais five months before, because they, too, were tired of the bad governance of the king and his council, and hoped perhaps the Yorkists would restore prosperity and peace to what had become a lawless land. The duke of York might yet be their savior, but still they were wary. Thus their cheers were less hearty than they might have been had their world not been turned upside down by these warring cousins.

Dickon had never seen the city of London before today, and it overwhelmed his senses. His ears were deafened by the hubbub on the streets: the pealing bells, the clatter of carts, and the barking cries from the hundreds of sellers of foodstuffs peddling their pies, produce and pigs. At the same time the smell of those pies, as well as composting refuse, horse manure and human effluence assailed his nostrils. His eyes took in the colorful clothes of the gentry, the red and black of the clergy, the green of the archers, and the brown of peasants, as well as the array of wares in merchants' windows tempting buyers inside to buy silk, spices, gold and silver. Dickon had never seen so many people—except on that day in Ludlow when the small town had been overrun by hundreds of soldiers.

His thoughts often returned there—almost a year to the day—but now he hoped for peace.

Dickon knew now why his father was returning to London, and it was not merely to be with his family. Seated on Edward's huge courser and securely leaning on his brother's strong torso, he was aware of hundreds of pairs of curious eyes watching the York party move up Chepeside, the soaring spire of St. Paul's pointing the way to heaven. The mood of the bystanders was a mixture of curiosity and suspicion, the number of enthusiastic cheers tempered by a few rotten vegetables and clods of earth thrown towards the Yorkist cavalcade. Two scurvy youths began taunting one of the guards walking beside the riders: "Ho there, White Rose! Where's your traitor lord?" The billman ignored them until one of them jostled him while the other ran past and seized Edward's bridle. "We don't want you here! This is Henry's capital," the man sneered at them and Dickon froze. Before Edward could react, the guard turned and caught the ruffian a blow to the head with the long handle of his bill and the lout loosed the rein and fell to the ground, moaning. Edward moved on as though nothing had happened and encouraged Dickon to wave and smile.

"Don't they want Father to come?" the boy asked, anxiously looking back at the fallen man. "I thought it was the queen they hated."

"Just as ours is, their loyalty is to the king," Ned told him. "They like Henry because he is saintly and kind, and they don't know Father. They don't know they can trust him. People will always take sides in a conflict, Dickon. That is why we have wars."

"York and Lancaster, the white rose and the red," Dickon said to himself. He was too young to see the irony that both boasted thorns sharp enough to draw blood.

The cheering increased at the great conduit on the Chepe when Edward was joined by Warwick and his father, also gorgeously clothed on their fully caparisoned mounts. Londoners had truly taken Warwick to their hearts, Edward noted, and was glad of it. He prayed those same loud shouts would later greet his father; it seemed Englishmen could waver in their loyalties as easily as the petals of a plucked red or white rose could wither and die. Would Londoners cheer or jeer his father? They must wonder at his purpose on returning from exile.

Dickon, less aware of the uncertainty, settled down to bask in the excitement of the moment, as clarion trumpets, shawms and drums gave notice they were nearing the Newgate past Gothic St. Paul's. Edward spurred his horse forward, anxious to be there at the western entry into London to greet his noble Father. "Hold on, Dickon! Judging from this din, our father must have already reached the bridge over the ditch before the Wall," Ned said, gripping his brother tightly and shouting to the crowd to let his party pass.

When Ned saw his father ride through the Newgate to join him, he gave a sharp gasp of dismay. "Bread of Christ, what does this mean?" he muttered, and Dickon turned his head to look up at him. Ned's stony stare scared him. Warwick's face was grave, too, and he raised an eyebrow at Ned.

"What does what mean?" Dickon asked, trying to see where his father was behind the lead rider carrying a huge broadsword pointed skyward.

"'Tis only a king who is permitted to carry an upright sword before him," Ned snapped. "And the banners—he uses the royal arms of England. Ah, Father, you swore not to claim the crown. What are you doing?" He urged his horse forward and forced a smile of welcome. York saluted his son with a raised fist, and when the two horses met, grasped Edward's outstretched hand. "Edward, my son! We meet again under happier circumstances." His exuberance was infectious, and the crowd reacted favorably to this greeting between father and son.

Dickon had almost forgotten what his father looked like over the year of separation, but seeing him now in the magnificent white tunic shot with gold thread on which was blazoned the York fetterlock, a new beard fashionably forked, and a blue bonnet stuck with a jeweled pin on his head, the boy was filled with pride.

It was a moment before Richard noticed his youngest son, but when he did he laughed in surprise, reached over and pinched his cheek. "You have lost your fair curls, my son," York said, ruffling the thick hair. "You are going to be dark like me. Good boy." Pleased with the compliment, Dickon forgave the reference to his childish curls, and chose to respond with the dignity befitting an eight-year-old.

"God's good greeting, Father," he said, brightly. "Are you the king now?" and he pointed to the knight carrying the upright sword.

Richard of York's eyebrows shot up, and Ned bent and whispered. "Keep your mouth shut, Dickon. Now is not the time." Ned grinned at his father. "You know Dickon and his nonsensical questions." And thankfully for a now mortified Dickon, his father laughed and turned his welcoming gaze on George and Meg. Easing his horse closer, he gave Meg a smacking kiss. "Go to the back and find your mother and brother," he directed George after slapping him on the shoulder. "You may both ride in the carriage." Only Dickon saw George's mulish expression as he turned his horse around. *He's jealous of me for once,* Dickon exulted.

York turned his attention to his brother-in-law, Salisbury, and nephew, Warwick. Warwick acknowledged York's hearty "God's greeting" with a stiff bow in the saddle, but his expression was somber. He drew his horse closer to the duke's. "Why this show, my lord? England has a king. You are defeating our purpose here." For a second, Warwick thought York would castigate him but instead the duke gave him a forced smile. "We will talk anon, my dear nephew," he said quietly, then motioning to Edward to join him, he spurred his horse forward.

Dickon was jubilant. He was not to be sent back but allowed to ride at the front with his princely older brother next to his father. With the cheers of the Londoners accompanying them, he thought this moment splendid. This must be what it feels like to be a king, he thought, proudly, as the impressive quartet of York, Salisbury, Warwick and Edward of March rode to greet the mayor and aldermen before turning west again to attend Parliament at Westminster.

In his jubilation, Dickon failed to feel the stiffness in his oldest brother's body, nor sense the chilly tension between the lords of Calais and their leader, the duke of York, nor hear the occasional jeer from the crowd. The earlier sun was now hidden behind darkening clouds, and the reason for this change in climate was the first of many quandaries that Dickon would soon need to decipher.

It was only later in the day, when Edward had relinquished Dickon to an escort who accompanied the younger York children back to Falstoff's Place, they learned from their mother's chief lady what had happened at Westminster to effect that change.

Richard of York, believing Parliament would welcome him as the savior of the realm and restorer of law and order, had dared to enter the hallowed chamber without invitation and deliberately place his hand upon the throne.

"He was wrong," Gresilde Boyvile said, wringing her hands, "so wrong. The Lords and Commons were aghast. It seems they saw it as an intention by your father to take the crown not protect it." She told them the archbishop of Canterbury had eventually stepped forward and asked if York sought an audience with the king.

"What did Father say?" Meg asked, fascinated.

Gresilde resorted to drama, mimicking the duke. "He shouted at them all, saying, 'I know no man in England who ought not rather come to see me than I go to him.' I don't know how he dared."

Meg gasped, George snickered, and Dickon said: "I don't understand what that means?"

"It means Father lost his temper, and he is probably in trouble," Meg told him, and Gresilde had bowed her head in sad acknowledgement.

The duke had then marched from the Star Chamber intent on seeing the king, virtually forcing himself into the royal apartments and sending the king to live in the queen's chambers instead.

"Your mother defended the king bravely," Gresilde told the children. "I know not what your father was thinking, but your mother was not about to treat that kindly, bewildered man uncivilly. Happily, the king went meekly to his new quarters on her arm—he obviously adores her, as he should," she said, loyally.

Dickon was now thoroughly confused. Hadn't their father told his children he had no designs on the crown? But he arrived in London with an upturned sword, went straight to the hallowed halls of Westminster and put his hand on the throne, as though he already owned it. The boy's confusion was further exacerbated by Dame Boyvile's next statement.

"We shall all be living in the royal apartments until your father's castle of Baynard is restored to him," she finished, feeling sorry for these oft-displaced children.

Dickon shook his head in exasperation. "By Christ's nails, not another move!" he spluttered.

"Dickon!" all three onlookers exclaimed in shocked unison at the unaccustomed profanity.

Another extraordinary event in the Star Chamber took place a week later. This time Dickon was a privileged witness.

Richard of York's rash act had had its effect after all. Several days and tense meetings later, he mollified Salisbury and Warwick, allowing the Yorkists to once again resurrect Richard's right to the crown before the lords and lawyers. Within a week, York's claim to the throne was finally legally recognized and a new succession drawn up: It was agreed by king, council and Parliament that Henry should wear the crown until his death when it would pass to Richard of York and his progeny.

Richard knelt and kissed Henry's ring as the king sat on the very throne Richard had dared to touch not twenty days before. "I swear to Almighty God and all His saints that I will honor you, Henry, as my sovereign lord until the end of your days, and that I shall do nothing to hurt or diminish your reign or royal dignity, nor do anything or consent to anything that might lead to the endangerment or ending of your natural life. So help me God."

It was the first time Dickon had seen King Henry since Ludlow. There at least, the king had looked like a soldier. Today, a thin, limp figure, with a passive face, and drab in his brown robes, he looked more like a mournful monk than a monarch. Young as he was, even Dickon could contrast the king with his magnificent subject Edward, earl of March, who now stepped forward and knelt. Ned looks like a real king, Dickon thought to himself, as his brother's strong voice echoed in the chamber while giving his pledge. It was odd he had not thought the same of his father.

Henry ratified the agreement in a soft monotone—*not like a king at all,* disillusioned Dickon thought. To Dickon the king seemed as dejected as the boy often felt when rebuffed by George or ignored by his father. Although he could not appreciate the ignominious position Henry had been put in, and how it was to the king's credit that his voice held no malice or bitterness as he disinherited his own son, Dickon felt sorry for him.

"I, Henry, by the grace of God, king of England and France and Lord of Ireland, do recognize the claim to the throne of Richard, duke of York and his heirs, which shall be theirs at the time of my death and not before." He looked up from the written statement, his sad eyes sweeping the chamber and coming to rest on the small boy sitting in the gallery next to his mother, the king's friend and sometimes champion. The boy and the king locked gazes for a second, and Dickon, moved by the king's focus on him, placed his hand upon his heart. *I am loyal to you, my sovereign lord,* the instinctive gesture seemed to say. A glimmer of a smile lit the king's face before he returned to his paper and continued to read:

"I charge all persons here to put it abroad that it shall be considered an act of high treason for any person to conspire against the said duke's life. And now, my lords, you must swear to uphold this agreement and all its particulars with the duke, as he must now swear to defend you from those who would object to it. Do you swear?"

With one voice the lords cried: "Aye, we swear." And Dickon, gripped by the stirring moment, could not help but join in with his own, "I swear!" much to his mother's amusement.

Richard, duke of York, was now rightful heir to the throne of England.

How easily men's loyalties wavered in those turbulent times, and Dickon was learning how an oath could be broken as well as made. He was now thoroughly unsettled. To whom was he to be loyal? The king or his father who, it was now said, should be king?

True, an oath had been sworn by the king, but it did not mean the fight for power was over, as the duke would soon discover.

Dickon saw Edmund mount the stairs to the roof of Baynard's one chilly morning, and wrapping his coney-lined cloak about him, Dickon hurried up the spiral staircase to join him. He liked this big, handsome brother with the gentle demeanor. Having spent those many months in exile with their father in Ireland, Edmund would surely settle the question of loyalty that had been gnawing at the befuddled young boy.

Despite the intrusion, Edmund's blue eyes twinkled as he gave Dickon a warm smile.

"Do you have time for me, Edmund?" Dickon asked and, after Edmund's nod of encouragement, he admitted: "I am so muddled up. Please can you help me understand why King Henry would give up his crown to Father when Father has said over and over he doesn't want to be king? And then one day Father is proclaiming himself king and the next minute he is back to swearing an oath to be loyal to Henry."

"I confess 'tis bewildering, Dickon. In truth, I had to come up here to ponder the puzzle myself. Perhaps it is not about wanting to be king but about wanting what is right for England. Father's Yorkist claim to the throne is better than Henry's Lancastrian one, but until Henry's many weaknesses endangered England, Father was content to serve at Henry's right hand. Perhaps that is what all this is about: his loyalty and duty to England."

"I hope you're right." Dickon nodded thoughtfully. "But he won't just snatch the crown away will he? King Henry is a good man—Father said so."

Edmund had to be honest with the boy. "I don't think he will, Dickon, but it worries me that he might. Father has always been loyal to the king, as we know. We have to trust Father, do you see?" He hoped he had answered some of the boy's questions, even if he had not answered many of his own.

"But how can Father be loyal to the king *and* claim to be king at the same time," Dickon persisted. "It does not make sense. I want to be loyal to the king *and* to father, but how?"

The earnest upturned face made Edmund smile. He reached down, picked up the boy and sat him in a crenel of the castle wall. "Always thinking, are you not, little brother? Nothing wrong with that, but for now I think we must just wait and see. Above all we must trust Father, and you do trust him, don't you?"

Dickon nodded vigorously. "Aye, I do." He looked up into the wintry sky as though searching for an answer from the heavens. "It's like trusting in God or believing in the Holy Spirit. To be honest, I am not sure about the Holy Spirit either, but Father Lessey has taught me to have faith in God and what I cannot understand. Father's real, so in truth it's easier to have faith in him, isn't it?"

Edmund hugged his brother warmly. "By all means believe, Dickon; it will help ease your mind."

Before vacating the royal apartments to return to Baynard's Castle, the family was joined by Cecily's brother one day after the noonday meal. Cecily and Richard were flanked by five of their seven children. As they all turned towards him, Salisbury thought he had stumbled into a painting. He was struck by the physical beauty of each one of them, and how impressive they were as a family. A royal family as it should be, he thought.

Cecily rose and held out her hands to him. "Welcome, dear brother. Come, take some wine with us. Dickon, give your uncle your seat." She was relieved to see no signs of worry on his lined face for a change. The frayed nerves of October had given way to a more tranquil November, allowing her and Richard to rekindle the passion of their youth in the days after the historic succession announcement and the restoration of their estates. It showed on her face, and Salisbury thought he had never seen his striking sister more beautiful.

"God's greeting, Uncle," Dickon said, effecting a graceful bow. "I pray you, take my seat," and he indicated the empty place on the bench. Dickon liked his Uncle Salisbury; certes, he was an old man to the child, but he had a kind face under his bushy beard, and he always had a sweetmeat or two to bring the children. In truth, the sixty-year-old earl was feeling his age and tiring of endless conflict. He was happy to relinquish power to his ambitious, capable son, Warwick.

"Is all well at the Erber?" Cecily asked, "or is this merely a social visit?"

"The latter, Cis." He turned to York. "I was dining with John Wenlock and heard an intriguing story that I simply had to regale you with."

"Please tell me that Margaret of Anjou drowned on her way to Scotland," York said, wryly. "I fear we shall not rest until she has expired. Word came that she had left Harlech."

"Nay, I know nothing more, except that Northumberland has been making mischief for us on the border, which is a little too close to the queen for comfort. If they join forces…"

"…'tis unlikely, brother. Now what is your tale?"

"It seems that as the Commons sat in the abbey's refectory arguing about the legality of your claim, the chandelier that is shaped like a crown loosed its chain and fell with an almighty crash in the middle of the floor, those present leaping aside to avoid it. "

The God-fearing York family all crossed themselves in unison, and Dickon muttered: "…'s nails!" which earned him a frown from his mother.

"'A portent for the house of Lancaster perhaps' one man had whispered, and a good omen for us," Salisbury concluded.

"Extraordinary!" York exclaimed.

"Poor Henry," Cecily said, feeling genuinely sorry for the innocent king.

When the talk turned to politics and armies, Dickon got bored. "George, I am going exploring," he whispered. "Will you come?"

George, for once paying attention to his elders, snapped, "Go and play by yourself."

Cecily, sensing her youngest's restlessness, gave an imperceptible nod toward the door and smiled at her son. There were times he was grateful to be small enough to slip easily from a room unnoticed.

He wandered down one of the long corridors that led away from the royal apartments, and the guards he encountered at strategic points grinned at him. "Having a look round, young 'un?" one said. "That way goes to the queen's chapel. 'Tis a wonder to behold, I have heard."

Arriving at a door that was more ornate than the others, the young York prince tried not to look lost. Two more burly guards with halberds stood to attention and bowed their heads.

"Can I go in?" Dickon asked timidly. "Your friend back there said it is 'a wonder.'"

The two men glanced at each other, their York livery making them more disposed to granting the young lord's request. "He be in there a long time," one of them said. "Could be 'e be done 'is interminable praying and has gone back to 'is chamber by the side door."

"Too true," his comrade grumbled. "And we get stuck out 'ere for hours when 'e's never even in there. 'Ere, take a peak and tell us if 'e be gone, there's a good lad." He gentled the latch open and pushed the heavy door ajar.

Dickon sidled in and saw instantly to whom the men were referring. "The king," he squeaked, and was about to turn and flee when Henry turned round from his cushion by the altar rail and spied him. It was too late to run, and the guards had hurriedly closed the door for fear of a reprimand. Much to Dickon's relief the king rose, smiling.

"Come here, young man. 'Tis Lord Richard, York's son, is it not?" he asked, a warmth in his voice not heard on that day in the Star Chamber. Dickon managed a low bow, then went on his knees before his king.

Henry shook his head sadly. "I remember you from Ludlow. Such a terrible day, and you saw such horror that no child should have to see. I pitied you and your brother and sister, although your mother showed extreme courage." Then he wagged his finger, "Ah! And now, I recall seeing you in the gallery at Westminster..." but his eyes clouded as he thought back to the Act of Accord, and his next comment was almost inaudible, "... on that dreadful day."

Dickon peeked up at the king who was staring down at him absently. The warm brown eyes reassured Dickon and he felt it safe to speak. "Aye, I was there, Your Grace, and I, too, swore my allegiance. If it please you, I am Richard Plantagenet. But my friends call me Dickon."

The lad's naturalness disarmed Henry, whose long face broke into a weary smile. "Well then, Dickon, if you are my loyal subject, come and keep me company. My conversations with our Maker are rather one-sided, although they do give me comfort." He sat in a pew and patted the seat next to him. "I hope you say your prayers each night."

Dickon hopped up and sat companionably beside the king. "Oh, aye, Your Grace. Every night. Mother would be very cross if I didn't." But then, not receiving a reply, Dickon lapsed into silence.

Henry noticed a likeness between father and this son that he found oddly reassuring. The hulking Edward of March had none of his father's fine features, but there were mannerisms that Henry recognized as York's. Henry was a little afraid of Edward, even though the eighteen-year-old had shown him nothing but respect in their rare meetings, perhaps because the young earl seemed to possess all the kingly attributes he himself was lacking: charisma; a striking physique; Plantagenet soldierly skill; brash confidence; and the ability, even at so young an age, to draw men to him. In one of his breaks with reality, Henry had clearly seen a vision of Edward wearing the coronation robes and being acclaimed by cries of "God save the king." He had never forgotten it.

"Do you think your brother will make a good king?" The question seemed to Dickon to come from nowhere, but to Henry it was perfectly logical, although he forgot he was speaking to a child.

"Ned?" Dickon queried, puzzled. "He is the best brother in the world—and the best soldier, after Father that is," he said, remembering to be loyal. "I think you mean Father, Your Grace, because Ned won't be king, will he? You have to die first and then Father will take your place. I know Father would be a good king," he hesitated, "but do you?"

Henry was astonished. The boy was certainly no clotpole and he deserved an answer. "Aye, I believe York would make a good one," he admitted reluctantly. If the truth be told, Henry wished he had never awakened from the bout with madness five years earlier that had left the government no choice but to ask Richard of York to be protector. Richard had accomplished the task well, Henry had later learned, but York never had a chance to prove his worth with Henry, for once Henry's sanity had returned, the duke had been immediately ousted by the queen and her sycophant counselors. Henry had no personal quarrel with York, but he could not deny his wife's fear or hatred of the man, and so the duke became their enemy.

As was this child, he thought sadly, observing the small innocent boy sitting with him. The saintly Henry could not help but cross himself as he thought, *Dear God, what kind of world is it we live in where even a child is an enemy?*

"Always be glad you are the fourth son, Dickon," Henry suddenly said. "It means you need never be king." Then his eyes moistened, and he said more gently, "'Tis a curse and a responsibility that is too heavy for one man. I am no God, although sometimes I must act as though I am." He shuddered. He thought of all the deaths he had caused, whether in battle or on the scaffold, and was certain he was destined for hell.

"What I mean to say is I have much to answer for as king, and it troubles me every minute of every day. 'Tis why I am here on my knees so much, praying for forgiveness from God."

Dickon heard the deep sorrow and remorse in Henry's voice, and, young as he was, he was greatly moved. Then when he saw tears in the king's eyes, his sympathetic heart wanted to comfort Henry but he dared not reach out to touch the long delicate fingers. They sat in silence for a few moments both contemplating the responsibilities of kingship.

Henry gave a long sigh. "Forsooth and forsooth," he went on, using his favorite expression, "how I wish I had not been born a king."

"Father always said that too—that he never wanted to be king. And neither do I," Richard declared. "It just does not seem to bring happiness, in truth, only trouble."

"You are quite philosophical for your age, are you not, Dickon?" Henry said, pulling himself together and brightening. "You must please your tutors greatly—or do you exasperate them?"

Dickon took this for a compliment, although he was not sure what philoso...whatever it was, meant. "I try, your grace," he countered, at which Henry gave such an extraordinary guffaw it startled Dickon until he realized the king was laughing. Then he laughed too and felt brave enough to confide, "And I am not good at Latin."

This caused Henry to turn serious again. "Read your scripture every day, and you will soon learn," the king said. "God's word in Latin is easier to understand than Caesar's Gallic Wars—and a lot less violent. Aye, I had to study all of that, too."

"But I want to learn to be a knight," Dickon said eagerly. "Father says I have a good eye for hitting the target with my arrow. He says I might go to my lord of Warwick's household to learn knightly skills. Doesn't that sound wonderful, Your Grace? Although," and he leaned in to whisper, "I am a little afraid of going into battle."

"I am too," Henry admitted, "but don't tell anyone." However, on sensing the boy's enthusiasm for being a solider, he added: "Although learning to be a knight is a noble goal, it is one that comes with a heavy price. You seem like a good boy, and you certainly have a quick wit. The Church has need of clever men, and younger sons often become churchmen. Do you remember your Uncle Beaufort?" Henry stared over Dickon's shoulder as though he could see the brilliant cardinal-politician who had guided his younger self for so many years. "How I miss him." He sighed so deeply that Dickon was afraid the king might weep again.

"The Church, Your Grace?" Dickon tried not to show disappointment. "But I'd prefer to be a knight."

"Some bishops do put on armor and go into battle, you know," Henry said, smiling. "So perhaps you might become a bishop-knight one day."

"Truly?" Dickon was thoughtful. He stared at the constant movement of the rosary between the king's fingers against the plain brown garb and well worn book of hours on his lap, and he suddenly blurted: "Is that what you would have liked to have been instead of king, Your Grace? A bishop?"

Henry put his fingers to his lips. "Forsooth and forsooth, you have the measure of me, Dickon, but it shall be our secret."

"Cross my heart and hope to die," came the boy's awed response.

"Before you go, Dickon, I must ask you something. Will you pray for me, even though we are supposed to be enemies?"

Dickon nodded vigorously. "I will pray for you gladly, Your Grace, but I hope we don't really become enemies."

Henry patted his hand. "I hope we don't either."

Dickon slipped off the pew to his knees and clasped his hands in prayer. Quietly, the king followed, and the two heads bowed reverently as Dickon's boyish soprano began reciting, *"Pater noster, ..."* and he was joined by the king's deep bass, now resonant in the beloved prayer, *"qui es in caelis..."*

After intoning the *amen*, Dickon said shyly, "I prayed we could be friends. Do you think we could?" Seeing Henry nod, he added, "That could be our other secret. In truth, I have need of a friend, and now that we have shared two secrets...."

Henry put his finger to his lips. "They are ours to keep forever. May God bless you, Dickon of York."

A vacant expression on his plain face, Henry watched the lad scurry away. How he wished the others in the boy's family were as easy to like.

Not long after the Yorks removed to Baynard's, a servant of the king's came to Baynard's Castle to deliver a gift to the young Lord Richard. As his family looked on, Dickon loosed the strings of the azure velvet pouch and reverently drew out a small but beautifully bound book, each page more elaborately illustrated than the next in dazzling gold, blue, red and green. Dickon looked up in amazement at his father and mother, who were watching curiously. "What is it?" York asked.

"A psalter, my lord," Dickon said, equally puzzled. "The king has sent me a psalter."

"If it please your lordship," the messenger said quickly, "but his grace our sovereign lord, also asked me to give you this." He handed Dickon a folded parchment.

Admiring the neat script, Dickon read aloud: "To my new friend Dickon. Please accept this gift to help you with your Latin. It was mine as a child." It was signed Henry R, with his distinctive curling tails on the "h" and "y."

Richard of York frowned. "What is this all about, young man? When did you see the king?"

Dickon grinned, hugging the book to him. "Recently, in the chapel, Father. And we became fast friends," he said airily, leaving his parents to exchange puzzled looks. "Oh, but," he caught himself, "it's supposed to be our secret."

A few days later, while racing Ambergris along the vast corridors of Westminster, Dickon turned a corner and collided with his father.

"Look where you are going!" Richard of York barked, thinking it was a servant, but on seeing his chastened son's hangdog expression, he chuckled as a long-ago memory popped into his head. Crouching down to the boy's level, he said: "Did I ever tell you about the first time your mother and I met?"

Dickon shook his head, his trepidation forgotten. In truth, he had always been more afraid of his mother than his father, her presence more frequent in the nursery, often to discipline one or another of the siblings. Even Margaret had not escaped the occasional slap for a transgression.

"Then let me tell you about it, but first, let us go somewhere warm. This palace is too drafty for a conversation, don't you think?" And so, with Dickon's small hand catching his, father and son went in search of the firelit sanctuary of York's office.

"The day I arrived at Raby—your grandfather Ralph of Westmoreland's home—your mother almost knocked me down with her reckless riding. That was quite an introduction. I was twelve and she your age, and—don't tell anyone this," putting his finger to his lips, "she was dressed like a boy."

Dickon's eyes were wide as he plopped onto a cushion. "B...but, isn't that forbidden?"

"Ssh, Dickon, God might hear," York whispered, albeit impressed by his son's liturgical knowledge. He grinned. "Besides she no longer does that," and he was heartened to see his usually serious son burst into merry laughter.

"Mother in braies? In truth, my lord, 'tis hard to imagine." Dickon could hardly believe his good fortune in having privileged private time with his father. And he took advantage of it. As children are wont, he never tired of gleaning any tidbit of his father's life. "Why did you go to live with mother's family so young?"

And so Dickon learned again the story of his paternal grandfather's treason and execution, and his grandmother's untimely death that left their five-year-old son alone. Dickon heard what it had been like to be an orphan until Richard of York had felt welcomed into Ralph Neville's family. "I was Ralph's ward and was treated with utmost kindness, and it was not long before he arranged the marriage between me and your mother. And, as you know, we have lived happily ever after." He grinned to himself knowing he was leaving out the many ups and downs of a marriage no matter how happy.

York was not prepared for the barrage of questions with which his son peppered him next. He was beginning to regret inviting the lad into his sanctuary, although he could not help feeling proud of Dickon's agile young mind.

"Father, all of these things have been puzzling me. Why is the king a prisoner, when he can walk about Westminster when he wants? Why is the queen somewhere else and not with him? Can a woman lead an army? If the king is not governing, why don't you take over? If your cause is just, why do people oppose you?" Dickon stopped to take a breath.

York held up his hand, laughing. "Sweet Virgin, do your questions ever stop? I can tell you that the king is not a prisoner; he is watched for his own protection. The queen is probably gathering an army somewhere in the wilds of Scotland, and we shall not worry about her until the time comes. And Queen Margaret has indeed led an army in her black armor, but she quickly retreats to the back as soon as any fighting starts. Ladies are not strong enough to wield a sword, my child, and they are better off looking after the home while their men are away fighting. That is a much more useful and necessary function for them." Cecily would praise him for that, he told himself. "And I cannot take over governing until Henry dies. I swore an oath, although I think I would be a better king."

"King Henry thinks so, too," Dickon remarked, and then covered his mouth.

York raised an eyebrow. "Does he indeed? Well, I think he is right. As for why I am opposed, it is because there are those in power now who know they would lose it if I were to be king. They have led the king astray and I would dismiss them. There now, are you satisfied?"

"Aye, my lord Father," Dickon said gratefully. He hugged his knees savoring the moment, but then noticing a large chart on the wall in front of him, he jumped up and pointed. "That is England and we are here," he said touching London. "And that is Normandy across the Narrow Sea. Have you been there, Father? Did you fight the French?"

York joined him and nodded. "For as long as England has been England, the French have been our enemies. Normandy has been joined to England since the Conqueror's time, but little by little the French have encroached on our territory until good king Harry the Fifth won it all back at Agincourt." Dickon's eyes shone at the mention of the great English victory, and he followed York's trailing finger across the chart to Rouen. "Your sister Bess and Edward and Edmund were all born there," he said. "I was Normandy's governor once, but I was then sent away to govern Ireland, where George was born." His mouth tightened into a thin line as he stared at the map. "Normandy should still belong to England. It was lost forever by this feeble Henry, his incompetent ministers, and his meddling queen."

Dickon had been taught how a weak king was a bad king, and he paused before pushing for a question that had been niggling him. "Surely King Henry is not your enemy, Father? He is my friend, and I think he is a good man."

York harrumphed. "Aye, too good. And easy for an ambitious woman to manipulate."

"Is that Queen Margaret?"

"Aye, she has been called She-wolf for her callous disregard for life," York said. "She is my bitterest enemy."

Dickon was confused. "Is she my enemy, too? And the king? What has he done to me? I like him."

York took Dickon by the shoulders. "By all that is holy, he is not my enemy. He is my king and as far as God knows, I have been loyal to him. But Margaret of Anjou turned the king against me, Dickon, and I can never forgive her."

"Is she French?" he whispered, now concerned by his father's seriousness. "Is that why she's your enemy?"

York pointed to a small province on the map. "Her father was duke of Anjou. The Angevin kings of France came from there—as did our own Henry II—and so Margaret is of an old royal French family, but she is not my enemy because of that." He was silent for a moment as he remembered the first time he set eyes on the fifteen-year-old put into his care for part of her journey to England to marry Henry. "By the Virgin, but she was beautiful," he muttered. "Spoiled and beautiful. But she was thought to be an excellent match for Henry—a political pawn in the game of thrones," he said bitterly and returned to his chair. "You will learn how important a wife can be, Dickon. Your mother was the best choice for me."

Dickon pressed on, thinking he might not have another chance like this. Boldly, he asked: "Will you arrange my marriage when I am older? I know I must not marry beneath me."

York chuckled. "Indeed it is high time your mother and I made provisions for all of you. Ned most certainly should marry soon—he needs to settle down. But the lady has to bring power and wealth with her. We must choose carefully for him." He looked at the intent young face taking all this in and decided not to complicate things further by mentioning love. He rose to end the interview. "Don't worry, lad, your turn will come, but I have more important matters to tend to at present. I will think on a suitable match for Edward in the New Year," he said airily, as if nothing could possibly stop that from happening; after all 1461 was only a few weeks away.

"And now, young Dickon, if you have no more questions, I must attend yet another tedious meeting, much as I enjoyed our little talk. I hope you did, too?"

Dickon solemnly shook his father's hand. "With all my heart," he said.

In early December, York was tasked with riding north and bringing order there. In London, a calm had taken hold of the city after the surprising turn of events in the matter of the succession in October. It was a deceptive calm. The Yorkist council was well aware that Queen Margaret was gathering with her allies over the border in Scotland, and they knew the She-wolf would not allow her cub to lose the throne without a fight. But when word reached London that Henry Percy, duke of Northumberland, was raising an army and spreading false rumors about Richard of York, Parliament had had enough. A show of force was needed to keep order and more important, prevent the Percies from joining the queen. Richard was deemed the man for the task.

Once again, Edmund would go with his father, while Edward was being sent west to the Welsh marches where the king's half-brother Jasper Tudor was brandishing his sword in support of the queen. Salisbury, too, would go with York, leaving Warwick to help govern in London. All knew the Londoners trusted Warwick—if they trusted anyone at all. In truth, Londoners were in an enviable position whether they knew it or not; they ruled themselves, and it was up to the king to treat with them or not. The Yorkists ruled the parliament but Lancastrian Henry was still the king for now. Holding many of the country's purse strings, bankers and merchants played a waiting game.

Family farewells were beginning to be a normal part of Dickon's life, but this one was far too soon after the reunion of September, he decided. It didn't seem fair, but then he was learning that life wasn't always fair.

Edmund lifted Richard off the ground to say goodbye and gave him a kiss, admonishing him to stop fighting with George and obey Meg. "When I come back, I shall expect you to hit the bullseye with two out of every three arrows. Do you promise to practice?"

"Put me down, Edmund," Dickon said crossly. "I am not a baby, I'm eight years old. And by the time you return, I shall be hitting the bullseye every single time *and* besting George with a shortsword."

"There is someone with fighting spirit," Richard of York remarked as he led his horse forward to the mounting block. Dickon flushed with pleasure. "It will not be long before you and George will be riding with us." He squatted down and tousled Dickon's hair. "Look after your mother for me while I am gone. You, too, George," he said, pulling his older boy into an awkward embrace. He loved all his children—especially Meggie, with whom he had already had a tearful goodbye. As well, the troops close by had already enjoyed seeing the passionate embrace of their lord and lady at the top of the staircase from the great hall half an hour earlier.

"Tell me, before I go, if you remember what is most important in this life, after loving a merciful God?" he asked his youngest sons.

"Our loyalty to England, the king and to our house of York," they chorused, and Richard nodded, pleased.

"And what is most dishonorable?"

"Betrayal of family and friends," Dickon piped up, eager for evidence of his father's approval.

"Well said, Dickon." Richard stood up.

"I knew that," George hissed at his brother, annoyed at his own hesitation. "Come, I'll beat you to the top," and he made for the spiral gatehouse staircase with Dickon in hot pursuit, George's new dog, Alaris, bounding between them and almost causing a catastrophe.

Standing on the flat roof, they watched the departure of the duke of York's retinue now marshaled into an orderly line in Baynard's courtyard. Cecily was already there with Meg by her side, her sable mantle wrapping her against a biting December wind. The boys ran from side to side, excited to see the knights, foot soldiers, horses, weapons carts, and even a cannon or two lined up to head north, or west with Edward. They would join the larger contingent of Yorkist forces camped outside the city walls.

"Who would you go with, if you had the chance: Father or Ned?" George asked his brother, at the same time making Alaris sit. "I'd go with Father. Ned's good fun, but Father is an experienced commander. I'd feel safer with him."

Dickon gazed down on his oldest brother's golden-red head, ramrod-straight and mailed figure riding tall in his saddle, shouting cheerful greetings to his men, and he knew in a moment of wisdom beyond his years that he would follow Ned for ever. "I'd choose Ned," he said solemnly. Then with an impish grin, he said, "If only to get away from you!" And he ran across to the other side of the parapet to avoid a jab to the ribs.

"Beast!" George laughed, running after him. They tussled in play briefly, the dog barking in excitement, before Cecily called a halt.

"By all that is holy, boys, can you not stop your rough-housing even for an hour and bid your father and brothers a dignified adieu?" As soon as the word left her lips, she choked, and turned it into "farewell."

"Goodbye Father! Farewell Ned and Edmund!" the boys shouted, leaning dangerously over the low wall. Cecily smiled her thanks as Meg hauled them back with a sisterly admonition. Edward blew a kiss to Cecily before signaling his retainers to follow him out of the courtyard and through the gate into Thames Street.

Then it was Richard's turn to depart, and Cecily took out her miniature version of the white rose banner and waved it in farewell as he preceded Salisbury and Edmund on their magnificent coursers through the archway beneath her. Richard lifted his sword to her and kissed its hilt, and Cecily stifled a sob. Saying goodbye to her husband had not eased one jot over the years.

"Farewell, Edmund," Meg called, and the boyish, fair-haired earl of Rutland looked up and waved at his sister. Dickon noticed his brother looked sad when his eye fell on his beloved mother. Edmund's hand over his heart seemed to have touching effect on Cecily, who placed her hand on her breast in answer. The gesture was all Edmund needed to know: *Aye, son, you do have my blessing,* and he smiled.

"Will Father have to fight?" Dickon asked as those siblings left behind clustered around their mother. "And Ned?"

"We must pray hard that the queen is sensible and does not provoke a fight, my son," Cecily replied. "Your father hopes that just by showing her his army, she will give up and go back to Scotland. Then your father and Edmund can come home safely again, God willing."

All four family members crossed themselves as they watched the last of the soldiers march from view.

Chapter Six
Winter 1460–61

It was yuletide, and even with his father and brothers away, Dickon was caught up in holiday preparations, including watching the huge yule log towed behind a horse across the snowy courtyard from the forests beyond London's eastern gate. Cecily had promised herself that those left at Baynard's would make as merry as they could during this festive season. She was as good as her word, and even Elizabeth, duchess of Suffolk, had traveled from Framlingham to join in the festivities.

A kind-hearted young woman, Lizzie's presence greatly cheered Margaret, and the two sisters were often seen arm-in-arm and tête-à-tête about the castle. She had hardly recognized the boys as it had been several years since she had seen them, and Dickon had no memory of her at all. He enjoyed her extraordinary yet infectious neighing laugh—the female mirror of their father's, and Lizzie's sunny nature was such that she often laughed, creating an atmosphere of jollity in the duchess's solar.

The relentless river wind whistled through the passageways of Baynard's that December, and even in front of a crackling fire, the family used mantles and shawls for extra warmth. "God help them in the north," Cecily said to Gresilde. "I have heard they are celebrating yuletide at Sandal Castle, a drafty place even in the summer, and blanketed in snow in the winter. My only consolation is that the queen and her foreign horde can be faring no better on the border. After the abominable summer and bad harvest, I wonder what our troops had to feast on for Christmas. The village of Wakefield cannot feed an army, God knows, and we do not have much even here in London."

One late afternoon as the twilight caused eerie shadows from the fire to flicker around the walls of the solar and Elizabeth brayed at one of Meg's whispered comments, George declared: "I miss Father."

"We all do, George," Cecily said, softly. "And we all miss Ned and Edmund, too."

"I miss Piers Taggett," Dickon said suddenly, and all heads turned in his direction. Dickon flushed. *Why did I say that?* he admonished himself. Would he be faced with retelling his grisly dream of the night before and be humiliated? It was the same recurring nightmare, always ending with the blood-soaked Piers falling into his arms. He had not owned up to having one since leaving Maxstoke in the spring and had learned to wake himself up somehow, lie in the dark—George snoring lightly beside him—and talk himself out of being afraid, with his father absent again.

A shadow flitted over Cecily's face at the mention of Piers, and she put down her needlework. Her youngest son puzzled her; he was a secretive little soul, albeit so loyal and eager to please, and she was surprised Dickon would remember the falconer after all this time. Piers's name reminded her of the greater loss of her beloved Constance that day in Ludlow, as if her daily prayer for the soul of her friend weren't reminder enough. "Whatever made you think of Piers?"

Dickon thought quickly. "When you mentioned Father, I thought of him and his soldiers up there at Sandal and ready to fight and it reminded me of the queen's soldiers at Ludlow and that reminded me of the king at the market cross and that reminded me of ..."

"We follow you, babble-mouth," George muttered under his breath, sensing his mother was close to tears. "No one wants to be reminded of Ludlow, so why don't you go and play with your marbles?" Then he gave Cecily his disarming smile. "Mother, I pray you," he coaxed, "can I interest you in a game of chess?"

"Gladly, dear child," Cecily replied, Dickon forgotten.

"You had another bad dream, didn't you?" Meg whispered to Dickon. "I had them when I was your age. They will go away one day, have no fear." She was wrong; she could not imagine how soon her own would return.

She put her arm around him, and he snuggled into her. Although she favored George for reasons unknown, Margaret had never been unfriendly to Dickon. She admired his stoicism and his ability to forgive George, but he was still a baby. Now she attempted to cheer him. "Do you wonder what gift we shall receive on the morrow? 'Tis the feast of the Circumcision, you know," she said. England had long abandoned the Roman tradition of celebrating the New Year on the first day of January and sensibly returned it to the vernal equinox, but the customary gift-giving of olden days had remained.

He knew he ought to wish for his father's safe return, but he was a boy with a more material dream. "A new longbow," he told his sister, adding proudly: "Master Blaybourne says I am too big now for my present one." Cecily had always measured her children at Christmas, and this year Dickon had grown two inches and George only an inch, a fact that had greatly relieved Dickon. "And you, Meg?" He grinned. "What a silly question. I would venture to guess you want a book."

"You read me like one, brother," Meg agreed, smiling.

She was not disappointed, and neither was George with his exquisite pair of kid gloves.

"Look, Dickon," George exclaimed, putting one on, "are they not handsome?"

But Dickon did not receive his wish. Perhaps she had misheard him, for instead of a bow Cecily gave him a large wooden bowl, "for putting your keepsakes in," she told him, equably. "Look, it has your initials carved in the bottom."

Dickon tried not to show disappointment as he cradled the bowl in his lap and stared at it. After all, he had been taught to be grateful for any gift no matter how small. "I thank you, Mam," he said so quietly, Cecily did not hear.

"What did you say, Dickon?" Her tone sounded irritable, so Dickon tried again.

"Th…thank you, Mother. It is a very useful bowl." He was chagrined to see George showing off his soft blue gloves to Meg and Lizzie and knew that his bowl paled by comparison. Well, what could he expect? After all, he was nobody's favorite.

"I think you had better go to your room and find things to put into your bowl, my lad," Cecily said sternly, "so I do not have to look at your disgruntled face. Run along now."

Dickon did as he was told, but he was puzzled to hear laughter from behind the door he had just closed. He hurried to his chamber, grateful to escape, but when he pushed open the door, he gave a startled cry as a gray behemoth bounded off the tester bed, knocked him on his backside and dislodged the new bowl from his hands. The young wolfhound then proceeded to give Dickon's face a thorough washing with its long, rough tongue. As he tried to sit up, Dickon knew this dog was not Ned's Ambergris nor George's Alaris, but all the same he tried the universal canine command, "Down, sir!" And immediately the dog quietened and lowered its lanky haunches to the floor in front of the astonished Dickon. "Traveller?" he said in disbelief, "Is it you?" Upon hearing its name, the dog's head tilted to one side and the long tail thumped an assent.

"*Tiens!* At last you have come, Master Dickon," Nurse Anne said, bustling in from an adjacent room. "I do not like the dogs on the bed, *tu comprends?*" she grumbled. "Her Grace tell me keep the monster here until you come. She say it was *une surprise. Nom de Dieu*, it was a surprise for *me!* And, too, I could not keep him from the bed."

Dickon gave the servant half an ear but was otherwise engaged in hugging the noble head and neck of his beloved abandoned dog from Fotheringhay. With all the family upheaval, he had never dared to ask for Traveller. It did not seem important, but during those eighteen months he had often wished for his dog. He had given up hope altogether when Ned had found Alaris abandoned and had given him to George. When Dickon had asked George if he didn't feel unfaithful to Captain, George had laughed. "It's just a dog, Dickon. Do you truly believe they would remember us now?"

"Dogs are the most faithful of creatures," Dickon had shot back, "and they never forget somebody's scent. I am sure my Traveller would know me."

"Pah!" George had been scornful and quickly transferred his allegiance to Alaris.

Traveller was now proving Dickon right, however, as the dog responded to Dickon's touch and leaned into his master. "What a beauty you have become. Are you really mine?" Dickon asked, half expecting the dog to respond.

His mother answered instead. "Indeed he is, my son." Her voice came from the threshold. "And the bowl is for his food. I am sorry I tricked you. Happy New Year, Dickon!"

She was rewarded by a sudden rush of love that flooded her as her youngest son's slate-gray eyes spoke volumes of gratitude.

No bad dreams interrupted Dickon's sleep for the next few nights, and his days were spent in the company of his new canine friend.

For once, George seemed genuinely happy for Dickon's good fortune. "At least Dickon doesn't follow me around all day now," he confided to Meg as they strolled for exercise around Baynard's impressive great hall, the early January sleet keeping them indoors. "Instead, he now knows what it feels to have someone dogging his heels. Oh," he exclaimed, pleased with himself, "that was clever, don't you think? I have to admit, Dickon is getting better at wrestling, though, and I think Father will be happy with his progress at the butts."

They watched as Dickon tirelessly taught Traveller to fetch a ball, his determination evident in his jutting chin. "When he sets his mind to something, there is no backing down," Meg observed. "I do wish he could learn to yield sometimes, or he will lose friendships when he is older."

"Aye, and he should stop always reminding people of what is right. It tends to ruin any amusement."

"You mean when he said you should return that poor stablehand's only boots you stole when the boy was told to muck out a stall?" Meg retorted. "Dickon was right to be indignant on his behalf. 'Twas unkind of you, in truth."

George chuckled. "I know, Meggie, but it was amusing just the same."

Meg cocked her head. "Can you hear bells? It sounds like tolling and not the usual calling to mass. Has someone died?" She gave an involuntary shiver.

All of a sudden Traveller dropped the ball he had just retrieved and barked. Those in the hall stopped their chatter as the others had heard horses in the courtyard. A servant ran to open the heavy oak door to let in the messenger, who was wearing the badge of the ragged staff on his heavy cloak. It was no ordinary messenger, however, as Dickon instantly recognized their cousin, Richard Neville, earl of Warwick, and gave him reverence. Usually affable, he paid Dickon scant heed today—although anyone standing close to him would have noticed that his grim face softened when he saw the children's expectant faces. "Where is the steward?" he barked. "Tell him I must speak with Her Grace immediately."

"What is it, my lord?" Cecily herself hurried in from the outer staircase, where she had seen the earl arrive. She was not the only one to have noticed the sharpness in her nephew's loud commands. Her children, huddled together sensing bad news, caught their breath seeing their stoic mother stumble as she went to greet Warwick, who reached out and caught her. "Is it the duke? Is it my husband? Has he been wounded?" she ran on. "We heard the bells…."

"Hush, my dear Aunt. Why don't you sit," Warwick said kindly, "I have much to tell you."

By now inquisitive servants had entered the hall. What with the tolling bells, the unrest in the north, and the absence of their lord, the household was more than curious: they were on edge. Aye, all of Baynard's wanted to know Warwick's news.

Cecily was helped to a bench, and the earl dismissed the others with an autocratic stare and a jerk of the head towards the door. Meggie pulled her reluctant siblings to the private staircase Cecily had just descended.

"But I want to hear …" Dickon protested, resisting her. His instincts told him Warwick did not bring good news, and he felt frightened.

Meg's instinct, however, told her to protect her two young brothers from any bad tidings that their mother alone should hear from Warwick. Shushing Dickon, she pushed him up the staircase in front of her.

A whole day went by, and the mood in the castle turned somber as the reason for the tolling bells and the duchess's collapse filtered along the long passageways, into the kitchens, and through the stables and to the castle's garrison. But although the whisperings had permeated the servants' quarters, the news failed to crawl its cruel way up into the children's apartments, where they resided separately from their parents. After the three children had left the hall and Meg had bullied the boys into their chambers, only Nurse Anne and Beatrice were left to see to their needs. Gresilde and Cecily's other ladies tended to their mistress, and no one thought to inform the children of the tragedy at Wakefield.

"We shall stay here until Mother tells us otherwise," Meg instructed her brothers sternly. "So refrain from squabbling, and let us wait for her peaceably."

"What do you think is the matter?" Dickon asked. "Our cousin of Warwick did not look normal."

Meg shrugged, although she, too, had a knot in her stomach.

"You should have let us stay to listen," George complained, and Dickon heartily concurred.

"Sweet Jesu, don't you think I wish I had, too?" Meg snapped back. "Do not blame me—you saw my lord Warwick's glare. I was not about to gainsay it. I have never seen him look so forbidding." Dickon had no response to that truth and continued marshaling his toy soldiers. George went to his sister and hugged her. "You are right; you had to obey him. I wish I knew where Mother was though."

When Cecily eventually entered the cozy, fire-lit chamber in time for the late-morning meal, they were shocked by her appearance, which verified that disaster had struck the family. Gresilde helped her mistress into the high-backed arm chair and fussed with Cecily's drab, gray overdress—a color reserved for dowagers and spinsters, not their fashionable mother. Cecily's face was blotched, and her eyes—usually a blue that matched the gentian flower of her native Raby—were swollen and bloodshot. Her fingers were wringing a lace kerchief, a sign of nerves the children had never seen from their imperturbable mother before.

They guessed her news before she opened her mouth: either beloved father or Ned was dead. None of them moved until Cecily had composed herself.

"Come here, my dears," she said, tears willed away as she faced her three youngest. "Why don't you sit on the cushions. Closer, come closer." She nodded an acknowledgement to Nurse Anne and Beatrice to sit, while she kept Gresilde standing by her, the older woman's hand steadying her shoulder. Then she drew a deep breath and told them all of the Yorkist defeat at Wakefield, which would not have happened but for an inexplicable, rash maneuver on her husband's part. Giving her audience the facts was easier; it was the personal details she would have loved to avoid.

"I know no other way to give you these terrible tidings, children, except plainly. Your beloved Father was killed in the battle, and Edmund..." she

choked on his name, and Meg gave a little scream when she told them, "…
Edmund was slain fleeing the scene."

"Not Edmund," Meg stammered, as tears overwhelmed her. "N…not
sweet Edmund."

Cecily nodded bleakly. What else could she say? Instead, she reached
out her arms and caught Meg and George, who sought her comforting
embrace. Meg sobbed and George whimpered, and over their heads,
Cecily saw Dickon's face, ashen white, staring in disbelief.

"Father is d…dead?" he whispered. He tried to go to his mother, but
his legs gave way and he fell to his knees, finally releasing a wail that
clawed at Cecily's heart. George turned and took his brother's thin,
shaking body into his arms and rocked him like a baby, a simple gesture
that finally undid Cecily, and, unashamed, she allowed her own tears to
darken Meggie's golden hair.

It was not until Cecily had fully recovered that she told her children the
details of their father's and brother's ends. As any mother knows, the
unknown is more fearful for children than the known, and Cecily was not
foolish enough to think Meggie, George and Dickon would be spared the
rumors, lies and fantastical imaginings that would be circulating about the
events at Wakefield.

Meg showed quiet anger at her father's demeaning death, and Cecily
admired her daughter's composure. How grown up she suddenly seemed,
and it filled Cecily with sadness that Richard would not see his favorite
daughter grow into womanhood. How Richard would have been proud
of her, Cecily thought. Anyone but Cecily might have recognized her own
indomitable spirit in Margaret, but Cecily was not so vainglorious as to
acknowledge it.

The boys too listened with mingled horror and grief to the the story
of the paper crown that was mockingly placed on Richard's head before
he was beheaded. Later, there came the impaling of the Yorkist leaders'
heads upon York's Micklegate. As though those scenes were not enough
to horrify the children, their reaction was mild compared to the terror and
outrage they expressed upon hearing of their brother's vile murder while
fleeing the battle.

"Edmund hid beneath a bridge but the soldiers found him and dragged
him out to face that devil's spawn Lord Clifford." Meg gave a little cry,

and George plugged his ears, but Cecily thought it best not to spare her offspring; it was the only way to prepare them for what life was really like. "Edmund pleaded for his life, as did poor, dear Master Apsall. What could a tutor do to defend them both, I ask you?" Why had Richard allowed the old man on the battlefield at all, she wondered. "Such senseless slaughter of innocents!" she exclaimed.

Dickon had buried his head in a cushion by this time, his mother's words conjuring the young billman who had expired in his arms at Ludlow from his hideous wounds. Dear, kind Edmund had died like that, Dickon realized, and so might he one day. He muttered a muffled, "Nay, say no more," but Cecily was relentless and could not stop now. "'Twas the cowardly Clifford's own hand that thrust the knife into your brother's innocent heart, declaring, 'This is for my father whom your father slew at St. Alban's.' And then he dispensed Master Apsall in like manner. What kind of man kills a defenseless boy and an old man?"

She did not accuse her husband outright in front of his children for allowing Edmund to fight. However, she would never stop blaming him for taking Edmund north. He was only seventeen, she kept repeating to herself. Her son's brutal death would haunt her dreams all through her long life.

The growing list of violent deaths in his family circle caused Dickon to spend long hours by himself with only Traveller for company. He pondered mostly the vengeful murder of Edmund by Lord Clifford's son. Neither had met the other before, Dickon knew, and yet John Clifford hated Edmund enough to kill him in cold blood to avenge his father's death. For five years the younger Clifford had nursed this animus and sought revenge. Was Ned now bound to go and kill Lord Clifford, Dickon wondered. Was he, Dickon, expected to carry on the blood feud? He tried to imagine himself saying, "And this is for my brother!" but could not.

The bigger question that confounded the boy was why Englishmen were fighting Englishmen? His military studies had taught him about fighting foreign foes, like King Harry had at Agincourt, the Black Prince at Crecy, even Caesar against the Gauls. But then he recalled learning about the Barons' wars in England two hundred years before, and about Stephen and Mathilda—he could not remember when. What was the term his tutor had used? Civil war—was that it?

Indeed it was, for if no one that autumn had publicly acknowledged a civil war was imminent, the battle of Wakefield confirmed it had begun.

The knowledge suddenly conveyed an awful truth to Dickon: his friend King Henry was now truly his enemy.

It was predictable that his father's and brother's deaths gave Dickon new nightmares, but he had become adept at waking himself before disturbing Nurse Anne or George. Trembling, he would lie in a cold sweat and will the grisly image of Edmund, his throat slashed and blood gushing, to dissolve with the help of prayers to the Holy Mother.

"Why do they put heads upon the city gates?" he had asked his father once. "It is a horrible sight, and suppose a boy like me sees his father's head there. 'Tis barbaric," he declared, pleased to be able to use a word he had learned the meaning of from one of Caesar's descriptions of barbarians.

"'Tis the custom to display the heads of traitors, Dickon. It reminds others they should not betray their king or country," Richard of York had explained. Then he added quietly, "I agree with you though. It is barbaric."

And now it had happened to his father, his brother, and his uncle. It was almost too much for him to bear, and thus he forced his thoughts down more rational pathways—a trick he was to use many times in his life. He knew his kin were not traitors, and he wept to think of these beloved men so cruelly treated. He could not bring himself to hate King Henry, because in his heart he knew that gentle man would not have ordered such a monstrous thing. It must have been the She-wolf, Dickon determined; it must have been that woman in black armor who has fangs like the beast she is named for. Margaret of Anjou now became the object of his hatred.

Saving his tears for solitary walks upon the ramparts, only Traveller was witness to them as the unhappy boy wrestled with his grief and human conflicts far too complex for his comprehension, though he did his best to understand.

When it was his sister's screams and not his own fear that awoke him one night, Dickon crept out of bed to investigate.

No one saw him slip into the room and hide behind the chair. Cecily, roused from a deep sleep by Beatrice, was sitting atop the downy bed and consoling her daughter. "Tell me about it, my dear," Cecily soothed. "'Tis not so bad if you talk about it. And it will not come to pass if you do."

"But it already has," Meg said on another loud sob. "Please take these terrible dreams away."

Dickon knew just what Meg meant. He wanted to leap on the bed and share in his mother's consolation, but he stayed silent, recognizing that tonight it was Meggie's turn.

"You know why your father and your brother died, Meg. They died to right a wrong done to our house, and your father knew full well the price we all might have to pay. 'Tis the price all those born of royal blood are in danger of paying. My dearest Edmund paid it, and you, too, must learn to sacrifice for your family—whether it be the house of York or that of whomever you wed..."

Sacrifice? The ominous word evoked for Dickon Abraham's son Isaac tied down on an altar on a mountaintop in some far desert land, staring in abject terror at the knife his father held poised ready to plunge into the boy's heart. As those biblical stories were supposed to do, it had put the fear of God into Dickon at too early and impressionable an age. He had never forgotten it.

So, he thought now, had Edmund been the sacrifice for his family? Their father had insisted his untried son must do his duty and fight, and Edmund had wanted to go—Dickon had heard him say it—but how much of his brave speech had been real and how much had been about not disappointing his father? The quick-witted boy now understood how often all of them had tried to please their father—even Edward. Who would they look to please now? He glanced up at his mother, always so self-assured, but she was his Mam, and he minded and adored her, but he instinctively knew he could never disappoint her. Whereas his lord father... he shuddered. His lord father was now having his eyes pecked out by crows and his face eaten away by maggots atop the Micklegate.

The gory image made him run all the way back to his bed before anyone could acknowledge his presence. He pulled the covers over his head and stopped his ears; but the ghastly, gory images of Piers, his father, and Edmund were blazoned in blood on his child's mind. For Dickon, his dream—and now Meggie's—only reinforced his own worst fears of dying violently, surrounded by menacing enemies, his entrails spilling out onto an already reddened battlefield.

The next day, despite the sleet outside, the sun came out briefly for the York family when a young messenger arrived with news of Ned and his army in the Welsh Marches. Dickon, George and Meg arrived in time to hear the herald say, "John Harper at Your Grace's service," as he went down on one knee before the duchess. "I have to report a great victory for Lord Edward seven days since!" he announced with relish, and a cheer rose from the assembled company. "At a place near Ludlow called Mortimer's Cross."

"I know the place," Cecily said, gripping Margaret's arm. She had been dreading news of Ned in combat, and thus her question was barely audible. "Does my son live?"

Dickon held his breath. Surely God could not be unkind enough to take Ned, too. he panicked. He closed his eyes and held his breath, sending a prayer to his favorite St. Anthony.

John Harper grinned. "Aye, he does, Your Grace."

Dickon exhaled. His imagination was fired by the tale the herald told. John Harper had a flare for drama, and as his audience grew, so did his enthusiasm for relating the thrilling details of how his master had won his first battle. It was on the feast of Candlemas, the herald said, adding that some were loath to fight upon such a holy day. "But just before the battle began, a strange happening took place that convinced our troops that Lord Edward would be victorious."

Dickon crept forward, seeing vividly the armored knights, weapons at the ready, the lines of soldiers, the ends of their long halberds planted on the ground, and Ned on his white courser riding up and down in front of them shouting encouragement. It must have been a wondrous sight, the boy thought, all nightmarish fears of dying banished for now in a view of his glorious brother in battle.

"'Twas close to ten of the clock," John Harper was saying, "and we were chafing at the bit waiting for the enemy to approach, when we noticed three suns in the sky ..."

"Three? Do not babble nonsense, man," Cecily snapped. "How can there be three suns?"

"I know not how, Your Grace, but I saw them with my own eyes. A fearful hush came over our troops and then Lord Edward turned his horse to us and cried: "'Tis the symbol of the Trinity, good faithful men—God the Father, God the Son and God the Holy Ghost! It means God is on our side! 'Tis a sign.' And we believed him then. He was so sure and so brave, and the light from the three suns shone bright on his gold-brown head, making him look like...like a young god," he cried, his voice ringing around the hall. Dickon fell to his knees and crossed himself.

Seeing Dickon on his knees triggered the natural response from the pious duchess. "My son is right," she called out, kneeling where she stood on the cold, flagged floor, "we should all give thanks." Dickon beamed at thus being praised, and he shot his mother a grateful look as the rest of the household followed his lead and Cecily's chaplain began the *te deum*.

When Cecily again stood, she addressed her steward. "Sir Henry, see to Master Harper's needs, but first, let us celebrate. Bring wine for the whole company! Our victory is sweet."

A cheer rose from the assembled retainers, whose very livelihoods were in jeopardy at this unstable time, and as the flagons of wine were passed, the shout of "A York! A York" rose in a hopeful crescendo, echoing off the hammered-beam rafters.

Dickon was thrilled to be allowed his first taste of wine, and he eagerly gulped down a mouthful as the company watched. He lifted his face in disgust. " Ugh. If victory is so sweet, my lady Mother, why does this taste so bitter?"

The Yorkist castle was gratefully relieved by the laughter that followed. Young Dickon, however, not grasping the humor, flushed with embarrassment. Cecily drew him to her and whispered: "They are not laughing *at* you, Dickon, I promise. Remember this, only the nicest people are teased."

CHAPTER SEVEN
FEBRUARY 1461

Dickon's prescient words were remembered two weeks later when the Yorkist army tasted the bitterness of defeat at the second battle of St. Alban's. Once again Dickon's life was plunged into uncertainty. He learned then how quickly the wheel of fortune turns. Not only had the all-powerful earl of Warwick lost the battle, but he had lost the king as well.

"Why did he take the king with him?" Dickon wanted to know. He was not going to betray Henry's confidence and tell Meg and George how the king hated fighting, but he was curious to know what role the king had played in Warwick's army.

"Henry is still the king, and I expect Cousin Richard thought showing him to the armies might stop the queen fighting," George said.

"Perhaps he wanted to prove that we Yorks are still loyal to our king," Meg offered.

"How could this have happened?" was the distraught Cecily's question when she heard of the defeat. Would Queen Margaret's army now sweep through London's streets burning, raping and pillaging as the earl of Warwick had described the Lancastrians' destructive march south through the English countryside. The She-wolf had never liked London, and the dislike was mutual. Never let it be said those same Londoners did not care for their king—they did; it was his wife and her counselors they despised. They had hoped the duke of York would bring about welcome change in the governing of the kingdom and bring stability to the city and its commerce—but now he was gone and they feared for their security.

In vain, Londoners had put their faith in the valiant and powerful warrior Richard Neville, earl of Warwick. So what had gone so wrong? With his superior defensive position inside the town, experienced commanders, new-fangled, sophisticated weaponry, and an army of ten thousand men, the formidable Warwick should have won a decisive victory. But in the melée of retreating Yorkists, Henry had been found laughing and singing under a tree. Perhaps his cheerful mood had reflected a thought of being reconciled with his warrior queen and their son, Edouard, prince of Wales. Or, people whispered, was it another bout of madness?

Mired in her own grief, Cecily of York had failed to notice that the loss of his father had affected her young nephew far more than he had admitted, and something of the Warwick fire had gone out of him. It seemed Richard Neville was better at planning grandiose schemes than carrying them out, and St. Alban's was the first example.

"Do you know who was the first to be knighted by Margaret's son after the battle?" Cecily was blazing now as she scanned a hasty letter sent to her by Lord Montagu, Warwick's brother, who had been captured during the battle. "That craven traitor, Andrew Trollope! If I ever get my hands on that man I'll string him up by his boll..."

"Mother!" Meg warned under her breath, dismayed by Cecily's outburst in front of servants. George and Dickon giggled. "I pray you, tell us where the queen is now? What should we do? Should we fortify the castle?"

Meg's brave reprimand took Cecily's anger off the boil, and she gave her daughter a rueful yet grateful look. "The queen must be near, and you are quite right, daughter, we should prepare ourselves for the She-wolf's entry into London. She will not waste time with courteous greetings." If the truth be told, Cecily was frightened and angry at herself for having no contingency plan in anticipation of this reversal of fortune.

She thought quickly now. Should the family take flight and leave the household to fend for themselves? Nay, that would be an act of cowardice she could not countenance, and besides she would get no mercy from the queen. *What would Richard do?* she thought. Images of Ludlow and her perilous march to the market cross flitted through her mind, but she forced herself back to the present. This time she would not leave the safety of the castle but fight for what was hers by right.

"Sir Henry, I pray you assemble the household in the courtyard within the hour, and I will address them." The man bowed and left the room. What she would say, she was not sure but her mother had always told her, "Servants do better when they have orders. They are more comfortable doing something." She would talk to the captain in charge of the small contingent of men-at-arms left behind to guard the duchess and her family. She nodded to herself. He could organize the small household in fortifying the castle; and she should send the kitchen boys out into the city to stock up on food in case of a siege.

What was she forgetting? Her eye fell on George and Dickon, watching her anxiously, and her heart stopped. Sweet Jesu, the boys! They were the most precious commodity in the castle, and they must not fall into Margaret of Anjou's hands. George was now second in line behind Edward to inherit the crown when Henry died, as had been laid out in the Act of Accord. Why had she not thought of this before? They were in extreme danger. (A more forgiving observer would have explained that her existence these past few weeks had been consumed by grief, to which Cecily would have roundly responded, "Pish!")

The wheels of her mind were turning as frantically as those that were lowering the portcullis at this moment. Where to send the boys? Anywhere north and west of London would be fraught with Lancastrian danger. Fotheringhay was too far—and they would risk running into the queen's soldiers—Elizabeth in Suffolk was a possibility, but Lizzie was expecting a child at any moment. Her other daughter, Anne, lived in Devon, but her husband was the hated duke of Exeter, one of Queen Margaret's adherents; nay, the boys would certainly not be secure there.

Sweet Mother of God, help me, she prayed fervently, looking out on the river, the small craft plying back and forth between the banks or down towards London Bridge and the larger ships in the Pool beyond readying for voyages to... and suddenly her prayer was answered. Why not send them abroad? English Calais, perhaps? But without Warwick there, could she trust that the garrison commander was loyal? She thought how lost she was without her husband, but Cecily had always undervalued her own intelligence for many of Richard's decisions had actually been made by her. She needed faith in that intelligence now...

"Burgundy," she exclaimed, startling those near her, "Duke Philip. Of course!"

"Did you say something, Mother?" Meg asked nervously from across the room. "Is there anything I can do to help?"

Cecily turned and smiled triumphantly. "Aye, there is, Meg. The boys must go away. Boys, come here!" she called. "Come here immediately."

Dickon stood perfectly still as he and George were given stern instructions to "pack some clothes, gather your cloaks, your boots and bonnets and choose one of your treasures to take with you. Margaret, go and help them."

"What for? Where to?" Dickon asked before George could open his mouth to ask the same. "What about Meggie?"

His mother held up her hand to stop Dickon's usual spate of questions. "Enough! I have no time to explain now. Just go!" Frightened into action, the three children ran from the room.

Arriving in their apartments, however, Dickon, now thoroughly alarmed, began to grumble. "You aren't packing, Meggie. Does that mean you are not coming with us? I don't want to go without you," and he clung to her arm. "Tell us. Where are we going?"

Meg shook off his hand. "You heard the same as I did, you simpleton." She was as perturbed as he was, but she would not show fear. "Mother knows what is best for us."

When Cecily finally swept through the door, a fur-lined cloak swirling around her trim, tall figure, she found her brood from oldest to youngest puzzled, sulky, and wary.

"Why is Meggie not coming?" Dickon tried again. "I don't want to go without Meg."

"It won't be so bad," Meg tried to sound encouraging, "and you will be back soon." She had no inkling that she would get her turn later to go to Burgundy, but as a bride.

On her way to the boys' chamber, Cecily had decided to make the hurried departure into an escapade. "We are going to outwit the queen. If she thinks she will find you here and capture you—just as your father captured the king—she will be disappointed, because you won't be here. You are going to escape the She-wolf's claws! Do not forget what she did to your father and..." She stopped as she now had the boys' attention.

"How clever of you, Mother," George said, grasping the urgency at once. "I am ready to go."

Dickon squeezed from his mind the gory image of his father's head on Micklegate and concentrated on his present dilemma. "But what about you and Meggie, and Nurse Anne, and Beatrice...." Dickon countered, obstinate now. "Why just us? I won't leave you behind. We walked together at Ludlow, and we will stay with you now. Father told George and me to look after you."

Cecily pulled Dickon to her, and he wrapped his arms about her. She was proud of her youngest and regretted bitterly that Richard would never watch the boy grow into a man. "We shall be fine, I promise, so please do as I say." She tweaked his bonnet. "'Tis not the first time you have been without me, is it? So be brave. For me. For Meg. For us all."

"'Twill be an adventure, Dickon!" George chimed in. "We are going on a real adventure."

Dickon tried to sound enthusiastic. "An adventure, but where? Will we be safe?"

"You will be safe where you are going, truly you will. And Ned will be proud of you," Cecily assured her youngest, although she had no idea how she was going to carry out this daring plan or if indeed the duke of Burgundy would welcome her sons. At least she had to try. One of her squires, John Skelton, had been entrusted with two hastily written letters, one of which would introduce him and her boys to the English Merchant Adventurers in Antwerp, and the second was to be delivered into no other hands but Philip of Burgundy's. She had to trust that young Skelton would carry out her instructions. It had tested her fortitude to consign the missives and this responsibility to the strapping squire, whose only outward sign of trepidation was a slight trembling of his hand as he had taken the letters from her.

Cecily knelt in front of her boys and explained. "'Tis for your own safety, boys. If something should happen to Edward—pray God it does not—then you and Dickon are York's heirs. And thus are heirs to the crown."

George nodded, understanding. "Where, Mother? Where are we going?"

Cecily straightened and told them they would be guests at the court of the mighty duke of Burgundy. Duke Philip of Burgundy was a friend to

England and had supported their father's cause. Burgundy was a friendly trading partner and would look kindly on two English princes.

"If you think the king of England is rich, you will be astonished by the magnificence of Duke Philip's court. You shall want for nothing." She laughed as their eyes grew large, but then she admonished them to mind their manners, study hard, and write to her often.

"Where is Burgundy?" George asked.

Dickon rolled his eyes. "Don't you remember from our geography lessons? It's across the North Sea, you idiot."

Seeing George take a menacing step toward his brother, Cecily admonished, "That's enough, George." Time was a-wasting, and she was impatient to leave. "Certes you will go by ship. Imagine, your first sea voyage!"

"A ship, Georgie!" Dickon cried. "We are going to sea, like the game we played yesterday!"

"Aye, something like that. I will protect him, never fear," George told his mother grandly.

"I am not afraid!" Dickon retorted. "I am a York. And us Yorks are never afraid!"

"There's a brave boy, Dickon," Cecily said, much relieved. "Now, both of you say goodbye to Nurse Anne and come with me."

"Are we to go alone? Who will dress us?" George suddenly asked as Dickon was enfolded in Anne of Caux's plump arms. The nursemaid had unaccustomed tears in her eyes as she hugged the thin little boy to her.

"One of the squires will accompany you. You know John Skelton?"

George nodded, reassured.

Cecily was about to cross the threshold into the passage when Traveller burst through the door, and she muttered a profanity.

Dickon cried. "Traveller! You have forgotten Traveller." He was clutching his dog's neck and announced stubbornly. "I am not going without him. You said we could take one treasure, and I choose Traveller."

"Don't be ridiculous!" Cecily cried. "It will be difficult enough to persuade the duke of Burgundy to take two small boys, but a wolfhound as well? The answer is *no*. Choose something else." Dickon stuck out his distinctive chin and refused to move. Nurse Anne held out King Henry's psalter, and Cecily nodded in approval. "Leave the dog, Dickon...*now*! Anne, put the king's gift in Dickon's bundle. Meg, take hold of Traveller, and you, Dickon, take hold of my hand." All of Proud Cis's children knew this was one of those times when she was to be obeyed, and thus a dejected Dickon loosed his hold on his faithful dog and grasped his mother's outstretched hand.

"I will take good care of him, never fear," Meg whispered to her brother. "Besides, Ambergris would be very lonely without Traveller, would he not?" Dickon saw the truth in this and sadly conceded.

"Farewell, dear friend," he said to the dog, who cocked his head and thumped his tail.

"Thank you, Meg." Cecily smiled wanly at her daughter. "Now let us to the wharf or we shall miss the tide."

They made their way to the castle quay, where Sir Henry had commandeered a boat without markings so Cecily would not be recognized lest some enterprising Lancastrian spot the duchess and her sons and thwart her plan. Undeterred by its lack of luxury or size, she saw the boys safely stowed with Squire Skelton and then sat herself in the stern. A harried Heydon took the bow seat, his white wispy hair clinging to his sweaty forehead as the boatman dipped his heavy oars into the water and pulled away from the pier towards the scores of ships moored in the Pool on the other side of London Bridge. Cecily sat with her black fur-trimmed cloak wrapped around her frightened children as they huddled together for warmth against the damp February afternoon.

Dickon twisted round to get a last glimpse of Traveller, each pathetic whine weighing on his heart, and wondered if they would ever be reunited. He knew he would miss the dog more than his mother; surely Traveller would miss him, too.

"I will be back with the tide, Meg," Cecily called to the desolate girl waving her brothers farewell. "You must take care of everything until I return. You can do it; you have learned well!"

Cecily suddenly felt tired. She was used to taking charge of her household and averting crises, but her grief had depleted her great reservoir of energy and making the decision to send her boys overseas was an enormous responsibility. Not for the first time did she resent her husband's leaving her alone to cope. But cope she must.

She turned to George and delivered another homily. "You are the older brother here, George, and you should think for the two of you. I beg you to stop your incessant fighting and be strong together for the house of York. Do you promise to watch over Dickon?"

Holding his hand over his heart, George replied: "I swear I will do my duty to you and our house," he said so solemnly, it made Cecily's mouth twitch. "I will let no harm come to Dickon, I promise."

"Spoken like a true son of York," Cecily said, kissing the top of his head. "And Dickon, do you swear to listen to George?"

"Aye, Mother," Dickon stated, trying to sound as grown up as George. "But...but how long must we be gone?"

"'Tis for your own good and the good of our cause," she hedged. "I promise to write to you. I shall explain everything then." She took his face in her hands. "From this day forth, you are no longer my little boy. It is time for us to stop calling you Dickon and use your given name of Richard. You will present yourself to the duke of Burgundy as Richard Plantagenet. With your dear father gone, you are the only one of that name now. Bear it proudly. Is that agreed?"

"Must I call him Richard, as well?" George demanded.

"Certes!" came the stern response. "It will take a little while to get used to, but it will give both of you more dignity at court." She looked up in time to see they were about to shoot through one of London Bridge's navigable archways. It was the most dangerous part of the course, with the narrow openings causing the river to sweep through at an alarming rate, and she held on to the gunwale. The boatman was used to it, and, swinging the bow into the rushing current, lifted his oars to the sky to avoid grazing the slimy, barnacled walls, safely bringing them into the calm Pool beyond.

"Your Grace," Sir Henry said, not betraying the concern he had for the duchess's harebrained scheme. "Do you know on which ship you wish us to set our sights?"

"You know full well I do not, Sir Henry," Cecily shot back. "We shall just approach the larger ones flying the Burgundian or English flags and pray someone takes pity on me."

"I see," said the steward, and only he could see the boatman lift his eyes heavenward. "Then, boatman, I would start with that one," and he pointed to a caravel flying the Cross of St. George. Unfortunately the captain was ashore, and no one else had the authority to take the boys on board. The next one was bound for Lisbon, and Cecily was beginning to worry, when they approached a carrack bearing the Flemish name of

Zoete. Sir Henry hailed a crew member dumping dirty water over the side. "Your captain, mariner? Where is your captain?" he shouted, and the man waved and ran off. A few moments later, as the boatman came alongside and grabbed the rope netting hanging from the gunwale, a burly man with a globe of a face appeared above them.

"*Ja?* I am ze captain, Captain Bouwen. Vat you vant?"

Relieved the ship was bound for Antwerp, Sir Henry stated his business and held up a pouch of coins that Cecily had given him. When the man knew he was in the presence of a noblewoman and that he might be rewarded even more for taking the two boys to Flanders, he nodded and grinned, calling over his shoulder to two of his sailors, who swarmed down the makeshift ladder like monkeys.

"Go with them, boys," Cecily commanded, her heart constricting under her high-waisted gown. She hoped she sounded more confident than she felt. As George and Dickon wobbled unsteadily to their feet, she placed her hand on each boy's head. "Go with my blessing. And may God keep you safe." Then she kissed them in turn and whispered, "Never forget I love you."

"I love you, too, Mam," George gulped, suddenly feeling very small and afraid.

When Dickon gazed up into his mother's anxious face, he realized she was as afraid as he was. It suddenly made her vulnerable, and, in a gesture older than his years, he patted her shoulder as he assured her, "We are big boys now, Mother. You need not worry. We shall pray for you every day and that God will keep you safe—and Meggie and Ned and Nurse Anne and you, Sir Henry, and Traveller and ..." at the mention of his faithful hound, he choked. Would he ever see any of these faces again?

"You must go, now," she said, grateful and proud, as she lovingly straightened his over-large bonnet. Turning to the sailors, she said, "*Merci, messieurs,*" hoping they knew French, "*Allez-y.*"

Clutching their bundles, the youngsters were hoisted onto the burly mariners' backs, who delivered them safely on deck. Then John Skelton, after securing their small chest into the netting, followed them on board.

As fate would have it, before Cecily could change her mind and order the boys back, a wake from a passing boat caused the boatman to let go of the rope and tend to his oars. The current quickly widened the gap between the vessels and soon Cecily was borne out of reach. It was probably just as well the boys could not see her tears or feel her doubt, or they might have jumped overboard and attempted to swim to her. Instead, they leaned over the side waving and shouting farewells.

As the figure of his mother receded in the distance and he turned to take in the unfamiliar surroundings and the strange, foreign sailors, young Richard unexpectedly found himself consumed with unbidden rage. He stepped back to wonder why instead of sadness and fear, he was feeling so angry. Nothing much in his life had angered him, until now. It took introspection and the two-day voyage to help him understand: He felt betrayed by his mother. He could not quite believe that the person he had counted on to safeguard him throughout his entire life had abandoned him on an unknown ship with strangers for companions, who did not speak English and who would take him to a foreign land where he knew not a soul. Before this act of betrayal, his mother had not given up on him. Ever. Not even through his difficult birth; nor when she had nursed him through several childhood illnesses at which doctors had thrown up their hands; nor when she had marched him through the enemy soldiers at Ludlow; nor as she held him when his nightmares woke him. Hadn't she restored Traveller to him when Richard had not thought to see the dog again? And even through that terrible day after Wakefield, when they learned of the loss of their father and brother, she had stayed strong for him. So why would his mother abandon him now? It was only after he returned from the short, forced exile to Burgundy that he had fully understood the sacrifice his mother had made.

But for now, his initial anger, like his father's, was short-lived, and by the time the anchor was hauled in, it had turned to melancholy. At one point, without warning, a greasy seaman pushed past him, leaned over the gunwale and dumped a bowl of chicken bones into the water from the galley. Richard's sad eyes followed the zig-zag sinking of the bones to the muddy riverbed, dredging up images of their watery grave. He even morbidly wondered where he might be buried one day—and whether anyone would care.

An old man's fear for such a young child.

A mere three months later, Richard—a child no more—returned to a London readying for a coronation. England had a new king: Edward the Fourth, oldest son of the late duke of York and his duchess—and

Richard's brother. The twenty-year-old Edward had been proclaimed king by Parliament and Londoners alike after routing the army of Henry and Margaret at the battle of Towton.

How proud Father would be, Richard thought as the city came into view. He was unsure how his brother and Henry could both be king of England at the same time, but he would worry about such a puzzle later. For now, his Burgundian adventure ended, he was overjoyed to return to his native land and the welcoming arms of his family.

Part Two

Duke of Gloucester
Warwick's Man

Leicester, September 5, 2012 — Eleventh day of the dig

At the trench, the DSP cameras roll as osteologist Jo Appleby bends down and removes a light covering of earth from the chest cavity and upper vertebrae. The spine has the most excruciating 'S' shape. 'Whoever this was,' she states, 'the spinal column has a really abnormal curvature. This skeleton has a hunchback.'...

Are they saying this is Richard? If this is Richard, how can he have worn armor with a hump on his back? I flop down onto the spoil heap behind me. I feel as if I've been hit by a train. The others want me to be excited because it looks as though we may have found Richard, but all I can hear is the pounding in my ears and the awful word 'hunchback' in my brain....

(Later) At the 12 September press conference, the University of Leicester confirms the discovery...On initial examination...it is revealed that the skeleton had acute spinal abnormalities, confirming severe scoliosis — a form of spinal curvature. This would have made the right shoulder visibly higher than the left, consistent with contemporary accounts of Richard's appearance. Finally, the skeleton did not show signs of kyphosis — a different form of curvature. The man did not have the feature sometimes inappropriately known as a hunchback, and he did not have a withered arm.

— Philippa Langley, The King's Grave

CHAPTER EIGHT
Summer 1461

"*Vivat Rex!* Long live King Edward!"

Jubilant cries mingled with the clamoring bells and rang around Edward as he rode through the welcoming London crowds on his way to the Tower the day before his coronation. To the strife-weary citizens, the young and handsome Edward of York gave them promise of better governance and a more stable way of life than had the weak, manipulated Henry.

Riding on a richly caparisoned black stallion alongside George in a place of honor directly behind Edward, Richard glanced left and right at the smiling Londoners waving kerchiefs and throwing flowers in the path of the riders, who were followed by the scarlet-clad lord mayor and aldermen and hundreds of London's most prominent men, uniformly dressed in green.

All the windows of the three-story merchant houses that lined London Bridge were flung open and jammed with spectators. A girl about his own age caught Richard's eye, and he could not help smiling at the frank expression on her pretty face, her amber eyes full of merriment as she waved to him—merely a face in the crowd today, certainly, but a face he was to come to know again intimately in only a very short time.

But now, the procession was reaching the Tower, its gleaming walls freshly limed for the occasion and the pointed turrets of the massive central White Tower festooned with banners. The fortress guardian of the capital city was ready to receive another king of England into its royal apartments for the traditional coronation eve. Richard was duly awed. His brother would be crowned on the morrow, and Richard was to be initiated into the Order of the Bath that very night.

How had Lady Fortune smiled on the house of York in such a short time? Richard pondered this question as he waved and smiled to the cheering citizens, as well as how Edward had miraculously come to be king at all.

Richard had been so happy to see his family again that in the euphoria of reunion he had suppressed his need to know how such a thing as two kings was possible. One day, kneeling beside his mother at prime when Edward was elsewhere, he whispered: "Don't cry, Mam. I miss Father, too, you know. God is looking after him now—and Edmund—and I pray for them daily."

Cecily turned her head and gazed thoughtfully at her son through her tears. "Thank you, Richard, I shall take comfort from that," she answered, reaching out and squeezing his hand.

As the small family group returned to the duchess's solar to break their fast, Richard sneaked his hand in Cecily's. "Tell me how Ned came to be king, Mother," he pleaded. "No one else will take the time to explain. Messire de Gruthuyse in Bruges told us Ned had won a victory, but what happened to King Henry? If the king was not killed, then shouldn't Henry still be king?"

It was a story Cecily never tired of repeating and one which, no doubt, had become embellished in her proud maternal mind. But before she could begin, suspicious George, who had noticed the tête-à-tête, had poked his head between them, asked: "Are you talking about me?"

"You are not always the center of our attention, Georgie," Cecily reminded him with a chuckle, unwittingly filling George with resentment. "Dick...I mean Richard was asking why your brother is now the king. I assumed you both had heard all about it at Duke Philip's court, but I am certainly happy to regale you further."

"I know the story," George boasted and stalked off, leaving Cecily perplexed.

She sighed and turned her attention to Richard. They walked to the river's edge and sat down to enjoy the warm June sunshine and tell her tale. And such a tale she told of thrilling victories for Edward at Mortimer's

Cross on the Welsh Marches and at Towton in Yorkshire, of a bitter defeat for Cousin Warwick at St. Alban's, and how the queen had failed to take advantage of her victory there to overrun London close by. "Instead, she rampaged north with her troops allowing your brother to follow and rout the royal army at Towton."

Richard's eyes shone. "Aye, my lady, I know about that battle on Palm Sunday. The king and queen ran away to Scotland. Is Henry no longer king because he ran away?"

"'Tis a mite more complicated than that, my child. Remember the oath Henry swore to your father that he 'charge all persons here to put it abroad that it shall be considered...'"

"'...an act of high treason for any person to conspire against the said duke's life,'" Richard finished for her with the exact wording.

Cecily proudly patted his hand. "That is correct, and by provoking your father to fight at Wakefield, his grace the king broke his own oath. It was enough for the Commons to acclaim Edward, as York's heir, king."

Later, Richard's memory of the conversation faded as he was prepared in the customary way to be made a knight of the Bath in a ceremony the boy would not soon forget. It was the first of many distinctions he was to be given during his brother's reign.

Together with Richard and George, twenty-six young noblemen were awarded the signal honor that night. Once again, he suffered a few regrets at being the smallest, but then he noticed the older boys were treating him with deference—a nicer side of being the king's brother, he decided.

Appropriately, the ceremony began with bathing as two king's knights intoned the rules and rites of this chivalric order. A priest entered the princes' chamber carrying a silver chalice. He blessed the water in it and sprinkled the cold liquid over the boys' heads and shoulders while giving a blessing for the purification of the two knight candidates. Then in complete contrast to the solemnity of the ceremony, the squires attending their knights began to sing and cavort about the tub—all part of the ritual, Richard realized, although he privately thought this silly. Then the two knights recited the chivalric oath, which the brothers repeated.

Later, clothed in white, Richard spent the rest of the night holding vigil and lying prostrate in the Tower's chapel with all the novice knights. The hours of humility in the silence had a profound effect on the boy, and for the first time he felt a spiritual connection with his God.

None had eaten since the previous day, and it was with a growling stomach that he rose and then entered the White Tower where Edward himself, his lords and councilors about him, was waiting to belt on Richard's first sword. Two gentlemen strapped on Richard's spurs, which made a satisfying clinking as the lad walked towards the king, who stood ready on a dais to dub him knight.

Edward's voice rang out clearly across the hall: "Richard Plantagenet, be thou a good knight and true," and as Richard bowed his head, his brother fastened the sword belt and scabbard around his waist. "I have no doubt that you will be true, Dickon," Edward murmured, covering Richard's hand with his own upon the sword hilt, "and I will put my trust in you."

Later that afternoon, clad in blue and white, the newly created knights followed behind Edward in the procession back to Westminster for the coronation. A cacophony of pealing bells and loud acclamations greeted the cavalcade from the Londoners, who gawped at the giant young god astride his white destrier on his way to be crowned king of England. Richard's heart could not contain an ounce more pleasure or pride in his family and country. He shouted: "God Save King Edward" as loudly as his compatriots. He could only imagine Ned's exhilaration at the prospect of being anointed and crowned before God. Surely he, Richard, would never surpass such a pinnacle of earthly man's success. For a second, he fancied the people were cheering for him and that it was he and not Edward who was riding to be crowned. *Addlepate,* the boy thought, *how could that ever be?*

No thoughts of "runt" crossed Richard's mind that day; he was a royal prince—a Plantagenet prince—and for once he felt every inch of it.

For the banquet following the long coronation ceremony in Westminster's Gothic abbey, the court moved into nearby Westminster Hall. The high, graceful hammer-beam roof was festooned with flags and banners dating back a hundred years. Colorful angels with golden wings were carved into each arched beam-end as if flying above mortals' heads. Thousands of candles illuminated the rich tapestries, and the scarlets, greens, blues and purples of the gorgeous gowns of the courtiers and their ladies crowding the spacious hall. Prominent everywhere, the white hart, heraldic symbol of the second King Richard, told of that monarch's hand in the renovations of this magnificent hall at the end of the previous century. A man of exquisite taste, it appeared alas he could not govern his kingdom; he was deposed by his cousin of Bolingbroke and died—they say of starvation—in captivity. Young Richard had been told by his father of this distant cousin's fate, and how the usurping Lancastrian Bolingbroke, crowned Henry IV, was somewhat to blame for the ensuing clash between York and Lancaster that finally had ended at Towton. Usurper was such an ugly word, Richard had always thought. Praise God, the strife was now over, and his brother wore the crown.

"A groat for your thoughts, Richard," George said. "Are you as excited as I am? Ned is king! King Edward! That makes me heir to the throne. I can hardly believe it." Grinning smugly, he added: "And now that I am duke of Clarence, you will have to call me 'Your Grace.'"

Richard's fists clenched in the folds of his azure short robe. He wanted to be happy for George, and he would have been had it not been for George's crowing from the moment he learned that he was now Edward's heir and had been raised to a dukedom. Richard watched as one by one people came forward to congratulate him, and George basked in the recognition. Indeed, Richard knew he, too, would have enjoyed the accolades had he been accorded a title, but he remained just Richard Plantagenet, and it just did not seem fair.

"I did not get a title either," Meg consoled him, leaning across George, "and I'm older than George." That made Richard feel better, until the next time George gloated. Yet Richard dared not ask Edward why he heaped honors on George and all his friends without giving one to him or Meg. Even plain Will Hastings, Edward's closest advisor, was now a lord. Nay, it did not seem fair at all.

Richard was standing near an ante-chamber and, wanting to escape from George, he slipped in and stood beside one of his fellow knights of the Bath. The boy put his finger to his lips and jerked his head towards the musicians' alcove. All of a sudden Richard was aware of a high, sweet voice fluttering on the edge of confidence rising above the gentle notes of a harp. He squeezed between two adults, whose attention was focused not on a boy soprano, which would have been usual, but on a chestnut-haired girl seated all by herself on a stool, the musicians having gone in search of refreshments. Had he been a little older, he might have noticed her beauty, but at eight he was more impressed with her daring.

Despite the din behind him in the great hall, all noise disappeared for Richard but the girl's plaintive song, and he was captivated by the sound. He had not shown talent for any instrument, despite the efforts of an accomplished music tutor, but he loved music. All too soon, the notes died away, and several spectators applauded. Seemingly unaware she had had an audience, the girl looked up and straight into Richard's smiling face. He would much later wonder if it had been his smile or her family's compliments that had made her blush so prettily.

"She's good, do you not agree," Richard's friend whispered. "I would not dare to sing in front of anyone."

Richard nodded. "Nor I. I wonder who she is." He was quite sure he had seen her before, but he had no chance to ponder the mystery as a fanfare behind him announced the coronation banquet, and the privileged guests hurried to find their places.

"The Lord Richard is it not?" a friendly voice stayed him as they moved into the hall. "Sir John Howard, at your service." Richard returned the bow, pleased to have been acknowledged by this well known loyal Yorkist and Edward's councilor. "Did you hear my young friend sing? A voice like an angel, did you not think? The lass is only ten, but by the Rood, with her looks, she will turn heads and make a husband happy …"

"Or be someone's leman," Will Hastings interrupted, chuckling. "She'd be wasted as a wife."

Richard was not sure what "leman" meant, but his beautiful mother was a dazzling duchess and had made his father happy, so why was a wife a waste? He had the sense to reserve that question for later, and besides he was hungry. He saw Edward beckoning to him from his throne upon the dais. Splendid in his ermine-trimmed royal purple, with the lions of England and his Sunne in Splendor badge decorating the baldachin held high above him by four knights of the Garter, Edward appeared the perfect model of kingship.

"I know you are disappointed not to be granted a title, Dickon," Edward said kindly, when Richard went down on one knee to his adored brother. Richard's guilty expression made Edward smile. "Never fear, your turn will come, I promise."

Richard daily imagined waking to find his new status as a royal prince was naught but a dream. He had yet to find a confidante he could trust. Everyone always seemed too busy for him.

Exciting though it was to be the brother of the king, he sometimes yearned for the less public life as a mere duke's son. Boating on the Thames or fishing from its banks was fun, but now he was forever stared at by the curious villagers, and learning the names of Edward's many councilors was as hard as any history lesson. But as he watched his charismatic brother win commoners and nobles effortlessly to his side, he felt increasing pride. Certainly it did not hurt that, at six feet and three inches, Edward stood half a head taller than most men and dominated a room with his golden good looks and charisma. But, truth be told, kindhearted young Richard did not give himself enough credit for attracting his own inner circle of pages, who liked him for his quiet humility and sense of fair play, whether practicing at tilting or archery, or by speaking up for them to their lords.

"He has Ned's common touch," Cecily remarked to Beatrice one day, as they watched the boys throw balls for Traveller, "although let us hope he does not forget he is first and foremost a royal prince. A pity he does not have a few more of Ned's inches."

"He is young yet, Your Grace. Wait and see; he will grow."

"The poor boy always seems to be in George's shadow," Cecily mused, as George snatched Richard's ball and threw it twice as far as his brother could.

It was during those idyllic summer days that Richard was enthusiastically initiated into the hunt, thrilling to his first sight of a wild boar bravely staving off attacks by the baying, snarling hounds. The animal, though dying of several well aimed arrows, was possessed with a will to charge his antagonist in one last desperate attempt to avoid death. True to its reputation, the beast's razor sharp tusks impaled one of the dogs and sent it flying into the air close to where Richard watched wide-eyed. The boar was finally defeated by a sword thrust through its heart. Despite his churning stomach, the boy experienced a rush of excitement, and he was forever captivated by the noble sport.

"How did you enjoy your first hunt, Lord Richard?" Will Hastings, Edward's newly appointed lord chamberlain, had sidled his horse next to the boy, noticing how well Richard sat his horse.

Richard nodded his head vigorously. "Very much, my lord."

As they watched the death throes of the boar and how the pewterers skillfully held the dogs at bay, Hastings remarked: "I have a great deal of respect for any creature who turns and fights when all seems lost. 'Tis why I follow your brother, the king."

Richard gazed curiously at Will, who towered above him on the handsome chestnut mare. He had heard people talking about Will Hastings and his bad influence on Edward, but the older man sounded sensible and sincere.

"My brother is the best soldier in the world," Richard stated. "When I am skilled, I shall follow him, too."

"Then he is a lucky man, young lord," Will said, grinning. "You will have to grow a little, 'tis true, but you appear a sturdy lad, and you already understand loyalty."

Richard thanked the chamberlain graciously, and as Will moved away, the boy wondered what the job of king's lord chamberlain entailed.

"Lord of the royal bedchamber," one of the pages enlightened him one day. "You know that men like to have women in their beds?" Richard was reminded of the conversation he had had while fishing with Ned that day at Southwark, and thus his blush told the page that Richard did indeed know. "The chamberlain finds ladies for the king, so I have been told."

Richard was shocked. "Will Hastings is the king's councilor. He helps Ned make important decisions. My sister told me."

His friend shrugged. "Decisions about women are important. I'm just telling you what I know."

"But what if a woman doesn't want to go?"

"All the girls want to be in your brother's bed, Lord Richard," Will's brazen young pageboy told him. "And my master likes to bed them afterwards."

This astonishing conversation would forever color Richard's judgment of his brother's best friend, even when he learned the real duties of a chamberlain. Much later, he would have to acknowledge Will as the most loyal of Edward's councilors, but for the time being he had his doubts.

It took Edward only four months to fulfill his promise of a title to Richard.

One blustery day in October, not long after Richard's ninth birthday, he received a letter with the royal seal of England and written in the king's own hand. That Edward would write to him personally, was almost more thrilling to the boy than the message it contained. But not quite.

"Meggie! George!" he cried, waving the letter at his siblings playing chess by the window in their solar at Greenwich Palace. "I am to be given the dukedom of Gloucester. I am to be a duke!"

Meg rose from her window seat and ran to hug him. "Good for you, Richard," she enthused. How could she not rejoice at Richard's good fortune, even though she, the oldest of the three, had been overlooked again. She hated being a woman—at fifteen she considered herself one—and too tall besides. Her only chance for a title was marrying one, as she knew only too well.

"George," she called now, "come and congratulate Richard. The two of you are equals now, so perhaps you will stop your squabbling."

George gave his brother a reluctant grin and shook his hand. "Gloucester? Where's that?" he joked.

Richard cocked a snoot. "At least it's in England," he retorted. "Everyone knows the Clare lands are in boggy, soggy Ireland."

"Oh no," Meg groaned as she watched the two boys wrestle each other to the ground. "When am I ever going to be rid of them," she muttered, picking up her book and leaving the room.

She did not have to wait long.

The royal trio was rowed up the Thames in the king's own barge, canopied in white and gold cloth, the royal arms decorating the streaming pennants on each corner. The oarsmen wore dark blue livery and pulled as one up the wide river, negotiating the dangerous surge on the rising tide underneath London Bridge and guiding their important passengers safely to the Westminster Palace pier.

Margaret lifted the hem of her red damask gown and took the boat master's hand to climb up the few steps from inside the barge and onto the wharf. Richard and George needed no help to nimbly transition to dry land.

Richard smoothed his rich, brocaded short cote, and fingered the sable hem. Other than at the coronation, he could not remember wearing anything as fine before. He was beginning to develop a taste for luxury even at nine years old, and it was one thing he and George could agree on: there was much pleasure in a fine wardrobe. Edward had sent Richard a handsome dagger to wear on this occasion, several semi-precious stones decorating its hilt, and Richard felt for it now.

"Straighten your bonnet." Meg could not resist acting the older sister, and Cecily had insisted that Margaret take the role of mother hen when Edward had given his siblings Greenwich for their new residence. "I will be staying close to Edward, my dear," Cecily had told her. "He needs my guidance in governance until he sees how the land lies."

"You will tell George and Richard they must listen to me, will you not, Mother?" Margaret pleaded with as much boldness as she dared. Proud Cis could be motherly when it suited her, but mostly she demanded obedience from her children.

As they mounted the spiral staircase on the river entrance to the royal apartments, Richard was losing his confidence. He was unsure what the ceremony would entail. Remembering the night-long rituals of the Order of the Bath, he prayed he would not be stripped naked again in front of the court. His upper body was developing outwardly, but he still hated his spindly legs.

He was relieved to see the sunlit audience chamber was only half-filled, and then there was Edward striding towards him, a smile of welcome on his handsome face. Richard went down on his knees at once and snatched off his hat. He should have known better than to speak before the king did but he could not stop himself from saying: "God's greeting, Your Grace."

Edward ignored the lapse in protocol. Indeed, since becoming king, he had shocked some old-fashioned nobles by resting a royal hand on some lesser man's arm, or even slapping a shoulder playfully. He was an amicable, friendly man, at ease with others and happiest in company. In only a few short months of kingship, he had earned the respect and devotion of many a hardened noble, and as well the commoners loved him, albeit for the blessed cessation of interminable warfare.

"My dear brother," Ned said warmly, raising Richard to his feet. "You look every inch a duke today, I might say. Will," he turned to his friend and confidante Hastings, "do you not think Richard will suit his new title?"

Hastings winked at Richard. "Every new inch," he said, reminding Richard of their conversation in the forest.

At last, the stiff little boy relaxed his face into a smile. "You really think so, my lord?"

"Aye, lad, you are growing nicely," Edward's chamberlain replied.

"Let us start the proceedings, shall we?" Edward propelled his young brother towards the dais. Standing on the steps, the king held up his hand, and at once the court fell silent. He motioned Richard to stand a step below him, and it was only then that Richard saw his mother standing quietly watching him from behind the throne. He bowed his head quickly, and she smiled at him. Jesu, but she is the most beautiful woman in the world, Richard thought proudly. Regal, elegant, her thick blonde hair now hidden under a hennin, her fashionably plucked brow accentuating her large, bright blue eyes, she wore her forty-seven years easily. And, no one would doubt that Edward, Margaret, or George were her offspring. Only Richard resembled his smaller, darker father.

"Cousin, welcome!" Edward's cheerful baritone carried down the hall to the figure now striding towards the dais. Richard Neville, earl of Warwick, was to read the proclamation announcing Richard as England's newest duke.

Richard was pleased to see the earl, who had played such a vital role in putting a Yorkist king upon the throne. He was known to prefer the north of England, and had even been absent for the coronation while he helped put down small rebellions north of the River Tweed.

"An auspicious occasion, *n'est pas?*" Warwick's familiar bark no longer frightened Richard, and he nodded earnestly and replied, "Aye, my lord."

"Your Grace, my lords, ladies....we are here to bestow the highest honor in our kingdom on our beloved Richard Plantagenet. From henceforth, he shall be known as Richard, duke of Gloucester, and shall receive all the benefices due to the holder of that noble name." An usher came forward with a velvet cushion on which lay a silver collar bearing a heavy badge emblazoned with the royal arms of the kingdom, differenced by a bordure argent. Richard was glad to see his other Neville cousin, bishop of Exeter and Edward's chancellor, approach the dais to bless the collar. *"In nomine patris, filii et spiritus sancti"* the bishop began, and all present crossed themselves.

Richard worried if he were old enough or wise enough to take on this great responsibility. No one had schooled him in what it meant to be a duke of a large area of the country with which he was not even familiar, but he knew he was every bit as capable as George. Besides, George's new title had not seemed to change anything about his brother's life yet—except make him more annoying—and so Richard assumed he would eventually learn what was required of him when he became a man. He bent his head as Warwick slowly placed the heavy collar over his shoulders and then solemnly grasped Richard's hand.

The earl turned back to the assembled court and in a loud voice cried, "Let me present to you his grace, the duke of Gloucester. God give him the strength to govern well."

When the trumpet fanfare's echo died, the hairs on Richard's neck prickled as he found himself moved beyond measure by this great moment in his life. He vowed to be faithful to God and true to Edward forever and always.

If Richard expected his life to change in that moment, he was to be bitterly disappointed. When would he be sent away to begin his knightly training, he wondered month after tedious month. It may have been named for the beauty of its gardens and aspect, but the Palace of Pleasaunce, as Greenwich was called, became synonymous with a luxurious prison for the young impatient Richard. *What's the use of being a royal duke if I don't even know how to defend myself, let alone my people?* he silently grumbled.

It did not help when, after a year of obscurity for the three siblings, George was called to Westminster to set up his own household at the king's side as befitted the heir to the throne. However, it was a relief not to have the daily reminder of "you forget I'm next in line, Richard," thrown in one's face.

George's arrogance aside, the thought that he was forgotten again irked Richard more as he chose to climb the hill to the ruined tower, once the pride of a previous duke of Gloucester, to watch George being conveyed up the Thames in the king's barge. He sat with his arm around Traveller's neck at the foot of it and gazed with longing at the far away spires of London. "I'll be stuck here forever," he told his faithful friend.

CHAPTER NINE
SPRING–SUMMER 1464

Richard had never been happier.

Many would have guessed it was because of the beauty of the wild Yorkshire landscape, the excitement of mastering a shortsword or dagger, the unaccustomed camaraderie of a dormitory filled with eager youths his age, or the bracing, clean air that filled his lungs and made him feel alive. Those were factors, it is true, but it was more personal than that: he was no longer compared with and tormented by George. No one here knew George, and he had, for the first time, known a freedom from family friction. Here at Middleham he could form his own opinions and become his own man. The thought had struck him one bright July morning as he rode out of the castle yard through the squared gatehouse with his friend Robert Percy of Scotton. He suddenly gave a gleeful whoop and kicked his mare's flanks into a canter.

The two youths had taken to sneaking in a daily early-morning gallop across the meadows behind the hulking gray castle, which dominated windswept Wensleydale for miles around. Emerald green fields dotted with sheep rolled over the hills to the bleaker moors beyond, meeting the unending sky in the middle distance, a landscape so empty of habitation its vastness reduced Richard and his horse to naught but specks.

Edward had described the region as "desolate and uncivilized" when he had given Richard the news that their cousin of Warwick had agreed to take on the task of training the youngest York son. But Richard, elated at the thought of realizing his dream of knighthood, not to mention escaping the confines of Greenwich or the Royal Wardrobe, where Edward had housed his siblings in the years since his coronation, paid no heed. He had broken with protocol and flung his arms about his idol and vowed he would be as fine a warrior as Edward when he became a man. "I will never let you down, Ned," eleven-year-old Richard promised. Much amused by this show of affection, Edward had turned to Hastings, and, as Richard ran off, remarked: "One cannot ask for more devotion even from a dog. I fear my pedestal is so high, you will need a ladder to reach me, Will."

Edward's description of the north had thus fallen on biased ears, and instead, Richard had fallen in love with his new home from the first moment he and his escort had their first view of Middleham more than a year before on the eastern road from York along the edge of the dales. He would soon get to know the elemental beauty of the area with its crystal-clear cascading waterfalls coming from the Pennines, its lush, upland, sheep- and cow-crowded meadows rising to the barren moorland hills, where the limestone, sandstone, and shale outcroppings had long lent themselves to ancient stone walls and isolated farmhouses. Richard learned that prehistoric man had lived there, trading the bronze and iron they dug from those hills, and much later the Romans had come, building a fort at Bainbridge, a few miles from Middleham. The upper dale was densely forested, creating perfect hunting grounds for a king—or in his absence, his cousin, the earl of Warwick.

It was into a forest to the west of the castle that Richard and Rob went riding that day, a groom following them in case of a mishap to the king's brother. Rob, the older of the two, was leading the way hoping to catch a glimpse of a small group of roe deer that had been spotted the day before near a tumbling beck well known to the henchmen—as Richard, Rob and the other noble boys in knightly training were termed. They were not permitted to hunt without adult supervision, but they were hoping to enjoy the sight of a fawn or two.

"Mayhap we will come upon old King Henry instead," Rob called in his pleasing northern brogue, "and then we would be exonerated from our escapade." Poor mad Henry had been separated from the Lancastrian forces after the battle of Hexham, at which Warwick's brother Montagu was victorious. The erstwhile king was rumored to now be roaming the Pennines as a fugitive.

"I feel sorry for him," Richard replied, remembering the gentle man in the Westminster chapel. "But he was not a good king—although my lady mother thinks he is a good man." Young Dickon had had trouble understanding this paradox, but now he knew that it was good governance and strength of character that made a king worthy to wear a crown, and he was very sure his brother Edward was suited to it.

A curlew's cry reached them as they plunged into the woods, and Richard had long decided it was the sound that would always remind him of his time at Middleham. He was only expecting to be a temporary resident while he learned the chivalric arts, but fate had other ideas for the young Richard as events in his life would bring him back time and time again.

The boys left their mounts with the groom and softly wended their way through the trees towards the familiar stream they could now hear spilling over rocks and fallen branches. Alarmed, its raised tail showing the white-heart mark underside, a doe bounded out of her bushy hiding place. Richard and Rob stood like stone statues and waited to see if she would be followed by her offspring. When none appeared, Richard crept forward again, almost tripping over a terrified, abandoned fawn, its dappled auburn coat looking like sunlight on dead leaves. Before he could alert Rob to witness it, the creature found its trembling legs, wobbled to its feet and tripped away.

"Such large, beautiful eyes!" Richard enthused. "In another moment, I could have touched her. Why would a mother leave her child in danger, I wonder? I notice there is no father to protect it either."

"I warrant the dam felt the fawn's coat would protect it more than she could, and so she drew our attention to her and away from it," Rob remarked.

"Perhaps," Richard mused. On this day, he was too rapt by the encounter to note the obvious irony. Later perhaps, the parallel to his own life would dawn.

Reaching the brook, they used stepping stones to reach their favorite mossy rock midstream and clambered upon it. Rob pulled out a hunk of bread and some good local cheese, the mixture of cow's and ewe's milk contributing to its characteristic blueness. Here was another reason Richard liked being in this place: He thought it produced the most delicious cheese he had ever tasted, and now he tucked in and observed Rob.

His friend was pleasing enough to look at, Richard thought, with ruddy cheeks and curly, light-brown hair, but he would not flutter the ladies' hearts, it had to be said. But Rob had been the first in the dormitory to befriend Richard, and Richard had been wary but grateful. It had taken him a few weeks to feel comfortable among his peers. Many avoided him, mistaking his shyness for arrogance. To be fair, they could not have known Richard had believed anyone who did speak to him was merely wanting to curry favor with the king's brother, and so he kept to himself in those first weeks. However, it was not long before the rigors of training put them all on the same plane, and competition among them sorted the strong from the weak, the loners from the team players, and the leaders from the followers. What was surprising to John Lacey, master of henchmen, was how quickly the smaller duke of Gloucester showed leadership qualities, with the older Rob Percy becoming his first follower. It is doubtful Rob was aware, but to the experienced Master Lacey, the situation was not unusual. Some people were born to lead, and, despite his apparent shyness, Richard of Gloucester was looking to be one of those.

"It is surprising how much you eat for a shrimp," Rob teased the younger boy.

Richard glared at him, the familiar shame flooding him. "If you and I are to be good friends," he snapped back, "I would ask that you not call me 'shrimp,' or 'runt,' 'small fry' or…or anything similar. Why do you think I eat so much? I'm doing my best to grow, and I will," he insisted. "After all, I'm only twelve and you are fourteen."

"Temper, temper! Aye, I see 'tis a sore subject," Rob replied. "It shall not happen again, and I will horsewhip anyone who mentions such 'shortcomings' in my hearing, I swear." He said with mock severity and winked at Richard.

Richard grinned. "You don't need to go that far, Rob—and I will excuse the pun this once," he said grinning, "but a black eye might be nice." He picked at the moss and admitted, "My brother George never let me forget how much smaller and younger and weaker and…oh, it doesn't matter. He is hundreds of miles away now."

Rob took note of the bitterness in Richard's voice and felt sorry for the boy.

Richard sighed. "For all Ned has given him, it seems George is never satisfied. Before I left London, he told me he resented my chance to learn from the great earl of Warwick and be far from Ned's huge shadow."

Rob aimed a stone at a cairn they had set up on another rock. "As the king's next brother, he is the heir to the throne, is he not? From all we hear in the north, he draws people like moths to a candle, and our sovereign lord allows him to live like a young king. What could possibly make him jealous of you?"

Richard smiled when he thought about his infuriating brother. "'Tis true, George can charm a bird from her eggs, has my mother's good looks, runs faster, throws better, and has mastered Latin more easily than I, but…" he paused and gave Rob a serious stare, "…can I trust you?" The other boy nodded and put his hand on his heart. "Ned favors me," Richard confided, "and I know not why. In the three years since he became king, Ned has honored me greatly, 'tis true, but, blinded by his own ambition, George cannot see that he has received far more." With exceptional maturity, Richard added: "It seems he is someone who will never be satisfied with his life, and I am sorry for him."

Rob reminded himself of some of Richard's enviable honors: not only knight of the Garter and the Bath; admiral of England, Ireland and Aquitaine; the county, honor and lordship of Pembroke; and several manors forfeited by the attainted earl of Oxford; but also the appointment as sole commissioner for several counties in the west, which had made Richard responsible for levying troops for Edward the year before. It was an impressive list.

"If I had not been so astonished by my good fortune that day Ned gave me both Richmond and Pembroke, I might have recognized George's look of…look of, um…disappointment," Richard finished. He could not bring himself to say "hatred," but that was what he had seen in George's face when Edward had bestowed the two counties on the younger brother. George had erupted. Richard had fled and had not been privy to the conversation that followed between his two brothers. A few days later, however, Richmond was whisked from Richard and given to George. Richard had been relieved, and accord had been restored—at least for a while—but resentments lingered.

Rob conjured a different picture of a scowling duke of Clarence and admired Richard's generosity. "George will be very surprised when you see him again after three years with Master Lacey, I'll be bound," Rob declared, brushing off the crumbs from his tunic and gingerly rising from the precarious perch. "And speaking of whom, we had better not keep old Blackbeard waiting, had we?" His feet finding the bank first, he reached out and grasped Richard's arm to steady his leap back beside him.

"My thanks, Rob," Richard said, and while Rob was not sure whether it was for the helping hand or words of encouragement, Richard was learning Rob Percy was someone to be trusted.

Trust became a theme of that first summer at Middleham for Richard. In the castle yard, where the young students practiced hand-to-hand combat with blunted weapons, archery, and tilting, Richard learned to count on his sword, his technique, and his instincts.

"On the battlefield, you must trust all those who fight with you—be they commanders, fellow knights or common foot soldiers," strapping and scarred John Lacey bellowed as he watched his charges thrust and parry, trip and fall down, get bruised and sometimes bloodied. "The chaplain will tell you to have faith in God, and I agree, but most of all you must have faith in yourself. If you cannot trust yourself, who will trust you?"

After a few weeks, the routine became second nature to the youths. Up with the lark, they attended mass before breaking their fast. Richard would laugh as Rob's stomach growled all the way through the service until they could fall on their breakfast of ale, bread, meat or cheese. Next there was food for their brains as they trooped into a wide chamber in the keep for serious studies that included not only the classics, French, law and mathematics, but the rudiments of music, dance and all the elements of chivalry. Being a knight meant more than mere skill with a weapon; it meant studying the great treatises of war and its tactics, and learning to have "all courtesy in words, deeds, and degrees. In other words," Richard groaned to Rob one day as they were struggling with the dense text of *The Government of Kings and Princes*, "we must be perfect."

By midday, they fell upon the dishes prepared for dinner, which the earl and his family took with the household retainers. The wealthy earl would regularly have several oxen cooked for the company, and that was not only when he was entertaining. Known for his generosity towards the peasants, he would send out daggers, speared to the hilt with meat, to the villagers waiting hungrily outside the kitchen door.

Richard particularly looked forward to this time in the day, and not just because of the food. As Edward's brother, he had a special place at Warwick's table and enjoyed feeling part of a family again. He never admitted it, not even to himself, but Richard was homesick for his own family—aye, even George. The earl had been absent often that summer. As governor of the north for the king, he had joined Edward to help keep safe the Northumberland border with Scotland. To tell the truth, Richard did not mind the earl's many absences, because he felt more comfortable with the female members of the Warwick family. Anne Beauchamp, the countess, was an unassuming woman with kind eyes, and Richard liked her. She looked to her husband in all things, unlike Richard's indomitable mother, yet Richard had noticed their marriage displayed none of his parents' mutual affection. That the countess reserved for her two daughters.

It was the eldest daughter, Isabel, who gave Richard's heart its first flutterings. About the same age, they sat next to each other at table, and Richard's pulse increased alarmingly whenever she turned to converse with him. A pretty blonde, Isabel had the palest of pale blue eyes, a pert mouth, and something that the pubescent Richard had recently begun to notice, breasts. Well aware of her charms at thirteen, she could have teased the young duke about his obvious interest. However, not yet experienced in the art of flirtation, she merely attempted to be nice to him, thus charming Richard further and increasing his timidity. He took to stuttering responses when she addressed him, which made the younger daughter, Anne, giggle. Isabel confided to Anne that Richard reminded her of a sad, bleating sheep. Most humiliating of all, Richard would wake up in the night and find his linen nightshirt wet after dreaming of the earl of Warwick's beautiful daughter.

Discovering Richard scrubbing his own shift one early morning, Rob Percy tried to hide a grin. "Stop spying on me," Richard commanded, trying to conceal the nightshirt behind the basin.

"Dreamt of Isabel, did you?" Rob asked casually, and laughed when he saw pretended incredulity on his friend's face. "It happens to us all, Richard. Every single one of us. No need to be ashamed; in fact you should feel proud. 'Tis the beginning of manhood."

Richard scowled. "Most unmanly and disgusting. I shall stop dreaming at once."

Rob guffawed and motioned for Richard to continue with his washing as he explained other bodily changes he thought Richard might be noticing. "Soon you will be desiring to touch females more often than you care to admit, and you must learn to curb those urges before they get you into trouble."

And so Richard listened to a much more pleasant—if less expert— explanation of the passage of boy to man than the usual father-to-son talk. He had not forgotten Edward's clumsy attempt to explain, but he recalled more vividly his conversation with Will Hastings' page. What happened when a man and a woman got between the sheets now became much clearer. He grinned at Rob: "Have you tried it yet?"

The ruddiness in Rob's cheeks, due to more than the Yorkshire weather this time, was not lost on Richard. "You have, you rogue! What was it like, Rob, you have to tell me. Who was it? Was it with…" he dared not breathe Isabel's name; he would die if it were Isabel.

"When you are thirteen, I will tell you, but not before, and certes," he retorted, guessing, "it was not with Isabel. Are you so ignorant? Girls like Isabel are not to be dallied with, and certainly not swived." Richard winced at the unpleasant peasant word. "Have you not learned anything from our lessons in chivalry about loving a noble lady? You speak prettily to her, write poems to her, sing songs to her, dance with her, but you do not bed her. That is reserved for her husband alone."

"Then I shall just have to marry Isabel," Richard declared, squeezing the rest of the water from his nightshirt.

"For you, 'tis not impossible, but until you are fully a man, you should practice on a wench beneath you," Rob told him, enjoying his play on words, which he saw was lost on Richard. "From all I have been told, lust comes before love. Although in my case…" he tailed off, a wistful note in his voice.

"Do you love someone, Rob? I think I love Isabel, but how do I know?"

Rob was tired of answering questions; typical of lads his age, he could be forgiven that he wasn't sure if what he felt for the gentle blacksmith's daughter was love or lust—all he knew was that he was happy when he was in her arms.

"Better hurry up and get dressed or we will be late for mass," was all Rob could think to say, thwarting Richard's desire to know more. Richard had observed his parents' great love: how they had often caressed each other even in their children's presence; the lingering kiss they used to share whenever they had to be parted; and the unbridled joy with which they reunited. Thus Richard had grown up thinking this was the normal way for a husband and wife to behave. After his conversations with Ned, and by eavesdropping on the older boys in the henchmen's quarters, he was learning that love could come from elsewhere besides marriage. It at once titillated and discomfited him.

At mass, he prayed he and Isabel might be wed soon, so he wouldn't have to choose.

"Ready!" shouted the indefatigable Master Lacey to the two squires at either end of the lists. Richard and Rob each lowered the visor on their helms, adjusted their wooden ecranches strapped on their left hands to shield their chests and held their lances raised to heaven.

"Charge!"

Urging his mount into a canter along the division between the paths, Richard began the graceful levée of precisely lowering his lance to be level with the torso of his opponent thundering towards him. He wished he could see more than Rob's hips astride the horse through the narrow slit in his visor, but using the skills he had been taught at the quintain, he knew how to balance his blunted lance and point it at a spot above what he could see to hit his target squarely. The idea was to deal a blow to shield or chest that would unhorse one's adversary, which would put a real knight in his cumbersome harness at a disadvantage on the ground. Often, the fight would continue on foot.

The thudding hooves echoed in his own beating heart, and he felt the blood coursing through his veins, his senses heightened both to hit the opponent and to brace for the impact to himself from the other lance. Rob usually bested Richard, being the more experienced and larger youth, but today Richard felt invincible. He tightened his grip on the lance, steadied his body in the cocooning saddle and smote Rob firmly and cleanly in his mid section, surprising his usually cocky opponent. Wobbling to his right, his lance missing its target, Rob slipped from his saddle and onto the ground, his horse cantering aimlessly away.

When Richard snapped up his visor, he was grinning. He wheeled his horse and trotted around the list to make sure his friend was uninjured.

Seeing Rob gingerly get to his feet, he said: "I took your advice, Rob. I decided it was time I became a man. Besting you was my first goal."

Rob lifted off his helmet and wiped his brow. "I wish you had started with a female conquest, damn you," he grumbled. "I think I have hurt my shoulder."

"At least it wasn't your pride," Richard replied, more seriously. "You hurt that every time you unhorsed me."

Muffled angry sounds gave Richard pause as he lifted his hand to knock on the earl and countess's solar door one September afternoon. He had been summoned.

Warwick had been absent for much of that summer, most of it helping to retake the Northumberland castles that guarded the Scottish border, and some of it in the south negotiating a marriage contract for the king with a French princess. He seemed indefatigable to Richard. The earl had ridden into the castle yard that morning and disappeared into his apartments without pausing to acknowledge the household dignitaries lining the steps to greet him. The uncharacteristic lapse had been reported to the henchmen after their training in the tiltyard and had given rise to speculation that the earl was on important business.

Probably relieved they were stationed on the outside of the carved oak door, the two guards stared stoically ahead as the young duke of Gloucester waited for a pause in the shouting before knocking. Eventually, he was given permission to enter the chamber with an impatient, "Come!"

An overturned chair and the shards of a Venetian goblet littering the floor, its ruby contents already soaked up by the rushes, also gave Richard an inkling that this was not to be a cozy afternoon of pleasantries. The hawk-nose stood out between scarlet spots of anger on Richard Neville's cheeks as he acknowledged the king's brother's deferent bow with a curt one of his own. Warwick's steward cowered on the other side of the bright solar, out of reach of anything else the earl might feel the need to hurl, and he also reverenced Richard, relieved for the interruption.

Dispensing with the usual niceties, Warwick launched the question like a bolt from a crossbow: "Were you a party to this? Well, were you, cousin?"

Richard recoiled as though struck by the imaginary arrow, a worried frown creasing his forehead. "Party to what, my lord?" he replied, as calmly as he could. His first thought was of the hawking expedition that Rob and another of the knight apprentices had gone on the week before without proper escort. *Sweet Jesu, someone must have seen me climb onto Rob's shoulders and slip through the small opening at the back of the mews,* he decided, and braced himself. But why had the rat waited a week...

"Your ungrateful brother has taken him a wife—in secret!" Warwick spat, stunning Richard into openmouthed astonishment. The man was beside himself with fury, and as his fist thumped the table the other goblets danced. "The king has wed a commoner—and without my permission."

"W...wed? Ned wed?" was all Richard could manage.

Seeing the bemused look on the youth's face, Warwick lowered his voice. "Your Ned has made a fool of me and a fool of England—nay, he has done worse than that: he has betrayed England and his crown. And all so he could poke his pestle in a paltry widow of no account."

Richard found his tongue and launched a barrage of questions. "Who is she? When did this happen? What did my mother say? Was he not intended for a princess of France—a match you had arranged, my lord? Is it not she?"

Warwick gave a short bark of laughter and endeavored to calm himself. "If I shouted just now, forgive me, Richard. I can see by your face and your stream of questions that you are as much in the dark as I was." Richard breathed more easily, but the lull did not last long before Warwick was railing at Edward again. "I put him on the throne; I brought the northern lords to him; it was my brother who turned the Lancastrians away once and for all; and I am the only one Louis of France will listen to." Warwick had no qualms about sounding his own trumpet, truly believing every word he said. Richard would later learn how inflated Warwick's truths were. The man was quite convinced he was the kingmaker that the common people had dubbed him. In truth, he was the most powerful noble in the kingdom and Richard's patron, and the impressionable youth was young enough to believe him.

The small door in the panelling beside the fireplace opened and the worried countess hurried in. "My lord, I regret I was not below to greet you. I was with the pantler," she said, going straight to her husband, who formally kissed her hand. "I heard angry voices and came as quickly as I could. Is all not in order?" Becoming aware of Richard's presence, she gave him reverence, but noticing the up-turned chair and broken glass, she gasped, "Who did this? What has happened, my lord? Were you not at Reading with the king?"

"Never fear, my dear," Warwick assured her, swiftly righting the chair, "all was readied for me here. It was my temper, 'twas all. I brought it with me, and it got the better of me. I apologize if I have upset you. And aye, I left Reading two days ago. God help me, I had to leave or I might have embarrassed myself." Seeing his wife's confusion, he patted the chair. "Why don't you take a seat. You might as well hear the story from the start along with Richard."

"Story? What story?"

Thus, as the steward stooped lower than his station to pick up the broken shards of glass, Warwick began to pace before the fireplace, stirring up the dust from the rushes so the particles danced in the sun's rays.

"The king, my cousin, the lecherous young fool, has succumbed to temptation one time too many, this time to dangerous effect. What is it they say: when the prick goes hard, the brain goes soft? Forgive me, Anne, my dear," and he held up his hand to ward off an admonishment. "It appears Edward's lustful eye fell upon a widow of no import standing prettily with her two little sons beneath an oak at her home in Grafton Regis."

"Is that not where Jacquetta of Bedford lives?" Lady Warwick interrupted, "that upstart Woodville's wife?"

Warwick nodded. "Aye, you have it right, my lady. The widow is her daughter. She is a beauty, in truth," he admitted, "but she is naught but a commoner's daughter, a mere baronet's widow, five years Edward's senior, and," his voice rose to a crescendo as he expostulated, "not fit for a king!" And he pounded his fist on the table again.

"Gently, my lord," his wife chided him, "we don't want the servants gossiping. Why do you not calm down and tell us how this came about. Richard here appears as perplexed as I am. This has come as a shock to him, too." Grateful for her concern, Richard nodded.

Warwick stood with his back to the fireplace, his restless fingers pulling at his lower lip as he stared into the middle distance trying to frame his thoughts.

"We had gathered at Reading for a Great Council mainly to discuss the scarcity of money in the mint. In the midst of what is being dubbed the 'silver' council, I was reporting on my progress with King Louis for Edward's marriage to Bona of Savoy when Edward, from the throne, held up his hand for silence. Stretching out those endless legs of his, an infuriating smirk of satisfaction on his face, he allows that he is grateful for all my efforts but that marriage with a French princess was out of the question because...and he does stammer a bit here, having difficulty hiding his own guilt as he confesses...'because I am married already.'" He watched with grim satisfaction as both Richard and his wife gasped in shock.

"Pandemonium broke out, as you can imagine," Warwick continued. "God help me, I stood there stupefied, my eyes bulging, my mouth opening and closing like some brainless carp."

"Jacquetta Woodville is of noble blood, my lord," the countess ventured. "Her brother is the count of St. Pol and she was duchess of Bed..."

"She married a commoner, madam," Warwick interrupted her rudely, "which makes her a commoner and all her brats commoners. He sank down heavily on the chair at the other end of the table, his shoulders slumped over his clasped hands. "'Tis the end of my influence with the king, I fear. He has made it clear that he intends to rule without my guidance. I shall support him, I suppose, but I can never forgive him for this humiliation of me."

Richard, shaken by the news, desperately tried to find an excuse for his beloved brother's thoughtless action. Despite his inexperience in politics and diplomacy, he knew Edward had transgressed by squandering an important alliance with Louis of France.

"I...I am sorry if my brother has offended you, my lord," he ventured, stepping forward. "For all the efforts you have made on the king's behalf, I thank you. I may regret Ned's action, too, but as his brother, I must forgive him." Richard so admired Warwick, who had risen from out of his father's shadow and who was now perceived as an even greater power than the king, that he feared he would be dismissed from Warwick's service before he had completed his training. "I apologize for my brother's disrespect to you, my lord, but please know that as long as I remain under your patronage, as I hope you will allow, you have my loyalty—as does Edward, our sovereign lord."

Warwick looked up at the slight young man and noticed Richard had grown in height as well as stature. Impressed by the earnest youth's directness, and his anger somewhat abated, he admired the boy. Here was someone he could trust, his instincts told him. "Well said, Richard. I own

I am proud to have you in my household." No fool, Warwick was aware of Richard's fear, and assured the youth: "You will serve out your three years here with my blessing." Richard's heart soared. It was one thing to have the grudging approbation of Master Lacey, but to earn the earl of Warwick's praise was quite another. "Now go and find my daughters. Is it not time for dance instruction? They will be in need of a partner."

"Especially little Anne," the countess agreed, relieved by the change of topic. "She has such affection for you."

Richard gave a slight bow, but he had every intention of asking Isabel to dance, not the baby, Anne. Although at this point, dancing seemed a frivolous pastime after hearing of Edward's reckless behavior. At the door, he turned: "May I know the name of my new sister-in-law?"

"Elizabeth Woodville," growled Warwick, "or the Widow Grey. Take your choice."

Elizabeth Woodville. A pretty enough name, Richard thought, as he quietly closed the door.

CHAPTER TEN
SUMMER 1465

Richard traveled down to London with the earl and his family for Elizabeth's coronation the following May. He was dismayed to see the poverty as they passed through the many villages and towns. Villagers stopped to stare sullenly at the richly adorned riders, while barefooted children hid behind their mothers' filthy skirts. Despite the relative calm of the new regime and with the exiling of most of the prominent Lancastrians, including Queen Margaret and her son, England had been stripped bare by the continual warfare between the houses of York and Lancaster. Maimed and disinherited soldiers had returned to find their homes burned, crops withered, or their disabilities preventing them from doing a day's work. Ragged bands of angry men skulked in the shadows of trees in the woods, ready to pounce on vulnerable travelers. Lords, however, still demanded taxes or forfeiture, and thus the forests had become home to these peasant outlaws.

Richard was glad of the relative security of the earl of Warwick's armed guard, and the journey was uneventful. In fact, it gave him the chance to ride alongside Isabel from time to time—although petite Anne was ever present seated in front and protected by her sister's arms. Richard was disconcerted by Anne's light brown eyes, fixed on him as he tried to make conversation with the older Isabel.

"I wish you wouldn't stare," he finally blurted, but then he felt churlish as Anne's eyes welled. The admonishment had the intended effect, and

Anne hung her head, focusing instead on her hands gripping the wooden pommel.

"Do you hear from George," Isabel was asking. "Does he write?"

Richard gave a scornful, "Hah! George put pen to paper? To me? Not a chance, I regret to say." He did not add that he hadn't written to George either. "But Meggie—my sister Margaret—writes. She tells me George is now considered fully a man with all the privileges of his own household. He will no doubt lord it over me when we get to Westminster."

"You don't like him very much, do you?" Isabel looked at him curiously. "I have met him on occasion and I find him perfectly amiable, and," she simpered, "very handsome."

A flicker of jealousy wrinkled Richard's pleasant morning ride through the farmlands of Leicestershire and Northampton. Isabel hasn't even really noticed me, he thought, his self doubt once again registering he could not match up to his more charismatic brothers. He gave Isabel a little bow and excused himself to ride on ahead.

Puzzled, Isabel watched him go. She liked Richard, but she found him enigmatic and a little secretive. Prettier, but not as clever as her younger sister, Isabel preferred the more direct, uncomplicated character of Rob Percy. However, she did selfishly enjoy Richard's attention, although he was hard work, she had once told Anne when they were walking in the walled garden. Anne had responded with astonishment: "But I understand him perfectly. He's the smallest, like me, and we are always trying to catch up." A remarkably astute observation for a nine-year-old, it must be said. "It is horrid of you to let him think you like him."

Flirtatious Isabel had merely shrugged. "Promise me you won't tell anyone, but Father thinks I should marry George." Anne's eyes had opened wide and Isabel had taken her sister's arm and hurried her away from the sharp ears of their nurse. "'Tis true. One day you will have to curtsey to me." Anne had shaken her head in disbelief then and laughed at her sister.

As Anne mulled over the possibility in her mind now, watching Richard ride ahead, a thought occurred to her. "Then why should I not have Richard," she muttered to herself.

Following Richard's progress to the head of the cavalcade that fresh May morning, Anne determined not to give up. One of these days, when she was older and Richard was a man, he would notice her, she was sure.

Who could blame the smitten girl for her plea to the Virgin to reserve Richard Plantagenet for herself?

In his confident new position at court, sixteen-year-old George of Clarence could afford to be magnanimous when the Middleham party entered the king's audience chamber a day or two after its arrival in London. George clapped his younger brother on the back and pumped his arm in friendly greeting.

"Christ's bones!" George exclaimed with a laugh, holding Richard at arm's length and subjecting him to scrutiny. "You have lost your baby face and developed some muscle," he said, squeezing Richard's bicep hard and nodding his approval. "The northern climes have toughened you up."

Richard grinned. "'Tis good to see you again, too, George. You must be glad to be on your own now. Meggie's happy about it. She told me in a letter you had become quite unbearable in your impatience to leave Greenwich."

It was George's turn to grin. "Aye, I was an irritant to our sister, I admit. But, as always, she has forgiven me." Richard said nothing. He knew all too well that George was Meg's favorite, but her letters had shown him that she had not forgotten her youngest brother and thus, he was now more inclined to shrug off envy. Besides, who could not be drawn to this tall, athletic young man, with a lion's mane of wavy golden hair, large sapphire eyes and sensual mouth? It was sadly obvious to Richard that Isabel was smitten, and when George turned his attention to his two female cousins, Isabel's cheeks turned the color of a Lancastrian rose. George also did not fail to notice, lingering over the girl's hand for just long enough to make Richard grit his teeth. He did not stand a chance with her, he realized, and his niggling resentment of George welled up again.

"As steward of England," George was boasting to Isabel as he put out his arm to lead her towards the dais, where Edward was in conversation with Warwick, "I am to preside over the coronation. After the queen, I will be the most important person at the ceremony."

Anne kept close to Richard. "What about the king?" she whispered, looking in awe at the sumptuously dressed giant speaking with her father. "Will he not be more important than George?"

Richard drew her hand under his arm and patted it kindly. "Court etiquette requires the king stay away from his wife's crowning, Anne.

Tomorrow is Elizabeth's day. But you are right, George is merely vaunting." As usual, he wanted to add.

Richard had yet to set eyes on the beautiful Elizabeth Woodville and, curious, looked about the room for her. When someone moved out of his line of sight, he knew he had found her. Her pale loveliness stood out from the frowzy, overblown peahens who surrounded her. Her waist-long hair was the color of moon-glow on water, her hooded hazel eyes dominated her heart-shaped face of smooth translucence, and her plump, cherubic mouth was asking to be kissed. He could not help staring. Always alert to ogling, as beauties are wont to be, Elizabeth soon noticed him and came forward to greet him.

"My lord of Gloucester, I presume? You are as His Grace the King described," she purred as Richard bowed and kissed her outstretched hand. Edward's showy sapphire gift overpowered her delicate fingers. Mumbling a response, he then presented Anne, who fell on her knees in awe of the vision before her.

A tinkling, silvery laugh made Anne look up surprised. "I am not queen yet, Lady Anne," an amused Elizabeth said as she raised the girl to her feet. The unusually sweet sound made besotted Edward take note, cutting short Warwick's rhetoric. Following Edward's gaze, Warwick stiffened. He watched the meeting between the queen and his daughter with barely concealed disdain, and annoyed he had lost Edward's attention, he scowled and went to talk to George and Isabel. The moment was not lost on Richard, but his face lit up as Edward approached.

"My dear Richard," Edward said, acknowledging Richard's low bow. "I see you have become almost a man in the year since you left us. I must commend Warwick for shaping you into quite the handsome youth."

Richard was so chagrined, he could not forestall a flush of pleasure. "'Tis good of you to say, Your Grace. I have been training hard." He noticed he was now at eye level with Edward's collar of gold "S's". I have grown, he thought pleased, I can remember when I only reached his waist. "And may I present the Lady Anne Neville, our cousin."

"I see you have made my Bess's acquaintance," Edward said after accepting Anne's reverence. He took his wife's hand and kissed its upturned palm hungrily. "Is she not the most beautiful creature you have ever seen?"

Richard did not want to contradict his brother, as how could this older woman compare with the exquisite Isabel? "Indeed, Your Grace."

"You were right, Edward," Elizabeth remarked. "He is solemn."

Seeing Richard's discomfort, Edward hurriedly added: "Solemn and loyal, my dear. Warwick has just been singing his praises."

"My lord father likes him very well," Anne suddenly offered. "He thinks he will make a fine knight. He told me so."

With so much approbation, Richard could hardly breathe. Then Edward, his huge hand easily enveloping Richard's shoulder, joined his wife's tinkling laugh with a delighted guffaw. The scene stopped the courtiers' conversations as all observed the genuine affection between the king and his youngest brother. It was a moment of glory for Richard in a room filled with important people. And what was more delicious: George did not appreciate Richard's easy intimacy with the king.

"What do you think of our new sister?" Richard asked Margaret a few days before the coronation. He had asked permission to stay in the Royal Wardrobe behind Baynard's Castle, where Margaret was lodged when not at Greenwich.

Enjoying the late May sunshine in the manicured gardens, Richard was demonstrating a recently learned thrust-and-parry maneuver with a stake he had pulled out of the flower bed. Margaret's shadow, a young dwarf named Fortunata, was teasing Richard by turning cartwheels just out of reach of his lunges.

"Do stop your swordplay, Richard," nineteen-year-old Margaret complained, shutting her book with a snap. "I cannot talk to you when you are cavorting like that." She may have sounded like an irritated older sister, but secretly she was impressed by his graceful movements and his confidence. This was no longer the mewling boy she remembered from the nursery, and she was glad; the past few days had revealed a Richard more willing to laugh, as he was doing now watching Fortunata's antics. "Fortunata," she called, "I pray you behave yourself. Go, fetch us some ale instead." She knew she indulged her beloved servant far too much, but the little Italian was clever, entertaining, and fiercely protective.

"*Si, madonna,*" the diminutive Fortunata replied, untucking her skirts from her belt and hurrying towards the house.

Richard sat down on the grassy exedra next to his sister and plucked a tiny daisy from it. "Now that we are alone, are you going to answer my question about Ned's wife?"

How much should she divulge, Margaret wondered. She had at first been on Elizabeth's side once her brother had taken her into his confidence and asked that Margaret be a friend to his secret wife. Indeed, Margaret was one of only a few who had known of the marriage. Later, he begged his dear Meggie to accompany Elizabeth to Reading, where he had revealed his clandestine marriage to the world and set the cat among the pigeons. Elizabeth had seemed humble enough and pleasant to Margaret and George, but now Margaret was beginning to suspect the woman was proving a negative influence on Ned.

Margaret stroked the smooth leather of her book pensively. "I should like to give her the benefit of the doubt, because Ned loves her so, and..." she tailed off, a tiny blush creeping into her cheeks. Richard did not need to know that she was in love with Elizabeth's handsome brother, Anthony. That was now her secret.

"...And what?"

"And nothing!" she exclaimed, and rose from the grassy seat. "You ask too many questions, brother."

Richard grinned. "That is what my lord of Warwick says, too." He twirled the pink-tipped daisy between his fingers as the next question came to him. "What did Mother say when she found out about Elizabeth? I wish I could have been a flea on Ambergris and heard her." He chuckled. "You know, I think even Ned is afeared of Mother."

Margaret stopped brushing down her skirts and with a wry smile confided, "George heard her recriminations all the way from the royal apartments to his own. She left Ned's side for Berkhamsted not long after without even a bow or bend at the knee, threatening never to return." The brother and sister shared a laugh, imagining their imperious mother stalking out of Edward's presence.

"I think perhaps Elizabeth is afraid of us all—of Ned's family," Richard decided. "Perhaps she is just a shy person, and one needs to get to know her."

Margaret harrumphed. "I can think of many words to describe Elizabeth Woodville—spoiled, proud, secretive, seductive, and ambitious perhaps—but shy? Never!" She leaned into him. "And heed my warning: never get on the wrong side of her."

Naively, Richard could not imagine how he would ever give her cause.

The opulence of the coronation and subsequent banquet told Richard his sister was closer to being right about Elizabeth than he had been by the way Elizabeth indelibly reminded her new subjects that day she was now queen of England. Hour after interminable hour, she made use of her new royal prerogative, forcing those once above her to kneel or stand to serve her. Richard saw with his own eyes that humility was not in her vocabulary nor in her character, and it made him wary.

As he watched her now, Richard had to admit that, seated alone on her splendid throne under a canopy of cloth of gold, her silvery hair flowing over her ermine-trimmed purple mantle, haughty Elizabeth looked regal enough. But her gaze was hard and her movements stiff, and she had none of Edward's easy air of kingship. The forty new knights, who had been created in her honor that day, knelt to pledge their fealty, and she self-consciously held out her hand for each to kiss without once softening her expression. Whether she was quaking in her elegant, crimson-silk shoes or she was nonchalant about her new status, it was hard for observers to decide. Only she knew.

At last the trumpeters sounded the end of the feasting, and Elizabeth processed to her apartments between two bishops, with the mayor of London carrying the voide—hippocras and wafers in case of hunger in the night—on a silver salver before them.

On the road back to the Wardrobe, Margaret was seething. "Did you see she had our brother-in-law Suffolk on his knees for two hours? She had better never try that with me. I shall refuse!"

Richard chuckled. "Seeing that you are a head taller than she and a good deal stronger, I would think she would not dare, Meg."

How wrong he was. A year later, after Elizabeth had given Edward his first (legitimate) child—a girl—she was churched with great pomp and accorded another elaborate banquet, where she was attended in silence by eight duchesses and thirty countesses. This time, the honor of serving the queen was given to the king's sister, Margaret, and Elizabeth's own mother, Jacquetta Woodville, both of whom had to kneel to serve her at each course and remain thus for as long as Elizabeth was eating. The meal lasted for three hours, and Margaret took ill the very next day.

Regretting he could not wait until Margaret had recovered, Richard had had to return to Middleham. Thus, he had been pleased to receive a letter from his sister upon his return. In dramatic fashion, she declared, *I wish I had died. Mayhap she would have learned her lesson.* But then she relented, *I cannot lie, dear brother, for she did visit me and profusely apologize. That was almost worth the cold bath they put me in to lower my fever. The only person Elizabeth is afraid of is Mother. She becomes the simpering miss whenever our parent comes from Berkhamsted or Baynard's to counsel Edward. Our lady mother is much versed in politics, I am beginning to realize, and Ned listens to her more than he does his precious Hastings. Do not misunderstand me, I like Will Hastings, but he and Ned are like peas in a pod when it comes to wine and women. I have to confess a slight sympathy for Elizabeth as Ned and Will spend many a night visiting the taverns in London or Southwark looking for amusement. And you know what Southwark is famed for.*

Richard did not know; he had been only a boy when he lived there in Falstoff's Place and so had never learned the words *whore* or *wagtail* growing up in the north. Her letter continued, *Mother was so angered with Ned one night when she caught him crawling home smelling of ale that she made him kneel down so she could box his ears. Her lady, Beatrice, told me the tale and that the Grey Mare stood aside openmouthed.*

Richard had laughed out loud. It was as plain as the horn on a unicorn that for all her airs —and her crown—Elizabeth was no match for Duchess Cecily. The letter finished with, *As for George, he has developed a bitter enmity for the queen for a reason he is not willing to share, but he should have a care, for the Woodville web is ever growing.*

Richard actually shivered as he folded Meg's letter. Although pleased to be away from court, he worried for his family, and for his eldest brother, burdened with this new responsibility—and a reckless heart.

CHAPTER ELEVEN
1466–1467

Ambitious Elizabeth was more than a match for the great earl of Warwick.

After returning to Yorkshire from standing godfather to Edward's first-born, Warwick again subjected Richard to a tantrum as he listed off the formidable favors Edward boldly granted the queen's large Woodville clan. Edward had no qualms about offending his exalted cousin, and the two men had become, even to a casual observer, further estranged during the earl's sojourn at court.

"The Woodville patriarch, a mere chamberlain when Jacquetta of Bedford's wandering eye caught his at her first husband's court, has been put on a rank with me," he said, in a tone hovering between menace and malice. "And no sooner had Edward created the man Earl Rivers than he took away that loyal supporter Walter Blount's position as treasurer of England and gave it to the wormy Woodville."

"My Lord Mountjoy?" Richard could not help interjecting. "But he was there at the beginning for us—I mean for Edward. How foolish to offend so faithful a friend."

Warwick nodded eagerly. "You see the way of it, Richard. And wait, there's more."

Richard stood aghast as the earl reeled off the important marriages Edward had apparently arranged for his new family: the young duke of Buckingham for one sister; the duchess of Norfolk for a brother; another sister for the heir of the earldom of Arundel; and the earl of Essex's son for a third sister.

"But Her Grace of Norfolk is in her late sixties," Countess Anne exclaimed. "That boy John is only twenty-one. 'Tis monstrous and…" she tailed off as she recognized signs of an outburst in her husband… "is there more, dear?" The whitening of Warwick's knuckles around the stem of her favorite Venetian goblet told his wife there was, and she tensed.

Too late, the twisted, colored glass snapped, and the bottom fell into the rushes. Lady Warwick sighed sadly, as the rest of the useless vessel was flung against the wall. Richard, on the other hand, was impressed. He had often been tempted to throw something in anger, but he was afraid the event would be reported to Blackbeard, and pleasing that exacting master of henchman had always suppressed his urge.

"The most heinous decision involves our family, my lady," Warwick was saying, sucking his bleeding finger. "You remember my brother's son—our nephew of Northumberland—was promised the hand of Nan, heir to the traitor Exeter's lands and fortune?" Binding her husband's injured digit in her kerchief, Lady Anne nodded. How could she forget? The mother of the girl was Anne, duchess of Exeter, Edward's oldest sister. "The ingrate Edward has now rescinded those thanks to please his queen," Warwick continued. "Instead, the king paid his sister, the duchess, a vast sum to buy the marriage contract for Elizabeth's wastrel and no-name son, Thomas Grey. It is an insult."

Richard could not help himself. He suddenly laughed. "That means Tom Grey becomes Ned's nephew as well as his stepson!" The innocent irony tickled him, but the earl glared at his young cousin, and Richard hastily covered his laughter with a fit of coughing. "It is an insult to our Neville house indeed, my lord," he demurred.

"And one I will not soon forget, my lord of Gloucester," Warwick assured him. "I hope your loyalties run deeper than your brother's. At least deeper than the length of a woman's passage."

"My lord!" his wife protested vehemently. "Curb your tongue, I beg of you. Would you use such description in front of our daughters? Nay, you would not! Richard is younger than Isabel and like a son to me. Now, apologize at once."

Astonished and warmed by the mild-mannered countess's defense of him, Richard found himself the recipient of a reluctant, none-too-sincere apology from the outraged earl. Hoping one day he might repay her, Richard bowed low over Lady Anne's hand. He gave his patron a more cursory nod and left the room.

His mind was in turmoil. He desperately wanted to believe the best of Ned, but his sense of justice understood how the earl might feel his honor had been violated. As well, he was beginning to comprehend just how much Edward was ruled by his sexual urgings, and this deeply disturbed him. Could his brother be losing his way?

In the years at Middleham he had become the earl's loyal servant as much as his brother's, and that his family loyalties might somehow be conflicted had never crossed his mind. He hoped he would never have to choose as he hurried to find Traveller, the one constant in his life and in whom he could confide without fear of judgment or recrimination. And above all, a creature he could trust.

Surprisingly, it was hard to find a contemplative spot in massive Middleham Castle, but Richard had found one not far from its walls. Early in his time there, when Traveller had bounded off after a rabbit, ignoring his master's commands to "Come!" Richard had followed him into the copse surrounding the rubble of the original castle on William's Hill a few hundred yards away. The ruin had become Richard's favorite place of solitude when he found the thick castle walls and bailey teeming with people suffocating.

The refuge called to Richard one spring day after a strenuous practice with the mace and war hammer. He actually preferred these effective weapons when in the saddle. There was something not quite right with his posture when he tried to wield a longer sword on horseback. The day after he had worked with the sword, he again noticed his back ached considerably, and Rob had teased him that he was getting old.

The meadows around Middleham were peppered with sheep, the frisky lambs gamboling near their dams. The faces of bright buttercups turned up to the sun as Richard sauntered through them. Traveller loped beside him, as happy to be outside the confines of the castle as Richard was. Richard breathed in the fresh air, expelling the stench of sweaty squires, horse manure, and effluence from the latrine chute nearby in the tiltyard, where the knight trainees spent their mornings.

From the top of the sole remaining but ruined tower, built in the time of the Conqueror, Richard could see the vast, forested, rolling dales beyond the Cover River valley, stretching forever to the south. Seated in a niche vacated by one huge stone that must have tumbled from the wall a century or so ago, he basked in the sun, idly swinging one leg to and fro. After a while, he drew a letter from his jacket.

How now, little brother, Meg began, her elegant script impressing Richard, *I trust I find you well. Perhaps you have not heard up there in the wilds that Ned may finally have succeeded in foisting a husband upon me.* Richard sighed. Poor Meg, Edward had offered her at least four other bridegrooms, but then, for one reason or another, the arrangements had come to naught. She was twenty-one, past the usual marrying age, and had decided, when last Richard had seen her, that she was destined for spinsterhood. He wondered who the lucky man was this time and read on. *It seems Ned has come to terms with Burgundy, much to French Louis's disgust, and I am offered to the widowed Charles, Duke Philip's heir.*

"Christ's nails!" Richard exclaimed to Traveller, sacked out precariously on the ledge beneath him. "My lord of Warwick must not be pleased." The dog did not raise his head or open his eyes but thumped his tail on hearing his master's voice. Richard knew the earl was at court at that very moment to advocate for an alliance with France. Warwick had seemed confident Edward would listen to his mentor this time and had ridden off with high hopes for a reconciliation. Burgundy was no friend to France, however, and Edward's design for Meg would thwart Warwick's plans once again. Richard frowned. He loved and admired both men and wished they could see eye to eye. The earl was older and more experienced, but Edward was the king and his own man. "And my brother," Richard said to himself, sighing. "Ned must always come first." But Ned did not make it easy.

He lowered his eyes to the vellum again and read on. *You may know that Antoine, the bastard son of Duke Philip, will come to London next month to take up the queen's Flower of Souvenance challenge made to him by our English Anthony—Woodville that is.* Richard had heard that the queen had revived the ancient tradition of asking a knight to carry out a deed of chivalry in her honor. Anthony had taken up the challenge, his namesake in Burgundy was to meet him in London for a joust. Richard did not have much patience with jousting, thinking his burgeoning skills as a soldier should only be exercised in real combat. "One should not use them to pretend to fight," he once told Rob, who had once again rolled his eyes at his sanctimonious friend.

Margaret's next statement surprised Richard as he well remembered her bemoaning that women had to marry where they were told. *Ned has not yet agreed to my marriage and, I am astonished to tell you, he says he will wait for my response before signing anything. It sounds kinder than it is in truth, for, as I write, French emissaries are in London to negotiate with Edward through Warwick to see if there is a better match to be made for me. Dear God, I feel like a ball being kicked around Europe until I score a suitable alliance. I want to ask you, dear Richard, if you remember Count Charles during your time in Bruges. Is he a pleasant man?* Richard cast his mind back to those months of exile in 1461 with George at Lord Gruthuyse's house, but it was only the bastard Antoine he remembered. Tall and proud, the duke's favorite son was far closer to his father's heart—and side—than the younger, legitimate, French-favoring Charles. He also knew, having been privy to yet another diatribe from Warwick the previous autumn about Edward's failed foreign policy, that Warwick had loathed Charles on sight. Probably not what Margaret wanted to hear, Richard decided. *All I know of him is that he dislikes his father,* Meg wrote on, *likes soldiering a little too much, and that he has a ten-year-old daughter, Mary. She has even been dangled in front of Edward for George, who stormed off in a fury when he heard.*

Richard chuckled. "Poor Georgie," he said out loud. "Serves him right." He doubted George would be satisfied being consort to a girl—nay, a baby—who would have to wait for her grandfather and father to die before he might attain title to Burgundy. "Poor Georgie," he repeated, with an unkind smirk.

He had not noticed Traveller's low-throated growl until a voice behind him said sweetly: "Why 'poor Georgie,' may I ask," and when Anne Neville revealed herself, the wolfhound stopped growling, thumped his tail, and raised his big head to welcome her.

Annoyed, Richard demanded, "How long have you been here? How did you know where I was?"

Anne flushed. "I...I always know wh...where you are, Richard," she stammered. "You come here often."

Richard rolled up the parchment and stuffed it back inside his jacket. "I come here for peace and quiet," he told her. "If I had wanted company, I would have asked for it." Damnation, he would have to find another more private retreat. Observing the downward turn of her delicate mouth and tears brimming, he was immediately contrite. "I did not mean to speak so harshly, Anne, but you do not need to follow me everywhere." He patted the seat. "I pray you sit down now that you are here. Is there some reason for seeking me out today?"

Certes, there was, she wanted to tell him. She would like to be near him always, but she knew he would not understand, and he didn't seem to care for her. If only she were as beautiful as Isabel... She pushed the thought aside and, tiny as she was, slipped beside him, the space only allowing her to have her back to the view.

"Do you have bad news from George?" she asked, eyeing the bulge in his jacket. "In truth it is about him I am come, Richard."

"Indeed?" Richard cocked his head, his gray eyes curious. He certainly was not revealing Margaret's information to the child and chose to answer her question with one of his own. "What has George done now?" It was then he saw fear flit across her face, and he patted her hand. "Tell me, Anne. I swear I will not repeat it."

"You know Father and the king have quarreled, don't you? I do not understand the politics and I don't want to, but it is on a more personal matter which they disagree." She hesitated, looking sideways at him for permission to continue. "Do you remember last Christmas at Warwick?" She saw him nod. "Did you know Father had invited George to come? I heard Father tell Izzy that he hoped to talk to George about a possible marriage between them. But the king found out about the invitation and denied George permission to visit us. Izzy told me George had written to her to say the king would never allow them to marry."

Richard was now staring across the Cover valley, chewing on his lower lip. So that was the way of it. He began to piece things together. *Christ's bones, no wonder George was angry when Mary of Burgundy might have been thrust on him. He means to marry Isabel, and Warwick wants the match!* The why of this escaped him for the moment, but whatever it was, it obviously had upset Edward enough to forbid the marriage.

For a moment, the part of Richard that disliked George gloated over his brother's lack of common sense. Why anger Ned like this? But then thought of Ned's displeasure was drowned in a flood of self-pity. *Isabel is in love with George! How stupid I have been thinking she could possibly* love me, he thought miserably, concluding Isabel would now never be his. A sigh escaped from him.

"Richard?" Anne leaned toward him and touched his shoulder gently, making Richard jump. He had forgotten Anne was there. Anne, however, had recognized the signs of agitation in her idol, and pulling his silver ring on and off his little finger was one of them. "I hope you are not angry with me. I only thought you should know."

Richard patted her hand. "You did right to tell me, little one. It explains much." He was suddenly struck how brave the girl was: she had in essence betrayed her father's confidence to him. And not just any father—Warwick was, after the king, the most powerful man in the kingdom. Richard bent over to kiss her on the cheek and was rewarded with a blush. Although only eleven years old, Anne had demonstrated more courage than he had owned at that age, he admitted. This was no mealy-mouthed girl, he could see, and he vowed to be kinder to her.

"Thank you. I will not forget this confidence."

"Promise me you will not tell Izzy?"

"I swear. Now, we should go before someone wonders where you are." As Richard moved to leave his perch, a painful twinge in his back made him wince, and he wondered, yet again, what part of all his exercising was causing him this discomfort.

June and July passed leisurely enough, and the great distance between the dales and London meant very little news from the south filtered northward.

All that changed when it was learned the earl was returning to Yorkshire at the end of July, and he wanted his household to remove to Sheriff Hutton castle, ten miles north of York. Countess Anne was puzzled; they always spent summers at Middleham. Packing and moving a household of hundreds would be even more irksome in the heat, she had told her girls.

"I don't much care for Sheriff Hutton," Isabel announced in response to this news. She put down her needlework and picked up her little dog. "It's always so windy there."

"Well I like it," Anne countered. "It's much smaller and cozier than Middleham, and so close to York. Besides, the wind will cool us."

Isabel ignored her. "What do you think, Richard?" She tilted her head and smiled at him.

Strangely, Isabel's flirting no longer excited her cousin; it had not done so since Anne had told him about Warwick's plans for George and her sister. He had been surprised, and a little dismayed, how swiftly he had been able to relegate the lovely, buxom young woman of his wet dreams to the rank of friend. *Is it that easy to fall in and out of love,* he had mused, sadly.

Unwilling to side with either sister, he diplomatically replied: "I could not say. I like both castles for different reasons." Both girls looked crestfallen, and the countess sighed to herself. She thought Richard a nice young man but enigmatic. Too serious and secretive were words she had used to her husband, and Warwick had laughed: "Nay, Richard is old beyond his years. He just thinks too much."

Richard was also perplexed by the earl's command to move, and later, as he and Rob walked the ramparts in the late evening sun, he shared this news with his friend.

"In truth, I should enjoy a change of scenery," Rob said. He had been disappointed the earl had not taken him to France with him, Warwick having told Rob that his training was nearly at an end and he could soon relinquish the title of squire and become a fully fledged knight. "Do you think the move is significant?"

Richard shrugged. "Countess Anne said they have always remained here in the summer."

"Perhaps it is the plague. I heard the court had removed to Windsor because of it. Sheriff Hutton is farther north."

Richard shook his head. "Nay, it is as though he is retreating farther from the king's reach. It causes me to wonder if the earl's embassy to France went awry. Or, more seriously, that Ned sent him on a fool's errand, and they have quarreled again." Richard pulled at his ring and stared over the treetops far below them in the Forest of Galtres. *Should I be sharing such thoughts with Rob?* He was a Percy after all, although not of the Northumberland Percies who favored Lancaster, but distant kin nonetheless. He looked at his friend who was busy pretending to pull back an arrow in an imaginary bow and letting it loose. Richard's hesitation made Rob look back at him, and he saw the question in Richard's gray eyes.

"Christ's nails, Richard, can you still not trust me after three years?" Swiftly unsheathing his dagger, he held the point at Richard's throat before laughing and taking the hilt to his lips and kissing the cross. "Dolt! You will always have my bond, my lord of Gloucester."

Richard relaxed. "My pardon, Rob. Aye, I trust you—although thousands wouldn't!" Grinning, he dodged a feigned blow from his friend. "I will confide that my lord of Warwick told me before he left that he was enjoying Ned's friendship again. I was much relieved. It is true that Warwick favors the French alliance and the king, Burgundy's, but I cannot believe Ned would have sent Warwick to France for nothing. And yet…"

Rob answered with a raised eyebrow. "Who knows? If you are right and Warwick lost his temper…" He grinned as Richard mimed their lord's propensity for throwing things.

"Then I would expect our patron needs to remove himself from court for a while," Richard finished for him. "*Et bien*, we shall know soon enough, I suppose."

Richard's logic had stumbled on the very reason for Warwick's retreat north. The king had used the earl's absence to forge ahead with his own diplomatic alliances without interference.

Within a week, the earl was greeting his family in the courtyard of Sheriff Hutton, pretending he had not a care in the world. But new furrows along the earl's brow and dark shadows under the piercing eyes told a different tale. The division between the kingmaker and his king had deepened.

Richard eyed with interest a youth quietly standing behind Warwick waiting to be presented. Richly garbed, an ostrich feather bobbing from a jewel in his velvet bonnet, his demeanor at once told of a confidence that could only come from his nobility. In truth, as Richard was to discover, the lad was rather shy.

"My lady, this is Sir Francis Lovell, or more formally Baron Lovell," Warwick informed his wife, bringing the boy forward. "He will join our household and train for knighthood with the others. The king has graciously given me charge of him."

Francis bowed and kissed the countess's hand. "My lady."

"You are right welcome, Francis. These are our daughters, Isabel and Anne." The countess watched as the dark-haired youth bowed to both girls before adding, "and this is our cousin, Richard…" she broke off amused as Francis eagerly finished the salutation.

"… of Gloucester. Your brother, His Grace the King, told me to seek you out particularly."

The warm smile and enthusiastic greeting made Richard like Francis immediately, and he grasped the boy's outstretched hand. "My brother was right to advise you thus, my lord. You will find a fine welcome in Yorkshire. The Lady Anne is kindness itself." He saw the recipient of his compliment smile and demur. "How did you leave my brother?" he asked.

"Your brother is as headstrong as ever," Warwick suddenly snapped, startling Francis into silence and causing the countess to wince. "Isabel, Anne, see to making Lord Lovell at home." He watched as the girls took Francis in hand followed by the long-suffering countess, then he glared at Richard and jerked his head towards the smaller of the two solars in the earl's apartments. "I would speak with you, my lord."

Richard had hoped to escape to his dormitory and did not like Warwick's formality. What now, he thought, as he dutifully followed his lord into the sparse solar that served as Warwick's office. The earl frowned as he realized his steward had not readied the room in time for his master's arrival, but he flung himself in the only chair, used the arm to prop his head on his hand, and left Richard awkwardly standing and fidgeting.

Richard waited. After a few moments, Warwick raised his head and looked wearily at him. "Your brother has betrayed me yet again. He has made me look a fool and for all his pleasant rhetoric about wanting my counsel, his sops—like putting Lovell in my charge and giving me more estates, shows he cares not a whit for the work I have done to ensure his place on the throne." He then rose so quickly, Richard took a step back expecting a blow. Instead, the earl brushed past him and went to stare out of the window.

"Because I value your loyalty to me and because of the friendship you have forged here with my family, I must tell you that I believe your brother is on the wrong course." Turning to face Richard, he confirmed, "Edward is in danger of becoming a tyrant, of not listening to those who are more experienced. His dismissal—nay, his contemptible treatment—of Louis's ambassadors was foolhardy. I am so close to a treaty with France because Louis trusts me, but he will now not trust Edward. France is a far more dangerous enemy to England than Burgundy, believe me. Oh, and while I was in France, Duke Philip died, conveniently sealing the tentative plan to have Charles marry your sister. As the new ruler of Burgundy, widower Charles needs a new wife—not to mention a male heir." He muttered something about fate that Richard did not catch, but then the earl continued with his indictments. "As well, your brother is not dealing with the lawlessness in his kingdom, and 'tis no wonder rebellions are beginning to erupt. God's bones, but he acts like a boy!" he cried. "All brawn but very little brain."

The earl turned back to the window, his hands clenching and unclenching behind his back. He was weighing how much to tell the young Yorkist duke, but he could not reveal his hand yet. He needed this boy on his side if he were to regain control of the king. And if not, well then, he had other plans.

"Not only did the king undermine my work with Louis by treating with Burgundy, but while I was gone on his business, he also signed a treaty with another of Louis's enemies, Francis of Brittany. Arrogant folly!" Warwick reached his hands either side of the casement and gripped the frame. When he spoke again, he was shaking with anger. "But most disturbing of all for me and my kin is that he removed my brother George Neville from the chancellorship last month. There was no reason for it, I warrant, and I am certain he only did it to spite me."

For all he was still unversed in the politics of the court, Richard was surprised by this news, but he did not believe his brother had no reason. He remained silent waiting for the earl to involve him in some way. As he gazed at Warwick's back, he briefly noted the window panes in this lesser-used of the Neville castles were still of polished horn and thus distorting Warwick's view—not unlike his perspective on Edward, Richard mused. But then, if he were honest, perhaps he did not know his oldest brother very well as yet, and perhaps Warwick did. Was Warwick right about Edward? It did seem to the thoughtful Richard that his brother was deliberately pushing Warwick away. But why, after all the earl had done for his king? For the first time, Richard allowed himself real misgivings about Edward's character.

Warwick swung round to face the wary Richard. "I think I have earned your loyalty, have I not? All of your family's loyalty if the truth be told. You know I want the best for York, don't you, Richard? Your brother George does," he inadvertently divulged. "He sees the unrest in the country; he sees the way the hated Woodvilles have usurped my proper place at the king's side; and he believes in my ability to bring peace to this troubled realm. Talk to George, he will tell you about Edward's indiscretions and how many other magnates are grumbling at his lack of judgment."

By now Richard's eyes registered his horror. Had he heard wrong? The earl's words were tantamount to treason. Was he expecting Richard to agree with him? Was the earl lying about George's support? Surely his brother would not turn on Edward; he might be vain, self-absorbed, and disaffected, but George was family. Richard's mind thrummed with questions, but his tongue suddenly did not seem to work although his mouth tried to move. Unfortunately, his silence led Warwick to believe Richard was in accord and emboldened the earl. "I want you to think on all of this, and tell me true: Might England be better off without Edward as her king? After all, there are two more-deserving York brothers to take his place—with my help. "

Now Richard's knees went weak, and he sank down onto the vacated chair. "Wh...what are y...you su...suggesting?" *Dear God, was that feeble squeak mine?*

Warwick decided he had planted the seed deeply enough for one day; he would wait until Richard saw the sense in his argument. He took Richard by the shoulders and said kindly. "'Tis a lot to digest, I know, Richard." He raised the youth up and said, almost as to a child. "Why don't you go and find young Francis Lovell and make him welcome in the henchman dormitory. He could not do better than have you as a mentor; you have all the makings of a great leader."

Richard was dumbfounded. In a shake of a lamb's tail, the earl had dared to speak treason and then, as though he had just remarked upon the weather, he had flattered his young charge so deftly as to make Richard disbelieve what he had just heard.

Richard pulled slowly away from the earl's grasp, executed a bow and removed himself from Warwick's presence without a word, revealing none of his feelings, now truly in turmoil. But the jut of the York chin and icy stare as Richard left the room registered the intensity of the young duke's fury. Treason would not win Richard to Warwick's side.

His head spinning, Richard descended the spiral staircase to find Francis Lovell. He almost knocked Anne over in his hurry, who was mounting the stairs to deliver a message from the countess to her father.

"Why so pale, Richard? Have you seen a ghost?" Anne enquired, smiling. "There is one in this castle, you know."

Richard was in no mood to play big brother to Anne Neville and tried to get by with a weary, "Not now, Anne," but Anne stayed him with her hand.

"So Father told you, didn't he?" she whispered, looking for anyone coming up behind her. "He told you, didn't he, that he and George have appealed to the Pope to help George marry Isabel?"

Richard froze. "What?"

Anne dimpled. "And if the Pope says yes, Father says he wants you and me to be married, too." Her pert smile vanished as she watched Richard's face fade from pale to furious white. "Are you all right, Richard? I thought you'd be pleased."

"For the sake of our friendship, I shall pretend I did not hear what you just said, Anne. Now, pray excuse me." And shaking off her hand, he brusquely pushed past her and sped down the stairs out into the balmy evening air.

Sweet Jesu, Warwick is seeking dispensation in secret against Edward's barring of the marriage, he thought. *Should I believe Anne?* Surely the earl would not get away with such a flagrant defiance of the king's command. The trusting boy in him did not want his hero to fall, and he was not yet mature enough to know that powerful nobles like Warwick would hold on to power regardless of cost. Richard had never yet experienced real power, and thus had not yet been seduced by it. Inevitably, all men of his high birth would at some time in their life feel its pull, and Richard would be no exception.

But for now, as he went towards the tiltyard to find young Lovell and, more importantly, Rob Percy, Richard's young heart felt as though a briar had wrapped its thorny vine around it. He faced a terrible choice. He had sworn fealty to Warwick as his lord until his apprenticeship ended, but he had also sworn an eternal oath of loyalty to his brother, the king.

For the first time since he had come north, Richard wished himself far away from it.

Chapter Twelve
Autumn 1467

Richard's wish was answered as though he had a direct line to God. Edward summoned him to London in September, and Rob Percy was given leave by Warwick to accompany Richard.

Warwick's parting words to Richard were curt. "Convey God's greetings to my cousin. Tell the king that I keep the north safe for him, but there are many disloyal to His Grace, as he well knows, including those Percies. Here is a letter I would have you deliver." He lowered his voice that now had a bitter edge. "I pray your brother heeds my warnings that by dealing with Burgundy and treating with Brittany, he may have trouble from Louis. He did not listen to me earlier this year, but perhaps he summons you to discover what the way of it is with me. Tell him the truth: I am his loyal subject." He paused and gripped Richard's arm. "And remember, you are mine."

"Your servant, my lord," Richard replied, bowing. "I will be honored to do your bidding." His face gave away nothing, but the unpleasant knot of conflict gripped his heart once more. Taking the letter, he stowed it in his saddlebag next to one Isabel had begged him to give to George.

Petite Anne stood holding the leading rein of Richard's horse, and as soon as her father mounted the steps to the hall, she braved: " You will be missed, Richard. When will you be back?"

"I know not, little mouse," he said kindly. "In truth, I do not know what my mission is with Edward. But when the king commands, I must go."

"I understand. And I suppose you must take Traveller, too." Anne stroked the dog's head, and Richard was amused that she stood not much higher than the seated wolfhound. He still saw a little girl, although Anne, who would never eclipse Isabel's beauty, was losing her baby face and becoming passably pretty. He bent and kissed her cheek. "I shall be back, never fear."

Besides Traveller, the only luxury Richard took with him was safely hooded and enclosed in a cage carried behind his groom. He hoped he could show George how well he had trained his hawk Phoenix when they had time to hunt outside London; besting George at something was a priority.

Once again, on the long road south, Richard observed with compassion the lot of the common folk. Villages with mud or wooden hovels disgorged ragged barefoot children eager for a glimpse of the finely arrayed horsemen bearing the ragged-staff badge of Warwick. Richard and Rob depleted their small coins before they were halfway to London, watching sadly as grubby fingers groveled in the dirt to find the treasure.

Richard could not help but wonder whether Edward was governing his people any better than good and saintly Henry, who had been removed from the throne because he had failed. It was the very same reason Richard's father had chosen to lay claim to the throne. "We did not depose a mad king to put a profligate on the throne," Warwick had said in a recent conversation, and Richard could not shake that thought from his head: his profligate brother. How could Edward not want to help his unfortunate subjects, Richard questioned. *If I were king, I would want all my subjects to have food, shelter and good laws. I would want them to know I cared for them.*

As they rode through St. Albans, the scene of two bloody battles in what was now being dubbed the "cousins' war," a woman—a merchant's wife, by the cut of her clothes—threw herself in front of Richard's horse, causing the animal to shy.

"Gently, Strider," Richard soothed his palfrey before calling out, "What does this mean, mistress? Are you hurt?"

"Nay, sir," the woman said, but she did not move.

One of the escorts dismounted and roughly pulled the frightened goodwife to her feet. "Be off with you," he hissed. "This is His Grace, the duke of Gloucester, now let us pass."

Richard heard the whispers of "'Tis the king's brother," and was dismayed by the scowls his name evoked. He was not exactly afraid, but his hand crept to the hilt of his shortsword as he addressed the soldier. "Leave her, sirrah!" More gently to the woman, he said. "We wish you no harm, mistress. I pray you, allow us to pass."

Seizing her chance, the goodwife ran to Richard's side and kissed his foot. "Help me, my lord," she begged, "please help me."

Richard frowned. He was not sure how to proceed; this was the first of such encounters for him. Protective Rob urged his horse forward. "Petition your own lord, mistress. His Grace is on the king's urgent business and cannot help you." He jerked his head to Richard to walk on, but Richard did not move. He looked down into the sorrowful face of the petitioner and was moved.

"What is your trouble? Has someone robbed you?"

The woman let go of Richard's foot and wrung her hands in her dirty apron. "My husband is awaiting trial for cheating a customer," she blurted. "He is in gaol and I am alone. My neighbors came and stole everything from us. There was nothing I could do. It was their right because my husband is accused."

Richard blinked. "It is their *right* to steal what is yours? I don't understand." He looked around at the now gathering crowd. "Where is your bailiff or alderman? Who is in charge here?"

A stocky, bald man with an enormous nose stepped forward and effected an awkward bow. "I be the constable, my lord. What Goody Wainwright says is true. If a man is accused but not yet indicted, his goods can be forfeit because there is no bail."

Richard glared at the man. "Do you know who took them?"

The constable shrugged, "Aye, but 'twere their right. 'Tis the law. Nowt I could do."

"Let us leave, Richard," Rob pleaded, noting the surly expressions on the restless villagers. "There's nothing we can do here. You heard the man, 'tis the law."

Observing Rob was right, Richard sighed. "Very well, but I shall look into this." He fingered a rose noble in the pouch at his waist, leaned over and surreptitiously pressed it into the woman's hand. "Hide this well, mistress. 'Tis all I can do…for the time being."

"G…God bless you, young lord," the woman stammered as the coin disappeared somewhere into the folds of her voluminous skirts. "I shall never forget this day. May the sweet Virgin watch over you, Richard of Gloucester." She backed away not taking her eyes off Richard as he clicked his tongue and Strider took his cue.

It was then Richard caught sight of a young man bent almost double over a crutch. His back was misshapen and his face twisted in pain. Richard noticed he was shunned by the rest of the villagers, and understanding that the Devil must have somehow touched the poor cripple, he crossed himself. He shifted in his saddle, his own back acknowledging the same dull ache that was becoming his constant companion. He vowed to double his prayers every night so that whatever was causing his discomfort never reached the level of this poor fellow's malady. He threw the man a coin and spurred on his horse.

"I am too busy putting down rebellions to worry about changing laws for the peasantry." Edward was condescending, dismissing Richard's plea and stinging the youth. "Mayhap you do not realize that my arse is not yet safe upon the throne, little brother. When I know my enemies are truly vanquished, I can look at the law." He took up his cup and swallowed the tawny contents.

Taciturn, Richard bowed his head and went to stare out of the window at the boatmen ferrying passengers back and forth across the Thames. He had been so full of righteous indignation when he arrived and sure that Edward would ease his people's lot, he could not now conceal his disappointment that his brother had not been moved by his example of injustice and sworn to act then and there. He would not dare suggest to this imposing king—brother or no—that perhaps it was precisely because Edward's subjects were unjustly treated by the law that they were rebelling. Could Edward not see that correlation for himself? But Richard was not king, and, young as he was, he could not imagine the weight of responsibility that hung on Edward's shoulders, however brawny.

The king fingered one of the pea-sized pearl buttons on his jacket and contemplated his young brother's back. Such an enigma, he thought, and though he had brushed aside Richard's ardent plea, he did admire that ardor. He coaxed the dejected Richard to face him.

"Do not think I did not hear you, brother. I did—and I do. But I am certain you are curious about my summons, are you not?" He was pleased to see Richard turn, his expression eased. "Let me be plain. I have called you south on your own to ask what you can tell me about my lord of Warwick's plans. He removed himself from London so quickly, I suspected he was fomenting a rebellion of his own." Edward grinned. "I am jesting, in truth. 'Tis not that bad, I trust?" But the lack of an immediate response claimed Edward's attention. "Is it that bad?"

Richard shook his head. "He is your loyal subject," he said, fulfilling Warwick's command. He was relieved that the summons was for nothing that he had done wrong, but he was unsettled that Edward expect him to act as his spy. While he was under Warwick's patronage, surely Edward knew that Richard owed some loyalty to the earl. What really confounded him was whether he should reveal Warwick's marriage plans for George and Isabel. What if Anne were wrong? Richard might look foolish to have listened to her; after all she was only eleven. Nay, he would hold his tongue until such time as he could verify the information. "He still believes you are wrong to treat with Burgundy and not with France," Richard offered.

Edward snorted. "Aye, that is the gist of his letter to me," he said, slapping the parchment on his lap. "Warwick does not see that he is but a fly in Louis' web. I refuse to be drawn in, especially when I heard the Spider was entertaining the She-wolf at the same time as the earl was supposed to be doing my business in Normandy. Did he tell you that?" He unfurled his long legs and rose to his feet. "I cannot believe that was a coincidence."

Richard was shocked. "Warwick and Queen Margaret? You must have it wrong, Your Grace. Warwick may feel slighted but he is still a staunch Yorkist. As is his brother, Northumberland."

"My lord of Gloucester is right." Will Hastings had entered the room unannounced, startling Richard. Richard was surprised how free and easy the chamberlain was with his king, although he knew Will was Ned's confidant. Richard had seen Will several times in the king's presence, but always in public. This was the first time he was witnessing the camaraderie between king and servant in private. "They are loyal to York, especially Northumberland," Will continued. "We would have lost much on the northern borders if not for John Neville."

"And yet another Neville turned his back on me last summer, and I had to remove the Great Seal from him, remember?" Edward snapped back.

"That Neville blood is as thick as the heather that covers their damned moors. I have no doubt that if Warwick turns, the others will follow."

"If I may say again, Your Grace," Will soothed, pouring his friend some wine, "my lord of Warwick is your loyal councilor; he is a proud man 'tis true, but he will do what is right for England."

Edward shrugged. "Aye, I believe he is loyal to England. In truth, possibly more loyal than my ambitious brother, George. I am not sure I trust that boy as far as Richard here could throw him."

Richard started. "George? He may be vain but surely he's no dissembler," he offered, feebly. He wanted to be fair, but even if he could forget the many slights and betrayals he had suffered at George's hands in their childhood, should he betray his brother now? What of the meetings he knew had taken place between the earl and George? And the secret letters between Isabel and George—one he was keeping inside his tunic at that very moment? This was more serious, and he had no proof. The imaginary scales in Richard's head teetered from one side to the other before he chose to hold his tongue for the second time in the meeting.

"I hope you are right," Edward mumbled into his well-padded jacket and, disappointed that Richard had no private information to share about Warwick's plans, he took a swig of wine and changed the subject. "How do you find my baby brother after three years in the Yorkshire dales, Will? Has he not become quite the handsome young man?" His lazy blue eyes smiled at Richard. "Have you discovered the joys of the fairer sex yet? You are not a man until you have, dear boy. Aha," he said, chuckling. "Look at those rosy cheeks; I warrant you have tasted such joys. Who is she, Richard? Your king wants to know."

"I thank you for your interest, but your brother does not wish to reveal the lady. 'Tis unchivalrous."

Will and Edward laughed heartily but wisely chose not to embarrass the lad further. When Richard's mouth was set in a line with his creased chin jutting out farther than usual, it was pointless to persist. "Stubborn," Edward had told his queen more than once, "Richard of Gloucester is stubborn." But Edward liked what he saw in the fifteen-year-old youth. He was growing into a man. The gray eyes were intelligent, steady and looked at him almost with adoration; the nose had grown with the man and was unremarkable; the mouth was a little thin and straight, giving its owner a sober mien; his hair had lost its childish blond and was now a rich brown, curling below his ears. *He is passably good looking*, Edward decided, *especially when he smiles.* He would never stand as high as he, Edward, or as Edmund, but he might surpass George. He felt at ease in Richard's presence, and he felt that he could trust this youngest York. In truth, the king was pleased to have his brother home. Edward would win him over into keeping an eye on Warwick, he was certain.

"Speaking of George, where is he?" Richard asked. "I thought he would be with you."

"He is probably consoling Meg at Greenwich. She is desolate that she cannot marry Anthony Woodville." Edward chuckled at Richard's startled, "Oh!" "She seems to have developed an infatuation for my striking, book-loving brother-in-law, who is, fortunately for England, married. She will have to marry Charles of Burgundy and seal that important alliance, and there is an end to it." He winked at Will and said behind his hand, "'Tis rumored Charles likes soldiering more than wenching. Spends nights in tents with his men. Poor Meggie."

Sir John Howard was announced, and Edward rose and went to greet the older man, an experienced soldier, king's councilor and one of Edward's knights of the body. He clapped Howard on the shoulder, a startling gesture for a king but Edward had won people to his side with it. "Sir John, I give you God's greeting. What brings you from your new wife's bed?"

Richard was embarrassed for the man, but Sir John merely chuckled.

"You sent for me, Your Grace," the stocky Howard reminded the king.

Edward pulled Richard forward. "So I did. Richard, do you know Sir John? He's too modest to say, but he is a distant cousin of ours (albeit on the bastard side)." Edward guffawed, and the councilor's mustachioed face broke into a grin of its own. "He tends to enjoy his Suffolk estates more than I would like, but when he is with me, he is one of my most trusted advisors, and you could do worse than be mentored by him."

Richard was puzzled; was he not already mentored by a far more powerful noble?

Jack Howard bowed low over Richard's hand. "It gives me great pleasure to meet you, my lord duke," he said. "Your brother thinks highly of you."

If Richard's cheeks had been rosy earlier, they grew fiery now. "I am flattered, Sir John," he answered. "I shall heed his grace's advice and learn what I can from you."

Anticipating his sovereign's every wish, Will handed Edward a goblet of wine just as the king said, "Christ's bones, but I need a drink. Come Jack, sit with us. I would ask that you take young Richard under your wing while he is in the south and see that he gets into no mischief. Then I will send him north again to see which way the wind blows, if you get my meaning."

Jack acknowledged with a nod. "With pleasure, Your Grace. I will be leaving Stepney—my London residence," he informed Richard, "for Suffolk on the morrow. Perhaps it would amuse Lord Richard to accompany Lady Howard and me. We could do some hunting."

Like it or not, Richard had to obey the king. He had hoped to spend time with George and Meg. Instead, applying diplomacy of his own, he smiled. "I should like it of all things, sir."

And so, the very next day, Richard set out with Rob and the Howards on a journey to Stoke by Nayland in the bucolic, wooded county of Suffolk, ostensibly to enjoy the hunt with his host. It would prove to be one of the most significant journeys of his life so far.

Compared with the formality of the Warwick household, Jack and Margaret Howard entertained the royal guest and his friend comfortably and with the friendliness of a host and hostess who treated the youths as they would their own sons. On the third day of Richard and Rob's visit, the boys were left to their own devices while Jack Howard went to Ipswich on business.

After enquiring of Lady Margaret if they might hunt, they set out early that morning, making for the extensive forest to the north of the Howard's residence of Tendring Hall, with their two grooms and several hare hounds from the Howard kennels. Richard stroked Phoenix's lustrous plumage as they bade Margaret farewell.

"We shall bring back something for the larder, madam, I promise. Wish us good hunting," Richard called, waving.

"Go north and keep to the main path, or you might get lost," Lady Margaret warned them, pushing a wayward strand of hair under her coif. How happy Jack had made her when he had taken her to wife after two miserable marriages, and now she was expecting his child. "Why do you not take Jack's groom, Wat, with you? He knows the forest." But being as headstrong and fearless as young men were, they waved off her offer, grinned at her motherly advice, and cantered up the drive. It would come as no surprise to Lady Margaret that by early afternoon, they had strayed from the path and lost their way.

At first Richard was unaware of their wandering for several miles, because the game was so bountiful. Rob felled a deer with his crossbow, a weapon he had become renowned for at Middleham, and Phoenix had delighted Richard by taking a hare the first time the bird was sent aloft, and an hour later the raptor had surprised an unlucky quail.

The huntsmen had ridden through several copses and crossed several clearings following another deer, but it was when they entered a particularly dense grove of trees that the two friends had to admit they were lost.

"'Tis Suffolk, not the wilds of Scotland," Rob said cheerily, "I shall go this way and find a path, never fear. You stay here and listen for my horn." A hare skittered out of the underbrush and, without thinking, Richard snatched the hood from Phoenix's head. Immediately seeing its prey, Phoenix began bating, impatient to be off Richard's wrist. Untying the jesses and flinging the bird aloft, Richard watched the elegant bird soar high above the tree tops, the telltale tinkling bell dangling from its leg.

"Christ's nails! What a fool," he muttered to himself. Had he not been taught that one should only release a hawk out in the open?

"Ho, Rob! Where are you?" he shouted. A wail from Rob's horn gave Richard a clue, and the dogs began barking and running in its direction. Twenty yards farther, Richard bent over his horse's neck to avoid a low branch and found himself in a clearing, unaware Rob and his groom were already there staring at a young woman attempting to hide behind her flaxen-colored horse.

Intent on reclaiming his falcon, Richard had eyes only for Phoenix, who had snared and dispatched the hare in its powerful talons, daring the dogs to come a beak's length closer. Richard whistled the bird back onto his wrist, hooded him and praised him before realizing he was not alone.

"There you are," he said, nudging his mount to join Rob.

It was then he saw her.

"Who is this?" Rob preempted Richard's own question and moved his horse closer, forcing the lovely young woman to back up into the woods, pulling her horse with her.

Richard sidled his mount between Rob and the anxious girl and assured her they would not harm her. Huge amber eyes gazed up at him with an intriguing mixture of fear and defiance, and he felt a strange jolt of recognition. Or was it something else? It was similar to the pleasurable rush of blood he used to experience when he looked at Isabel, but this seemed to take the wind from him. He drank in the wild mass of bronze hair, the freckles on her straight nose, the generous mouth, and the long fingers clutching her jennet's leading rein, and he was entranced. He had thought Isabel beautiful, but she was but a spring windflower to this summer rose.

He found his voice again, telling Rob, "Leave her be. Maybe she knows the road to Stoke."

It seemed Richard's calm reply quelled her fear for she suddenly smiled at him. Again a flash of recognition allowed him to smile in return. "Do I know you, mistress? I am…" He was about to give his formal title when something made him hesitate. Would it make her uneasy or, worse, run away? He wanted to stay and take in the beauty of her for ever. However, sensing Rob was about to reveal his identity, he quickly introduced himself as Dickon, "and this is my friend Rob. I confess we are lost. Perhaps you can help us."

He was right; plain "Dickon" unbound her tongue.

"I am called Kate. Katherine Haute, an it please you, sirs." More at ease now with the two young men, she chattered on about being new to the county, having recently arrived from Kent with her husband.

Husband? The word took Richard aback. Kate looked only about a year older than he was—about Isabel's age, he thought, although her figure was more fully formed. It also meant she was spoken for. *Spoken for? What am I thinking?* Judging by her clothes and her lack of escort even by a groom, she was obviously beneath him socially, so why should her status matter? His mind was sorting out these details until Kate mentioned a name he recognized.

"Martin Haute? Is he not a retainer of Sir John Howard?"

Kate nodded eagerly, happy to have recognition from this kind, good-looking youth. Richard's first instincts had been correct; he had encountered Kate Haute before somewhere, but he could not call it to mind. Kate, on the other hand could; she remembered he was not plain Dickon, but Richard, duke of Gloucester, who had heard her sing the night of King Edward's coronation. She was not, however, about to spoil the excitement and confess. Agreeing to lead them back to her husband's home in Chelsworth a mile from where they were standing, she assured the two young men her mother-in-law would put them on the right road to Stoke.

Richard was elated. The ride to Chelsworth would give him more time to observe this enticing creature, and, transferring Phoenix to his groom's glove, he dismounted to help Kate back onto her horse. Before he could remount his own palfrey, Kate wheeled hers round, and plunged back into the woods.

It was all Richard and Rob could do to keep up with her, as she galloped across meadows, her mane of hair streaming behind her, until a modest manor house on the edge of a village emerged in the distance.

"I'd follow her anywhere, wouldn't you Richard?" Rob said breathlessly, a gleam in his eye.

His friend nodded silently, and, as though in a daze, he muttered, "and I must."

Although he did not yet know it, fifteen-year-old Richard Plantagenet had fallen in love.

Before dispatching Richard north again, Edward had signed a treaty of perpetual peace and league with Burgundy, lifting the trade restrictions on Burgundian goods coming to England, and signing Margaret of York's marriage alliance with Charles the Bold. It was the most overt slap in the face to the mighty earl of Warwick Edward had yet dealt, and Richard did not relish facing his patron with this news.

Edward's actions may have pleased Burgundy, but they incensed the London merchants. And when Duke Charles failed to revoke his father's edict against the importation of English cloth, as Edward promised them Charles would, their faith in their king was lost.

Thus, it was an even more hostile countryside that Richard and Rob had to face on the road home. He was glad of the armed guard Edward had sent to accompany them.

Riding north through the gold and brown of autumn, Richard put the politics of London behind him and could not help but see Kate Haute in everything he observed. He likened her hair color to the bright auburn clouds of robin's pincushions, her eyes to the amber beechnuts, her merry laughter to the many babbling brooks the riders forded, and her singing voice to the larks which rose high above the meadows. And he hadn't, until then, even cared for poetry.

Rob was, at first, amused by his companion's infatuation, but then he became weary of hearing the paragon's name. "Aye, she is a beauty. Aye, she has a pleasant manner—although methinks she talks too much—and aye, I think she was taken with you, too, but I pray you, stop prattling on about her or I will continue north home to Scotton and leave you to ride to Sheriff Hutton alone. You cannot pursue her, so what is the point?" Seeing the expression of dejection, Rob, as he was always able to do, made Richard laugh then by recalling the moment when, back at Chelsworth Manor, they had eventually revealed their true identities to Philippa Haute, Kate's mother-in-law."Did you see her eyes? They were as big as communion plates," Rob said, chuckling. Then poker-faced, he declared: "It was hearing that you were a duke and the king's brother that made Kate turn her attention from me to you."

Richard launched a glove at his friend, whose groom scrambled off his horse to retrieve it from the dirt. "Liar! She only had eyes for me from the first moment," he retorted. "But I promise to stop talking about her—at least for five minutes."

They shared a laugh and urged their mounts into a faster canter. The long ride was getting tedious, and they longed for strong Yorkshire ale, some deliciously smelly cheese, and a soft bed. Hardy northerners were wont to sleep under hedgerows when on the road, using their saddlebags for pillows, and although Richard now looked on himself as a man of the north, tomorrow night, God willing, they would find themselves in the luxury of Sheriff Hutton castle.

"What do you think Warwick is hatching?" Rob asked later, when they had slowed to climb a steep hill, jarring Richard out of his reverie about Kate. "I heard it said at Westminster that he had had audience with exiled Queen Margaret in Rouen. Is it true, do you know?"

Richard stretched out his aching back, dismayed by the increasing discomfort. "'Tis true that she was in Rouen as Louis's guest, but I could not say if Warwick actually spoke to her," he hedged. Edward had made it clear that no one outside the privy chamber must know that the two had met and talked. Richard had been so honored to have been included in the private conversation with Hastings and Bishop Stillington, the new lord chancellor, that he would never divulge this information, not even to his closest friend. Richard was learning not to trust anyone in this world of politics and power. Later in his life, breaking this rule would have disastrous consequences.

He frowned now when he thought of Edward's parting words: "I would that you return to my lord of Warwick, say nothing of why I summoned you, and report to me anything that even hints at disloyalty. Will you uphold me in this, brother?" Richard had nodded and placed a hand on his heavy heart. "I will."

Richard shook off the memory as his eye was drawn to something metallic in the hedgerow. "Look yonder," he said pointing. "What is it?" He signaled to one of the escorts to fetch the object, and they all recognized a half-rusted sallet. The man also found a broken sword and, buried in the grass and earth, a halberd, its wooden pole so rotten, it fell apart in the soldier's hand.

"Good Christ," Richard exclaimed, watching Traveller disappear through the hedge. "What is this place?"

"Towton," Rob shouted from farther down the road, where a crude sign pointed the way to the village. "We are at Towton field."

They all crossed themselves, and Richard dismounted and walked to a gap in the wall and stared down the long, steep field to the beck at the bottom, where more than five and twenty thousand Englishmen had given their lives six years before. He whistled to Traveller, not wanting the dog to disturb the dead.

It seemed to Richard that the earth might suddenly erupt and disgorge the uncomfortable, telltale mounds of buried bones and armor, the newly sprouting grass on top like whiskers on a young man's chin. He shaded his eyes and imagined his golden warrior brother on the other hill across the little stream shouting orders to his army as the flying snow blinded them all. He fancied he could hear the whirring sounds of arrows shot from lovingly crafted longbows, the mainstay of the English foot soldier, and remembered now that the strong blizzard had cut short the Lancastrian arrows' flight, allowing the Yorkists to collect and redirect them back, slaying the bowmen on Henry's side of the hill with their own shafts. He thought he could hear the agonized cries of men dying, see the blood-red beck filled with bodies that their comrades used to ford the flooded stream and flee the field. Like other soldiers from time immemorial, something in his blood stirred, and he found the handle of his shortsword and gripped it instinctively. When would he see battle? Part of him longed for it, longed to show what he had learned in three years under Master Lacey, longed to right a wrong, fight on the side of God, Edward and England, and taste the thrill of victory. But part of him did not blame those poor yeomen on Towton Field who had turned and fled instead of standing only to be cut down by the enemy. Which way would he turn? Was he old enough to fight like a man, he wondered? How old must one be?

"Sweet Jesu," he said out loud to the now silent, empty field. "I am fifteen today!"

"Are you, by God!" Rob's voice startled him. "And you still have never felt the joy to be had between a woman's legs. We must do something about that, my friend."

Richard grinned, slapping Rob with his glove. "You, Sir Robert, are naught but a libertine!"

The bigger of the two, Rob laughingly wrestled his friend easily to the ground. "Bite your tongue, my lord," he mocked, and balling up his wool liripipe, he covered Richard's mouth with it. At once, Richard was transported back to the most frightening scene of his boyhood, and a surprised Rob was thrown several feet to his left with tremendous force. Richard now knelt astride him and, with his grim face two inches from Rob's, he snapped, "Never do that again, do you understand. Never!" Puzzled, Rob nodded.

Standing, Richard suddenly winced in pain and fell to his knees. His squire quickly helped him up again, while Rob brushed himself off, looking askance at his friend.

"Too many days in the saddle," Richard muttered by way of explanation. "Let us not waste time in this unhappy place."

The specter of the Towton battlefield clung to Richard as they approached York, the massive Minster dedicated to St. Peter dominating the skyline behind the gleaming city walls that, for two miles, encircled the castle, town, and its many churches. He had often passed under the Micklegate during his time in the north, but today, he could not help but look up at the barbican and imagine his father's bloody head, mockingly crowned with paper, atop a spike. He crossed himself and offered up a prayer for his namesake, whose face had all but faded from his memory. He only remembered the voice, the kindness with which he would speak to his youngest son, and his loud, neighing laugh. "Loyalty above all else should be your watchword," Richard could hear his father say now. "Most of all to family, king, and God." *Aye, Father, but at what cost?*

"We have time to make confession at St. Peter's," Richard suddenly decided. Rob, sensible to his friend's mood since leaving the battlefield site, had refrained from speaking along the way. Now he bowed his head respectfully. "As you wish, my lord." It was time he atoned for the maid he had enjoyed during their brief stay in London anyway, Rob admitted to himself.

"Father forgive me for I have sinned," Richard began the rote prayer to the shadowy figure on the other side of the grille. The detour had been a spontaneous decision brought on by a jumble of guilty thoughts of the thousands of deaths his father's fight for the crown had wrought; his disloyal censure of his brother's failure to bring about peace and justice to the kingdom since winning that crown; and the knowledge that he was about to spy on the man who had treated him like a son for the past three years. So many problems to worry about, none of which was in his control to change. At these moments, only God could alleviate his anxiety.

"Bless you, my son. Confess, and your sins shall be forgiven."

But when Richard opened his mouth, the previous thoughts were pushed aside as he surprised even himself with his guilty admission.

"I have lusted after another man's wife." Surely that was not his feeble voice? "I covet my neighbor's wife."

The priest allowed himself an indulgent smile. He had seen the serious young man on his knees in front of an alabaster figure of the Virgin Mary, and Richard's very youth led the cleric to believe the lad had not yet seen enough of life to have sinned too greatly. He wanted to simply tell his supplicant that all boys of his age lusted—usually after an older woman who was inaccessible—and it was perfectly natural. But his faith and responsibility as confessor instead gave the stock pronouncement: "You must resist temptation, my child, and turn towards the Lord our God for temperance. He will guide you from the path of sin and one day He will bless your marriage bed. Fornication is a mortal sin, as I am sure you know."

"I do, Father. How can I atone for my transgression?"

"Remember the scriptures: He that hideth his sins shall not prosper, but he that shall confess and forsake them shall obtain mercy. If you are truly penitent, by the power invested in me, I can forgive you."

"O God, be merciful to me the sinner," Richard muttered, and after receiving his penance, he thanked the good father and returned to kneel in front of the Virgin. Being in God's presence never failed to move Richard and restore order. Thus, he resolved to put Katherine Haute from his mind.

It would prove an impossible task.

During the hour Richard and Rob had tarried at the Minster, a small group of armed men in the king's livery must have overtaken them, as Richard's meinie soon caught them up on the road to Sheriff Hutton. Observing that one soldier was leading a horse on which a sorry-looking fellow sat with wrists bound and tied to his pommel, Richard slowed his group and rode forward.

"Good day, captain," he addressed the lead rider. "I am Richard of Gloucester, the king's brother. May I know your destination and the prisoner's crime?"

The captain thumped his chest with his fist. "God's greeting, my lord duke. I am taking this measle to my lord of Warwick on command of our gracious sovereign lord, the king. As for his crime, I regret I am ignorant." He slapped his saddlebag. "I have letters from his grace to the earl."

Richard rode closer to the scruffy, terrified prisoner. Judging from the broken nose, black eye and split lip, Edward had had the man roughed over for information.

"I've been wrongly accused, my lord," the man objected. "I was just a messenger."

"No doubt," Richard said, skeptically. "But I will know your business shortly and judge for myself. If you are innocent, you will find Lord Warwick a fair-minded man."

He turned his horse around and signaled to his group to pass the king's men and take the last two miles at a canter. Richard wondered why Edward had sent a prisoner all that way to appear before Warwick, and he was determined to be at Warwick's side when all was revealed. He grimaced. Something else to worry about, he mused.

"Me consorting with Margaret of Anjou?" Warwick bellowed, purple indignation matching his short houppelande. He was garbed to be as intimidating as possible, the baldric across his chest boasting his order of the garter and various precious jewels, and his enormous black felt chaperon and trailing liripipe framing his furious face. He glared at the kneeling messenger-prisoner, who, Richard learned, had been captured at Harlech castle purporting to have heard from French spies that Warwick was conspiring with the exiled Queen Margaret to incite rebellion against Edward.

The telltale marks of recent torture on the man's bruised face did not move my lord of Warwick, the vibrations of fury emanating from the earl almost tangible. The anger felt genuine, Richard was bound to admit, for if Warwick were guilty, this playacting was brilliant. Although Richard pretended outrage at the accusation, and in truth he was inclined to think it was a lie, he knew this was not the first time Warwick's name and the queen's had been linked. Could there be any truth to this whey-face miscreant's words? Or had Edward sent the messenger with false information to test Warwick? He had no time to answer his own questions, however, before Warwick raised his arm and struck the unfortunate messenger a blow to the head that toppled him sideways to the floor. Richard's instinct was to help the man, but he resisted.

"How dare you accuse me, you odiferous, rumpfed villain! Who paid you to speak treason against me?" Warwick demanded of the trembling prisoner, now nursing an already bloodied nose.

"No one paid me," he whimpered painfully, attempting to right himself. "'Twas but a rumor, my lord, whispered by sailors lately come from France, as I did tell the king."

"Lies! All lies!" The earl swiveled, turning his fury on the king's startled brother. "And what do you suppose my reward would be for treating with her, pray? Does Edward have some punishment in store for me? Is that what you have come to tell me, Gloucester?"

Richard could not restrain his own angry outburst. "How should I know, my Lord Warwick?" he lied, his fists clenched in the folds of his tunic. "As you know, I have been upon the road for the past sennight and have had no knowledge of this pitiful pumpion or his rumors until now."

Both men stared each other down, but not wishing to give the king's emissary fodder to take back to London, Warwick grunted an acknowledgement and then dismissed the captain and his prisoner. "You may tell his grace, the king, that I have not treated with Queen Margaret, nor would I have reason to. England's interests—and thus mine—lie only with King Louis of France."

When the two had gone, Warwick roamed around the hall in silence, leaving Richard to wonder if he, too, should leave. He longed to go straight to the chapel and ask God to forgive his lie, the first one he had spoken in his new role as spy. He did not care for the ease with which he had told it, and more unsettling was that it would likely be the first of many in the service of his brother.

But Warwick had not finished with him. "Were you privy to the summons the king sent me last week to attend him on this trumped-up charge of conspiring with the She-Wolf?" Seeing Richard shake his head, he continued: "I refused to take the accusation seriously and so made my excuses." He jerked his head toward the door through which the prisoner had just exited. "Did Edward think that by sending me the man who had falsely denounced me I would change my story? How stupid does his grace think I am?"

"If your conscience is clear, my lord," Richard replied, not fully understanding Edward's motives either, "then you have nothing to fear."

"Fear!" Warwick exploded again. "Fear! It is he who should fear me. I put him on the throne, but the young puppy ignores my experience and insults me with this feeble charade."

"Edward is the king, my lord," Richard said quietly. "He has not acted gracefully, but there is nothing any of us can do about that. He wears the crown and is our sovereign lord."

Warwick stiffened, and Richard steeled himself for a roiling. Instead, the earl accepted the reasoned response with one of his own: "Certes, you are right." His anger abating as quickly as it had arisen, Warwick appraised the young duke, liking his thoughtfulness and admiring his composure. "If I may say so, my dear Gloucester, you would make a far better king than your brother—as would the heir presumptive, Clarence. In fact, he and I spoke of Edward's faults during our time together this summer hosting the French ambassadors. He, too, sees the wisdom of siding with France and eschewing the Lancaster-loving, self-interested Burgundy."

Richard felt cold fear grip him. What was the earl insinuating, that Edward's brothers might conspire to unthrone him? He blinked once or twice, but, not wanting to reveal his discomfort, he attempted a stoic stare. He could not wait to be dismissed.

Warwick quickly regretted his words and sought to diffuse the awkward silence. "Don't look so serious, Richard. You know I was speaking in jest," he said, gently grasping the youth's shoulder. "You must be tired from your journey. Why not change out of your riding garb and join the countess and me for supper?"

"I thank you, my lord." Richard bowed away from the unwelcome hand. "Until then."

With a mixture of sorrow and unease, the earl watched his protégé leave the room. George might be easily swayed with the right incentives, but Richard was far more complex. What was more, Richard had integrity. He had to admire that, even if he could no longer count on the lad.

Richard was even more disturbed by a piece of information idly given by Isabel soon after his return.

"How long does it take to get to Rome from here?" she asked the Italian dance master, who was teaching the young apprentices the newest haute danse, which required the Neville daughters to participate. Richard observed that Isabel was in high spirits, her cheeks glowing, and her chattering excited. Anne was but a pale, mouse-like shadow beside her, although those, like Richard who knew her well, could see Isabel's exuberance was trying the younger girl's patience.

"*La bella Madonna Isabella va a Roma?*" Maestro Bassano enquired, lifting her lithe body off the floor for a beat of the music. "*Perché?* Why?"

"The Pope is there," Isabel replied, landing like a feather. Seeing Richard watching her, she covered her indiscretion by laughing it off with a flippant, "Why does anyone want to go to Rome?"

As Richard circled Anne's waist to emulate the movement so deftly executed by their teacher, his partner whispered: "My uncle, the archbishop, has sent a messenger to the Pope, and Isabel is certain 'tis about her and George. She is simply guessing," she scoffed. As both girls grew older, Anne knew the time would soon come when they would be separated, and, despite occasionally squabbling with her older sister, she dreaded that time. "If the king has forbidden the marriage, Father would not disobey, would he? Isabel is being silly."

But Richard did not think Isabel was silly at all. Was Warwick seeking dispensation? He decided he should pass on this tidbit to Edward, for what it was worth.

CHAPTER THIRTEEN
ADVENT 1467

Celebrating the yuletide season with his family again was mostly on Richard's mind as he rode at Edward's command to Coventry with an armed escort. So bad was the crime now in England that even Edward had to travel with more than a hundred bodyguards wherever he went.

Richard thought back on those happy Christmas reunions of his youth at Baynard's, Fotheringhay and Ludlow, where the temporal music, dancing, and mummery blended with the moving, sacred ceremonies of the holy season. Now watching Traveller lope beside his horse, he remembered December of 1460 when the dog had finally become his. It was probably the moment when he had loved his mother the most. Inevitably, that New Year brought back the painful feelings of emptiness and sorrow at the loss of his father and brother and of witnessing his mother's terrible grief—grief that had perhaps allowed him his first glimpse of the special love between a man and a woman. He pondered whether he would ever know such love, and the thought predictably took him back to the lovely Kate Haute. Just thinking of her gave him pleasure. When would he ever see her again? He could not imagine it. But Rob had once said to him, "… until you are fully a man, you should practice on a wench beneath you." All well and good, Richard thought now, but would Kate be willing. And where could they be private together?

Why not ask Sir John Howard if he could hunt at Tendring again? Had Kate not said something about her father-in-law being Howard's retainer?

Nay, you fool, that was her husband. God's bones, the husband! He slumped down in his saddle and stared at the bleak landscape that was lacking a white mantle so far that winter. *Why does there have to be a husband?* The idea of consorting with another man's wife had never crossed his mind. Indeed it was anathema to him, although he knew it happened. *Control yourself,* Richard thought. *The whole notion is hopeless,* and he reluctantly put Kate from his mind.

The young duke had left Warwick Castle on the banks of the River Avon earlier that afternoon, where the earl and countess were holding their own yuletide festivities, and was relieved to escape the earl's anxious eyes. Coventry was a mere twelve miles away, but when Richard saw the massive red sandstone walls of the city, with its many towers and gatehouses, and the soaring spire of St. Michael's on the far, flat horizon, he let out a heartfelt, "At last!" and the worry over Warwick fled his mind.

Spurring his horse into a canter, he rode through the Cheylesmore Gate and up to the modest but beautiful manor house of the same name, nestled just inside the city wall. Richard understood why Edward needed to be in Coventry, because it was the center of the kingdom, and in these days of unchecked lawlessness, a king might feel more able to put down insurrections from that vantage point. But arriving at the handsome, half-timbered Cheylesmore Manor, Richard could also understand why Edward liked being there. It was a charming place.

A roaring fire in the newly constructed fireplace welcomed the youngest York into the hall, where a scene of domestic tranquility greeted him: Edward was dandling a cherubic blond toddler on his knee; George and Meg were absorbed in a game of chess; and their mother, Duchess Cecily, was dozing on a cushioned settle. Edward's wife and her handsome brother, Anthony, were conversing at the other end of the hall, but all looked up when Richard was announced, and, to her credit, the elegant Elizabeth rose and was the first to greet him warmly.

"Well met, my lord," the queen said, motioning to a servant to take Richard's long velvet cloak.

Richard bowed and kissed her outstretched hand. "Your Grace, God's greeting to you."

A smiling Anthony Woodville, now Baron Scales, grasped Richard's arm in friendship and also bade him welcome. They were indeed two of the most striking Woodville siblings at court, Richard noted, and, like his own, they had a strong family bond. Richard allowed Elizabeth to lead him to where he could give Edward reverence.

"Up off your knees, Richard," Edward cried, hoisting his young daughter into the crook of his arm and getting out of his chair. "'Tis good to see you, little brother. Bess, you remember your Uncle Richard, don't you?" The blond curls bobbed and Richard leaned forward and kissed his niece. She held out her fat little arms to him, and delighted, Richard took the child from her father and bounced her gently up and down.

"You are a natural," Meg teased him, leaving the chess table and kissing his free cheek. "Too young to be a father yet, but I can see you will be a good one some day."

Richard chuckled. "I shall have to find a wife first, Meggie," he whispered. "But Edward has to get you married off before he can look for a mate for me. I hope yours is a giant," he teased her.

Meg made a face. "Charles—the Bold—they call him. I hope he's only bold in battle." She took wriggling Bess from him and the child reached for Meg's jeweled headband.

"Do you have a greeting for me, my son?" Their mother's familiar voice interrupted the siblings. "They all think I am asleep, but I never miss a thing. You have grown and grown handsome, too, Richard. I am pleased."

She held out her hand to be kissed before pulling her youngest into her arms. Despite his fashionably padded jacket, she could feel the increased muscularity in his arms and shoulders, although it seemed to her one shoulder did not feel quite symmetrical, and she frowned. Mayhap he had developed more muscle in his sword arm, and as Duchess Cecily was not one to let her imagination run away with her, she thought no more of it. Richard's mother was, of course, correct. Richard's spine was growing crooked.

"And you are still the most beautiful mother in the world," Richard said, "although I suspect Elizabeth is as close a second as a lily is to a rose." Two women complimented in one sentence he marveled, surprised at his own skillful diplomacy. Although he disliked engaging in this conventional flattery, it was all part of his chivalric training. Elizabeth bestowed one of her dazzling smiles on him, and his mother remarked, "Nicely done," before subsiding back onto the settle. Richard made a silent note: flattery may be false, but it can work.

"What? No greeting for me, George?" Richard called across the room. "Were you finally winning a game from Meggie, and my arrival interrupted you? Too bad!" George pretended not to hear the taunt and kept his eyes on the ivory figures. Richard tried again as he moved to the chess table. "We shall have to play while I am here. I believe I have improved, at least that is what Isabel says." *Aha,* Richard noticed, *that's got George's attention.*

Without even bidding Richard a good day, George was all impatience. "Do you have a message for me?" he muttered so the group by the fire could not hear. "Ned doesn't let me out of his sight, so if you do, slip it to me later, there's a good lad."

Richard frowned, bristling at George's imperious tone and belittling "lad." "What have you done to irk Ned?" he shot back. "It must be more than your dalliance with Isabel."

"That's irksome enough, you simpleton," George snapped. "She is *Warwick's* daughter."

Richard just stared at him. Not for the first time did he wonder at all the secrecy. Isabel Neville was the most eligible, and richest, young noblewoman in all of England. Besides, if truth be told, Richard did not think Edward could question the match given that he had squandered himself, and England, on a nobody like Elizabeth Woodville.

But before he could voice these thoughts, Edward's resonant voice interrupted them.

"What are you two scheming over there? Come take some wassail with us before we sup, and then I would have a private audience with both of you."

His tone was affable, but something in Edward's look made Richard tense.

An hour later, George of Clarence, not as astute as his young brother, sauntered casually into Edward's ante-chamber, a full wine goblet dangling delicately between his fingers. Accompanied as usual by Will Hastings, Edward stood waiting, backlit by the fire, his face in shadow. Richard chose to stand to the side, resting his fingertips on the parchment-strewn table.

"Now pr'haps you can tell ush why we were royally shummoned here, Ned." It was clear this was not his first goblet of the night. "I had t'decline an invitation to shelebrate Christmas with the Talbots and come here to wash your Woodville relations lord it over the household. Christshnails, the arrogance of 'em!"

Richard held his breath. Edward remained dangerously quiet: not only had George insulted Edward's in-laws, but the Talbots were not exactly in favor with Edward.

Oblivious, George persisted. "Were you sent a similar shummons, Richard?" He chuckled on a hiccup. "I like alliteration, don't you? Shlips off the tongue."

That tongue will get you into trouble, Richard thought, willing his brother to notice Edward's darkening face. "I was to spend the season with my lord of Warwick, aye, but I confess I am happier with my own family and welcomed the chance to leave," he said calmly. *Let him soil his own braies,* Richard decided, disgusted by George's behavior. "I am grateful to you, Ned, for asking me to join you—Woodvilles or no. Besides, Elizabeth has been more than civil, has she not?"

Edward abruptly took a long stride forward and poked Richard in the chest. "Stop chattering like a jay. You have not been forthright with me, have you little brother."

Taken completely off-guard by Edward's vehemence, Richard's throat constricted, as he searched for any reason for his brother's outburst. "Wh... what do y...you mean, Ned?"

"Did I not ask you to report on Warwick's actions and intent?" Edward growled. Richard nodded dumbly. "Then why did you not inform me that the earl had sent an emissary to Rome? Why did you not inform me that your brother here and Warwick's daughter were secretly meaning to wed? Don't look the innocent, Richard!" He pulled Isabel's letter from his jacket and waved it in Richard's face. "Did you not carry this missive with you, intending to pass it to George?"

The guilty flush on Richard's cheek affirmed Edward's suspicions. At the same time, Richard was furious that Ned would stoop to searching his baggage. He balled his fists and confronted his angry sibling. "I admit I did carry the letter, aye. Isabel is my friend, and I saw nothing wrong carrying a letter for her, in truth. And, and..." He fumbled for the right words, wishing to defend himself yet not wanting to betray Isabel or Anne. Most of all, he did not want to break his chivalric bond with Warwick. He had planned to tell Edward of Anne's whispered words of the possible dispensation, but not like this. Not in front of George. And not under coercion. Besides, Edward would not believe him now.

"And what?" Edward menaced. "I am waiting."

"I was waiting for a private audience, Ned, to report what little I know…"

Surprisingly agile for one in his cups and finally sensing the danger he was in, George sprang forward, rudely shoving Richard aside, and snatched the letter from Edward's fingers. "If that letter is intended for me, then I should have it!"

Already wound tight as a silk thread on a spindle, Richard instinctively drew back his arm and punched George hard in the gut, emptying the air from his brother's lungs. "May that be the last time you push me, George!" he warned.

Somehow still holding onto his goblet, George flung the remaining contents in Richard's face. "You would betray me, would you, babykins?" he snarled, the slurring vanishing, "and the earl, who has done his best to make a runt into more than the puny prince you are? Good Christ, he has wasted his valuable time!"

"Take back your words or I will mar your pretty face so Isabel will shun you forever," Richard shouted, advancing on his brother.

"Enough!" roared the king, his long arms spanning the gulf between the brothers and grasping each by the front of their pourpoints. He pulled them to within a nose of each other and hissed, "By God's holy mercy, neither of you will consort further with my lord of Warwick. Do you understand? There will be no marriage between you and Isabel, George—not ever. And you, Richard, will henceforth remain at my side. As of this moment, your knightly training is at an end. I have need of both my brothers by my side and on my side." He let them go and watched them step back and glare at each other. "We are a family. We are Yorks. We are our noble father's sons. And we will behave as such. Just because I wear the crown today does not mean I will wear it tomorrow. There are rebellions in the air, traitors to be dealt with, and Lancastrians on our doorstep. Do I have your solemn oath that you will abide by my edicts." Richard nodded. George looked sullen but reluctantly inclined his head. "No more consorting with Warwick unless it is to ride by his side in my royal train. No more love letters to the lovely Isabel. You best not have given your heart or—God help you—your promise, George, for you will not have her. And no more private time with the Nevilles, Richard. I have come to believe your patron and I cannot agree on policy, and I sense a parting of the ways. He must not take either of you with him."

"Well said, Your Grace." Hastings' voice startled Richard, who had forgotten the chamberlain was even there. "Let us give a toast to York. A York!" and he passed some wine to Edward, who grunted.

George turned on his heel and letting the empty goblet fall to the floor, left the room.

As Richard brushed the spilled wine from his clothes, Edward put his arm around his brother's shoulders. "Let him sulk, Richard. He is just a lovesick pup. He will get over it. Now what more do you have to tell me of Warwick's intentions. I can count on you for the truth, can I not?"

"With my whole heart, Ned," Richard replied sincerely; he never again wanted to feel pulled in opposing directions. It was far too nerve-wracking. "You can always count on me."

Richard wandered up to the bedchamber he was sharing with George, brooding on the ugly scene, but before he could step over the threshold, he felt the front of his jacket grasped and he was flung rudely to the floor. George stood over him, eyes bloodshot from wine and anger.

"You traitorous bastard!" he cried, and kicked Richard's side hard while trying to retain his balance. George's squire attempted to steady him, but George thrust him off. "Leave us, Godfrey," he commanded. When the door was shut, George watched as Richard crawled to his knees and hauled himself onto the bed, rubbing his sore ribs. "You betrayed me to Ned, you flap-mouthed measle."

George was unprepared for Richard's newly muscled body and doubled over with a groan as Richard came off the bed, head lowered, and barreled into George's midriff. George found himself flat on the floor with strong arms pinning his own and Richard's angry face three inches from his.

"You betrayed yourself, George Plantagenet," Richard sneered. "'Tis a wonder Ned has not locked you up before now. I know how many times you have consorted with Warwick behind Ned's back. You are playing a dangerous game, brother, but you are not playing it with me. You are playing it with the king."

"You told him about Isabel," George whined. "You gave away my secret. My own brother!"

Richard was suddenly transported back to a day long ago, the last time he had seen Fotheringhay. "Then consider this payment for your betrayal of me when I was much younger and had no defense. You gave me away about Traveller all those years ago, and I have never forgotten." He let go of his brother's arms and stood up. "We are even, and if you want some advice, take Ned's warning to heart. Give up the idea of Isabel." He picked up his fallen bonnet and went to the door. "Never fear, I shall seek more accommodating quarters tonight."

The two brothers avoided each other for a day or two, but then George said something that made Richard laugh, and the two agreed to shake hands. "Now Meg is not here, I shall have to teach you how to win at chess," George said. "I swear, neither of us will ever be as good as she."

When the temperatures plunged at night, most chose to enjoy the warmth provided by another body under the covers. Even so, it was awkward for Richard and George to share a bed again. Richard resented the drink-induced snoring of his older brother, which gave Richard restless nights that yuletide. His childhood nightmares even returned, and one night he shouted so loudly, George came out of a deep sleep to shake his brother awake.

"You must have evil thoughts to be thus inflicted by demons in your sleep," George grumbled. "You know what they say: no peace for the wicked."

"Go to the Devil yourself, George," Richard snapped, wondering himself why his sleep was so disturbed, "and stop your snoring! 'Tis your conspiring with my lord of Warwick that gives me bad dreams."

"Pah!" George rolled over and muttered grumpily, "Next time I shall simply let you thrash around in your sleep and hope whoever is chasing you, catches and silences you for good."

Richard ignored him. George had said worse to him over the years, and he realized his brother was half asleep. Besides, he knew that nothing had been chasing him in the dream: it was some terrifying monster inside him who was trying to push his ribs through his back. In the dream his right side was growing more and more misshapen as the demon used Richard's spine as a brace for its feet so it could thrust the ribs farther and farther out from under his shoulders. Richard shuddered and, as he had been doing for the past few weeks now, allowed his trembling fingers to feel his backbone; it was definitely crooked. Right in the middle of his back, he could feel where it turned sideways.

"Richard," Rob had said to him one day in summer when all the squires had stripped naked and were refreshing themselves in Aysgarth Falls. "Is there anything wrong with your back?"

Richard had frowned. "Only a few twinges now and again after a long ride," he admitted. "Why?"

Rob had thrown him his shirt. "Perhaps I am become too familiar, but your back looks askew. Perhaps you should find a mirror."

Later, Richard had slipped into Anne and Isabel's chamber where he knew there was a polished brass mirror and, locking the door behind him, had lifted his shirt and tried to see his reflection. Rob was right, it was hardly noticeable, but there was a slight list to his body. After that, he had tried hanging by his arms from a tree branch, had favored his left arm during wrestling, and focused on building up the muscles of his left side by doubling the weights he lifted.

When did this happen? he asked himself again now. The vision of the cripple outside the church came to his mind, and he choked down a shudder. *I am deformed,* he thought. What had he done to deserve this? He pondered his many sins: He had cheated at cards when young Francis Lovell was set to best him; he had left the henchman's dormitory several times to go hunting when he should have been studying; he had refused to dance with Anne on occasion because he had wanted to dance with Isabel; he coveted another man's wife; he secretly hated George; and worst of all, he had betrayed Lord Warwick's faith in him. Was God punishing him? Was his deformity indeed a sign from on high? He had been taught long ago that a crooked body came with a wicked mind. Had he been touched by the Devil? Was he capable of evil? The thought was unbearable, and he crossed himself and begged the Virgin Mary to intercede for him. Vowing to live a less sinful life, he found solace in prayer and eventually some rest that night.

The court at Coventry was merry that Christmas, and Richard became acquainted with more of the Woodville siblings, whose numbers seemed to grow daily. He met the once-beautiful matriarch Jacquetta, who took Richard's face in her pudgy fingers and kissed him square on the mouth. "York's youngest boy," she purred; her slanting almond eyes also reminding him of a cat. She called over her shoulder to Richard's mother, elegant in blue silk. "My dear Cecily, what a sweet child." Child? Richard thought bitterly; the woman had not kissed him like a child.

"I am fifteen, my lady," he said politely but firmly, and gracefully removing one of her hands he bowed over it. "Richard of Gloucester, *Madame*, an honor to meet you."

Cecily glided up to Jacquetta, revealing that, despite their same birth year, the duchess of York's tall, lithe figure had weathered the years more elegantly than the shorter, fleshier duchess of Bedford's. "Have you not made my son's acquaintance before, my dear Jacquetta? He was at Elizabeth's coronation, you remember." She took Richard's arm possessively. "This is my kind-hearted son who would like to right all the wrongs of the common folk. Aye, Richard, Edward told me of your passionate appeal. You will learn that it is not good for the people to desire more than their due, is it, Jacquetta? It just leads to violence, exactly as is happening in the kingdom today. Do peasants believe they can govern themselves? Nay, they are incapable. 'Tis why we must lead the way."

Richard had not heard his mother so openly defend her privileged rank or seem to mock him, and he was taken aback. Another time, he might have kept silent, but his youthful indignation and new found confidence spurred him now.

"Did you know our English laws are all written in French or Latin, Mother, which means no one except priests, lawyers and we of the nobility can read or understand them? Do you think that is fair?"

He had not realized he had raised his voice enough to quell conversation in the hall and stop the musicians mid-phrase. All eyes turned to Edward, who momentarily paused in his stroking of his wife's full breasts that were bulging invitingly over her low-cut gown. Turning to the trio by the fire, he made a mocking gesture of futility with his hands and waved on the music. "Richard is lecturing again," he whispered to Elizabeth.

"Have a care, my son," Cecily warned Richard. "Keep your radical thoughts to yourself—until *you* become king." Chuckling at the impossibility, she took Jacquetta's arm and drew her away. "This is what comes of allowing him to play with the yeomen's children at Ludlow."

Richard was disappointed. Had Cecily Neville forgotten her own intercession forty years before when she had rescued the youthful Piers Taggart from the life of an outlaw? She had been just as outraged then at the injustice of the young peasant's plight as Richard was today, and she had taken pity on Piers and given him a position in the York household. But years as a royal duchess and now mother of a king had detached the once compassionate Cecily from commoners.

Richard's awkward moment with his mother was averted by a loud knocking on the manor's stout oaken door. A harried messenger, snow still clinging to his sodden cloak, was ushered in and fell to his knees in front of Edward.

"What means this, sirrah?" Edward demanded. "You interrupt our festivities."

"I come from the Lord Rivers' estate in Kent, Your Grace," the exhausted man mumbled. "I would speak to his lordship."

"I have no secrets here." Edward's debonair father-in-law stepped forward, and bowed to the king. "By Your Grace's leave." Edward gestured to Rivers to question the man, who revealed that a mob had attacked the baron's manor in Kent and that he, the messenger, had ridden hard for two days to report the incident. Jacquetta and Anthony hurried forward and plied the man with questions.

Edward walked to Richard's side and, sotto voce, admitted, "I like not this news. I heard another such attack took place in the north a few days ago—Warwick adherents all."

Richard stiffened. Four years of serving the earl faithfully made him loath to accuse his patron, despite growing suspicion that Warwick was on the verge of turning his coat. He came to Warwick's defense. "How can you be certain these are Warwick's men, Ned? Where is your proof? I left his lordship in the bosom of his family preparing for the season not a fortnight ago."

"We will see. 'Tis time we summoned the mighty earl to speak for himself. If he is responsible, I shall expect him to apologize to Lord Rivers and his family for this outrage." Edward pulled Richard into a shadowy corner of the room to whisper. "My kingdom shall never be peaceful until Richard Neville accepts my wife as my consort and her family as my family. I must have them reconcile."

Richard well knew the disdain in which the noble Warwick held the Woodvilles: "upstart nobodies with greedy ambition," he had said of them, but Richard could not bring himself to betray that confidence to Ned now, although he had questions of his own about Ned's unsuitable marriage. Wisely, Richard decided now was not the time. Besides, he did not want to jeopardize this flattering confidence Ned was placing in him, and Edward's idea of an accord seemed sound.

"When the earl obeys my summons, and I have effected a reconciliation," Edward continued, "I will inform his lordship that your apprenticeship with him has ended. You will be gracious in your thanks, as will I. You will finish your education under my roof, where you belong."

At once, the view of the countryside from Middleham ramparts flooded Richard's mind. Then beloved, familiar faces floated across his vision: cheerful Rob Percy; the young, devoted Francis Lovell; gruff Master Blackbeard; the kindly Lady Warwick; lovely but faithless Isabel; and, unexpectedly, the childish, doting Anne. Was he not even to say farewell? A pang of longing made him wince, but his duty was to his brother, and he bowed acquiescence.

"Do not look so miserable, Richard," Edward chided, making Richard flush. His brother's blue eyes gave the impression of a wandering interest, but in truth they were as watchful as a falcon intent on prey, unnerving many a courtier who wrongly assumed the king's mind was elsewhere. "I will have need of you before long, and perhaps George will work harder at pleasing me now he will have competition for favors."

Seeking to assure his brother, Edward made to put his arm about Richard's shoulders. In an-other time, Richard would have craved attention from Edward, but now, he could not bear to think his growing crookedness might be obvious to his brother's touch. On his part, Edward was surprised when the young man evaded his grasp. Guessing it was to avoid looking like a child, he did not force the gesture. With a glint of mischief as he asked, "Did you leave a sweetheart in the north country, my lad? I hope you do not begin a new chapter with your virginity still intact? Don't be glum, there are too many young ladies here to woo to waste time on one so far away."

"You are mistaken, Your Grace," Richard affected nonchalance at this trivial sexual banter. Was it all Edward could think about at such an important time? "There is no one in the north who awaits my return." Except perhaps Anne, he thought diffidently. He quickly changed the subject. "Do you have a role for me at your council table, Ned?"

"Not yet, but it has occurred to me that you might benefit from time at Lincoln's Inn. Your interest in legal matters shows an aptitude for the law, and I can arrange for an article of clerkship for you. It would serve me well—and you, too, when you are fully in charge of your estates."

Excited, Richard stepped to face him. "I would like this of all things, my lord, except for proving myself as a soldier. If I can continue in that training as well, you will have a most contented and devoted brother."

Edward was satisfied. He had successfully extricated one brother from Warwick's sticky web. Now for the other.

Almost before the final feasting of Epiphany had time to settle on the court's stomach, Edward's angry voice was again heard throughout the small mansion. Richard hurried down the stairs to find Elizabeth pacing and muttering in the hall, her brother Anthony watching her from a high-back settle. The queen scowled at Richard.

"Your high and mighty lord of Warwick has refused Edward's summons—again!" she snapped, accosting him. "His minions are spreading rumors about an imminent Burgundian attack, and that Charles has overturned his treaty with us and is now conspiring with Louis against us. 'Tis no wonder the king is unhappy."

Even angry, Elizabeth, in pale blue satin, was a very beautiful woman. "This is old news, Your Grace," Richard retorted, asserting himself and enjoying the inches the last step of the staircase afforded him over her. "What was my lord Warwick's reason for refusing to come?"

Anthony Woodville stepped between his sister and Richard, his prudence calming the stormy exchange. "Temper your tone, Bess. Richard is not to blame."

For the first time, Richard saw Meg on the shared settle seat and noted the tender expression on her face as she watched Anthony. So this is the man Meggie's in love with, he thought, but had no time to ruminate on it as Elizabeth was expostulating again. "The man is insulting," she raged at her brother. "He had the gall to call us his enemies and demand that I and our family be removed from this house if he were to deign to make an appearance. His king demands his presence and the man refuses. Why, 'tis tantamount to treason!"

Richard suspected something more than Warwick's enmity for the Woodvilles deterred him, but Richard had seen the earl on his high horse many times. And there was his insufferable pride.

"My dear Elizabeth," he began and smiled. "May I call you Elizabeth? If you recall, our cousin of Warwick is a Neville, and just as my Neville mother is proud, so is her nephew. He will bend and he will come, I have no doubt."

"Well said, brother," Edward's voice from the other side of the room made them all start. "I shall bide my time, but he will come."

CHAPTER FOURTEEN
1468

With a magnanimity born of stubbornness and naïveté, Edward did exactly as he had confided to Richard. He summoned Warwick again to his council at Coventry in early February and insisted on a reconciliation with the Rivers family, father and son. Blessed as he was with an almost exuberant optimism, however, Edward badly misjudged the overly sensitive Warwick. While the earl smiled benignly, he was forming his own plan for England, one that did not involve Burgundy—or Edward. Oddly, for one who was so decisive on the battlefield, the young king disliked conflict and tended to procrastinate on matters of governance. Some might even have seen him as duplicitous, or even lazy, while others praised his ability to charm his way out of confrontations. These traits and his hedonism were to plague his reign, and on his death leave England in a dangerous state of instability.

In the spring of 1468 and for the next few months, however, to all but the keenest observers, it seemed as though the king and his noble cousin Warwick were hand in glove once more.

Meanwhile, Richard was to once again be a guest at Jack and Margaret's charming manor of Tendring. The Howard party left Coventry following the reconciliation and wended their wintry way to Suffolk.

Once there, Jack Howard was helped from his saddle by his squire and a groom. He still had a great deal of pain in his leg from the goring he

had suffered during a boar hunt several months before. Richard slipped
gratefully from his horse and gave the reins to his own groom. After a
four-day ride from Coventry, made longer by Jack's handicap, Richard had
so enjoyed the councilor's jovial company that he had hardly noticed his
own physical discomfort.

Besides, Richard was delighted to be spending a week with the
Howards because it meant he might, if he were fortunate, renew Kate
Haute's acquaintance. The very thought gave him a pleasurable rush. He
cleverly raised the subject at the private supper later in the Howard's solar.

"I met Martin Haute when I was in London last summer," he began,
pretending to focus on cracking a filbert instead of the Haute family. "He
is your neighbor, is he not? A pleasant gentleman, I found. I told him how
his daughter-in-law had rescued Rob and me in the forest last autumn. You
remember the day you went to Ipswich, Jack? His son is in your service,
I believe." Whatever he was he blathering on about, he could not seem
to stop.

Jack appeared not to notice and unwittingly pursued the topic. "Aye,
young George Haute is, like you, a knight in training under the duke of
Suffolk's banner. His grace was decent enough to have taken him in at my
behest." Then he shook his head. "I fear he is not made for soldiering like
his father was—seems to enjoy gaming more than tilting, but out of respect
for Martin, I cannot bring myself to dismiss him." This tidbit was music
to Richard's ears. *Thanks be to the Virgin, George Haute is no paragon and so
does not deserve a faithful wife like Kate,* he thought. It also helped Richard's
dislike of the fellow that he had the same name as his least-favorite brother.

"Besides," Jack went on, patting his wife's plump hand, "Kate,
George's wife as you know, was a blessing at the time of my little Cat's
delivery last October. Martin, George and Kate were here when our babe
came early, and Mistress Lackseat's way with herbs and kind heart saw
Margaret through. We are forever grateful, are we not, my love?" Margaret
nodded, her mouth full of venison.

"Mistress Lackseat?"

Jack regaled Richard with Kate's ignominious arrival in London at the
time of the coronation, when her horse had unseated her right at Jack's
feet. "Such a bold-faced wench, I have to say," Jack said, chuckling. "Upon
our short ride to her accommodations in the Chepe, I gained a hearty
respect for her spirit."

"Aye, I, too, noticed it," he said a little too enthusiastically for sharp-eared Margaret. It sounded to her as though Richard of Gloucester had a great deal of interest in young Kate Haute. Embarrassed by his own fervor, Richard hastily added: "Rob Percy and I both noted it."

Later, behind the heavy curtains of their tester bed, Margaret said to Jack: "We should invite young Mistress Haute for a visit, don't you think? There is no one here of Richard's age, and he must be bored with us old folks."

"What are you up to, my wily wife? Think you Gloucester lusts after our beautiful Kate? The king did confide in me that he fears his brother has a dull, moral streak and has eschewed the pleasures of the flesh—if I may be so profane—and Edward could wish he would unbend somewhat." He propped himself up on one elbow and allowed Margaret to twirl his long mustache between her fingers. He would do anything for her when she gazed up at him lovingly from the pillow. "But, come, come, my dear, Kate is wed. Should we be encouraging adultery? And they are so young!"

Margaret's deep-throated chuckle always aroused Jack, and he reached under the covers and fondled her breast.

"Trust me, Jack, I know more than I am bound to divulge now about Kate and her so-called husband," Margaret said on a sigh of pleasure. She pulled his face to hers and gave him a kiss full of promise. "Let us invite her and see where it takes them."

Raucous cock-crowing awoke Richard a few dawns later to a typical East Anglian winter day. The sun had disappeared into a gray, damp mist for a week now. Even hunting was unpleasant in the snow-melted mud and leafless forest. He was in no hurry to leave his warm, downy bed.

But then he remembered: Today was the day Kate would arrive.

He sat up, flung the curtains aside, and slipping off the high bed, nestled his toes in the rich Turkey carpet. Was he ready to face Kate again? He had carried the precious few memories of her in his heart for months now. His excitement mounted as he splashed his face awake, hardly noticing the thin film of ice that had formed in the washbasin. But along with his excitement came the usual qualms of an inexperienced fifteen-year-old—and especially one whose insecurity about his body was already taking hold. Would she find him attractive? What would he say to her? Would she even like him? What would they talk about? They had very different lives. And would his crookedness be noticeable? His fingers crept back there, and he grimaced.

His servant scrambled off his pallet to tend to Richard, who insisted on scraping the meagre beard he had now managed to produce. That had been another worry, as Rob's had come in dark red when he was only thirteen, and Richard had begun to doubt his would ever sprout. Warwick had spotted Richard feeling his chin for it one day and remarked: "'Tis only peasants who have beards before fifteen, Richard. It will grow. Just as you did. Have patience."

Richard was in his chamber following the prayers at sext when Jack's booming greeting told him Kate and her odd-looking servant girl had arrived. He straightened his padded, black fustian jacket, fashionably short to show off a man's shapely buttocks and muscular legs, and checked that all his points were tied—how horrifying if one of his stockings were to slip down his leg. He ran a comb through his thick, chin-length hair and then, silently standing on the landing, observed the scene below.

Despite her sodden appearance from the drizzly day, Kate's beauty glowed. At his shadowy post, Richard took full advantage of his view of her. She was as lovely as he remembered. From the tendrils of chestnut hair curling around her cheek from under her simple caul, the adorable freckles on her nose to her merry eyes accepting the teasing Jack was giving her, he was in her thrall. He allowed his gaze to take in her ripe young body, and to his horror felt himself go hard. Mortified, he turned away. But merely imagining the horror had his erection been seen magically reversed it, and, relieved, he was able to casually stroll downstairs.

"Who is your guest, Jack? May I be introduced?" He could have sworn he had said something, but the thin, inaudible voice surely wasn't his? *What a stupid question,* he told himself upon seeing the astonishment on Jack's face. *What is happening to me,* he wondered? His astute host, however, had immediately grasped an infatuated youth's distress and pretended to do the introductions. It helped that Kate seemed surprised by his presence and appeared to falter in her curtsey. How charming, Jack thought, wishing Margaret could see how perfectly her plan was working instead of supervising the servants in the pantry.

Richard lifted Kate's hand to his lips. "I am right glad to see you again, Dame...."

"Mistress Haute, Kate Haute, my lord," came the quiet response. Kate was acutely aware of Richard's warm fingers wrapped around hers.

"My friend Rob will be envious we are reacquainted, mistress. We dubbed you 'the Lady of the Forest,' that day," Richard said, releasing her hand, and then cursed himself for mentioning Rob's name. He need not have worried; Kate was too busy trying to calm herself. She had thought of the young duke many times in the loneliness of her unhappy marriage, and he was the last person she had expected to see today. He excited but unnerved her at the same time. However, thanks to her resilience and quick tongue, she rallied: "The Lady of the Forest is happy to see you again, too, my lord." And her voice, she was pleased to note, sounded almost normal. "What brings you into Suffolk at this dreary time of year?"

Seeing the two young people now comfortable with each other, and feeling superfluous, Jack Howard sneaked off to fetch Margaret just as the dinner bell rang.

Once the rain stopped, the afternoon was spent with the gentlemen of the house enjoying friendly sport at the archery butts while the women dallied with their needlework, usually an excuse to gossip.

Richard shone at archery and proved it by besting all but one in the group in the first two rounds. However, at that moment he was only aware of the proximity in the house of the lovely young woman from Chelsworth. Glancing up at the solar window, where he imagined the ladies were plying their needles, he was sure he could see those amber eyes watching him. He quickly looked away as Jack called for his next shot, which flew wide and surprised even him.

"Come, come my lord," Jack teased, "one would suspect your mind is on cupid's bow, not on your own."

Richard's attempt at astonishment made Jack laugh. "'Twould be a fool who did not see the lady pleases you," he said, conspiratorily. "Who could blame you. If only I were younger..."

"Sir John," Richard protested, pulling another arrow from his quiver. "Let me demonstrate that my mind is indeed on our sport." He took aim and his arrow found the bullseye with a thud. "Observe, Sir John, I shall prevail yet. Wait and see."

No doubt you will, young man, Jack thought with amusement. No doubt you will.

Richard sat entranced.

Jack and Margaret had persuaded Kate to take up her harp and sing as they all gathered in the Howards' private solar. "You must remember her, my lord, from Westminster? At the coronation feast? You were there in the room when she sang."

"Certes! I knew I had seen you before, Kate," Richard had said happily and was rewarded with a smile. "Why did you not remind me? Aye, please sing for us again."

It was a cozy family scene, with Jack lounging on damask cushions at his wife's feet as she rocked their baby daughter in the cradle while two of Margaret's gentlewomen sat apart diligently embroidering in the light of a small candelabra.

Kate's pure voice and eerie tale transported them all to an imaginary king's hall where the ghostly voice of his drowned younger daughter miraculously rose from the strings of a harp standing by itself in front of the king. Betrayed and murdered by her sister for the love of *sweet William*, the harp revealed the tragic story, finally accusing *the false Helen* in the last melancholic minor notes.

The company sat transfixed for a few moments until Jack said quietly, "'Twas well done, Kate. You have moved us all."

Kate glanced up at Richard and was taken aback by the intensity of his expression. Humbled, she lowered her eyes and carefully wrapped her harp in its velvet covering. Richard said softly, "Mistress, you have a rare gift. My compliments." How he managed to keep from reaching out and touching her he did not know. Every fiber in his body yearned to know this woman. This felt different from his childish infatuation for the untouchable Isabel. Could this be real love?

An explosive snap from the dying fire startled everyone, and heaving himself to his feet, Jack pronounced it time to retire for the night. "Come, Margaret, we should leave our guest his room. God give you a good night, Kate."

Clutching her harp, Kate dropped a curtsey not daring to look directly at Richard again. After the women had gone, Jack turned to Richard to bid him goodnight. "I believe my cursed leg is healed enough to hunt on the morrow. If it dawns fine, we should go."

"Tell me of your injury, Sir John. 'Twas a boar charge, was it not?"

"I pray you call me Jack while we are privately at Tendring. And aye, it was a boar. A noble beast, in truth, which, in the agony of dying, will make one last charge at its adversary." He chuckled. "Alas, that was me."

It cannot be said that Jack Howard's praise of the fearsome wild boar that night inspired Richard to choose the animal for his badge, for he had been pondering a choice ever since Edward had given him leave to order new livery for the small household he was setting up for himself, but he now decided the beast would serve him admirably. One of York's enemies, John de Vere, earl of Oxford, had used the Blue Boar as his cognizance until his execution at Edward's hands, thus Richard came to choose the white, *Blanc Sanglier*, which was to be associated with Richard throughout his life.

Not a half hour later wild boars and badges fled his mind as soon as he blew out the candle hanging on the bedpost. His thoughts were all of Kate and how much time he could snatch with her the next day. For once, his desire to hunt was doused by a fount of passion for the enchanting young woman sleeping not thirty paces away.

The very next day, Richard lost his virginity. As he lay back on the bed in Kate's small chamber, he marveled how easy and how natural it had been. No wonder Edward was so addicted, he shamefacedly admitted.

There had been a little awkwardness at the start when he struggled to undo his straining codpiece, but Kate had known what to do and with nimble fingers loosed the ties, impatiently allowing him to enter her. The pleasure was exquisite but short-lived as the climax was alarmingly swift. The coupling had lasted mere seconds, he was sure, but even so he felt unusually drained of energy as well as filled with amazement. When he turned to look at Kate's perfect profile and make sure the pleasure had been as extraordinary for her as it had been for him, he was horrified to see her tears.

"Did I hurt you, Kate? You cried out, and I was selfish..."

She smiled then. "Nay, you did nothing wrong. My silly tears are happy ones." She hesitated, but her joy could not be hidden. " May I confide in you, my lord? You did think I was experienced, a twice-married woman."

Aye, and thus no virgin, Richard had supposed. He was astonished when she told him about her first marriage at thirteen to an old man unable to bed her as he had dearly desired, and who, in fact, died trying. Her second husband, George Haute, she revealed with a mixture of sadness and anger, preferred his own gender. "And so, Richard, this, too, was my first time," she told him with a rueful smile.

A wave of relief washed over Richard. Although they had known their mutual desire would lead to adultery, Kate had assured Richard before they gave in to their passion that the blame would be hers as she was the married partner. Guiltily, Richard had not protested too much; he found the urge to lie with her had quelled all rational thought.

Now he understood. Although in the eyes of the church she was guilty of adultery, Kate's two marriages had not been consummated. Hard for her to prove and thus outwardly she was culpable, but here was an instance when Richard refused to let worry take control.

"In neither case have you been truly married, sweetheart." Where had that endearment come from? The word had never before come out of his mouth. But with Kate, it seemed perfectly natural. "God will forgive us, if we confess."

Kate laughed and ran her hands over his chest and shoulders. He caught his breath; for the first time in their nakedness he thought of his misshapen back. Had Kate noticed? She must not have or she would have surely turned away in disgust. He drove the thought from his mind and succumbed to her caress.

"And so," she answered slyly, "if we do confess later, what is the harm in doing it again?"

"And again, and again…" Richard whispered, surprised at how soon his body was able to respond to her touch. "But let us not rush it this time, if 'tis possible."

Kate leaned over to kiss him, her impossibly long and lustrous red hair spread like a veil of satin over him. "Then let us learn together, my lord. At this moment, we have no one but ourselves to please."

Ignorant of such matters as they were, the last thought they had was of consequences.

As a result of an afternoon of pleasure and more later that same night, Richard was to learn painfully of its uninvited fruit.

The few lines of untidy scrawl in between ink blots came soon after his first letter to Kate. Her elegant dexterity with the harp did not spill over to the quill he noted with a grin, and he loved her the more for it.

My dearest love, I, too, yearn to be with you once more. And more so now that I am with child.

Richard smothered his gulp with his hand and read the announcement again. Could this be true? They had only made love three times in the space of a mere twelve hours. Sweet Jesu, he was to be a father? Surely he was too young? His seed not ripened? Fifteen was young to sire a child, wasn't it? And yet he did not doubt his beloved. He read on: *My mother Haute knows, but she believes it to be her son's.*

Thank Christ, Richard thought and then crossed himself. "Forgive me, Father." he mumbled, not meaning to take the Lord's name in vain, especially not in the matter of bastardy.

Tell me what more I should do and when I shall see you again, Kate wrote. *And fear not, for I am well. Your faithful Kate.*

Richard knelt at his little prie dieu, and stared at the exquisite painting of the Virgin and Child in the well-used prayer book King Henry had given him. "Help me to be the man I need to be for my child, sweet Mother of God," he said, feeling the comforting mantle of childhood slip away. "Help me shoulder this new responsibility. I shall not abandon the babe— nor Kate."

He bowed his head, turned the page, and prayed.

PART THREE

Lord of the North
Edward's Man

Leicester, December 7, 2012

Dr. Jo Appleby had undertaken the osteology examination at ULAS (University of Leicester Archeology Services) and was waiting to reveal the results to us .... together with Dr. Piers Mitchell, a scoliosis specialist...

The remains would be on a table in the centre of the darkened room, positioned on a specially designed light box that would illuminate them gently from beneath. ...the remains would be given as much dignity within the analysis as possible.

I don't remember the opening words of the session. All I could see was the box that illuminated Richard, his washed bones bright against the darkness. To me he seemed unprotected and I felt like a ghoul invading his privacy....

...Piers Mitchell explained the scoliosis. He had measured the remains...the curvature could have been as much as 80 degrees in life. ...It was idiopathic scoliosis, that is, of no known cause: he hadn't been born with the condition. ...It was most likely progressive and may have led to a shortness of breath, due to increased pressure on the lungs. ...The curve was a "C" shape in the upper torso, and would have made the right shoulder appear higher than the left. ...the right clavicle was a different size and shape, much bigger than the left.

—Philippa Langley, The King's Grave

CHAPTER FIFTEEN
SUMMER 1468–SPRING 1469

London had never looked so festive as it did on the day its citizens bade a bittersweet farewell to one of England's most precious assets: the king's youngest sister, Margaret. The cheering throngs were sending the twenty-two-year-old princess on her dutiful journey to Bruges as bride of the powerful duke of Burgundy. It was said to have been one of the greatest matches of the century, and it may have been that Londoners understood its significance even then. Whatever the alliance may have been deemed later, Edward appeared mightily pleased with it then.

Richard slapped a bluebottle off his soft kid glove as a plague of them continued to worry his horse. The animal's tail swished them from its rump and its shaking head kept Richard busy with the reins. It was unbearably hot that June day, not a cloud in the sky, and the scent of so many garlands and strewn blossoms, mingling sickly sweet with the masses of sweating bodies, horse droppings, and general London filth, was overwhelming. He saw one old woman swoon onto the dirt and called to an escorting guard to fetch water for her.

He was riding side by side with George, and although both regally robed in royal purple doublets with white slashed sleeves, Richard knew most eyes were on his handsome, garrulous brother, who flung coins into the crowd and bent to accept nosegays from giggling maids. Richard sat his horse quietly, hoping the tailor had adequately padded his jacket so his uneven shape would not show. They did not know him here in London, and most stared at him curiously. He knew he should wave, but his horse was skittish, and he kept his eyes on Warwick, who, astride an enormous black courser, was leading the procession with Margaret riding pillion, her scarlet cloth-of-gold gown draped artfully over the horse's back and tail. Somehow from the February fracas to this auspicious occasion, Warwick and Edward had darned the hole in their former friendship, and Warwick had agreed to be Margaret's escort. Richard was much relieved; perhaps now he could resume relations with the earl.

Richard had not been privy to the discussions Edward had held with Warwick in February at Coventry, to which the earl had been persuaded to attend by his brother, Archbishop Neville. Warwick had reluctantly reconciled with two of his adversaries, but he would not keep company with the Woodvilles. Edward also refused to take warning from the earl's ire that he had forged alliances behind Warwick's back with Burgundy and Brittany against France, leaving the earl to keep his own counsel and the wounds to fester. How the two men arrived at this day of unity was testament to Edward's naive dealings with the powerful Warwick—of which the earl would fully take advantage in the not too distant future— and Warwick's arrogant belief that he was the power behind the throne.

Was it Richard's imagination or were the Londoners cheering Warwick as much as Meg? He thought he heard, "à Warwick" in the cacophony of voices, trumpets, and bells, and he observed how the earl smiled and bowed left and right, throwing coins into the crowd. Richard had often admired his mentor's ease and generosity towards the Yorkshire yeomen. Warwick seemed to reserve his arrogance for the nobility below him and not for the commoners. Edward would do well to copy him, Richard thought, for once Warwick and Meg's horse had passed a well-wishing group, the cheers became less enthusiastic for Edward following them.

Halfway down the Chepe, Margaret caught Richard's eye and blew him a kiss; without a moment's hesitation, Richard looked over at George. Surely it was for him, Richard thought, but George was busy bussing a plump woman's blushing cheek, eliciting catcalls from the fishwife's intimates. Richard pointed at himself, and Meg nodded and blew him another. She looks so confident, he thought. Happy almost. She was sitting tall and proud behind the earl, waving to the wish-wishers lining the windows, doorways and street. But Richard knew Meg was dreading going "to her fate" as she called her arranged marriage.

"'Tis my duty," she had told him. "As a woman, I was born to be of use to my family. This is what I am useful for, like it or not." Richard understood duty only too well and had acquiesced. If only Edward had considered duty before marrying Elizabeth, he thought. Although consumed with passion for Kate, Richard knew their love could not lead anywhere; his duty would not allow it.

A cry of "God bless our own Lady Margaret!" from a group of nuns jolted him back to the present, and he remembered learning how Meg spent hours of her time nursing the sick and giving alms to the poor in this overcrowded, plague-ridden city. He would miss Meg. He felt pride for his generous, intelligent sister, and wished instead it were George leaving to be married to young Mary of Burgundy—an alliance that had come to nothing.

He shifted in his saddle and turned to watch a juggler fling balls high in the sky. *Is that what Edward must do as governor of his people,* he idly wondered. *Keep so many balls in the air?* All of a sudden he recalled the conversation he had had with poor King Henry about the burden of kingship, and now Richard thanked the saints he was not destined to wear a crown.

One-by-one her family said goodbye to Margaret in the hall of the archbishop's palace at Canterbury, where they had all stopped for the night to pray at Thomas a Becket's shrine. Edward, Elizabeth, George and Richard each presented her with a parting gift, while Cecily, stoic as always, took her daughter aside into an adjoining room and gave her a mother's blessing.

Watching Meg's carriage and her entourage move slowly out of the courtyard on its way to Margate, and hence by ship to Flanders, Richard, standing with George and Edward, felt a real sadness at her loss. He had been touched when she sought him out at her wedding festivities at Stratford Langthorne Abbey to whisper that she had divined who was his lady love. "Such a beauty, Richard. And she is with child, is she not?" Meg had asked. Richard had known his flush confirmed her suspicion. He had inveigled Jack Howard to bring Kate to the abbey, amusing the older man who could not refuse. "Even if she were not such a beauty, I would not blame you for having fallen in love with her voice," Meg had told him. "It is surpassing heavenly."

Indeed, Margaret's cheerful attitude throughout the week-long pre-marriage proceedings had impressed Richard so much, he had at one point actually concluded that Margaret would have made a better leader than the men in his family. Her regal bearing—at five-foot eight inches—and her ability to converse as easily with men about policy as with women about fashion would endear her to her new Burgundian subjects in a very short time, Richard had no doubt.

Edward suddenly cried: "Farewell, Mistress Nose-in-a-Book!" The friendly nickname Meg had earned for her love of books made Richard forget his sadness and cheerfully chime in.

Hearing this annoying endearment for the final time made Margaret lean out far enough to see her beloved family get smaller and smaller under the palace gate. She had never felt so alone. She knew it was the last glimpse she would have of them for years—perhaps for ever. Her tears ran unabashed down her face, and she clung to her wolfhound Astolat's neck, as her faithful servant, the dwarf Fortunata, patted her mistress's knee.

"Farewell, England," Margaret sobbed into the wind. "And God save the house of York."

It was an astute plea as Margaret was leaving an England in turmoil and thus the crown in danger. Indeed, on several occasions during the week-long bridal journey, Edward had received alarming information of incidents that were rumored to include Lancastrians, Margaret of Anjou and, most lamentable for the Yorkists, my lord, the earl of Warwick.

Edward took the arm of each brother, turned them around and marched them back inside the archbishop's palace, where they proceeded to drink heartily of the strong apple cider for which Kent was famous.

"I think we gave our sister a royal send-off, do you not agree?" Ned asked after the second pouring. "Let us hope Charles recognizes how fortunate he is and treats Meg with the respect she deserves." He chuckled. "He will regret it if he does not."

His brothers laughed in agreement and raised their cups. "To Meg!" George cried, and all three downed their cider.

Edward beckoned to his brothers to lean in over the table. "Did you notice who I sent with her as her champion and my representative? Our sister is enamored of Anthony Woodville, and I have a suspicion the feeling is mutual. What irony that her lover should give her away to her husband, don't you think?"

Richard did not think it was irony; he thought it was cruel, but he said nothing and tried to join in the laughter. Also, he was not as familiar with the apple liquor they were downing with alacrity as he was with ale or wine. Hiccuping loudly after his third helping, he banged his cup down and watched Ned go in and out of focus at an alarming rate. "What'sh in this?" he slurred. "I shwear I haven't had mush."

Ned grinned and winked at George, who was also doing his best to stop his own body from reeling. "Poor little Dickon," the oldest York teased. "He's been too long in the north where the strongest liquid they have to offer is ewe's milk. 'Tis time you learned to drink seriously, my lad. Especially if you are to be with me more often." He reached for more cider and began to pour. "Will and I are wont to frequent the city taverns when we can; the wine and women are more plentiful and accommodating than at Westminster."

Edward's words struck a raw nerve with Richard. He had parted from Kate at Stratford with a heavy heart. She was radiant in her pregnancy but had welcomed him to her bed during the few nights the royal party had feted the bride. In whispered conversations after blissful lovemaking, the lovers had told each other of their hopes and fears, and Richard had promised to support Kate and his child, when it came. They had shared gifts—his a gold filigree ring and hers a French écu on a leather lanyard. "My father gave it to me. It came from Agincourt," she had told him, slipping it around his neck. "It has brought me good luck. Mayhap it will bring you the same." He had kissed her and told her he loved her. Coward that he was then, he had not told her he would always be faithful. It would have been cruel to explain about duty at such a sweet moment. He had made love to her instead. But Richard swore to himself that he would remain steadfast until such time as he would make a marriage befitting his royal status, which now brought him back to Ned.

Richard stared at his brother and did his best to concentrate, as one does knowing one is inebriated, but the drink also gave him unaccustomed daring. "Have you no shame?" he answered finally, not realizing he was shouting. "You leave your wife's bed to go whoring? Is that the way a king behaves?"

The momentary silence hung like lead in the small solar. George instinctively shrank back in his chair, a small smile curling his mouth; for once it wasn't he who had angered the king. Edward's eyes glittered as he raised them from the jug to Richard, and the set of his jaw told of his ire.

"You presume to accuse me, your king, of bad behavior, my lord?" Edward's measured tone fooled Richard for a second and gave him license to continue.

"Aye, Ned, I do. You told me once you loved Elizabeth. Seeking pleasure elsewhere does not bear out that love. You pledged your troth before God..." He got no further. Edward suddenly stood up, knocking over his chair and thundered his fists on the table.

"You insolent pup!" he roared, leaning in. "Drunk or not, how dare you! My marriage is none of your business. I am King of England, and shall do as I please." He glared down the table at his youngest brother, who had initially flinched, but now rose to face Ned, the drink giving him courage.

Holding firmly to the table edge to steady his legs, he told Edward exactly what he had been thinking about his big brother. "You have been my idol all these years, Ned. I looked up to you—we all did. None was prouder of you on your coronation day than I, except perhaps for Mother. I have wanted to be like you all my life, but now...now I am not so sure. You seem to care more for your own pleasure than you do for the welfare of England. How can you set a good example as king when you have no morals?"

George gasped, and Edward took a step back. Not even his mother had given him a dressing down such as this, although Edward knew she had been close—especially after the revelation of his secret marriage. He considered Richard for a prolonged moment, watching his brave little brother squirm on drunken legs awaiting his fate. Ah, the power of kingship.

"Have a care, Richard," Edward said finally, the measured tones returning. "I should have you put in chains for speaking thus to your king. But you are my brother first and so I shall demand your apology instead. I hope 'tis the drink that has addled your brain or I would take you for a fool or, worse, a prude. Therefore, I shall forgive your outburst. But hear me well, Richard, I will not countenance another."

Richard felt for his chair and sat down, but his eyes never wavered from Edward's. He knew he was in the right, and although he wanted to do nothing now but run to the garderobe and lose the contents of his stomach, he said: "I apologize, my lord, but I must stand by my words."

"Fair enough," Ned said, relaxing. "Spoken like a York. What say you we find some food."

And just like that, Edward's anger died. The next day, he was called away to London on urgent business and took Richard aside. "Do not imagine I have not thought on your words of last evening. But bear in mind, my boy, don't think I'm ignorant of your dalliance between the sheets with a certain young lady, who," and he paused meaningfully, "who, I believe is married and with child. Be careful you are not called hypocrite." He chuckled as he saw Richard's chagrin and pulled him into a brotherly embrace. "You, too, may find one day that passion trumps duty."

Never, Richard thought. *Not ever.*

Richard's resolve may have wavered a little when he was sought out by Kate's father-in-law, Master Haute, one day in early October, as Richard was returning to Baynard's from his daily studies at Lincoln's Inn. Ned had been as good as his word and arranged for Richard to study the law under Justice Markham, known as "the Upright," and Richard's first foray into the law courts was to watch Markham try several instigators of a plot to bring back Queen Margaret from France. Those first months, Richard had struggled with the Latin, but as he read more and strived to understand the English laws, his fluency improved. *"Dei verbum est legis,"* he was able to tell his chaplain a few months later. "Indeed the word of God is the law," the delighted cleric had responded.

The affable Martin Haute nodded when a page pointed to Richard seated under a tree, reading a page from a sheaf of papers. A tall athletic man in his late forties, the gentleman from Suffolk bowed and begged a moment of Richard's time.

He cleared his throat. "Your Grace, I am Martin Haute of Chelsworth. My daughter-in-law is Katherine Haute." He wished he had not acquiesced in seeking out the duke of Gloucester with Kate's news. Why would the young man care, he had argued, but his wife, Philippa, had reminded him that Richard had been a guest in their home briefly and that Kate had come to know the duke at Sir John Howard's manor. She had seen no harm in

Kate's friendly request. "'Tis an opportunity for you to be known to the king's brother, Martin. It cannot hurt your career at court."

Now facing the young duke, who had risen quickly at the mention of Kate's name, Martin thought his mission foolish, but there he was. "Kate wishes to be remembered to you," he said, "and she thought perhaps you would be happy to know her news. She has given us a beautiful granddaughter, born two weeks since. We insisted the babe be named Katherine after her mother."

Richard felt as though he could float off the ground. A child? He had a child—a daughter. It took all his resolve to calmly put out his hand to shake Martin's and say, "My congratulations to you and to your daughter-in-law, Master Haute. I trust Kate and her babe are well?" What he really wanted to do was dismiss the man and give out several shouts of joy. Instead he listened as Martin described young Katherine and how she was the image of her mother. *May the saints be praised*, Richard thought. The Hautes mercifully thought the child was their son George's, who was blond-haired and blue-eyed.

The bell for terce rang and seeing Richard gather his papers, Martin bowed and politely excused himself. As he rounded the corner of the nearest building, he could have sworn he heard whooping.

With his obligations to both Edward and Warwick and his work at Lincoln's Inn, it was six months before Richard could excuse himself to ride to Suffolk and meet his daughter. He had, however, made good on his promise to Kate to help provide for the child. An annuity of five pounds was entered in Richard's household accounts in Katherine Haute's name, with no explanatory footnote.

Kate had moved from her in-laws' house in Chelsworth and was the proud owner of her own small house, given to her by Margaret and Jack Howard on their property in Stoke by Nayland. Only they knew of little Katherine's paternity, and removing Kate from her in-laws lessened those good people's chances of discovering it, too.

Richard and his squire, a young man named John Parr, rode fast out of the Aldgate, joined the Colchester Roman road and thence onto Stoke. With every passing mile, Richard's anticipation grew. He wondered if motherhood had changed Kate in some way. Would she still be beautiful? Would she still care about him? Her letter-writing was sporadic, and he could see she labored over the penmanship. He loved imagining her chestnut head bowed over a parchment, her generous mouth screwed up in concentration, and her ill-sharpened quill leaving splotches on the page. Would the baby scream if he picked her up? At least he knew that George Haute would not be there—he had gone with Jack Howard and Warwick to Calais.

As they cantered through the village of Stoke towards Tendring Hall, Richard wondered if he should have alerted Kate first, but he wanted to surprise her. It had been a spur of the moment idea, and so he had decided to inform only Lady Howard of his visit. The kindly Margaret was waiting for him and, after giving him refreshment, sent Wat the groom down to Dog Kennel House—the name Jack had given Kate's new home—saying she wished to see Kate. A true romantic, Margaret was relishing the clandestine meeting between the two young people.

Margaret was discreet enough to have left the tower room when Kate arrived looking for her, so she did not witness the passion with which Richard and Kate were reunited. She did watch and smile as they trotted down the long drive to the cozy cottage on Richard's horse, Kate cradled in front of her lover. Margaret knew full well what love was; she and Jack had found each other after previous marriages, and she had never been happier.

Once upstairs in Kate's fire-lit chamber, Richard could not believe the entrancing little person swaddled in her cradle was his. He gazed in wonder at the cherubic face framed in wisps of copper-colored hair, the baby's tiny mouth working on her thumb as she slept. "She's perfect!" he said. "I cannot believe she is mine." He pulled Kate to him and whispered, "Oh my dear, my heart is so filled with pride and joy. How can I ever thank you?"

Smiling seductively, Kate responded by drawing him to her bed.

With Richard's knightly training complete, he was released from Warwick's charge and was a frequent guest at Edward's council table. The rumors of rebellion were rife in April, and Edward had not lost time executing several Lancastrian lords for treasonable treating with Margaret of Anjou. The previous autumn he had allocated money to local sheriffs for the purpose of spying on the suspected families in their district. It was the first spy network set up in England, and the resulting arrests had revealed to the council the precariousness of Edward's hold over the kingdom. Richard was dismayed to learn how many times the earl of Warwick's name had been associated with some of the accused troublemakers.

What was worse in Richard's eyes was that George's name was being more and more associated with the earl. He feared for the stability of his family, let alone England.

"Why do I hear nothing but praise for Warwick when he is clearly undermining his king?" Edward complained to Richard one day. "Just because he dispenses leftover victuals to the commoners outside his door does not mean he is an upright man." Richard bit his tongue as he had seen how Warwick drew the people to his side through his even-handed and strong governance.

"Perhaps if you showed more compassion for your subjects—stopped taxing them with so many benevolences, heard their grievances with respect to outdated and unfair laws—they would rally to your banner, Ned." Richard was becoming more at ease in his role as advisor to his brother, and Will Hastings had more than once complimented Richard on his maturity and common sense. Knowing how much Edward favored Will, Richard was gratified to have earned the older lord chamberlain's approbation. The young duke still did not approve of the unfortunate influence the hedonistic Hastings had on the king, but he had begun to understand that Ned was just as guilty. It was as well Richard had earned the councilor's trust, for in a very short time the two would need to work in tandem on behalf of Edward to avert a regnal crisis.

In January, Richard had served on a special commission of oyer and terminer for the first time. Presiding alongside several other nobles, Richard watched as the judge and jury found two traitors guilty of being in league and plotting "the final death and destruction of the Most Christian Prince Edward IV…"

He did not, however, choose to witness the cruel hanging, disemboweling and quartering of the accused. He was not so naive as to think he would never have to see such a death—it was part of everyday life in that day and age—but this was his first time of pronouncing a death sentence, and he chose to leave Salisbury before it was carried out. *Am I a coward?* he worried, remembering how he had vomited upon seeing poor Piers Taggett's violent death. He had been spared seeing bloodshed in the years since Ludlow, but he did not doubt that at some point, he would have to put his knightly skills to the test and spill another man's guts without benefit of choice. Today, he had had the choice, he reassured himself, and he was about to urge his horse into a canter when he fancied he heard his father's voice asking the same question: "Are you a coward, my son? That is what others will think when you are absent from the punishment you were responsible for meting out." Richard gasped and clutched his chest, the blood pounding in his ears. *Is that what they will believe?* He could not tolerate that he—Richard Plantagenet, son of York—might be branded a coward.

Reining in his mount, he glanced about him, wondering who was watching. Only a washerwoman hanging clothes raised an eyebrow as the young noble, grimly talking to himself, made an abrupt turn and galloped back to the market square.

By the time the third man was quartered, the horror of the cruelest of executions eventually allowed the bile to settle back into Richard's stomach. The young man was becoming hardened to his station in life, like it or not.

An uprising in Yorkshire was reported in early April, led by an activist calling himself Robin of Redesdale, and although Edward trusted in Warwick's brother, John Neville, to rout the rebels, which he did with little or no resistance, it unnerved Edward that Neville agents were said to have incited the unrest.

"At least I can count on one of our Neville cousins," Edward remarked to Richard. "John seems to understand loyalty better than his brother."

"Be not so quick to condemn my lord of Warwick," Richard replied. "We only suspect him of turning his coat. I still cannot believe it of him. This rebellion had naught to do with him."

Edward grunted. "I pray God you are right and that this is the end to the troubles."

It was not.

Two weeks later another "Robin," this time of Holderness, gathered followers in the East Riding of Yorkshire, who seemed bent on restoring Henry Percy to his rightful earldom of Northumberland. These ragged men threatened at the very gates of York until once more John Neville, who had, ironically, been given the very earldom in question by Edward many years since, put this rising down as well. However, a revival of Redesdale's movement occurred almost immediately in Lancashire, and his army grew. It was time for Edward to leave the comfort of Westminster and deal with the insurrection himself.

It was also time, Edward said, for Richard to get a taste of combat. "You will come north with me, brother. Go muster your men."

Muster his men? How? Richard, in his seventeenth year, had only a few retainers at his disposal. His squires, a few servants, and his friend Rob Percy, who had chosen to join Richard's household from Middleham. Certainly, Richard had others he could call on from his several land holdings scattered around England, but Edward was leaving immediately. Richard also found himself low on resources to pay those he could muster. It was an embarrassing situation to be in for a royal prince, he fumed, but he did not dare complain to Ned. Instead he asked for a loan from a trusted friend, who had once asked a favor of Richard.

On June 21, the two brothers rode out of London towards Bury St. Edmunds and Walsingham, where they would pray for guidance in their mission at the two world-renowned shrines. The journey was uneventful except for an unexpected reunion with the indomitable Kate. She had talked her way into riding to Bury alongside Margaret Howard, who was to meet Sir John there. Kate had an inkling Richard might be in Edward's party, and she had been right.

Somehow the two lovers were able to escape for an hour or two one afternoon, and, consumed with passion and overheated in the hot June sun, they had thrown off their clothes and plunged into the nearby river. Like two children released from supervision, they frolicked in the cool water until, excited by the delicious exploration of each other's submerged bodies, they made love in rhythm with the gently moving stream.

"Perhaps we have made a son, today," Kate whispered after they climbed out onto the bank and lay naked on the green moss to dry in the sun. "I shall pray to Saint Catherine that we have." Gentling him over onto his stomach, Kate stroked the slight protrusion and enlarged clavicle.

"Does it hurt, my love? It looks as though it must hurt."

He tensed. "Only when I have sat my horse for too many hours. But I have worked long and hard to compensate," he told her. He could not see her expression from his position but, certain it reflected disgust, he tried to roll back over to conceal his flaw. Kate resisted him and then, with a tenderness that moved him greatly, she kissed the shoulder.

He sighed then, understanding that she was unperturbed by his imperfection. "I am fearful of it being noticed. Any enemies I make will be sure to blame the Devil and call me a monster. I do fear that I have displeased God in some way," he confessed. Then turning over and taking her hand to his lips, he asked, "Tell me true, my rose, does it notice when I am not prancing about naked."

Kate smiled and shook her head, her curtain of wet hair sprinkling his chest with cold drops of water. "You have no need to trouble yourself, Richard. Only I know what is beneath your shirt. Well, me and Rob Percy, I suspect."

And perhaps Mother, Richard thought, remembering the concerned look on Cecily's face the last time they had embraced. "Aye, Rob knows and certes, my squire. I could not bear for others to know, so I beg you never to disclose my secret to…"

Kate stopped his words with a kiss.

By the time Edward reached Lynn, he had gathered more than 200 men to his banner. It has to be said that Edward did not appear in any great hurry to quell whatever annoying rebellion had erupted in the northern "wilds" of his kingdom, more's the pity. Richard silently took offense to Ned's ribbing of his preferred part of the country, but as he had similar feelings for the self-important southerners he ignored his brother's taunts.

They had taken to the waterways of the fenlands after leaving Bishop's Lynn and the little army ventured all the way to Fotheringhay on the winding River Nene. Seeing his birthplace for the first time since he had left it at seven years old, Richard remarked it did not seem as imposing as it had been then. Even so, the keep rose high on the motte with the York banner floating over it, and it was comforting to see not much had changed in almost ten years.

Richard watched with an ache of envy as Edward dismounted in the inner bailey to stride eagerly across the cobbles and take his wife in his arms. Elizabeth had accompanied her father and two brothers to meet Edward on his march north, and they had mustered more men to Edward's side. How he wished he could take Kate as a bride, but the idea was absurd and he put it from his mind.

Although more troops and supplies arrived during the last two weeks of June, Edward was disappointed he had not been joined yet by the earls of Pembroke and Devon. He moved out of Fotheringhay and rode unhurried to Nottingham castle, where he dug in and waited for news.

Edward blanched, reeled backwards and collapsed into a chair when he read the missive that he now crumpled in his clenched fist.

"What is it?' Richard and Hastings asked in unison. Elizabeth quickly poured some wine and offered him the cup.

Edward downed the contents in one long swallow. All eyes were on him as he handed back the cup to Elizabeth, who was now kneeling by his side. "What is it, my dear lord?" she asked.

"The worst of news," Edward's flat monotone belied the words, but all could see he was in shock. "Not only is my cousin of Warwick preparing to turn his coat, but it would seem my brother George has done the same."

It was not a complete surprise to anyone in the room, but all gasped just the same. Richard felt the bile in his throat as all the years of friction and suffering at George's hands rose to sour his senses. He could not speak he was so overcome with a heady variety of emotions: anger, disappointment, scorn, sadness, deliverance, and loss.

"'Tis said Warwick has not only promised Isabel to George but my crown into the bargain," Edward growled, rising and pacing about the room.

"The crown?" Earl Rivers shouted. "Has the man gone mad? 'Tis not his to give. It is time for you to cut off his haughty head, Your Grace," he counseled Edward, who turned his back and stared silently out of the window. It was clear to Richard that Ned was in no mood for discussion.

Richard seized a moment of silence and faced the handsome patriarch of the Woodville family, who was decidedly overstepping his bounds albeit he was Edward's father-in-law. "My brother and I wish to be alone, if it please you, my lord. I pray you, take no offense, but George's defection is a family matter, and we would be grateful for time to discuss it between ourselves."

"I am Edward's wife," Elizabeth objected. "I should stay."

Richard smiled and, in a rare gesture for him, went to Elizabeth and lifted her hand to his lips. "He will be with you shortly, Sister, I promise. Just allow us this moment, I beg of you." What he wanted to say was: *Much of what ails us is your family's fault. You have all set yourselves up above those who are far nobler than you. Your influence with the king has repelled those who would give experienced counsel — including Warwick, hence distancing himself from good governance.* Instead, he simply opened the door.

The queen had no recourse in the face of such diplomacy and flounced from the room, followed by her family and Will Hastings, who acknowledged Richard's wise decision with a quiet, "'Twas well done, my lord."

When the door was closed, Richard waited for Ned to say something— perhaps even reprimand him. He suddenly noticed Ned's shoulders were shaking, and thinking his brother was laughing, he took a step forward. "Ned," he said, "Ned? Are you all right?"

But when Edward turned to face his brother, Richard was horrified to see that Edward was weeping. "Dear God!" Richard exclaimed, and the youngest York took the eldest into a close embrace and let his big brother cry.

"They have twice as many men as we have, Your Grace," Will Hastings informed the king a few days later. He cursed the slow intelligence of the rebels' movements, but when the hoped-for reinforcements from the earls of Devon and Pembroke did not appear, the usually even-tempered chamberlain was nervous. "If you want my advice, you will send your in-laws away. They are part of the grievances laid out by Redesdale and his followers. Aye, even Elizabeth. You have allowed her family to exploit their position, and their presence is only aggravating resentments here."

Richard had become accustomed to the familiar way Hastings addressed the king. He recognized the informality came from the same degree of trust he himself had in Rob Percy.

"I agree, Ned. Let the people see the Woodvilles have no influence. Listen to the people's grievances," Richard begged, "they do not want to fight. They complain they have fought too many battles already for a cause that is not their own. They have been forced to leave their homes to fight those battles, paid too many taxes to fund the fighting, and have no food to feed their families. And they blame the Woodvilles. They have had enough and are wanting you to listen."

Edward studied his steepled hands and nodded slowly. "Elizabeth will not like it, but I will send them away." He looked up at his two advisors. "What then?"

"I cannot believe Warwick wants to attack you," Richard said, "and I do not think you believe it either, Ned, or you would not have just put him in charge of our fleet to ward off the French. He is patrolling the Channel protecting us. It does not make sense."

"Astute thinking, Richard," Edward said, grateful for this brother's wisdom and loyalty. "We know the rebels are led by Warwick's adherents, so who do you think is giving them their orders?"

Richard shrugged. "There are so many Nevilles—from both branches of the family," he said. "Perhaps these are from the Stafford line not our Beaufort one."

But all three men knew in their hearts that Warwick was the culprit, although the earl's two cousins wanted desperately to believe otherwise.

"Perhaps," Edward humored his brother. "Then all we can do is wait here in safety for Pembroke and Devon."

They waited in vain.

In the meantime, and unbeknownst to the Yorkists at Nottingham, the earl of Warwick, his wife and two daughters, George of Clarence, and Warwick's brother-in-law John de Vere, earl of Oxford, had sailed from Sandwich to Calais, where, on the eleventh day of July, Archbishop Neville performed the marriage ceremony between Isabel and George.

There was now no doubt of Warwick's treasonable intentions. The next day, Warwick and his followers issued a manifesto to Parliament in the form of a letter denouncing the king's willful exclusion on his council of *...princes of royal blood, in favor of the deceitful, covetous rule and guiding of certain seditious persons.* In particular, they mentioned Earl Rivers, his wife and sons, and the earls of Pembroke and Devon. They did not dare include the queen. *They have caused our said sovereign lord and his realm to fall in great poverty of misery, disturbing the ministration of the laws, only intending to their own promotion and enrichment.*

Warwick declared his intention of returning to England to lay these grievances and proposals of reformation before the king.

How ironic that ten ~~years earlier, Richard~~ duke of York, Edward's father, had set sail from exile in Ireland with exactly the same goal in mind: To reform the bad governance of a king.

Cut off from the south by the rebels, the king was unaware of these developments, all too easily—and expediently—choosing to believe that the silence from Pembroke and Devon meant they were making their way to Nottingham.

Twice Richard attempted to rouse his brother to be more aggressive in his intelligence gathering, and twice he was rebuffed. To Richard the silence was ominous, but Edward scoffed, "You are too pessimistic, Richard. If we are so outnumbered, why have the rebels not attempted to reach us? Where are they?"

Richard could only demur, but he was anxious to leave the castle. Part of him longed for his first foray into battle, and so far he had seen nary a sword unsheathed nor a cannon ball fired. But he was convinced Edward needed to gain the trust of his subjects again, and he would not do that by cowering behind castle walls.

Hastings spoke up then, voicing what Richard was thinking. "Go among your people, Edward. You are your own best advocate. I've seen you charm the surliest of men with a warm greeting or a friendly slap on the back. Be the people's king once more. Dare I say, but you have lost the common touch that endeared you to all, which has allowed Warwick to exploit and gain from it."

It was a bold pronouncement that earned Richard's admiration, but both waited apprehensively for the king's reaction.

Again Richard was impressed by the trust the king had in his lord chamberlain, because Edward finally nodded and said, "Aye. I see that now," and rose with more purpose. "Let us make plans to find Devon and Pembroke."

At the end of July, Edward finally received word of the two earls' progress, and heeding Hastings' advice, he marshaled his meager troops and began the march south to join them on July twenty-ninth, a much happier Richard by his side.

The mood would not last long.

Once again Edward's intelligence was tardy, for on July twenty-sixth Devon and Pembroke, commanding two separate forces, did not make their rendezvous somewhere in Northamptonshire before being outmaneuvered by the rebel force and vanquished in the battle of Edgecote Field. Both earls were sent before Warwick and executed.

Not far from Northampton, a messenger from the royal force reached Edward with the bad news. Upon hearing that the rebels were at hand and had already defeated their comrades, Edward's small army dissolved like a summer's mist, leaving the king and his small entourage marooned in the middle of nowhere.

Richard could not believe his ears.

"You are my prisoner," the earl of Warwick told the angry Edward at Olney, where the earl had cornered the helpless king and his few men, who were seeking to ride back to Nottingham.

Like a wounded dog, Edward turned his horse around to face the earl and snarled, "Nay, my lord, you are mistaken. As soon as I return to Westminster, 'tis you who will be tried for treason." He attempted to unsheathe his sword, but Warwick's henchmen had hedged him in and one wrenched the weapon from his grasp.

"I think not, Your Grace," Warwick almost purred at Edward. "As you can see, you are greatly outnumbered. I am here speaking for your subjects who seek naught but a way to lay their grievances and the need for reform before you."

Richard observed several heads nod in agreement and sheathed his own sword. He suddenly saw Francis Lovell among the earl's knights and lifted his hand briefly in salute. Poor Francis had no choice but to be at the earl's side, Richard knew, for he was Warwick's ward. The youth's shoulders shrugged a reluctant response. It was then Richard determined he would make his protégé one of his household when the present debacle was resolved. It was clear Francis wanted none of this treason.

However, more important matters concerned Richard here at hand, as he watched Edward use his intimidating strength to push away the guards and move his horse closer to the earl's. "So what do you propose, cousin. That you take my place as king, or…." Suddenly Edward caught sight of George, skulking behind Warwick's brother, the archbishop. Kicking his horse's flanks viciously, he jostled Warwick and rode straight at George, purposely allowing his mount to rear up and stop a precise few inches from the startled duke of Clarence.

"Did Warwick promise you the crown, my lord duke?" Edward cried, and he slashed George across the face with his rein. "Over my dead body, traitor! My own brother. You are lower than the muck in a gong-farmer's barrow. Aye, turn your face away in shame. I have no wish to see it ever again." And he wheeled his courser around and rode back to Warwick, Richard, and Hastings. "Keep him from my sight, do you hear me, my lord."

Warwick nodded and glanced at Richard. Despite his enmity towards Edward, the earl still felt an affinity for Richard, whose eyes spoke of betrayal and sadness as they held Warwick's for a moment, and Warwick had the grace to lower his gaze and incline his head in a tacit understanding of the young man's conflict.

"What do you intend to do with me, pray?" Edward was bold despite the danger. "Am I to suffer the same fate as my ancestors Richard of Bordeaux or the second Edward, shut away to be forgotten until discovered dead?"

"You are still the king, cousin," Warwick assured him. "But your power will be greatly reduced—at least until I and my council believe that you have accepted our manifesto."

"Pah!" Edward harrumphed. "So another Magna Carta. I think you overestimate your sway with my people, my lord." He looked around hopefully at the soldiers but saw nothing but surly faces. Thus powerless, Edward gave himself up to the earl, who told him to choose from his retainers to accompany him to his confinement at Warwick castle, where, the earl assured the king, he would be housed in comfort.

Hastings moved his horse towards the king, but Edward gave an imperceptible shake of his head. "I trust you have no quarrel with my chamberlain or my brother, Gloucester?" Edward asked Warwick. "I will be content to have two gentlemen of the bedchamber and my secretary to take with me into this 'confinement.'"

Warwick bowed. "As you surmise, Your Grace, we have no quarrel with Lord Hastings or Richard." He emphasized Richard's first name purposely. "They may go where they will. Fare you well, my lords."

Hastings leaned over to Richard and muttered. "I'm for Lancashire," where Richard knew Will had large land holdings, "and may I suggest you find Jack Howard and keep me apprised." Richard nodded, and after saluting Edward and ignoring Warwick, Will and his men cantered away.

"Find Elizabeth and tell her the news, Richard," Edward commanded, only now choosing to dismount. "I am sure this 'confinement' is a temporary inconvenience. Am I right, cousin?"

Warwick said nothing and watched as Richard followed the king out of the saddle and Edward took his brother in a warm embrace. "Don't let him get away with this," Edward hissed in Richard's ear. "Gather support and we shall defeat these rebels ere the rising of the next moon. Now get you gone from here at once, before the traitorous whoreson changes his mind about you."

CHAPTER SIXTEEN
AUTUMN 1469–SPRING 1470

Bemused and silent, Richard rode from the extraordinary scene towards London. He kicked his horse's flank into a gallop, intent on putting as much space between himself and Warwick as possible. Trusty Rob Percy was at Richard's side, and he was also rendered unusually speechless by the disaster that had befallen the king. With only their squires attending, they followed Watling Street and covered the first ten miles on that old Roman road in record time, and, upon reaching the town of Stony Stratford, reined in their mounts. As the sweating beasts gratefully slowed to a walk, their riders guided them over the River Ouse to an inn hard by the Eleanor Cross.

"What happened back there?" Rob wondered aloud as he wolfed down a pigeon pie. "Has our former patron committed treason? He has taken up arms against the king."

Richard shook his head and cradled his cup of ale. "It seems Warwick would rule the king who would still rule the kingdom. He does not see himself as traitor, I'll warrant. What I need to discover when I reach London is if the council is for Warwick or for Ned. If Jack Howard is there and active, then I cannot believe he sanctioned Warwick's actions. But we don't know. We could ride into a trap and end up in the Tower. Then I am of no use to Ned." He chewed on his lower lip. "I need some time to think—and get a message to Howard."

Rob was concerned for his friend. Like Richard, Rob had learned to put his faith in the earl of Warwick for many years. Now it seemed the earl was wanting complete control of the government with a puppet for a king. And, worse, the man appeared to also be pulling the strings of Richard's only other brother. It was a catastrophe, Rob thought, and he doubted Richard knew how or was influential enough to play politics.

And Rob had another concern. He knew Richard could be rash when he lost control of a situation. He had seen it at Middleham when Richard had accused one of his fellow henchmen of letting Traveller loose while Richard was in the tiltyard. The dog had disappeared for hours, and Richard despaired of ever seeing his faithful friend again. The accused youth had been seen near the kennel where the wolfhound was kept, and Richard had flown at him in a fit of rage and given him a black eye. He would not even hear the henchman's protestations of innocence, he was so distraught. After searching in the village and surrounding fields, Richard eventually returned only to find Anne standing sheepishly with Traveller next to the kennel. She had "borrowed" him to keep her company in her chamber for the afternoon. Master Lacey had censured Richard for his rash behavior and made Richard curry the abused victim's horse for a week.

Richard was certainly not in control now, so Rob decided to step in. "Who can you trust to help, Richard? You cannot do this on your own."

Richard shrugged, despondent. "I seem to only have you."

Rob suddenly snapped his fingers. "I have it! Your mother! Duchess Cecily! That's where you should go," he cried, pleased with his solution.

Richard lifted his head and his face brightened. "You are right, my friend," he answered, slamming down his empty cup. "Few would think to look for me at Berkhamsted. Mother spends her days in prayer and has not been seen at court since Edward's Mary was christened two years ago. I will send John Parr ahead to warn her of our coming."

Enjoying feeling like a child again, Richard gave himself up to his mother's maternal ministrations. He was not surprised that she already knew of Edward's capture by Warwick. Ever since she had been widowed, Cecily had learned to think and act independently, and using spies was not beneath the duchess to protect her family.

Cecily motioned to her son and his friend to sit. When Richard sat across from her at the table, she smiled. "You cannot imagine how like your father you are to look at, and he always led with that chin, as well. When you walked in just now, I could almost have thought it was my dear lord, may he rest in peace." She was glad to see Richard's face light up at the compliment. Her startling blue eyes now roamed over Richard's tired body and once again settled on the minuscule rise in the right shoulder. Only a mother or a lover would notice the list, and Cecily determined to consult her physician while Richard slept.

"You need rest, Richard, and you too, Sir Robert. You both look as though you could do with a hot bath and soft bed." She nodded to her young page. "Remove their boots, Harry, and then find my chamberlain."

Soon the two young men were devouring fresh trout, jugged hare and custard tarts at the table in Cecily's solar. "I had forgotten how much boys eat," Cecily said, chuckling. "My ladies and I have the appetites of sparrows, I confess. Comes from growing old, I suppose."

Richard smiled fondly at his mother. "You don't look a day older than when you birthed me," he teased, although he found the widow's wimple that hid Cecily's glorious hair too severe. He whispered behind his hand to Rob, "She is nigh on fifty-five, you know."

Cecily feigned a reprimand. "Enough of your flattery, young man. Certes, wheedling a meal from your old mother is not the reason for your sudden arrival. You need my advice, I warrant, and I shall freely give it." She frowned. "Edward was not one to take it, but then you are not Edward."

"Nor charming George," Richard added quietly, "and now not-so-charming George."

"George will wave in whichever direction the strongest wind blows, my dear Richard. If there is one thing I have learned in my dotage, it is that we all spoiled that boy. But he is the least of your worries at present. He will do whatever Warwick tells him; thus it is my nephew of whom you must beware."

As if I did not know that already, Richard thought, but he held his peace. Was he wasting precious time being cosseted at Berkhamsted? But then Cecily allayed his doubts and demonstrated why her husband had so often counted on her common sense and intelligent insight in times of crisis.

"Warwick may have the respect of the common people, but he does not have that of their leaders—the nobles, if you will. He has not wooed them to his side the way your brother has these ten years. They see Warwick as power-hungry, arrogant, and a turncoat, and wonder where it will all end. He is a fool if he thinks he can rule through Edward, and he is a fool if he thinks that he can murder him, win the hearts and minds of Englishmen and then put George on the throne." She paused and requested wine. "It is curious the man does not seem to want the crown for himself, is it not? But it is as clear as a day in May to me he wants it for his daughter."

Richard gave a low whistle and replenished Cecily's cup. "Isabel. Of course. So he believes, if he disposes of Ned, he can rule through his daughter and thus through her husband—George." It suddenly occurred to Richard that Warwick had been planning this coup for a long time. "How blind Ned was—I was," he admitted. "I have known about the plan to have George wed Isabel for more than a year. I kept turning a blind eye." True to his nature, Richard took the blame. "I should have warned Ned sooner, but I trusted the earl."

Cecily patted his hand. "Your loyalty to your lord was admirable, Richard. But 'tis good that you now know where those loyalties lie. Your father would be proud," she told him, "as am I, my dear boy. But for the present, I shall send you both to your bed. Sir Robert...Rob, I bid you a goodnight. I would have a last word in private with my son."

Richard cocked an eyebrow. "What is it, Mother?" he asked as Rob took his leave.

Cecily came around to where he sat slouched on the bench. She gently put her hand exactly on the rib protrusion, and he froze. "Since when have you had this affliction? I am your mother; did you think I would not see?"

Richard moved away from her touch, ashamed, but he knew her concern was genuine. He rose and walked to the window. It would be a relief to talk about it, perhaps. Kate knew, but she had not questioned him. When he was with her he forgot about it. Now, he took a deep breath: "For a year or more I have felt something was amiss. Rob noticed one day after our exercise, but it was when I needed harness before last yuletide that I became concerned. The armorer told me it would have to be bespoke due to the slight curve." He turned, stricken. "I fear God has forsaken me, Mother," he admitted suddenly. "I have tried to be righteous, I have attended to my prayers and the scriptures, but there is no doubt that I am crooked. Is the Devil in me?"

He was unprepared for his mother's fierce embrace and gave in to its remembered comfort.

"Never use Lucifer's name in this, Richard, I beg of you," Cecily said when she eventually loosed him. "It is a dangerous thing to say, and if you have enemies in life, they will surely use it to bring you down. You will see Doctor Cooke in the morning who is sure to be able to fit you with some sort of brace that will help." She did not mention the other remedies Constance had described many years ago, including a contraption like the rack that had sometimes been employed for spinal ailments she had seen while studying in Padua. "We must not question why God has chosen to afflict us," Cecily soothed. "You are the very model of a good man and must put guilty thoughts aside."

Cecily's mind raced back to the hour of this son's difficult birth, but with Constance and her favorite midwife at Fotheringhay present, Richard had been born healthy, if a little small. She thought of all the times George had knocked him down as a boy, wrestled too hard, tied him to a tree as a "prisoner" in the games he played with the older boys. Then there was the time Richard had fallen off a hay wagon and landed hard on his backside. He had complained of pain for a week or so but was soon running and climbing as before. Surely these were normal incidents in a family of boys, she reasoned, and not to blame for Richard's crookedness.

Cecily turned him around. "With a little more padding in your pourpoint here," and she smoothed the quilted back of the jacket, "the bulge will not be noticeable. And I promise I shall tell no one, except the doctor."

Richard nodded his thanks. "And pray for me, Mother. I ask that you pray for me."

"Aye, I shall. Remember, Richard, God tests the faith of those he loves the most. Take heart."

The doctor's plump fingers probed Richard's back for several minutes, tut-tutting as he went. They were behind a screen in Cecily's solar with the duchess plying Dr. Cooke with a myriad of questions, the most embarrassing of which was "Will he be able to sire children?" He wanted to cry out: "I already have, Mother!" but he thought it wise to keep his mother in the dark about his romantic life—he was certain it would elicit outrage in his prim parent.

"I am afraid the...ah...the affliction," the doctor settled on a less ugly word, "is too far grown for a brace to make any difference, Your Grace," he explained to Cecily, as though Richard were not there. "I can try, but I do not guarantee it will lessen the ....ah...the outgrowth." He stared with medical curiosity at the upthrusted ribs attempting to burst through the skin on the underside of the scapula and forcing the right shoulder higher than the left. "I can concoct a potion to slow the growth of your bones, my lord, but it will affect all of them."

Richard paused before deciding. "I am low enough to the ground already compared with my brothers, so I will decline your offer, Doctor Cooke. But I thank you for your expertise." The doctor had said nothing to advance the layman's prognosis Richard and Rob had discussed in private. Richard vouchsafed to keep his secret to a few trusted souls and shoulder the burden of hiding this defect solely on himself. He would put one of the Middleham armorers, an Italian, on his personal payroll and employ an unmarried tailor who would keep his counsel and not tattle to a wife. He hated to believe it, but women were more likely to gossip. The fewer people who knew the better.

Armed with his mother's love and a letter from her to the steward at Baynard's, giving Richard permission to muster men from its garrison on Edward's behalf, Richard set out for London. He had no clear idea what he was supposed to accomplish, but the knowledge that his brother was being held against his will at Warwick's pleasure and was counting on him was enough to plunge the young man into the first really important political enterprise of his seventeen years.

In the autumn of 1469, the kingdom was once again in crisis, and loyal Richard could not bring himself to blame it on his beloved brother although he feared it was so. History would later support him: through bad governance, Edward had lost what, a decade earlier, he, his father and his family had achieved in claiming the throne for York.

Cecily had been right. Despite his bravura performance at Olney, Warwick was unable to win the nobles or council to his side, and Edward's seeming willingness to play the captive lulled the earl into believing the king was complacent and in his power. But suspicious of the earl's intent and his lack of a plan, the common people, having grumbled enough at the king's lack of governance to cause previous rebellions, now found themselves wishing for the stable authority the king had nevertheless brought to the realm. Having chosen to try and rule from the north, Warwick lost control of London and the south. Indeed chaos now ruled in the capital.

Unable to subjugate Edward—or his subjects—Warwick was forced to admit he had lost the advantage and allowed Edward to address the city elders in York and then ride on to Pontefract. It was a mistake. On that bright morning in September, as Edward rode up to the fearsome fortress, its ten tall towers and double bailey wall straddling a craggy hill, the small Warwick party was confronted by a sizable force led by William, Lord Hastings and Richard, duke of Gloucester.

"Well met, brother! And Will!" Edward called, spurring his horse towards them. "I am right glad to see you—and you too, Jack Howard," he cried, spotting the portly Howard grinning from under his raised visor. He shouted more loudly for the benefit of a disconcerted Warwick, "It seems I am prisoner no more," and as a few cheers rose from those crowding the battlements above, he smiled and waved. Then he turned and bowed to his captor. "I thank you for your hospitality, cousin," he joked, "but I am for London with my trusty youngest brother and Lord Hastings. I must undo the mess you have wrought in my forced absence, my lord, and bring law and order back to my kingdom."

What now? Richard thought. Would London make Edward welcome again? After seeing the city in such disarray in the few short weeks when he was gathering support, Richard was not sure. *Ned needs to change his ways. Pray God he has learned his lesson these past months. And,* he wondered, *what would be Warwick's punishment?*

Once safely on the road south, he asked. Edward's answer was unexpected.

"We shall reconcile with Warwick once we have regained control of the government," the king told him. "Warwick has taken his revenge on his enemies, so I have heard, so it will not be an easy task, but I am determined to be a better governor, and he and I shall be reconciled."

Richard was astonished. "After he took revenge and executed Elizabeth's father and son?" Something stopped him from remarking that a vengeful queen would not be eager to talk reconciliation. *Besides, look where your last attempt got you, Ned,* he thought.

Hastings, doubtful that Edward would succeed yet admiring him for trying, asked: "And what of Clarence, my liege? Will you make your peace with him as well? If I may say, he deserves to be horsewhipped at the very least."

Edward sighed. "George is my brother and still young, Will, so I must forgive him. Nay, it is Warwick who's to blame, in truth." He neatly slapped a fly on his hand and it fell, squashed, to the ground. Will muttered that he would have dealt with the arrogant, traitorous earl of Warwick in the same way, but Richard thought George should be the fly. "My cousin now knows where he stands, I trust" Edward continued. "It is by my side as loyal councilor, or else he will be stripped of any power and isolated. But I am determined upon reconciliation. After all, we all desire the same thing: a peaceable kingdom with a York upon the throne."

"Not just any York, Ned," Richard rejoined. "You are the only rightful king."

Edward grinned at his brother and eased his horse closer. "I have had time to think while idling at Middleham. I discovered you certainly made your mark, Richard. Young Anne dotes on you as do half the servants, so as soon as we are back at Westminster, I am naming you constable of England. Since my father-in-law's untimely demise, the position lies vacant."

Richard almost fell off his horse. "Me, Your Grace? But what have I done to deserve the honor?" A flush of excitement colored his cheeks.

"The more I heard of you at Middleham and the more I have watched you these many troubled months, the more I could trust you. Loyalty must be rewarded, and this is your just due."

"I know not what to say, Ned, except that," and he put his hand to his heart, "I am your very true and loyal servant."

By November, the king was in command of London once more, and he would spend the winter months regaining the trust of his nobles. Astonishingly, not only did the earl of Warwick meekly agree to reconcile along with Clarence, but Edward did not even punish him.

"A mistake, if I may say so," Jack Howard confided to Richard as they sipped wine by Jack's fireside at Tendring. "You can see the bitterness in Warwick's face. I would not trust him with any task that sent him even a mile from where I sat. He likes not his new minion status after tasting the power of the crown."

Although Richard had doubts about his old mentor, he knew the earl was, at heart, a decent man. Certainly his actions in the summer were not those of a trustworthy one, however. And George... He shook his head. "I pray to God daily that my brother George has learned his lesson. Why he believed Parliament and the people would have accepted him as king with Ned still alive, I cannot imagine. I would love to know how Warwick had planned to bring that about?" He looked at Jack in horror. "By murdering Edward? Surely not?"

Jack chuckled. "My lord of Warwick may now look a fool, but he is not that foolish, Richard." He now chose his words carefully. "Have you ever heard any untoward rumors about your brother Edward's legitimacy?"

Richard was aghast. "His legitimacy? You mean his legitimate birth or his kingship?"

"Aye, his birth. It was whispered that Warwick was prepared to declare Edward a bastard, and...." Jack quickly put his hand on Richard's arm to stop the angry younger man from leaping to his feet. "Now calm down and hear me out."

And so Howard revealed the rumor that Duchess Cecily had dallied with an archer in Rouen while her husband was fighting the French at Pontoise, because Edward was born only eight months after York had rejoined her.

Richard was scornful. "Mother and ...*an archer?* You have to be in jest, Sir John. 'Tis a monstrous lie, and besides, who would believe it?"

"Edward's enemies—York's enemies, it matters not. The record stands: Your father was not in Rouen at the usual time of conception."

Richard gulped. "My mother an adulteress? I don't believe it." He thought of the reaction Cecily would have to such a story and shuddered. Then he shook his head. "'Tis impossible. She and my father were truly in love. There must be some mistake."

Jack shrugged. "Sadly, people believe what they want to believe. I too think it absurd, but if the rumor persists, I would not discount Warwick's using it to depose Edward and set George on the throne." He could not tell Richard that when he had first heard the story he had briefly considered it; after all Edward stood six feet and three inches of pure muscle, a giant in those days, golden fair with bright blue eyes. Richard of York had been of below-average height, slight, dark-haired with brown eyes. But Edward had his mother's Neville features, and Plantagenets of the past had been imposing. Didn't Jack's own son outstrip him by several inches and have his mother's flaxen hair? Thus Jack had dismissed the idea within a few moments of hearing the fable.

Richard played with the ring on his little finger and sat staring at the fire. "I would like to believe my brother George would never be complicit in such a monstrous plan," he said. "But I don't know him anymore, in truth. Perhaps he does covet the crown."

"And you, my lord?" Jack's quiet words hung in the air like a puff of smoke down-vented from the chimney.

"It has never crossed my mind," Richard replied, turning to hold Jack's gaze. "I was the fourth son. I did what I was told—supported my brothers and did my duty by my king." He was suddenly reminded of his conversation in the chapel with King Henry, and he chuckled. "I was told once I would probably be a churchman—a bishop. But all I wanted from a young age was to be a knight. Besides, I now know I would hate to be a king."

Jack smiled. "Then I shall have no worries about your craving power, young man. In the meantime, may I congratulate you on your appointment as constable of England, a high honor indeed, and well deserved. Your brother has the measure of you."

Richard inclined his head in acknowledgement. He had underestimated Edward's confidence in him, but he was pleased. Prone to undervalue his own strengths, Richard was eager for others' approbation, which later in life—and especially in times of crisis—would render him vulnerable to flattery.

Jack looked up as he heard women's voices on the staircase landing above them. "Margaret, my love, Lord Richard and I are lacking your company. Come warm yourselves."

Richard jumped up then, and Jack noted the flush of pleasure on his young friend's newly bearded cheeks as Richard watched a pregnant Kate follow Margaret Howard down the stairs.

"When is it due?" Jack asked in Richard's ear.

"March, I think," Richard said, grinning happily. "I pray it is a boy this time." He had been overjoyed to hear that his and Kate's tryst in the river near Bury had been fruitful. The news of the demise of Kate's husband at the hands of outlaws later that summer had also greatly relieved him. The child could certainly be Master Haute's, but the jealous husband could no longer treat Kate so cruelly.

Having been faithful to two wives, Jack's first instinct, upon learning from Margaret that Kate's child was Richard's, was to upbraid the young man—a mere boy, in truth—but he was disarmed by the couple's deep devotion, despite long separations. But it did occur to Jack that promiscuity might run in the York family.

There was no doubt Jack was quite taken with the youngest York and was gratified Richard had sought to spend more time with him, discussing policies and asking for explanations after council meetings. Richard's devotion to his brother, his paramour, and little Katherine showed the older, astute councilor a strength of purpose and sense of duty in the young duke that he had not seen in Clarence—nor, in some instances, in Edward. It was in these intimate conversations around the fire at Tendring, when Richard fled the hated halls of Westminster for a few days, that their friendship burgeoned.

In late November, as the newly appointed constable, Richard received his first proper military command to depart into Wales and recapture two important castles from Warwick's rebels.

Richard relished his first taste of combat only a month after his seventeenth birthday. He rode out of London with a goodly body of men at his back, determined to swell the numbers along the route. Rob Percy kept him company, and behind followed Richard's squire John Parr and his newly appointed secretary, John Kendall, whose father had given so many years of loyal service to Richard's father.

Winter in Wales was even colder than at Middleham, Richard decided, as his army climbed into the Welsh hills towards Carmarthen, an early snowfall mantling the landscape. Certainly the wind blew cold in Yorkshire and snow was no stranger, but this chill was damp and seemed to penetrate his bones and make his back ache more. He scanned the untidy hills for signs of rebels and marveled that he was now appointed surveyor and steward of this beautiful but untamed land with its mountains rising in the distant north, where he was also chief justice.

Richard could now see the stark silhouette of his goal dominating the steep bank of the River Towy to its south, the castle's keep rising above the high crenelated walls, and a shiver of anticipation ran through him.

Carmarthen was a mighty fortress, and he was supposed to capture it. How many men and how much artillery would he be facing? All he knew was the Welsh were fierce fighters and had resisted invading armies time after time in their long history.

The duke's small army heard the faint wail of a shawm announcing the enemy's arrival, and as he drew closer, Richard saw men clambering around the castle ramparts readying for an attack.

"Remember our training," Rob told Richard. "You were good at strategy in Blackbeard's classes. Our intelligence is that the ap Griffiths have split their forces between here and Cardigan. Capture Carmarthen and the other will quickly follow."

Richard climbed to the top of a knoll and took stock of the castle and its high wall. As well as the castle, Richard could see the whole town was also walled, which gave him an idea. "What if we, too, split our army," he said to Rob and his other captains. "We send the artillery to bombard the closest castle wall together with enough of our force to fool them into thinking it is a simple frontal attack, and the rest of us conceal ourselves right under the town wall and, keeping it close, we circle to the back of the town and enter there. Chances are the constable will concentrate his efforts on the army he can see." He pointed to the city wall that stretched away into the distance. "You see, if they are short of soldiers, they cannot man the town walls as well. We shall attack the postern gate. I warrant one battering ram will suffice."

As the cannons began pounding the thick castle wall and arrows flew back and forth between the well populated ramparts and the troops on the ground, it became clear that Richard's plan was sound. No one noticed the rest of the army stealthily creeping around the city wall until a few good runs at the postern gate with the battering ram alerted the terrified townsfolk to a rear assault. It was too late. The splintered door yielded and gave Richard's soldiers the access they needed to swarm through the small town and threaten the northern side of the castle.

Now the arrows came thick and fast, and Richard heard cries from his men as they were felled by the vicious flights, but being attacked on two sides proved too daunting for the Welshmen. Besides they were no match for the English longbowmen's deadly aims over the walls and into the defending soldiers, and when Richard's cannons breached the wall, the fight was all but over.

Not before Richard had made his first kill, however. He saw the pikeman run at him, and bringing his years of practice in the Middleham yard into play, he judged the man's weapon to within a few feet and stepped sideways, swung his sword high and brought the blade down upon the man's neck. He was momentarily surprised how easily his sword had sliced through flesh and bone, but he had no time to contemplate the taking of a man's life before he had to maneuver his weapon again to thrust it into another Welshman's belly. This time he felt the jarring in his arm as he tore through the man's tight muscle and gristle and hit the spine, and the terrifying sound of the man's death cry sickened him. He swiftly pulled the sword out and watched the fountain of dark red spout from the wound as the man fell like a stone.

Richard's blood sang and his senses seemed heightened as never before. He was able to ascertain what was transpiring with great clarity, and he began shouting orders, as well as again and again lifting his deadly broadsword. The whole battle lasted no more than half an hour, when Willam ap Thomas ap Griffith surrendered the castle to the young English duke. Looking around at the carnage, Richard was relieved to see most of the dead were rebels. Rob Percy joined him, his tunic stained and his mail nicked, and the two comrades locked relieved looks at seeing each other alive.

Richard gave orders for the proper burial of the dead, rounded up the rest of the rebels and penned them up, well guarded, for the night. He and his captains feasted on what the kitchen staff had abandoned when the battle began, and slept on trestles in the great hall along with their retainers.

"Why not seek Thomas ap Griffith's bed, Richard?" Rob said, peeved. "They must have better beds than these in the lord's private apartments?"

Richard shook his head. "Our men have marched and fought alongside us and are just as weary. No need to play the lordly one tonight, my friend."

Rob should not have been surprised by the reply; it was all part of Richard's drive to understand the common man, which Rob thought somewhat eccentric. He himself had spotted a well-endowed Welsh girl and would probably find solace in her arms. "Suit yourself, Richard," he said, chuckling. "I'm off to find a softer cushion for my head, and a warm port for my..."

"Aye, I know what for," Richard laughed. "No need to explain."

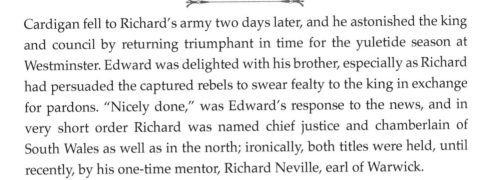

Cardigan fell to Richard's army two days later, and he astonished the king and council by returning triumphant in time for the yuletide season at Westminster. Edward was delighted with his brother, especially as Richard had persuaded the captured rebels to swear fealty to the king in exchange for pardons. "Nicely done," was Edward's response to the news, and in very short order Richard was named chief justice and chamberlain of South Wales as well as in the north; ironically, both titles were held, until recently, by his one-time mentor, Richard Neville, earl of Warwick.

However, despite Edward's magnanimity towards Warwick, Clarence and their faction, and Edward's determination to govern his realm better, trouble was always bubbling north of the Trent. The month of March saw Richard back in Wales and brought fresh outbreaks of rebellions. Once again it became clear that Warwick and Clarence were the instigators.

It seemed Edward had learned his lesson, and this time he moved quickly to suppress the uprising. Richard was relieved when he got the news of Edward's victory at Empingham, a battle later dubbed Losecote Field for the numbers of rebels who tried to shed their Warwick liveries and be spared by Edward. Thinking Edward had matters under control, Richard went about his task of holding several oyer and terminer sessions, pardoning some and imprisoning or executing others for their part in the Welsh defection to Warwick.

A man had been caught with an incriminating letter about raising men for the rebel cause destined for a Welsh lord. The man was clearly guilty of treason, and it was Richard's duty to condemn him. Owen Rhys was the same age as Richard and had his whole life ahead of him. He was brought before Richard, his heavy chains clanking on the stone floor, his face bloodied and bruised from bullying guards, and flaunting a defiant stare that hardened Richard's heart.

"You have been found guilty of treason, Master Rhys. You shall henceforth be taken to a place of execution where a priest will hear your confession before you meet your Maker. Do you have aught to say before you are taken away."

Several lawyers looked startled, and one whispered to another, "'Tis not customary. He will say his piece on the scaffold."

Richard held up his hand. "My brother, the king, is perhaps more merciful than you are used to here in Wales," he said equably. "Let us give this man a chance to defend himself once more." He rose and approached the prisoner. "Do you deny you aided the cause of the king's great rebel, my lord of Warwick? Perhaps you were coerced?"

"I deny nothing," the man snarled in his sing-song Welsh and suddenly spat on the ground. "And that is for your English king, look you."

All pity vanished from Richard's thoughts. "Then take him away," he commanded the guards, "and may God have mercy on his soul."

Richard found he could now wall off his personal feelings about taking a man's life. It became all about his duty to his brother.

And duty called soon after, when Edward found himself chasing Warwick and Clarence southward, who were making for the coast and an escape to France.

"God's bones, Ned!" Richard cursed, reading the latest missive a messenger had just delivered. "What a fool you are."

Rob and a new member of Richard's circle, Sir Richard Ratcliffe, looked up from their game of cards. "What now, my lord?" Rob enquired. "Are we called to action? I am bored to tears in these dreary Welsh hills."

"I do not doubt we shall be called now. You will not believe it, but the king has returned Northumberland's earldom to Percy, stripping the loyal John Neville of his prized possession."

Ratcliffe whistled through his teeth. "'God's bones' indeed, my lord. Warwick's brother has remained the one loyal Neville until now..." he did not dare voice what the other two were thinking.

Richard nodded. "Just so, Sir Richard." He snatched up his bonnet, stuffed the letter into his doublet and went to the door. "Come, friends, I believe I need to muster the troops. For all he is doing the chasing, I fear the king will be needing our help."

Poor Anne, Richard thought, riding hard for Southampton, his soldiers now mingling with Edward's. The king's army had discovered the rebels' destination upon arriving at Warwick Castle, where the earl had gathered up family once again and continued south.

Anne must be fourteen now, Richard mused, remembering fondly shared times with her at Middleham. She was a kind-hearted girl and did not deserve the turmoil in her young life that her father had thrust upon her. He supposed the same could be said for his own father's actions back in 1460, but he had an inkling it might be harder on a girl. She should be betrothed by now, he thought, but who would choose the daughter of a traitor—albeit a rich one? And perhaps she had no wish to give up her allegiance to Edward and have to follow her father. Poor Anne indeed.

Her sister Isabel had married for love, but that love was a millstone as well. The king had been told at Warwick Castle that her grace, the duchess of Clarence, was heavy with child. What an abominable journey for George to inflict on his wife, Richard fumed, but at least they would be together. Part of him prayed that George would come to his senses, forsake Warwick, and return to the family fold—but perhaps he did not deserve to, Richard's less charitable side decided. Aye, George is just as traitorous.

Richard's back was hurting him, and the road seemed interminable, despite the blossoming countryside along the way. The blooming of wild daffodils, cowslips, oxlips, dandelions, primroses, not to mention the *plantagenista* or broom, for which his royal house was named, had all caused Duchess Cecily to dub April her "golden month." It was not long before thoughts of Kate filled Richard's head and took his mind off his discomfort. As itinerant as he had been in the past weeks, he knew news from Tendring might be greatly delayed. Their child should have come by now, he calculated, and although he prayed nightly for mother and babe, he surmised it would be many more weeks until he would see them. Although he rejoiced in being a father, it saddened him he could not share in the children's daily lives. One day, he promised himself, he would see to their well-being.

All should have been well, once Edward's great rebels—as he had taken to calling Warwick and Clarence—had sailed off from Southampton. Unfortunately, he was only given that summer of 1470 to take stock of the turmoil the rebels had left behind before the news of a possible invasion sent the country reeling once more.

Who could have guessed that, being denied entry to Calais, Warwick had managed to evade both English and Burgundian fleets to find safe haven in France in May, where his old ally, Louis the Spider, sat waiting to lure him into his scheming web.

Richard reeled in shock two months later as he listened to the envoy from France tell Edward what had transpired there in June. They were clustered in a small audience chamber at Westminster, for once the thick stone walls useful for keeping out the summer heat. Edward was glowering at the quaking messenger.

"M...my lord of Warwick has entered into an alliance with...with Queen Margaret, my liege," the elderly diplomat said. "Warwick has pledged his support for an invasion that will place King Henry back on the throne."

He shrank back, waiting for the explosion, and he was not disappointed. Edward slammed his hands down on the arms of his chair and almost levitated from it, shouting: "You lie, you spawn of ...of ! Warwick and Margaret? It is not possible. Tell me you are lying!"

The man fell to his knees, his bony fingers clutched around his hat. "I swear on my father's grave I tell the truth, Your Grace. King Louis has promised to help the two of them, if they will support France against Burgundy and Brittany. Th...they agreed." He suddenly smirked and added: "Queen Margaret made my lord of Warwick kneel to her for a full fifteen minutes before she would speak to him."

Richard thought he saw Edward's mouth twitch, but the king was too worried and angry to appreciate the image of Warwick's humiliation at that moment. Richard's own mind was trying to process this extraordinary news and what it meant for England and the Yorkists, when the envoy stammered: "Th...that is not all, if it p...please you, my lords."

Will Hastings growled: "Out with it, man. What else, pray?"

"The earl agreed to and has betrothed his younger daughter to Henry's heir, Edouard of Lancaster."

It was Richard's turn to leap up. "Anne to wed Margaret's whelp?" he cried, horrified. "Over my dead body! He is a degenerate—caring only for his weapons and harness who talks of nothing but cutting off heads or making war. Why, 'tis monstrous!" He began pacing in front of the window, chewing on his lip and picturing Anne being pawed by the brutish Edouard. He was surprised at the emotion evoked in him at thinking about his little Middleham friend's helplessness. But if he were honest, Richard had another reason for abhorring Anne's marriage to Edouard: Lately he had begun thinking about his own need for a consort, and Anne Neville's pedigree and wealth had reluctantly stolen into his consciousness. If the Pope had given George and Isabel dispensation, why not him and Anne? Now Louis, Warwick, and Margaret of Anjou had thwarted his plan. Damn them.

"Louis of France is a cunning bastard," Will broke into Richard's musing. Taking off his bonnet and scratching his thinning scalp, Edward's chamberlain commented: "He is shoring up Margaret's support by offering her Warwick's in case Henry should again sit on the throne. He thinks Warwick will not forsake the Lancastrians now and betray his son-in-law. He's clever—even for a two-faced Frenchie."

"Devilishly," Edward agreed. "Is there any other tidbit you have left out, Master Pomfrey?" he demanded, drumming his fingers on the table.

"I know not if you were told the news, Your Grace, but when Warwick was denied entry to Calais in April and was forced to put back to sea in a storm, the duchess of Clarence was in childbirth. So great was her discomfort and labor, the babe did not survive."

"Poor lady," Richard sympathized, crossing himself, "what she has suffered at her husband's and her father's hands is pitiful." He could not bring himself to feel sympathy for George, who he believed had put Isabel in mortal danger. *He does not deserve to be a father*, Richard adjudged. He conveniently chose to ignore his own shortcomings in that regard. His and Kate's son, John, had duly been born in March, and Richard had not yet set eyes on the child.

"So Master Pomfrey, it stands to reason we should expect an invading army sometime soon, if Louis holds his two pawns' feet to the fire. Am I right?" Once again, Edward's temper had died as quickly as it has risen, and he sat down, steepling his fingers and training his watchful blue eyes on the man.

Master Pomfrey nodded vigorously, happy to see his king calm again and back on his chair. "The fleet is victualing at La Hogue, I believe. I returned here through Calais as soon as I could. But if I may be bold enough to say, my lord, an invasion would be nigh impossible because, as you have commanded, our own fleet, together with Burgundy's, is keeping the French pinned in their harbors all along the coast."

"Ah, I knew I could count on Jack Howard," Edward said to Will. "He does like riding the waves, in truth."

"'Tis good to know our brother-in-law Charles is also keeping his end of the bargain, Lancastrian lover though he is," Richard commented.

"With Meg at his side, he could hardly not help us, could he?" Edward allowed himself a pat on the back. "I was right to forge that marriage alliance. Well, Master Pomfrey, you may retire and know your task is well done."

"Christ's nails! But this is a holy mess," Richard cried as soon as the door closed. "Just when we thought all had settled. What will you do, Ned?"

Edward made a shushing noise and smiled at his brother, who was wound up like a spring. "Calm down. You heard the man, Richard, Warwick cannot sail from France because of our naval advantage. Refitting the ships will take weeks and then the winter storms will prevent them crossing. But if it makes you happy, I will set up lookouts along the south coast and you, as chief constable, will assign more guards at the Tower to keep Henry well and truly safe from any attempts to reunite him with the She-wolf. Then we will go north to show we are serious about putting down rebellions. Will that satisfy you, little brother?"

Richard did not appreciate being patronized. "If you want my advice, you will strengthen the garrisons on the south coast and send me to muster the troops again in Wales. What say you, Will?"

Will chuckled. "I agree with my king, my lord, from whence cometh my next meal. Seriously, it does seem unlikely that Warwick and Margaret will really fight on the same side, and I think there will be so many arguments between them, they will never organize an invasion."

Richard shrugged. He thought differently, but he was not the king. "And what of George?" he asked. "Master Pomfrey never mentioned George. It cannot sit well with him that Warwick is pledging to put Henry back on the throne when it was promised to him. What will become of him?"

Will harrumphed. "He should have thought of that earlier. I doubt his vanity will allow him to be passive."

"If only we could win him back to us," Richard remarked, "but would you forgive him now, Ned. It would seem he is well and truly hoisted with his own petard."

"I'd forgive him," Edward said, rising and walking to the door. "He is family." He turned to Will. "This news has given me a thirst, and, with Elizabeth pregnant and unwilling, another urge that needs to be satisfied. Shall we ride into London tonight?"

Richard was indignant. "Is that all you can think of at such a time? England is in danger!"

"Rubbish!" Edward retorted. "You are far too serious for your own good. Come with us!"

Richard's response was a curt bow and silent exit.

Edward should have listened to his "serious" brother. Wending his way slowly north to show himself to his subjects and punish the rebels, he was still in Yorkshire in September when he received news that Warwick had landed in Devon with a force and was on his way to London, winning people to his new cause: the return of King Henry VI to the throne.

"How could this have happened?" Edward demanded of his council.

Richard resisted the temptation to snap back: "I told you so." Instead he said: "We must reach London before the earl, or all will be lost."

CHAPTER SEVENTEEN
1470–71

For the second time in his eighteen years, Richard found himself an exile, staring glumly over a carrack's gunwale at England's receding shoreline on his way to Burgundy. How did it come to this? Over and over again, he had asked himself the same question during the three weeks between Warwick's landing and the king's inglorious flight. At the outset, Edward seemed to have been well received on his journey north, notably for his merciful treatment of the rebels (excepting the very worst offenders), and relative calm had returned to the northern regions of his kingdom.

However, Richard rued now, his brother had more than once ignored the intelligence from his brother-in-law, Charles the Bold, that Warwick was on the brink of invading. And he invaded. Moreover, despite hearing that Warwick and Clarence were on the march for London and had been joined by Oxford, Jasper Tudor, Shrewsbury, and Lord Stanley, Edward had still not moved—until it was too late. And then, when he did march south, he hesitated near Nottingham, looking for John Neville, Lord Montagu, to bring his force to join him. *How could Edward not guess that his bad judgment regarding Montagu would provide this final ignominy,* Richard wondered. For Montagu, still smarting from the loss of the Northumberland earldom, had turned his coat and become Edward's enemy. It could have been another "I told you so" moment for Richard, but watching his brother visibly crumple in his saddle as the messenger breathlessly relayed the news, Richard had instead urged his horse beside Edward's and laid a brotherly hand on the king's shoulder.

"It was bound to happen, Ned," Richard had said, "but for now, we need a plan."

"Aye, we do," said Will Hastings, who had ridden up on Edward's other side. He was joined by the remaining lords in Edward's party, and with their encouragement the king had made the only sensible decision. Just as his father had done at Ludlow ten years earlier, he had been forced to choose flight. "We must go if we are to gather our strength again and defeat Warwick and Margaret. We must sail to Flanders," the king told the group. "Where is the nearest port from here?"

Anthony Woodville had spoken up then: "Bishop's Lynn is close to my wife's lands, and I am well known there."

"What is that noise?" Richard recalled saying. His sharp young ears had heard something more ominous to the west of them. "Good Christ, can that be Montagu already? We must go."

Always best in a crisis, Edward, made a quick decision. He shouted thanks to his soldiers and told them to return to their respective homes. He also dispatched a messenger to his queen at Westminster to tell her to take sanctuary in the abbey. He appeared composed, but his eyes had been alive with adventure when he wheeled his horse around to face east and led his party of nobles and squires in a gallop across the flat countryside of Lincolnshire to the North Sea. All they had to do was cross the treacherous body of water known as The Wash, which had swamped many a vessel and drowned many a sailor in its unusual tides over the centuries, and reach Lynn.

Richard frowned as he remembered watching helplessly when one of the small boats had indeed capsized as the Wash claimed yet more victims, dragged down by their mail. Bedraggled and exhausted, the small royal party had clambered aboard the two merchant ships turned over to the king at Lynn and almost immediately set sail with nothing but the clothes on their backs.

Richard turned to look at Edward now, standing alone in the bow of the larger of the two vessels and staring disconsolately at the unending sparkling waves that stretched on and on to meet the sky. How low he must feel, Richard mused. All that was missing was an attack by pirates!

The ships that appeared from nowhere were not pirates, but almost as dangerous.

"Easterlings!" the boy in the crow's nest cried to his captain. "Off the starboard bow!"

"Hard to port!" the captain shouted. "We shall make for Holland and not Flanders."

Edward walked unsteadily along the rolling deck to Richard. "God is not on my side this time," he groused. "My trade policy towards the greedy Hansards has made them enemies of a sort. They have been attacking our ships to spite us. 'Twill be ironic if I am carried off as their prisoner to some godforsaken German hellhole after all this."

Richard grinned. "In some perverse way, I hope they do catch us just to see the look of surprise when they realize who is on board. But, it seems our ships are lighter and faster. See the gap widens between us, praise God."

"The optimist for once," Edward said, putting his arm about his brother's shoulder. "Sweet Jesu, but this has been a trial. Let us hope Duke Charles can give us all shelter in Bruges."

The trial was not over, however, because upon reaching the flat sandy shore of Holland, the English ships' entry into Alkmaar harbor was prevented by the low tide. Thwarted, it looked as though the pursuing Hansards would indeed capture them. But at last God smiled on the English king and gave them a rescuer. Louis de Gruthuyse, Duke Charles's governor in Holland, happened to be visiting Alkmaar and upon hearing the English king was trapped off his shore, sent small boats to deliver him safely to dry land. It helped that the seigneur was the same man who had generously housed the young York princes, George and Richard, in Bruges ten years before. Richard was delighted to greet the elder statesman again, albeit with a measure of embarrassment that once more members of the York family needed a refuge, and further, they were penniless. Edward had only his fur-lined cloak with which to pay the ship's captain. The wealthy Gruthuyse, however, gladly provided for his royal guests and offered to escort them to The Hague.

"Your sister, our beloved duchess Margaret, will repay me, I have no doubt," he told the king, chuckling. "She and I have books in common, and I am sure there are one or two she would relinquish in exchange for my hospitality to you."

Thus, forced to accept Gruthuyse's kind offer, Edward, Richard and others of the king's closest adherents, spent the winter in The Hague in relative luxury, all the while plotting their return. The bad news from England those first weeks under the new Warwick-Henry regime told of riots in the cities and a much-angered merchant body in London. King Henry reigned, but Warwick ruled.

The exiles then learned of their attainders. Warwick now deemed that Edward was King Henry's "greatest rebel and enemy, usurper, oppressor and destroyer of our said sovereign lord."

"Such a hypocrite," Edward had scoffed when he heard, and Richard had to agree; how had it all come to this?

Then, in November, came good news. After three daughters, Elizabeth Woodville had borne Edward's son and heir in Westminster sanctuary. "At last," Edward rejoiced and promptly spent the evening carousing with Hastings in the taverns of The Hague. This time, Richard happily joined in the celebrations.

As the tavern wench refilled their tankards, Richard tapped the side of it with his heavy signet ring, claiming Edward's attention from the serving girl. "I have been saving something of my own to share at the right moment," he said, "and this is as good a time as any. I have two children. A daughter, Katherine, and my son, John, was born last March."

Had Richard been in possession of an apple at that moment, he could have easily stopped Edward's open mouth with it. "You had not guessed? I know you suspected I had a paramour, Ned. You even asked me about Kate the night she sang at Margaret's farewell banquet. You were right, she is my love."

Edward closed his mouth and shook his head, his long locks swinging freely. "You sly fox, and, I might add, hypocrite; my lord of Warwick has nothing on you, brother. All those homilies about my wanton ways, and you sit here calmly telling me you have sired two bastards already at eighteen?" He chuckled and then he laughed. "And there I was thinking you were a sanctimonious prick. Why have you not sought my permission to wed? At least I wed Elizabeth so I could bed her."

Richard had the grace to look sheepish. "Kate is the daughter of a Kentish farmer—although her mother is vaguely related to the Hautes— the Richard Haute who owns Ightham Mote. She knew when we first...

er...when...well, you know," he tailed off awkwardly. "She knows 'tis impossible, and that I must take a wife one day who befits my rank. But unlike you, Ned, I have been loyal to only her."

Edward let out a low whistle. "Then I admire you, little brother. To have found a paramour as lovely as your Kate—remember her, Will? She of the long russet hair who sang like an angel. Nicely done, Richard. I envy you."

Richard shot back, "Why should you? I thought Elizabeth was your love and your wife. 'Tis why I have a hard time understanding why you... er...why you wander." Richard wondered if he had gone too far, but Edward was in his cups and in a benevolent mood.

"To each his own needs and desires," Edward said, raising his cup and scanning the room. "Now where has that little baggage gone."

Richard gave up and gave in to his own cup of wine.

"This is good news, Ned. You can be sure Meg had a hand in it," Richard surmised, when the brothers had been given leave to meet with Duke Charles in Aire. Formerly a staunch Lancastrian supporter, the duke had been forced to change his allegiance now his enemy Louis was hand in glove with Lancastrians against him. "I am looking forward to seeing our sister again tomorrow, are you not?"

Edward harrumphed. "She can be a force, I have to confess, but aye, 'twill be good to witness Meg in her new role. And I shall expect an impassioned plea from her on behalf of George. Poor George, he must be much disillusioned by all of Warwick's false promises."

It was Richard's turn to harrumph. "Poor George indeed!" he spat. "He is not a charming child anymore, Ned. He grew up getting his own way so many times, he never learned how to handle disappointment well. I will wager he is knowing it now. He is his own worst enemy."

"Careful, little brother," Edward warned. "Your jealous side is showing."

Although Edward came from the meeting with an agreement from Charles to fund his return to England with men and ships, it took another six weeks to ready his little flotilla. Unfortunately, a storm blew the ships off course, separating them. When the mortified master of their ship informed Richard they were making for a little-known spot named Ravenspur,

Richard's grin astonished the captain. "Just like Bolingbroke!" he cried. "We are landing in the same spot as the fourth Henry did when he came to depose his cousin Richard back in..." he frowned trying to remember the date.

"1399," John Parr reminded him as the captain looked blank. "'Tis a good sign, my lord."

"Sweet Virgin, I hope you are right," Richard replied, scanning the horizon. "Although where Ned and the others are now, is anyone's guess, God help us."

As luck would have it, all of Edward's commanders were separated in the storm, but his little army of five hundred, now on foot, were joined the very next day by Richard, Rivers, and Hastings with their companies. Just as Henry of Bolingbroke had experienced, no welcoming peasantry greeted them as they began to march into the heart of Yorkshire, and in fact the town of Kingston on Hull refused entry to the former king. It was when Edward chose to use exactly the same ruse as that distant cousin that he gradually began to win people to his side.

"I come not to claim the crown," he cried at each market cross, "but to claim what is rightfully mine: the duchy of York." And he would proclaim in a loud, clear voice: "I am King Henry's loyal subject. God save the king."

How short men's memories were, Richard thought, for just like Bolingbroke, the ruse worked. And thanks to the grateful earl of Northumberland's northern influence, the path to York was cleared and he began to gather men. However, York was the only city that opened its gates, and then allowed only Edward himself to enter, insisting the army remain a safe distance away. "As long as you are simply reclaiming your duchy," the mayor told Edward, "you—and a few of your lords—are welcome."

Richard was dazzled by his brother's talent for seducing an audience. He knew he would never be an orator like Edward nor have the physical stature to impress, but he watched and learned. So regal did Edward appear to the crowds curiously watching him ride through the gate, they did not question the three-ostrich-feather emblem of the prince of Wales he wore as heir apparent.

"Will that not enflame them, Ned?" Richard had asked.

"King Henry promised that a York would follow him to the throne that day in the Star Chamber, did he not?" Edward had replied. "You were there. Father is dead, and if I am no longer king, then I am still heir to the throne—still prince of Wales."

Richard had laughed outright. "But we are all attainted, Edward. You have no claim to anything."

Edward grinned. "Wait and see, little brother. I will have them eating out of my hand."

And he did. A few hours later, Edward's army was permitted to enter the city and avail themselves of a decent meal and beds for the night.

"Long live King Henry!" Edward cried as he stood outside the mighty minster and addressed the crowd before attending mass. "I am here solely to reclaim my duchy of York. Who will join me?"

By the time Edward marched on Nottingham, he had a veritable army in his wake.

Drawing near to Coventry a few days later, where Edward knew his adversary Warwick was trapped in its castle, he stood up in his stirrups and addressed his troops. "I am now convinced King Henry and his mouthpiece, Richard Neville, earl of Warwick, are not fit to rule our fair land," he cried. "Let it be known far and wide that I, Edward of York, now challenge the earl to come out and fight me man to man for the right to rule." Shouting above the cheering, he added: "I shall seek to reclaim the throne of England!"

Not surprisingly, Warwick stubbornly refused to take up the challenge.

"He is waiting for Clarence," a spy from the castle told Edward. "He expects the duke to join him with his army from the west."

"George," Richard said under his breath. "I was wondering where he was."

"And how close is my brother?" Edward demanded.

The nervous man simpered. "The last I heard, he was at Banbury, Your Grace."

Edward gave the man a coin and dismissed him. To Richard, Hastings, Rivers, and three other commanders, he ordered: "To horse, and arm yourselves. You will ride with me."

Richard rode up alongside his brother a mile distant from the army, the raised visor on his helmet revealing anxious eyes.

"What are we doing, Ned? We are but eight against an army we know not how large."

"Never underestimate the element of surprise, Richard," Edward said, a gleam in his eye. "Did you not learn that during your henchman days at Middleham? George may know we are at Coventry and think he can pin us between his army and whatever force Warwick has inside the castle. I would wager a jewel from my stolen crown that he will not be expecting me alone." He chuckled, scratching his nose. "Still puzzled? Then I will enlighten you. Despite his association with Warwick, George, as we have surmised, must be deeply disillusioned with the earl by now. I am hoping that by appealing to him in this way he will see that we—you and I—still think on him as our brother, as family. I think he will not raise his sword against us when we have no army at our back."

Richard gave a low whistle of understanding. "You hope to use him, but will you forgive him? Will he even believe that?"

"His vanity will believe it, my dear Dickon. You, on the other hand, have never needed flattery for me to win you to my side."

Richard grinned. " But it helps," he said. Hearing his childhood name so warmly spoken had nevertheless touched Richard deeply. George wasn't the only one Edward could charm.

And what further awed Richard was that Edward's plan worked brilliantly. As soon as he saw the small group led by Edward and Richard, George slipped out of his saddle and in front of his troops knelt in front of his brothers and begged forgiveness. Had Richard been in Edward's place, he would have been less inclined to grant it, but then he had seen Edward be merciful time and time again with his enemies not to mention George— sometimes to his cost—and knew it was in his nature to be so. He admired Edward for it, but he did not always agree. He would have found a way for George to pay for his treason; he did not think he would be merciful.

With his arm around both brothers, a much relieved Edward grinned. "On to London, boys! Oh, won't Mother be pleased."

Despite the turmoil the fleeing Edward had left behind in London the previous year, the capital city gave the Yorkist king a triumphant welcome. Henry was safely back in the Tower, the saintly, frail monarch deprived of his crown for the second time. Ever the conciliator, he had shown no rancor when Edward met with him at the archbishop of York's episcopal palace, where Henry had been the guest of the archbishop, George Neville. "My cousin of York," he had said to Edward, "you are very welcome. I know that in your hands my life will not be in danger."

Although the words had disarmed him, Edward had no choice but to confine Henry in the Tower alongside the archbishop and several other lords and bishops. As the reinstated constable, Richard saw to it that the deposed king was made comfortable in his new quarters.

"You have grown into a fine young man," Henry told him as Richard turned to leave the chamber. "I trust your Latin has improved."

Richard could not forbear to smile. "Thanks to your treasured gift, my lord, it has," he said. "As well, my time at the law courts forced me to apply myself." He bowed. *"Usque ad alteram diem."*

"Amen," the weary Henry replied. "I pray there *is* another day."

If Edward had been careless enough to lose his crown the previous September, he was not about to allow Warwick to outwit him again. Richard marveled at how his brother could be indolent, profligate, and imprudent one day and resolute, valiant, and in control the next. Crises fueled Edward's natural leadership skills; routine bored him into inaction.

There was no inaction now, Richard confided to Rob as they rode out of London the day before Easter. Richard's White Boar adorned the murrey-and-blue standard that stood stiff from its bearer's staff and marked the duke of Gloucester's troops in the long procession. "'Tis said Warwick, Montagu, Oxford and the rest have a force of twenty thousand and are at St. Alban's. Even with the arrival of many of our supporters in the last two days, we cannot be more than nine thousand. And within a day, here we are marching to do battle," he said proudly. "But then, Ned does believe in the element of surprise. He hopes Warwick will expect us to stay put in the city for the Easter celebrations, and he would be wrong. That would be the old Ned."

Rob tried to relieve an itch under his layers of protective clothing and squirmed in his saddle. "Won't Warwick be astonished. But his grace, your brother, is right. Had we stayed in the city, a force that large would overrun London and leave us fleeing yet again."

Richard agreed. "Only this time, George would come with us, not against us," he said, nodding his head to where George rode alone nearby. George had hardly spoken to Richard since returning to the family fold, and Duchess Cecily, who was in residence at Baynard's and had welcomed her boys home, had spent many an hour with her wayward son, lecturing and praying.

"Have pity on him, Richard. It was a lot of pride he had to swallow," Rob counseled.

Richard shook his head. "I cannot pity him. He rebelled against his king—his own brother." Then he chuckled. "But I don't envy him all those hours of tongue-lashing from our lady mother."

At that moment, Edward himself left the head of his troops and cantered back to Richard.

"My lord of Gloucester," Edward called so the men who marched under the White Boar could hear. "If we engage tomorrow, you are to command the van. You have more than earned the honor. I pray you, make our father proud."

Richard flushed first with pride and then felt something more akin to fear. Leading the vanguard meant engaging the enemy first and setting the stage for the rest of the fighting. His own acceptance of the command was drowned out by the rousing cheers from his men—many of them veterans from Richard's forays into Wales—who chanted "A Gloucester, à Gloucester!"

Rob reached over and slapped him on the back. "'Tis well deserved, my lord."

Edward saluted his brother, wheeled his horse around and cantered back to his place. Richard could not help but glance at George, whose humiliation at being passed over for his younger brother showed in his ramrod posture and steely eyes fixed on the road ahead. A small part of Richard felt a modicum of pity; most of him felt justified.

Richard was not alone among Edward's commanders who thought the king had taken leave of his senses, but Hastings was the only one who braved the question: "Advance in the dark?"

Edward's spies had revealed Warwick was on a ridge straddled across the Great North Road half a mile from the village of Barnet. Clearly, Warwick was ready for Edward, but, expecting the Yorkist army to rest the night in the town and advance at first light, he was unaware that Edward's nine thousand men were creeping forward in the dark and silently settling down right under the earl's nose. There would be no campfires for the Yorkists that night.

The morning mist rising with the soldiers at dawn was a mixed blessing on that Easter Day. Assuming Edward would be advancing from the village but not being able to see through the brume, Warwick began to fire off his cannons and other artillery in the direction of St. Alban's. The missiles sailed over Edward's army, already close, and harmlessly exploded too far. From the other side, Edward's all-important archers were not given leave to fire for fear of hitting their own men, so close together were the armies in so dense a fog.

Richard could barely see as far as his sword point and was thus dismayed to realize his van first needed to wade through marshy ground at the foot of the rise to attack. It was not the last time a bog was to play a part in his life in the winning or losing of a battle. On this day, it was the making of his name as a soldier; he fought valiantly and his troops held the line for Edward, which was no easy task.

In the dark the night before, however, Edward had overestimated the position of Warwick's left flank, under the duke of Exeter. He had positioned Richard too far right, so that Richard's men were advancing up the hill without Exeter facing them and thus leaving the Yorkists with no one to attack. Peering through the murky miasma, Richard could hear the cries of Exeter's soldiers to his left, and realizing what had occurred rallied his own men to swing around and attack the side of Exeter's force. Squelching through the mud, he raised his sword and shouted, "à York, à York!" so many times, his lungs hurt. He began thrusting at the men who came out of the mist to attack him.

Both armies had made the decision to fight on foot, which meant hand-to-hand combat was slow and exhausting. Time and again, Richard cried out to his men to follow him and with superhuman strength, he never gave in to the larger and more organized force that Exeter was commanding. At one point, as he sliced a man's gullet with one expert move, he remembered that Exeter was his brother-in-law—a vicious brute who had abused Richard's sister, Anne, before they were estranged. He looked for the standard of the three royal lions passant, near which Henry Holland would most likely be, but in the fog he could only see the enemy within his sword arm and so he kept swinging.

Rob was close by as was one of Richard's Welsh retainers, John Milewater, both covered in blood and breathing hard. An enormous yeoman, his leather helmet lost and his eyes filled with blood-lust came charging at the lanky John with an axe, sliced off the man's arm and then split his skull in two. Richard groaned as memories of Piers Taggett flashed into his mind, and giving a shout of anger he lifted his sword with two hands and brought it down on the surprised assailant's head, spilling brains onto the bloodied mud.

For three hours the battle raged, and Richard's line never broke. He had no idea what was happening elsewhere in the field, but suddenly he heard angry shouts of, "Treason! Treason!" and wondered which side was committing it. At that moment, Edward's messenger managed to find Richard and gave him the king's command to hold on as the battle was turning in their favor. Momentarily distracted, he failed to notice the billman to his left, who wielded his deadly hooked pole with enough power to cut through Richard's mail and heavy padded gambeson and into the flesh of his left arm. He cried out in pain, but pivoting with his sword sweeping sideways in a wide arc and with such force that he almost sliced the unfortunate man's torso from his legs.

"You all right, Richard?" he heard Rob call. "Aye, 'tis a scratch," he lied, feeling the blood dripping out of his sleeve. "Sweet Jesu, I am tired. How much longer can we hold?"

And as though the Almighty had heard his plea, a cry went up from the enemy's ranks, "Montagu is fallen! Warwick flees!" and trampling over their dead comrades and throwing down their weapons, the Lancastrian soldiers took flight. A shout of triumph erupted from the center of the melée, and Richard heard the words in his heart of hearts he had dreaded hearing. "Warwick is slain!" *You could have avoided this, cousin,* he thought grimly. But then he recognized his brother's jubilant voice: "The battle is won, lads! God is with us!" and all thoughts of Warwick were put aside as he and his exhausted soldiers took up Edward's cheer.

Richard, too, praised his men: "Thanks to you, the battle's won. Thanks to God for taking our side." He walked slowly through their ranks, a smile here and a slap on the back there, asking his men to hold their dead comrades in their prayers, and sending up an ave for John Milewater and the others he had lost that day. And then he sought medical help for his own flesh wound. *Where is Constance when I need her?*

It was on the march back to London that Richard asked Edward: "And what of Warwick, Ned. How did he fall?"

Edward's face was stern. "I had given the order to take the earl, not murder him," he growled. "Some enthusiastic lads took matters into their own hands when they saw him running for his horse and brought him down. They disobeyed my order and will be punished, I can assure you. I was too late to save him, and when I did arrive on the scene, the man was already stripped naked."

Richard was silent. For some reason, he was imagining Anne Neville's sadness upon hearing of her beloved father's death. "Did they have to despoil him? Such an undignified end for such a noble man." He shuddered, praying his own misshapen body would never suffer that ignominy.

"He was a traitor, Richard!" Edward snapped. "Had I caught him, he would have been publicly executed." He wiped his sweaty face with the back of his hand and looked surprised when it came away scarlet. "We must be thankful George was not among them, or I would have been faced with condemning him as well."

Richard glanced back over his shoulder to where a weary George was riding with his own cronies further back in the cavalcade. He frowned. "Knowing you as I do, Ned, I feel sure he would have found forgiveness from you yet again. Certes, you must be a better man than I, because I know I would not have forgiven him. Of all of mankind's failings, surely disloyalty is the most abhorrent."

Richard, weakened from his wound and bone-tired, was never so glad to see anyone in his whole life as he was to see Kate, who was anxiously leaning out over the second story balustrade in Baynard's inner courtyard. He had smuggled her and his two children into the castle a day or two before the battle when his mother was at prayer. Their reunion had been sweet, and made all the sweeter for the presence of little Katherine and one-year-old John. He had not seen his son since the child's birth, and his delight in the lad was heartwarming for Kate. He had not been able to stop dandling the child and marveling. John, unlike Katherine, who resembled her mother, had Richard's own chin, gray eyes, and straight dark hair, although the boy had Farmer Bywood's solid build.

"A Bywood and a Plantagenet," Kate had remarked. "Good solid stock, I would say."

Now collapsing onto the soft feather bed after Kate had lovingly removed his blood- and sweat-stained clothing, he wished she were truly his wife and helpmeet. Kate inspected the wound and sent her servant, Molly, to fetch her traveling supply of potions together with a needle and silk thread. He winced as she expertly sewed up the ugly gash. "You told me you hated sewing, my love," he teased, "and that you are the worst seamstress, yet this looks to be skillfully done."

"Fiddle-faddle!" Kate retorted, as she dipped her finger in a mustard-colored ointment. "Now hold still, this will hurt."

Richard fell asleep almost before Kate had finished, but when he awoke much later and the castle still slept, he was overjoyed to find Kate snuggled against him. She felt him stirring and was immediately awake.

"How many men died at Barnet?" she whispered. "Was there anyone I knew…" She had been afraid to ask earlier in case she recognized names. "…Jack Howard? My father-in-law?"

"All in all more than one thousand fell," Richard said, his heart heavy from all the carnage. "But Jack Howard lives to fight another day. I promise to enquire about Martin Haute for you."

He rolled onto his back and stared into the darkness, Kate tucked in the crook of his arm. His mind could not help but return to Warwick. "Poor Anne," he whispered. He felt Kate stiffen.

"Why spoil our time together, Richard," she complained. Anne Neville's name had come up before in their infrequent meetings, and Richard had admitted that for some time he had considered making Warwick's daughter his wife. "Why must you always mention her name? You know how much it hurts me."

At once contrite, Richard turned on his side and pulled Kate to him, careful to protect his arm. "I have always been honest with you, Kate. You know that my duty is to wed…"

"I know, I know—'someone of my rank.' But it does not hurt any the less to know that one day you will have to give me up." A note of pleading came into her voice. "You would not have to, in truth, even if you were married."

Richard sighed. "You know me well by now, sweet Kate. You know that cannot be."

"Aye. Your morality will not allow a mistress, will it? Sweet Jesu, sometimes I wish you were not so God-fearing!" She stroked his cheek and sighed. Then she giggled. "We shall just have to make the most of our times together, won't we? And thank the Almighty for sending Edouard to wed Anne, which will delay our parting—at least until someone else acceptable comes along."

Richard pulled her close. "Until then, my dearest rose."

Every scrap of clothing Richard wore was thick with the dust kicked up by four thousand men marching at double quick time in pursuit of the enemy. This time it was the Yorkists' original enemy, Margaret of Anjou and her commanders, Somerset, Lord Wenlock, the earl of Devon, and her son, Edouard.

"My crown is not safe unless we prevent the She-wolf joining forces with Tudor in Wales," Edward had said to his own commanders upon hearing the news that Queen Margaret had landed in the west country and was gathering men to her banner in that Lancastrian part of the kingdom. He sent out commissions of array to fifteen counties, and by the time his army marched out of Windsor on the twenty-fourth day of April, he had amassed a considerable force. History would show that Edward acted decisively and with intelligence in his bid to thwart Margaret's effort to reclaim the crown for her husband and son.

By this time, Edward's troops would have followed their magnificent leader into the regions of Hades, and at the wicked pace up and down the Cotswold Hills, they had an inkling of what those hellfires must be like. Both armies raced against time—Margaret to cross the Severn somewhere and find safety in Wales, and Edward to stop her. Although on horseback, Richard often chose to dismount and march alongside his tired and thirsty men. Rob teased his friend: "Why must you show yourself no better than they? The common folk probably think you are as foolish as I do."

On the evening of the third day of May, after a grueling thirty-six miles, the royal army camped a few miles south of where the Lancastrians had taken up a defensive position near Tewkesbury. The only way to cross the Severn was a ford that was tantalizingly close.

"Gloucester, you will command the van," Edward told his brother, as they studied his battle strategy. He once again excluded George, who pretended nonchalance. "George you will ride with my center, and Lord

Hastings has the right flank. Aye, we are tired, but the enemy is more so—my spies tell me they have marched relentlessly for a full day and a night. And thanks to my commanding the constable of Gloucester to refuse them entry, they have had no supplies since Bristol. We shall have the edge." He drummed his fingers on the table, making the small pieces of wood representing his divisions jump up and down. "You know our aim: we must remove the threat to the crown permanently. We must kill or take Edouard of Lancaster or there will never be peace." He leveled his gaze at each of them in turn until they nodded. "Now get some sleep," he ordered.

Richard and George left the tent together. "You know I could command as well as you, don't you?" George said.

Arrogant prick, Richard thought. "Aye, I do not doubt you think that, George, but you have no one to blame but yourself, and I cannot pity you. Do you blame Edward for wanting to keep you close? To me you are no less a traitor than Warwick." He strode off to his own tent.

George glared after his younger brother. "Runt," he muttered, "and a deformed runt at that."

The battle of Tewkesbury, with the magnificent abbey standing sentinel a half mile away, was a decisive but bloody climax to the quarrel between cousins. Edward's four thousand Yorkist soldiers crushed Lancastrian Henry's five thousand commanded by the duke of Somerset.

Once again, Edward owed much of the triumph to his youngest brother, Richard, whose force at first was taken by surprise by Somerset. But Richard held on valiantly, thanks to some two hundred spearmen concealed in a copse to his left, who at his command suddenly emerged from cover and scattered Somerset's right flank. As the fleeing Lancastrians raced for sanctuary in the abbey, George and some of his men caught and killed young Edouard, giving George something to crow about and earning Edward's gratitude.

"He whimpered like a pup," George told the group gathered around Edward when the fighting was over. "He cried for his mother, poor baby. I killed him in revenge for Edmund."

"Good for you, George," Edward said. "But now, we must find Somerset."

Richard caught George's eye and acknowledged the revenge with a respectful nod before following the king and others in a search for the

Lancastrian leaders. Most had taken sanctuary, but Edward, uncaring of his mortal soul, had them dragged out of the church and put in chains. This time Somerset and his cronies could expect no mercy from Edward, who had pardoned them for previous rebelling. Subsequently the next day, Richard, as constable of England, together with the earl marshal, Norfolk, tried them all for treason and had them executed in the town square. Richard stayed to watch, his heart hard, as one by one the heads rolled. "They should be shown no mercy," he told Edward. "Not this time."

His victory complete and his throne secure, Edward could afford to be magnanimous. He prohibited the rebels' bodies to be quartered and exhibited in public places as was customary but instead had them buried in the churchyard. In deference to his rank, their prince, Edouard, was entombed in the abbey's nave.

"This business is not finished until we find Margaret," Edward declared, "but we go north from here. There is more trouble brewing."

Richard wearily climbed back into the saddle and joined Edward on the road to Coventry. He was not so much thinking about Margaret as wondering what had become of Anne, who was last known to be in the deposed queen's company. It had occurred to him the night before, as he lay under the stars unable to sleep, that she was now a widow and free to remarry. Despite her childish peskiness at times, he remembered her fondly. They had liked each other then, but would she want him now? Had she loved Edouard in the end? He even wondered if she might be with child. He had sat up then with a "nay!" on his lips. She was not even fourteen, he recalled, so surely the marriage could not have been consummated. And yet...*I was only fifteen when Kate conceived our very first time....*Then he had a more disturbing thought about Anne's possible pregnancy: Her child would be the Lancastrian heir and mean Edward's hard-fought victory at Tewkesbury would have been for naught. He wondered if Ned had contemplated such an unpropitious circumstance, and if so, would the child even be allowed to enter a Yorkist world. In truth, he thought not. Time alone would tell.

Richard would never forget the triumphant entry into London on the twenty-first day of May, for Edward had given Richard the supreme honor of leading the procession. Londoners were greatly relieved that Edward's victory at Tewkesbury had also put paid to the recent Lancastrian attacks on their city. With news that northern dissent had also dissolved with the intervention of the earl of Northumberland, there was nothing or no one now to stand in Edward's way of reclaiming his throne. Tower-bound King Henry had no one to rescue him now.

With Richard rode William Herbert, earl of Pembroke, who had also distinguished himself at Tewkesbury. The two men were about the same age, and Herbert would become a staunch supporter of Richard's in the years to come. The roar of the crowd as they emerged from under the Bishopsgate caused their horses to shy and the pair exchanged surprised grins at the cheering throngs.

The colorful cavalcade was pelted with flowers—mostly white roses—and the air was filled with clarions and trumpets and the ear-stopping roar of "God save the king," almost drowning out the pealing of hundreds of church bells. Riding in full armor upon a colossal gray courser and carrying a vicious war hammer, Edward's majesty was almost mythical. It was as though Thor himself had come amongst them, although no one still believed in the old pagan gods.

Somewhere behind his brothers, George sulked, once again eclipsed by Richard at the head of the procession, and his resentment grew.

It was then Richard saw Kate at the front of the crowd, John clinging to her neck, and Molly holding Katherine by the hand. The little girl was jumping up and down with excitement, and his heart leaped at the sight of his little family. Kate took John's hand and waved at Richard, who grinned back at her.

"Who is that?" Herbert asked. "She seems to know you."

"She is an acquaintance of Margaret Howard's 'tis all. I met her at Tendring," Richard said with a shrug. A pang of guilt assailed him as he watched Kate. Could he not even acknowledge her or his children to William, who probably had a mistress of his own? He grimaced. What a coward!

But his guilt had more to do with his all-consuming thoughts about Anne Neville at the present moment, which he knew would hurt Kate far more than pretending to Pembroke she meant nothing to him. Once Margaret of Anjou and Anne had been captured following the battle, Richard had been relieved to discover that Anne and Edouard's marriage had not been consummated. Not only would there be no rival heir, but Anne was free to marry again and would need a husband. Richard was now determined to woo and win her. Soon, his time with Kate would come to a close.

Without warning, there was a change in the crowd's mood, and jeering replaced the cheering. "It must be for the She-Wolf," Richard muttered, sorry that he had not prevailed to have Anne ride separately from the erstwhile queen. How shrewd of Edward to include Margaret in the procession, he thought. *I warrant she wishes the carriage curtain sides were rolled down.* He also wondered if George were wishing himself far away from his former ally. What would have been his fate had he continued to throw in his lot with Margaret of Anjou?

"I wonder if she will be allowed to reside with Henry in the Tower," Richard mused aloud. "She needs to be locked up on a remote island somewhere and the key thrown in the sea. As for poor Henry, he will never be a danger to anyone as long as Margaret is under lock and key."

"I do not pity the man," Herbert said. "He was good for nothing."

Richard nodded. "He should have been a monk. He told me so himself. My wish for him is that he may while away the rest of his days in prayer."

"Amen to that," Earl William replied, smirking.

"Are you certain, Your Grace?" Richard tried to steady his voice, but he knew it wavered. "You are commanding me to order regicide—and indeed to commit my soul to the devil."

Edward glared at him, his mouth set in a tight, straight line, his fingers gripping the arms of his throne. "You are constable of England, are you not, my lord of Gloucester? I seem to remember your having no qualms about accepting that honor."

"I am, Your Grace," Richard replied, quickly organizing his thoughts, "but I understood my duty is to bring the accused to trial and, upon that person being found guilty, to mete out an appropriate punishment. May I ask the nature of Henry's crime, and how long will I have for a fair trial?"

It was a bold rebuttal to Edward's appalling command to rid England of Henry and the Lancastrian line. Richard could not believe his brother's request, and although the others in the small, secret council nodded, they would not lift their eyes from the floor. Even Archbishop Bourchier did not condemn the order. What a lickspittle, Richard thought angrily, and a hypocrite. He looked at George to see if he perhaps would stand up to their brother, but of course George had every reason to acquiesce. Nay,

George was not going to risk provoking the king again. Richard's only hope was Will Hastings, but he seemed to have found a wayward thread on his elegant sleeve and was busy trying to break it off. Besides, Will had possibly suggested the outrageous solution. Richard was on his own. How he pitied the former king. He had been saddened by the grief Henry had expressed upon learning of his only child's death. *In truth, what does he have to live for*, Richard thought now.

"There will be no trial, Richard," Edward answered. "As constable you have the right to administer punishment without one. You will arrange to end Henry's life in the kindest and most discreet way possible. I want no signs of violence upon the body, do you understand. It must look like natural causes. Use money from the privy purse if you have to, but you will do it tonight." He rose from the chair and towered over his brother. "I am the one whose soul may see hellfire, not you. You have but to obey an order from your king—the Lord's anointed. For the peace of the kingdom, I must sometimes act in God's place." Then putting his hand on Richard's arm, he said, "Come, let us pray together for you to have strength to do was is right for England."

"I don't need your prayers," Richard snapped, shaking off the unwanted hand. "Save them for yourself, Your Grace."

It was with heavy legs and an equally heavy heart that Richard climbed the spiral staircase to Henry's apartment in the Tower. Richard had had no trouble finding an assassin within the Tower dungeons to carry out Edward's bidding, and with a promise of freedom and a few guineas, the unsavory-looking man was now keeping a respectful distance behind his savior.

Upon seeing Richard, the guard outside King Henry's room unlocked the door and bowed. "Wait downstairs for me," Richard commanded, taking the flambeau from its sconce, and the turnkey gladly sauntered off, hardly giving the other man a glance.

The former king was housed in a large, well furnished room and was lying in the bed, a black velvet blanket covering his thin frame. *He almost looks like a corpse already, poor man*, Richard thought, ashamed. Could his prayer have been answered so soon? He had spent the past hour on his knees in the Tower's chapel trying to think of a way out of this dreaded responsibility, and begging God to simply strike Henry down with some natural cause.

Henry's eyes flew open at the light and locked on to Richard's troubled ones. As Richard secured the torch, Henry suddenly saw the ruffian in Richard's shadow. The man was clutching a cushion from the only chair, and the king blanched. "So is that the way of it?" he asked so quietly he unnerved the already-tense Richard. "I am a nuisance and must be eliminated. Is that it?"

Richard could not lie. "Forgive me, Your Grace. I am but my brother's messenger," he murmured. "If I had my way, you would be allowed to end your days in a monastery. I hope you believe ..."

"Enough talk!" the assassin hissed and lunged at the bed, shoving the drowsy king back down and pushing the cushion onto Henry's face. It was a clumsy attempt at suffocation, and Richard had cringed when he had instructed the convict in the manner of the murder. "No wounds," he said. "We shall hope he is asleep and you can smother him quickly." He could not believe he was subjecting gentle Henry to his own worst nightmare, and the bile rose sourly. He stepped back and turned his face away. He wanted to run, or at least leave the room and the murderer to his business, but he knew he must not. He must witness this heinous, unnatural execution.

But it seemed Henry would not exit this life as weakly as he had lived it. His body, now desperately awake, took on superhuman strength and began flailing wildly and clawing at the pillow and his killer. Richard knew exactly what Henry was experiencing and involuntarily gasped for air.

"Good Christ Almighty!" the hoodlum cried, fighting off the terrified king's blows and scratches. "You told me he'd be asleep and weak." He tried in vain to hold the cushion in place. "Hold still, you feeble-minded bastard!"

Richard could bear the scene no longer. What a hideous way to die, he raged inside. Henry did not deserve to be so ignominiously treated, and with great force he grabbed the felon by the scruff of his neck and threw him out of the room, slamming the door shut. "You have your freedom," Richard shouted, "now go to hell."

He could hear the man trip and stumble down the stairs as he turned to face Henry, who was now on his knees, eyes turned to heaven. Only his torn chemise, shallow breathing, and disheveled, lank hair gave proof to what had just happened. What impressed Richard most was Henry's calm: he had his rosary between his fingers and was telling the black beads as though nothing had happened.

It was in that quiet but ghastly instant Richard knew what only he must do—and, moreover, quickly and cleanly. He moved behind Henry and put his hands on the king's shoulders. Only then did Henry tremble.

"Lord God Almighty, take me to Your bosom quickly," the condemned man whispered, "for I have no wish to live in a world without my kingdom, queen or son. And forgive this man his transgression as I forgive him."

With tears very close, Richard took Henry's head between his hands, the head that had once worn the crown of England, and snapped the thin neck with surprising ease. "Good man that you were, may you now rest in peace."

He laid the king's body gently on the bed and covered it in the blanket. Then he prostrated himself on the floor, tears wetting the cold stone, and prayed for his own soul.

The story that was put about in the days and weeks to come was that when King Henry, sixth of that name and last of the Lancastrian Plantagenets, heard of the disaster at Tewkesbury, he died of a broken heart in his Tower prison.

Richard did not understand until much later why he had decided to do Edward's bidding himself, but at the time he only knew he could not have lived with himself had the murder of saintly Henry been carried out by that criminal in such a dishonorable manner. He felt ashamed he had given so rash a command, and a mantle of guilt settled permanently on his heart. 'Twas badly done, Richard, he told himself.

Only his confessor ever knew of his sin.

He would never forget the deadly sound that had put an end to the strife between the cousins and given England a dozen years of peace. He knew it would haunt him for the rest of his life

As he buried his face in Traveller's comforting neck after the awful deed, he had let go of his self-control and wept. All vestiges of his youth and belief in a merciful world had died in one sickening crack.

Part Four

Lord of the North
Anne's Man

London, 16 January, 2013

Finally to see the face of the last warrior King of England, the man I had sought for the last four years, would be the culmination of a long and difficult journey. It would also be an enormous personal relief since after all the research it would have seemed wrong not to proceed to the project's visual conclusion.

...The reconstruction then followed a process based on the anatomical formations of the head and neck, where scientific standards are used to interpret the facial features....

The reconstructed head was set up in the centre of the main archeological Institute, University College London. To enable DSP* to record me meeting Richard for the first time, I was asked to close my eyes as Simon Farnaby led me in. After a few moments' hesitation, I opened my eyes. Richard's face took me completely by surprise. I don't know exactly what I had expected but it wasn't this....it was the face of a young man who looked as if he were about to speak, and to smile. I searched in vain for the tyrant. I can't describe the joy I felt. I was face to face with the real Richard III.

—*Philippa Langley,* **The King's Grave**

*Darlow Smithson Productions, the documentary filmmakers of the **Looking for Richard Project.**

If Richard had assumed the mantle of manhood, it was time for him to take a wife.

"In truth, you above all men have deserved my gratitude," Edward told Richard in a private meeting at Windsor early in the autumn. "Not satisfied with being constable and admiral of England, great chamberlain, chief steward of Wales and all the other honors I have bestowed on you to show it, you now want to wed Anne Neville." He harrumphed. "George will not be agreeable."

Richard gave a snort. "Annoying George is only part of my reason for wanting Anne's hand." He stuck out his chin, clueing Edward that Richard had made a decision. "I am determined to wed her, but I need your support, Ned. Besides, you owe it to me." Richard would never let his brother forget that he had carried out the orders for Henry's execution, although Edward was not privy to the how and who. The king was unaware of the dark shadow that had descended on Richard's very soul from the moment he had ended Henry's life.

"To soften George, I suppose?"

Richard nodded.

When Anne had been captured along with Margaret, she had been placed in her sister Isabel of Clarence's household, which in essence meant George was now Anne's guardian and entitled to revenues from her estates. He now controlled both sisters' vast Warwick inheritance as well as their mother's Beauchamp manors. It was George, not Edward, who had the right to give Anne in marriage.

"How does the lady feel about it? Is she not grieving for her husband? You will have to wait for the year of mourning, you know."

"Of course. But she writes that she desires our marriage above all things." Richard felt his cheeks flush. "She says she has loved me since she was a girl."

"And you, Richard? Do you love her?" Edward laughed. "Cock's bones, it doesn't matter if you do or you don't. Besides, I know you have given your heart elsewhere."

Now Richard laughed, too, enjoying this rare intimate moment with his brother. "You know too much, Ned. Am I still transparent? Ah," he said, seeing Edward nod, "then I will not lie. I shall always love Kate, but I also care for Anne—like a brother, 'tis true, but it will grow deeper with time, I have no doubt. I remember her as a sweet, kindly soul—although she can be…um, spirited." He was recalling their last meeting when she was brought to Coventry after being captured. Far from falling into Richard's arms, she was brave enough to publicly decry George's vicious killing of Edouard when the battle was already won. Richard had been impressed, and doubly so when, in a less public moment, he had asked her, in the most tactful way he could for a man, whether she carried Edouard's child. Anne had slapped his face. He grinned now. "Aye, she definitely has pluck."

"Then I shall not stand in your way," Edward said, "and I will support your suit. But mark my words, it will be messy." He rose from his chair. "After all this talk of wedding and bedding, I think I will go and find my beautiful Bessie. My cock is crowing."

Richard winced.

Feeling the confidence of Edward's backing, Richard rode past the many mechanical cranes standing along the wharves on Thames Street and into the large courtyard of Coldharbour, the Clarences' London house. He tossed a coin to the groom who helped him dismount and lead off his horse. He glanced up at the impressive facade of the fortified mansion that had belonged to the dead and attainted duke of Exeter and caught sight of Anne's pale face at a window on the second floor. He waved, but from his distant position he was not able to see her change of expression from anxiety to one of joy as she shyly waved back.

He ran up the graceful staircase to the studded front door, which had already been opened for him by the steward. "My lord duke, we are honored," the grave, bewhiskered old man said, bowing low. "My lord of Clarence is expecting you and will receive you in Duchess Isabel's solar, if you will follow me."

"I know the way," Richard said kindly, making a note to tell George his steward was getting too old to climb all those stairs in the three-storied townhouse. "I can announce myself, Sir John."

A young page was on duty outside the door, caught picking his nose as he waited for something to do. He scrambled to his feet and bowed, recognizing his lord's younger brother. Richard tousled the lad's hair and knocked on the door before entering.

Anne was still at her window seat, George looming over her, and it disturbed Richard that George was gripping Anne's delicate shoulder a little too tightly. Frowning, Richard wondered whether George had guessed the reason for this visit?

"Good afternoon, Brother." Lovely as always, Isabel glided forward to greet him, and he lifted her hand to his lips. She leaned toward him and kissed him on the cheek. "For old times," she whispered, taking Richard by surprise. Then more loudly she said. "We are glad to see you, are we not, George?"

"If you say so, my dear," George replied, but his expression was wary. He left Anne only then to stand by his wife, who entwined her fingers in his and rested her cheek on his sapphire sleeve. "Have you come as Edward's mouthpiece, my lord, or as my brother?"

"Oh, George, my love, I beg you..." Isabel pleaded, and Richard was heartened to see George's expression somewhat soften.

"I am always your brother," Richard answered him and went towards Anne at the window seat. Smiling, he held out his hands. "Lady Anne, how good to see you again."

Still petite, her face had lost its girlhood plainness and might now even be considered pretty, he noted, and her body had filled out nicely in womanly places. Now if her nature had not changed, Richard decided he would be very fortunate to claim Anne as his wife. Clearly, the blush on her cheeks and the adoration in her eyes gave Richard confidence that this was no grieving widow. He took her hands in his and kissed her boldly on the mouth. Much to his surprise, he felt his desire stir.

"I have missed you, cousin," he said, leading her to a place next to Isabel on the cushioned settle. "I trust George is seeing to your needs?"

Was that a flicker of unease that Richard observed on her face? But she answered cheerily enough: "His grace, the king, was kind enough to place me in Isabel's care. George has more important things to concern himself with than my well-being, I'll be bound. And Isabel and I are happy to be together again."

Isabel patted her sister's knee. "We are, we are," she said.

"So, what is the purpose of your visit, Brother?" George interrupted the banter. "You could have had news of Anne from me in council meetings any day last week."

Pleased that Anne had clearly kept their correspondence a secret from her guardians, he asked that he might have a private word with George. Once behind the closed door of George's cabinet, a magnificently paneled room overlooking the gardens reaching down to the river, he chose flattery to open his suit with his vain brother. "Marriage agrees with you, George. You and Isabel seem very happy. I envy you."

George was surprised by the warm comment, and he motioned Richard to take a seat as he himself sat down. He lifted the elegant pitcher to pour a glass of wine for his brother, when Richard came to the point.

"I have come to negotiate with you for Anne's hand."

George's aim wavered and he splashed some claret on the rich Turkey rug covering the table.

"Christ's nails!" he swore, slamming down the jug and shoving a pile of blank vellum out of the red rivulet's path. "Look what you have made me do."

Richard tensed, but chose to tread carefully; he needed to win George over. "I did nothing of the sort, George. Why does my proposal upset you? You have found happiness with Isabel; why would you resent my finding mine with Anne. She is free, and I already know her mind about this."

"How?" George snarled, rising from his seat and using a beautifully embroidered kerchief to mop up the spill. "How do you know what Anne wants? I have hardly allowed her to leave the house since she came under my charge. She is my dependent, by Edward's order. I shall not consent, and there is an end to it."

Now was the time for anger, and Richard felt it mounting as he stared at his feckless sibling. He leaned forward on the edge of his seat and pointed an accusing finger. "I know why you do not sanction the match, George. I can see right through your greed and your trumpery. You are as false as you are shallow. As long as you control Anne, you own both Neville sisters' inheritance. Do not lie, you dog in a manger!"

George sneered. "Be careful of hypocrisy, Richard. You want Anne for her inheritance, too. Don't deny it. And it would please your sanctimonious little mind to deprive me of it. Why would Anne want to wed a crookback like you, anyway?"

George was unprepared for Richard's sudden lunge and even less prepared to ward off the blow to his cheek from Richard's fist. Reeling back, George hit his head against the mantle and howled in pain. "You arse-licking puttock!" he shouted. "Get out of here! You will not have her now—or ever."

Like his father's, Richard's anger died quickly. He made sure George wasn't bleeding, went to the door and shot his final dart. "I have Edward's full support in this request. After your treachery last year, you might not want to test our brother's indulgence again too soon."

For the first time, Richard wondered at his motives for wanting Anne. Was George right? How would people interpret this betrothal? He shrugged it off. Why should he care so much what other people thought. After all, this issue was minor when compared to the dark deed he had perpetrated in the Tower that haunted him every single day. He had begun to believe, after that, he could handle anything Fate might throw his way.

He strode back to the wharf, satisfied he had Anne's consent and dismissing any doubts he could not accomplish this next step in his life, despite George's threats.

Richard confided in Rob that George might stoop to anything to thwart Richard's plan to win Anne. "I did not like the way he treated her. She was intimidated—almost fearful. Poor girl, she was manipulated by her father, forced to marry Edouard, and now she is under George's controlling thumb. I doubt he will let me near her again."

Rob was thoughtful. "You say Isabel greeted you warmly? Why not enlist her help? Surely she wants to see her sister happy?"

"You may be right. Isabel might champion us. Sweet Jesu, I am glad I was not born a girl. The fair sex may seem to us to have an easy life, but in truth they are shackled to the will of whichever man has charge of them. No wonder so many of them end up taking the veil."

Rob guffawed. "Ever the philosopher, Richard." More seriously, he offered, "Shall I be a go-between for you? I could pay my respects to Anne and find out when George may be away from home."

Richard and Rob had not counted on Isabel's loyalty to her husband, and she would not send for Anne when Rob turned up on Thames Street. "My husband has gone to Bisham," she said, referring to one of the inherited Warwick manors. "You must treat with him when he returns, Rob. Forgive me, but I know my duty."

"Will you give Anne a letter at least? I wish to extend my condolences to her on the loss of her husband." Rob's innocent expression convinced Isabel, and she nodded.

"I will send for parchment and quill," she said, "and then you must go." She stood to the side as he put pen to paper, but when he stopped mid-greeting and stared at her, she shrugged and went to the door. "Thank you for your visit, Rob."

As soon as she had left, Rob scribbled the requisite few lines of sympathy, but then folded Richard's letter inside his own and put his seal on it. At least Anne would know that Richard cared. How this was to be resolved, he had no idea, but he was well acquainted with Richard's stubbornness. Glib, shallow George was no match for Gloucester's level head and determination.

Dearest Richard, Anne wrote in her tiny, neat script, *if you are as determined to have me as I am determined to have you, then God will help us. We will all be together at yuletide, as the king has invited us to Westminster, so we can meet there. George will not dare refuse to let us talk with Edward watching, will he?*

Richard agreed, but Christmas was a good month away, and he was tired of George's bullying. He had stayed away from Coldharbour House for long enough, he thought, as he was ferried to Thames Wharf one chilly November day. Pushing off from Baynard's wharf, he was reminded of the scene there many years ago when he and George had fled to Flanders and Meg stood with a distraught Traveller watching them go. *Traveller! Dear old Traveller, I hope one day we will be reunited in some pleasant place,* Richard thought sadly. He had nursed his faithful old hound who had succumbed to a sudden sickness in the bowels not three days since. Richard had stayed with him all night and had finally administered the deadly tincture that had put the suffering animal to sleep. "Who shall I confide in now, dear old friend," he had whispered, cradling the dog's big head in his arms one last time; the wolfhound had given comfort during those black moods for many months.

Richard forced his focus back to his journey. He worried that his brother would take out their quarrel on poor Anne. His protectiveness towards his young cousin was something he curiously had not felt with Kate, who had demonstrated her independence well enough. He had arranged for an annuity to help with expenses for the children, and he was grateful for Jack and Margaret Howard's generosity towards his beloved mistress. He begged God nightly to forgive him his illicit love for Kate and for the lie they both had lived in allowing Kate's wastrel husband to believe the two children were his. Richard knew he must honorably dissolve his liaison with her, but, as with most young men, a divided heart was a guilty obstacle.

It was easy to blame a sudden shivering on the cold wind, but it more likely came from a dread of confronting this unpleasant task. He must do right by Kate and tell her in person, but how much simpler to write a letter. He had to admit that, as well as their physical passion, he would miss her sunny nature and fearless candor. She was the only woman who made him laugh out loud, and her loving acceptance of his growing deformity allowed him to forget the cursed affliction if only for a few hours. And how he treasured her badly written letters. He smiled to himself; if only she could write as well as she sang, and—made love. He sighed. Nay, the passionate letters must stop once he married Anne; he would restrict himself only to those that concerned their children's welfare. He was confident Kate understood their love affair was destined to end, and he vowed to resolve the matter. He must go to Anne's bed with a clear conscience and stay true to his matrimonial oath. But could he free his heart from Kate? At least, unlike Edward, he had stayed true to only one mistress.

Seeing Coldharbour's towers now peeking over the leafless willows by the river reminded Richard of his mission and that George, for all his faults, had been faithful to Isabel and also frowned on Ned's lusts. It was one of the few things they had in common these days, Richard thought ruefully. For the rest, they could barely be civil together.

By the time he clambered out of the boat and walked through the mansion's gardens undetected by the Clarence's steward, he had made up his mind that if all went well with his quest to wed Anne, he would send for Kate. Having negotiated to rent a magnificent townhouse of his own from a wealthy merchant in Bishopsgate, he was looking forward to setting up his own household. He could safely talk to Kate there.

Plainly garbed to avoid attracting attention on his short journey, Richard entered Coldharbour by a lower back entrance. He had chosen the dinner hour to visit, knowing the occupants of the house would be too busy to notice his arrival. No one hindered his climb up the narrow spiral staircase to the great hall, and he stood unheeded, observing the servants to-ing and fro-ing from the kitchens and buttery with plates of food and pitchers of ale. George and Isabel were seated together at a table on a raised platform, enjoying their meal, but, oddly, Anne was not with them. Richard frowned. As the duchess's sister, she should have been there. He scanned the long table stretched in front of the duke but she was not there, either.

Something made George look Richard's way. The speared chunk of suckling pig froze halfway to his mouth, and he slowly rose from his chair. Richard hurried forward before the ancient steward could heave himself from his seat and attempt a formal announcement. Richard patted his arm and told him remain where he was.

"You were not expected, my lord," George said civilly as dozens of pairs of curious eyes watched intently; he knew servants loved to gossip. "Will you take some ale with us?" George offered his brother, pointing to a seat. Richard ignored the gesture and remained standing.

He noted that Isabel's face had drained of color, and he felt a frisson of anxiety crawl up his spine. "Forgive my intrusion, Your Grace," he addressed Isabel, hoping he sounded nonchalant. "May I ask where is the Lady Anne? I have some news for her."

"You may give it to me," George snapped before Isabel could speak. "Lady Anne is unwell and asked to dine in her chamber."

Richard heard a gasp behind him and knew George was lying. Richard smiled and shrugged. "Then I trust you will tell Anne I came. I will await word from you as soon she recovers. I don't think my news will comfort her, so it can wait. I beg your pardon for interrupting your dinner."

Before George could object, Richard bowed, turned on his heel and hurried back to the staircase. But instead of going down, he ran lightly up to the ducal apartments on the second floor and, finding no one monitoring them, began to look for Anne. His fear mounting, he threw wide the final door to a small but sunny solar. He found a servant girl spreading fragrant rushes on the floor, who dropped her basket and curtsied.

"Do you know where the Lady Anne is housed, girl?" he barked a little too harshly.

"This be her chamber, my lord, but she be no longer here. Been gone a sennight."

"A week?" Richard cried, now very much alarmed. He could see the room had been stripped of anything belonging to Anne and the bedclothes had been removed. "Where did she go?" he demanded, grabbing her arm. The girl shrugged, tears starting. "Every...th...thing be gone," was all she could stammer.

Frantic, Richard retraced his steps to the staircase, bumping into Isabel at her solar door. She gasped. "You are still here?" She glanced anxiously over her shoulder.

Richard gripped her elbow and pulled her inside the room. "Where is she, Isabel? Tell me. Where is Anne?" His face was hard, his gray eyes boring into hers, as he now held both her arms and was shaking her. "Tell me! What has George done?"

Isabel began to cry. "I know not, Richard, I swear. Please, you are hurting me."

Richard let go and Isabel stepped back rubbing her arms. Her expression defiant, she said, "She disappeared several days ago. I think she ran away. George sent someone to look for her, but..."

"I don't believe you," Richard snapped, grasping her again. "Why would she run away? And to where? She is a fifteen-year-old girl, for God's sake, and all alone. Tell me what George has done with her?"

"I will thank you to unhand my wife." George's voice behind Richard startled him, and letting Isabel go, he swung round to face his brother, fists balled, but George's larger frame made Richard step back. "Isabel is right," George confirmed, smoothly, "she ran away. I sent two of my gentlemen to search for her to no avail. Most likely she has gone to find her mother at Beaulieu. There is a horse missing from the stable, and that is all I can tell you."

Richard was dumbfounded. "What did you do to her to make her run away? It has been a week! Did she take her maidservant? Did no one in the stable hear or see her go?" His voice shook with anger. "This story is preposterous. Why did you not report her disappearance to Edward—or me? You will answer for this, George, as soon as I have found Anne."

Then shoving George out of his path, Richard ran down the stairs and out into the garden. There he stopped, his heart pounding and his mind a jumble of possible theories. That she had run away by herself he dismissed; Anne was too timid. Besides, surely someone in the house would have noticed Anne taking the horse and carrying her belongings. Everything had gone from her chamber, that seemed certain. She must have had a helper, and that someone might talk—with a little assistance from a rose noble.

It was only on the way back to Baynard's that Richard was consumed by self-reproach. He had stupidly put his trust in George, which once again George had betrayed. Richard blamed himself for postponing a decision to fight for Anne, and now he had put her in danger.

"A curse on my brother," he muttered under his breath, "and may he get what he deserves."

Richard enlisted the help of the newest member of his growing group of adherents, Lord Lovell. After Warwick's death at Barnet, the young Francis Lovell had been without an overlord, and Richard was happy to have the intelligent seventeen-year-old as part of his inner circle.

"As a newcomer to London, no one will recognize you in the Clarence household. The last time Isabel saw you, you were a boy," Richard remarked, as he, Rob, and Francis sat discussing Anne's fate beside a crackling fire in his private office. Duchess Cecily had allowed Richard to adopt her late husband's treasured sanctuary at Baynard's while he awaited his move to Crosby Hall. Richard could feel the duke of York's presence every time he entered the room, making him want to impress his late father.

"We must find Anne, and I am convinced someone in the house knows where she is. Rob and I have a plan for you, Francis. You will go there disguised as a squire come from the duchess of Warwick with a message to her daughter, Isabel, concerning Anne."

"Then what?" Francis looked perplexed. "Am I going to interrogate every one of the servants—there must be dozens."

"That should not be necessary, Francis," Rob said, "A cleverly jingled purse will bring someone forward. Money talks, as the saying goes."

"You will have my undying gratitude if you are successful, Francis," Richard said. "We must find Anne. It may take you a morning, but I'll wager that, by terce, you will be handing out a noble."

It took less than an hour for Francis to discover that Anne, dressed as a scullery wench, had been secreted from the house one night and hidden in the kitchen of a nearby tavern or inn, the name of which was the only piece of information still missing.

Richard was incredulous. He stared at Francis for a full ten seconds before hurling a filigreed silver cup across the room, stirring a memory of a similar scene with Warwick at Middleham. Francis winced, the cup having missed him by the width of a broadsword's blade, and Rob suppressed a smile.

"This is too outrageous to be true," Richard fumed. "Is there no code of chivalry left? Do you have reason to doubt your informant, Francis? Perhaps 'tis a lie fabricated by George."

Francis scratched his wispy new beard. "Nay, my lord, I swear the man was telling the truth." His hand went to his dagger and he grinned. "A little persuasion along with the noble went a long way to extracting the truth," and he then put his hand to his codpiece. "The man seemed to want to hold onto his jewels." Rob sniggered, but Richard was in no mood for humor, so Francis continued, "It was he who had smuggled the kitchen maid's attire to George's squire and helped dispose of Anne's wardrobe."

Rob snatched up his bonnet and crammed it on his head. "Let us not waste time talking about this, lads. We must find the poor lady as fast as we can."

Richard nodded, buckled on his shortsword and grabbed a fur-lined cloak hanging on the peg. "Onward!" he cried, flinging open the door and calling for his squire. "Fetch our horses immediately, John," he commanded the brawny young man.

Soon the trio was cantering out of Baynard's courtyard and onto Thames Street. They began with the area adjacent to Coldharbour and shocked several tavern owners by sweeping into their modest establishments demanding to search the kitchens. Each time, they found nothing, and Rob began to think this a fool's errand. And then their luck turned. At an inn at the top of Bread Street, the landlord, on seeing the three noblemen enter, was clearly flustered.

Richard took the man by the arm and led him to a secluded corner. While Richard interrogated him, Rob and Francis moved quietly through the archway that led down to the kitchens.

"Do you know who I am?" Richard demanded. The frightened landlord, his rheumy eyes darting in all directions, shook his head at the grim young duke. "I am Richard, duke of Gloucester, brother to his grace, the king," and he grasped the small man's stooped shoulders to make sure he was paying attention, "and brother to the duke of Clarence. Has a servant of his placed a kitchen maid in your employ recently? The man would have worn the bull badge of Clarence."

The unfortunate landlord trembled and was silent. He had been paid handsomely for taking on the useless wench. It was clear she had never washed a dish in her life nor cut open a fish, and it was only the promise of more reward for silence that had prevented him from turfing her out.

"Well?" Richard barked, forcing the man's arm behind his back. "Answer me, you fool, or I will break your arm!"

Luckily for the landlord Rob's excited voice broke in from below: "My lord, she is here!" Richard threw the man onto a bench and growled, "Don't move," before hurrying down to the kitchen, where the rest of the servants stood gaping.

Anne was huddled on a stool sobbing, Francis crouched beside her offering his kerchief. When she saw Richard, she ran into his arms. She reeked of onions and fish. Her long, light-brown hair was matted with grease, her hands raw from cold and lye, and her homespun gown stained with blood and gravy. No semblance of the noble lady remained in the waif, who clung to her savior with such desperation, her red, swollen eyes framed by dark hollows.

Richard stroked her face and whispered her name, trying to calm her. "Anne, Anne, hush, sweetheart. Never fear, I am here, and you are safe now." He turned to the curious onlookers. "Away with you! All of you," he commanded, and the servants scurried away.

Her sobs abating, Anne spied the landlord creeping up the stairs, and pulling away, she pointed at him: "George paid him to take me, and he has treated me abominably," Warwick's daughter cried, regaining her composure. "He beat me and threw me to the ground. I have bruises…"

The landlord was clearly terrified that the lazy girl's accusation could get him arrested or worse, and he attempted to defend himself. "I was paid to take a servant who they said was soft in the head. They said she would pretend to be a lady." He feigned bravado as a last resort: "Ha! look at her. Does she look like a lady to you?"

He was unprepared for the fist that hit him square on the jaw. "This is the Lady Anne Neville, widow of Prince Edouard," Richard hissed over the pathetic figure on the ground, who spat out a bloody tooth. "Rob, send someone upstairs for the sheriff. This man should be in irons."

The blubbering landlord crawled to Richard's feet, begging for mercy, for which he received a swift kick. "You are no better than a dog!" Richard snapped. "Come, Anne. Let us away."

Anne was too grateful to be shocked by Richard's violent behavior, but she wondered later at the change in him. He was still her beloved Richard, although a black cloud seemed to hover about him, but perhaps her predicament had angered him, and she could only be secretly thrilled.

Gentling his cloak about her pathetically thin shoulders, Richard led the way out to the street, leaving Rob behind to deal with the landlord. "Francis, all is arranged with sanctuary at St. Martin's?" he asked.

"Aye, my lord," Francis answered his lord, whom he revered. It would be many years before he would allow himself to acknowledge the growing friendship.

"How can I ever thank you?" Anne said, melting into the safety of Richard's protection.

Richard smiled. "Marry me, my lady," he said simply.

"With all my heart," was Anne's happy response.

Anne's devotion to him and the gallant way in which he had sought her out led her to assume that Richard returned her feelings. She never considered the young man's understandable ambition to marry into the wealthiest family in England, and, just as her sister had been for George, Anne Neville was the best match for a brother of the king. But for Anne, she wanted only to wed the man she loved.

Three steps lay in Richard's path to the altar, and only two were legal obstacles: George's sanction and the Pope's dispensation. The third was a task Richard dreaded: bidding Kate farewell.

She arrived with the two children at Crosby Hall during advent. As well as delighting in being a father, Richard's passion for his beautiful mistress kept him away from Westminster night after night while he imprinted on his mind the image of her naked body rising above him, lying beside him, or thrilling him with every caress—memories that he hoped to carry with him forever. How he wished he could take her to court, show her off, and introduce his family to three-year-old Katherine and baby John. But Kate had begged to remain anonymous, high-born gossiping a real fear. "I would embarrass you," was her excuse, and so Richard had kept his promise to her. Later he would also keep his promise to acknowledge the children by placing them in noble houses. "Let them never forget they have a royal father," he begged of her, "and one who loves them."

"This is farewell, is it not?" she whispered into the dark, fingering the écu talisman she had given him and that was always about his neck. "Can I guess? You are to be married? Is it…will it be …soon?"

"'Tis not settled yet, love. I have Edward's permission at last, but my brother, George, is opposed, and there is much dissension between us. You see, I hope to marry his sister-in-law…"

"…Anne Neville." Kate's tone made Richard wince, but he would not flinch from his duty.

"Aye, 'tis Anne and no surprise. You must know that I marry for other reasons than love."

He explained as much as she needed to know about the obstacles he faced and the intricacies of why Anne was the right consort for him, but he hastily promised his tearful mistress: "It has nothing to do with my heart. You have that, I swear. How could I ever forget our precious times together. You have taught me what true love is by loving me despite my having to forsake you now. But to honor both you and Anne, I must foreswear our liaison. One day, I promise, Anne will know of my love for you—and our children—and she will have to accept that I have a divided heart."

"I think I understand," Kate answered, sadly. "But I cannot help hoping my part of your heart will be the larger."

Richard smiled in the dark, took her in his arms and cradled her to sleep. He wondered if the honorable Kate would love him still knowing he had so recently committed regicide. He prayed fervently that no one but he and God would be privy to his crime and closed his eyes.

"Let me dress you today," Kate pleaded the next day, as they bathed together. "I want you to go to court with my scent upon your clothes."

He kissed her trembling mouth, tasting tears. This would be the last time they would be naked together, and the ache in his heart almost translated into tears of his own. He touched the new ring he had given her; delicately filigreed in gold, inscribed with his chosen motto: *Loyaulté me lie*—Loyalty binds me. "Know I shall not forget you, Kate. And if you have need of me for anything at all, send me this ring and I will answer."

"Fiddle-faddle!" Kate retorted, bravely. "Why would I ever need you, pray?"

When she had lovingly clothed him in his finest velvets and satin, he left her standing proudly in the middle of the room clutching the first love poem he had ever written. Before he could change his mind, Richard fled. So long as Katherine and John lived, he knew his love for their mother would never die. It was also a sad certainty that this was, for him, the close of a chapter.

CHAPTER NINETEEN
1472–1473

Edward watched his two brothers with growing impatience. His admonition to them during yuletide appeared to have kept the peace for the season, but the two dukes had circled each other for most of the festivities like a couple of rival tomcats.

The court had removed to Sheen, a favorite palace of the queen's, and Richard's fight for Anne had reached a climax. Still stuck in sanctuary, the pawn in the two men's game awaited her fate, although her confidence in Richard never wavered. "'Tis what I like about her," Richard had admitted to Rob after yet another visit to St. Martin's in early February with no news of his success. "Her loyalty to me has not diminished despite my inability to win her. I must not let her down."

Now George goaded his brother, sarcasm dripping like goose grease off greedy fingers. "Such the gallant lover, aren't you? Anne must be loving her cold little cell at St. Martin's while you sleep on a featherbed under a coney coverlet. At least she has no excuse to spend as much time on her knees as you do, *O perfecte quidem pie hominem.*"

George believed Richard's Latin was as bad as it had been in the schoolroom, but Richard surprised him. "I am no 'perfectly pious person,' George. *Pietate autem Diabolus esse melius quam,*" he retorted. "And you are no better than a devil. Anne is safe, warm and cared for, which is more than can be said for her time at Coldharbour."

Edward got to his feet surprisingly swiftly for one so large and bellowed, "Enough of this!" causing his new wolfhound pup to disappear under the chair. "I have had enough. You are both equally to blame that this dispute is now public gossip from Carlisle to Cornwall. You have become an embarrassment to me and to the crown, and we will have no more of it. You will both appear before my councilors here at Sheen in two days and put your arguments before them. Mark my words, you will abide by their ruling and this quarreling will stop." He turned to Elizabeth and held out his hand. "Besides, your bad behavior upsets Bess at this precarious time. Come, my love, you are looking peaked. Perhaps you should rest and leave these tiresome young men to their incessant squabbling."

The queen, heavy with her fifth child by Edward, allowed him to help her to her feet. She glared at George, and Richard was glad the venomous look was not aimed at him. He had long suspected Elizabeth blamed Clarence's treason for the deaths of her father and brother following the battle of Edgecote, and she barely spoke to George when they were in private. That the Woodvilles wielded too much influence over Edward was the only issue Richard and George agreed upon, but for now it appeared they had nothing on their minds but dividing up the Warwick inheritance.

Elizabeth then demonstrated why she could be so dangerous. Just as the sun can transform in an instant the darkness cast by clouds, she transformed her sneer for George into an angelic smile for Richard. Startled, Richard had no idea why he had earned the queen's favor. As he kissed her hand, she whispered: "I am on your side, my lord. I abhor George's treatment of innocent Anne."

In the end, and in front of Edward's council, George gave in. But not before both brothers had dazzled the learned councilors and judges with their impassioned arguments. For every glib, affable and urbane remark of George's, Richard impressed with his knowledge of the law and his logic: George's heart pitted against Richard's head.

Richard was surprised to see the queen in attendance, and several times he saw her whisper behind her hand to Edward. When the verdict was given by Edward that Richard was free to wed Anne, he wondered how much influence Elizabeth had wielded. It was wise to be wary of her, although she had sided with him this time.

George walked away with the earldoms of Warwick and Salisbury as well as manors and lands, and eventually insisted that Edward award him the title of great chamberlain of England, taking it from Richard. Thus in the end, through the skewed division of property and titles, George of Clarence became the wealthiest magnate in the kingdom after the king himself, all this for a man whose treasonous ambition had sent his brothers into exile and caused a rift in noble loyalties that only Warwick's death had overcome. How Edward could have rewarded George so richly when he had turned against his brother, coveted his crown, and caused so much bloodshed was the question that gnawed at Richard. He harbored so much ill-will towards his brother, it frightened Richard.

But for now Richard feigned contentment. He had achieved his main goal, permission to wed Anne, which meant he too would profit from her inheritance and that of the countess of Warwick, her mother. The latter prize was not his to win nor Edward's to give, however. The Beauchamp inheritance, which included the vast Despenser lands, belonged to Countess Anne, and Richard, through Edward, was depriving her of it— illegally. But who would gainsay the king? It was one of the only times in his life that Richard was to behave dishonorably towards a woman, and his conscience may surely have pricked him given the kindness Anne Beauchamp had shown him during his years at Middleham. He finally shook hands with George but only after hours of debate and arguing. Was he as greedy for power as George? Nay, Anne may have been a great heiress, but she was the only noblewoman Richard wanted as wife, and in time he would learn to love her.

He looked into George's face, studying the handsome, vain man standing before him. George's smugness infuriated Richard, just as the jealousy and bullying had when they were young. Richard knew his brother had not changed, and he felt a lifetime of anger and resentment rise to the surface. Turning away abruptly, he bowed to the king and queen and quit the chamber without saying another word.

Edward's magnanimity toward his faithless brother disturbed Richard. Did Edward not see how shallow George's loyalty was? Richard had made up his mind long ago never to trust George again, family or no, and in some part of his heart it saddened him. Not for the first time Richard wished his father had lived a long life; York would not have allowed his three sons to fracture the family as they had.

If only Richard could have foreseen the future, he might have warned Edward of George's lack of scruple, for, as the fable goes: a leopard does not change his spots.

Instead he went straight back to London to give Anne the good news, but not before securing Edward's signature to petition Rome for a papal dispensation allowing the marriage between the cousins, who shared two sets of common ancestors.

"I care not one whit about dispensation, Richard," Anne said, happily, in the cloister of the sanctuary church of St. Martin le Grand a few days later. "We will receive it eventually, just as George and Isabel did, but I beg of you, let us be wed tomorrow."

Richard chuckled at her enthusiasm. "What, no special gown? No elaborate ceremony? No nuptial feast? What kind of woman are you?"

"One who loves you and has since I first saw you." Her disarming answer made him encircle her waist and draw her to him. "I have dreamed of this day for too many years, Richard." She paused and gripped his velvet jacket tightly. "Especially that awful day when my father made me plight my troth to Edouard. It feels as though I have held my breath from then until that day you rescued me from my misery in the tavern kitchen. I am finally alive again, thanks to you."

Richard pulled her onto a bench and took her hands in his. "I shall do my best to make you happy," he told her, "and if there is aught I can do for you, you have only to ask." He wished with all his heart he could offer something more than brotherly affection, but for now, that would have to suffice. Anne seemed no more than a child needing his protection. And his heart ached for Kate.

"Take me back to Middleham," she begged, "I have no desire to live in London. It does not suit me."

Relieved she had not requested a declaration of love, Richard readily granted her wish. "I, too, feel like a dog up a tree here, and to breathe the clean air of the dales again is perhaps what I need to banish the foul stench of dissent between George and me. Aye, we can live in Middleham."

He was startled when Anne loosed her hands and, putting them either side of his face, drew him into a hungry kiss. Her lips parted, inviting him into her mouth, and thus taken unawares, he found himself responding. When they separated, Anne blushed and hung her head.

"Forgive me, Richard, but I simply could not wait, for, after these last two years, who knows what life has in store for me. I hope you are not ashamed of me?"

Richard laughed out loud for the first time with Anne. "I do believe the mouse has roared," he marveled, reaching for her hand and kissing it. "Far from being angry, I am much in awe. I fear there is a touch of wanton in you, Anne," he teased, and she blushed again.

Middleham in June meant larks in the meadows and wild thyme on the hills. Anne eagerly pointed out her favorite dropwort among the tall grasses, their white and pink bulbous buds ready to burst into starry white flowers with showy yellow-green stamens. Richard was amused by his wife's girlish delight in the colors of the countryside; he didn't know a dog rose from cow parsley, but he sensed Anne would teach him. The many towers of Middleham soon rose on the horizon, and Anne sighed happily: "Home. We are home, my dearest husband."

Husband? Richard had not grown used to the idea after only a week, and except when he had sworn to take Anne as his wedded wife in front of the priest at St. Martin's, he had not yet referred to her as "wife."

It had been a simple ceremony, with only Anne's gentlewoman, Rob, and Francis as witnesses, because Richard did not trust that George would not again interfere. He had persuaded Anne to wait for the dispensation—holy law was strict regarding consanguinity—as he told her gently: "When you know me better, you will understand I am loath to break God's law." The words had almost stuck in his throat. *What a hypocrite you are, Richard. Break God's law? Haven't you spent these past months trying to bury the memory of regicide in the depths of your unhappy conscience?* But once again he pushed the guilt away.

Anne had been disappointed to wait, but by April the vital piece of paper had arrived from Rome and the young couple had breathed a sigh of relief.

"With this ring, I thee wed," Richard had said, placing the gold band on Anne's finger. Her hand trembled and without a second thought, he had clasped it in both his and taken it to his lips. Her eyes sparkled as she finished the pledge and happily promised to love, honor and obey her husband from that day forth.

It was done, Richard thought now. Anne was the consort he deserved and a woman he would come to love. He had tried not to think of Kate as he gently broke Anne's virginity on their wedding night, and her eagerness to please had touched him. Was it possible to love two women at the same time, he asked himself. It was a question for an intimate evening with Rob and a good claret sometime soon. He was glad Rob had chosen to stay in his household; he was now Richard's most trusted councilor, and as soon as Francis could take care of business at Minster Lovell, the young nobleman had promised to join Richard's council for as much time as his baronetcy allowed. Francis, for all his youth, was proving a valuable friend to Richard; in fact he and Rob were the only two of his gentlemen who knew of his growing affliction (he refused to call it a deformity, which he viewed as Satan-sent), besides his trusted squire, John Parr.

His back ached now after so many days in the saddle, but he endured the discomfort for fear of seeming weak. That first night with Anne in his big tester bed at Crosby Place, he had come to her fully clothed as she sat waiting for him, dressed in a simple shift, her long hair draped over her narrow shoulders. When John had helped him out of his tight, cleverly padded pourpoint and his hose, Richard, carrying two cups of malmsey, dismissed the squire and came to sit on the bed. Anne smiled at him over the sweet, herbed wine, and he had toasted his new wife.

"We can sit and sip for as long as you like, Anne. We have a lifetime of bedding each other, and I am in no hurry if you are not ready." He had been more nervous than he wanted to admit, but he knew he must tell her about his back before she discovered it and might recoil. Her dismay at his reluctance made him realize she misunderstood him, so he hurried to explain. "Dear Anne, you shall be bedded tonight if you wish, but before you do, I need to reveal a secret."

"I know about your mistress and your bastards, if that's what you mean," Anne interrupted, hurt clouding her face. "How could you speak of them now? I did not take you for a cruel man, Richard of Gloucester."

Richard had almost choked on his wine. "You know?" he sputtered. Sweet Jesu, but this was not going well. He gathered his wits. "My dear, I am sorry that you have heard of my liaison from another and not me; I intended to wait for a more appropriate time to tell you. Certes, I would not be cruel enough to speak of it tonight. All I will say is that she is part of my past, but you are my present and my future. Please believe me."

He had reached over and stroked her cheek, holding her eyes with his for a long moment before slowly drawing his shirt over his head. "My bigger secret is this," he had confessed, turning his torso so that she might see the unsightly protrusion below his shoulder. He heard her soft gasp.

Swiveling back to face her, he had said. "I was afraid you would not marry me." He lowered his eyes, expecting her to ask what sin of his was so dire that God had punished him thus. But Anne was silent for a moment and then she had thrown herself into his arms, saying: "Do you think you are the only one with a flaw in your body, my dear? It is you I love, not your back. None of us is perfect, Richard; my breasts are too small, and I have my father's nose." When Richard laughed, Anne had chided him. "Did you think I was such a whey-faced milksop that I would flee from you for this? You must learn to have faith in me, my dear. I am not Isabel; I am more my father's daughter than she is. Trusting me with your secret only means I will love you all the more."

Then they had embraced and caressed each other until Anne pulled away and removed her shift. "I want you to make love to me, Richard. I want you to truly be my husband." She had put one of his hands on her breast and sighed when he fondled the pert nipple. The rest had been easy and natural.

How grateful he was as he now watched her canter away to be the first reach her beloved Middleham. He must not ever betray Anne's trust, he vowed.

Riding into the familiar courtyard, Richard could not help but remember the happy years he had spent training as a knight under the castle's hulking walls. How would he be greeted by Warwick's servants? Were they still loyal to the earl? Would they reject and resent their new lord, especially as Richard had been Warwick's enemy at Barnet? He sat straight in his saddle and rode up to the long steps leading to the great hall. Anne had already dismounted and was being fondly greeted by Middleham's long-serving steward. Richard waited his turn. He was Anne's husband now, and lord of Middleham, and yet he was unsure of his own welcome.

Suddenly the bailey was filled with cheering yeomen—guards, armorers, blacksmiths, farriers, potters, fletchers, cooks, almoners, pantlers, and others who support the daily living of a massive castle like Middleham. Two strapping young men ran forward and touched their forelocks. "We be glad to see you, my lord," one said to Richard, "do ye know us?"

Richard recognized the grooms immediately. "Tom! Jake! I am right glad to see you," he cried, expecting one of them to take his reins. Instead, coming to help him dismount was old Blackbeard himself, the master of henchmen, his lopsided grin revealing empty spaces in his gums.

"My lord of Gloucester, welcome!" Master Lacey cried, taking the reins. Then, surprised at seeing Rob and Francis close behind, he could not help but laugh. "My three worsest students," he teased them all. "Have ye come back for more training? By all the saints, I done my bestest."

The trio joined him in merry laughter, and Richard knew his worries had been for naught. "You were right, Anne," he murmured, seeing her eyes brimming. "This is where we belong and where we shall, God willing, stay."

"Aye, Richard." She stood on tiptoe and whispered, "And have our first child."

Richard turned his happy shout of "God be praised" into "God bless you all," as he lifted Anne's hand to the sky.

Nothing could console Anne when, three months into her pregnancy, she lost the child. There seemed no reason for the loss except that perhaps her despondency during the past two desperate years had led her to become malnourished.

"Some bracing Yorkshire air, nourishing Wensleydale cheese, and plentiful game will soon put flesh on those bones," the physician told her after an examination. "There is no reason you will not be with child again soon, your grace." His prediction, however, was stalled until the following March, when a wicked north wind forced even stoic Yorkshiremen and women to spend more time than usual huddled beneath blankets. Thus Richard and Anne's little son was not the only babe to come into the world at yuletide that year.

All through the summer months, Richard went back and forth to Nottingham, where Edward was holding court and where Richard and George still disputed their respective claims. George was angry when Edward decided to restore the coveted Beauchamp inheritance to the duchess of Warwick, depriving Isabel and Anne of it for as long as their mother lived. Imagine if you will, George's fury when Richard, in decisive

preemption, sent his retainer James Tyrell to Beaulieu Abbey to take
Countess Anne from sanctuary and convey her to Middleham. Mother
and daughter were happily reunited, and grateful for his protection and
for installing her at her favorite residence, Anne Beauchamp chose to turn
over her entire inheritance to Richard and Anne—with Edward's blessing.

It was clear to any with an interest in the matter, that the king had
favored his brother Richard, and it was no wonder there were rumors that
George of Clarence was stocking arms and would soon declare war on his
younger brother.

The happy result of the wait for their firstborn was that Anne had her
mother by her side as she labored on Christmas Eve. "This will be a special
child. A Christmas child," Richard told her before being shooed from the
birthing chamber. "I shall pray for his safe delivery for as many hours as
you must labor, my dear Anne, and I shall think of a suitable name."

Anne smiled weakly at him and then waved him away. "He will not be
called Jesus, despite your love of Him," she stated firmly. "Now go, before
the midwife chases you out."

Richard had not known those times when Kate had gone into labor for
her two children, and thus he had not yet felt the terrible anxiety and guilt
that a man experiences during his wife's travail. He knelt in Middleham's
little chapel until his knees told him to take some exercise around the
ramparts. He had prayed hard, *Do not blame Anne for my guilt, dear Lord,
and in Your gracious mercy see her safely delivered of her child—our child,* he
corrected. He gingerly made his way along the castle wall, watching for
icy patches on the walkway, and once, when nearing the tower that housed
Anne's apartments, he heard her muffled screams. Shuddering, he gazed
over the snow-covered meadows south of the castle feeling completely
helpless. In the distance stood his one-time favorite sanctuary, the bare
trees exposing the ruins to the elements, and, after a moment's hesitation,
decided he needed to be there now.

Donning his heavy, fur-lined cloak and whistling to his new wolfhound
pup Rufus, so named for the reddish tinge to his coat, Richard trudged
purposefully through the ankle-deep crusty snow. The unexpected noise
startled two hares, who loped off as fast as their long legs could propel
them from the excited hound, whose own overgrown legs skidded on the
slippery surface. Richard had purposely waited before choosing another

dog; none could have bested his first dog, but Rufus's grandsire was Captain and, like Traveller, had been born at Fotheringhay. Traveller would have known exactly where Richard was headed, but Rufus approached the old stones only when Richard began clambering over them, and then he bravely made his mark. Several ungraceful attempts later to follow Richard higher, the dog eventually gave up, taking shelter under a crumbling arch.

On his usual perch that bitter winter day, where Richard had always felt close to God, he had never felt so distant from the Almighty. The bleak, pristine-white landscape, the winter quiet and the wide gray sky reminded Richard how vast the universe was that God watched over and how small and insignificant he was. And yet he knew God saw into every single heart and observed every living creature. Richard had no doubt that his heart was of special interest to his Maker and was why he had been punished with a crooked spine. The burden of his great sin weighed heavily on him, and he pulled his cloak tighter. He nevertheless bravely begged the Almighty to bless his union, bless the child that would come into the world on such an auspicious day, and watch over his beloved wife in childbed. Dare he even hope that the loss of their first attempt might have been atonement enough for Henry's death? He chose to believe it today, and murmured his thanks for his good wife and the child she bore. So, for a few pleasant moments he allowed himself to bask in his blessings.

But he could not banish the darker thoughts that crowded his brain every day. He had established himself as Lord of the North with relative ease, and had won praise for his generosity, not only for protecting his mother-in-law but for taking in as his ward the son of the traitor, Montagu. He was proudest of his rapprochement with the unpredictable lord of the borderlands, Henry Percy, the earl of Northumberland. With the two of them working in tandem to keep the peace in Edward's northern territories, the often rebellious natives had gladly settled into a period of calm.

Richard still questioned some of Edward's policies—especially the power the king had afforded his wife's ambitious family, the Woodvilles, even superseding Richard's jurisdiction in Wales. Elizabeth and her brother, earl Rivers, had taken over Ludlow Castle to establish the household of young Edward, prince of Wales. The prestigious position of governor of the prince was also given to Rivers, which Richard had the foresight to recognize was a dangerous move. Richard determined to tell his brother about the hostility the rest of the peerage felt towards the queen's family, for it seemed Edward was oblivious and firmly under his wife's thumb.

Puzzled why Elizabeth would put up with Edward's infidelities, Richard harrumphed loudly, startling Rufus. He slapped his forehead. "Of course," he muttered, "she lets him have what he wants in exchange for what she wants. And she wants power. How stupid of me."

Frowning, his thoughts turned, as they always did, to the division in his family. Why did George persist in provoking Edward? And now it would seem Richard himself had become an object of George's enmity, for during those summer and autumn months he had been laying up arms. Would George actually try to do him harm? Or his foolish brother might again be thinking of colluding with Lancastrians against Edward. No one, not even Richard, dared voice the treasonous insinuations, but he did not doubt the possibility. Rumors had even circulated that George's name was associated with a failed invasion by the Lancastrian earl of Oxford in September, although nothing was proven. Even so, Richard pondered, did the foolhardy George still believe he could unseat his brother and take the crown?

Richard shook his head. How could he make George see the futility of his ambition and bring him back to the family fold? He was forced to acknowledge he actually did not want to; he could care less what happened to George. He sighed deeply, feeling helpless and angry at the same time; besides, he did not dare to ask God for any more favors at this point.

The loud wail of a shawm shattered the silence, and Rufus barked. For an instant Richard thought it came from heaven, and he crossed himself. The logical instinct was to reach for his sword, but certes, he had left without it. Was there an advancing army? Was it George? *Nay, you fool,* he realized happily, *it must mean the babe has come.*

He scrambled down from the ruin and ran as fast as the snowy ruts allowed him back through the postern gate, up the Round Tower's steps to Anne's chambers. He was met by his mother-in-law, wreathed in smiles. "Where have you been, Richard? Your son was born an hour ago, and you were nowhere to be found. I had to sound the alarm! But rest easy. Mother and child are well, and Anne was very brave."

Richard let out a whoop, gave Countess Anne a smacking kiss, and barely knocked on his wife's door before bursting in. A moment later he held his little son, swaddled up to the chin, and marveled at the perfection of the child, who stared placidly up at his father. Richard swore later that the baby had smiled. "He knows me," Richard enthused, "and, I cannot believe this, but he looks like … someone, I could swear."

Anne chuckled wearily. "Let me help you, my dear. He took his time, seemed quite content to come into this world, charmed everyone, and took to the breast like a duck to water." There was a glint in her eye. "I, too, was reminded of someone."

Richard laughed out loud. "Edward! He reminds you of Edward."

"And so, with your blessing, we shall name him for his royal uncle," Anne declared, and addressing her son, added, "How do you like it, Edward of Middleham?"

There, snuggling into the richly hung tester bed, the fire crackling in the hearth, Richard held his wife and son. He had never been happier, but he did not dare to hope God had smiled on him.

CHAPTER TWENTY
1475–1476

Usually a bucolic spot dotted with sheep, Barham Downs was now teeming with soldiers, horses, carts piled high with harness, artillery, and tents as far as the eye could see. Richard arrived with his army from the north, an army he had been mustering for several weeks now. He gazed south to the coastline and the silvery sea. On a clear day one could see the faint line on the horizon that was France.

Edward was going to war with Louis. Over what, Richard had not quite understood when he had received the command to bring troops to Kent to support an invasion of their long-time adversary. He had been pleased to have raised three hundred more men than Edward had demanded. Richard might not have admitted it, but it spoke highly of his popularity in the north country.

For close to three years, he had been content to carry out his administrative duties as Lord of the North, hear petitions, mete out justice and settle land disputes, as well as maintain good relations with the northern nobles and keep a watchful eye on the Scots. It may have been coincidence, but Richard's good governance of the north paralleled his father's ability to bring the rival Irish factions together during his lieutenancy in Ireland twenty years earlier. By only rarely moving among his castles of Middleham, Sheriff Hutton, Richmond, and Pontefract, Richard was able to be an attentive father and faithful husband. Young Ned was the joy of his parents' life, a happy, energetic toddler beginning to babble his first words. Standing on the steps of Middleham, it was with reluctance that he bade his son and anxious wife farewell to go to war.

"Come back to us, Richard. Come back whole," Anne whispered as he kissed her. "We shall pray for you hourly." Eighteen-month-old Ned giggled as his father nuzzled his neck, and Rufus pinned back his ears and regarded Richard with soulful eyes.

"I shall be back soon," he told them all, bending down one more time to pet his dog.

After seeing his men billeted on a decent patch of the grassy hillside, he went off in search of Edward's contingent. The lack of the royal banner told Richard that the king must be housed in greater luxury elsewhere—no drafty tent for Edward, Richard thought scornfully. News of his brother's continuing descent into hedonism had disappointed Richard greatly and made him ever more determined to steer a righteous path and follow his father's example. Richard of York had been a capable Protector during Henry's madness, and progressive, steady lieutenant governor of Ireland before Richard was born—those troublesome subjects still harboring goodwill towards anyone bearing the York name.

As he stepped between groups of soldiers seated or lying back on the chalky grass, some preparing a meagre meal or polishing a blade, he paused to greet a billman here or an archer there or admonish two that were brawling. "Keep your fighting spirit for those Frenchies," he said, pulling them apart. When they recognized his White Boar on murrey and blue, their eyes widened and they fell on their knees. Richard grinned at them and gave them both a friendly cuff. "I know 'tis tedious waiting, but you'll be glad you rested once we face the enemy."

"That's Gloucester! They say he be a good commander," Richard heard one in the group say as he moved off. "Better him than his prick of a brother, they say. Clarence only cares for hisself." It was only too true, but Richard was sorry to hear it from the yeomen.

"Lord Gloucester!" the booming voice of Jack Howard hailed him from farther up the hill, and he hurried down to meet Richard as fast as his stocky legs could carry him. "Well met, my lord. With your northern troops assembled, I can send word to the king that we are all mustered. Did you know he is sending me as envoy to treat with Louis first?"

Richard grasped his hand, glad to see his old friend, although Jack would always bring thoughts of Kate to mind. "You are just the man I wanted to see, Jack. Perhaps you can explain the logic behind this invasion—the king has failed to enlighten me."

Jack laughed. "Invasion is a lofty word, in truth, although," and he waved his arm in the direction of the coast, "the Conqueror undertook a successful one a few miles from here, did he not? My role is to persuade the Spider to give up what was ours by right (thanks to that same Conqueror). I shall leave on the morrow with Lord Stanley. But to answer your first question, we aimed to use our alliance with Charles of Burgundy to force Louis to return Normandy and Gascony to us. The king and council believe that, by mustering an invasion force and having Charles's army ready to join us across the channel, Louis will give in." He furrowed his brow and kicked at a stone. "However, we had not reckoned with the self-interest of our ally Charles. They do not call him le Téméraire for nothing. His rashness or boldness, or whatever it means, has led him to ignore our treaty obligations and lay siege to some no-account city for so many months that we cannot hope for the full army he promised."

Richard was dumbfounded. "So without our ally's support, how can we defeat France with these?" He indicated the English troops. "If Charles were not to be counted on, why muster our troops? Surely 'tis a futile campaign and Edward should abandon it."

"What? And infuriate the people of England? The poor bastards had to find money they did not have in the first place to fund this war. Can you imagine the fury if we return empty-handed having never fired an arrow? They won't be refunded, you know. The king has enough disaffection on his hands now; he was counting on reclaiming the French crown to warm Englishmen's hearts. Nay, we have to go."

Richard nodded although now this expedition seemed like mere folly to him. "There are still those who remember Agincourt and the honor King Harry brought back to England. In truth, it was a blow to my father's pride when Somerset lost France—he spent many a year in Normandy holding it safe for Henry." He was always hoping his own chivalry both in war and at the council table measured up to his father's high standards. In his wishful thinking, he wanted to believe Edward, too, was living up to it with this venture. "'Tis a worthy cause, I warrant—and if Charles is there, albeit with a smaller force, it is attainable."

"He will be there," Jack assured him, "and we have St. Pol's and Brittany's support as well. Edward's plan is that Louis will be squeezed between the borders of Burgundy and Brittany."

Richard pondered all this as he watched the many ships bobbing like toys in the faraway bay. His own ship *The Mayflower* was anchored somewhere in the flotilla, he knew. He had held the position of admiral of England since his tenth birthday, even before Edward made him Constable of England. It meant he drew income from the posts, and when he came of age at sixteen, he had been presiding over both courts whenever possible.

Jack Howard was used to the young duke's way of sizing up a situation and waited patiently. Finally Richard asked: "Why is Edward wanting you to treat with Louis? What is he expecting to achieve? Let us set sail and get the business done—or is my brother afraid?"

"King Edward is afraid of nothing, Your Grace," Jack assured him. "I was with him at Towton, Barnet and Tewkesbury, and in truth he is a fearless fighter. If I may speak frankly," he paused to get Richard's nod, "his weakness is indolence and too great a taste for fine living. He now prefers governing from a throne..." he refrained from adding "or a bed," "than from the back of a horse."

Richard shook his head. "I am sorry to hear you say this, but I, too, have worried. He did not learn it from our father. Let us hope he proves us wrong, and we will soon engage the French in our rightful cause."

He walked off troubled by Edward's decision. What could he do? Edward was king by God's grace, and his word was thus the law.

Knowing how scornful Richard was that he was negotiating with Louis rather than fighting, Edward left his brother out of the group of high ranking nobles to meet the French king at Picquigny. The scene had not been pretty, and for once George had gained Edward's favor by being the first to step forward and join his brother in the decision to pull out of France—provided Louis gave them incentive.

"Where is our honor?" Richard had demanded of those gathered at the council meeting in Amiens in mid-August. He could hardly contain his disgust. "Where is England's honor in this? We have sat upon our backsides since crossing to Calais two months ago. Two months! And not a shot fired nor an arrow loosed. I am ashamed, and," he dared to add, "our father would have been ashamed."

Edward glowered at his brother, drumming his fingers on the arms of his chair, while his commanders and fellow lords uncomfortably observed the stand off. George stood so close to Edward he must have felt the heat of anger coming from Edward's rigid body. He awaited the predicted eruption with glee though not a muscle of his face revealed any emotion at all. Here was his chance to supplant sanctimonious Richard in the eyes of the king.

"Does anyone else stand with Gloucester?" Edward growled. A few men shuffled their feet, and three stepped forward, but as none was of great account, Edward waved them off. "The majority wins," he announced, rising. Richard's strong stance had surprised Edward, but due to the high opinion Edward had of his brother's honor, he attempted to appease Richard. "Without Charles's help and now that St. Pol has once again turned his coat from us, we are at a disadvantage. Our spies have reported how Louis has ravaged the countryside from Paris to Picardy to keep us from resupplying our troops. With hungry soldiers, how are we expected to defeat the superior French army, brother? Besides, I have it on good authority that Louis would prefer not to fight and will even give us all pensions to leave."

"Pay us? Pay us!" Richard was outraged. "Pay whom, may I ask? Pay the soldiers who have languished here since June earning a pittance when they could have been at home working their farms and feeding their families? By wasting so much time, you have eaten through the hated benevolences you taxed them to fund this so-called invasion. You have even denied them the chance to reap the usual spoils of victory. What of them, Your Grace, and you, my lords?" he turned in a circle accusing all those who stood with Edward. "How can you look your men in the eye and send them home empty-handed while you line your pockets with French crowns?"

"Stop there, Richard!" Edward commanded. "You will abide by our decision, and you will sign the treaty with Louis. As your king, I command it."

Richard's gray eyes glittered black as he bowed to his brother. "I will do as you wish, my lord, but I want it known I will have no part in Louis' peace pension," and he backed from the room.

Not a few of the men who watched him go admired the determined duke, one of them being Will Hastings, who was to receive the largest pension from Louis after the king. Will attributed Richard's refusal to the high-minded principles of youth; the older and more jaded one became, the more pragmatism wins the day, Will thought ruefully. But he pocketed the pension anyway.

Richard, however, left the meeting with bitterness for his brother's lack of moral courage. The glorious, golden brother of his childhood had once again disillusioned Richard, and for the first time in days, that heavy disappointment in his heart caused his crooked back to ache and his shoulders to sag under its weight. He wished he could be spirited back to his Middleham solar, his wife quietly sewing next to him, and his adored young son bouncing on his knee.

He could hear the raucous results of Louis's generosity to Edward's commanders emanating from the Amiens' alehouses, but he was in no mood for celebrating that night. He would take his pride, discontent, and his empty pockets back to his own rooms and confide in Rob and Francis. He would not even trust Jack with his frustration, for he knew even the ethical Lord Howard had accepted the French bribe.

"Devil take him," he muttered as he made his way through the dark, muddy streets to his quarters. "Devil take 'em all."

No one was surprised at Richard's absence among the richly arrayed nobles who accompanied King Edward to the staged meeting of the two kings upon a bridge at Picquigny.

King Louis, having heard of Richard's rejection of any monetary payment in the peace contract, and knowing how well regarded the young man was among his peers, invited him to dine a few days later. With the treaty a fait accompli, and his temper having cooled, Richard thought it churlish to refuse. When Louis presented him gifts of two horses and some silver plate "as a courtesy to the king of England's youngest brother," Richard's usual scruples did not prevent him from accepting them. They were merely gifts, he rationalized, not a pension.

By Richard's high principles of chivalry, the invasion of France was not Edward's finest hour. History, however, would applaud Edward's choice to negotiate and commend him for preventing a costly campaign that he may or may not have won. His bravado had upheld England's hunger to humble France, and he had come away with a sizable pension that would eliminate the need to tax his people further—although the common soldier returned to England empty-handed but for the usual daily wage. The invasion did, however, prove to be the last time Edward would ride at the head of an English army.

Richard left France beginning to question the long-held belief that a king was all-powerful on the Ladder of Being, as decreed by God. In this case, Edward was plainly wrong, he had concluded.

On the long journey back to Yorkshire, Richard had time to spend in quiet solitude having dismissed his troops to their homes. He knew they were resentful returning without the rewards known as the spoils of war, but Richard knew they did not blame him. Nonetheless he felt responsible for their loss and bitter towards Edward.

Anne was overjoyed to see her husband home so soon, "and without a scratch for a change!" she cried, clasping him to her. "I must thank Edward the next time I see him." She was nearly as excited at Rufus, who attempted to leap into his master's arms with the exuberance of a pup.

Richard responded to Anne's questions with platitudes. Not wanting to burden her with details, he often kept matters of policy to himself. His habit of protecting her led him to misjudge her ability to grasp complicated issues. He should have remembered lessons learned in childhood from Constance and his mother and given Anne credit. But keeping his domestic life tranquil and simple was a panacea for his many complex duties as Lord of the North.

Thoughts of his other children now interfered with his domestic bliss, and a few days after his homecoming that autumn, he chose to open his heart to Anne. "I swore to you then and I swear to you now, I came to you free of Kate, Anne. But I cannot neglect my responsibility to those two children I sired with her. I promised Kate that I would provide for them. My sister, Lizzie, has agreed to welcome Katherine at Wingfield. She has such a big brood she will not notice another, I suspect." He watched Anne's soft brown eyes lower to her lap, where her hands were clasped tightly, and he let the idea sink in before broaching the more delicate subject of John.

"I know it pains you to talk about my children, but I must be honest with you. These children will never come between us, Anne, you do believe that don't you?" He was cheered to see her nod. "But they are mine, and as such are also of Plantagenet blood. I must do right by them. 'Tis a matter of honor." He paused, watching her nod. *Now for the hard part,* he thought. "I would very much like my son John to come and live here, if you could see it in your heart to take him in. He will soon be ready to be a page, and once he is old enough to be sent to learn his knightly skills, Francis Lovell has offered to mentor him just as your father did me."

Anne continued staring at her lap, idly turning Richard's betrothal ring. In a very small voice, she said: "I knew this day would come, Richard, and I cannot refuse your request. It would hang like a veil between us. Eventually, we would grow distant. I could not bear that, my love. Thus, I consent to your sending for your son. Besides," and she looked up, tears close, "Ned needs a brother as I do not seem to be fruitful."

Richard went down on his knees and gathered her to him. "You see why I love you, my dear. You have the most generous heart, and I thank you with all of mine." He kissed her sweetly on the lips, and wiped away her tears with his thumbs. "I shall wait until the spring to do it, when John will be five, but for now we need speak no more of it."

Anne stroked his hair and smiled, her eyes now full of passion. Thus encouraged, Richard picked her up as though light as goose down and carried her to their bed.

"Perhaps tonight will bear us fruit," he said, teasing her nipple. "At least we'll enjoy trying."

After such an uneasy conversation, Richard was relieved to hear a seductive chuckle.

The mile-long cortège snaked its way at a snail's pace throughout the midlands' countryside the following summer. King Edward had finally decided to honor the remains of his father and brother, killed at Wakefield and buried at Pontefract, by reinterring them in the church of All Saints at the house of York's principal seat of Fotheringhay.

The funeral carriage began its ninety-mile journey at Pontefract on Monday, the twenty-second day of July and ended a week later, stopping each night at a designated church where the coffins would be carried into the sanctuary, accompanied by a local procession of town elders and churchmen.

Showing that Edward had lost none of his regard for his youngest brother, despite their disagreement in France, the king had chosen Richard to act as chief mourner. Cloaked and hooded in black velvet, he followed immediately behind the unwieldy funeral vehicle in which an effigy of the deceased duke could be seen by the bystanders through the struts of the carriage. The seven horses pulling it were draped to their hooves in embroidered caparisons bearing Edward's sunne in splendour badge, the white rose of York, and the royal arms. Behind Richard rode three bishops, abbots, and many of the northern barons. Far ahead of the clumsy carriage, the slow beat of tabors and loud bleat of trumpets preceded heralds and pursuivants carrying York's arms, all announcing the procession's arrival in several towns from Doncaster to Stamford and finally, to Fotheringhay.

Riding alone, Richard had had many hours to ruminate on aspects of his life, his family, and his sins. He spoke directly to God on occasion, acknowledging his imperfections and taking full responsibility for King Henry's death. On some days he was unapproachable, even by his friends riding behind him. It was somewhere between Grantham and Stamford when his conscience began to ease, and he believed the Almighty's grace might allow him to move on with his life. Feeling some redemption, he resisted looking for Kate among the silent spectators in Stamford, even though he had asked her to meet him there. God must know his motive was honorable, he hoped.

A most magnificent hearse awaited the duke of York's coffin inside All Saints at Fotheringhay, whose candelabra atop intricately carved and gilded wooden towers almost reached the church beams. Twelve servants who had served Richard of York placed his coffin and effigy on the black velvet cloth in the center of the extravagant monument. Painted on the underside of the hearse's ceiling was the figure of Christ seated on a rainbow; the eyes of Richard of York's effigy could therefore stare heavenward and see his savior. Edward, dressed in a blue velvet mourning gown as befitted the king, was waiting with George to receive the coffins along with chanting monks and nine bishops. Edmund of Rutland's hearse was also elaborate and was in place in the Lady Chapel, where the young earl's remains would be buried.

Edward sat apart from the other mourners, the most important of whom had the honor to flank York's hearse for the duration of the mass, including the dukes of Clarence, Gloucester and Suffolk, Lord Hastings, and four earls. Soon the church was full to stifling from the hundreds of candles and scores of sweating worshippers on that hot July day. Outside in the village and crowding into the castle bailey were two thousand participants in the reburial ceremonies. Edward was to feed them all and many received alms monies in remembrance of his father.

Sixty-year-old Duchess Cecily, regal in mourning gray, was given a seat in an alcove to the side of her husband's hearse, and Gresilde Boyvile, perspiring profusely herself, was fanning her mistress with a rush fan. No one could blame the bishop of Lincoln for hurrying the *placebo* and *dirige* that sweltering afternoon, knowing the next day held the prospect of three more masses for the souls of Richard's father and brother.

Richard wept as he thought back to the last time he had seen his father, the day the duke had ridden out of Baynard's and towards his death. "Tell me, before I go, if you remember what is most important in this life, after loving a merciful God?" he had asked Richard and George. "Our loyalty to England, the king and to our house of York," Richard recalled was their answer. "And what is most dishonorable?" York had persisted.

Richard swallowed hard, glancing across at George on the other side of the hearse. Had George forgotten or merely ignored the answer: "Betrayal of family and friends."

Before the final feast, as many sought their beds for an afternoon nap or took a walk along the river, Richard, Rob and Francis went riding. It was not for mere sport, however, as Richard had the assignation in Stamford with Kate. He would gain custody of his son that day, and the anticipation of seeing the boy again after all this time made him anxious. Would the lad accept him? How would Kate handle the parting? She had written to tell him that she had seen Katherine safely into the duchess of Suffolk's hands, as he had requested, and that Katherine had already settled into life with her cousins. Richard was certain John would come to like his new home, too. He worried how Kate would fare alone, but he was convinced he was doing the right thing by his children.

Even with all his mental preparation, he was unprepared for the heartbreaking parting between mother and son on the road outside the town, where he caught up with them. It took all his resolve not to gather Kate to him and comfort her. His time with little Ned had taught him much about fathering, and so he was able to kindly but firmly reassure the sturdy, dark-haired John that not only would he live like a prince, have a new brother to play with, but he would be free to see his mother as often as possible.

"I will look after him, Kate, I promise," Richard swore to her as John said his farewells to Kate's servant, Molly. "And I will make him write to you." He stepped aside as John ran headlong into his mother's arms again, and she clutched her son hungrily. But a prolonged parting was only more painful, Richard guessed, and so he gentled John away from Kate's embrace.

"Forgive me," he mouthed to the anguished Kate and, swiftly carrying John to his horse, Richard settled the boy on the saddle in front of him and cantered off from those heartbreaking sobs, without a backward glance.

"This is your son?" Edward was amused and curious. "Aye, he has your serious expression and your coloring, but he is of sturdier breeding, I reckon. Kate's father was a farmer, I remember." He turned back to the little boy, still on his knees but gaping in awe at the magnificent giant of a king, and said: "I am your Uncle Edward." Then he bent and whispered, "but when we are not alone, you should call me 'Your Grace.'"

Five-year-old John blinked and turned to his father. Richard nodded, "He won't bite you, Johnny. Just try saying 'Your Grace.'" When John mimicked the salutation, Edward smiled and raised him to his feet. "Good boy. Brother, why don't you take him along to meet his cousins? My two boys are with their mother in our apartments." Richard was grateful Edward had not seen fit to comment on John's illegitimacy; he was unsure yet what John understood.

As John stared about him at all the darkly clad men crowded around the king, he suddenly felt alone, afraid, and wanted his mother. He had had enough of this "adventure" that had been promised. Tears began to form, and he wailed, "I want my mother."

Richard reached down and took his hand, remembering well what the need was like.

"You will get used to being here, son, I promise. Now, let me introduce you to another important member of the family," he said, snapping his fingers at his wolfhound. "Meet Rufus, and tell him to sit. He will, you know."

Richard could not have known that John had left a much beloved litter of pups in Suffolk, but he was pleased when the boy's his eyes lit up.

"Sit, Rufus!" John ordered, and his wailing changed to smiles when the huge dog obeyed.

The queen was less accepting. She looked down her perfectly pert nose at the small boy, her large eyes taking in every peasant inch of him. She refused to acknowledge he was also a Plantagenet. "He looks strong," was all the goodwill she could manage. She pointed to her sons playing with toy soldiers in the corner of the large solar. "You may go and play, if you wish," she curtly instructed the lad, who clung to his father's hand.

John had never seen such fine toys, however, and, happy to see children his own age, finally let go of Richard's hand and cautiously joined his cousins.

"I am glad to have this chance to talk to you, Brother," Elizabeth said, suddenly becoming charming as she took his elbow and guided him to the window seat. Richard stiffened. Why, he could not say. She had never been impolite to him, nor dealt with him in the haughty manner in which she had just treated John. She had even sent an exquisite, silver baptismal cup to Ned.

"How is Anne? I trust she and your heir are well. A pity they could not be here for this important occasion." She chattered on for all she and Richard were good friends. "But I hear from your mother that Anne may be with child again and thus was wise not to make such a journey."

Richard acknowledged that they were indeed expecting another child. "But Anne is quite well, I thank you. She wanted to come, but it was I who dissuaded her. We have waited too long for another babe to take any chances."

He never failed to be astonished by Elizabeth's beauty. At forty, she had weathered two marriages and seven children well—and the Grey brothers were already adults. He was not to know, as he pondered this, that Elizabeth was in fact carrying her eighth child. He inclined his head and asked, "You wished to talk to me, Your Grace?"

"Call me Elizabeth, Richard. You are always so formal." Her famous laugh again disarmed him, and he smiled. "There, that's better. You are quite handsome when you smile."

What do you want, Richard wondered. The last time they had met, she had shocked him by remarking, "I must say, your tailor does admirable work hiding your hump," before scooping up her little dog and gliding from the room. He had not even disclosed his problem to Edward, but, with all the comings and goings in the many castles he visited, he guessed a servant or two must have gossiped. Not his servants; he could trust them, even Signore Vicente, Middleham's master armorer, who had had to make him a new bespoke harness for the France enterprise. Elizabeth's remark had made him self-conscious for the next few months, however, causing him to always stand or sit against something, and he took to wearing a short mantle to change his silhouette. Today, however, Elizabeth was being warm and friendly, which made him wary. He waited.

"I do not trust Clarence, do you?" the queen eventually asked as casually as she could. *Where is she going with this?* Richard asked himself as Elizabeth continued: "He preens around the court for all he is heir to the crown and fawns on Edward, who is still foolishly blinded by his charm. It does not fool me, and I detest him. I warned Edward not to forgive him the first time he rebelled, or the second when he murdered my father and brother, but he believes George's ambition died with Warwick at Barnet. I do not." Elizabeth was leaning so close, Richard could smell the rosemary in her hair. "I am watching for him to put a foot wrong, which I wager he will do e'er long. What do you think, Brother? I know there is enmity between you and want you to know I share your suspicions." She placed her delicate hand on his, and he was trapped. He felt the threat in her touch; she was out to avenge her family's deaths and would use him, but Richard was not to be used again for dark deeds—especially not by Elizabeth Woodville.

He wanted to get away, but he patted her hand indulgently. "Dare I say you have an overactive imagination, my dear Sister. Despite his bravado, George is chastened I assure you. Besides you now have two healthy sons in anyone's path to the throne. You should not worry yourself any further about George."

"You Yorks!" Elizabeth snapped, snatching her hand away. "Loyal to each other in the extreme. It seems you're as much a fool as Ned, Richard," and she stalked off towards the children, her warmth dissolving rapidly into a chill wind.

Richard watched her with interest. It was as though she was waiting for George to blunder so she could pounce and bring him to his knees. Richard thought about warning his brother, but later upon joining George and Edward cordially drinking and sharing family anecdotes, he decided Elizabeth was no match for the York brothers and foolishly dropped his guard.

CHAPTER TWENTY-ONE
1477–1478

In December of 1476, George of Clarence lost his beloved Isabel in childbirth together with the newborn, and from the first week of January, events further spiraled down for him. Richard, too, had grieved for his first immature infatuation and had written a letter of sympathy to his brother, who he knew had loved Isabel as much as George would ever love anyone but himself.

When the shocking news came that Charles the Bold had been killed while besieging snow-covered Nancy, Edward called for his brothers to join his council at Westminster and debate the implications for Burgundy. Richard reluctantly left his family at Sheriff Hutton, Anne having suffered yet another miscarriage at yuletide, to travel through the snow and ice to London. He took only a group of ten with him, it being easier to find suitable lodgings along the way for such a small number. Even so, the roads through the midlands were treacherous, and the horses could only be ridden at a walk. The journey took them more than a week.

"You understand our concern, Richard?" Edward said at a private supper with his brothers in his apartments as soon as Richard arrived. "We must heed Meg's appeal."

"But we are at peace with France now," Richard said, frowning. "If we send troops to Meg, we will be breaking our treaty with Louis." And you will lose your pension, he wanted to say but didn't. "How else then can we help?"

Edward's chair groaned as he shifted his considerable form. Richard had been shocked to see how much weight the king had gained even since the previous summer. Edward's face was florid, and his once lively blue eyes had all but disappeared between his fleshy cheeks and brows. The ever-present goblet of wine was cupped in his fingers, which now resembled large sausages, and rested comfortably on his shelf of a belly. As ever, Will Hastings was at hand to pour more wine and add commentary when appropriate. Richard had begun to resent the jovial chamberlain, especially when he heard the man had produced yet another mistress for the king.

"Margaret, as dowager duchess, needs to find a strong husband for Mary," Edward was saying. "As you realize, it is not wise, in view of Louis of France's ambitions to break up Burgundy, to allow a woman to rule, let alone one as young as Mary." He looked over at George. "How old is she? Twenty?" George was slumped in his chair, already the worse for drink. He nodded. "Tell Richard Meg's idea, George," Edward went on. His silky, easy-going tone did not fool Richard. Something was afoot.

"She wanted me to marry Mary and frighten Louis. But my dear brother has refused," George responded, wine-fueled anger in his tone. "He doesn't want me to be happy."

Richard smirked. The last time Mary had been offered to George, he was insulted.

Elizabeth had been quietly watching the trio from her seat in the shadows, but now she raised her voice and spoke her mind. "Pah! Your happiness be damned. You are not to be trusted, and Edward is too kind to tell you so."

George feigned ignorance. "What do you mean, I am not to be trusted? I have proved my loyalty over and over," he expostulated, his hand shaking enough to spill wine.

"Ha!" Elizabeth snorted.

"Enough, Bess," Edward growled, "and I am not too kind—I have already told George my reasons, and that is why he is sulking."

George downed his wine, and rose unsteadily to his feet. "Have a care, Elizabeth," he warned, leaning on the table and glaring at her. "You think you rule the roost here, but I have heard a certain Mistress Shore now holds more sway in my brother's bed. And she is a lot younger and prettier than you."

Despite her swollen belly, Elizabeth rose quickly from her seat and flung her cup at the retreating George. "Get out!" she screamed. "Out!"

Will jumped to her defense, surprising Richard for he thought Hastings detested Elizabeth. "The queen is right. You are insolent as well as treacherous, George. I would leave if I were you."

Elizabeth pushed past him and commanded, "Edward, tell him to get out. Now!"

Edward sighed, dreading having to placate his irritable wife. "I think 'tis best you both leave us," he said to his brothers, too sluggish to raise his voice. "George, I expect you to apologize to Elizabeth on the morrow, do you understand? You are beginning to irk me. Richard, take your brother to his room. God give you a good night."

George effected a semblance of a bow and allowed Richard to lead him from the room. "Didn't I tell you to beware of Elizabeth, Brother? Your turn will come, mark my words."

Anne had another miscarriage in June, and Richard was plunged into a dark mood that caused servers to tiptoe around the great hall at Middleham during the midday meal and Richard's retainers to grumble at his testy commands. Only Rufus dared be with him and licked his hand as if to say, *I am here, you can count on me.*

"It is nothing new. These moods began only after he knew his spine was crooked," Rob Percy reassured John Kendall a week later, once Richard's talented secretary had been ushered from the duke's presence with an ink pot thrown at his head. "He believes his ailment is a sign that God is displeased with him. When something else is visited upon him—like Anne's several miscarriages—he is certain God has abandoned him, and he goes into a solitary, black place in his mind. The man has such faith in the Almighty—indeed, enough faith for the three of us combined—and I cannot convince him that perhaps it is not he that God is punishing but Anne being punished for the sins of her father. He will not hear of it. As far as he is concerned, Anne is a saint."

John Kendall dabbed at an ink stain on his fustian pourpoint with a wet kerchief and offered his assessment. "The Lady Anne is a sweet soul, but she is frail. Childbearing may not suit her and that is all there is to it. Duke Richard is a good man—is usually a good master," he said, looking up from his cleaning task and shrugging, "but I am warning you, I would not go in there today."

"Bad news? I mean besides losing the babe?"

"Aye, he will tell you I have no doubt, but it seems his brother Clarence has properly cooked his goose this time."

Rob's eyebrows shot up. "Christ's nails, what now?"

They had not heard the latch click open on the office door and were startled when Richard's voice interrupted: "He has accused a servant of poisoning Isabel and her child, which is ridiculous, and has had the woman hanged without trial and without Edward's knowledge." Rob let out a low whistle, while the other two men crossed themselves in remembrance of Isabel and her little son.

"Why is that such bad news, my lord?" Rob asked, crushing a lazy flea between his thumb and finger and flicking it to the floor. "Perhaps my lord of Clarence did have intelligence that they were poisoned by the woman—whoever she was."

"Her name is unimportant, but George's accusation that she was acting on the Woodville's instructions is significant."

Rob's whistle was more pronounced this time. "I see where you are going with this, Richard. Coupled with George's anger that Edward refused to allow him to wed Mary of Burgundy, which would have created a possible danger to the English throne..."

"...and then he found out Anthony Woodville was put forward by Elizabeth as a bridegroom instead," Richard took up the story, "which sent George into a vengeful fury against Elizabeth. Hence the unprovoked and cavalier condemnation and meting out of justice for poor Ankarette Twynyho with no proof." He looked at his two companions, his face grave. "He acted as though he were king, and that is tantamount to treason." He let the word hang in the room for a few seconds before adding, "My brother has been arrested and placed in the Tower."

Rob had no more wind for whistling as he stared open-mouthed at Richard.

"Whatever should I do?" Richard asked looking from one to the other. "George has brought this on himself, and I cannot condone his actions, yet it is hard to think of him languishing in a Tower prison." He expelled a dispirited sigh. There was a time when he might have written an appeal to Edward, but that was long ago and before George's many betrayals had hardened Richard's heart.

Richard made the journey to London in January to attend George's trial. As well as the Twynyho incident, more treasonable actions would be laid at George's feet during it: A servant in his household was accused, tried, and executed for purportedly agreeing to use necromancy to bring about Edward's death; rumors of Edward's bastardy were circulated by his followers; George had assisted in yet another rising against the king that came to naught; and the final straw for the benevolent Edward was getting word direct from King Louis that George had planned on using his marriage to Mary of Burgundy as a stepping stone to the English throne. Richard was appalled and lost any shred of sympathy he might have once had for his wayward brother.

"How could Parliament not try him, Richard?" Edward said, clearly disturbed. "'Twas they not I who decided on that, but it is I who must condemn him or not. Jesu, what should I do?"

Richard steepled his fingers, deep in thought. He could not believe it had come to this. George's life had begun with all the promise of privilege, charm, intelligence, and a happy marriage, but he had squandered a goodly, noble life for vainglorious ambition. His own antagonism towards George notwithstanding, Richard was angry at George for putting Edward in such an atrocious position. Fratricide must surely rank among the very worst of sins, and yet it would seem Edward had no choice but to condemn his brother. As well, he was adding that sin to regicide, Richard realized. Thoughts of Henry returned him yet again to the hideous scene in the Tower. It was true the regicide was on his hands not Edward's, but he had chosen not to inform the king of the fact. *Let him believe he is guilty,* Richard thought spitefully, *he deserves to carry the weight as well.* Once again, he was reminded of his boyhood conversation with King Henry about the responsibilities of kingship. *'Tis a curse and a responsibility that is too heavy for one man. I am no God, although sometimes I must act as though I am.*

Richard glanced at the gray-faced Edward, looking years older than thirty-eight, and knew now what the dead king had meant. His stomach churned at the thought of Edward's terrible burden. Aye, Henry was right, *I am glad I am the fourth son; I could never be a king.*

Will Hastings approached with a pitcher to refill Edward's cup, and the familiar ritual suddenly struck a wrong note with Richard. He did not doubt Will's loyalty, but he abhorred his immorality. It was said that when Edward tired of a mistress, Hastings would then enjoy her. What had his glorious, golden god of a brother degenerated into?

Richard shot out a hand and stopped Will's pouring. "My brother needs a clear head, my lord. I thank you not to add to his already troubled mind."

Will was clearly offended, but he stepped back and looked to Edward, who, however, seemed preoccupied. "What must I do?" the king asked with desperation in his voice.

Richard took a deep breath and stated: "He is our brother, but he is a traitor. If I were the judge, I would condemn him."

Edward slowly nodded. "I have done my best to save him all these years. Our mother has been here begging for his life in the names of our father and dead brother, and Meg's pathetic letters have been arriving weekly since December."

"I, too, might have asked mercy for him, Ned, but when I think of all the ways he has threatened the safety of the realm and tried to seize power for himself, I find I have no pity left for him."

Edward looked intently at his youngest brother, surprised by the cold assurance of his tone. Richard had always been passionate about justice and the law, Edward knew, but now he could see why the Lord of the North commanded such respect. Richard might be smaller in stature, but he now stood shoulder to shoulder with Edward, and the king was glad of such support.

"I will review the trial transcripts once more, and then I will sign the death warrant."

"Will you not see him first, Ned?" Richard asked. "I am in no mind to go, but 'tis my duty, and Father would have wished it."

"I went," Edward said, dully. "It was a waste of time. George was pathetic and I had to leave. May God have mercy on his soul. And on mine."

And on mine, Richard thought. *Please, Lord, on mine.*

With rheumy eyes that Richard could not tell were from weeping or from wine, George gazed at his detestable younger brother. "Come to gloat, babykins?" he sneered. "Good little Dickon come to say farewell? Always did want to do the right thing, didn't you? Always seeking approval, aren't you?" He lurched at Richard, who neatly stepped aside and watched as George tripped on an uneven flagstone in the Tower room and landed on his knees.

Richard smirked. "Always in your cups, aren't you?" he mimicked, letting George clumsily right himself. He was shocked how callous he had become and that he cared not now whether his brother lived or died. "Always thought you could charm your way out of trouble, didn't you? I doubt you can charm you way out of here, my dear George. You have given Edward no choice." George slumped onto the bed—one too luxurious by far for someone supposedly in prison for treason, Richard thought. "You are right, I have come here out of duty," he continued. "You lost my respect many years ago when you treated Anne so abominably. I was hoping, perhaps, I might eke an apology out of you on behalf of my wife. Anne does not know how to hate—as I do—and she deserves your respect in this."

George guffawed. "'Tis you who owe me an apology, Master Crookback, for stealing my wife's inheritance...." But Richard had unsheathed his dagger and had it at George's throat before he could finish his sentence.

"Call me 'crookback' one more time, and I swear I will spare the executioner his work," Richard snarled, angling the point of his knife under George's bearded chin. "Now apologize, you adder-tongued, two-faced coxcomb."

George spat in Richard's face. "There's your apology, my lord. Go and ball yourself."

"Guard!" Richard shouted, wiping the spittle from his cheek. "May God have mercy on your lily-livered soul, Brother," he said under his breath, locking eyes with George's sapphire ones. Richard saw no remorse in George's, and George found no forgiveness in Richard's.

The harsh grating of the door hinges broke the momentary silence before Richard turned on his heel, exited the room and never looked back.

"Bye-bye babykins!" followed him down the stairs and out into the snowy half-light.

Although not far from it, Richard was not present at George's execution. Unbeknownst to Richard, the two men Edward had hired had been instructed to administer poison to the hapless Clarence in answer to a desperate request by Duchess Cecily that her son not die publicly nor by the traditional beheading. "I am afraid he will not behave correctly and be scorned," she had confided to Edward. "I could not bear that. He has had nightmares about a clumsy executioner. Let him drink himself into a stupor and then poison will allow him a death sleep. Do this for me, Son, I beg you."

Cecily would have been devastated had she been able to read Richard's mind when he learned of the plan. All the wrongs George had done the young Dickon had been festering and now blossomed into one wicked thought: *He does not deserve to die kindly. He deserves to be suffocated, just like he attempted to do to me. He deserves to suffer.*

"They are late!" Richard was pacing the audience chamber in Westminster a mile upstream of the Tower wondering what could have gone wrong. George's guards had been told to ply George with his favorite malmsey until he would be oblivious to the poison. It sounded like a simple plan, but Richard had been skeptical. "What if the guards bungle the task? Can we trust them not to have been charmed by George?" Edward had dismissed his brother's doubts.

Now Edward sat silently on his canopied throne awaiting the return of the assassins, fingering a silver adornment on his pourpoint. His calm unnerved Richard, who had joined Queen Elizabeth and Will Hastings in keeping the king company.

After what seemed like an age, the two men were finally ushered in and knelt, keeping their eyes on the ground and kneading their coarse felt hats. They were clearly on edge, but then who would not be, Richard mused, having executed a fellow human being. *How well I know the feeling.* But when the bigger man began to stammer, it was not from any empathy for the dead man but from fear of repercussions for an assignment gone awry. Richard's heart sank.

"Is he dead?" Edward asked, rising and approaching the men. "Speak! Is the deed done?"

"He is dead, Your Grace," the man answered, nodding. "B...but n... not in the man...manner in which was ordered." He cringed, expecting a blow, but Edward quietly told him to tell the truth. "The d...duke dr... drowned, my lord. We had to hold his head in a butt of wine."

"You drowned a royal duke?" Richard blurted in horror. *Sweet Jesu, I should have insisted on a proper execution. What a shambles!*

"Hush, Richard," Edward admonished him. "Give the man a chance to speak." Clearly rattled, he encouraged the guard. "Go on, sir, tell me what happened. Leave nothing out."

Responding to Edward's tone, the man took a breath and continued. "He knew summat was up because the good Father came in with us. He would not drink the poisoned wine and threw the cup at us. He began a-blubbering and went on his knees begging Father Lessey to save him. The duke was making so much noise, we had to drag him to the barrel and...." he raised his hands and shrugged. When everyone gasped in shock, the man became defensive. "Well, we couldn't think of nothing else, with the priest there an' all. We did carry out your orders, Your Grace. You'd said 'no blood, let him drown in his beloved wine.' It seemed the only way."

Sweet Jesu! I wished him an unkind death, Richard thought mortified. *Am I to feel yet more guilt, Lord?* Should he have begged Edward to forgive his brother? He had considered it, but had done nothing. Aye, the Almighty had seen right into his heart then—even to the blackest part—and Richard knew he would pay.

Will Hastings stepped forward holding a bag of coins, and with a dagger at the lead assassin's throat, he threatened. "Go! Both of you, and say nothing of this or I will kill you myself. Understand? I know where to find you." Nodding vigorously, the men fell over themselves to exit.

"Did you order this as they accused, Edward?" Richard demanded.

Elizabeth sprang to Edwards' defense. "'Twas meant in jest, Richard. But in the end it was what he deserved. Even you believe that."

Do I? Dear God, do I? Aye, I do, Richard had to admit to himself.

Richard did not grieve for George, but once he was safely in Anne's comforting arms, they both mourned the two orphans George and her sister had left behind. Little Ned, sensing his parents' melancholy, climbed between them as they lay on cushions by the fire and gave them both kisses.

The nursemaid came to find her charge and carry him off to bed, but Anne waved her away. "We will keep him with us, tonight, Matty. He will be quite safe."

Safe. Richard liked the sound of the word at this moment. With George dead and his rebel adherents without a leader, perhaps England would be free from civil strife, and Edward could focus on protecting his kingdom from foreign interference. Moreover, Elizabeth could focus on mothering her growing brood instead of plotting to destroy George. The more Richard thought of Elizabeth's words, the more suspicious he became that she had somehow orchestrated George's downfall. It was a feeling, nothing more, and he dismissed it. Elizabeth was not worth his thoughts at this tender moment with the people he loved. How grateful he was for his gentle wife, his happy home, and his precious son.

He nuzzled Ned's dark curls and looked across at Anne, watching him with such devotion, and he finally said the words he had been unable to say truthfully all these years. "I love you, Anne. I love you with all of my heart."

Elizabeth Woodville gave birth to another son on St. George's Day and ironically named him for that dragon-slaying patron saint of England.

Not three months later, and not satisfied that George's death had made her husband's and sons' crown safer, she turned her malicious thoughts to the last of the York sons, convinced that Richard of Gloucester would seek power for himself and take arms against the king. It was hard not to blame her suspicions after George's clear designs on Edward's throne, but to turn on Richard was purely vindictive. She lived in perpetual fear of losing her own status as queen as well as her children's right to the crown.

Richard had sensed he was in danger as early as the summer of George's arrest and imprisonment. In an unusual move when war was not imminent, he had called upon all his tenants in the bishopric of Durham to swear an oath that they would do him service in time of need. He was expecting the queen to turn on him, and he would be ready. Disturbed by George's grisly death and convinced Elizabeth's revenge was unassuaged, he could be forgiven for overreacting.

But for now, Richard returned to his duties. He tried to forget the execution and forgive Edward for allowing it. That George deserved his fate there was no doubt in Richard's mind, but he still believed his brother should have been beheaded in the proper manner of a noble, and only he could have ensured that end. How he loathed not having had control over the situation, as he would have done as Lord of the North. Over and over again, he chastised himself for not fighting harder for a better death for George. Yet another burden to bear, he thought grimly.

It was perhaps more guilt after the botched execution that gave him the impetus to endow a new chantry college at Middleham, which housed several priests and choristers who prayed and sang masses daily and exclusively for the saving of the souls of not only himself and Anne, but for his family, both living and dead. These acts of piety somewhat salved his soul and made him less afraid to confront his Maker or his confessor. Moreover, he was often seen slipping into a side chapel during a mass. On his knees, his eyes firmly fixed on the crucified Jesus, he hoped to ease George's troubled soul to heaven. His own guilty soul, he had no doubt, was destined for hell.

CHAPTER TWENTY-TWO
SUMMER 1482–SPRING 1483

The ramparts of the high bastion that was Berwick Castle were bristling with soldiers, the July sun glinting off helmets, shields and weapons and the calm sea beyond. The pale, crenellated curtain wall that encompassed the town swooped down the steep hill and into the estuary like a giant staircase, ending with a square tower jutting into the water, making the castle all but impenetrable. It was easy to see how besieging the fortress on its hill from land or sea had failed many times in its three centuries.

"Whoreson thistle-arses," Richard muttered under his breath to which insult Henry Percy, earl of Northumberland and Richard's lieutenant, grunted an assent. His other lieutenant, Lord Stanley, actually guffawed. "If it is the last thing I do, I will take back Berwick for my brother," Richard vowed. "After Queen Margaret lost it to the Scots twenty years ago, 'tis a matter of pride."

The three men sat their coursers not far from the drawbridge but out of range of any projectile that might be hurled from the town gatehouse. Behind them, the twenty-thousand-strong English army awaited commands, among them Queen Elizabeth's oldest son, the marquis of Dorset, and Richard's friends, Rob Percy and Francis Lovell.

Set a little apart from the trio in front, a stocky man with startlingly red hair and dark red beard watched Richard anxiously. Alexander Stewart, duke of Albany, was counting on the young Gloucester to help him unseat his brother, the weak King James III, and take the throne of Scotland for himself. Berwick was the first test along the path, and he was eager to know if King Edward's trust in his younger brother was well placed. Little did Albany know that Richard of Gloucester had thought it a harebrained scheme of Edward's from the start.

"Remember George?" Richard had warned Edward at Fotheringhay a month earlier. Albany had signed a pact with Edward that Scotland would support England against any threat from France, if Edward put Albany on the throne of Scotland. "Another ambitious, perfidious brother, if you ask me. If you are worried about James being manipulated by Louis of France, why not simply show him you are serious with a proper campaign over the border. I have the troops, let me do the job."

"You may lord it over the north, Richard, but you may not lord it over your king," Edward had snapped back, surprising Richard with his vehemence. "James broke his truce in '81 and his raids into Northumbria grow more daring and troublesome. Putting Albany on James's throne will put paid to Louis web-spinning, and I can concentrate on my unhappy subjects." He gave a long sigh. "I weary of governing them. We have had eleven years of peace in this kingdom. Can they not be satisfied with that?"

And although Richard would have dearly loved to give his brother some reasons why his starving people were unhappy, he had acquiesced in taking Albany with him into the borderlands. England and Scotland were many centuries away from uniting; even the Romans had failed to join the two peoples and had had to construct an impressive wall to achieve a semblance of peace.

Richard refocused on the town in front of him, not relishing the task of attacking the innocent resident English citizens in order to storm the castle on the hill. Northumberland raised an eyebrow and addressed his commander-in-chief. "What now, my lord duke?"

Before Richard could answer, the town gates swung open to allow a contingent of town elders to emerge. He frowned. He had anticipated the Scottish defenders would man the town walls and at least put up a fight. It seemed it was not to be, for in a very few moments the mayor of Berwick fell on his knees in front of Richard and explained the town was surrendering. "Mayor Holtham, if it please you, m'lord," he introduced himself, in his broad northern accent. "It is gradely to see you." He was in awe at the mass of fully armed men swarming the meadows before the town. "It seems all the soldiers living amoong us have been summoned to defend the castle. Those boggin' oat-eaters had nae stomach for a fight once they saw your noomber. Canna say I blame 'em," he said, showing gaps in his gums as he grinned.

But Richard was all business. "What food supply is there, Mayor? I can pay a fair price."

Holtham lifted his shoulders and spread his hands. "Nowt, my lord. Our people are starving."

Richard thanked the man and dismissed him. He made a quick decision. "We camp here for the night, and move on to the border at first light," he cried to his captains. He turned to Stanley. "You, my lord, will remain here and lay siege to the castle. Starve them out if you must, but I have no doubt it will fall if we persist. Percy and I will defeat the Scots and return to help you do it."

Thomas Stanley bowed. Not yet entirely certain of Richard, Stanley had grudgingly agreed to accept him as his commander. But now he acknowledged that the young duke had been entrusted with the Scottish campaign not merely because he was the king's brother but because he had a strategic military brain. Surprisingly, Richard was a leader of men, Stanley observed, despite a lack of his older brother's stature and charisma. Stanley's wife, the formidable Margaret Beaufort, who despised the York brothers, had warned him not to trust either of them, but he had so far not seen anything to distrust in Richard.

A scout cantered through the town streets to where Richard and his commanders were lodging for the night and gave Richard the information he needed. "The Scottish army is moving south and is at Haddington, my lord duke. If they keep moving, I warrant it is three days' march to catch them—if the weather holds."

The English troops were primed for action, and with relative ease, they swept through several towns and villages in southern Scotland leaving them still burning. Richard ordered the fields stripped of all their harvest, and the English army left devastation in its wake. All this was a provocation for the Scots, but Richard was puzzled when he encountered no resistance.

In the middle of the second day, a dusty horseman galloped full speed down a heather-laden hill to Richard. "I come from Lauder, my lord, a village not ten miles from here," the man in Lovell livery said, "where I witnessed an extraordinary scene: The Scots had arrested their king and proceeded to hang his...um...his *favorites* from Lauder bridge right in front of him." It was these foppish young men's influence on infatuated James that had incensed the other nobles.

Surprise greeted this news, and Francis asked, "What did they do to James?"

"He is their prisoner and is taken to Edinburgh, and the army has turned back."

"Now what?" Northumberland asked. "We have them on the run."

Richard was quiet for a moment. He had hoped to engage the Scots in the lowlands; he knew the closer to Edinburgh they went, the rising topography would be a less desirable battleground.

"Let us double our efforts to reach the lily-livered rabble," he declared. "Let us march on."

Their small tastes of victory soon paled as they passed by the unfortunate favorites, swinging from the bridge. Richard ordered them cut down and buried. Confounded again to meet no resistance at all, he rode unopposed into the capital city of Edinburgh two days later. The Scottish army had not only retreated to Haddington following their seizure of James, but Richard was greeted by a message from the enemy commanders begging for a truce.

They declared that 'the war was over' in their missive, Richard wrote to Edward later. *What war? I have had more difficulty snaring a lame rabbit than I had taking Edinburgh!*

With James in his nobles' power, it seemed that Albany's way to the throne was assured, but after a week or so it became crystal clear to Richard that the Scots had no wish for Albany to rule them either. Instead, the unhappy man was granted a pardon for his treasonable behavior if he swore allegiance to his brother and would never vie for James's throne again. Before he left Edinburgh, Richard made Albany sign an oath that England was released from the contract to support him.

Just in case! Richard continued to his brother after describing the scene. *The numbskull even accused me of betrayal. These uncivilized people vacillate in their allegiances like waving wheat. I shall march back to Berwick and with God's help—and some well-aimed cannons—I shall take the castle back.*

He could not take all the credit, however, as Lord Stanley's men had worn down the defending Berwick garrison so that they threw down their arms and surrendered as soon as Richard's army reappeared. Nevertheless, once back in London, and at Edward's behest, Richard rode through the streets to receive the accolades of the people—and the gratitude of his king.

It was the first time he had been hailed a hero in his own right by his fellow countrymen, and he was proud to hear his name shouted from the rooftops. What enhanced Richard's honor was that he had resisted a victor's usual temptation to destroy the city of Edinburgh. Instead he had reconciled peaceably with James's council and withdrawn his army without burning a house or killing a citizen.

Other than the brief visit following the Scottish campaign, Richard was not seen at Edward's court much in the years after George's death—years in which, as Lord of the North, he heard appeals, dispensed justice wisely, mended bitter rivalries between Nevilles and Percies, kept the peace, and maintained border fortifications, earning the deep respect of northerners. His only domestic disappointment was Anne's continued inability to bear another child.

"It is God's will," he had told his weeping wife, when yet another miscarriage laid her low. "We have Ned, who is a good boy and strong, and John is turning into a fine young squire. My dearest Anne, we have an heir and should be grateful. Let us count our blessings."

Richard thought of that scene now as he watched his beloved heir from a viewpoint above the tiltyard and again gave thanks for the boy.

"Look, Father! Look at me!" Ned cried with delight as he trotted on the back of a cream-colored Welsh cob. The pony was a perfect size for the nine-year-old Edward, who had been taught to ride almost before he could walk. The boy adored horses, and just as his father before him had loved the kennels as a child, Ned spent hours in the stables, giving the horses treats and helping the grooms curry the beasts and muck out their stalls.

Ned wielded a long baton and when it was his turn, he kicked his horse's flanks, lowered his weapon and galloped towards the target, a small wooden shield attached to a swivel arm on a post. Ned timed his tilt perfectly, and the quintain swung away allowing the rider to pass. The other boys whooped and their instructor nodded his satisfaction, but it was his father's approval Ned sought, and he trotted up anxiously to where

Richard was watching proudly from a platform above the yard. "Did you see, Father? I hit it well, did I not?" Ned crowed, waving his stick.

"Aye, you did, my son," Richard said, truthfully, "but you must learn not to boast of it. Wait for a compliment, because there is always more you can learn. Humility is a better teacher than pride." He bent down and tousled Ned's light brown hair, loving the way his son's expressions mirrored Anne's. Disappointment shadowed the boy's face though, stirring Richard's heart. "You are the best of the boys, Ned," he said quietly. "John has taught you well." Ned rewarded Richard with a smile that never failed to wilt his father's determination to be stern. "Now cheer your comrades on."

Ned trotted off and was soon applauding the efforts of others. Richard knew he ought to be looking for the right nobleman to mentor his son, but Anne could not bear to part with her only child yet, and Richard could not bring himself to dishearten her. The couple had sadly given up hope for more children, simply treasuring the one they had. Having no siblings to compete with for attention, Ned was growing up fearless and carefree, and, unlike Richard's lot as a boy, Ned's childhood had been free of upheaval and violence.

But for how much longer?

Richard had returned from London in February concerned for his brother's health, the growing worry of an invasion from France after the Burgundians signed a treaty with their old enemies, and the continued depravity of Edward's court. He prayed daily for his brother's immortal—or he should say immoral—soul, and he shuddered now remembering the unfortunate meeting he had had recently with Edward's latest mistress, Jane Shore.

He referred to her as "the Shore whore," as he had no doubt she must also be warming Will Hastings' bed, judging from the way Will looked at her. Indeed, their only meeting had been at the Tower where he had caught Jane coming out of the room where the lord chamberlain was being held as a temporary punishment. Edward had blamed Will for a diplomatic mistake he himself had made that had led to the treaty of Arras. The king's subsequent depression had resulted in unfairly slapping Will with a month's prison term. It was Richard who had seen the injustice of it and persuaded Edward to lighten the sentence.

Now back in the north, Richard dwelled on other problems to do with the well-being of England. No further rebellions or in-fighting between noble families had surfaced recently, and now, two weeks after Easter, he felt his territory was secure enough for Edward. As was his wont during these reflections, George's ghostly face would invade his thoughts, giving rise to a guilty relief that he would no longer have his brother scheming behind his back. *Good riddance*, he found himself echoing Elizabeth's words, and forced George back into the grave.

Richard returned his attention to the quintain exercise. Next to tilt was John, who had taken to the martial arts like a cat to cream, and was tasked already with mentoring some of the younger boys. Ned cheered the loudest for his stepbrother, and John winked at him before lowering his lance and charging. The two boys were a complete contrast in physique, though both showed an aptitude for athletics. Ned had inherited his and Anne's slighter build, but John was everything Richard had wished himself to have been at thirteen years old: strong, outgoing, and confident, although Richard wished John would apply himself more to his studies.

"A groat for your thoughts, Richard," Anne Beauchamp's warm voice interrupted his musings, and he turned to his mother-in-law with a smile. She had aged greatly. Life had not dealt kindly with her since her husband's treachery, and her time in sanctuary had caused her to become a shadow of herself. The Yorkshire air had restored some of her health, and, remembering her many kindnesses to him, Richard had always treated Warwick's wife with love and respect. He knew the rumors had made him seem a grasping son-in-law, and indeed he had benefited greatly from her fortune, but he hoped that he had given her a warm welcome in his—and her erstwhile—home.

"I was thinking how fortunate I am with my family, 'twas all," Richard told her. "Your grandson shows good progress at the quintain, my lady."

Spotting his grandmother on the platform, Ned waved enthusiastically and the countess waved back. "I do not doubt it, my dear Richard, but I have come to speak to you of my other grandchildren." Countess Anne had chosen her moment carefully, not knowing if Richard harbored any ill-will to George's orphaned children. "Would you consider allowing little Margaret and her brother to come north to join your household? I do not think his grace, the king, is unkind to them, but I am sure they are easily forgotten among the Grey Mare's brood."

Richard chuckled. "How Elizabeth would hate to hear herself called a brood mare. In truth, I do not think the orphans are ill-treated—my nieces Bess and Cecily are delightful girls—but let me consider your request, Mother. 'Twould do Ned good to have cousins his age about him, in truth, but I must consult..."

He broke off as a shout floated from the ramparts, "Riders approaching—fast." Bowing to the countess, he hurried down the steps to the yard and disappeared into the inner courtyard. His mother-in-law stared after him; it was when he was in a rush and unheeding of his posture that his crooked back became more evident. When she had first mentioned it to Anne, her daughter had admonished her: "Never mention it to him, Mother. He only trusts a very few of us with the truth. It is a burden he bears with great humility and anxiety. Whenever Richard is angry—I mean really angry—I know it is because his back is troubling him." She had then whispered, "He fears he has displeased God. I think it is why he sometimes seems obsessed with morals and piety. He also believes God's displeasure has prevented our having more children."

The countess now turned her gaze on Richard's young bastard John, and she frowned. No wonder God was displeased with Richard, she thought. She had been insulted on Anne's behalf to learn of his liaison with a common peasant that had produced this boy and the beautiful Katherine, now one of Anne's own ladies. The countess saw them as a sad reminder to Anne that she had failed to give Richard more children. Sighing, she climbed up stiffly onto the ramparts, inhaling the sweet April scent of flowering thyme from the meadows below. How peaceful it all was here, she thought, and sent up a quick *ave* that tranquility would last.

But all was not peaceful in Richard's office next to the great hall. The news the messenger had brought was devastating: the king was dead.

Richard paced up and down along the same tiles that Warwick had worn down, his mouth set in a grim line in his pinched face. Francis and Rob watched him anxiously, and Anne, attempting to stop his pacing and calm him, was brushed off. The messenger in the Hastings' livery was still on his knees but had backed himself into a corner fearing the duke of Gloucester's ire.

Richard turned suddenly and proceeded to loudly berate the poor man: "How is this possible? He was only forty! How did he die? 'A cold,' you say? You lie! No one dies from a cold. How long was he ill?"

"'Tis all in the m...missive, my lord," the man stuttered and bowed himself away.

As though frozen, Richard stood holding the letter from Hastings, his mind reeling. "Perhaps he was poisoned," he suddenly posited. "Who would want him dead? Louis of France!" he answered his own question, preposterous though it was. "This will mean war," he shouted. At this point, his legs were visibly trembling and had Francis not pushed a stool behind him, he might have fallen to his knees. He reached out for Anne, and as she ran to hold him, Rob quietly indicated to Francis that they should leave the room.

Once the couple was alone, Richard indulged his grief. As is human at the loss of a loved one, he could remember only the magnificent, golden king of his youth, the valiant soldier, and the generous big brother, and he could not imagine his world without Edward. At that moment, he forgot all of his brothers faults, including the heinous deed Edward had demanded of him that lived on in his nightmares.

It was as well Anne could soothe him, because Richard was soon lamenting the dangerous position in which the king had left his crown and his kingdom. For Richard it meant more uncertainty, because, according to Will Hastings' missive, on his deathbed Edward had relinquished the protectorate of the new king and the realm to his younger brother. For so many years, Edward had counted on Richard; now, Richard thought somberly and the enormous responsibility loomed, England would have to count on him.

PART FIVE

Richard, Protector and King

Sunday, 3 February 2013
A sample of Michael Ibsen's DNA had been taken at the beginning
of the dig and [Dr. Turi] King had sequenced it in her labs, identifying
its particular code. If Richard's DNA matched that of his alleged
seventeenth-generation nephew [Ibsen], it would be the final piece of
evidence that the Greyfriars remains were those of the king. The test
would also check for the male Y-chromosome ...

Michael Ibsen had asked for the result of the investigation to be
revealed to him first privately. Turi King met him in an office in the
university then brought him to meet Simon Farnaby, Richard Buckley
and me.

As Michael entered he was in shock, his face ashen. King began with
the news that a Y-chromosome had been found...She then revealed that
the mitochondrial (female line) DNA was a complete match...

Was I surprised the DNA was a perfect match? Yes and no. The
project had run so smoothly, from the finding of Richard's remains on
the first day, exactly where I thought they would be, to the carbon-14
date, the osteology, scoliosis, insult wound and facial reconstruction.
Although I believed from the very beginning that the remains were
those of Richard, I had been assailed by fears and doubts throughout the
process...

At 11 a.m. on Monday, 4 February 2013, Richard Buckley made the
historic announcement: "It is the academic conclusion of the University
of Leicester that the individual exhumed at the Greyfriars in August
2012 is indeed King Richard III, the last Plantagenet King of England."
—Philippa Langley, The King's Grave

CHAPTER TWENTY-THREE
APRIL–MAY 1483

In the bat of an eye, Richard's ordered life was at an end.

He knelt at his prie dieu and opened the little book of hours King Henry had given him—still a favorite and which forced him to pray for the murdered king nightly—and found a prayer for the dead. As he recited its comforting words, images from his childhood with Edward were conjured, and it suddenly struck him that only three York siblings remained, and he was the only male. Edmund, George, and now Ned had all deserted him, overwhelming him with melancholy.

Protector. The word at once thrilled and terrified Richard. It was not lost on him that his father, too, had been the protector of the realm in the '50s, when King Henry had lost his mind for almost a year.

Richard's charge was only twelve years of age, and, although Prince Edward was said to be "ripe beyond his years," he was a minor. Having spent the best part of the last six years at Ludlow, under the governance of another uncle—Anthony Woodville, Lord Rivers—young Edward had not much been in Richard's company. Richard knew the younger boy, another Richard, better and appreciated the mischievous lad's merry temperament. "My mother says he reminds her of Ned at that age," Richard had told Elizabeth once, in a rare intimate moment.

When the shock of his brother's untimely death had abated, Richard found himself irked that the king's council had not formally sent him a message about the king's passing and his appointment as protector. At this point in time, however, he had no reason to suspect it was a calculated omission and, knowing the funeral would be long over before he could arrive for it, he tarried in the north long enough to hold obsequies for his brother in York Minster.

The consequences of this delay changed everything for Richard.

For now, Richard took Hastings at his word—after all Will had been Edward's closest friend and advisor—and so he had accepted that he, Richard, was the logical choice for protector. As such, he immediately wrote to Rivers at Ludlow, pledging his allegiance to young Edward and requesting their itinerary and route for London. *The king and I should meet at Northampton and enter London together on the thirtieth day of the month,* Richard instructed Rivers. He had then written a sympathetic note to Elizabeth on her loss and again pledged to protect the crown for her son.

"Should you not go immediately to London and make sure your position is recognized," Rob asked him. "Why have you not had a formal appointment from the council?"

Richard shrugged. "Perhaps they have been preoccupied with laying Edward to rest with appropriate respect and ceremony. As soon as I have honored my brother at York and required all the northern barons to swear an oath of fealty to my nephew, I will make my way to London."

"Rob is right," Francis chimed in. The two friends were used to speaking their minds to Richard. "You should not delay. I fear the Woodvilles will take control of the government—they and their adherents are in the majority in London. You don't know what they are planning."

"Planning?" Richard asked, irritated now and anxiety rising. "What would they be planning, pray? A coronation no doubt, but they would not dare organize that without me. Away with your fear-mongering, my friends," he countered, but, seeing their chagrin, he relented. "As you will. I shall write to the council that I know of Edward's last wishes and will dutifully take up my appointment when I reach London. Does that reassure you?"

His two friends exchanged worried glances but murmured their acceptance.

Reminding the council of his lifelong loyalty to his brother, and in accordance with Edward's decree that he be protector, Richard sent a firm letter to Westminster in which he asserted his continued loyalty to the young king, his nephew, and requested that, *any new government be conducted according to the laws of the land.* His inference was clear. Legally, once a king died, his councilors were no longer a valid body. The new king would then appoint his own advisors. But it seemed this council had conveniently forgotten the custom and were acting as though Edward still lived—the queen merely taking her husband's place. Richard must make sure he was the one to advise the young king on his appointments to the council, not Elizabeth Woodville.

Richard went about his usual business of leaving his own affairs in his administrators' capable hands during his absence. "Not knowing how long I shall be gone, I beg you consult with her grace, the duchess, who will remain here."

Then he went to the small private chapel tucked in the castle wall and prayed for guidance. He thanked God—and his brother—for the existence of a suitable heir. Young Edward was an upright lad, he had heard, and Richard had only to hold his leading strings for two or three years until the young king could take his proper place at the head of the government as an adult. "Give me the patience, the steadfastness, and the justice to discharge my duty to my nephew with integrity," he pleaded, "and let me choose my council wisely." Jack Howard would be at the top of the list, followed by Rob Percy, Lovell and Ratcliffe. He would add Northumberland and a couple of churchmen, like Canterbury and Lincoln, and Stanley would back him, Richard was sure of it.

Then Hastings' face floated into his mind and he hesitated. Aye, the man was as loyal a friend to Edward as could be found; he was intelligent and understood the workings of government; and hadn't he been the first to send for Richard and keep him abreast of the queen's deeds? But the baron had also led Edward into gluttony, drunkenness, and debauchery. Not surprisingly, the first item on Richard's list as protector would be to clean up his brother's court. It was no place for a twelve-year-old boy, he had decided. His hardest task was how to deal with Elizabeth and her family, but he would wait until he reached London and could see the look of things for himself.

By the time he rode out of the castle and onto the road to York a few days later, he was satisfied he was prepared for the new role his brother had bequeathed him.

"It is unfortunate that Ned saw fit to place his heir in Woodville hands," Richard said to Anne, as she tweaked his black doublet and brushed some lint from it before they set off to observe the obsequies for Edward at the Minster. "Poor boy will not know which uncle to listen to once we get to London. And Elizabeth is bound to want control, too."

"You have two boys of your own, my dear, and John is almost the same age as young Edward. Just talk to him the way you do John."

Richard gave a reluctant smile—he found it hard to smile these days—and agreed. "As well, I know what it is like to lose a father as a boy, so I shall be easy with him."

He wished his work could be as simple as being kind and mentor to the lad—he would enjoy that, but he was well aware that the Woodvilles must be worrying about their position at court now Edward was gone. As they should, he thought, but that makes them dangerous. He felt his own anxiety mount at the thought. Of one thing he was certain: he would not sanction any interference in his governance of the young king from Elizabeth or her family. But with what consequences? Richard knew he was one point of a triangle of power: himself in the north; the new king under a Woodville in Wales; and the council in London under the Woodville queen determined to be regent. He needed to find the right balance between respecting maternal instincts and removing the boy from the overly possessive, power-hungry woman that Elizabeth was. And he had to gain young Edward's trust to carry out the task fairly. He tried to assess who on the old king's council would support him, but other than Hastings and Jack Howard, he had no real idea how the others viewed him. Yet more doubts to unsettle him.

"Stop fiddling with your ring," Anne said, slapping his hand playfully. "You are such a worrier." When he did not smile, she looked at him anxiously. "What are you fretting about now, my love? Until Edward is old enough to take the reins, you will have all the power."

Richard pushed his fears aside and gave his wife a kiss. He would not speak of his concerns to Anne, but he wished he had at least one prominent nobleman he could fully count on to back him up in council.

"Harry?" Richard murmured when he saw the golden knot of Stafford emblazoned on the messenger's tunic. "What does he want?"

He soon knew. The letter Richard read from his cousin—his only royal cousin—was, in essence, an answer to his prayer for help. Henry Stafford, third duke of Buckingham, had been shunned by Edward for most of the previous decade, which must have peeved the arrogant young duke greatly. He had never forgiven Edward for pandering to Elizabeth and bestowing her younger sister, Catherine, on him as a bride at the tender age of eleven. He had whined to Richard that he should have married far above a Woodville and held a high office in Edward's court. He greatly resented Elizabeth's influence on the king, and Richard was sure Harry hated the Woodvilles even more than Hastings did.

Edward had dismissed Harry as a "vain and officious buffoon," but in February 1478 the king had given the buffoon the temporary title of Lord High Steward. Thus it was from Harry's mouth and not Edward's that the pronouncement of death for George of Clarence had been made. "He griped about that, too, saying it would be the only thing history would remember him for," Edward had said. "Ungrateful ass. Elizabeth warned me not to treat with him—said he was cruel to Catherine, and in truth, I think I would have wrung his neck if he hadn't disappeared back to Wales for long spells."

Richard thought of that conversation now as he re-read Harry's friendly letter.

Richard, duke of Gloucester and cousin, I greet you well. First, my sincere condolences on the death of your brother and my cousin, the king. It has been a shock for us all, but we must not allow our grief to cloud our judgement on how to proceed from here. I was glad to know that you are named protector, cousin, for you possess an exemplary character to counsel a king. I hereby give you my promise of support. I have no doubt you will be in need of friends with those wily Woodvilles ever ready to seize power, and, if I may be so bold, I am offering my help. It is time for my royal blood to be recognized and to take my rightful place by your side. I can muster a small force to meet with you along your route if you tell me where to make our rendezvous. Let us keep this discourse between ourselves. We do not need to give our enemies any cause to evade us, for I believe their thirst for power is a dangerous threat to you, and they will want to hold young Edward close.

Written this seventeenth day of April at Brecknock by your humble and loyal cousin, Henry Buckingham.

Richard let out a low whistle and handed the missive to John Kendall. "Write to my cousin Buckingham and ask him to meet me with his men at Northampton in ten days' time. Tell him no more than three hundred men will be necessary, and I will bring the same. Oh, and thank him graciously for his advice."

Enemies? He had always hated the word. Of course Richard had had to deal with enemies since he was a boy. He had grown up learning that King Henry was an enemy, but Richard could never bring himself to call the saintly, gentle man a foe. Whenever Richard went into battle, and even though he had been on the other side of the field from Warwick and George, he had never believed they were fighting to kill him personally but rather fighting for a cause, as was he. But now Cousin Harry was intimating that Richard himself could be at risk from the Woodville faction. He had felt trepidation then, and an even greater foreboding overtook him when yet another missive from Hastings warned him to come quickly. The queen and her adherents were ignoring Richard's role as protector and arranging the coronation for the young king on the fourth of May with or without Richard's presence.

He needed to move quickly now and cursed his previous tarrying.

Buckingham had grown stouter since Richard had seen him last at George's trial. But Richard greeted his cousin gratefully when he arrived at the largest inn at Northampton on the twenty-ninth of April with his three hundred men.

"Where are Rivers and the king?" Richard asked his cousin, surprised not to see them. "I requested they should meet me here."

Buckingham escorted Richard into the landlord's private chamber on the first floor and shut the door. The inn must be popular, Richard thought idly, looking about him and noting the velvet bed hangings, Turkey carpet, and a large silver pitcher in lieu of the more commonplace pewter. Buckingham handed Richard a cup of ale and sat himself down on a cushioned stool, leaving the best chair for Richard.

Richard eschewed the seat and the ale and began his customary pacing, which Buckingham found unnerving. "Mayhap he did not get your summons, Richard. Or the king took ill on the way from Ludlow. They will be here, mark my words. If he received it, Rivers would not dare defy your command."

"I know he left Ludlow six days ago. Ample time to get here, but," and Richard's tone was harsh, "when one is dragging two thousand men and cartloads of weapons, it will slow one down."

"Two thousand? And *weapons?*" Buckingham expostulated. "Is he looking to do battle with you? I warned you to be careful. We should have mustered more men ourselves. I only brought close to three hundred." Finding the stool uncomfortable, he transferred his bulk onto the chair. "We should march out and confront them on the road," he announced. "Bar their way to London. They have no right…"

Richard held up his hand. "And turn the people against me, Harry? Nay, we shall show unity when we all meet. There must be no sign of conflict. Young Edward should be greeted joyfully by his subjects, and I will be the first. Rivers will have no choice but to fall in behind me, and we shall proceed to London and show the citizens, council and parliament that I have already taken on my new role."

"Let us hope Rivers and his two thousand men agree with you, because…" Harry got no further as the door suddenly burst open and an agitated Francis went down on his knee to Richard.

"Something is amiss, my lord," he cried, just as Rob and Sir Richard Ratcliffe, both out of breath, followed him into the room. "We have come from seeing to the horses and discovered that my lord Rivers and the king were here yesterday and left. They were making for Stony Stratford."

"They were *what?*" Richard bellowed. "On whose orders?" His heart was racing and he felt control slipping. Why had Rivers not stayed in here Northampton and waited for him? It was clear to Richard that unless he entered London at the side of the young king, he might never gain access to the boy. He must secure Edward, and secure him quickly. "Spit it out, Francis, what has happened?"

"We were told that the town was full to overflowing with Rivers' troops ready to spend the night when the queen's son, Richard Grey, arrived in a great hurry from London," Francis, now on his feet, replied. "Soon after, the whole company was on the march south again."

Richard acted decisively now. "Harry, you and I will ride immediately and catch up with them. You three," he nodded to Francis, Rob, and

Ratcliffe, "make sure our troops are camped here outside the walls at the south end and await my orders."

As they crossed the taproom to the inn's entrance, a group of horsemen trotted into the yard and to Richard's astonishment, Anthony Woodville, Earl Rivers, was at its head. The tall, handsome brother of the queen dismounted and strode up to the doorway as Richard emerged. He gave Richard elegant reverence. "My Lord Protector," Rivers said amiably, and Richard noted the use of his new title. Perhaps he would not have to fight for it after all. "I bring you loving greetings from your nephew, our sovereign lord Edward. He is tired and has sent me in his place. You must have been expecting me to meet you here, but I doubted the town could hold both our retinues so I moved the king on to Stony Stratford leaving you sufficient room. I trust you approve."

Almost charmed by the earl, who was known as an erudite scholar, exceptional jouster, and penitent pilgrim, Richard was startled by Harry's whispered, "Dissembler." When Anthony smiled at him, Richard was suddenly so reminded of Elizabeth, his stomach knotted and his fists clenched. He wanted to wipe the smile from the supercilious man's face, but he needed time to think.

"I accept your consideration, but I am very disappointed not to find my nephew here. I was looking forward to greeting him and pledging my allegiance. We had an agreement to meet—here." He, too, could dissemble, Richard thought as he beamed a beatific smile. "You must agree that, as protector, I should be the one to accompany him to London." Did he see a flutter of anxiety then? And instead of a pleasant, "aye, my lord," Rivers' gaze slid to the earth, and he felt for the rosary always clipped to his belt. The man seemed suddenly nervous. Was he lying? Richard would find out. He decided to test Rivers and detain the man to ensure he did not try and move the king even closer to London. "'Tis too late to return to Stratford now, Anthony," he said affably. "Why not join us for supper, and Sir Robert here will secure you all suitable rooms for the night."

Rivers was perplexed. He had orders from the queen to approach London as quickly as possible, but he did not want to arouse Gloucester's suspicions. He wished he had listened to his nephew Grey's instructions and not ridden back the thirteen miles to Northampton to reassure the duke. But he could not refuse Gloucester's invitation now or the duke might suspect the truth.

"I accept with grateful pleasure, Your Grace," he said, executing a flourishing bow. He beckoned to his squire and, unbuckling his sword in a gesture of conciliation, he turned his back on Richard and murmured a few words to the man as he handed over the weapon. Then, although feeling trapped, he followed the two dukes inside, satisfied they had accepted his explanation.

Supper was surprisingly jovial, with the landlord plying his important guests with the best wine in his cellar. The eloquent Buckingham parried with the erudite Rivers; Francis, Rob and Ratcliffe provided laughter and even a bawdy song. Richard sat quietly at the head of the table, playing with his food, chuckling at the jokes, and occasionally contributing a witticism. No one would have doubted the camaraderie among the diners. Finally, in the early hours of the morning, Rivers rose somewhat unsteadily and declared he was for bed.

"God give you a good night, Anthony," Richard said pleasantly.

"And t'you, Richard," Anthony replied and laughed. "I shall shleep like a babe, but I 'spect my snores may d'sturb my fellow guests."

Richard turned to Ratcliffe. "Go with him," he murmured, "and see him safely housed and make sure he does not attempt to leave."

Rivers was led away by Sir Richard and soon strains of a slurred "Summer is icumen" floated up from the courtyard. Waiting until the noise quietened, Richard deliberately removed the wine and cups from the table and made sure the door was firmly closed. Puzzled, Harry, Francis and Rob looked at him expectantly, their focus none too sharp either.

"I do not like our situation," Richard declared. "Something is awry. For all he seems innocent—and drunk—enough, Rivers is concealing something from us."

Rob shrugged. "He did not appear ill at ease to me. What can he be hiding?"

Forcing his head to clear, Harry leaned forward and thumped the table. Here was his chance to get back at the hated Woodvilles, who he believed had influenced Edward to keep him from the king's council. "By the Virgin, you are right to be suspicious, cousin," he menaced. "He is a Woodville, and not one of them is trustworthy. They remind me of Cerberus—many headed and ready to strike at any who disturb its hellish lair."

"Anthony Woodville is known for his chivalrous deeds," Francis retorted. "What was it he said that alarms you, my lord? He has always seemed the least ambitious of the family."

Richard toyed with his ring. "His ability to mask his ambition is what makes him dangerous, Francis. My brother once told me that Anthony was one of the most intelligent men at his court. An astute politician, Edward said, and widely read. 'Twas why he chose Anthony to guide and govern his heir. I do not trust him."

"Nor do I!" Harry blurted. "And if I were you, I would not allow him to come anywhere close to our young sovereign until we are safely installed at Westminster. We should stop him from leaving tomorrow."

Rob and Francis exchanged a look, both wondering to whom the we referred. In only a day, Richard's two closest friends had united in disliking the conceited young windbag of a duke. Perhaps it was understandable that they saw Buckingham—with his royal blood—coming between them and Richard.

But relieved that he had someone of his own rank advising him in this crisis, Richard forgot Edward's unfavorable opinion of Harry and nodded in agreement. The more he thought about Rivers' odd action, the more it disturbed him. "I believe there is a conspiracy to prevent my joining the king, which can only have come from Elizabeth," he said. "God's bones…"

He was interrupted by the sudden entrance of Ratcliffe, who looked pale.

"What is it?" Richard demanded. "Has something happened to Rivers?"

Ratcliffe took his seat and collected his thoughts. "I stayed with him long enough to ensure Rivers was readied for sleep, but then I concealed myself in a niche near his room in case of any attempt to sneak away. Not fifteen minutes later, a man ran up the stairs and entered my lord's room. In a great hurry, he carelessly left the door wide enough for me to hear him say 'I have delivered your message, and your nephew, Sir Richard, bids me tell you they will make for London when the cock crows.'"

Buckingham jumped to his feet. "But this is treason." He turned to Richard. "As protector, you speak for the king. Rivers is directly flouting you. The Woodvilles aim to secure the boy."

"Calm down, Harry," Richard said, although his frown increased. "To be fair to Rivers, treason is a stretch. I have not formally been appointed protector by the council yet. But I agree, the Woodvilles conspire to keep the king from me, that is clear. Friends, how do you see it?"

"What I perceive is that you are in grave danger," Rob warned. "I am inclined to agree with my lord Buckingham about the Woodvilles. If you do not apprehend Rivers now and defend your protectorate, you could risk either civil war or losing your life."

Losing my life? Richard thought, taken aback. *But I am the Lord Protector. Surely Rob exaggerates.* But the fear was planted, and Richard's anxiety mounted.

"Arrest the man!" Buckingham growled. "If you allow him to get word to Stony Stratford again, his troops would turn and massacre us—they outnumber us two to one. Why do you think Rivers brought all those weapons?" Buckingham added, and the others loudly concurred.

Richard held up his hand. "If we are all agreed that there is a plot afoot to prevent my protectorate, then I have no choice but to arrest Rivers and Grey and seize control of my nephew."

"Now you're talking," Buckingham enthused.

Richard rose. The decision was made, putting him back in control. "Then Rob, take an escort and rouse the earl. Hold him here until I send word. The rest of us should prepare to ride before dawn to stop the march south."

The thirtieth of April was the last night of freedom for Anthony Woodville, Earl Rivers. The more he tried to weakly plead his case with the two angry dukes, the more they became convinced that he was conspiring against Richard. Leaving Rivers under guard at Northampton, Richard, Harry, and a few others rode south to Stony Stratford to head off the king.

Just as the sun rose over the horizon, the six horsemen galloped along Watling Street past the camp followers at the back of the army that was already on the march, scattering the rank and file of soldiers in their path. The cloaked and hooded riders clattered into the market square surprising the group of nobles beginning to mount their horses. One slight rider was already astride a huge gray courser, his good looks, golden-red hair, and noble carriage instantly recognizable as the dead king's son. Richard was the first to slide out of his saddle, discard his hood, and go down on one knee in front of young Edward. Buckingham followed a few seconds later.

"My liege," Richard said loudly enough for all to hear. "I am your uncle of Gloucester and lord protector come to escort you to London and to pledge my allegiance to your noble Majesty."

A gasp rose from Edward's retinue as they realized who had interrupted their departure. "Gloucester!" Sir Richard Grey hissed to the young king's elderly chamberlain, Sir Thomas Vaughan, who was bemused by the arrival. He had expected to see Lord Rivers. And indeed so had the new king.

"Where is my Uncle Rivers?" Edward asked, trying to sound imperious. "It is he who was to escort me to London, my lord, on the queen, my mother's orders." He hesitated, not knowing what to do without his guardian instructing him on protocol. He decided to bow, knowing his Uncle Richard was important.

The queen's younger son by her first marriage, Richard Grey, stepped up quickly to take Edward's bridle and stand between Richard and the king. Good-looking and over-confident, he dared Richard to displace him. "In my uncle's absence, I am in charge of his grace, my lord," Grey proclaimed, searching the faces of Richard's group for Rivers. "I, too, would enquire why Lord Rivers is not with you."

By this time, word had been passed back through the ranks that Richard of Gloucester had arrived, and soon the marketplace was thick with spectators.

Ignoring Grey, Richard swung himself up easily into his saddle, settled his horse down and addressed the throng. "Loyal Englishmen, as decreed by my brother, our dear late king, I am protector of our new sovereign lord and of his realm. I thank you for your duty and service in escorting him thus far, but it is time for you to return to your homes. His grace of Buckingham and I shall safeguard the king's triumphant entry into London. Now I charge you all to pledge your allegiance to our new sovereign. Long may he reign." He turned to Edward. "God save the king!"

"God save the king!" rose from the throats of the thousand loyal Englishmen as they all knelt to give young Edward homage. Richard Grey and his entourage could not but warily follow suit.

"Gentlemen," Richard instructed Grey and Vaughan, "take me and my nephew back to your lodgings." He moved his horse close to Edward's. "Your uncle is safe, but I will explain why we must detain him."

Edward's face registered uncertainty and even fear. He did not know his Uncle Richard well, but he knew Rivers very well. One could not blame the boy for wishing his erstwhile guardian there. Richard recognized the boy's dilemma instantly, and leaning over to him, he patted Edward's hand. "I see it is a surprise to you that I am to be in charge. 'Twas your father's wish that I be protector. Your mother and your uncle were fully aware of this royal appointment, yet they did not see fit to tell you, did they?" He saw Grey and Vaughan exchange meaningful looks, which, to Richard, verified their duplicity.

Edward shook his head. "I had not heard. Mother said she would help me rule, with Uncle Rivers and my stepbrother Dorset to help." He stuck out his chin defiantly. "I am the king, and I want my other uncle to ride with me, my lord."

Richard took a deep breath; this was not going to be easy. "Let us remove to the inn where we can speak in private," he coaxed. Then he turned to Rob. "Take Grey and Vaughan back to Northampton and keep them locked up with Rivers."

Edward protested when he saw his stepbrother and chamberlain removed and guarded, but again Richard assured him it was for his own safety. "What will become of them," Edward whimpered. "They have done nothing wrong."

"Ah, but they have, Your Grace," Richard said respectfully, leading Edward's horse back to the inn as Rob's group rode out of the town. "I don't expect you to understand now, Edward, but they look to their own selfish needs and not for the good of England." He could not believe how agitated he was, wishing he could disappear as he was wont to do at Middleham. He thought a few quiet moments might calm him. "Please go with my lord Buckingham," he told Edward, "and I will see you shortly." He watched Harry put his arm about the young king and lead him into the inn.

He walked around the side of the building to think. It was only then that he fully comprehended the real danger he might have been in had he not acted quickly. All the stress in his body seemed to shift to his right side and into his crookedness, and he leaned against the wall for support. Why did this all have to be so conflicted? Again he found himself questioning God's plan for him. Despite his prayers, penances, and generous presents to the church, Richard still felt God's displeasure every time he was helped into his cleverly fashioned doublets and harness, tailored to hide his affliction in public. Could not this transition of kingship go smoothly? So far, it was hell. Who could blame Richard for believing he was being tested yet again. He kneaded his stiff shoulder and, feeling the bony protrusion under his fingers that had worsened in the last year, he grimaced.

Was the groan he let out then for the pain in his back or for the ache in his heart?

After a small repast, Richard tried to mollify the young king. He first expressed his own sadness at the death of his beloved oldest brother and expressed his deepest sympathies for the loss of the boy's father. "I was a little younger than you when my father was killed, and so I know what a shock it is to lose a father. Your grandfather York was a wonderful man, and he would have been proud of you, I am sure." He saw a glimmer of interest in the young king's eyes. "He taught us that the most important virtue in life is loyalty. Loyalty, by the grace of God, to family, king and country. It is why I chose *loyaulte me lie*—loyalty binds me—as my motto." Edward had listened attentively, and Richard was cheered.

"Aye, my lord," the new king replied, "I have heard say that your loyalty to my father has never been in doubt. I hope I may expect the same from you." Then he braved, "My loyalty is also to my family, which includes my Uncle Rivers and my two stepbrothers, and after so many years at Ludlow, I have learned to trust my uncle. Although my lord father was the king and so had my allegiance, I hardly ever saw him. Neither do I know you, my lord, so why should I trust you more than my Woodville kin?"

Richard was impressed with the lad's reasoning. He spent the next hour trying to convince the youth of his good intentions, of Edward's trust in him to take charge, and how thus he was surprised Earl Rivers had contravened Richard's instructions to meet at Northampton. He explained how solemnly he took his duty to the crown and to England, and it was why he had had to detain Rivers and Grey, even though he liked both men.

"When you take the oath and are anointed with the holy oil, your life will be one with England. Aye, loyalty to your family is important, but there will be times when you may have to choose England over family. That is what I had to do today. Thanks to your noble father, the throne now belongs to York, descendants of the first Plantagenet. It does not belong to the Woodvilles, but it is my belief they would try and rule England through you. Things are complicated, nephew, but I swear to you I will help you to the throne and guide you to the best of my ability."

At the end of the hour, Edward began to unbend and, realizing there was much for a twelve-year-old to absorb, Richard engaged him in lighter conversation.

"I suspect you are looking forward to seeing your brother again, are you not," he said, smiling, and offering the lad some ale. "I warrant you and he fight and wrestle as I did with my brother at your age." At this critical juncture, he allowed himself a little white lie. "Oh, and I forgot. I also bring you greetings from your cousin, my son Ned. Aye, yet another Edward. 'Tis complicated with so many Edwards in the family, is it not?"

Edward, now fully relaxed, chuckled. "You forgot Uncle George's son is also Edward. I swear I will not call a son of mine Edward. I will think of something completely different, um," he thought for a moment, "like Cuthbert!"

Richard was relieved they were both laughing when Buckingham returned with food. The first hurdle seemed to have been vaulted.

The good humor did not last long.

When Richard told Edward that Rivers, Grey and the old chamberlain Vaughan had been sent north under armed guard, the king rounded on Richard, panic in his face.

"What have they done, my lord?" he cried, tears close. "I forbid you to detain them! Where are they? I want to see them. They told me not to trust you. They said you would lie to me."

Harry spoke now. "Who? Who told you Duke Richard would lie?"

Richard held up his hand. "Enough, Harry. It is not important."

"It *is* important," Harry retorted. He turned to Edward. "It is your *uncle Rivers* who lied, Your Grace. He told us he had *no* good reason for evading our request to meet you at Northampton. The truth is he had no intention of meeting us, because your mother had instructed him to ignore your Uncle Richard's request to rendezvous so you would get to London ahead of us. Do you see?"

"Easy, Harry," Richard warned, seeing young Edward's mulish expression; his cousin's aggressive tone was not helping. He pulled up a stool to sit and face Edward. Richard wanted to be kind, but this was a time to be stern. "Now you know the full story, can you blame me for assuming Lord Rivers and your mother had plans to usurp my lawful position as your protector and take power for themselves? I promise you, protecting you is what your father wanted. I am simply abiding by his wishes. Do you understand?"

Harry exploded then. "By God, their action is tantamount to treason!"

Edward jumped to his feet. "How dare you!" he yelled, clenching his fists and moving towards Harry. "My uncle is no traitor."

"Leave us, my lord!" Richard barked at Harry, angry at his cousin now. "You go too far."

Harry slammed the door behind him in disgust. A short silence followed during which Richard went to sit on a stool to wait for Edward to compose himself.

"Certes, your uncle was acting on your mother's orders, but until I am assured he was not plotting to take you to her without me, I must detain him—and your stepbrother," Richard said, quietly. "It is clear that Sir Thomas, as your chamberlain and close confidante of Rivers, must have been party to it all, so he must be remanded too. They will be comfortably housed out of reach—but guarded. Once we are in London and I have talked to your mother, we shall see about releasing them." He chose not to complicate matters by explaining he had separated the three conspirators to his three major castles—Sheriff Hutton, Middleham and Pontefract, which would make it more difficult for the queen to stage a rescue.

Edward's lower lip trembled, but he bravely looked Richard in the eye. "I don't think I want to be king, uncle. All this talk of power. I don't even know what power means. Uncle Rivers didn't teach me about that. We learned about chivalry, poetry and how to dance. Sir Thomas taught me Latin and French, but no one taught me how to be a king." He was close to tears now, and clearly exhausted, he blurted, "Oh, I just want to go to London and see my lady mother and my brother."

Richard nodded. How could he tell the lad that his mother was poison? Not for the first time did he curse Edward's stupidity for his choice of queen. "Aye, soon," he replied. "Let me send in my friend Lord Lovell to tend to your needs. He is a good fellow and one your father liked well."

Richard bowed and left the room.

The two messengers sent from Northampton to the council in London told very different stories of the events on the last day of April. The lord protector's missive spoke of a perceived plot by the Woodvilles to take control of the king, and that instead he now had charge of the king and would be escorting Edward to London. He begged the lords and council to support his protectorship. His private letter to Hastings was joyfully received.

But whatever Sir Richard Grey's squire had conveyed to Elizabeth was different enough to cause panic at Westminster. At midnight, the queen and her children gathered some belongings and ran the hundred yards across the courtyard into the sanctuary of the abbey. From there, Ellizabeth's eldest, Dorset, sent appeals to the council and clerics to intercept Richard on the road to London and seize the king from the protector and the duke of Buckingham. As if her flight did not arouse suspicion enough, she sent Dorset, as constable, to the Tower to fetch the royal treasure, half of which had been appropriated only the day before by Elizabeth's youngest brother, Edward, when he had sailed with his little fleet into the Channel. "For safe keeping," Elizabeth had said after giving both sons the command. History might well ask: for whom?

All this was enough to sway those uncommitted councilors to Richard's side, convinced the Woodvilles had effectively incriminated themselves. Certainly it was Richard's perception of the events; the Woodvilles, however, may have seen things differently. Once Richard had thwarted her plan to secure the young king, Elizabeth's flight into sanctuary smacked of a guilty conscience as far as Richard was concerned. *She was afraid to meet me,* he thought, *as well she might be.*

Richard could not tell if the young king was aware or not that this day of triumphant entry into London was to have been his coronation day. Richard chose not to remind him. The lad greeted the flowers flung, the excited cheering, and the pealing bells with gracious smiles, waves, and handfuls of coins tossed among the thousands of well-wishers along the Chepe. Any misgivings he may have had about his unexpected escort was hidden in the perfectly polished facade he had been taught to show in public during his upbringing at Ludlow. Richard was impressed; the little he had seen of him, Edward had the makings of a good king.

Richard gave Buckingham the honor of leading the procession and thus could not see the puffed-up young duke smiling and waving as though he were king. He blew kisses to the women who hung from upper-story windows and was more than generous with his seemingly unlimited store of farthings. Behind him, carrying an upright sword, was York Herald, his surcote emblazoned with the late king's rose en soleil. Richard well remembered the awkward tension of his father's faux pas all those years ago. It had not helped York's cause then. He must be careful as protector, he thought, not to behave like a king.

The lord mayor, with the aldermen, burgesses, and members of the guilds, met the procession at the widest point in the large cobbled thoroughfare by the Chepe Cross. Forming colorful blocks of scarlet and blue among the drab browns and grays of the common folk, the leaders of London threw back their hoods and knelt in unison to swear an oath of fealty to their sovereign.

Then a fanfare of trumpets caused a hush in the crowd, and Richard dismounted and knelt before Edward. He had chosen this moment to swear his own oath to Edward in front of the greatest number as possible of the young king's subjects. Already Richard had heard rumblings that his wresting of the king from and arrest of his guardian smacked of a power play. He wanted to squash those false rumors. What did they think he would do? Take the crown for himself? "'Tis the last thing I want," he had told Francis when the whisper had reached him at Barnet the day before. "'I have to play God betimes,' King Henry once told me, and that the responsibility was too great for one man. I have never forgotten it." Except for his Maker, Richard had never told a soul that he had played God once.

"I swear to you on my life that I shall be faithful to you as my lawful sovereign for as long as I shall live, God save Your Grace," Richard declared in a loud voice.

"I thank you with all my heart, my uncle and lord protector," Edward cried, doing his part. "I also thank you right well, Mayor Shaa and your company for your loyalty." He maneuvered his horse around in a circle to encompass the throngs gazing in curiosity at their new king and shouted: "May God bless you all. I promise, under Duke Richard's guidance and with God's help, to fulfill my duty to you as your king."

As he got to his feet, Richard caught Edward's eye and gave the lad a quick smile and an imperceptible nod of approval. *He is just like his father,* Richard thought wistfully. He has them in his thrall. *Jesu, how I wish I had half of Ned's presence or George's charm. Instead I am pinch-faced and crookbacked.*

CHAPTER TWENTY-FOUR
JUNE 1–15, 1483

Despite the lack of funds due to the Woodvilles' thievery of the king's treasure, Richard was able to demonstrate his administrative capabilities within the first few days. By the time the council formally proclaimed Richard protector and regent, he had won most of the members to his side. Jack Howard called him "masterful" to his son, Thomas, who was also appointed to the council. Richard gave the chancellorship to John Russell, bishop of Lincoln, and soon the rest of the spiritual lords ranged behind Richard's protectorship, including Bishop Stillington of Bath and Wells, once a close friend to George of Clarence. Only one, John Morton, bishop of Ely, equivocated.

As with any change in government, guarding a kingdom's borders was paramount, and Richard quickly gave his northern ally, Henry Percy, earl of Northumberland, captaincy of the Scottish border. Then he sent a naval force into the Channel to find Edward Woodville's fleet and offer his mariners a pardon if they abandoned Woodville. Most of the rebel fleet gladly complied, preempting any threat of a Woodville alliance with France.

A new date for the coronation was set for June twenty-second, and to keep Edward safe from any possible Woodville coup, Richard moved the king and his servants to the royal apartments in the Tower—the best garrisoned palace in London. In truth, Richard made the decision, but it was Buckingham who proposed it. More and more, Hastings and Richard's close friends watched jealously as the royal cousin wheedled his way into Richard's confidence.

Of all, the loyal Will Hastings had the most to lose with Buckingham's ascendancy. Was it then that he began to question Richard's motives? Or shore up a future for himself? At first he had been the most ardent supporter of Richard as protector, but as an older statesman, he perhaps believed by counseling Richard he would retain his close position to the throne and thus the young king. It was this expectation that made him send for Richard in April in all urgency, and Richard had duly rewarded him by according him governorship of the royal mint and the captaincy of Calais—no paltry offices. Surely, Will had thought, his loyalty was unquestioned, and thus he would also remain as chamberlain to the young king and on the protector's council. He had expected the inexperienced Richard of Gloucester would gratefully seek his guidance upon arriving in London. Instead it seemed the now-mature Lord of the North had a mind of his own. As well, Richard's generosity towards his young cousin threatened those expectations, and thus Will was wary of Buckingham.

Following one of the many council meetings in May, in which he had played a major part and was beginning to relax his guard, Will strolled over to Richard expecting an acknowledgement of his invaluable insights.

"I thought that went well, Lord Gloucester," he offered. "If there is anything else I can do for you..."

He was rudely cut off.

"There is, Lord Hastings. You can kindly remove the whore Jane Shore from the house my brother, in his folly, thought necessary to give her. And she must return any jewels she was gifted," Richard said, coldly. "They all belong to the crown, and, if you have not noticed, we have an innocent child as king, my lord, not a Caligula. I will not allow my nephew to have his father's mistress sully his young reputation by allowing that woman to publicly flaunt her former liaison with my brother at court. She must go. Do you understand?"

Stunned, Will went pale but for two pink spots of anger on his cheeks. "Jane Shore is a decent, kind woman," he asserted, "and, what is more, your brother loved her."

A long time ago, Will and Edward had decided Richard was a prude, but even so Will had not been prepared for Richard's contempt now. "It does not surprise me that you defend such a woman, my lord," Richard parried. "You are as debauched as she is. I pray you, have her removed immediately from the house and the court or…"

Furious if not not a little uneasy, Hastings shot back, "…or what, my lord duke?" This conversation was not going at all as he had anticipated, and he began to be concerned. What if Richard knew that Will himself had taken Jane as his mistress, having loved her throughout her time with Edward? *Perhaps Richard already knows,* Hastings thought, alarmed.

"Or I shall question your loyalty to me and our new king," Richard said evenly. "I am determined to purge this profane court, and I consider you to be at the center of its immorality." And he walked off.

The viciousness of Richard's attack made Will realize that not only had he lost the power he had held under Edward, but he might well lose his position on the new king's council entirely.

After safeguarding the kingdom from any possible attack and assigning the new council their roles, Richard turned his attention to the stubborn queen, who refused to leave sanctuary. He assured Elizabeth that he held no animosity towards her and attempted to persuade her, in vain, to rejoin the court. He was met with dramatic tears and an emphatic rejection of his offer.

"She is convinced I wish her and her children harm," he confided to Buckingham. "At least that is the excuse she is giving the other mediators I have sent to her. 'Tis as clear as a mountain brook that her refusal to leave is proof she is guilty of conspiring to keep me from my duty." He did not voice his fear that only by his demise could she keep him from his duty. "But to the people, it merely looks as though she is afraid of me, and that does my standing with them no good. Ah, but the witch is a wily one."

Richard rubbed his right jaw, where a molar was screaming for a clove tincture. It made him irritable and impatient, but Harry was impervious to anyone else's moods.

"Witch? I would more likely call her a bitch," Harry said, wringing his bonnet as though it were Elizabeth's delicate neck. "Let her rot in sanctuary with her brood, I say. But with Dorset in there with his mother, I would keep an eye on them. Why not send your man Catesby to watch the abbey and report on who comes and goes."

Richard nodded slowly. "Good idea." he said. "Incidentally, I don't think I have expressed my gratitude yet for coming with me to London of your own accord. It could have been dangerous for you to ally yourself with me so soon. You have my thanks and will be rewarded. Trust me."

"Oh, I trust you, Richard," Harry said, unable to hide the greedy gleam in his eyes.

It was thus that Henry Stafford, duke of Buckingham, became the virtual viceroy of Wales, one of the most important regions in the country. And, much to the annoyance of Jack Howard, who believed the task belonged to him as lord high steward, Buckingham was put in charge of arranging young Edward's coronation. Others on the council were watching and waiting to see how the protector would fare, some still on the queen's side. Ignored all those years at court by King Edward, there seemed no heights to which the young duke of Buckingham might rise. Richard had observed Harry's conceit, but he was willing to overlook it in his need of a powerful royal cousin as ally, as Warwick had been for Edward. So, for the time being Harry's assets overcame any doubts Richard had as he felt his way forward.

It did not occur to Richard to express any trust issues with others in his circle, assuming they were as wary as he, but Richard knew Buckingham and Will Hastings had formed a mutual dislike of each other. Will's staunch loyalty to Edward had always appealed to Richard, and Richard hoped he could count on that loyalty going forward with Edward's son. He would, however, expose the young king as little as possible to a man Richard considered immoral. Therefore, for the moment and perhaps unwisely, Richard got into the habit of excluding Will from private conversations with Buckingham, fanning the flames of Will's discontent. As well, when Richard went to the Tower to confer with the young king, it was Buckingham who accompanied the protector, not Hastings.

As protector, Richard was legally responsible for signing court documents in the king's name, and after the crowning, Richard was determined to begin the transfer of power to the boy; for now, however, let him enjoy what remained of his boyhood for a few months longer. Edward had a quick mind and would learn fast, and Richard would be glad to relinquish his protectorate and eventually return to the relative peace of Middleham.

"Where is my lord Hastings?" the young king asked Richard one day when Richard had gone to explain a detail of the coronation. "He was my father's councilor and should be here."

An awkward silence followed. "I will bring him next time, Edward," Richard promised. *Just as soon as Will proves his allegiance by ridding the court of Jane Shore and her ilk, I'll take him back into my confidence,* he thought. Hastings still had much support on the council, and Richard could ill afford to lose it.

Richard was not to know that, on his part, Will was having misgivings about the protector's motives based on Richard's puzzling attitude towards him. Was Richard pushing him out, Will wondered, to take sole control of the king? Or was he seeking the crown for himself?

Richard was not sleeping well and, lying alone in the downy bed, he had too much time to brood. Although he was demonstrating his administration abilities in the council and had won support from many members—at least he thought he had, he was unsure of himself. As a northerner, he was looked upon as an outsider in London, and he was doubtful whom to trust. All smiled and nodded, appearing acquiescent to his demands, but how much was fawning, he could not tell. It seemed to Richard that his northerners were more plain speaking and did not dissemble nor put on airs like the courtiers who had surrounded Edward.

Richard was so different from his affable, backslapping brother that the council, for its part, was wary of him. But he was optimistic that by showing good judgement and listening well, he would win the skeptics to his side. Unbeknownst to Richard, several of the barons had been shocked when, a few years before, a report had filtered to them that he had sided with a man of York—a yeoman—in a judicial dispute with one of the northern lords over land rights. Richard had found the baron guilty and fined him heavily. "If he takes the word of a commoner over a fellow nobleman," Lord Stanley had remarked to Will, "what does our rank protect?"

One sleepless night, after going over the day's events for the third time, he turned to where Anne should have been lying. *I miss you, my dear wife,* he thought, and in that moment he made up his mind to call for Anne. He needed her, and he hoped he could persuade her to leave Ned in safety at Middleham. After all, she deserved to be with him at the coronation.

A gray drizzle greeted the small procession of riders as they entered the city from the north, and Anne was glad she was on horseback as she watched the townsfolk teetering on their pattens picking their way through the mud. The damp did not suit her, and her persistent cough had worsened since leaving Barnet earlier in the day. Of course, Anne had been to London before with her father during her childhood, but it had been many years since she had been persuaded to leave her beloved Yorkshire for this god-forsaken, overcrowded, and stinking city.

Francis Lovell proudly escorted the protector's wife along Chepeside towards Bishopgate and Richard's domicile there at Crosby Place. "Gloucester's lady," somebody cried out recognizing the white-boar cognizance, and once the word was passed that the Kingmaker's daughter was in their city again, Londoners flocked into the Chepe to cheer her. Despite his treason, they still had a fondness for the deceased Warwick. It warmed Anne's heart to hear the shouts of welcome, thinking it was due her as Richard's wife. She waved and smiled shyly, recognizing the important role she now played, but she hoped Crosby Place was not much farther.

She caught sight of two lovely women standing by the conduit, looking past her to someone in her entourage. One of them in a widow's wimple looked familiar, and Anne frowned trying to remember where she had seen her before. She turned in her saddle to ascertain who they were focused on and saw it was Richard's son, John. All at once, she knew. "Kate Haute!" she murmured, dispirited by the widow's beauty despite the unattractive head covering. She was Richard's leman and mother of John and Katherine, who was now one of her ladies and the image of her mother. No wonder Richard had tumbled Kate, Anne thought, as she noted the remarkable amber eyes in the heart-shaped face that were fixated with longing on John. A momentary pang of sympathy for the widow engulfed the gentle duchess as she imagined the pain of having to give up Ned.

When she was lifted down into Richard's loving arms at Crosby Place, Anne forgot Kate. It was Anne's first visit to the large, gothic mansion. "It is magnificent," she enthused, noting the ceiling-high windows of colored glass, gilded carved beams overhead, and the red-and-blue tiled floor in the great hall. A servant removed Anne's soggy velvet cloak and hood, and she shivered. Richard looked anxiously at her, for she had lost weight and dark smudges ringed her eyes.

"Are you unwell, my dear?" he asked, leading her along a passageway to her chamber, where he had thoughtfully ordered a fire to be lit on this dreary day. "I will order you a hot bath after you have rested. Perhaps I was selfish to ask you to come." He smiled, and Anne noticed he had lost a tooth. "Aye, it had to be removed last week. I regret I could no longer withstand the pain."

He took her in his arms and sighed with pleasure. He had been right to send for her; how he had missed her steady, loving presence. All the stresses of the past month were released in that sigh, and Anne looked up, concerned. "I swear you look ten years older, Richard," she murmured, stroking his back. "Has it been aching more than usual?" Anne was the only person he allowed to mention the evidence of God's displeasure that protruded below his shoulder; he knew he would never atone for King Henry's murder, but he could not tell Anne that.

"Aye, I get tired more easily now. Standing as straight as I can and doing my best to conceal the monstrosity puts a strain on my whole body." He kissed her mouth softly and felt himself aroused, but now was not the time for seduction; now was time for her to recover from her six-day journey. "How is our son?"

"He wanted to come so much, but Mistress Idley will keep him occupied until we return or send for him. He sent a million kisses. I worry he will forget me."

Richard chuckled. "Have no fear, he won't. If truth be told, I expect he will miss John more than us. And speaking of John, did I tell you that Francis is ready to take him on as squire now. 'Tis time the lad flew the coop."

Anne smiled. "You indulge both your boys, Richard, and do not lie, you are besotted with your daughter."

Richard grinned. "You've noticed? I shall try and be impartial from now on. But she is a beauty, is she not?"

Just like her mother, Anne wanted to say. "Pah! Impossible," she said instead, giving him a gentle swat. "In truth, it is your kindness to the young ones that I find so dear."

A tap on the door meant an end to their privacy, and giving Richard a peck on the cheek, Anne called, "Come." One of her tiring women came in with Katherine in tow, and on seeing her father, the auburn-haired fifteen-year-old forgot all decorum and threw herself into his arms.

"Father! I am so happy to see you." As she pulled back, she studied him. "Are you unwell, my lord? You look tired."

Richard smiled, adoration in his eyes for his comely daughter, reminding him daily of Kate; she was filling out a little more rapidly than an anxious father would have liked, he admitted. "I am tired, poppet. Tired of waiting for you all to arrive," he teased, and hoped he did not look as bad as his wife and daughter made him feel by their concern. "I thought you would never come."

Richard recalled his father's long-ago remark, "Being born noble means to court an early death," as he rode through the city on his way to Westminster, and his eyes darted right and left anticipating danger. Despite Anne's calming presence at Crosby Place, Richard still worried about his personal safety in light of the Woodville ambition. It did not help that one of the prelates who had gone to negotiate with Elizabeth to leave sanctuary had given Richard disturbing information. The queen had commanded her astrologer to chart Richard's birth stars. Nay, he had not exactly seen it, the bishop had said, but he had heard rumor there was one. (Superstition held that a death date could be predicted from the charting—or in the case of the black arts, a death date could be manipulated.) It was no wonder Richard tossed and turned at night. His back had never pained him as badly, and he would wake up with one arm stiffened. His superstitious mind questioned whether Elizabeth was dabbling in witchcraft—after all, she was descended from the water-witch Melusine—and, together with her astrologer, was perhaps plotting his death. Richard's superstitions had grown with his fear, which made him testy and unapproachable.

Thus when Buckingham gave Richard the news that Hastings had flouted his orders to dismiss the Shore whore, and worse, he had taken her to mistress himself, Richard flew into a rage.

"Did the lying dotard think I would not discover this? Now I know he is truly depraved and certainly not to be trusted. Can he believe I will entrust him with any position around my nephew? Over my dead body!"

Quickly Buckingham pressed his advantage. "Then wait until you hear this. Guess who Catesby spied going in disguise to visit the queen," he said, mentally rubbing his hands. "None other than Jane Shore."

Richard stared at him in astonishment, and then he frowned. "What possible reason could Jane have for visiting the queen? It is common knowledge Elizabeth hates the woman."

Then Harry whispered the words Richard had tried to suppress in consideration for Will's friendship with Edward. "I think there must be a conspiracy, and Hastings' mistress is involved."

Or Hastings himself, Richard thought, as he lost control of his ring and it fell with a clink to the floor.

He confronted Hastings at Crosby Place in mid-June after a supper with Buckingham, Jack Howard, and his son Thomas. Catesby hovered around his master, ready to do Richard's bidding at the flicker of an eyelid. Jack Howard had long decided Catesby looked like a weasel and hoped he was less devious than his animal counterpart. A brilliant young lawyer and one-time servant of Will Hastings', Catesby had inveigled himself onto Richard's council by dropping Will's name, making Richard believe he had come with the councilor's blessing. Worrying for Jack, the man had already impressed Richard with his legal mind and become a member of the inner council. Keen to trust anyone with no ties to the old regime, like Buckingham, Richard had gladly accepted him.

Richard soon turned the conversation to the queen in sanctuary. "We must persuade her to release my other nephew or we cannot have a coronation. The people would not sanction it, and Edward is demanding to see his brother." The others nodded in agreement. "Master Catesby here has kept me informed of any unusual visitors to my sister-in-law. I was not surprised to learn that Margaret Beaufort has been, as has her friend my lord bishop of Ely."

"Lancastrians both," Buckingham grumbled.

"Let us not forget the Woodvilles, too, were red-rose wearers until Towton," Jack Howard offered. "Margaret is godmother to one of Elizabeth's daughters, I believe, so perhaps she went to pray with the girl." The group chuckled at the reference to Lady Stanley's famous piety. "But Morton is two-faced and often in the Beaufort woman's company. I would not trust him as far as I could launch his paunchy body across St. Paul's yard."

"I would not lose sleep over those visits, my lord duke. They seem innocuous enough," Hastings remarked, picking up a plum and biting into its juicy flesh.

Catesby glanced at Richard, whose frown silenced him. Richard turned to Hastings and controlling his rising anger, he said: "I thought I could trust you, Lord Hastings, but you have disappointed me in the matter of Mistress Shore. I had asked that you dismiss her."

It was an odd non sequitor. Hastings was taken aback but, unsuspecting, he swallowed the piece of plum. "I regret I have not had a moment to explain, my lord, but be assured I have procured her a new house with my own funds," he said, and as if to prove he was not underhanded, he took a chance. "She is now my ... well, you know, er..." *Dear God,* he thought amused as Richard's face showed no emotion, *do I have to spell it out for the man?* Still seeing no reaction, he explained: "She is now under my protection and no longer the crown's concern," and he waved his hand airly. "Rest assured, this has nothing to do with my loyalty to you or the king, Lord Richard. You can trust me."

"Trust you, Lord Hastings? I think not, " Richard snapped back. "You must truly believe I am a fool. I also do not trust your whore. You have lied to me about her, have you not?"

"I would trust Jane Shore with my life!" Will cried, bristling at the ugly moniker. "She is a good woman. Why do you bring her into this, my lord. Jane is an innocent."

Richard gave a derisive snort. "An innocent? Your idea of innocence is obviously quite different from mine, my lord. I give you a goodnight." He gave Will a long, unwavering look before pushing his chair back, rising, and ending the encounter. He would let Hastings sleep on the matter, he had decided. It was the best he could do for the well-respected chamberlain. Perhaps Hastings would make a clean breast, avert a plot, and Richard could bring the man back onto his side.

Puzzled, Hastings bowed and returned the salutation. Turning, he asked the Howard men: "Shall I see you at meeting in the Tower on the morrow, gentlemen? Splendid. Then may God give you all a good night." Buckingham held the door for him and soon after, Jack and Thomas bowed their way out, leaving Richard still nettled.

"Good evening, my lord bishop." Richard heard the muffled greeting through the open door, and he frowned. Who would come here just before curfew? He hoped it wasn't Morton; he could not abide the man. He sighed, wanting nothing more than to shut out the world and his daily cares and hide himself in Anne's comforting arms in their soft tester bed. But it was not to be.

"His lordship the bishop of Bath and Wells, my lord," William Catesby announced, as the elderly prelate shuffled in. After bowing to Richard and Buckingham, Stillington moved to the fire to warm his bony fingers.

Richard raised an eyebrow. "My lord, what may I do for you?" The cleric hesitated, his gaze shifting from Buckingham to the unfamiliar face of William Catesby. "You may speak freely," Richard assured him. "I have no secrets from my advisors. What brings you here at this hour? Speak, I pray you."

What the priest did say was to drain the blood from Richard's face.

"A pre-contract? My brother was previously spoken for before Elizabeth?" he demanded in as loud a whisper as he dared. "By all that is holy, it must be a lie!" He pulled his book of hours from under a pile of signed letters and held it out to the bishop. "Swear you are telling the truth."

Surprised, Stillington placed his hand on the book and swore. "The lady's name was Eleanor Butler—Talbot that was—the daughter of the old earl of Shrewsbury. 'Twas some time before the late king wed the queen. The lady took the veil and is long dead, my lord. She cannot make trouble, but I could not in all good conscience keep this secret to myself now that King Edward is dead. It means that the new king…"

"…is a bastard," Richard breathed, his heart pounding. He did not add: *and so cannot wear the crown.*

The news was stunning. Richard had so many questions for the old man, which he answered without hesitation, swearing that he was telling the truth. He caught Buckingham's eye and Harry pursed his lips in a silent whistle. The implications of the revelation were enormous.

"I witnessed the plight-troth when I was an archdeacon," the bishop told the astonished group, "and as you know a plight-troth made with a witness is tantamount to…"

"… the giving of a ring," Catesby interrupted. "The king's marriage to Queen Elizabeth was thus invalid."

Richard was regretting he had not dismissed Catesby. Could he trust the lawyer yet? He had not thought Stillington had anything of such importance to divulge and had wished merely to test Catesby's loyalty with whatever insignificant item the bishop disturbed them. Who could have guessed it was this monumental?

As Richard put the pieces of the puzzle together, the truth became horribly clear: Edward had given Stillington a bishopric to buy his silence. But why had Eleanor not come forward and denounced Edward when he and Elizabeth first revealed that they had been secretly wed? *Certes,* he realized, *she would have been laughed out of court. Who would have believed her—a widow woman with no man to fight for her? No wonder the poor lady took the veil! God's bones, Edward,* Richard thought, *what an unholy mess you have left me.* Yet how typical of his reckless, wayward brother.

"Who else might know of this, my lord bishop?" Richard demanded.

Stillington shrugged, but tiny pink patches appeared on his cheeks that alerted Richard. "You told someone else, did you not?" he pressed. "I can see it on your face. Who, who?"

The protector's irritability was new to the bishop, and he trod warily. "It was my understanding that the Lord Hastings was in the king's confidence. And…" he broke off, obviously riddled with guilt and weighing whether to confess to Richard's scowl. He was regretting he had come for he did not like the look in Gloucester's dark eyes. "…And, I foolishly made mention of it to Duke George of Clarence, b…but I paid for that folly with a t…term in the Tower," he mumbled.

Stunned, Richard now realized the condemned George must have threatened Edward. Could that have been why Edward had chosen not to pardon his brother for a third time? He needed to be rid of George. George had already cast aspersions on Edward's own birth—the rumor of bastardy with which Warwick had tempted George. That conjecture was ludicrous, but this new one may well have been the final straw for Edward. Richard shook himself. What devilish dark thoughts of Ned were these? He ought to dismiss the accusation outright. But the temptation to believe that Hastings might have known of Edward's bigamy for all these years and had kept silent was too great.

"Hastings knew?" he snapped, and the bishop nodded. "'Tis hard to believe he has not come forward since my brother's death to prevent a wrongful crowning. It was his duty."

Catesby suddenly stepped forward. "May I suggest that this is why Jane Shore was seen at Westminster, my lord. Could he be in league with the queen and sent his mistress as a go-between?"

"Hastings despises Elizabeth more than most," Richard retorted, twisting his ring. "Why would he choose to side with her rather than with me?"

The lawyer's mind saw a plausible reason. "Perhaps he resents your new order, my lord," Catesby ventured, braving his lord's displeasure. "You have chosen my lord Buckingham as your second in command, easing out Lord Hastings from the position he held with the late king. Since my lord bishop's story has revealed that Hastings has known all along, he may want to offer his help to the queen to oust you and, as a reward, become the new king's close advisor."

Richard noted Catesby's easy betrayal of his one-time mentor, but all that consumed him now was the lawyer's implication. If Hastings aided the queen and together were able to get possession of the young king, Richard would lose everything he had strived for. They could easily silence Stillington—and him. Buckingham and Catesby would be finished without him, and no one would listen to them. Then nobody would know the truth. He stared at the floor, but aware all eyes were on him, he rose and began to pace.

Buckingham, who had no love for Hastings, broke the silence by bringing his fist down on the table, making everyone start. "By the Virgin, the man has threatened the royal line by remaining silent. If young Edward is a bastard, he should not be king. Hastings has deceived you, the council and the whole kingdom. He is a traitor and should be punished!"

Richard thought so too, but not so much for keeping silent as for plotting to oust the rightful protector. In Richard's eyes, the man's loyalty was now doubly suspect. At the May council meeting, Hastings had sworn to uphold Richard as protector and regent until Edward was crowned and able to assume kingly duties. Richard was king in all but name. But now it seemed, just as Rivers, Grey, and Vaughan had attempted to deny Richard's right as protector at Stony Stratford, Hastings was plotting to do the same.

Richard made up his mind. He must do what was right for England, and he must protect himself and his family from whatever Elizabeth Woodville was conspiring. That very night he had John Kendall write an urgent letter to York, beseeching the loyal city to give him aid: ...*we heartily pray you to come unto us to London in all the diligence you can after reading this, and with as many as you can defensibly array, there to aid and assist us against the queen, her blood adherents and affinity, which have intended, and daily do intend, to murder and utterly destroy us and our cousin of Buckingham and the old blood of the realm...* John Kendall paused in his writing and looked up. "You are certain, my lord?" he asked.

Richard nodded. "It has come to my attention that the queen's astrologer has been busy plotting my chart, and you know they are not doing it to pass the time." He did not mention his excruciating back pain at night and his suspicions that the queen was putting a curse on him.

Kendall gave a low whistle of surprise. "Then let us hurry and finish this," he said, dipping his quill in the ink.

"I will send Ratcliffe to York, so they know I am serious," Richard said. He dictated a few more lines and subsided into his chair, listening to Kendall's scratching. His mind wrestled with all the pieces of information he had been given in the last few days and where it all led. He suddenly saw clearly what should be done.

Hastings must be punished.

"What will you do?" Anne asked, her face pinched with worry. "Hastings served Edward loyally. Are you accusing him because he took a mistress? Be careful, Richard. You, too, committed adultery."

Richard swiveled to face his wife. "How dare you! Are you calling me a hypocrite?" he demanded. "Are you still jealous of Kate? After all these years? Nay, do not answer that, the subject is not important." He ignored her tiny gasp of hurt. "What is important is how I deal with this new information and how I lead England out of a morass. This news will cause a crisis of the monarchy. According to English law, young Edward cannot be king and Hastings knew it and said nothing. He was willing to keep silent so that he might stay in power. And worse, he has been plotting to undermine my position as protector by going to the Woodvilles. I cannot allow him the freedom to continue down this path. He must be contained—nay, detained."

Anne had retreated to the bed and was watching him stalk up and down. What had happened to the man she loved who had ridden grieving from Middleham not six weeks before? She had been stung by his retort, but she recognized he was merely lashing out at the nearest person because he was angry and afraid. She decided to appeal to his fair-minded, honorable self.

"I understand now why you are upset, my dear, but do not let your anger impede justice. William Hastings should be given the chance to defend himself in a fair trial. You will grant him that at least?" she implored him. "If not, what will people think of you? What will God think?"

"God knows I am right!" Richard shot back and then mumbled, "if He is even listening anymore." Nothing Anne could say would change his mind. Hastings' silence and subsequent plotting was a treasonable offense. "I must do what is right for England now," he told his alarmed wife. "You can pray for me if you want, but I can no longer wait for His counsel."

"My lord, I am innocent of treason, I swear!" Will Hastings cried, his ruddy face ashen with fear. "I have no knowledge of any plot to overthrow you. Whoever says so is a liar."

Unmoved, Richard watched as the big man wrestled out of the guards' hold to go down on his knees and beg for his life.

Despite telling Anne to the contrary, Richard had spent hours on his own knees the night before, but not only did his aching back interfere with his prayers but voices from his past insisted on whispering in his ear, tormenting him and shutting out anything God might have advised.

"He was my most loyal servant and friend," Edward's ghost reminded him.

"A good man and true," Warwick's agreed.

And even George from his grave had admonished him: "Don't blame Hastings, blame the Woodville woman." But then Richard of York's face, all bloodied, its head crowned with paper, spoke, "Remember your duty, my son, to God, to England and to York."

"It is what I am doing, Father," Richard had whispered into the darkness. "I am trying to uphold my position and govern my nephew and England as faithfully as I can. But I fear betrayal—betrayal by those I thought were friends."

"Then you know what you must do." His father's words reverberated in Richard's exhausted brain as the image faded. But it was the last voice he had heard last night that made him cringe. "Sometimes you must play God, Richard Plantagenet," the murdered King Henry murmured. "You played it once before, remember. Now you must do it again for the good of England. I said 'twould not be easy."

Richard banished Henry's ghost now and, clearheaded, he glared at Hastings. "Take him away," he commanded the guards. "Let him be shriven, but then execute the traitor!"

The others in the meeting room gasped as Hastings was pulled to his feet.

Jack Howard stepped forward. "Without trial, my lord? Where is justice in such haste? What is proof of his treason?"

"Aye," Thomas Stanley, Margaret Beaufort's husband, agreed, "we must have proof."

"Look to your wife," Richard spat at him. "She is not innocent in this." And Stanley cowered in his chair. His fellow councilors, Lord Chancellor Rotherham and John Morton, bishop of Ely, remained silent. Richard knew why—they were complicit, he felt certain of it.

"As protector and chief constable of England I do not need to answer to any of you, but I will tell you that Lord Hastings has been dealing secretly with the queen to plot my downfall."

"'Tis a lie!" Hastings cried, now terrified. "Why do you accuse me of this?"

"Your mistress was seen visiting the queen in sanctuary. Prove to me you did not send her. 'Tis certain the two have been practicing witchcraft to aid my demise," and he held out his stiffened arm. His superstition blamed witchcraft at this volatile time instead of a perfectly natural result of sleeping heavily on one side of his body. "Do you see their work?" he shouted. "Witchcraft, I tell you, and I have sent Tom Howard to convey Mistress Shore to prison for it."

Richard was surprised by the anguish in Hastings' face. The man is in love with the harlot, Richard realized. Was she really so desirable, or did the woman's witchery entrap her prey, including his brother Edward, which had led to his demise? She was immoral and a necromancer, and he was right to arrest her. All of these thoughts further enraged him. "If that is not enough for you, my lord," he continued, loudly, "then shall I accuse you of withholding a secret from me and the council that would put the monarchy in jeopardy. You have such a secret, do you not? And by not confiding it to me, you have betrayed your country and your king."

With this damning disclosure Hastings knew he was doomed. He knew exactly to what Richard was referring. As Richard divulged to the others the devastating secret as reported by Bishop Stillington the night before, Hastings' legs crumpled under him and he fell to his knees. The councilors exchanged worried glances, and Jack Howard sat down hard.

Frantic, Hastings attempted to defend himself. "I was always faithful to your brother, Richard. 'Twas his secret I held, God help me." He appealed to the group, wringing his hands. "My lords, you know me. You know my loyalty is to the king! I implore you, speak for me now. I am no traitor."

Either in fear that they might be the next in line to face Gloucester's wrath or they were too stunned, no one spoke. Hastings tried again: "Richard, for the love of God—and of your brother, punish me for immorality, for lacking in judgment, but do not accuse me of disloyalty." When Richard turned away, in desperation Hastings raised his voice. "Remember your oath, Richard of Gloucester!" he cried. "You pledged to protect your nephew's throne. Some protector! I believe you are only serving yourself." Now petrified and with nothing to lose, he warned the others: "Mark my words, my lords, Gloucester seeks the crown. He destroys me for no other reason."

Richard's fist smashed down on the table and shouted, "The reason is treason!"

At that, more guards rushed into the room causing the councilors to leap from their seats in surprise. They were even more surprised when Richard ordered the arrest of the three unsuspecting of them he believed were Hastings' and Elizabeth's co-conspirators: Rotherham, Morton and the loudly protesting Stanley.

Hastings, now firmly held by his guards, cried triumphantly: "You see, my lords, I was right. The lord protector has his eye on the crown."

"Away!" Richard shouted, pointing towards the door to an outer stair. "Find a block and execute him at once."

When the prisoners were removed and Hastings' loud protestations could still be heard, Jack got down on his shaking knees. "Come, my lord, the least we can do is to pray for Will Hastings' soul." Only his long association with Richard gave him the courage to suggest this generous action. "You know in your heart he deserves our prayers."

But Richard was in no mood. He had yet another violent death to beg God's mercy for, and this one would surely lie as heavily on his heart.

"You pray for him, Jack," he said as he left the room. *I'm beyond prayers now,* he thought. *I fear no prayer can bridge this chasm between me and God. Nay, I will answer to no one but England now; it is she alone in whom I must put my faith. She is my religion now.*

CHAPTER TWENTY-FIVE
JUNE 15–JULY 7, 1483

"Hastings is dead!" The cry rippled out from the Tower down the narrow lanes and alleys of the city and sent the citizens into the streets in alarm. They were used to seeing the genial Hastings alongside the king enjoying an ale at one tavern and a wench at another. "He was one of us," an innkeeper told his neighbors as they hurried to the standard on the Chepe, where important announcements were made. "What has he done? Better be ready for trouble," he said, picking up a stout stick. Others brought their tools and weapons with them, shooing children back indoors. They needed answers in these uncertain times. Questions were being asked as to why the queen remained in sanctuary and refused to let her younger son join his brother in the Tower. What was it about the protector that frightened the woman enough to choose to stay at the abbey in relative discomfort? Already he had postponed the much anticipated coronation twice in his six-week term as regent. The most suspicious of them whispered that the king's uncle might have designs on the throne himself. "Just like his brother Clarence," they said.

At the standard, a trumpeter silenced the rowdy crowd that was shaking staffs, knives, pikes, and fists. A herald rode forward and read the proclamation from the royal council: "In so much as William, Lord Hastings has been discovered plotting with her grace the queen and others of her affinity to destroy the lord protector and my lord Buckingham so as to rule our sovereign Edward and the king-dom at his own pleasure, the charge of treason warranted his immediate punishment. The said Hastings was also charged, with his co-conspirator and concubine Jane Shore, of bringing about the demise of the late King Edward through their immoral and licentious way of life. Therefore, Lord Hastings was executed in the Tower this day, the thirteenth day of June, by order of the lord protector, his grace the duke of Gloucester."

The mayor ascended the Chepe Cross steps: "The government, our city, and the kingdom hav-ing thus been secured, you are required to return to your homes and put away your weapons."

Apprentices, mercers, butchers and bakers, goodwives, weavers, tailors and wherrymen stood for a moment to absorb the extraordinary news before an excited buzz of conversation supplanted the silence as they dispersed. Most accepted the lord protector's action as necessary—if sudden, but others of a more cynical nature had to ask, if the popular Lord Hastings could be despatched so swiftly, was anyone safe?

When Thomas Grey, marquess of Dorset, escaped from sanctuary the very next day, Richard was further convinced he had been right about the conspiracy.

"We must increase security at the Tower in case he tries to capture the king," Richard told the council in the Star Chamber two days later. "After all, until I relieved him of the post when he went into sanctuary, he had been constable of the Tower and thus is well known there. He will be seeking to join with his mother's followers, so we must find him quickly. My lord Buckingham, I shall count on you to spread a net throughout the city."

Whether Richard noticed the subdued demeanor of the members was doubtful given his heightened anxiety. With Hastings executed and Stanley, Morton, and Rotherham still in custody, the rest of the council members feared for their own safety and so watched Richard warily.

Surely of all the items needing discussion that day the pre-contract was the most important, and yet Richard hesitated to give it voice. Of those present only Harry, Howard, and Ratcliffe knew of it, although rumors were surely rife, but those three were loyal, and Richard decided it must wait. Before he could proclaim the news publicly, he was determined to make sure he had custody of the king's younger brother in case of any insurrection following the announcement. He spoke slowly and deliberately hoping to sound in control. But Richard was far from being in control. In fact, he decided, his labored speech might easily have been mistaken for inebriation. He explained why it had been necessary to put Hastings to death, and although there were murmurings and surreptitious glances, no one dared interrupt the protector. The time was ripe for Richard to make his move.

"Regarding the preparations for the coronation," he continued, more naturally now, "it is my certain belief that Edward cannot be crowned until Richard of York is retrieved from his mother. He is heir to the throne and must be under my protection. With the escape of Dorset, we cannot afford to take any chances with the boy. I am afraid we shall have to resort to force if necessary."

Several members nodded, but Francis was perturbed. "Force, my lord? In sanctuary?"

"The archbishop assured me that because the boy is not there of his own volition nor has he done anything wrong to warrant his being there, it is within our legal right to remove him. It is not the way I would prefer to proceed, but if we want a coronation, we must secure the heir." Richard's tired back had begun to force his head forward, but to his audience it merely looked like bullheadedness. They stayed silent. After what had happened to the respected Hastings, who could blame them? "Sir John, I trust you can arrange to accompany the archbishop with an armed escort. Now, if you will excuse me, gentlemen."

Richard rose painfully from his chair, unwilling to answer possible questions about any rumors of the pre-contract. *Later,* he thought, *I will tell them later.* His discomfort was overriding his usual logic or he might have understood that the longer he waited, the more his detractors would view him as coveting the crown.

Fortunately, no one was surprised when he left the meeting early. It was true, Richard did not look well; he had hardly slept since the execution. He had taken to downing several cups of wine to help make him drowsy, but it just gave him headaches in the morning.

"I am haunted by bad dreams if I do manage to sleep. Ah, Anne, how I wish we could just ride home to Middleham," he confessed later that night. "How I long for the life we had there, away from such turmoil."

"Aye, and to see Ned," Anne agreed. She rubbed willow-bark balm on Richard's back and massaged his tense muscles. If the truth be told, she was frightened, but she would not let Richard see her fear. Katherine had told her of the whisperings among the servants: that the lord protector sought the crown for himself. "Make sure you tell them it is not true, Katherine. Your father just wants to safeguard the king and his realm from those who would do harm to both," she had admonished the girl and then had tried to allay her own fears.

"What is next, my love?" Anne asked Richard now.

"Canterbury will be removing Richard of York tomorrow. I wish you would come with me when I take him to be with his brother. The boy will be afraid, and the way I look now, I don't blame him. Edward greets me cordially enough—he is a very self-assured and intelligent boy—but not with any affection; he still pines for his Uncle Rivers. Perhaps you can change that, my dear. I would be grateful if you would try."

Thus, Anne was by Richard's side two days later when the two brothers were reunited in the royal apartments at the Tower, and Edward thanked Richard graciously for arranging it.

"I hope they are looking after you well, my dear Edward," Anne said, gliding forward and putting her arm around the boy, "and the food is to your liking?"

"Too much fish!" cried the rambunctious duke of York, riding his wooden hobby horse around the room. "It's always fish, fish, fish!"

Anne and Richard glanced at each other and burst out laughing. And Edward joined in. "He must have driven my sisters mad in the abbey," he whispered to Richard behind his hand. "Maybe I will not be thanking you at this time next week, Uncle."

"There, you see," Anne said as they walked towards their waiting mounts after the visit. "Edward is warming to you. And the way Richard hugged you when you lifted him up to say goodbye is a very good sign."

"I hope you are right, Anne, because when I have to tell Edward he cannot be king, I do not want him to look on me as a monster."

"Not if you choose your words kindly and truthfully. Imagine you are speaking to Ned."

With the younger prince safely under his protection, Richard could procrastinate no longer and called another meeting of the full council to inform them of Stillington's staggering news. He could almost feel Edward's looming presence over him as he explained his brother's misjudgment. For the first time since embarking on the difficult task of overseeing the government, Richard felt disloyal to his brother's dying command to protect the crown for young Edward. His only consolation was that not telling the truth would betray his fellow Englishmen. He tried not to be judgmental, but he did despair of his brother's foolishness. "When the prick goes hard, the brain goes soft," Warwick had told him once when the earl was railing against Edward during those early days at Middleham. Edward's brain had gone soft during much of his scant forty years, Richard lamented.

"My lord Bishop, I pray you tell your colleagues exactly what you told me." Richard left the dais and approached Stillington, who had hoped to avoid directly addressing the council. The cleric's right hand nervously grasped the large silver cross around his neck as if to ward off any verbal attacks, but Richard believed the gesture served to sanctify Stillington's oath.

"So it would appear the children of the late king and his queen are bastards," the bishop finished. As expressions of disbelief began to supersede the initial openmouthed reaction to the momentous news, he flushed and stepped back.

Again, suspicious glances were sent Richard's way, but before any questions were asked of him or Stillington, He returned to sit down on the same throne his father had so unwisely touched in his bid for the crown all those years ago. "I leave it to you, gentlemen, to draw your conclusions."

Pandemonium broke out around him as the twenty or so members each jockeyed for his opinion to be heard. Finally, Buckingham marched into the center of the room and cried, "For heaven's sake, my lords, you are behaving like spoiled children. Let us debate the issue in more discreet tones as befits a royal council."

If the moment had not been so tense, Richard might have smiled. His cousin's bulk and loud voice could certainly claim attention, but then Harry could also woo a treasure from a reluctant merchant with his silver prose. Let Harry lead the debate, he thought, listening intently but saying nothing until Harry said: "It would seem we are all agreed that we do not have a king to crown. I propose we cancel the coronation."

"I second that." Richard had not meant to speak, but his exhaustion made him careless.

Seizing the moment, Buckingham went down on one knee to his cousin. "My Liege," he cried, sweeping off his hat. A shocked silence followed, and Richard saw the accusation clearly in some of the members' looks: *Is he stealing the crown?*

Horrified, Richard leaped up and pulled Buckingham to his feet. "You go too far, my lord Buckingham," he countered. "We must first try and find more proof of this story. Perhaps my lord bishop misremembered …"

"…but he swore on your holy book of hours that it was true," Jack Howard broke in, and Stillington nodded vehemently. "I witnessed it, my lords. I do not believe the bishop is lying."

Buckingham murmured. "Leave this to me, Richard." He turned to the company. "Let us allow the lord protector to go on his way while we have a conference to determine a course of action. Do you agree?"

"Agreed," they chorused.

Grateful, Richard made his way to the door of the Star Chamber, where he turned and bowed. "May God help you make an honest decision, my lords. I am putting my trust in you. Now forgive me, it is my duty to inform the king…I mean Edward…that there will be no coronation."

Instead of taking the royal barge straight to the Tower, Richard made a stop to prepare his mind for revealing the brutal truth and unfair consequences of the princes' father's indiscretion those many years ago. Whenever Richard felt helpless or needed to clear his head to solve a problem, he found solace in exercise. Over the years that his spine had begun to twist and push, he had dedicated a good portion of his daily training routine to strengthening his arms and shoulders to ensure he was fully capable of swinging his favorite weapon, the war hammer, to maximum effect. Determined to overcome his handicap, he never missed a day of vigorous training.

Richard had a personal combat instructor, another of the very few who knew of Richard's physical condition, and Walter Woodman traveled with Richard's household along with a personal armorer, an Italian master named Signore Vicente. A knight's harness must fit its wearer's body exactly or chafing would cause extreme discomfort during combat, and thus Vicente was now intimately familiar with his master's body as was Richard's tailor.

That morning upon leaving the council, Richard went to Baynard's Castle where the enclosed tiltyard afforded him privacy while he trained with Walter. Duchess Cecily she had again made her favorite London residence available to her youngest son. *Take advantage of its proximity to Westminster, the garrison, and its high walls, my son,* she had written to him from her Berkhamsted retreat. *You may need it.* After the unrest over Hastings' death, Richard had reluctantly moved Anne and their households to the Thames-side fortress. "'Tis for your own safety," he had told a disgruntled Anne, who had grown to like the modern comforts of Crosby Place. "Just until we untangle the knotty problems threatening our monarchy, I promise. I would caution you to stay within Baynard's walls until we do."

Despite his back pain, which seemed to have diminished after the fateful council meeting in the Tower, Richard spent an hour lifting weights and challenging Walter to quarterstaff combat. It was a hot day, and soon he felt the sweat trickling down his back and through his heavily padded jupon. Walter soon overpowered him, and Richard put up his staff and his hands. "Forgive me, Walt, I cannot concentrate today." Blaming his performance on his back, he did not tell the goodman that he was anxious about the coming interview and still reeling from Hastings' treason. He walked away to the changing area as Walt watched with consternation; he had never known Richard to lose to him with a quarterstaff. Did the duke ever sleep, he wondered. It would appear not, judging from the dark rings under his eyes.

Francis and Rob had also been watching and stood ready to help him out of his jupon, douse him with a bucket of water and towel him off. The inward curving from ribs to waist on Richard's left side, starkly evident when he was naked, followed the rightward curve of his spine. Francis often wondered how Richard managed to best most of them in many of the martial skills required of a knight; he was weakest when not mounted and needing to make upward thrusts with a sword. It puzzled Francis why fatigue set in so much faster with Richard, who appeared fitter than most. Richard would complain that his lungs were constricted, and he would find himself fighting for breath. Much later, doctors would understand why this occurred, but Richard only understood it was just another punishment sent by God that he must overcome.

It never failed to astonish both of his most loyal retainers how uncomplaining their lord was about his affliction, although they worried Richard was relying on wine a little too much of late—to dull the back pain, they believed. Always contained in public, even his friends were unaware of the turmoil inside the protector.

As they waited for Richard on the wharf to ride the tide to the Tower, Rob remarked to Francis on the pitiful condition of Richard's body. "He has great forbearance, it is true, but I notice how he draws his strength from those he loves best. His mother loves him in her own stiff way, although I doubt she has seen him unclad of late. Kate gave and now Anne gives him constant devotion. I hope he never doubts our devotion, and I believe we have served him with affection."

"He knows he has our loyalty, Rob. I would follow such a man anywhere," Francis declared. "It appalls me to hear people accuse him of seeking the throne from pride or ambition. He already has more power than he has ever asked for, has he not?"

Francis shrugged. "Unfortunately, there are those who will judge Richard based on their own jealous desires. For some, there is no such thing as too much power."

"Talking about me again?" Richard startled them as they stood by the boat, their words drowned by the lapping waves. "Come, friends, let us get this over with."

Once Richard began the difficult conversation, he found it easier than the anticipation of it. He sat between his nephews on the large tester bed, and it so reminded him of his quiet bedtime talks with Ned that he found his words coming more easily.

"I regret to have to bring you news that will affect your lives, my dears, but it is of such importance that you must only hear it from me. A long time ago, before your father met your mother, your father made a promise to wed another woman. The promise is called a pre-contract and is legal and binding in the eyes of the church. Unless the two people ask to be released from it, they are considered married. Your father broke that promise when he married your mother instead."

He paused, upset that the younger boy, Richard, was already crying. He was the same age Richard had been when the dreadful news of York's death had changed his life, so he did not blame the boy for shedding tears; as well their father's recent death was still an open wound. Richard took out a linen kerchief and gently wiped the boy's face allowing Edward to gather his thoughts.

Edward picked at his fingers. "What does this mean exactly?" he demanded. Why was this uncle always against him? Nothing good had happened to Edward ever since Uncle Richard had come into his life at Stony Stratford, and, at twelve, he was learning to be suspicious of people—even his own family.

Richard took a breath and answered as simply as he could. "It means your parents' marriage was not legal, because your father was not free to marry. And for you boys, this is the upsetting part. One must be lawfully married in the eyes of the church before having children, or those children are not legitimate—legal. It does not mean your mother and father did not love you or each other, because they did," he hastily added, "but it means you have no legal rights—including," and he drew another deep breath before pronouncing, "your not being able to be king, Edward."

Richard was expecting Edward's anger. "How do I know you are not lying, Uncle?" the boy cried, jumping up from the bed and kicking over the pewter jakes. "You lied when you told me my uncle Rivers would be released. He hasn't, has he? I don't trust you. And I don't want to be called 'bastard.' I want to be called king." He rounded on Richard, his fists clenched and looking so like Edward, Richard's stomach contracted. "Why are you lying to me? You swore to protect me and uphold my kingship not three weeks ago. Do you break your oaths so quickly? I had heard you were my father's loyal brother, but now I am not so sure."

Richard winced, but he let the boy vent. Edward had every right to do so; his father had betrayed him after all. He was quite eloquent for his age, and Richard sadly regretted the lad would not be king. Rivers had schooled him well in rhetoric and logical argument; he would have made his York family proud as king. But it was not to be.

"How I wish it was not so, Ned. I am so sorry," Richard told the older boy standing stiffly by the window. He gave the smaller boy a squeeze and kissed the top of his golden head. Poor boys, one day king and heir and now reduced to bastardy.

"I understand your feelings, Ned, and you have every right to question me. But it is your father who was at fault, not I. It is he to whom you should address your anger." Richard rose and went to Edward's side, pretending he had not seen the few tears that had spilled down the lad's cheeks. "I swear to you, that I am not lying in this. Everything I have done since your father's death I have done in accordance with my oath to you for the good of England. I cannot break my promise to England that I will defend her crown to my dying breath, and I would break that pledge if I said nothing and allowed you to be crowned. Would you have me break my pledge, Ned?"

Edward hung his head. He understood. "Nay, I would not," he murmured.

With the worst of the interview over, Richard went on to reassure his nephews that no matter their status, his and Aunt Anne's affection for them would not change, and that whenever their mother chose to leave sanctuary, they would be able to live all together at Elizabeth's family home in Grafton. "You will be welcomed at court, but I doubt your mother will want to be there." He paused, watching them anxiously. It was a lot to absorb, he knew.

Edward stared out onto the green where, less than a week ago, Will Hastings had lost his head. Dear God, Richard thought horrified, had the boy witnessed the execution? He would have to ask the usher. But he did not have to, Edward's quick young mind had gone there, too.

"Why did my father's best friend lose his head?" Edward asked in a dull monotone. "Was it he who told you of the pre-contract? My Uncle Rivers called him immoral and a bad influence. My Uncle Rivers did not like Hastings. Did you?"

Richard was flabbergasted by the boy's adult questions. He struggled to give the lad a good explanation of his decision about Hastings, but first he suggested that little Richard go and ask Lord Lovell for a ride on his horse. The boy did not hesitate and ran off.

"It was not a question of whether or not I liked Hastings, Ned. It was a question of high treason. He was a faithful friend to your father, 'tis true, but sometimes lying for one's friends has larger consequences. There was more to the decision than that, however, but I will tell you all when you are older, and we have put this behind us." Richard would not add to the boy's burden now by implicating his mother in the plotting.

"I watched him die, you know," Edward said, quietly. "He was very brave."

Richard groaned inwardly. "If it is any consolation, Ned, I have honored Lord Hastings' wish to be buried at Windsor near your father."

"It is," the boy replied, sadly. "They were such great friends." He turned his back on Richard, and, with dignity, he said, "I would have you leave me now, my lord. I wish to be alone."

"You must take the crown, Cousin," Harry of Buckingham insisted at the next privy council meeting. "It is your right and the kingdom needs a king."

How Richard had dreaded this moment. In truth, he had anticipated it, but he still was not prepared to think about wearing the crown. Anything he said now was likely to be whispered outside these walls and misinterpreted. Indeed, anything he did from now on would be recorded for posterity, and the burden was heavy.

He looked around at the expectant faces of the men he hoped he could trust and wondered if they thought he had planned it all. He decided to bury any speculations without delay. Rising, he announced, "I swear to you that I have never sought nor do I now seek the throne." He paused, letting the faces register surprise or guilt. He was suddenly aware that he must sound exactly as his father had sounded when York had vehemently denied seeking the throne. *Dear God, is this a case of the sins of the father...? Nay, 'tis nothing of the sort, merely an extraordinary coincidence,* he told himself. Putting those thoughts aside, he continued, "Those of you who know me well—Cousin Buckingham, Lord Howard, Sir Francis—can tell you this is true. Sweet Jesu," he sighed, "how much simpler for all of us had my brother's secret died with him." The lords then heard a sincere desperation in his question: "Gentle lords and friends, is there no other way to solve this?"

Seeing Richard's disquiet, Jack Howard stepped forward and laid a fatherly hand on Richard's arm. "Who else is there, my lord? With the boys declared bastards, and Clarence's son attainted through his father's treason, you are next in the York line and the rightful heir."

"If you don't want it, I'll take it," Buckingham quipped, but the jest flopped as flat as a cow's turd, and the faces on the other councilors registered horror at his poor timing. Less shocked, Richard nevertheless glared at him. Sometimes he despaired of Harry's judgment, and certainly his lack of tact. Had Edward been right not to give their cousin a position on his council? But Richard's moment of doubt passed, and he let the gaffe go, unaware that later he would live to regret it.

"I will consider accepting the crown but only if I have Parliament's and the people's blessing. This must not look like a *coup d'état*, my lords. If I do my duty, it must be seen as England's choice not mine. And it must be a peaceful solution, do you understand?" *Remember my father,* he was tempted to say. "If you are agreed we can discuss ways to bring this to a satisfactory conclusion." He sensed the only reluctance coming from Archbishop Rotherham, but Richard did not blame him; he was a churchman who had sworn an oath to uphold young Edward's claim—as had Richard himself. He changed the subject.

"I must report on further mischief by Thomas Grey, marquess of Dorset. I have intelligence that he is still at large and plots to 'rescue' his half-brothers from the Tower and assassinate me, to which end he has been in secret communication with his imprisoned brother and uncle in Yorkshire. As I would prefer not to part with my life as yet, we must find him, my lords." Taking a deep breath, he again courted controversy. "And now, if you indeed wish me as king, then I would have the right to end Rivers' and Richard Grey's continued treason, would I not?"

There was a gasp from the clerics Rotherham, Bourchier and Russell, but Stillington merely nodded. Certes, Richard knew he could count on Stillington to support him now, if the man wanted to keep his position on the council. Henry Percy, earl of Northumberland, and no lover of Woodvilles, was the first to say, "Aye," and the others followed.

Richard hid his relief, but he would not rest easy until he knew his enemies were dispatched. He was sorry Earl Rivers had tried to trick him at Northampton for he had always admired the handsome, erudite Anthony, as had Edward, but a traitor must be punished; Richard did not see the man as anything else. And so once again, Sir Richard Ratcliffe was sent north, but this time to give the order to execute the oldest brother and youngest son of the queen.

Despite the unknown whereabouts of Elizabeth's first-born, Richard slept soundly that night for the first time in weeks.

Bastard slips shall ne'er take root, was the theme of that Sunday's sermon at Paul's Cross outside the Gothic cathedral in the heart of the city. Coached by the duke of Buckingham, Father Shaa, brother of the mayor, delivered an oration to a huge crowd that hung on every word of the scholarly cleric's declaration that of the three adult sons of Richard, duke of York, the one most deserving of inheriting the crown was his youngest, the lord protector. Extolling Richard's virtues, Ralph Shaa also pointed out that when King Edward had married Elizabeth Woodville, he had failed to disclose a previous contract with another.

The ensuing buzz among the spectators had to be silenced by a loud drum roll. At the side of the cathedral, seated on his horse and next to Buckingham, Richard scanned the crowd with apprehension, knowing Londoners eyed him with suspicion. How would the people react? Would there be a mandate for him to take the crown, or a bloody insurgence? He had been against Harry's bold suggestion from the start to make a public announcement of Edward's infidelity, of his betrayal of a vow, and worse his keeping this damning secret his whole life, jeopardizing his heirs and the country. Nay, Richard had told Harry, it was too humiliating to broadcast, but, sweet Mother of God, it was happening. He barely listened to the learned father explain Richard's right to the throne, extol his upright nature, his piety and morality. He wanted it to stop.

"He is the true son of his noble father, Richard of York," Father Shaa droned on, "whose direct descent from Edward the Third has never been questioned. The lord protector is the spitting image of him. Not so his brother and our former sovereign Edward, whose mother herself once acknowledged he was not York's son, and thus did he doubly stain the throne with bastardy."

Richard held up his hand to stop the man's lies to little effect. The crowd, titillated by the idea that Edward might have been a bastard, turned restless and angry, and to his intense shame he could not summon up the courage to defend his proud mother. He hissed at Harry: "I suppose I have you to thank for this? Publicly insulting my mother was not anything we discussed. I am leaving."

As he gentled his horse around, he caught sight of Kate in the crowd, standing with Margaret Howard and staring straight at him. Why was she there, he wondered as his heart lurched. Her eyes were full of compassion, but, thoroughly disgusted with himself now, he could not bear to accept even a modicum of goodwill, and, turning his back on her and the still-blathering preacher, he made for Baynard's.

The castle yard was empty; everyone had been given leave to hear the sermon, and so he spent the next half hour stabling his horse to work off his frustration. How humiliating to be under his mother's roof and hear the defamation of her ringing in his ears. *Thank the sweet Virgin, she is at Berkhamsted,* he thought. It was no work for a duke, but mucking out the manure and piss-soaked straw seemed to him to be exactly what he deserved at that moment. I am no better than shit, he decided, noticing his fine leather boots were ruined. The task may have served as a penance, but it also put him in the mood to confront his presumptuous cousin.

"Never plan any public action without consulting me first," he railed at the astonished Buckingham, after having downed two cups of wine. "I assume I have you to thank that my noble mother was slandered. How dare you! How are we going to undo that wrong?"

Buckingham shrugged. "You worry too much, Richard. You do not seem to understand, it doesn't matter. *Alea iacta est*—the die is cast, and you will be king. If you had stayed you might have seen how Shaa turned the crowd around so skillfully—'England needs a man not a boy' he told them. They were moved to shout your name. The people want you as their king."

"Harry, you are exasperating," Richard growled. "I never know when you are lying. Besides, how many times have I told you, I really do not want to be king."

"God's bones, Richard, why so reluctant? You will not be alone, Cousin," Harry said eagerly. "You will have me at your right hand advising you. Together we shall be invincible."

"I'll have a whole council to advise me, Harry. So what do you propose to do next? I will accept nothing without the consent of Parliament, and we postponed that session when we cancelled the coronation." He picked up his square velvet hat, and went to the door. "As you are so keen, you deal with it. I shall go and find Anne."

"You do that, Richard. Leave everything to me," Harry reassured him. There were skeptics who would not have credited Buckingham with a plan, but it seemed Harry had it all worked out. "I am doing this for you, Cousin—all for you."

"For me? I have told you before I never wanted this. I am doing my duty for England, and that is all," Richard snapped and turned away.

But nothing could deter greedy Henry Stafford now with so much power within his grasp.

In fact, Buckingham comported himself brilliantly for the next three days, giving elegant voice to Richard's claim to the throne and the country's need for an adult leader. "'Tis never wise for a king to leave a boy as his heir," was the main thrust of his argument after touting Richard's legitimate claim. He well knew that the bastardy story had preceded him, and he doubted only a few of the dignitaries of, first, the lords, then the Guildhall and finally Parliament—or rather, a large enough gathering of that body to warrant it being deemed Parliament—had not already heard the news. Those present tasked with chronicling events for posterity would say that the duke of Buckingham's words were *so well and eloquently uttered, and with so angelic a countenance,* that no one had ever heard such an oration before nor did they question its sincerity. One scribe even mentioned that the duke was able to talk at great length *without taking pause to spit.* Buckingham was in the ascendant and even began to refer to himself a kingmaker. "Like my lord of Warwick," he boasted to Francis, who ominously retorted, "Let us hope you, too, don't turn your coat like he did."

It was as well that Richard stayed away; he would not have sanctioned the zest with which Buckingham denounced Edward's numerous indiscretions and his disregard of duty. No matter how exaggerated the lords and commons had found Buckingham's claims, however, the outcome was inevitable: Richard was their unanimous choice for king.

The days dragged by for Richard, and Anne attempted to calm and comfort him. At night, he took solace in wine, and yet he still could not sleep. He spent time with his inner council and had even invited several to stay at Baynard's, including Jack Howard and his wife, to facilitate frequent meetings. He was getting used to the fact he might be king, and he noticed how much more his councilors deferred to him.

One evening, after a walk around the ramparts with Anne to enjoy the balmy June air and the late summer light, Anne related a difficult meeting she had had that afternoon. She tried not to sound accusatory, but she could not hide her hurt. "Did you know your erstwhile leman was staying here with Margaret Howard?"

"Kate?" Richard stopped and turned to her. And then he remembered seeing Kate at St. Paul's. "I did not know she was at Baynard's, I swear. 'Tis true I told Jack that he and Margaret were welcome to stay, but I knew nothing of Kate's presence." He frowned. By God, this was awkward. Why, he might have run into her himself. He would speak to Jack directly.

"It seems Katherine asked her mother to come to the small solar, and I cannot blame her for that. I went in there unannounced and was confronted with mother and daughter talking and laughing. It was…uncomfortable," Anne said, staring over the wall towards London Bridge farther down the river. "Both Mistress Haute and I were civil with each other, but I let her know that I did not believe you would condone such an ill-judged visit—and in my own solar." She paused. "I want to know that I can trust you, with her being so close…"

Richard took her hands. "I swear you have no need to worry, my dear. When it comes to trust, I well know how hard it is to be betrayed by someone who swears to it, but I would hope by now you know that I love you and would never be unfaithful."

Anne smiled. "That is enough for me, my dear."

Richard pulled her to him. "Sincerely, I am sorry for your discomfort, Anne, and you are right that Katherine should have known better, but you are wrong that I would have denied the girl a chance to see her mother. I am certain Kate still pines for her children, and I am sure you can sympathize with her need." Despite being distressed for her, he felt the necessity to explain. "I cannot deny having loved both of you, can I?" And he let go of her to entreat her with his eyes.

Anne shook her head and drew his hand to her lips.

Richard grinned. "I cannot forbear to ask, were there no kind words spoken between you?"

"I invited her to sit, and we made conversation—for the sake of Katherine." She gave a reluctant smile. "I know now where Katherine gets her unruly tongue. And yes, at the end, when I succumbed to my usual coughing, Mistress Haute gave me the receipt for a posset to ease it. She seemed concerned," she had to admit.

"Then I am glad of that, Anne." He kissed her. "I have wondered at her bitterness. It wasn't easy for her to give up her children." He did not add, *and me.* "Come, let us go inside. I fear our peaceful hours together now will be few and far between, and I cherish them too much."

The very next day, Richard was proved right for his peace was shattered.

He was unprepared for the numbers of men who pushed their way through Baynard's gates and thronged the courtyard. Buckingham had informed Parliament that Richard must be persuaded to take the crown, and that the protector would only have the decision from the members themselves. It appeared the duke's gift of persuasion was boundless.

"As God is my witness, I did not ask for this nor do I want it," Richard told Anne, watching the scene below them from a window. " But I am going to have to accept it, am I not? For England."

For once, Anne could not mask her own nervousness. She was visibly pale. "I think so, Richard, but I am afraid." He drew her close and kissed the top of her head. Filled with misgiving, he had spent the best part of the night in the private chapel on his knees praying for guidance. He often avoided speaking directly to God now; the Virgin had a kind face and was easier to address. During these past few weeks, Richard had shunned their bed, so bad were his dreams. When the great bell at Bow Church had rung for prime, he had gone to break his fast no more able to accept the inevitable than the night before.

"I must go and greet them, Anne. Will you come with me?"

Anne shook her head. "It is you they want, not me. Go now, and hold your head high," she told him, trying to make him smile. "You are Cecily Neville's son after all." She pushed him towards the door leading to a platformed stair descending to the courtyard. Far from reassuring him, her kind comment took Richard back two dozen years to another terrifying moment in his life when his mother had made him and George walk through a scene of carnage and jeering soldiers to the Ludlow market cross. Strangely, he felt Cecily's presence with him at that moment, and remembering her courage, he unlatched the door and stepped into the sunshine.

"Richard of Gloucester!" Harry cried loudly, holding a roll of parchment in his hand. "Come forth and be recognized."

Richard approached the railing on the platform and held on to it like a lifeline. He scanned the upturned faces and recognized many from the weeks of meetings at Westminster, but many more were merely curious citizens who had pushed their way into Baynard's yard. His gaze settled on Buckingham, whose bright blue hat, golden curls and angelic smile reminded Richard of an oversized cherub. "I am here, my lord Buckingham. At your service," he said, surprised his voice sounded so strong. "To what do I owe the honor of these distinguished visitors?" Harry was grinning now, and Richard began to feel a little ashamed of the way Harry had planned this theater.

"My lords, members of the council, members of the commons, citizens of London and all present shall bear witness that this day Parliament petitions that the most mighty Prince Richard, the lord protector and duke of Gloucester, take to himself, as is his right, the crown of England." He read on from the parchment, a more formal version of Father Shaa's sermon, and ended by going down on one knee to declare: "Beyond this we consider that you are the undoubted son and heir of Richard, late duke of York, truly inheritor to the crown and royal dignity of England."

Despite his apprehension, Richard found himself moved to tears by the thunderous accolade he received at that moment. As the cries died down, Buckingham held up his hand for silence. "My lord of Gloucester, will you accept the crown?"

The crowd held its collective breath as Richard removed his hat and held it against his heart. He could still refuse, he told himself, and hesitated. But then, as he gazed down upon his cousin and the expectant faces of the onlookers, they melted into an earlier time in that very courtyard—a day when he had seen his father for the last time. He clearly saw his father walking towards him saying, "Now there is someone with fighting spirit." The memory faded instantly but the words had inspired him, and his voice rang out over the people: "I accept your petition. I will be your king, and I do it as my duty to my country." *Do I have enough spirit for you now, Father?* he thought, gazing skyward.

Anne came forward to join him, and they stood side by side thrilling to the shouts of, "God save the king! God save King Richard!"

"You are a good man, Richard, and you will make a good king," Anne whispered.

"Only with God's blessing," Richard answered. He was uncertain he could count on it.

In the dimly lit crypt, Richard knelt at the altar rail and contemplated the crucified Jesus, ghoulishly fashioned with hollowed eyes, a shrunken bloodied face, and a cadaverous body. His hands and feet were a gruesome pulp, cruelly caused by the crude, oversized nails.

"Richard of Gloucester," a voice spoke to him from the figure, "do you know me?"

As Richard watched in horror, the skeletal form disengaged from the cross and moved towards him. Richard shut his eyes and sank lower on his knees, praying hard.

The voice commanded: "Look at me! Do you know me now?"

Richard dared to look again and gasped. The face was King Henry's, and the bony finger, so often telling a rosary, pointed straight at Richard. "Aye, you do know me. See these bruises? They are from your fingers, the fingers that murdered an anointed king. And now you will be king? Why, you are not fit to wear my crown!"

Terrified, Richard rose and tried to make his feet move backwards, but someone was standing right behind him. He swiveled and came face to face with Will Hastings, whose bloodless lips pulled over his teeth into a grisly grin. "Aye, you might as well have held the axe, Richard Plantagenet, for you alone did murder me. Was it to take the crown?"

This time Richard lifted his hand out to ward off the specter. "I did it for England, my lord, I swear," he pleaded. "Leave me be, both of you."

"Are you trying to usurp my son's throne, Brother?" Edward's resonant voice accused as the larger-than-life figure of the late king glided towards Richard on ghostly legs. "You betrayed me and my son! Usurper!"

"Nay! Nay! I did not!" Richard shouted. "God knows, I did not!"

"Richard! Richard! You are having a bad dream," Anne's voice broke through his nightmare, and he sat up in bed with a start his nightshirt drenched in sweat. "Hush, my love, 'tis but a bad dream. All is well, I am here."

Richard was trembling. He fingered the cross and écu coin around his neck, hoping both charms would protect him from such hellish images as he had just seen. He had never been able to tell his wife about his part in King Henry's death. It was hard enough for him to own, much less expect his wife to understand or forgive. It must be his burden alone. "I dreamed I was accused of stealing the crown," he admitted. "Jesu, 'twas frightful. Should I refuse it even now, tell me truly?"

Anne slipped out of bed and opened the heavy shutter to reveal the dawn breaking. She hoped the light would chase away the dark demons of the night and of his dreams. She watched as Richard poured himself some wine and walked towards the daybreak, taking deeps breaths of cooling air. "There, that's better, isn't it?" She stroked his perspiring brow, noticing even more furrows than had been there before the news of Edward's death had changed their lives. "You have been working too hard and have so many responsibilities, 'tis no wonder you have nightmares. I will ask the doctor for a physic to help you sleep. We do not want to see the haggard shadow of a king mount the stairs to be anointed at his coronation, now do we?"

Richard attempted a smile, and gave himself up to her comforting arms. "I don't know what I would do without you, Anne. I do not deserve such devotion."

"Pish-tush," Anne scoffed. He wanted to laugh but could not; at that moment he thought he could never laugh again.

After Parliament set the date for the coronation as Sunday, the sixth of July, Richard went about his duties in a daze. He saw himself sign petitions and proclamations with his new signature Ricardus Rex; he assigned roles for the coronation; he conferred the dukedom of Norfolk on Jack Howard, and titled his son, Thomas, earl of Surrey; he bestowed honors on others who had supported him; and spent an hour with his nephews. Through it all, he was numb, barely discerning young Edward's reserve.

The one ceremony which brought him back to reality was the taking of the royal oath in Westminster Hall. He was fully aware of the enormity of the occasion and forced himself to appear kingly and robed in royal purple. He had witnessed Edward take his oath in 1461, and Richard felt a proud connection to his brother. Solemnly seated on the marble King's Bench, Richard was now officially named England's chief justice. After swearing the oath, he addressed the crowded hall:

"To all my judges and lawyers, I command you all to justly and duly administer the law without delay or favor. And to you, my lords," he addressed the barons present, "I require you, following the coronation, to return to your own estates and counties and make certain they are well governed and the people treated fairly and without extortion. It is my wish that my subjects know I am on the side of the law, and no matter if a man is rich or poor, he will receive justice."

The murmur of approval softened Richard's expression a little. So far, he had heard no jeers, and he began to believe he might be acceptable to the people as their king. Then he called Jack Howard to his side. "Go into the sanctuary and summon Sir John Fogge to come to me here," he commanded. Jack looked askance for it was well known Fogge, a former Lancastrian, was Elizabeth's closest advisor and had been on young Edward's council in Ludlow. He had insisted on accompanying the queen into sanctuary within the first week of her fleeing there. "Tell Sir John he need have no fear of me, but that I wish to see him."

A buzz of curious conversation greeted Jack's departure and filled the silence while Richard waited. Within ten minutes, the portly Sir John, looking puzzled and wearing a somewhat moth-eaten surcote, shuffled into the hall with Howard at his elbow. He bowed stiffly and gave Richard a haughty stare. "My lord?" he said, refusing to address the king as "Your Grace."

Jack was attempting to have the old man kneel, but Richard stayed him, rose from the chair and welcomed the Woodville favorite with a, "God's greeting to you, Sir John." Turning the astonished knight to face the crowd, he said: "You are free to go to your home and family without fear of reprisal. I would ask, however, that when you bid farewell to my brother's widow, you will take my promise that should she, too, decide to leave the abbey, she will be welcome at my court." Richard could no longer address Elizabeth as queen, now that her marriage had been deemed unlawful, but it would be a long time before he would demean her with her old title of Dame Grey. He may never have trusted the woman, but he believed she had been ignorant of the Butler pre-contract. That was all on Edward's head.

Richard accepted Sir John's surprised, conciliatory thanks. But immediately he wondered whether God could be appeased as easily? Richard could not say, but he hoped for some atonement.

Francis and Rob praised the Fogge conciliation as a brilliant signal to those dubious about Richard's election. He was beginning his reign on a generous high note. "I pray some of his tension slackens now," Francis muttered to Rob. "He has been tied tighter than the gordian knot of late."

Rob grunted an assent. "He threw a cup at a lackey yesterday and glared at me when I upbraided him. And he drinks too much."

"At least he still listens to us," Francis said. "Instead of widening his circle now that he is more comfortable with the council, it seems he has closed it. I just wish he could see what we see wrong with my lord of Buckingham."

"Softly, Francis," Rob murmured. "The pompous fool may hear you, and with his undue influence on Richard, we could be sent home with our tails between our legs."

In their eyes there was no end to Buckingham's rise, and they feared Richard was unable to refuse the glory-seeking duke the honor of assembling the coronation procession, which was by heraldic right the duke of Norfolk's purview. It was a slap in the face to Jack Howard, newly named to that dukedom, but Jack had amiably stepped aside. What other protocols was Richard willing to ignore to satisfy Buckingham's ambitions?

If there were doubters about Richard's path to the throne, it did not affect the huge numbers of visitors who poured through the city gates to enjoy the coronation festivities. Inns were even renting out stable stalls, makeshift camps were set up outside the city walls, and arguments broke out in the hundreds of taverns between well-aled customers, who had nothing to do but amuse themselves the days before the event. Richard was glad that the northern army he had sent for in a panic earlier in the month had eventually arrived, with Northumberland at its two-thousand-strong head.

Despite the Londoners' distrust of anyone north of the Trent, they tolerated the army's presence in Moorfields that ensured a trouble-free coronation. Who knew if the Woodvilles might attempt to disrupt the ceremony or even take the opportunity to steal into the Tower and abscond with the two boys? For this reason, Richard ordered his nephews be moved from the king's apartments into the queen's rooms in the well-guarded Lanthorne Tower and forbade their servants from allowing them to sport in public on the Tower Green. "At least until after London has emptied again," Richard commanded, "'Tis too risky. Out of sight, out of mind, I can but hope."

He and Anne went again to see the boys before the coronation, and this time both youths were ill at ease. Their guardian told Richard that the lads had received a few visitors, "including the Lady Stanley, my lord. Lord Edward said she came bearing loving messages from their mother, the queen, but I noticed a change in the lad's demeanor following her visit. He became angry with one of the gentlemen of the chamber and demanded to be taken back to his former lodgings."

Richard soon discovered why Edward had reacted so to Margaret Beaufort's visit. The boy confronted Richard, boldly. "Lady Stanley and my lady mother have heard you plan to send us away. She also warned us you may want to do us harm. Would you do us harm, uncle?"

Richard was appalled. "Do you harm? Why would I want to do that, pray?" Richard asked, gently holding him by the shoulders. "Fate has taken an unfortunate turn for you and Richard, but as soon as your mother leaves sanctuary with your sisters, I will return you to her side. This I promise."

On the day prior to the crowning, as had every king since the Conqueror before him, Richard journeyed with his court from the Tower to Westminster in a spectacular procession. Somewhere along the road through the city, he was suddenly reminded of the boyish fantasy he had had all those years ago as he rode to Edward's coronation. No longer a fantasy, it was indeed he who was riding to the great abbey to be crowned, and he reverently crossed himself.

Anne was seated in a litter carried front and back by two beautiful white palfreys, and all of her and Richard's henchmen wore scarlet satin with white cloth-of-gold mantles as they rode beside the royal couple. Behind them the cavalcade stretched for half a mile, buoyed by trumpets, shawms, sackbuts and tabors as the crowds thronging the route showered flowers and cheers upon the glittering column of riders.

Instructed by Anne to remember to smile and wave, Richard was complying with effort. A little girl bravely ran out among the horses and reached up to him with a nosegay of meadowsweet and cornflowers. Genuinely touched, he bent down and said: "I thank you kindly, sweeting, but I would like my lady to have them. I pray, will you give them to her?" Flushed with pleasure from getting a word from the king, she scampered back to Anne's litter with her gift. Anne took the bouquet with a smile, inhaled the sweet scent, and then asked one of the henchmen to lift the little girl into the litter beside her. The spontaneous gesture was greeted with a roar of approval from the Londoners. On turning to see what the fuss was about, Richard once again praised the Virgin and her mother, Saint Anne, for having given him the consummate consort.

Putting one bare foot in front of the other, Richard trod the cold, ancient flagstones of Westminster Abbey almost in a trance. Flanked by two bishops, he could see the archbishop of Canterbury and other clerics awaiting him and Anne at the end of a long tunnel of dazzlingly arrayed guests. Unlike the poor showing of nobles at Edward's coronation, Richard's was attended by every one in the realm, with the exception of those few who were minors. He heard the sublime voices of the choir raised in the *Te Deum* as if indeed they were far away in heaven, but the only thoughts crowding his brain were of how much he did not deserve this supreme honor. Aye, despite the many times he had bared his soul to his confessor and done penance for it, nothing could take away his dread of hellfire for committing a mortal sin; the guilt of Henry's death would always suffocate him.

But there was no turning back. So he kept his eye on Bourchier and somehow reached the high altar, upon which were laid the ampulla filled with anointing oil and its accompanying spoon. As soon as Anne's procession reached the steps, she joined her husband in kneeling on cushions, where they bowed their heads in private prayers. Anne managed to entwine her fingers in his as Cardinal Bourchier addressed the congregation.

"Sirs, I here present unto you King Richard your undoubted king: Wherefore all you who are come this day to do your homage and service, Are you willing to do the same?" Richard was startled by the shout of "God save the king" from a thousand throats. He rose to acknowledge his people's affirmation and take the coronation oath, which, at his insistence, was in English for the first time.

It was not until he was seated in St. Edward's beautifully gilded throne with the heavy crown placed on his head that Richard truly appreciated the sanctity of his new role. "Dear God, save the king," he pleaded, watching Anne being anointed beside him. "I pray You protect my family, and I promise to wear this crown with all honor and do my duty."

CHAPTER TWENTY-SIX
JULY 1483

July was stifling in London, and the city was stifling Richard.

The first thing he did after the coronation and its following feast was to pack up his household and move down the Thames to Greenwich, away from any threat of plague. The Palace of Placentia was indeed a pleasant place to live with lawns running down to the widening river. It had been Elizabeth's favorite residence.

As the oarsmen expertly guided the royal barge to the familiar wharf, Richard recalled his time there fondly while he had waited for King Edward to send him to Middleham. He also remembered it was the last time the three youngest York siblings had been together. They had all been so young and innocent in those first months of Edward's reign. Now George was dead and Meg, the dowager duchess of Burgundy, was far away in Flanders. Richard suddenly wondered if the news of Rivers' execution had reached his sister, rumored to have had a dalliance with the handsome earl. Another person to hate him, he mused with resignation. The longer he was king, the more that number would grow. He sighed.

For the first time in a week, Richard sat down to eat in the privacy of his own small hall with Anne and Harry as his sole companions. Still showing favoritism to Harry, Richard had given him the added titles of great chamberlain and constable of England and promised him the enormous earldom of Hereford, making Buckingham, in all but name, king of Wales.

Ironically, he did not fully trust Harry, but he needed him. Besides, Harry knew how to get things done.

With Howard now duke of Norfolk, Richard felt East Anglia was his, Stanley was strong in the midlands, and Northumberland could be counted on in the north. It was only in the south and southwest where Richard lacked a following, and he hoped by good governance to bring those provinces around as well.

Anne was complimenting the garrulous Harry for carrying off the coronation arrangements with aplomb, and they gossiped about some of the lords and ladies present at the festivities. Richard retreated into himself as he twirled the goblet carefully in his fingers watching the burgundy liquid spin. He was remembering a sweet moment during the presentations at the feast when he had come face to face with Kate again. He had indulged his daughter's request that her mother sit with her to watch the crowning, and she was presented to him afterwards.

Anne suddenly reached out and touched his left hand that was resting on the spotless linen cloth, and he looked up guiltily, as he did whenever thoughts of Kate trespassed on his mind. "Working on another problem, my love?" she asked, gently. "Come, why don't you leave those headaches for tomorrow. Harry is our guest and deserves some of your attention. He is tired of my appraisals of everyone's gowns, are you not, Harry?"

"Your taste is impeccable, my dear Anne, and so matches my own," he boasted. He turned to Richard. "Is there aught I can help you with, Cousin? I have spoken with Lawyer Lyneham about Jane Shore's punishment, and her penance will be carried out next Sunday."

Anne gave a little gasp. "Penance? Punishment? What kind of punishment? And for what? You told me there is no evidence of witchcraft."

"Aye, that appears to be the case," Richard said, his face darkening. "But she must pay for her harlotry. Not only did she lead my brother a merry dance, but she went straightways to Hastings' bed as soon as Edward was in the ground."

Anne winced at Richard's crassness, but she knew how much he blamed both Hastings and Jane Shore for Edward's demise. "What is her penance then?"

At Richard's hesitation, Harry gleefully enlightened her. "She will walk the streets barefoot around St. Paul's in naught but her shift and carrying a large taper. All of London will bear witness to her shame."

Anne said nothing. She stared at Richard, her eyes revealing her disappointment in him. She rose. "Goodnight, Harry. I hope you find your chambers comfortable," she said and excused herself.

Richard's gaze followed her from the room, knowing there would be more to say later. For now he changed the subject. "What do you know of Morton? I hope you have a good guard on him at Brecknock? I do not want him to have any chance to communicate with the Beaufort woman."

Harry smirked. "Fear not, Richard. His lordship of Ely is well guarded and, isolated as my castle is in the Welsh hills, he can have no contact with Lady Stanley. By the bye, it was a brilliant idea of yours to allow her to carry Anne's train at the coronation. If anyone believed that you suspected she was involved in the Woodville plot with Hastings, showing her such favor would have surely dispelled those ideas. It was a signal honor, and her husband was mightily pleased."

"Have I ever told you that I would not trust Thomas Stanley to take off my boots?" Richard replied, pouring himself more wine. "We must watch him and his wife carefully. Remember, she is the mother of the so-called claimant to the throne, albeit my brother was astute enough to exile the brat to Brittany." Richard sipped the ruby claret, savoring its sun-drenched bouquet.

"Henry of Richmond is no threat to you, Cousin. The Beauforts, by decree, cannot inherit the crown. You have more to fear from your brothers' sons than that Tudor spawn."

Richard stopped mid-drink and put down his cup. "My nephews? Why should I fear them? I am king because they cannot be. What nonsense is this, Harry?" Richard pushed his cousin to know why he would even mention the boys.

Harry poured more wine. "I know Stillington swore they are bastards, but suppose Dorset succeeds in securing them and whips up sympathy for their cause. There are still those who believe you were seeking the crown from the moment you took Edward at Stony Stratford and that Stillington was paid to lie."

"Christ's nails!" Richard exclaimed, rising from his chair. "I thought we were long past those rumors. *You* do believe Stillington, don't you? You were there when he came. I believe him, because Edward's lust makes that pre-contract with the Butler woman plausible. Did you know, by the way, that Elizabeth held him at knife's length before she got his promise to wed? If it weren't so tragic, 'twould be funny."

"I do believe Stillington, Richard, but there are enough who do not. Those boys are your blood and thus your greatest threat."

"Well, my lord Buckingham," Richard snapped, tired of the subject, "what do you expect me to do? Maybe you could, but I can't murder my own flesh and blood!" Hadn't Henry shared his blood? *Christ, it always returns to Henry,* he thought. He gripped the silver goblet hard and focused on the present. "Should I send them away—somewhere secret until my reign is more established? I do not want England to face yet another civil conflict." He looked directly at Harry. "Aye, mayhap that is what I should do. When Anne and I are well on our progress, and London is quiet again, it would be easy enough to send them somewhere remote. Now that Brackenbury is constable of the Tower, he must know a safe place north of the Tees to house them."

Harry shrugged. "Why don't you leave it to me to arrange. You have enough to occupy you before you set off."

Richard nodded absently. "I would be very grateful."

On his way to Windsor, where the court would gather before setting off on the progress, Richard took a detour to Chertsey Abbey. Shooing away the shoeless pilgrims from the modest tomb Edward had given King Henry in 1471, the abbot groveled his way in front of Richard when he was told who the plainly dressed man was riding up with several escorts. Richard gave the monk a weighty purse for the upkeep of Henry's grave and begged to be left alone with the former king's remains. He was not surprised by the number of pilgrims gathered there, as the abbey had become a shrine to the pious monarch, with even a miracle or two credited to Henry.

Waiting until the church was emptied, Richard prostrated himself in front of the cold, gray, stone tomb. "Forgive me, Your Grace," he began aloud, but fearing eavesdroppers, he fell silent. *Forgive me my dreadful sin,* he begged the king. *A day does not pass that I do not think of what I did. You are with the angels and have left me with hell on earth and worse to follow in Lucifer's domain. I pray that you will intercede with Almighty God for mercy, for I cannot believe He has forgiven me.*

An hour later, he emerged into the July sunshine and the queue of pilgrims fell on their knees in deference. As he went to retrieve his horse, he heard a man say to his neighbor: "A bit of a short-arse for a king, ain't he. And crooked into the bargain."

Richard winced, but kept walking.

The noisy, colorful cavalcade stretched along the roads and lanes of England for miles, following the new king as he showed himself to his subjects. Leaving Windsor on the twentieth of July with an impressive array of bishops and nobles, Richard was buoyed by the welcome he received as they passed through hamlets and villages and on to towns like Reading and Oxford. Having watched how Edward used pomp and ostentation to his advantage, Richard spared no expense on his jewels and clothing nor on his generosity to the towns he lodged in. In Woodstock, where, discovering that Edward had annexed a large tract of public parkland for his own hunting enjoyment, Richard returned the land for the use of the people once again. It was one pleasure of kingship, he thought, that he could redress some wrongs.

On those first days of his travels, he could truthfully say he was happy for the first time since consenting to be king. The delight and enjoyment of others who feasted at the many banquets he funded or who benefited from his gifts to the cities enhanced his own good humor. The king's party was entertained by Francis at his luxurious ancestral home, Minster Lovell Hall, alongside the pretty River Windrush. It was Francis who rode alongside him most days, Buckingham having taken leave to remain in London until the progress reached Gloucester. On the night Richard rested at the hall, he created Francis viscount as well as chamberlain of the king's household and chief butler of England.

"I am greatly honored, your grace," Francis publicly declared, but later in private he admitted to Richard, "I am overwhelmed."

Richard grinned. "It is the least I can do for one who has never let me down, Francis. I should be thanking you. As soon as Rob joins us, I will tell him he is to be my comptroller of the household and thus keeper of the privy seal. I think he will be pleased. I need my friends close." He helped himself to wine and stretched out his aching body in a high-backed arm chair. "I confess I am bone weary already. This progress is more exhausting than doing battle. But I am pleased with our visits so far. What do you think—and I pray you be honest with me."

"Then I shall be frank, Richard. When you are without Buckingham, you are easier to be with and, if I may say, you make better decisions. I still wonder why he chose to remain behind as he does enjoy showing himself off, you have to admit."

Richard was startled but attentive. "He is doing my business," Richard said, but gave no explanation. "So, he irks you that much, Francis? Do others feel as you do? I did not realize I indulged him or behaved any differently around him. I have to admit that I benefit from his influence with council, you must see that, but I will consider your advice about my judgment. Bad judgment makes a bad king, and I aim to be a good king. I hope you believe that."

Francis nodded. "I do, Your Grace. But there are times when I—and certainly Jack Howard—have felt pushed aside, not by you, but by Harry. I would just ask you to be cautious in your favor with him, 'tis all. Your position now is strong, but..."

"...there are those who call me usurper, I know, I know," Richard finished for him. "I need Harry to hold Wales strong for me, so giving him the Bohun Hereford estates seemed like a good idea. But I will take your words to heart, Francis, and watch myself with Harry. I thank you for your honesty." He lifted his cup in salute. "Here's to Gloucester on the morrow. I have proudly carried the name for all these years, and I hope the citizens will welcome me, despite my absences of late."

"You should have no fear of failure there, Your Grace," Francis assured him, "Gloucester will welcome you with an open heart."

Gloucester was to mark the end of the honeymoon of Richard's three-week reign.

The day began benignly enough with a walk along Ebridge Street to the market place where trumpets sounded his arrival and the mayor and aldermen knelt to their duke, now king. After several florid speeches of welcome, Richard addressed the crowd at the High Cross in his pleasant tenor.

"I would not be standing here today if your mayor and aldermen had not barred the gates to Queen Margaret's army a dozen years ago. Loyal to me as your duke, they obeyed my desperate request that she not be allowed access to the city. That action allowed my brother, the late King Edward, to array his troops at Tewkesbury instead of the more difficult and destructive military maneuver of besieging this city. For this I must thank you all, and in gratitude, I have granted your city a charter of liberties." A roar of approval met this statement, for the people knew that the arbitrary taxation and fines carried out by kings before Richard would no longer apply to Gloucester if it had its own charter. He also offered the mayor money to distribute among the citizenry, at which the mayor, consulting with his aldermen, declared: "We will not accept the money, your grace, for we would rather have your love than your treasure."

When Richard asked: "Is this true?" he was gratified by the unanimous shouts of "Aye!" from a thousand throats. "Then you have my undying love always," he declared.

It was an hour after the feast when the duke of Buckingham was announced, surprising Richard, who had withdrawn to his private office in the castle. Richard rose to greet his cousin with a smile and a slap on the back. "I am right glad to see you, Harry. I was not expecting you. I hope all is well or has London Bridge fallen down?" he joked, but seeing how flushed Buckingham was and that he was clearly withholding some news, Richard asked, "What is it?" and sat back down in his chair. This time it was Harry who took to pacing.

"You remember our conversation about removing your nephews from a possible rescue?"

Richard nodded. "We talked about sending them north, and you were going to speak with Brackenbury. I trust you communicated this plan to Sir Robert, and that he has a solution?"

Harry lowered his voice to an excited whisper. "Better than that, your grace, you need never again worry for your crown. I have taken care of the boys. They pose no threat to you anymore. They are with God."

They are with God.

As the awful truth sank into Richard's brain, the smile vanished from his face and, as the bile rose, it turned his color to a green-gray and his eyes to blazing orbs of fury. "Are you mad!" he cried in a hoarse whisper. "Did the Devil himself spawn you? The boys cannot be dead. They were under *my* protection," Richard rose and menaced his cousin, who stared at Richard aghast. Richard grasped Harry's arm and jerked him as far from the door—and unwanted ears—as he could.

The bigger man, Harry threw off Richard's hand and felt for his dagger. "I did it for you, Richard. I did this for you! I thought 'twas what you wanted," he cried. "You said you could not kill your own flesh and blood, and that you wanted me to kill them. You told me to take care of them. Good Christ, I thought you would be pleased." Sweet Jesu, he could see from the murderous look in Richard's eyes that he had read his cousin wrong. He desperately tried to think of something clever to say, but his silver tongue betrayed him into a babbling of excuses and blame. "It was Brackenbury's idea," he finally lied in desperation.

Outraged, Richard propelled the bulky Harry into the garderobe out of anyone's earshot. "Sit down," Richard commanded, and pushed Harry onto the wooden seat. "Do not lie to me," Richard threatened. "Brackenbury would never risk his eternal soul by sanctioning or committing such an act. But it seems you would, my lord. Now tell me exactly what you have done."

Little by little Richard coerced from the nervous duke the details of how he had so easily taken possession of the boys, being that he was the mighty duke of Buckingham and was acting on the king's orders. Thus who would not have believed him? Richard listened in horror as Harry described duping the boys with a story that he was sent by the king to rescue them from people who wanted to harm them, and that their Uncle Richard would protect them. Richard gasped at the lie. His nephews went to their deaths believing he had ordered this atrocity. Dear God, how much more could he take? But for his nephews' sake, he would hear the whole sorry story. He grasped the neck of Harry's doublet."After you lied to them about me, what then?" he demanded.

Harry forced Richard's hand away. "I had to lie to get them to come. Besides, 'twas not a lie," he retorted. "You were going to send them away."

"Not without a proper, carefully devised plan sanctioned by the council," Richard snapped. "You acted alone, my lord."

Harry tried again to turn the tables. "It was a misunderstanding, cousin; I thought I was acting on your orders."

Richard snorted. "Enough of your excuses. Continue with your execrable story."

Harry stared at the floor as he related how he had hurried the boys away in the middle of the night in a small boat and rowed them to a wooded place upstream from Westminster. "I knew those woods were thick and no one would hear or find them. I urged them to rest under a tree as we had a long journey the next day..."

So outraged, Richard had to interrupt. "Those poor children. They must have been terrified. What kind of a monster are you? And you a father yourself! Go on, give me the rest of it. God help me, I am listening."

"I swear they were not afraid. Edward believed I was taking them to Wales—to safety—and he calmed his brother. Said it was an adventure. When they were asleep, I...er," and he was barely audible now, "...I smothered them, took off their rich clothing, covered them up with ferns and branches, and rowed back to the city."

Richard slid down the wall to a sitting position, his head in his hands. For the first time since taking the reins of state, he felt powerless and utterly alone. Appalling images flooded his mind of the boys enduring the same terror and blind panic he had known with George and the cushion, and seeing the abandoned bodies of his brother's children either decaying or being eaten by animals. In disbelief he asked, "You did not even bury them? How cruel and how stupid. Someone will discover them, and you will be found out."

A gleam of hope made Harry lift accusing eyes to Richard and he rose from the debasing seat. "But I will tell them I was acting on your orders, Your Grace. That I was merely your instrument. Do you know how many who already think you usurped the crown will believe me? I warrant a lot." He was not prepared for how swiftly Richard could move until the fist hit him square in the face, and he fell back onto the seat clutching a bloody nose.

For once Richard knew Harry was right. What was he to do? He alone was responsible for raising up his cousin to lofty heights. All had witnessed that the two were hand-in-glove from the moment they arrived in London from Stony Stratford with young Edward. Harry had been a comforting voice and right-hand man since then, and he had welcomed his only royal cousin to his side. So who would believe that Harry had acted on his own? No one. And if he did accuse Harry, very few people would believe the two of them had not planned this heinous act together. Why else would Buckingham have stayed behind in London and not taken his place on the progress? He could hear the accusations now: "They have murdered innocents," and he put his fingers in his ears. It would be his word against Harry's, for surely Harry would swear Richard had been complicit. Had he really led Harry to believe he had intended such a monstrous act and would have issued such an order? Nay, surely God knew he had never had such an evil thought.

He stood over his cousin staring at him with new eyes, knowing now he had been wrong to trust Harry so blindly. The image of little Richard wriggling in his sleep to catch a breath as Harry held his hand over the pert nose and cherubic mouth sickened him so painfully that he had to puke. He shoved Harry off the garderobe seat and vomited down the chute.

Buckingham crawled out of the confined space and was attempting to stand, when Richard once more pinned him against the wall. "Christ's nails," he spat in Harry's bloody face, "I trusted you, and you have betrayed me." He grasped his cousin's elegant jacket and pulled him closer. "Hear me well, my lord, for this is what you will do. You will leave immediately and finish what you started, you monstrous murderer of children. Do not return until you have properly disposed of the bodies, do you hear?" Harry nodded obediently, and Richard released his grip and walked past him into the office. "God damn you, Harry," he lamented, "you have made both of us complicit, and thus you have consigned both our souls to hell. God knows I shall never rest again." He pointed to the door. "Now, go! Get out of my sight!"

Nobleman that he was, Harry held a kerchief over his nose and left the room in a dignified manner, but he seethed. Hadn't Richard secretly desired the boys' deaths? Harry had not enjoyed the act of killing them; in fact it had been repugnant. But he was an ambitious man, and if the two brats were a threat to Richard's crown, then they were a threat to Harry. Richard should be grateful to him for taking on the task, not insulting him. He was a royal duke after all and did not deserve such treatment. As his self-esteem fell, his resentment mounted, and once out of the city gates, Harry did not hesitate. He urged his horse into a gallop and took the road west to Wales and home, ignoring the royal order to return east to bury the boys. "Let them rot," he said into the wind.

Inside, Richard was slumped in a chair weighing the enormity of the crime his cousin had committed *in my name,* he bemoaned. The murder of innocents was the most heinous of sins, so the scriptures taught. *Even worse than regicide,* he never needed to remind himself. He imagined his own little Ned being so callously smothered, and he groaned. He rose and locked the chamber door, not wanting to be disturbed while he knelt and prayed for the souls of his brother's sons.

He remembered young Edward's telling words from their last meeting, asking, "Would you do us harm, uncle?" Richard shook his head violently at the memory. *Nay, Edward, I swear I never meant you harm, so help me God.* But no comfort came, and he knew he did not deserve any. God had truly forsaken him. His chest heaved with dry sobs as he begged his brother's forgiveness. They were gone; Edward and Elizabeth's beautiful young sons were gone.

Francis was glad when Rob Percy joined the progress as they approached the great abbey at Tewkesbury, where Richard had a mass said for the souls of George and Isabel, buried together in the Clarence vault. Contemplating George's ugly death did not lighten Richard's black mood, but he thought how fortunate George was that he had died before Edward left England in such scandalous turmoil. *And now I have Edward's sons' souls to atone for,* Richard reflected somberly.

"How long has he been like this?" Rob asked Francis as they waited outside for Richard to emerge. They stared south across the fields where, a dozen years before the decisive battle took place that vanquished Lancaster once and for all, or so they had thought then. The prince of Wales, Edouard, had been killed fleeing that field and was buried somewhere inside the majestic church. It was said George of Clarence had killed the prince himself, and if so, then there was irony in both men lying side by side in death.

"It began the day Buckingham arrived in Gloucester then just as swiftly departed. Richard locked himself in his room for several hours, and I was told the duke had ridden off in a fury." Francis shook his head. "Richard has not made mention of Harry since. It is passing strange."

Rob chuckled. "Good riddance, I say. How long have we wished the clown would be humbled? Perhaps Richard finally saw through his guise. He knows our opinion of the duke, and mayhap he spares himself an 'I told you so' from us. 'Tis as well we go to Warwick next. I have seen to it that the queen is comfortable there, and she awaits Richard eagerly."

"Anne will buoy his spirits, I have no doubt," Francis agreed. "And Richard will be even happier when Ned is reunited with them, although I wish it were sooner than a month hence."

When they asked, a few days later, if Buckingham would catch up to them, Richard gave a terse response.

"Perhaps," he said and mounted his horse.

Richard had never been happier to see Anne, and she was elated to have such a positive effect on her husband. The first night of feasting at her father's favorite castle was boisterous, full of music and laughter, helping Richard to relax and his two friends to breathe more easily.

But Richard's first nightmare came that very night. In his cups and unable to bring lovemaking to a much needed climax, he fell into a fitful sleep. His flailing awakened Anne as the watch cried out the hour after prime. She lit a candle and shook him. It was a hot August night and her nightshift was damp with perspiration, but Richard's was drenched. She thought he had a fever.

"Wake up, my love," she urged him. "You are dreaming. No doubt you had too much wine."

Richard shuddered. "Not wine, Anne, but fear. Fear for my immortal soul."

Anne held her breath. What could be troubling him so? She rocked him but wisely kept silent; he would tell her when he was ready. As long as he still loved and needed her, she did not care to know his every secret, she had long ago decided. It was sometimes best for secrets to remain secret. But Richard was clearly in distress, so she gently prodded him to unburden himself.

"Tell me what ails you, Richard. There is nothing that would shock me anymore," she said, teasing. "Unless you have found another mistress." She could have bitten off her tongue as Richard roughly pulled away from her. "Forgive me, that was foolish. But tell me Richard, I insist."

Richard began pacing the chamber, hugging his arms to his chest. He wanted to tell her, but his guilt was so profound, he doubted even Anne would understand or forgive the morass he found himself in. Nay, Anne was too kind and gentle to hear a tale of such appalling cruelty. And so he told her a half-truth.

"Harry and I have quarreled, Anne. More than quarreled; I am not certain we can be reconciled. You only need to know that I was in the right, and Harry would not accept it. He betrayed my trust, and that is all you need to know."

"He will recover," Anne said, brightly. "He likes his position near you too much to stray."

Richard returned to his place beside Anne and stroked her sandy-colored hair. "I expect you are right, my dear. Now, let us try and sleep."

The farther north the king traveled the more rapturous his reception became. Pageants and plays were presented to him in Leicester and Nottingham before the royal procession crossed into Yorkshire and on to Pontefract. The extensive and many-towered castle, once called the kingdom's most fearsome fort, was visible for miles, and it was difficult to avoid noticing the spiked heads of Rivers, Grey and Vaughn so recently set above the gate. Richard and Anne spurred quickly across the short drawbridge and rode under the gatehouse to the best of all welcomes.

"Mother! Father!" Ned's happy cry reached their ears as he raced across the bailey to greet them. Anne turned shining eyes to Richard and mouthed, "Thank you," as the castle residents—Yorkshiremen all, who possessively looked on Richard as their own lord—cheered the returning couple. Originally, Ned was to have met them at York, but Richard thought to surprise his road-weary wife, who had had to resort to riding in a litter for many of the miles since Leicester.

Richard had already dismounted when Ned, with Rufus at his heels, flung himself into his father's arms. It was hard to say who was more excited to greet him, Ned or the wolfhound. Smothering the boy with kisses, Richard hoisted him in front of Anne, who wrapped her hungry arms around her son. Holding the rein, he lead his little family to the steps of the turreted keep set high on the motte. Richard greeted his subjects as Anne and Ned were helped off the palfrey.

"I have never been more pleased to see Yorkshire again than I am now," he told the exuberant crowd. "Although I am your king and have my duty, you here in the north have my heart."

Ned was a joy to be with for the weary Richard and Anne. He had grown an inch since Richard had left Middleham, and his parents were pleased with his progress in Latin. They were even more delighted to witness the real affection he and his half-siblings demonstrated upon being reunited. Richard could not have been prouder as he sat and watched his children laugh and chatter together. Katherine, at nearly fifteen, was a lovely young woman and, more disconcerting for a protective father, a honeypot for the young men in his train. Perhaps it was time to think about a husband for her. As she filled out, she looked less the image of Kate and showed some of his own expression, so Anne said. Nevertheless, Katherine was a daily reminder of his first great love, which at once continued to comfort and discomfit him.

And then there was young John. Confident, friendly and intelligent, he could go far, although he would always be hampered by his bastardy— just like his nephews would have been, Richard thought with chagrin.

If Richard felt fêted enough over the past six weeks, he was to be overwhelmed by his homecoming to York. The citizenry was dressed, according to the mayor's edict, in blue, violet or grey. All the arras and tapestries in the city had been collected and were decorating buildings and stages, where pageants played out, and music floated up from every street corner. Tumblers tumbled, children strewed flowers, and young girls danced through the streets, ribbons and tresses flying behind them. Richard was enchanted as he rode at the head of this most splendid of retinues.

When the mayor, extolling the new king to the townspeople, presented him with a golden cup filled with marks, Richard came to a sudden decision. He would not wait until returning to London to invest Ned as prince of Wales, he would do it here in York. In an astonishingly short time, a delivery of countless garments for his household, coats of arms, banners, pennons and White Boar badges fashioned for the ceremony arrived from the keeper of the Wardrobe in London.

And in the magnificent minster on the eighth day of September, the investiture of Edward of Middleham as prince of Wales took place to the great rejoicing of the city. On the same day, he acknowledged his love for his older son, John, by knighting the suitably awed thirteen-year-old. It has been said that the investiture and subsequent banqueting was even more lavish than Richard's own coronation. And by formally crowning his heir, Richard's reign appeared to all to be stamped with legitimacy and blessed with longevity.

Knowing how valuable his former position had been for Edward, Richard formed a new Council of the North, putting his oldest nephew, John de la Pole, the earl of Lincoln, son of his sister the duchess of Suffolk, at its head. He decided Northumberland was best positioned in command of of the important Scottish marches. Richard established this second royal household at Sheriff Hutton and put his other nephew, George's son, under Lincoln's guardianship. Although he had stood next in line to the throne after King Edward's sons, young Warwick was also ineligible to wear the crown due to Clarence's attainder. But Richard had anticipated the danger of an enemy using the lad as a figurehead for a possible uprising, and he hoped the Yorkshire moors might put the boy out of sight and out of mind.

Anne asked to return to Middleham with Ned for a period, and although Richard was loath to say farewell, he knew she would regain her strength there and granted her request. Besides, he needed to go south and quell a new rebellion before it spread. How quickly his euphoric but ephemeral reception in the north had evaporated. As well, he was perturbed that Harry had never returned or sent word that his grisly mission was accomplished. It had been reported to Richard that the duke was now spending time on his estates in Wales. "Sulking, I expect," Anne had said.

"I am trusting you to look after your lady mother, Ned," Richard told his son, who was seated beside Anne in the horse litter. "You are near to ten years old and almost a man."

Ned held himself erect. "I shall do my duty, as you have taught me, but when shall I see you again, my lord Father?"

"Perhaps we can share the yuletide season together in London." Richard smiled at Ned's excited nodding. "We shall have a Christmas fit for a king." Both Anne and Ned laughed at the joke.

"Something to anticipate, is it not, sweeting?" Anne said, leaning back on the cushions as the horses began to move away.

"Aye," Richard said, blowing them a kiss. "Only three short months."

His last view of them as they disappeared through the castle gateway was of Ned leaning out of the litter and waving gaily.

Richard knew he had stayed away from London too long when he heard even more worrying news, this time from the duke of Brittany. It had to do with Margaret Beaufort's exiled son, Henry Tudor, earl of Richmond, the pretended Lancastrian claimant to the throne. All those years ago, Duke Francis had promised to house Tudor for Edward in exchange for Edward's support of Brittany against any possible war with its neighbor

France. King Louis was now threatening war with Duke Francis unless Tudor was handed over to the French.

"Brittany is so certain I fear Tudor that he expects me to send 4,000 archers to ward off the French. " Richard told his privy councilors upon arriving at Lincoln. "My brother may have feared a Lancastrian challenge, but Richmond is a Beaufort and, as such, has no right to the throne."

Lawyer Catesby felt obliged to remind them all: "By decree of Richard the Second, upon legitimizing John of Gaunt's Beaufort bastards, they should never be eligible to wear the crown."

The other three nodded remembering that Henry of Bolingbroke had ignored the decree, usurped the crown as Henry IV in 1399, claiming right of conquest, and then begat the Lancaster line. It was a sobering reminder for the group.

"Is anyone else concerned about Henry of Richmond," Richard asked, feeding the faithful Rufus a tidbit from his discarded plate of roasted rabbit, "or shall I tell Duke Francis to heave the annoyance over the French border?" He motioned to one of his gentlemen to pour him some wine. Without Anne to admonish him, he was drinking more heavily to alleviate the tension of each day.

"I think we have more to worry about on our own doorstep," Francis said. "Who do you think is behind this latest incursion? Surely, with Elizabeth guarded at the abbey, her cohort Hastings dead and buried, and no sign of her son Dorset..."

"The degenerate!" Richard interjected. "I have it on good authority he has been bedding Mistress Shore. That woman has an appetite for trouble. I had all but cornered Dorset after his failed attempt to rescue my nephews, but he has fled London. He can be of no help to Elizabeth now."

"The merry mistress conquers anew," Rob chuckled. "I can't help but admire her initiative."

Richard grimaced. "I fear I shall have to prosecute her again, this time for harboring a fugitive." He went to the window. "But let us focus on the problem of unrest. Do we believe the trouble has arisen over my kingship or does the discontent stem from Edward's mismanagement?"

John Kendall looked up from the sheath of papers he had on the table next to him. "If I may interrupt, Your Grace, but here is a letter from Queen Elizabeth." He handed it to Richard, who broke the seal and scanned the unruly writing.

I am writing to beg you to allow my sons to join me here in sanctuary. I have heard rumor that they are dead—murdered in the Tower by your own hand. I do not believe it, and thus, appealing to you as a father and my erstwhile friend, I request you prove me right and bring me my boys. I remain, your brother's faithful wife and queen, Elizabeth.

Richard paled. If the rumor of the boys' death had reached Westminster sanctuary, then it must have spread throughout London—and thus, how far outside? Was this what the rebellion was about? Then it was a lot more serious than mere discontent over taxes.

He stared out of the window weighing if he should tell these few loyal friends what Buckingham had done. He had confessed harboring the secret to his chaplain, but no one else knew the atrocious truth—except Buckingham, of course. How long before the man's silver tongue divulged the deed and then blamed Richard? *Dear God, I could be brought down by such a lie!* He resolved to reveal the secret now. How much better for his friends to hear it from his lips than to discover it for themselves upon their return to London. Besides, he needed help to handle the unrest.

Rob broke into Richard's thoughts. "What does the Grey Mare want now, Your Grace?"

"She wants her sons restored to her," Richard said quietly, still with his back to them all. "It is the one thing I cannot do for her, God help me." He turned and dismissed the gentlemen of the chamber so that only Francis, Rob, Will Catesby and Ratcliffe remained, all staring at him curiously.

"Why is that, Richard?" Rob spoke first.

Richard rasped in a low whisper, "Because they are dead." Crumpling the parchment, he threw it on the floor. "They are dead, God forgive me."

After the initial shock, the close-knit group of loyalists debated a course of action. It was Catesby's nimble mind that latched onto the one possible, plausible pathway to dispelling the rumor. "You said Buckingham told the boys' servant that he was taking them to safety at your behest, am I right? Then who are we to deny that 'truth?' You sent Buckingham to remove them in secret somewhere—let us say 'abroad.' At that point, Buckingham must see, like the worm he is, he will be off the hook and acquiesce to save his arse. Who will dispute you? You are king, and who will dare demand of the king to show the lads' faces?"

Francis let out a low whistle of admiration. "If that story is circulated immediately, no one will believe Harry if he now comes forward to say you had him murder the boys. It will sound ridiculous."

"'Tis a plausible story indeed, William," Rob Percy agreed and grinned at the young lawyer.

Richard smiled for the first time in days, and he slapped Catesby on the back. "I am grateful for your legal mind, Will, and I think your idea may save the realm from further conflict. I will summon Buckingham to return and tell him in person. He must agree for his own good. It must be the same tale: the boys are somewhere secret and safe. I will even write to Brackenbury and thank him for allowing Harry to take the boys from the Tower on my behalf."

Then he shook his head sadly. "Foolish Harry truly believed I would be pleased by what he had done and was confounded when I was not." He nodded at Catesby. "'Tis a masterful solution, and I hope I can persuade Harry to share in it—and return to the fold." He harrumphed. "That is when he has finished brooding in Brecknock."

Richard could never have anticipated what happened next: Henry Stafford, duke of Buckingham, turned his coat.

Not two days later, Richard received the intelligence that Buckingham was the acknowledged leader of the rebellion that had interrupted Richard's progress.

As though he had received the shock physically, Richard doubled over in pain as Jack Howard's son relayed his father's urgent message from London. Thomas, now earl of Surrey, quickly handed the king a cup of ale and suggested that Richard sit. "Allow me to tell you what we know, Your Grace," he said, as the room began to fill up with advisors, stunned by the news. The young man could not guess that Richard already knew the real reason for Buckingham's defection, and that his letter to Harry had been too late—or ignored.

Surrey's father was holding London against Kentish and Sussex rebels, while in the west and Wales, Buckingham was at the head of the rebel force intent on combining forces with the eastern contingent. Jack Howard believed the Woodvilles and their allies were to blame for the rebellion. "Margaret Beaufort has been seen at the abbey visiting the queen, and we intercepted a message on its way to Wales for John Morton, bishop of Ely.

The two have been in correspondence it would seem and, with the queen, are plotting to remove you."

Thomas paused, watching Richard slide his ring on and off his finger as he processed the information. Suddenly, Richard made a sound that was part laugh, part growl. "And here is irony. I sent Morton to Brecknock so he could whisper treason in Harry's ear," he said. "*He* is the one I should have executed, not Hastings. Let me borrow from my ancestor, the first Plantagenet, who famously said, 'who will rid me of this meddlesome priest.' Morton the manipulator; Morton the flatterer; Morton the deceiver; he is the snake who has bitten Buckingham and infused him with poison." His control slipping and his voice shaking, he muttered, "I pray you excuse me, gentlemen, I need some air. Thomas, continue with your intelligence so Kendall here can chronicle it."

"Your Grace, would you like me to accompany you?" Francis offered, stepping forward.

"I thank you, nay," Richard answered, walking slowly to the door, his head heavy on his crooked shoulders. Harry's betrayal was too great to comprehend, but he needed to be alone to try.

He trudged up the spiral stairs to the ramparts with only Rufus for company and faced the glorious west front of Lincoln Cathedral a few hundred feet away high on the hill, its soaring central spire reaching to heaven. Richard hardly noticed its beauty as the cool, damp October air reflected his gloom. Two guards were making their crossover on the northern wall; otherwise, he was alone.

Angry thoughts of his cousin raged around his brain like untamed animals, but all eventually returned to one place: betrayal. What had pushed Harry to treason? To break his sacred oath to his king? Richard recalled Harry boasting one night of taking a leaf from Warwick's book: "I am a kingmaker," he had crowed. *Aye,* Richard thought, *and like Warwick you have betrayed your king.*

He groaned. How had he come from Edward's death to crisis after crisis in only six months? When he had started out from Middleham that bright April day grieving for his brother and intent on being a strong protector of the young boy king, he had felt confident, sure of his purpose in life, and a happy family man. Fortune's wheel had spun him around so many times since then, he was dazed. Sometimes it felt things were not happening to him at all, that he was floating aloft watching himself react, no longer in control of anything. Harry had had a hand in turning that wheel, he could see that now, and Richard had gone along with him, reluctantly at times. And now Richard was king with too many deaths on his conscience already. Guilt and despair gripped him with icy fingers, and he steadied himself against the battlement.

Turning and leaning over a crenelation, he glanced down from three stories to the grassy banks below. He immediately felt a queasiness and instinctively stepped back. Something intangible tempted him to look out again, and this time saw in the green carpet beneath him a possible end to his terrible turmoil. If he could just let himself float down into its soft embrace, his trials, his sorrow, and his wretched life would be over in a second. *Sweet Jesu, let me end my misery. I am already damned to hell, so what is one more sin?* Summoning the courage to indulge himself in ending it all, he leaned out over the wall farther, sending a shower of loose stones cascading to the ground. How easy it would be to follow them, to know no more...

"*And You would leave Ned and me alone, Richard?*" Anne's voice in his brain was as clear as the shout of warning from one of the guards that jolted him from his self-destruction. Rufus gave a responsive bark, and Richard jerked himself erect. He waved off the guard and quietened the dog.

He shivered. How close had he come to self-slaughter, he wondered, dispirited and afraid. He slid his back down the damp wall to sit with Rufus, who nuzzled his master's wet face.

"Good dog," he praised him, and then looked up to heaven. *Tell me this, Lord, were You not content enough to give me this pathetic body? Have You not denied Anne and me more children? Taken my brothers from me? Have You given me this crown as reward or curse? And now You have Harry betray me*" He gave a harsh laugh. *Ah, and lest I forget. What punishment will You give me for the deaths of my sweet nephews. I know I shall take the blame.*

Aloud, he cried: "Dear God, have pity on me! How much more must I endure to satisfy You? In Jesus's name, I can bear no more." He buried his face in Rufus's rough fur and let the dog's devotion ease his broken heart.

Little by little, as the drizzle turned to rain, despair turned to resolve, and Richard's spirit began to revive. He lifted his face to the heavens and made a heartfelt promise: "I will be a better king. I will take care of my subjects, if You will take care of me and mine, O Lord. Let me atone for my past sins by ruling well. I vow I will be strong and do my best for England."

CHAPTER TWENTY-SEVEN
WINTER 1483

The old Richard was back.

At least that was how Francis and Rob perceived their friend and king following Richard's decisive action to suppress the widespread rebellion. They had cheered when Richard had returned from the rooftop and declared: "First things first, I will rid the kingdom of its traitors and in particular my cousin, surely the most untrue creature living."

He had issued a proclamation that denounced Buckingham as a rebel and traitor, ordered the Great Seal to be delivered to Richard in its white bag, and called his loyal subjects to arms. With two of his great lords, Northumberland, and Thomas, Lord Stanley, he moved to Leicester, where his troops were mustering, and pondered a move to defend London. When news came that Jack Howard had neutralized the East Anglian and southeast insurgency, he marched in the pouring rain to Coventry, intent on sweeping the southwest and Wales clean of rebels, including their leader, the perfidious duke of Buckingham. Others declaimed were Thomas, marquis of Dorset, the queen's brother; the bishop of Salisbury; and one of the chief plotters, John Morton, bishop of Ely, who had ridden with Buckingham from Brecknock.

But two women were also colluders—two mothers in fact—each believing her son was the center of the rebel cause, so Richard learned. It was clear to him that Elizabeth must believe young Edward was alive, and he came to the swift decision that she did not deserve to hear the truth from him. *Let her believe the boys had been sent away.* Margaret Beaufort, on the other hand, must know they are dead from Morton and Buckingham, and so her cause was simple: to set her son Henry on the throne. For a moment, Richard felt sorry for the queen; the cleverer Beaufort woman had tricked Elizabeth into supporting Buckingham, promising that he would return the crown to young Edward. By this time, Richard was convinced Harry's only goal was to take the crown for himself—his claim, in truth, was better than Tudor's. "Batfowling scoundrel," he muttered, "and bloody fool."

A few days later, Richard issued another proclamation hoping to avoid as much bloodshed as possible: *The crown promises to pardon any man who was duped into following that great rebel and traitor the duke of Buckingham, and the bishops of Salisbury and Ely, or the marquis of Dorset, whose damnable maintenance of vices make them traitors, adulterers and bawds.*

Thomas Stanley chuckled. "I assume you are referring to the adulterer Dorset? Isn't that language a little strong, my lord?"

Richard did not hesitate. "That is what he is, Lord Stanley," he snapped. "Do not forget he was mentored by Hastings to lure my brother into debauchery, and he is bedding my brother's whore. I would prefer my court to be safe for virtuous and God-fearing people once more."

Northumberland suppressed a smile. While Richard was Lord of the North, the earl had become used to Richard's moral preachings. Stanley could only grunt an assent; he was not about to argue with the king when he himself was already under suspicion by virtue of his wife's involvement in the rebellion. It was as well Stanley had been with Richard since leaving Yorkshire and had mustered a goodly number of troops to Richard's banner or he, too, might have been suspected of abetting Margaret Beaufort and John Morton.

"We march on the morrow, my lords, despite the foul weather," Richard told them. "We should have news of where the bulk of their force is by then."

Never was Richard more thankful for the disagreeable English weather than he was that October. Perhaps God had heard him on the Lincoln battlements. The rivers to the west swelled and overflowed to bog Buckingham's reluctant, resentful troops in the mud, and storms in the Channel forced Henry Tudor's small invading fleet back to Brittany. Unable to unify, the rebels scattered and fled. By the time Richard and his force reached Salisbury, the rebellion was over "with nary a drop of blood spilled," as he proudly told Anne later. Much of the success was attributed to Richard's leadership. He had acted quickly and decisively.

"I shall have only the captured leaders executed, all the rest, the commoners, are pardoned. Let them go back to their homes with my blessing," Richard told his new constable, Sir Ralph Assheton. "It was always my brother's custom to spare the commoners."

Two days later, on All Hallow's Eve, as news of the fate of the other rebel leaders filtered into Richard's council chamber in the cathedral close and after ten executions had taken place, Francis barged into the room to announce: "Buckingham is taken, he is being led to gaol as I speak!"

Richard leaped out of his seat, elated. "Where was he found? Who can I reward?"

How glad was Richard to discover that Buckingham in his turn had been betrayed. "Now perhaps you know how it feels, Harry," Richard muttered under his breath, "and how fitting it was done by a servant." He turned to Assheton. "You will try him on the morrow and give me a report. I have no doubt his lordship will wet the axeman's blade before this week is out." This time, there would be no quibbling as to the king's meaning.

Any mercy for his cousin Richard may have held in his heart was expunged when he heard that it had taken only the threat of torture to convince Harry to deliver up his fellow rebels. Richard felt relieved and disgusted. Harry begged his guards to take him to the king, and when Richard refused to see him, Harry then sent his cousin a pathetic, pleading letter.

> *I appeal to your goodness, your mercy and your renowned sense of justice to spare my life, Cousin. I pray you remember our friendship, my invaluable support, and our many shared ventures on your path to the crown. Have you forgotten our shared blood? I beg of you to reconsider having my death stain your conscience...*

That was enough reading for Richard. *Damn you, Harry, murderer of children,* he thought, *if you believe I will count your traitorous death among my many sins, you are even more foolish than I now know you are.* And he flung the letter into the fire.

The garrulous, vain and once-powerful duke of Buckingham was led to the scaffold the very next day. Visibly terrified and surrounded by jeering townspeople, he stumbled up the hastily constructed stairs to face the hooded executioner. Shivering in his fine lawn shirt against the cold November air, he fell on his knees to be shriven by the priest before gingerly placing his neck upon the block. His treasured glossy curls, always so meticulously coiffed, fell over his face, hiding his shameful tears. Then his nerves took hold of his body, and a guard had to steady him as the axe was swung high and swiftly brought down to end Henry Stafford's faithless life.

Watching from a window, Richard did not flinch.

With the rebellion quelled, Richard turned to governing in earnest. He first sent out a summons to all the lords and commons to convene at Westminster for a session of Parliament in late January.

Returning to London in early December, it was clear to him from the reception he was given by the grateful citizens that he had been accepted wholeheartedly as king, especially as, with her complicity in the rebellion acknowledged, Londoners had lost all sympathy for Elizabeth Woodville.

Richard welcomed Anne to London for Christmas but was disappointed that Ned was not well enough to travel through the cold and snow.

"It is nothing serious, Richard," Anne assured her husband as they snuggled together on her first night in London. "I would not have come if I thought our son were in any danger. He had the croup—he has had it before, but it takes a week or two to subside. Never fear, Mother will take good care of him."

"Has he grown? Does he miss me? Can he hit the quintain squarely?"

Anne was amused. Richard was so full of questions, the way she remembered him from their childhood, that her heart glowed. She stared up at the beautiful canopy above the bed in the spacious firelit chamber at Westminster, the tapestry depicting a scene from the story of Ruth, and answered every one. Later, she whispered that she preferred Crosby Hall's intimacy, but that "this is more comfortable than drafty Baynard's." She began to caress his chest and tease his nipple, which soon achieved the desired effect. "Never mind Ned," she said seductively, sliding her petite body on top of his. "Have you missed me? Or have you found a mistress while I was away."

Richard smiled and took her face in his hands. "If only I had had the time," he said, feigning regret. "And even Jane Shore is no longer available. Oh! Would you believe she has conquered yet another willing fool—this time my own solicitor, Thomas Lyneham. He was supposed to prosecute her but he fell in love with her instead. They are to be married."

Anne's laughter roused Rufus, curled up on the Turkey carpet. He put his whiskered nose on the bed and wagged his tail.

"Lie down, Rufus," Richard admonished him, and, chastened, the old dog padded away. "Now, my dearest wife, where were we?" He slipped Anne's chemise over her head and pulled her to him. Soon the rediscovery of familiar urges and intimate places put all but pleasuring each other from their minds.

Their passion slaked, Anne lay content in Richard's arms. She sighed pleasurably. "I love you, Richard," she whispered. "The Virgin help me, but I love you more than God."

Richard stiffened. "Do not say such things, dearest. You need not bring down His wrath on you as He has on me."

Anne sat up and turned to him. "What now, Richard? What do you think you have done now to displease Him?" Richard would not meet her gaze and instead tried to pull her close again, but she resisted. "Can you not be happy for once? I pray you, tell me your troubles. How can I be a good consort if you can't entrust your worries to me? If you won't trust me, then I cannot be happy. 'Tis as simple as that."

"'Tis not so simple, my precious wife," Richard replied. He rolled awkwardly onto his right side and then to a seated pose next to hers. Their shadows in the candlelight flickered eerily on the curtain, and he flung it aside. *She is right, we must trust each other,* he suddenly decided. And so he confided in her the tragic tale of his nephews' deaths at the hands of Buckingham.

Anne stared open-mouthed at her husband, and then she reached out and took his hand. "You have lived with this since July, Richard? How have you borne it, my love? 'Tis no wonder you are not sleeping and are afraid for your very soul." Tears rolled down her cheeks as she imagined the plight of the two innocent boys. "'Tis monstrous, and Harry deserved to die."

"You must swear to keep silent, Anne. Most believe they are sent far away to safety. Let them think that, and soon the lads will be forgotten— except by you and me, and a few close friends." And he spoke their names.

"Poor Edward, poor Richard. Those boys had done nothing to deserve such a fate...other than being born royal," Anne realized and shivered. Both knew they were thinking of Ned.

Richard then spent much of December dealing with the continued harassment of English shipping by the Breton fleet. With the capable Jack Howard as admiral of England commanding the English Navy, Brittany was quickly subdued, and Duke Francis eventually signed a new treaty with Richard, admitting his error in having supported Henry Tudor. Before Duke Francis could hand the young earl over to the English, however, Henry escaped and found refuge in France.

"*Bon débarras!*" Richard told the council. "Good riddance."

With rebellion dead along with its self-proclaimed figurehead—Buckingham never ceased thinking to the end that it was all about him—the court settled down to celebrate Richard's first Christmas as king. He was determined to make it a merry one, and he chose to hold it at Baynard's instead of at the vast palace of Westminster. Duchess Cecily had been invited to join them, but she claimed that a dislike of traveling in winter prevented her presence. To tell the truth, Richard was relieved he did not have to answer any awkward questions his mother would have asked.

Even though the death of his nephews haunted him daily, it surprised and saddened him that they seemed to have been forgotten elsewhere. No one spoke of them anymore; it was as though they had never existed, he thought. *And, God help me, I am not about to remind them.*

Two days before Twelfth Night, Richard received another surprise—this time one that pleased him.

He had chosen an eminently suitable husband for Katherine, and knowing Kate was staying with the Howards at their Stepney town house, he wanted her to meet their daughter's bridegroom. Although it had been sporadic, Richard and Kate had exchanged a few letters about their children over the years. Their bond had turned into one of deep friendship, and he wanted to honor her now. He sent Rob Percy down the river to fetch Kate and then paced in his privy audience chamber awaiting her arrival.

Her lovely face fell when she saw him, and he was concerned. "Are you ill, Kate?"

She shook her head. "Nay, Richard, not I. But I see that you are. You appear to have had no sleep for several days."

"Weeks, if truth be told," Richard admitted. "I look that bad, do I?"

Kate nodded. "Do you have something important to tell me, Richard. You have never before summoned me. Has it to do with John or Katherine?"

Richard smiled. "Aye, but I think you will be pleased. I have found a husband for Katherine. William Herbert is the earl of Huntington and a loyal Yorkist."

Kate's eyes lit up. "An earl? Can this be true? My Katherine?" Then, in her inimitable frank fashion, she added, "but does he know she is a bast....?" and immediately clapped her hand over her mouth.

Richard chuckled. "Aye, he knows of her birth, Kate. But as he is an impoverished earl, he will be glad of the dowry I will bestow on my beloved only daughter. She is a beautiful and kind young woman, and we should be proud of her."

"I am," Kate replied, "and I always have been. She was created with much love." She lowered her eyes to her hands, wondering if she had overstepped a line. Richard watched her absently turning the gold filigree ring he had given her the day they had parted. Suddenly looking up, her eyes met his, and as if he were reading her thoughts, Richard pulled out the écu on its leather cord. "Aye, I still wear it." He hesitated, averting his troubled gaze. "Although I am not certain it has always brought me good fortune."

Kate felt emboldened to go to him and take his hands, encouraging him to talk as they had done so many times during their affair. She gently removed his soft velvet hat and stroked his dark hair, noticing its flecks of grey. "What is it, Richard? What is worrying you? Tell me."

Feeling her so close again and sensing her love for him, he broke his resolve and allowed her to lead him to the window seat. He could trust so few these days, but Kate he trusted with his life, and so, with difficulty, he disclosed the fate of the young princes to her.

Certainly Kate was not unmoved by the tragedy. "'Tis one of the most hideous tales I have ever heard," she pronounced, but her concern was all for her beloved, and she guessed he did not need her sympathy; he needed her counsel. She took his hand. "Richard, you must not brood so," she began. "Do not allow your enemies to see you so low. 'Twas not your fault. Lord Buckingham's evil is not yours."

Richard jerked up his head. "God knows I did not order their deaths, but because Harry did it for *me*, I must carry the guilt. Do you see?" He implored her to understand. "It will always be *my* fault."

"Stop this, Richard!" Kate said, shaking him. "God *knows* you did not order their demise, you just said so. You must put it behind you. It is over, and you are king. Nothing will change that now, and so you must get on with the business of governing. Your people need you; they need to know what a good and just man you are."

Despite his present self-loathing, Richard was desperate enough to listen. Kate's advice was sound, and her passionate conviction that he was indeed a good man helped convince him. He patted her hand. "You are right, my rose. I do need to look to England's welfare. Doing my duty has not been easy, I admit, but I have sworn an oath and I must fulfill that promise. I thank you for reminding me." He smiled for the first time.

Kate smiled back. "That's better," and she changed the subject. "Indeed, 'tis I who should thank you for the mercy you showed my cousin Haute for his part in the rebellion. How can I ever show my gratitude?" She picked up his hand and kissed it.

"You have given me two beautiful children, Kate," Richard said softly. "That is payment enough," and gently releasing her hand, he rose to pace, heartened by their talk.

"Three…" Kate said without thinking. "Three children."

The king stopped mid-pace and stared at her. "What are you saying?" He went to her. "Three? Tell me truly, was there…*is* there a third child?"

As his reaction was sheer loving surprise, Kate continued, "Aye, I bore you another son six months after your marriage to Anne, and he is named for you. Please do not be angry with me." Flustered by his silence, she plunged on. "You were not to know you got me with child on our last night together, and I chose not to tell you because I knew you had promised God you would go to Anne with our affair at an end. I could not burden you with having to lie to her."

Richard sat down hard in his chair. He had another child—another son. "Does Johnny know? Katherine? They have…they have never said aught about another brother. All…all these years and nary a word…sweet mother of God…"

Kate chuckled at his stunned stuttering. "Dickon was born in secret at my family home in Kent. The children did not know. As you must recall, my husband died before John was born, but his family believed our two children were their grandchildren. They never knew the truth about us, and they had been too kind for me to visit this scandal on them—that this child could not have been George's. I traveled to Kent before my belly gave me away, stayed until I gave birth, and my brother John and his wife agreed to raise our son as their own." She sighed. "He does not know me, and only my brothers and the Howards know of him."

Richard was speechless. Kate had given up her child to protect him. He could not conceive of such selflessness. It took him a moment before he spoke. "Jack Howard knows how to keep a secret, in truth. I am profoundly sorry for your sacrifice, Kate. What can I do to help the boy? Tell me."

"He is better off thinking he is a Bywood. I, too, have felt guilt that I have never even seen him since he was a baby, but I have sent what money I could. Lately, I arranged with my brother Geoffrey, who is now the schoolmaster in Ightham, to teach Dickon his lessons, although," and she smiled, "it would seem he prefers woodcarving to Latin. The boy is very happy, truly he is."

"Dickon," Richard repeated, a soft smile on his mouth. "'Twas my name as a child. He is in Kent you say? Then I must do what I can for him." He could almost feel his spirits lift. "Can I see him? Is it possible?" He saw her frown. "I promise not to reveal myself to him."

Kate hesitated, but seeing how Richard's eyes had lost some of their sadness and his face its careworn expression, she could not refuse him. "You swear Dickon will not know you as his father."

"I swear."

"Then I will write and warn Geoff to expect you."

Dickon was another secret Richard kept from Anne. He was consumed with curiosity about the boy in Kent, and he soon found an excuse to travel to Thomas à Becket's shrine at Canterbury to ask the saint to bless his first session of Parliament. En route, he bore off towards the village of Ightham, where Kate had spent some of her childhood. He went alone with only a groom in attendance as he did not want to attract attention. Even so, his clothes spoke of wealth, which brought the villagers out to stare when he asked the way to the schoolmaster's residence.

Although Geoffrey Bywood had been very young during Richard and Kate's liaison, he knew immediately who the man was who slipped off his horse to the frozen ground outside the modest cottage where Geoff lived with his young wife. He began to kneel, but Richard murmured that he did not want to arouse suspicion. "Call me Master Broome," Richard told him, liking the simplistic translation of Plantagenet. "I do not want Dickon to be afraid. Say I am a merchant who has heard of his skill with a knife and might perhaps buy one of his woodcarvings."

"Come inside, Your Gra...Master Broome. You must be cold," Geoff said, ushering the king into the cozy but plainly furnished kitchen parlor, where the family spent most of their day. Through the door into the adjacent schoolroom, Richard saw an orderly row of desks empty of pupils at that hour. A roaring fire drew Richard to warm his hands as Jane Bywood entered. Richard observed she was taken aback by their visitor, and he silently admired Geoff for keeping Kate's secret.

"Dickon!" Geoff called up to the second floor, reached by a sturdy open staircase. "We have a guest. I pray you come down, and bring some of your carvings."

Richard's heart beat a little faster as he heard his son's footsteps hurrying to the stairs. He could not remember being so nervous when he had met Johnny. Would the boy look like himself at ten? Would he be short and thin like Ned or stocky like John? He was therefore, surprised to see a mirror image of Katherine at the same age descend the stairs. An almost girlish face peered over the banister: freckles smattered over a small nose; a generous mouth; and a mop of thick auburn hair that reminded Richard of Kate's magnificent mane. The familiarity immediately put Richard at his ease.

"Dickon, please greet our guest the way you have been taught. Master Broome has ridden here especially to see some of your work," Geoff said sternly.

Dickon gave an awkward bow and stared openmouthed at the man by the fireplace. Despite trying to dress quietly, Richard's deep-blue surcoat bordered in fur, his long leather boots, and beringed fingers, dazzled the young country boy. "G...God's greeting, sir," Dickon managed to stammer. "I am Richard Bywood, if it please you, but I like to be called Dickon."

It gave Richard a start to see the boy close and recognize his own serious, dark-grey eyes looking back at him. He smiled. "Then Dickon it shall be. Why don't you show me what you have made, Dickon?"

He winked at Geoff, who drew Jane into the schoolroom to leave father and son alone.

The boy displayed half a dozen exquisitely carved figures of animals of the forest for Richard to peruse. "Do you like them, sir?" Dickon asked eagerly.

"I like them very much, Dickon. Would you permit me to buy one?" He picked up a fox and could almost swear the animal's brush tail was real. "Because you have red hair, like a fox, this one would remind me of you. How much would you like for it?"

Dickon's mouth opened and closed. "I d...don't know, Master Broome. How much will you give me for it?"

Richard laughed. "Good answer, Dickon. Remember, everything worthwhile is deserving of negotiation, and this little fellow is certainly worth it. How about a penny? Oh, I see that is not enough. I apologize, then would a groat suffice?" And he reached into the pouch at his belt and drew out the silver coin.

Dickon's eyes glowed. "I thank you, sir," he said, holding the money in the palm of his hand as though it were gold. "I am saving up for more tools. You see, I want to be a mason when I grow up. Do you think that is possible, sir?"

"If you want something badly enough—and you work hard, pray to God every day, and obey your uncle—anything is possible." He tucked the fox inside his shirt and chuckled. "I shall give this to my son, Johnny. 'Tis said he behaves like a fox in a hen house when he is around the young... not that you would understand, young Dickon," he hurriedly added.

"Fiddle faddle!" Dickon retorted, grinning and for a moment forgetting Richard was a guest. "Of course I know."

Richard was so unnerved to hear Kate's favorite expression, he rose and picked up his cloak.

Dickon blanched, suspecting he had upset the grand visitor. "I b...beg your pardon, sir. Did I say something to offend you? My father always said my tongue would get me into trouble one day."

Just like your mother, Dickon, Richard thought, amused. His heart ached for Kate at that moment, but reaching out and chucking the boy under the chin, he said kindly, "I am not offended, Dickon. Far from it. You have lightened my day. Now run along while I talk to your uncle."

Geoff was astonished by the generous stipend Richard promised to send every year to help with the boy's board, lodging, and education. "See to it that he finds a good mason to apprentice with, Master Bywood. The boy has a true gift."

Richard rode on to Canterbury, his mind going over the extraordinary encounter. He did not blame Kate for keeping knowledge of the boy from him. After the turmoil of his own life as a royal prince, he envied Dickon his simple life. If only he, too, could have been an ordinary man. He patted the fox hidden in his jacket and marveled that he and Kate had produced such a prodigy. Had the lad been forced into the royal household, his talent would have been stifled. He decided to honor Kate's wish that he not interfere in the boy's upbringing except for the monthly stipend. How he wished he could have put his arms about the innocent lad just for a moment—his own flesh and blood.

Suddenly, his thoughts were all of Ned. His unruly hair, his lopsided smile and cheerful nature. He realized then how very much he loved and missed his heir and vowed to send for him as soon as the snow was off the northern moors.

Richard's only Parliament opened on a frosty day in late January with a lengthy oration from England's chancellor, John Russell, bishop of Lincoln, who proudly praised the body politic that was Parliament but that, under Edward, had lost its way. "Like the lost tenth coin of the woman in Christ's parable, we look to our new sovereign to cleanse our house and recover what was lost: good governance and fairness for all people."

Seated on his throne, Richard observed the depleted ranks of barons and bishops ranged around the bright walls of the Painted Chamber, with the commons crowded in on benches in the center of the room. His family's war with Lancaster had certainly taken its toll on the nobility, he realized. He was not naive enough, however, to guess the failure of some to attend was a lack of support for his claiming the throne. As well, some of the dead nobles' heirs were still in swaddling clothes, but it was a poor showing of the lords indeed. No matter, he was determined to enact the reforms that he and his council had labored over for weeks.

But first there was old business.

In a move guaranteed to please the new king, William Catesby had been appointed speaker of the house by the commons. He began by reading a document entitled Titulus Regius, an act of settlement or formal ratification of Richard's right to rule by the three estates of the realm: the lords spiritual, temporal, and the commons. With Richard's insistence that any one of his subjects should be able understand the document, it set out in English many of the justifications for Richard's crowning that Buckingham's proclamation had made the previous June at Baynard's.

As Catesby's somewhat nasal reading went on, Richard, anxious to get beyond this part of the proceedings, wondered what the many members staring motionless at the floor were thinking. He knew many men had questions as to his own motives and actions and what had happened to the two boys, and he had heard the malicious monikers. He looked calm, but he felt far from it. Every day he feared that the tide could turn on the shifting sands of men's loyalties and at any time someone might leap up and shout "usurper" or "murderer." He knew rumors abounded about another possible Tudor attempt to invade and claim the crown; such unease haunted him day and night. Richard had to consolidate control, and he hoped to God this Parliament would ratify his right to rule.

However, all was proceeding smoothly, and he breathed more easily as he heard the final statement of the important document read:

And over this, that, at the request, and by the assent and authority abovesaid be it ordained, enacted and established that the said crown and royal dignity of this realm, and the inheritance of the same, and other things thereunto within the same realm or without it, united, annexed, and now appertaining, rest and abide in the person of our said sovereign lord the King, during his life, and, after his decease, in his heirs of his body begotten."

Catesby then moved on to the bills of attainder for the autumn rebellion. Buckingham, Dorset, John Morton and more than ninety others were attainted, and all of Margaret Beaufort's estates were confiscated and, rashly Richard thought, put in the hands of her husband, Lord Stanley.

Last but not least, the bill addressed Queen Elizabeth. As soon as Richard had been informed that a secret marriage contract between Henry Tudor and Elizabeth's oldest daughter, Bess, had taken place at Rennes— on Christmas Day of all days—Richard had lost all patience with her. "It means Elizabeth must now believe her sons are no longer alive," he deduced, grimacing as he talked with Francis. "She is seeking another way to regain power."

"Now you have lost me," Francis answered. "Why should betrothing young Bess to Henry help…. Christ's bones! I see," he cried, slapping his forehead. "If Henry does invade and capture the crown, then Bess will be queen of England! By all that is holy, the Grey Mare's a canny one." He paused and then blurted: "But why does that mean she believes her boys are dead?"

"Because, muttonhead, if Henry does become king and goes through with the marriage, he will not agree to wed a bastard and have her crowned," Richard explained. "He would have to legitimize her and…"

"…I have it!" Francis interrupted, excited. "It would make all of Elizabeth's children legitimate and thus, if young Edward were still alive, he would be the legitimate king!"

Richard nodded. "Ergo, Elizabeth must believe the boys are dead."

Attempting to cheer Richard, Francis had said, "But their plan has only an outside chance of succeeding. Tudor cannot have the support he needs to overthrow you—not while he has spent the last decade abroad and you are here, the anointed—and chosen—king of England."

But Richard, in a dark mood and doubting God's favor, had harrumphed. "Anything can happen—as I well know. Poor Bess, I warrant she had no choice in the matter. A sweet child with a witch for a mother."

And thus, as punishment for her part in siding with the exiled Henry Tudor, Elizabeth—like Margaret Beaufort—had all her lands and titles stripped from her, relegating her to plain Dame Grey.

"'Tis fortunate for both of them that England does not execute traitors of the fair sex," Francis remarked, "for both of them deserve it."

The most important business to be debated in the three-week parliamentary session were the laws and reforms Richard was proposing. Thanks to his stint in the law courts and his many years meting out justice as constable of England, no one could question Richard's ability to draw up fair and just reform, even though he must have angered some barons and merchants in the process.

The first act, however, was enthusiastically received as Catesby read: "The king, mindful that the commons of this his realm have been enslaved by intolerable charges and exactions as the result of new and unlawful inventions and inordinate covetousness, contrary to the law of this realm, and in particular by a new imposition called a benevolence..." He looked up and saw astonishment and approval on many faces. King Edward had imposed these so-called benevolences upon his people, which was nothing short of robbing the poor to feed the king's coffers for possible use in war. Richard remembered how unpopular the collection of them was for the foolish French campaign. Unlike borrowing from bankers or the rich merchants, Edward had impoverished his subjects and pocketed a pension from King Louis into the bargain. Richard was determined to end the practice.

As Anne told him, after he had outlined his reforms to her one quiet afternoon spent in her solar, "You will be remembered for protecting the poor and the powerless. Surely many of these acts—how many are there, fifteen?—will end the many injustices inflicted on commoners that you have talked of. I am so very proud of you, my dear." Richard was grateful for her support, but he knew he would lose favor with those corrupt officials who had benefited from these taxes. He just hoped the commoners would thank him.

Certainly, they would benefit from another reform he was proposing in the jury selection process, in which he insisted that a man must now be judged by property owners of upstanding character who were respected and invested in the community and not by just any vagrant, paid lackey, or warm body brought in to stack the jury. This law, it turned out, would stand for centuries.

Later in the session, Richard was to receive approbation for a statute that had been in his mind for several years—ever since he had encountered the distraught woman in St. Alban's on his way to London. The law had said her husband's property could be forfeit as soon as he was taken into custody yet was not formally indicted of a crime. Richard's new law decreed that bail be made available to someone in custody before being indicted, in the same way that a man ready to face trial might be. If a man were innocent, he could return home knowing his property was intact.

The final decision he made after all the new bills were ratified was that they be written down in English so all, from high to low, would understand.

Richard hoped God was taking notice. *Am I atoning for killing a king— who was a good man but a bad ruler?* It was the only way he thought might appease the Almighty now.

In the middle of March and after many assurances that she would not be punished further for her part in the rebellion and could return to Grafton, Dame Elizabeth Grey agreed to leave sanctuary with her daughters.

"I am sorry for you, Elizabeth, but you cannot deny you deserved it," Anne said to her sister-in-law the day before Elizabeth was to finally quit sanctuary. "You gave Richard no choice. It was treason, Dame Grey. If you had been a man, you would have lost your head."

"Pish!" Elizabeth said dismissively as she contemplated the new queen. Anne was a good match for the under-sized, misshapen Richard, she thought. Small, attractive, but not beautiful, Anne had always appeared a bit childish to the older woman—wishy-washy even. However, her new power had given Warwick's daughter confidence; confidence enough to scoff at Elizabeth's new loss of prestige. Elizabeth shrugged. "Believe what you want."

"'Tis not a question of believing," Anne insisted, "it is a question of knowing you plotted with the Beaufort woman and that odious bishop to put Henry of Richmond on the throne. You even agreed to betroth your daughter, Edward's beloved Bess, to that Lancastrian upstart."

"Do you blame me? He promises to legitimize my poor children," Elizabeth shot back. "I do what I can for them. Is that not what we mothers all do? And, may I point out, Henry Tudor is no parvenu; he is the Lancastrian heir to the throne." She sat back, a smug smile on her face. She doubted Anne knew yet, as they bickered here, that another attempt at invasion was being planned for the spring. Elizabeth would take her daughters home to Grafton Manor, the only residence left to her now, and await the event. With help from the French and those exiles gathered with Henry—including her son, Dorset—she had no doubt Richard would be deposed in short order. She wished she had proof he had killed her boys, but all she knew was they were no longer alive. Her son, Dorset, had heard it from the now-executed Buckingham. *Hearsay is all it is now,* she lamented.

Anne regarded the still-lovely widow with a mixture of sympathy and disdain. Anne was not a woman to hate easily, and Elizabeth had never done anything to hurt her. But she knew she had the upper hand and was emboldened to state: "Edward would never have condoned such an unholy alliance, and you know it. Where is your loyalty?"

"Pah! You speak of loyalty in the same breath as my philandering, lying husband—oh, no, I am forgetting, he was not my husband, was he?"

Elizabeth's claws were showing, and she needed to control them before Richard changed his mind about allowing her to leave. Because she could, Elizabeth chose to bring tears to her blue eyes. "How would you feel if Richard had lied about loving you all these years? That he had secretly loved someone else so well he had pre-contracted with her?" She was so self-absorbed, she failed to see Anne wince. "And now I am left with nothing to offer my six daughters. Can you not see, Anne? I had to at least help Bess to a future. And what about my boys...my poor *bastards*..." she broke off, dabbing at her eyes, "I have lost my boys ..."

"Aye, you have my heartfelt sympathy for them, Elizabeth," Anne broke in not unkindly. Best not to travel that path, she thought. "but you must look to your daughters now." She could not blame Elizabeth for wanting what was best for her children. Would she not do the same for Ned? She softened her tone. "As I said, I am sorry for you, but I am here to tell you that Bess and Cecily are welcome at our court, and Richard has promised me that he will find suitable matches for them—and your other daughters when they are of age, if you will allow him to help you." She looked across the refectory where the two older girls sat quietly sewing and pitied the boredom they must have endured shut in a cloister for almost a year. "I must commend you, they are exquisite."

Elizabeth inclined her head at the compliment. She knew this was not a suggestion from Richard but a command. Richard would need to keep Bess close in case Henry Tudor spirited her away, married her, and used her to shore up Yorkist support.

Elizabeth rose. "Pray tell the king I will consider his kind request," she said. "If that is all, then I shall wish you a good morning." She made to leave, but seeing Anne's raised eyebrow, she asked, "I beg your pardon, did you have anything else to say?"

"Only that one does not usually rise before the queen and dismiss her," Anne said evenly. The quick flush of embarrassment on Elizabeth's face gave Anne immense satisfaction.

But Elizabeth's bravado only lasted long enough for her to concede that Richard's offer to protect her daughters was both generous and a relief. The dreary life in sanctuary was grinding her resolve down, and once accepting that there was no chance her boys would suddenly reappear, she gave her girls permission to leave. She grunted her reluctant admiration as she read a transcript of Richard's oath taken in front of the lords: *I, Richard....promise and swear that if the daughters of Elizabeth Grey, late calling herself queen of England...* She paused to mutter before moving on, "but I *was* anointed queen," *... will come to me out of the sanctuary and be guided, ruled and conduct themselves after me, then I shall see that they shall be in surety of their lives, have them honestly and courteously treated...and to have all things requisite and necessary for their exhibitions and findings as my kinswomen....* The next sentence finally broke Elizabeth's reserve: *I shall arrange marriage for them to gentlemen well born, and give every one lands and tenements...* Elizabeth sighed. "Where would I now, as disgraced Dame Grey, look to find husbands for my beautiful girls," she moaned to her last faithful lady. "As innocents, they deserve nothing less than what Richard offers."

Richard also extended Elizabeth an adequate annual stipend, which would allow her to return to live quietly at her manor of Grafton if—and the written declaration made it clear—Richard never heard any reports of duplicity or disloyalty from her.

Being a schemer, Elizabeth looked for a motive behind Richard's seeming generosity. The only feasible reason was that he intended to keep a close eye on Bess in case Henry Tudor decided to snatch her and make good on his Christmas promise. But, she sadly admitted to herself, Henry had had ample time and an easier opportunity to carry out an abduction from sanctuary and had made no attempt in that direction.

"It is the best I can do for you, my dears," she told her five older daughters. She had decided the baby, Brigid, would stay with her.

Thus, with the glimmer of hope that one day Bess would be queen, Dame Elizabeth Grey conceded defeat. She emerged from the abbey a suffocating year after seeking its sanctuary. She would have been mortified to see how quickly her daughters embraced life at Richard's court.

By mid-April, Richard's fear of an invasion from across the channel compelled him to move north to Nottingham Castle, an impressive stronghold perched on a promontory, centrally located and giving him a commanding view to the south and west. Underneath, and dug into the bared sandstone hillside, ran a labyrinth of tunnels up into the castle, useful for an escaping royal in times past.

"How I envy you your return to Yorkshire, my love," Richard said, kneeling to remove Anne's tiny green slippers. After being readied for bed by their servants, taking off Anne's shoes and stockings had become a tender task Richard had long ago insisted should be his. The intimate gesture often led to lovemaking that Anne looked forward to whenever they shared a bed.

"I am glad you will soon be with Ned," Richard continued, stroking her thin calves as she caressed his bent head. "Do you realize it has been six months since I saw him, more's the pity. 'Tis too long. I pray every day that whatever ailed him this winter will see him healthy now spring is here, and he can soon join us."

"Mother says he is growing, so I am not concerned. Perhaps the sea air in Scarborough will do him good. I will take him there when it is warmer." She yawned, pushed her husband away and got into the comfortable downy bed. "I confess I cannot keep my..." She did not finish as they heard unexpected sounds of an arrival in the courtyard.

"Who can that be at this hour?" Richard muttered, going to the window. His nerves always on edge, he assumed the worst: Henry Tudor, earl of Richmond, had landed.

But the news was far worse.

Francis Lovell knocked on the door requesting immediate entry a few minutes later. Anne slipped on her bedrobe while Richard flung open the door. Francis and a muddied messenger in Richard's own livery stepped into the room and went down on their knees.

"What is it?" Richard demanded, noting Francis's pallor. "Is it Richmond?"

Francis rose and glanced at Anne in the bed. Her eyes spoke of concern but not fear, he noted, and he took a protective step towards her. The messenger, astonished to find himself in front of a king clad only in his nightwear, looked up and cleared his throat. "I...I have a message for you, your grace, from...from Middleham," he stammered and handed Richard a letter. Clammy fingers wrapped themselves around Richard's heart as he tore open the letter and read the few devastating lines from his steward at Middleham.

Anne flew to his side. "What is it, Richard? Is it Ned? Sweet Virgin, is it Ned?"

The floor was moving beneath him, and Richard was no longer able to stand. "Oh God," he groaned, falling to his knees and reaching for Anne.

"My dearest wife, brace yourself." He pulled her close and held her face between his hands. "Our little Ned is gone. He's dead!"

Anne screamed, "How? When? Tell me!" A vile taste invaded her mouth, and she puked the bile onto the blue and white tiles, smattering Richard's nightshirt.

Richard tenderly wiped her mouth with the towel Francis had found for him, and when Anne insisted again, he told her: "It seems he took ill of a fever a few days ago and nothing could be done to cool the heat in his blood." He watched her tears fall, and cradling her to him, he, too, began to heave with sobs. "He is dead, Anne, our precious son is dead."

Francis touched the messenger on the arm and jerked his head towards the door. The man, open-mouthed at the openly weeping royal couple, gladly got to his feet and preceded Francis out. Francis gently closed the door on the tragic scene, allowing husband and wife the privacy to grieve.

Richard lifted Anne onto the bed, spread the coverlet over her shaking body and drew the heavy curtains around her. Trembling, he knelt at his portable altar and found a prayer for the death of a child in Henry's holy book. As he stared unseeing at the page, his anger built, until he snapped the book shut and flung it away. "I see You are not keeping Your end of the bargain, are You?" he accused the Almighty, his voice shaking. "Or will You not be satisfied until You have taken everything from me?" Another heart-wrenching sob from Anne gave fuel to his ire. "Never mind me. What about Anne? What has she ever done to displease You?" and he raised his fist and shook it at the painted crucifix on the altar. "She has done nothing, I tell you, nothing at all!"

As Anne drenched her pillow, Richard knelt by the bed and, holding her hand in his, he gave his own pitiable blessing to his beloved son. He left God out of it.

Part Six

Last of the Plantagenets

O most sweet lord Jesus Christ, true God, who was sent from the bosom of the Almighty Father into the world to forgive sins, to comfort afflicted sinners, comfort the sad, and to console those in grief and distress, deign to release me from the affliction, temptation, grief, sickness, need and danger in which I stand, and give me counsel. And you, Lord, who reconciled the race of man... and who made peace between men and angels, deign to make and keep concord between me and my enemies...

Even so lord Jesus Christ, deign to free me, your servant, King Richard, from every tribulation, sorrow and trouble in which I am placed and from the plots of my enemies, and deign to send Michael the Archangel to my aid against them...

By all these things, I ask, you most sweet lord Jesus Christ, to keep me, your servant, King Richard, and defend me from all evil and from all peril present, past and to come and deliver me from all tribulations... in the name of all your goodness for which I give and return thanks, for all those gifts and goods granted me...

The Prayer of King Richard, from his Book of Hours

CHAPTER TWENTY-EIGHT
LATE SUMMER 1484

Despite Richard's anger at his Maker, he tried once again to appease Him.

After burying Ned in the little chapel at Middleham, Richard and Anne wanted nothing more than to leave. The boy was imprinted on every inch of the great castle, and Anne expected him to come around a corner at any moment. So they traveled east with their court and spent July and August at Anne's favorite castle on the cliffs of Scarborough.

What can I do to satisfy you, Lord? Richard asked his Maker for the thousandth time, morbid thoughts returning, as they always did, to the scene in King Henry's Tower chamber. *Henry, Henry...* Then all at once he knew what he must do to help salve his soul: He must re-inter Henry's bones in a more appropriate site than insignificant Chertsey Abbey, Edward's choice of resting place. He would pay for a royal reburial in St. George's Chapel, Windsor. The gentle Henry had seen many pilgrims come to pray at his grave over the years, and, after miracles were reported, there was even talk of sainthood. Perhaps Richard saw a chance to make amends, as well as placate those pilgrims.

"That chapel was his pride and joy until my brother won the crown and made it his own," Richard told John Kendall as he dictated the order. "It is only fitting that Henry lie there. He was, after all, an anointed king and should be buried with all the respect due him."

Although little Ned's mother and father would never recover from losing him, they attempted to quarantine their grief in the privacy of their curtained tester bed. There, listening to the waves of the North Sea rhythmically rolling over the beach below them, they exchanged remembrances of their beloved child, alternately laughing and crying. Richard spent other nights drinking himself into a stupor, while Anne gave up eating all but what would minimally sustain her, the seamstresses toiling to alter her gowns. She would spend hours sitting on the grassy cliff edge staring out to sea, and when Richard became concerned she might throw herself off, he ordered that she be accompanied at all times by at least two of her ladies and a groom.

A king's duty, however, could not be put aside, and first he needed to shore up his throne and name a new heir. The latter was an easy decision: he named his older sister Elizabeth of Suffolk's son, John de la Pole, the young, vigorous and capable earl of Lincoln, and already Lord of the North; he was next in an unquestionable Yorkist line of descendants of English kings.

It was a tribute to Richard's thoughtfulness at this unhappy time, that he remembered to pay attention to his remaining children—illegitimate though they were. The beautiful Katherine bade a tearful farewell to her father when she was escorted to her new home in South Wales that summer, where she became the bride of William Herbert. "He is one of my loyal supporters, Katherine, and we shall see you often, I am certain," Richard told her. He took her chin in his fingers. "And I believe you were not displeased with my choice, am I right?" He laughed when he saw her blush. "Aye, poppet, you will soon forget me and embrace a new life." He had winced when she clung to him and called him "her dearest Father." They were only sixteen years apart in age and yet he felt many more years older.

Fourteen-year-old John, already captain of Calais, was knighted by his father during a visit to Scarborough with his lord, Lovell, who told Richard that John was quick-witted and an able soldier.

"He needs to curb his lust, however," Francis had said with a grin, but Richard was not amused. "Give the boy a chance, my lord," Francis teased. "Remember his mother? You were about the same age when you seduced Kate."

"Was I?" Richard mused sadly, not rising to the bait. "It all seems so long ago now." And in truth he did not seem like the same man who had loved so passionately and recklessly in his youth. He had sighed deeply and moved on to other issues. "I am glad you are here, Francis. I may have need of you before long. Those perfidious Scots are rattling their claymores again."

During those long, hot days of summer Richard tried to fill his days with his royal duties, which included outfitting the fleet for a possible invasion from Scotland. He threw himself into preparations including adding new artillery to his inventory. Also fearing another attempt by Tudor to invade, Richard ordered cannons be mounted on the walls of the Tower of London to fend off a southern attack. Breton pirates were causing trouble in the Channel again, taking advantage of a new regime in England, and Richard sent a flotilla to worry them off the Breton coast. It seemed as though he was beset on all sides by conflict, not the least of which battled in his own mind. He knew he did not have Edward's way with people, but the more he tried to please his subjects, the more they viewed him with suspicion. Even his personal intervention in a woman of York's law suit against an unscrupulous relative could not erase the words "usurper" and "murderer" from tainting the twelve months of his reign and burrowing into his unhappy heart.

"What is it this time, my dear?" Anne asked wearily one evening. She wanted to support her husband, but her own need for strength always threatened to overwhelm her frail spirit. Anne's apathy in the world around her had forced Richard to keep politics from her door. Should he bother her with the latest from Brittany? At first it had been good news; Richard's action along the coast had resulted in a diplomatic victory as Duke Francis, fearing for his duchy's security, agreed to hand over Henry Tudor and his fellow Lancastrian exiles. But then…

"I have received bad news, I am afraid, but you do not need to concern yourself, sweetheart."

She smiled then, warming to the endearment. "I do need to hear. I pray you, tell me."

He poured himself another goblet of wine, causing her to frown, but she had lost her energy to chastise him. "Very well. We had almost bagged Henry, but Duke Francis's bootless minions were too slow to catch him before he crossed the border into France." He crashed down his fist on the table, making Anne jump. "We have lost him, God damn their eyes and lazy arses! A few minutes would have changed everything."

Richard could have uttered no truer words, for the capture of the Lancastrian claimant to the throne would have changed the course of English history.

"Do not fret so, Richard. We don't have Louis to deal with anymore, and perhaps the new French king will be more reasonable. Offer to treat with him." After a pause, she suddenly asked, "How did Richmond know Duke Francis was coming for him?"

Richard stared at her, impressed by her insight. Anne was right, someone must have leaked their plan. Someone must have betrayed him—again. He frowned as he pondered the probable culprit. "Stanley," he said under his breath. "Stanley knew. He was at the council meeting. He must have told his scraggy wife, the Beaufort woman..." He paused, drumming his fingers on the chair arm, his expression darkening as he worked out the chain of events, "...and she told that traitor Morton in Flanders. He must have sent the message to her son." He began twisting his ring. "Edward told me once that Thomas Stanley was a survivor in the game of polity. I see that now. If I did not need him on the council for his power in the northwest, I would confront him." He put his head in his hands. "I'll have to keep an eye on Stanley. I wonder who else is with him? Christ's nails, can't I trust anyone anymore?"

Anne went and knelt beside him. "Certainly you can. There's Francis Lovell, Rob, Richard Ratcliffe, your lawyer friend Catesby, and what about dear Jack Howard and his son?" She pulled his hands away from his face and stroked his stubbly cheeks. "And for what 'tis worth, you have me. You will always have me."

Richard kissed her hand tenderly. "Aye, I will always have you. You mean the world to me."

Richard did win one victory for his efforts to safeguard the country that summer. The Scots were soundly defeated both on land and, commanded by Richard himself, at sea. King James III conceded defeat and, in a diplomatic ceremony in Nottingham's castle, treated for a three-year truce.

"I don't even like the man," Richard grumbled to council as they watched the Scottish contingent file out of the great hall. "For all his flowery language of peace, I would not trust him as far as I could toss a caber."

"I would not be surprised if half of his men sailed for France rather than support this treaty. He is not popular with either his lords or his subjects," Thomas Stanley remarked, an edge to his voice, and even though he had not addressed Richard personally, Richard wondered if the equivocating earl of Derby was also referring to him.

By Christmas it was clear even to the most unobservant that Anne was dying, but Richard refused to accept it.

"She is still grieving, 'tis all," he firmly told the doctor. "She needs some gaiety and an end to all these tinctures she is drowning in. What she needs is good mulled wine and yuletide reveling."

He turned to his chamberlain, Francis. "This season will be the merriest yet. I command it," he said. "My young nieces will cheer Anne. We will have mumming, my minstrels will play for dancing..." and he suddenly had an idea, "...and a masquerade," he cried. "I attended one in Bruges during my exile with George. A masked pageant."

The doctor's bushy brows shot up in horror. "But her grace should not leave her bed, look you," he said. "She is trop malade."

"For pity's sake, cease with the faux French, Doctor Gruffydd," Richard snapped. "It does not suit you. Everyone knows you were born in Cardiff, look you."

The man bowed and muttered an apology into his gray beard. Francis quietly shook his head, wishing Richard not be so brusque, but he understood the enormous strain his friend was under—and had been for six months now. He ushered the Welshman out and turned back to discuss the Christmas season. But when he saw despair in Richard's slate eyes, he put his hand on his friend's shoulder and squeezed it. "She will recover, I am certain of it."

Desperate, and out of character, Richard grasped Francis to him and whispered, "Don't let Him take Anne from me, too, Francis. Promise me."

"Who?" Francis replied, taken aback. "Doctor Gruffydd? He is a good man, you know..."

"...not him," Richard said, desperately. "Him," and he pointed to heaven. "I am talking about God. He will not be content until he takes everyone from me." He disengaged himself and sank into a chair.

"You think God is punishing you? For what? You have led a God-fearing life ever since I have known you." Francis pulled up a stool. "Fate has been cruel, I grant you, but you are no better nor worse than the next man, and you are a damn fine king."

Richard looked at his friend and wondered if he could finally reveal his guilt for Henry's death to someone other than his confessor. *Nay, why should I burden Francis?* Instead, he said: "Not good enough it seems," and changed the subject. "Now, let us plot some merry-making."

For the days leading up to Advent and on to Christmas, politics, conflicts and talk of invasion were set aside while Westminster readied for the most joyful, lavish yuletide season ever witnessed. Even Richard was seen smiling and laughing as Anne and his nieces paraded their gowns and King Arthur-themed masquerade costumes for him to admire. Pink roses began to color Anne's cheeks once more and Richard knew he had been right. He was also pleased to see the friendship that was developing between his wife and nineteen-year-old Bess. Not only was his niece lovely, but Richard was struck by Bess's extraordinary gentleness and warmth, unlike her unruly sister, Cecily, who was perhaps even comelier but whose boldness reminded him poignantly of Kate.

His first love had begun to creep into his thoughts of late since Anne had begged him to keep to his own bed while she coughed her nights away. It did not help his natural achings that Bess went out of her way to please him, calling to him to try a sweetmeat or asking his opinion on a new headdress. Richard wanted his nieces to feel safe and welcome in his household and thus he indulged them, and he felt gratitude to Bess in particular for her kindness to Anne. Unaware that the young woman, very ready for love, had developed an infatuation for him, he was too caught up in trying to lighten the dark days of winter for Anne to anticipate the difficulties of such an attraction.

When the day of the pageant arrived, the excitement in the palace corridors was palpable. At great expense, thousands of candles helped light the reception chambers and magnificent great hall, and the cooks spent days concocting elaborate dishes to put before King Arthur and his court, which at Richard's command had been transformed into Camelot. Richard had had his tailor craft a costume the silver sleeves and leggings of which, visible under a richly decorated long tunic, cleverly resembled armor. An ermine collar on his purple velvet cloak masked his higher shoulder, and as Arthur he wore a high gold crown made of parchment in the style depicted in tapestries.

After knocking on his robing-chamber door, Anne entered to admire his costume. "Do you mind, my lord? I could not wait to see my noble Arthur."

At first, he was glad to see that his wife, all smiles and giggles, was entranced by her flowing gown, its sleeves brushing the floor. But as she tweaked a tuck here and a fold there in his costume and straightened his crown, Richard could not bear to hurt her by pointing out that white satin only accentuated her pallor, and the golden belt was pathetically clinging to her bony hips. With her already-graying hair pulled starkly into a long braid and crowned with white and red silk flowers, she resembled a ghostly wraith rather than a buxom, healthy Guinevere.

"Come in, come in, Bess," Anne was calling as Richard kissed her hand. Excited, she told him, "We decided you should have two Guineveres to take you to the masque." Going to the door, she pulled Elizabeth Woodville's lovely daughter into the room, and Richard gasped. Bess may indeed have been clad in the identical gown, but there the similarity with Anne ended. Her regal carriage, glowing rosy skin, abundant red-gold hair cascading loose around her plump shoulders and voluptuous breasts all painfully emphasized who was to be queen of the night. She was the glorious sun to Anne's pale, waning moon, and Richard, at a loss for words, could not prevent a frown.

"You don't like it, Uncle?" Bess asked. "I did say to Aunt Anne that…" but she faltered.

Anne stood defiantly in front of the nervous young girl and chastised Richard. "It was my idea. If you are angry, be angry with me and not poor Bess, who falls over herself to please you."

Richard's gentlemen of the chamber, who had withdrawn to the other side of the room, stared at the odd scene. They were no doubt thinking about a rumor that Richard may have been eyeing his niece with something more than avuncular kindness. He would need a new wife, would he not, and one who could give him an heir?

Anne took her husband's hands, her hollowed eyes brimming. "I knew I would not have the strength to dance with you, my love. I wanted you to have a surrogate Queen Guinevere. Please say you are not angry."

Richard looked into her anxious, innocent face and realized suddenly what he had been denying. *What a fool I am! She is dying,* he thought.

Sweet Jesu, how much he was going to miss his gentle, principled consort. He could not let her guess his fear, and his frown melted into a smile. "Certes, I am not angry with you or Bess. It was a thoughtful gesture, and I thank you." He looked across at Bess, wishing she did not so resemble her beautiful mother. "If my niece does not have ideas above her station," and he winked at her, "I shall be honored to be escorted by two such fair ladies." Oblivious of his niece's heightened flush, he lightly kissed Anne on the forehead. When they had donned their masks, he took both women by the hand. "Let us join our guests, my queens. Perhaps this Guinevere," and he turned to Bess, who blushed again, "will find her Lancelot tonight."

Anne's happy laughter quickly turned to coughing. "Silly of me to get so excited," she apologized, accepting a kerchief from her attendant. "It will pass."

As the halcyon days of that yuletide season became a poignant memory and the harsh winter of 1485 turned to spring, Anne's pallor became indistinguishable from her bedsheets. More and more often a crimson spot spoiled their pristine whiteness, telling the physicians that their royal patient was suffering from the same consumptive disease that had taken her sister. The doctors forbade Richard close contact with her as they believed the condition was contagious.

Missing his wife's presence, Richard spent many of the dark winter evenings in conversation with his four nieces, including a newcomer to his household, Grace, one of Edward's by-blows. In an extraordinary, and surprising, act of magnanimity for the usually selfish Elizabeth, she had agreed to take in the young woman, who was a little younger than Cecily. *It was a promise I made to Edward on his deathbed,* she had written to Richard, *and with the income I am expected to live on, I must now ask your help in providing for her. Have no fear, she is as quiet as a mouse.*

Before Anne had permanently taken to her bed, she had begged Richard to allow Grace to join her older cousins at court. "If I can take in your Katherine, then you can do right by Edward's Grace. I pray you, do this for me. She will be a companion for young Cecily." And as Richard could deny his beloved wife nothing at this point, he agreed.

Besides finding the girl no trouble to protect, it cannot be denied that Richard found solace in helping his brother's children, perhaps to staunch the heinous whisperings that he must have killed his two young nephews.

Wanting to be a benevolent uncle to his nieces, he failed to listen to his usual rational self and the quartet of councilors he trusted most, Francis, Rob, Ratcliffe and Howard, that he was causing gossip by being seen too often in close company with Bess. If he had heard their counsel, his moral self was so appalled by the thought of wooing his own flesh and blood, that he had dismissed the warning as ridiculous. *Why must I always be misconstrued?*

"I *will* go in, Doctor Gryffud," Richard insisted, pushing the good doctor aside. "Never fear, I will not go close, but my wife will not die alone."

He crept to the end of Anne's bed, rendered vast by the skeletal figure lying in the center, her once-brown hair a snarled confusion of gray on her damp pillow. Anne had always been so meticulous about her appearance that seeing her thus disturbed him greatly. He turned to find one of her women, but they were huddled in a corner, weeping and afraid to go near her. He snatched a comb from the table of potions and bowls, and, fearlessly sat down beside Anne and began to gently untangle her hair. She did not move. He thought she was unaware of his presence, when her skeletal hand fluttered above the coverlet and found his leg. He stared at it aghast. *How could skin be so transparent?* He dared not touch it but was comforted that she knew he was there.

"My dearest Anne," he whispered, tears he had kept in check for these past weeks slipping down his cheeks. "They would not let me see you. Pray forgive me for my cowardice. I should have come sooner."

Her sunken cheeks, eyes deep in their dark sockets, and parched lips drawn away unnaturally from her gums gave the impression of a skull already, and he could no longer see the dear face he had lovingly kissed only a few months before. The first memory of her standing in Isabel's shadow returned to him. Aye, she had always been there in his life, quietly loving him. Even knowing about Kate, she had loved him. "I am sorry I did not see you, sweetheart," he confessed and wondered when was it that she had stepped out of Kate's shadow and into his view and his heart? He could not remember now; it seemed forever ago. He thought of the years Anne had suffered from his selfishness: his youthful adoration of Isabel; then his affair with Kate; Anne's many miscarriages—his desire perhaps the culprit—although Anne had never accused him of those. Indeed, hers was a life of untimely loss: her father, her only sister, her only child, and finally and cruelly, her own life. This birdlike creature had borne them all so stoically. Richard was in awe of her spirit.

He continued combing her long, fine hair and spoke to her. "Ah, Anne, you promised you would never leave me. You have not deserved such suffering, and yet you suffer. What, pray God, has brought us here? Oh, my dear, how do you expect me to go on living without you and our beloved Ned? You were always so good, so true, and so wise. Dear God in Heaven, what will I do without you?"

Richard broke down then and, gently gathering her precious body to him as though he could transfer his strength to her, he willed her to live.

Roused by her husband's grief, Anne managed to say, "D...don't cry, my love I c...can't bear to hear you cry. You have been my strength, my rock, my love..." Her little speech gave way to a spasm of coughing, and Richard reached for a kerchief. Carefully wiping her mouth, he was appalled by the scarlet stain that spread over it. She closed her eyes, exhausted.

"Do not try and talk, Anne. I will not leave you again, and I pray to the sweet Virgin Mary that you will find her loving arms when mine can no longer hold you..." He forced himself then to summon the chaplain to perform the last rites. It was no good hoping, no good praying any longer. There would be no miracle—it was the ides of March after all—and his wife would die.

Dawn was just breaking on that cold day when a strange orange light set the roofs of London aglow. Citizens crossed themselves as they emerged from their doorways and glanced up at the heavens. As the sun rose high in the sky, a black orb began to slide across its golden surface and a shadow fell over the earth just as, at the palace of Westminster, the light of Richard's life also began to slide away. He murmured the *non nobis, Domine,* as he felt the soul slip from Anne's frail body, and all of London was plunged into semi-darkness. *It is a sign,* he marveled and bowed his head. *Sweet Jesu, receive her soul, and I pray You do not forsake me now, for I am truly alone.*

Kind hands gentled him away from Anne's still form, and, as Anne's women prepared her body for burial, he allowed himself to be led from the darkened room to his own chambers. There, Bess was waiting to greet him with soothing words and comforting arms. He saw his son John among the other councilors watching him anxiously, and Richard reached out a hand to him behind Bess's back.

Taking the hand, the young man said, "Courage, Father. We are here to give you courage. The queen would have wanted that, and England needs you."

Richard nodded. "Thank you, John." But privately he thought, *England can wait.*

Chapter Twenty-Nine
1485

Anne Neville, daughter of the earl of Warwick and queen of England, was given a resplendent funeral and buried on the southern side of the high altar in Westminster Abbey. Richard's spirits were so low in those weeks following Anne's death that he could not bring himself to commission a tomb and effigy yet. He could not have known his procrastination would mean Anne's grave was never marked.

"Have you lost your wits?" Richard spat at Catesby, who cringed at his king's fury. "I shall do no such thing. Now leave me, all of you."

All but Francis bowed and retreated. He put up his hand to stop Richard's admonition and put his finger to his lips. "My lord, Your Grace, I beg of you hear me out. But first, I pray you lower your voice. These are dangerous times."

Richard snorted. "You are telling me? What with the Tydder lusting for my throne and the news that Oxford has escaped from Hammes and has joined with him, and wondering who will betray me next, I am well aware of the danger, I thank you." Richard had, Francis noted with relief, taken his advice and spoken more quietly. "But I will not believe that anyone thinks I poisoned Anne in order to wed my niece." He shuddered at the word. "Why, 'tis monstrous. And the council wants me to make a public statement that I won't commit what I consider to be incest? By denying it, I will surely give credence to it, will I not." He calmed himself, but he was greatly perturbed by this turn of events. "Francis, how can anyone think I would plot to poison Anne? Poor lady, she suffered enough and for long enough to be able to rest in peace now. Tell me, whence comes this tale about Bess?"

Francis pulled a chair forward and encouraged the pacing Richard to sit. He noticed the dark rings under Richard's eyes, and it seemed to Francis that the weight of Anne's death had given his old friend an even more pronounced stoop. "I warned you before Christmas that people talked of your favor towards Bess. I know, I know," he put up his hand, "you were just being kind to her, but vicious people love to gossip and her attraction to you was evident." He drew a letter from his pocket, and Richard frowned. "Read this, Richard. It was written to Jack Howard and, dismissing it at first, Jack then decided to give it to me. I was not aware Bess and Jack were that much acquainted, but it seems she trusts him."

Perturbed, Richard nevertheless unfolded the parchment.

To my lord of Norfolk, my friend and my uncle's trusted councilor, I greet you well. I write to beseech you to intercede for me with my dear uncle, that if he has a mind to marry again after the queen's passing, I am willing—nay, desirous... Richard looked up aghast: "By Christ's nails, what is this? It is fabricated, forged, fraudulent! Bess seeks to replace Anne, and so soon? She insinuated herself into Anne's kind graces and all the time wished she were dead? She is not so unkind. It has to be a forgery. A monstrous jest!"

"Read on," Francis insisted. "Bess is not false-hearted. 'Tis a girl infatuated, nothing more."

Richard continued reading. *He is my dearest love, as I have told you...* "Damnation," Richard interjected again angrily, "Howard knew this before and did not tell me? I'll have his guts for garters." He read on, *... and I believe he has a fondness for me.* "I did, I did," Richard mumbled, "but as I have a fondness for all my nieces. Why must my actions be so misconstrued?"

He threw the parchment on the table and speared it to the table with his dagger. "Am I to be hounded even in my hour of grief. I must send Bess and her sisters away. Out of my sight and out of people's minds." He looked across at Francis who was shaking his head. "You don't agree? Then what, pray, does Lord Lovell think I should do?" he snapped. "Poison her as I did her brothers?" And he grabbed an inkwell John Kendall had left open on the table and flung it at a valuable tapestry.

Francis bided his time as Richard stalked to the window to stare out at the mantle of daffodils below him in Westminster's well-kept garden.

"It is the view of your privy council that you make a public denial of this rumor. It is the only way to put it behind you."

He stopped there. Francis had been Richard's friend long enough to know that, after an explosion of ill-judged temper, Richard had to process information before he could be reasoned with. Usually, he was reasonable, but Richard was not himself these days—Francis had not heard him laugh for weeks—and so he braced himself for the next onslaught. Richard suddenly swung round and said coldly, "I will not do it, and there is an end to it. Let the rumor-mongers go to hell."

Francis bowed and quietly left the room. Richard was wrong, he knew, and needed time to calm himself. In the meantime, he went to find Jack Howard.

Richard stood by the fireplace and turned the delicate gold-filigree ring around the tip of his finger, wondering what had prompted Kate to send the keepsake back to him. When he had given it to her those many years ago, he had made her promise that if ever she had need of him she would send it and he would see her. Jack Howard had delivered it from Suffolk the day before, saying Kate had accompanied him and was now a guest at his townhouse in Stepney.

Reasons for her having sent the ring raced through Richard's mind as he waited for her. Did she need money for Dickon? He doubted it for he had been true to his promise to Geoffrey Bywood to send a generous stipend to cover the boy's provisions. Perhaps she had found a suitable husband? But why would she need his permission? Perhaps a relative had been unjustly accused and she was seeking his intercession?

The rap on the door startled him, and he dropped the ring in the rushes. When Kate came in, he was down on one knee searching for it, and she could clearly see the outline of his crooked back through his doublet. She felt a pang of sympathy; the last time she had seen him he had hidden that side from her. The protrusion was far more visible after all these years, she observed sadly.

As soon as Richard looked up and saw her, his spirits lifted, and he could not help smiling. Francis, who had stayed long enough to usher Kate through the door, hurried out with relief.

Kate curtsied as Richard, having retrieved the ring, stood up, but her face fell when she saw the reddened eyes, the shadows of grief, and new deep lines of worry etched on his face. She went to him then and, cradling his head between her hands, kissed him tenderly on both cheeks. "How truly sorry I am, Richard," she said, "about Anne."

Tears pricked, but Richard allowed himself to be gentled into a chair. She knelt on the floor beside him as she had done so many times. Although he would not touch her, he experienced a calmness he had not felt since Anne's healthy days.

"Is that why you came, Kate?" he finally asked, toying with the ring in his palm. "Did you think I would not receive your condolence unless you sent the ring?"

"Oh, no, Richard, it was not that at all. I could have sent you a letter if I had only wanted to express my sympathies." She rose, agitated now, as her mission was far more sensitive. "I came because I hear you have been somewhat...um...contrary of late. 'Tis hard to gain an audience with you, I've been told, and then it's not pleasant. In truth, I should be flattered you agreed to see me."

Richard looked surprised but then gave a reluctant grin. "Is that what they say? I suppose 'tis true." He motioned her to sit on a stool. She listened quietly as he spoke of his grief and, hard though it was for her to hear, of his love for Anne. "But after all my many sins—and there have been some heinous ones, including wishing for your arms about me more times than I care to admit—I truly believe God has forsaken me. He took Ned, he has taken Anne, and soon Henry Tudor will take England from me. I know it."

"Fiddle-faddle, Richard!" Kate retorted. "I cannot speak for God, but I hear what people say in villages and towns, where you cannot go. They praise you for your concern of us, the common people. They will not want the unknown Tudor who has not set foot in England for nigh on fifteen years. Your throne is safe, I am certain of it, and you are loved."

Richard smiled at her naïveté, but he did not contradict her. Instead, he gave her back the ring and asked: "Enough of my woes. So why are you here, Kate?"

She took a deep breath, replaced the ring on her finger, and started slowly. "The reason is important, or I would not have come. There are rumors...I have heard...it is said..." she struggled for the words and finally settled for, "...it is said you have in mind to wed your niece, Elizabeth."

Richard let out a harsh laugh. "Aye, so I have been told. And the rumors are false." He was curt now. "But why should this concern you?" He cursed himself for his cruel tongue, but he was tired of the subject. "They are just rumors. Ignore them, as I am trying to do."

Kate leaned forward, her expression earnest. "But you should not ignore them, Richard. That is why I am here. You should listen to your good friends like Jack, Francis, Rob Percy and the rest of your trusted advisors. You need to *deny* the rumors not dismiss them."

"Why should I deny them?" he shot back, and sprang from his chair. "Why not Bess? She was the one who wrote the letter; she was the one who started this," he railed at her. "How dare they ask me to make a public denial. I have done nothing wrong. Nothing!" and he pummeled the paneled wall in frustration. Kate was distraught by his uncharacteristic anger. This was a Richard she had never seen before.

A door flew open beside the fireplace, startling Kate into knocking over her stool. Will Catesby entered, dagger drawn, only to be told: "Get out! Out I say!" by his king. The man hurriedly bowed and retreated.

"God's nails, can a king not have any privacy?" Richard complained, glowering at the door.

"Calm yourself, Richard, I beg of you," Kate implored him, trying to understand the complexity of this man she had loved for so long. He must truly be mad with grief, she reasoned.

"Calm myself, you say. As if it were that easy. I shall never be calm again," he said, his voice rising. "I am doomed, 'tis certain." He lifted his eyes to the ceiling. "God in heaven, I never asked for this. I sought only to serve my country, and I have tried to expiate my sins. Why do You hate me so?" he cried, sinking back into his chair.

Now Kate was truly worried. She had known him to be angry at injustice and treason, but never this disconsolate. His grief had led to self-hatred, she believed, and time alone would heal him. But Kate, like Anne, had never known the deeper reason for Richard's belief that God had forsaken him. No one but God knew the terrible burden he carried. For that sin, Richard would never forgive himself, but he had hoped that, in His infinite mercy, God had.

"You have every right to be angry at God, my dear Richard," she said, kneeling beside him again and taking his hands. "But your subjects need you. The council needs you. Even though you are innocent, you must let them know you have no intention of wedding your niece. Only then will you quell the rumor."

He stared at her for a few moments and held onto her loving fingers while he fought the urge to deny her request again.

"Please, Richard. It is the right thing to do," she whispered. "Please think of Anne, think of our son and daughter and the hurt it would cause them. And think of the peace of England. I beg of you, deny it."

Without warning, he pulled her to him and kissed her hard on her mouth, taking her breath away. It was the kiss of a desperate man, she knew, but she allowed herself to caress his head and hold him close one last time.

"I will think on it," he murmured. "You are perhaps right. For now you have my thanks and my love." He held her head between his hands. "You know I will always love you, Kate."

It was Duchess Cecily, the indomitable York matriarch, who finally swept into Westminster's draughty corridors and convinced her son of the need for a public denial.

"Your morals have been impeccable until now, Richard. You did right by Anne at the time of your marriage and gave up your leman—aye, I knew about her from the moment she played her harp for us at Margaret's farewell. Since then you have wisely learned to conceal the passionate nature you had as a boy." She paused to chuckle. "Always asking questions; always loudly championing the peasantry; even lying for George because you could not bear to be disloyal; and announcing your displeasure to the wrong people when injustice had been done."

"I have tried, Mother," Richard said, annoyed at her ability to reduce him to a little boy when she leveled her gaze at him. "I have tried to rule as Father would have done had he lived to wear the crown." At that, he saw Cecily's face soften and knew he had disarmed her, which he hoped might temper the sermon he was expecting. After all, she had just ridden all the way from Berkhamsted, when she had not even left her seclusion to attend his coronation. But now the York name was being besmirched, and the lioness had come to correct her cub.

"Your father would have been pleased to see the man you have become, Richard, a man worthy to wear the crown. It has become clear to me since you became king that you are perhaps the best of our sons. You are certainly a better king than Edward and certainly a better man than George. Edmund had promise, so I cannot compare you with him, struck down so cruelly and so young as he was." Cecily noticed how straight and tall Richard was standing now. "Your father would have been so proud of you." She hesitated. "Until now. He would never have countenanced a scandalous rumor to have spread about his son and his granddaughter." The very idea was abhorrent to her that she had to pause for breath. "You must rectify this matter now, Richard," she commanded.

All the way to London, Cecily had been weighing how to threaten her son should he exhibit his usual stubbornness. "You must make a public denial of this vicious rumor," she persisted, "or I will expose you as a liar."

Richard was dumbfounded. "A liar?" he protested. "How could I be a liar if I have never even expressed a wish to wed Bess?"

"That is not the lie I am speaking of, my dear Richard," she replied, deliberately inscrutable. When she purred, Cecily was at her most dangerous, and Richard knew he was about to be scratched. "Did you or did you not instruct Doctor Shaa to proclaim Edward a bastard at that infamous oration from Paul's Cross?" Richard paled, but she continued. "Aye, that disgusting slander announcing to the world that I had cuckolded my husband—*your* father. You are the king—some say usurper—and thus you can say whatever you wish..." She saw the fleeting wince and pounced. "Ah, I see that you are not insensitive to others' opinions of you. You do not like that word 'usurper.' Well, I don't like the word 'adulteress.'" Watching him avert his gaze, she pushed on. "Suppose I expose your lie? How many lords' support do you think you might lose, most of whom have never had cause to doubt my word? You cannot afford to lose any, Richard, but if those lords believed you had lost my support, I wouldn't like your chances."

"It was Buck..." Richard tried to interrupt, but he was cut off.

"Do not pass the blame, my boy. You could have stopped Shaa there and then!" Seeing him sufficiently chastised, she softened. "It could be that all the good work you have done so far—and you have done good work, my son—will go down the garderobe chute." She sighed but reiterated: "Deny the marriage rumors, Richard, and I shall return to Berkhamsted and resume my silence."

Richard was dumbfounded. Perhaps he had never fully comprehended his mother's intelligence and power all these years, yet he had observed before her strength and wisdom in a crisis. Cecily's ploy was a master stroke, but he could not help being angered by it. "Well played, Mother," he said, wearily, "It would seem you have me by the...."

"...short and curlies, my boy," Cecily finished, approaching him and taking his stiffened shoulders. "Do the right thing, Richard. If you do not want to do it for yourself, do it for Bess. Don't let this rumor fester so that it ruins her life. Say nothing, and no one knows for sure and people's salacious imaginations will see you in bed with her." Richard sagged, and she caressed his cheek. "You are grieving still, and in that state, one says and does things without fully considering the consequences." She sighed. "I should know. Believe me, the Dickon I know who braved Ludlow, stood up to the great Warwick, and stayed loyal to Edward throughout his short life would have done the right thing."

Richard had long awaited such words from his mother, and now they consoled him somewhat. However, his guilty conscience knew he did not deserve all this praise. He gently extricated himself from her hold and turned away. "I have done things, Mother, terrible things..." he began.

Cecily waved him off. "I do not want a litany of sins, my boy. We have all done things we regret, but it doesn't make us evil. I know you are a good person, Richard, and God knows it, too." She changed the subject. "I apologize for not coming to you sooner after Anne's tragic death. I am much moved by how devoted you have been to her. I see it in your face, heard it in your voice. I have been too wrapped in my Berkhamsted cocoon to care about my life—or anyone's—much anymore. I am seventy years old next week, and I have lived through more upheaval and unhappiness than most people, and I needed to withdraw from the world. But I should have been here to support you in those demanding times after Edward's death." She went to the window to let in some air, her figure still elegant if a little stooped, Richard noted. "I tried to help Edward at the beginning, but he was headstrong and we quarreled. Then I did not want to interfere when it seemed you were handling everything so well."

Richard harrumphed. "If only you knew, Mother. In truth, I would have been glad of your counsel, but events happened so fast, I did not think to consult you—especially during those first weeks of upheaval."

Cecily turned back to him. "You need to know that I do not believe the hideous rumor that you had Ned's boys murdered. You have the courage to render justice, but it is not in your nature to callously execute innocent children, and your own nephews at that." She shook her head. "Impossible. Whatever has become of them—and their demise is certainly one very real option—I can believe that ambitious Margaret Beaufort had a hand in it. Even my nemesis, the other Margaret, might have had she lived. Elizabeth Woodville, too, would stop at nothing to secure her family's power..." She paused and chuckled. "Listen to me disparaging my own sex. In truth, we can be as ruthless as men when we feel our families are threatened."

"Is that why you threatened me just now, Mother?" he asked with enough of a hint of sarcasm to flout his mother before he continued more seriously: "I swear to you on my wife's grave, that I had nothing to do with the boys' deaths..." he caught himself, but Cecily was too quick.

"So they *are* dead? Dear God!" she exclaimed and crossed herself. "How? Those poor boys."

Richard lowered himself into his chair. "It was Buckingham. Even worse, he did the deed himself and came gleefully back to me expecting my gratitude. Gratitude? I almost ran him through there and then." Richard began pacing, remembering the scene. "Instead, I sent him away, and..."

"...he turned against you and rebelled," Cecily finished the sentence for him as the truth dawned. "You did right to execute him," she said vehemently. "At least his crime died with him. But why did you not get a signed confession? And, more important, why did you not reveal his crime when you had the chance?"

"Because I thought no one would believe me," Richard muttered, shamefaced. "I had elevated him so high, if he fell I was going to fall with him. I regret I did not have the courage or the wisdom to reveal the truth for the peace of England, and, selfishly, for the peace of my own soul. And now...now..."

"...it is too late and history will say you are guilty," Cecily once again finished for him, fingering her ebony and pearl rosary.

"'Tis a curse to be born royal," Richard said angrily. "There is always someone behind you ready to stab you in the back. I am trying to make amends by ruling justly, and I only hope history will record that fairly."

The duchess went to the door. "You have the measure of it, my son. And now I would counsel that you grieve for Anne apace longer, but then you must turn to the future. I know about the Tudor threat. Make ready and make it known. Ha! Margaret Beaufort's son is no match for the best of mine." Then she lowered her voice. "You do need an heir, 'tis true," and she shook her finger at her youngest, "but not with your niece! End this rumor about Bess. Promise your aging mother."

Richard kissed her hand. "Aye, Your Grace," he promised. He opened the door for Cecily and bade her farewell, giving her a low, respectful bow; she would never ceased to awe him.

"Come and see me, Richard. Let us get reacquainted," she urged over her shoulder. He nodded, not knowing the last sight he would have of his mother had just disappeared in a swirl of mauve silk.

In a loud, confident voice Richard told the mayor and aldermen of London, the lords and priests, the officers of his household and his council gathered at the beautiful great hall of the Priory of St. John, that he had no, nor had he ever had, intentions to wed King Edward's daughter, Elizabeth. The chroniclers duly wrote it down for history to judge whether Richard was telling the truth. What their version did not record was that this unfortunate rumor was just one of many aimed at Richard by a burgeoning number of Tudor followers, who meant to undermine his rule and stall any progress Richard sought to make for the kingdom.

Even more difficult than the humiliating denial was his subsequent meeting with Bess. He owed it to the girl to tell her himself he had no feelings for her, other than those an uncle might have for a favorite niece.

"I pray you to forgive me if I, in any way, led you to believe otherwise, my dear Bess," he told her gently in Anne's sunny solar, where he now spent most of his leisure time. He could see Bess had been crying, and he felt sorry for her, but he dared not lay a comforting finger on her in case she misinterpreted the action. "You must see how wrong any arrangement between us would be. I am your uncle and the king."

"And I a bastard—so they say," Bess gamely retorted through tears that sparkled on her lashes. "I understand the king cannot wed one, but would you have considered marrying me had I not been, my lord? Could I have hoped?"

Had she been his daughter Katherine thus heartsick, he would have taken her in his arms and soothed her. Instead he rose abruptly and turned his back to her, not wanting to hurt her further by his grim resolve to end this foolish fancy. "Nay, Bess, I have never desired you, and I would never have wed you. It may be that I will be counseled to take a new wife, but it will not be before I have ended this Tudor threat and found a suitable alliance for England." Now was not the time to raise the topic of her so-called betrothal to Henry, although later he would request that she promise never to see it through. He turned back to her, his expression impassive. "My devotion was always to Anne from the day that I married her until the day she died. I dare any man to say I was untrue to her—and especially with you. You must forget your childish infatuation."

With tears running down her face, Bess shook her fist at her uncle."I hate you, Richard, I truly hate you!" She jumped up. "I will marry Henry of Richmond, and won't you be sorry!" she cried and ran from the room, leaving Richard cursing himself for his cruelty. He moved to the bed and sank into its softness, wishing for the thousandth time that Anne was still there. He stared at the flowers embroidered on the silk canopy above him and pondered Bess's final remark. Should he not make her unavailable to the Tudor wretch? He sat up. Aye, first he would send her with the youngest members of the family to Sheriff Hutton for safe-keeping and then he would find her a suitable husband. There was no doubt that she might be a rallying cry if a promised alliance between York and Lancaster were used to attract supporters to the Tudor cause.

Henry Tudor himself must have been relieved upon learning of the public denial. While he may have urged his English supporters to vilify Richard with the false rumor, surely he would not have sanctioned pushing Richard and Bess together to his own cost?

Richard was determined to stamp out the spiteful falsehoods that were spreading throughout the kingdom, vowing to punish anyone caught perpetuating rumors of any kind or who published seditious articles about him or any of his household.

A man named Colingbourne was given the grisly traitor's death of being hung, drawn, and quartered for attempting to send a message to Henry Tudor in France encouraging him to invade England, and for having written the malevolent couplet tacked to St. Paul's door slandering Richard's closest friends:

The Cat, the Rat, and Lovell our dog
Rule all of England under an Hog.

Richard wrote furiously to his friends on the York city council urging them to *apprehend the bearers of false rumors for divers seditious and evil-disposed persons enforce themselves daily to sow seeds of noise against our person... to abuse the multitude of our subjects and avert their minds from us...*

In the quiet evenings now spent alone, Richard's spirit flagged. He was losing the will to fight for his throne. "Without a wife, without an heir, what is the use?" he muttered into his wine one fine April evening, pushing away a half-eaten mutton pie. The news from France was also not good: Henry was gathering friends among the new king's courtiers. Together with Oxford; the exiled, wily bishop, John Morton; Dorset; and Henry's uncle, the troublesome Jasper Tudor, he had convinced the new French king to lend him support for an invasion.

A knock on the door jarred Richard from his reverie and he slurred, "Come in." It was Rob Percy, back from his estates in Yorkshire, where he had been commissioning troops. All up and down England, Richard had sent out commissions of array, and he had resurrected the beacon system of alarms that had worked so well for Edward.

"Your Grace," Rob began, going down on one knee. Richard waved him into a chair. "We have just had news from Calais. The queen's...I mean Dame Grey's son Dorset has forsaken Tudor and attempted to return to beg that he be readmitted to court."

"You astonish me, Rob," Richard said, attempting to clear the wine fog from his brain. "Is he here now? I am glad to hear it, but I cannot say I trust him."

"Unfortunately, he got no further than Compiègne before being apprehended. Henry has him well guarded I have no doubt."

Richard drummed his fingers on the table. "Why now? Perhaps Henry has lost favor with the French king, and Dorset ..."

Rob shook his disheveled head. Richard loved that his old friend had never adopted the Londoners' fussy fashions. "Nay, it is simpler than that. It would seem your inviting Elizabeth to return to court, coupled with the decisive way you quelled the ugly rumor about her daughter, has prompted her to urge Dorset to return and make his peace with you. It will be a blow to Henry's ego if he thinks Elizabeth has withdrawn her support for his betrothal to Bess to side with you."

Richard felt as though some weight had been lifted from him. *If Elizabeth has eased her mind about me, then she cannot believe I murdered her boys*, he thought. "This is good news," he agreed, "the first in a long time."

He may have sounded glad, but Richard had learned not to let down his guard. He had been misled by his too-trusting nature so many times he could not find it in his heart to believe his clever sister-in-law did not have ulterior motives in this apparent reversal. After all, he reasoned, she would win either way—as a family member again at his court or, God forbid Henry Tudor did invade and take the crown, as mother of a queen.

He shivered. It was as though someone had walked over his grave.

CHAPTER THIRTY
SUMMER 1485

Richard the king marched through the balmy days of May and June fulfilling his duty to defend his kingdom from the invader. Richard the man wafted through nightly mists of grief and bad dreams, sleeping fitfully and waking wearier than when he had put his head down the night before. His physician prescribed a potion of chamomile, hawthorn, and linden flowers, and it brought him some relief, although he wanted to ask the doctor if he had a cure for heartache.

At the end of May, he held his last council meeting in London and moved on to Windsor. Confident of an easy victory against any invasion, Richard had persuaded the merchants and Italian bankers in London to extend him loans to pay for a royal army. "Help me stamp out this arrogant canker once and for all," he had persuaded them. "Henry will see who is rightful king of England."

At the council meeting, he ordered Francis to depart for Southampton and organize its defenses; Jack Howard and his son, Thomas, were to return to East Anglia and await commissions of array; Brackenbury was to stay in London and keep it safe with the new artillery installed at the Tower; and his supporters, including Richard's son-in-law in Wales, were told to remain vigilant.

"Only the northeast is doubtful," Richard observed quietly to Chancellor John Russell. "Can I count on Stanley or will he and his brother risk splinters in their arses by sitting on the fence?"

Russell smiled at the imagery. "Lord Thomas has been a good member of your council and your trusted steward of the household, Your Grace, so why the concern now?"

"Because he and his brother—indeed his family—have always managed to end up on the winning side. If you notice, Thomas rarely makes an opinion contrary to the majority on the council. I also have good cause to be wary of his wife, as you know. It is impossible to believe he cannot be privy to any communication between her and her son." Richard tapped his temple. "Nay, my lord bishop, I shall use my head this time and take Stanley and his son, Strange, with me to Nottingham. I want my eye on them."

"Very wise, my liege," Russell replied.

Nottingham.

The castle on the rock dragged his memory back to the awful day when he and Anne learned of Ned's death. "My 'castle of care,'" he said to Rob Percy, as they rode under the portcullis. Rob was one of only a few of his closest advisors, with Catesby and Ratcliffe, to accompany Richard.

"I am surprised you returned, Your Grace. And I am even more surprised you are come without an army. Is this wise?"

Richard smiled. "Thank God for your northern candor, Rob," he said. "I get tired of flattering fawners. All is ready around the south and east coasts for any sightings of Richmond, and Neville has the fleet patrolling the French coast for a possible French flotilla. With commissions of array in every part of the country, I am thinking I can have an army assembled more quickly where it is needed rather than have all of it here and have to march to the other end of the country as a whole."

Rob nodded his approval of the strategy. "Always thinking, aren't you, Richard?" he teased, evoking similar conversations from their days at Middleham. "What about Stanley? Should he not be mustering on his estates, too?"

"Stanley stays with me for the time being," was all Richard would say.

Richard had been watching Stanley grow more and more taciturn since learning the king wanted him to stay close. Stanley was no fool. The earl realized his loyalty was in question, but there came a day in late July when he could no longer remain obediently at Nottingham.

"It has been many months since I oversaw my affairs on my estates, Your Grace," Stanley said, affecting a pinched grimace of pain "Besides, I have not been well of late. I beg your leave to return home where I can recoup my strength and prepare my own troops to support you."

Richard stared long and hard at the fifty-year-old earl of Derby, his sharp features, wispy gray hair and drooping mustache and beard making him look like an aging weasel. Stanley attempted to hold Richard's eyes, but his lie forced him to avert his gaze. Finally, Richard spoke. "I will let you go, my lord Derby, on the condition you leave Lord Strange with me."

Stanley looked startled. "My son? What for, may I ask?"

"Insurance, my lord," Richard told him coolly. "And you know very well why."

Two men-at-arms stepped forward to flank Lord Strange, who seemed perplexed. "Insurance against what, Your Grace? Surely you do not question my loyalty or my father's? We have served your family well."

Richard inclined his head. "And so you have, George. Up until the autumn of 'eighty-four, I had no worries as to your family's loyalty. As I say, 'tis merely insurance."

Stanley sighed. "I understand. It is my wife, is it not? Very well, I will take my leave and prove my loyalty to you by bringing a sizable force whenever you summon me."

"I hope that you do, Thomas. Your son's life depends upon it."

Lord Strange suppressed a gasp, but Richard was gratified to see Stanley's hand waver as he fumbled his hat to his head before bowing stiffly.

It was then that Richard called for the Great Seal to be brought to him from London and under it, he issued a proclamation calling all to resist the man Henry Tudor, earl of Richmond, *who is descended of bastard blood and claims the royal estate of this realm where he has no interest, right or colour.* It denounced all who would support him or *other divers rebels and traitors.*

Richard prayed he had won his people's trust and that they would honor this decree. Unfortunately, the people were tired of war and even more tired of the barons who fought it, and they still did not entirely believe that Richard's path to the crown had been innocently paved. His people were not privy to Richard's inborn sense of duty, however. He would never betray England's trust, although there were many who still could not trust him.

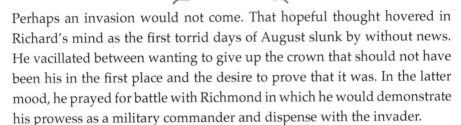

Perhaps an invasion would not come. That hopeful thought hovered in Richard's mind as the first torrid days of August slunk by without news. He vacillated between wanting to give up the crown that should not have been his in the first place and the desire to prove that it was. In the latter mood, he prayed for battle with Richmond in which he would demonstrate his prowess as a military commander and dispense with the invader.

"I would rather die in battle as king of England than lose the crown and live," he confided to Rob one day when he was being fitted for a new cuirass. Having assessed the increased curve in Richard's back, Signore Vicente had tactfully suggested a few months earlier that Richard's old armor had been irreparable after the Scottish campaign and that he needed to craft new harness. Richard now praised the faithful craftsman for his meticulous work, never suspecting the true reason for the beautiful new backplate. "It almost feels like a second skin," Richard told the delighted man. "He is a genius," Richard murmured to Rob as they left the armory and went to the training yard for their daily workout. "With this harness, I shall send Henry packing!"

"Pray God you will not have to, Richard," Rob said, vehemently. "I would like to die from old age rather than a sword thrust," and the two friends went, chuckling, to pick up their weapons.

When Richard finally learned of Henry of Richmond's landing in South Wales, he was almost relieved: the long wait was over. Richard was well represented in Wales, thus he had no doubt the Tudor upstart would never make it across the Marches into England. Nevertheless, he sent out messages to all awaiting his command to array, and then he went hunting.

"I have done what needs doing to prepare," Richard announced to his household. "It is the feast of the Assumption, and thus after honoring the Virgin, let us enjoy some sport at Bestwood while we wait further news, rather than wearing out the tiles here with our pacing. I warrant a brave stag will show more courage than Henry Tudor."

His retainers gave a cheer—albeit half-hearted.

"It is not your lucky day, Lord Strange." Richard's voice dripped with sarcasm as he kept the young man on his knees. "It would seem your father has been taken ill of the sweating sickness. How curious that this new ailment seems to have arrived along with the invaders. Now, how do you suppose he contracted it?" Richard had been disgusted at Stanley's lame excuse for why he was not already on his way to Leicester with his force. How stupid did Stanley think his king was?

"I would have gladly let you join your father, had he obeyed my command and sent me a force. Now, I am obliged to retain you further. This time I will have no doubt about my condition for his presence at Leicester. If he does not join my army, you will be sacrificed."

George Strange assumed a stoic expression, but he gave a nod of understanding. "My father will not betray you, your grace, not while I am here."

"For your sake, I hope you are right," Richard said, and left the room. He had no doubt that Stanley—and his brother, William, who had apparently not stopped the invaders on their way through his territory in Wales—would play a waiting game. He had no tolerance left for anyone who bore the Stanley name.

Lord Strange attempted to escape that night and having been thwarted, the unfortunate heir to the vast Stanley estates found himself under heavy guard.

Richard's army began the move to Leicester, where he had ordered his commanders to meet him to do battle with Richmond and his followers. Although men joined his ranks, it would seem that England was tired of war and weary of watching the crown move from Lancaster to York and back again, because by the time he reached Leicester, Richard had far fewer troops than had fought for Edward at Barnet.

Richard rode alone at the head of the column, listening to the jangling and clanking of an army on the move and was suddenly catapulted back to that day in Ludlow when he had first heard the sound. He could hear his father's voice clearly ordering the flight of the Yorkist lords in the middle of the night rather than face defeat by the royal army. He grunted at the irony that another Richard of York was readying to do battle with another Henry of Lancaster, but this time, the roles were reversed: York wore the crown and Lancaster mounted the challenge.

With Northumberland trusted to bring several thousand to swell Richard's force, and Stanley another five thousand or so, Richard hoped that this Henry would turn tail and run, but a dark cloud of treachery hung over Richard as he contemplated the recent intelligence that Northumberland had failed to muster any men in York, citing plague as an excuse. York was Richard's stronghold, and thus he had managed to impress upon the mayor the urgency of his need for loyal men. At the last minute, York had done its best to answer the call. There was, thus, a niggling doubt in Richard's mind about Henry Percy, earl of Northumberland, and an even larger doubt about Thomas and William Stanley. He knew between the two brothers there were four thousand men at somebody's disposal; his gut told him he could not count on their being at his.

Richard entered Leicester by the Gallowsgate on Friday, the nineteenth day of August, and was greeted by cheering citizens and throngs of soldiers from all parts of the country shouting his name. The sight gave him tremendous confidence, and he began to believe his crown was secure. He reined in his great white courser along the route to the castle to address his faithful followers.

"I thank you from my heart for this welcome, good people of Leicester. I well remember my warm reception here after my crowning. It is good to know I have your loyalty in the face of the invader, and, as loyalty is *my* watchword, I give you my word I will beat him back into the sea from whence he came and keep our kingdom safe. It is my sacred duty."

"God save King Richard! God save the king!" rang from the rooftops as Richard proceeded through the narrow streets to the castle overlooking the River Soar. Waiting for him were those he trusted most, and he slid off White Syrie's back to greet his heir, earl of Lincoln, Francis Lovell, Jack Howard, Robert Brackenbury, Lord Ferrers, and his own son, John, the lad's eyes shining with pride.

After thanking them all for heeding his call to arms, Richard led the way inside the castle to be briefed. As they crossed the great hall to the smaller audience chamber, Richard drew Francis aside. "I have a favor to ask," he said. "I would be grateful if you kept my son out of the fighting this time. He is only fifteen, and although eager to prove himself, he is too young for battle. Besides, his mother would never forgive me if aught happened to him." Francis grinned and agreed.

Jack Howard opened the strategy meeting by ruefully admitting: "Richmond has gathered a goodly number on his way, our scouts report. More than we anticipated. They are two days' march from here, led by Oxford."

"Where is Northumberland?" Richard asked.

"On the road south, I am informed," young John of Lincoln replied, eagerly, "with more than five thousand."

Was he the only one who questioned Percy's loyalty, Richard wondered, but he nodded. "That is good news. And what of my lord Stanley?" He hoped he sounded nonchalant.

Silence.

"God damn him to Hell!" Richard shouted and his fist hit the table. "Not even a word?" Jack slowly shook his gray head.

Always able to calm Richard, Francis Lovell stepped forward. "It is not to say he won't be here, Your Grace. We should not count him out—yet, although we know his brother did not hinder Richmond in Wales."

"Such perfidy," Richard muttered and turned to John Kendall. "The charts, John. Let us look at our battlefield options."

A few minutes later, the lords were gathered, heads bent poring over the map, when Rob Percy entered the room and whispered in Richard's ear.

"Excuse me, my lords," Richard said, and exited with Rob, who gave him the thick envelope, bowed and left.

Instantly recognizing Kate's untidy lettering, he frowned; he had no time for anything but the upcoming fight. Curious, however, he opened the crudely sealed parchment and Kate's little gold ring fell into his palm. What this time, he wondered.

I must see you, Richard. I beg of you, do not deny me, although I know you are occupied. I am staying with Master Roger Wygston on Church Lane. I await your summons. Yours truly always, Kate.

Richard folded the paper and smiled to himself. *Aye, you have always been true to me, Kate. But what, in Christ's name, are you doing in Leicester?*

"Get out!" Richard's voice carried into the great hall, where several of his friends exchanged meaningful looks. His raised voice was becoming an all-too familiar sound as Richard's knights went about their business, some checking their weapons and armor or giving instructions to their squires, and others writing letters to their wives.

Into the hubbub walked John of Gloucester escorting his widowed mother to see his father. Kate hesitated on hearing Richard's repeated "Get out!" as a clerk escaped from the audience chamber on the run, clutching his bonnet.

"Fear not, Mother, he will see you," John reassured her, "although your news will not make him any less quarrelsome."

"Kate! Kate Haute!" Jack's warm baritone made her turn only to find herself in a fatherly embrace. "So, my bold girl, you made it here safely," Jack said, releasing her. "I was not pleased you left Tendring with only two escorts at such a dangerous time, but then Margaret and I have known you so long, why should I be surprised at anything you do, Kate. I do not envy you having to face," and he jerked his head towards the audience chamber, "*him*. Sadly, he is not the cheerful young man I remember. Your news can't wait, I suppose? Nay, it cannot," he agreed as she shook her head.

"Keep yourself safe, Jack Howard," Kate said, kissing his cheek. "Margaret is waiting impatiently for you to come home. And then, no more fighting."

Jack forced a laugh. "I promise you, this is the last time, my dear Kate."

John boldly knocked on the door and ushered Kate through to the untidy office. Richard swiveled round, a frown creasing his face, but when he saw Kate, deep in her curtsey, he bent and raised her to her feet, his frown erased.

"I think I shall have to claim this ring now," he said, holding it out to her. "God's greeting, lady. You are a sight for this soldier's tired eyes."

"And greetings to you, too, my lord," she replied, replacing the love token on her finger. "Forgive my untimely visit, but this could not wait."

He drew her to a bench, and they sat down. "What is it, Kate? You've been crying." And then he knew.

"Is it Katherine? Is she ill? I heard she was with child. Has she lost it? Speak, please."

Kate nodded. "Aye, it is our daughter, Richard. I am so sorry to tell you that she died in my arms a week ago." She waited for a reaction, but Richard just stared at her, unseeing, his crowded brain and empty heart unable to process more ill tidings. "I could not merely write to you of this, could I? I had to come in person." She took his hands. "She was so precious to you, I know, and I could not bear to have you hear the dreadful news on your own or from someone else. Selfishly, too, I needed to share my grief with you."

Richard clutched at Kate's hands, and his throat constricted. He wanted to weep for his beautiful daughter, but it seemed he had no more tears. Kate gently opened his hands and put into them a folded strip of velvet containing a long lock of shining auburn hair tied in black ribbon.

Richard gazed at the glossy tress and touched it reverently. "Ah, my sweet Katherine! Never was a father prouder of his poppet." He looked up at the mother of his beloved child and asked, "How did she die?"

"'Twas the sweating sickness. She came to visit me from Wales and apparently she brought it with her..."

"Aye," Richard interrupted harshly," I know all about the sweating sickness that Richmond's mercenaries carried with them. Now I have even more reason to run the bastard through." He looked down at the auburn tress and carefully folded it back in the material, tucking it into his doublet.

"Wear it for luck when you fight, Richard. Katherine will keep you safe."

She moved closer and rested her head on his shoulder, and there they sat for a few quiet moments mourning together until, with growing fury, Richard pushed her aside, picked up his crown and flung it at the crucifix on the wall. Fearful, Kate rose and backed away.

"Richard...Richard I beg of you...Contain yourself! What has happened to my gentle Richard?"

"What happened?" he spat back at her. "What happened?" He picked up the dented circlet and shook it at her. "This happened! This crown has brought nothing but death. First Ned, then Anne, now Katherine." His heart was cold stone, and his back ached. He kneaded his shoulder with his thumbs. "Now I know I am cursed. God has marked me, and I am finished trying to appease him." Confronting the emaciated Jesus whose hollowed, agonized eyes bored into him from the cross. Richard snarled, "Look not on me thus. I, too, have sacrificed and suffered. I suppose You will not be satisfied until I am dead? I wish Richmond would walk in here this minute and put an end to me." He gave a harsh laugh. "Then I could join Lucifer in the flames of hell, where I belong."

Kate dared to touch him then, but he flung her aside, needing to be alone.

"You are not cursed, Richard." Desperate, she tried again. "You are a loyal and dutiful servant of God—and England. God cannot...He will not forsake you." She boldly ran on, "You have a son who adores you and looks to you as an example. He is right outside. Be strong for him. He will not forsake you, and neither will I. Someday Dickon, too, will know the truth, and be proud. You cannot go into battle from such a dark place in your heart. It only tempts Fate." She wrung her hands. "Damn my rashness. I should not have added to your burdens by coming here. I should have waited until after your victory. Forgive me, my love! I beg of you, forgive me."

With supreme effort Richard pulled himself together and turned to her, his torment plain. "Nay, 'tis you that should forgive me," he said, carefully placing the crown on the table. He took her hands in his, unable to resist her pleading eyes. "Know this, Kate Haute, that you have always owned a piece of my heart." He reached inside his undershirt and pulled out the écu. "You see, you are always with me, God help me. And every time I saw Katherine or John, you were with me." He replaced the coin and patted his heart. "You and Katherine will ride with me on the morrow, and thus protected, I cannot lose." He paused. Despite his words, he suddenly felt fear, and, cursing, he turned away to hide it. She should not have come, and yet he hated his weakness for needing her.

With his back to her, he gently but firmly said, "Now please go. I have more pressing matters to attend to." He felt cruel, but she, too, had been cruel coming with such news on the eve of what would more than likely be the most important day of his life. "Go!"

Kate swallowed a sob and left without a word. He sank down on the bench, pulled out his daughter's strand of hair and finally allowed tears of sorrow to darken its green velvet covering.

Richard tried to concentrate on billeting and the mustering of troops that continued to arrive, but thoughts of Katherine clouded his mind. By the time he had laid his head uneasily on his pillow at the Blue Boar Inn, he could not remember any of the orders he had given nor what his scouts had told him. (It did not help that he had consumed an entire gallon of claret, hoping the ruby elixir would work as a sleeping draught.) Was Henry two days or one away from the royal army? How many did they say the earl had brought with him? Where was Stanley? And had Northumberland come? Instead of conjuring those crucial answers given him by manly voices, he heard Katherine's sunny laughter and oft-repeated, "Don't you know, 'tis you I love best, Father?" When he closed his eyes, he saw so vividly her jaunty smile and toss of the head that the image made him open them quickly to confirm she was not real. Soon Katherine's face dissolved into Kate's youthful one, and his mind returned to a day by a stream where, naked, he and Kate had frolicked in the icy water and conceived John. He banished the vision, immediately remorseful for the unkind way he had dismissed his erstwhile mistress that day.

Before the wine did its soporific work, he put out his hand to feel Anne next to him and touching nothing but a cold sheet, he turned in that direction, willing her come to him. "I think it will not be long before I shall join you and Ned, dear Anne," he murmured. "I pray that through your goodness you have interceded for me with God Almighty, and He will welcome me to Heaven."

A sudden shocking thought occurred to him and he abruptly sat up. "King Henry!" he moaned into the darkness. *Christ's pity, Anne, he thought, you must now know my fearful secret, and I beg of you to understand that I performed the execution myself out of respect for the harmless, saintly man. Edward commanded it, and therefore it would have been done—one way or another. Better I than some paid, sadistic henchman.*

Tucking his body around the pillow, he held it as if Anne were giving him comfort. Finally he slept.

CHAPTER THIRTY-ONE
AUGUST 21–25, 1485

On Sunday, the twenty-first of August, hundreds jammed the road out of Leicester over the Soar heading west. Word was that Henry Tudor, earl of Richmond, was camped along Watling Street near the village of Atherstone. This meant he could either evade the royal army and march quickly south to London, or—and the honorable thing to do—he would advance and engage with Richard. The scouts further reported that Lord Stanley had reached the area and was encamped at Stoke Golding, with his brother a stone's throw from there. They had not joined Henry's force, and Richard's commanders breathed a sigh of relief, but Richard was less easily fooled.

When the news was given at the final briefing before the lords and knights of the household donned their armor and joined the procession, Richard had grunted, "I cannot trust Thomas Stanley. Why did he not obey my command to muster here? Send out an advance to keep an eye on them." He then looked around the room making eye contact with his commanders as he thanked each one for their loyalty to England. "I will be honored to fight alongside every one of you, and I pray that you may honor me by wearing this token on the field." He nodded to a young squire, who with great solemnity, had handed each commander a silver boar badge.

First to cross Bow Bridge across the Soar was Richard's vanguard, jointly formed by the Howards' forces, father and son. Thomas Howard, earl of Surrey, led the procession, guiding his snorting courser out of the castle yard and onto the road over the river. Richard saw that he was wearing the little silver badge on his tabard and was pleased. After a thousand troops had kicked up the dust far into the distance, it was time for Richard's middle guard to move out of the city.

Richard stepped onto the mounting block and was helped into the saddle by Francis and Rob.

"Don't forget to wave," Francis teased, earning a grin from his sovereign. Handing Richard the helmet encircled with a dented, golden crown, he cried, "Listen, my lord, they cheer for you."

Indeed they did cheer. The townsfolk crowded the entry to the castle, trying to get a glimpse of their king, but they fell back to a respectful distance when he emerged from the gateway, trumpets blaring, heralds and pursuivants carrying colorful pennants and banners behind him, and the arms of England and France fluttering above him on the standard borne by Sir Percival Thirwell. "God save King Richard!" the citizens cried, and some even shouted, "Death to the Tudor traitor."

Riding either side of Richard were his two other battle commanders: Jack Howard, duke of Norfolk, and the latecomer Henry Percy, earl of Northumberland, who would command the rearguard. Northumberland had not been present at the final meeting, having arrived too late; he too had received a silver badge but had chosen not wear it. Richard hoped the omission was not deliberate. Burying the doubt, he concentrated on acknowledging his subjects' good will.

As he neared the end of the stone Bow Bridge, he suddenly spied Kate, her long chestnut hair flowing free of the customary widow's wimple. Reining in his mount, he sidled up to her. "Shocking, bold lady!" he murmured, his fingers itching to touch the glossy tresses. "I did not think to see you."

It was then that a single magpie alighted a few feet in front of them. Kate gasped. Was it an omen? Richard crossed himself as Kate muttered in superstitious country fashion: "Good morning Mr. Magpie, how's your wife." As their eyes met, Richard instinctively reached for the écu on its lanyard. He suddenly realized this might be the last time he saw her. He pulled out the talisman, untied it and bent down to give it to Kate. He heard Northumberland grumbling behind him, but Richard decided to let him wait. I waited long enough for him, he thought.

"Nay, nay, Richard," Kate protested. "You will need it now more than ever."

Richard smiled. "I have Katherine's lock of hair, remember. You must give this to Dickon. It should go back to a Bywood, and he will have something to remember me by." He bent down to her, dropped it into her outstretched hand and whispered. "Forgive me for yesterday. Farewell, my rose."

Kate reached out her hand and caressed his cheek. "God keep you, Richard."

As he eased his horse away, his mailed foot caught the bridge abutment, and he saw Kate recoil in fear. He was momentarily curious, but their brief interaction being over, he set his horse once more on the path to Henry Tudor and forgot the incident.

Finally alone in his pavilion and with several black hours of waiting ahead of him, Richard had whiled away one of them ruminating on the twists and turns his life had taken to this point. Holding King Henry's gift in his hands, he tried to concentrate on the text and accompanying illuminations, but, as always, the memory of the dark night in the Tower returned. Why he had not divested himself of the prayer book long before now, he could not imagine, but perhaps it was God's way of holding him hostage to his guilt for all these years. *God's bones, why can I never forget?*

Richard began to wish he had taken more wine to drown any such maudlin thoughts, but instead he wondered how a man who cherished his wife and children and worked to improve the common people's lot as he had could have callously ordered the hideous deaths of brilliant men like Anthony Woodville and William Hastings? How could such good and evil abide in the same man? *I thought it was my duty to protect the crown. Woodville had weapons on those wagons at Stony Stratford. He would have used them against me had I let him reach London with young Edward. Hastings!* He sighed for he had always thought well of Hastings. The man had betrayed England by keeping so dangerous a secret as the pre-contract. *I have no doubt either that he was plotting against me. Certes, there were other rebels who deserved their deaths just as much,* he mused, *for a traitor must always die horribly. Buckingham, the sad, sorry and untrue creature, should have been quartered as well as beheaded. I was too kind to him for what he did. Dear God, those poor boys.* "I hope he rots in hell!" Richard cried aloud. "'Tis where all rats must go."

"Your grace requires something," one of the knights outside the king's tent called back.

"Nay, Sir Robert, I was talking to myself. What time is it?"

"'Tis five hours to lauds, my liege."

"Instruct the chaplain to come to my tent at prime. We will hold mass here before we arm."

He knelt at the portable altar, the candles in sconces either side of the crucifix dripping wax onto the grass, and opened his well-worn book of hours to the last page. He whispered the words he had written himself not long after Anne's death and which had been added to the prayer book: "I ask you, most sweet lord Jesus Christ, to save me from all the perils in which I stand and, by your love, deign always to deliver and help me, and after the journey of this life deign to bring me before you, the living and true God, who lives and reigns through Christ our Lord."

And then he prayed for a victory for England. "Should I win, I shall know You have absolved me of my sins, which are many and for which I have tried to atone many times. I gave You my promise to rule my kingdom well, and I believe have kept that promise." The candlelight illuminated the gold and enameled cross, as well as the delicate portrait of the Virgin and of Richard's favorite St. Anthony on either side. His voice became more urgent. "Now, in the name of the holy Mother, of Saint Anthony and of your Son our Saviour, show me the way to victory."

The candles flared suddenly, and the altar vanished, dissolved in the sudden brilliance of the light. Richard, as in a dream, fully armed on White Syrie, found himself galloping down a hill alone while all around a battle was silently raging. Far ahead he saw his quarry, Henry Tudor, cowering behind a giant of a man and the standard bearer. Tudor's banner, emblazoned with the red dragon of Wales, waved tantalizingly at Richard. *He waits for me. He sits there and waits for me.* Joy and divine confidence filled Richard's chest as he unsheathed his sword and heard himself cry, "For York, God and England! Death to the invader!" The sure-footed courser navigated the steep hill and carried Richard forward as if on wings. He could hear nothing else but the wind whistling past his helmet and his pounding heart. Closer and closer he rode, brandishing his sword and easily slaying two knights in his path. The goliath moved towards him and raised his deadly mace. With God on his side, nothing could stop Richard now, and he engaged the knight, slicing so powerfully through the vambrace protecting the man's forearm that the weapon fell harmlessly to the ground, still gripped by the severed hand.

Now Henry was alone, and even with his visor down, Richard could see the terror in the pale blue eyes. "It is only you and me now, my lord!" Richard shouted. "Unsheath your sword, or do you want to die without a fight? If you want my crown, come and get it." Before Henry could properly adjust the grip on his sword, Richard urged White Syrie sideways, the horse's armored shoulder unbalancing Henry's horse. Henry fell out of his saddle and onto the ground, knocking off his helmet.

"Did you not learn in the art of war, as I did, that being unhorsed and losing your helmet is the killing blow for nobles, my lord?" Richard gloated high above the trembling Henry, who was begging for mercy. "You should have heeded the lesson. Now make your peace with God!" As Henry prayed, Richard raised his sword and brought it down.

The light guttered suddenly and the kneeling Richard started. He knew then this victory had been but a vision, and, marveling, he crossed himself. Vision or no, he now finally believed God was with him. He would win this battle.

Dawn broke on that twenty-second day of the month, and when his chaplain entered the tent just before prime, he found Richard prostrate in front of the little altar, fast asleep, the candles long since extinguished.

"There is nary an Englishman with Tudor, they are mostly Frenchies. Will you let those Frenchmen over there beat us on our own soil?" Richard asked to shouts and boos of "Nay! Never!"

Francis stood awed as Richard addressed the troops assembled on Ambion Hill. He did not know what miracle had led Richard to seem to tower above all others, his voice strong and confident as he roused the thousands of men to fight for him, but he was grateful; the miracle was much needed. After weeks of depression and self-pity, Francis worried Richard had harbored a death wish.

Now in his gleaming harness, the arms of England brightly displayed on his tabard, the crest on his crowned battle helm streaming his white boar pennon, Richard was magnificent, ramrod straight in his cleverly fashioned cuirass; no one who did not know the king would guess it hid a curved spine. White Syrie was a fearsome sight, plate armor covering his face and flanks making him appear larger than life. He snorted and pranced along the ranks of horsemen of the household who surrounded Richard on the hill, anticipating the coming battle like the superbly trained warhorse he was. Richard seemed unconcerned that Henry of Richmond had stolen a march on him and had already chosen more solid ground past the somewhat boggy terrain to the south. He let them come and deliberately continued his delivery of thanks and encouragement to his mustered troops.

"I had a sign from God last night," Richard told them. "I had a vision that I slew the Tudor in a great victory. Let us now fulfill that destiny. I am ready!" he shouted. "Are you ready to end the strife that has near destroyed England for thirty years? Let our enemies hear your resolve! Let me hear you now—are you ready? "

The roar of "For England! For King Richard!" that echoed over the plain inspired his army to raise their weapons—English longbows, crossbows, halberds, bills, lances, swords, and battleaxes—and shake them at the Lancastrian troops assembled in front of them. Compared with the mile-long line of royal troops facing them bristling with weaponry, the Lancastrian force appeared small, boosting the morale of Richard's army.

Richard gave the order to the extensive artillery to fire. The first thundering booms from the serpentines and bombards were the signal for the archers to loose their deadly arrows skyward and commence battle. Jack Howard advanced the van, and soon he and Oxford were lost to Richard's sight in the vicious melee. *God keep you, Jack,* Richard thought.

His gaze swept the rest of the battlefield from his vantage point, noting where Richmond's strengths and weaknesses lay. The terrain was not ideal, he knew, as he watched Oxford's van carefully maneuver round a large patch of marshy ground, forcing Norfolk's soldiers to tread it.

Richard became focused on two forces a half mile hence, both close to the village of Dadlington but set apart and seemingly rooted to their spots. "Stanleys," he muttered, angrily. "Fence-sitting Stanleys. Let us finally see where their loyalties lie." He had despatched a messenger half an hour before to order Lord Stanley's force to move towards Norfolk and attack Oxford's flank. Thomas Stanley had not yet moved a muscle.

Richard turned to look over his shoulder to his other worry. So far to the rear had the earl of Northumberland chosen to station his force, Richard could only glimpse the glinting of sun on steel. *Will he or won't he obey a summons when the time comes,* his king wondered. He looked back to his right and was dismayed to see Norfolk being hard pressed by Oxford. *Rally them, Jack, rally them now!* He looked again at Lord Stanley's thousands-strong force and growled, "Move your arse, Thomas." But when he saw his messenger returning at full speed, he guessed that the older Stanley brother had turned his coat. The other, he knew, would follow his senior brother's lead. It meant five or perhaps six thousand men were lost to him. He knew then what he must do. It was time to be unmerciful. He summoned an esquire waiting for a command. "Return to camp and tell Sir John to execute Lord Strange. His father has turned traitor." The young man wheeled his horse around and galloped off. Richard never knew that the knight guarding Strange had been forewarned that the Stanleys would enter the battle on Henry's side, and he made his choice: He ignored the king's command, later earning a Tudor pardon for himself.

"Norfolk has fallen!" Richard heard the cry and turned his attention to the mass of men below him slashing, slicing and piercing each other while tripping over those bloodied, mutilated bodies already littering their path. He could no longer see the red and white of Norfolk's banner. *It cannot be true!* Richard thought grimly, *he is the best of men.* Jack Howard was a seasoned fighter, but he was no longer in his prime. When the king heard several shouts of, "Howard is slain," his anger at Richmond rose. "Stay your course!" he yelled, "reinforcements will come," but his words were drowned in the battle cries, screams from horses, and the agony of the mortally wounded.

It was then that Richard saw Henry's standard move off to the left of the main battle with only a handful of escorts and seemed nonchalantly to skirt the marsh near Fenns Lane. Richard frowned. Where was Richmond going? *Most likely to parley with the Stanleys directly in front of him,* he fumed. A blinding flash of sunlight on a distant breastplate dazzled him momentarily, and the shimmering memory of his battle dream rose before him and made him gasp. It was the same scene: Henry almost alone and vulnerable. Richard did not think twice. God was speaking directly to him, he was certain of it: *I have not forsaken you, Richard, and here is My proof,* the Lord seemed to say.

Without warning his retinue, Richard gathered his reins in his strong left hand, unhooked his war hammer and lowered his visor. He spurred White Syrie into sudden action, and charging down the hill with only his standard bearer by his side, he skirted the battle and thundered along the path known as Fenns Lane and across Redemore towards the red-dragon standard and his enemy. He had no fear, had not thought of the risk, because he had a divine purpose. God was carrying him along to put an end to all the doubts and struggles of his reign and cement his right to the throne once and for all. He was in a state of euphoria: he was riding to his destiny.

Behind him, Rob and Francis called desperately for him to stop or wait for them. When Richard ignored their plea, they quickly decided that Francis should assume command of the main battle to bolster the flagging van. Rob and John Kendall then ordered others to join them, and they took off after Richard to stop his foolish charge. But by now Richard had a good hundred-yard lead.

"What is he thinking?" Rob yelled, and then he saw. "Good Christ, he is making for Richmond! Is he mad? He is acting like Achilles charging down on Hector. We must stop him, John! Christ's nails, look!" And he pointed to William Stanley's force moving towards Henry. "We cannot think Stanley is going to *Richard's* aid now, can we? Richard is in mortal danger! Faster, faster!"

The first knight to block Richard's lethal charge hardly registered with him so intent was Richard on reaching Henry. He brought his hammer up and smashed the man's skull as though brushing a fly off his nose. The next man thrust a sword at him, and Richard easily parried the blow with the cannon of the lower vambrace of his superior armor, and smote the soldier so hard it knocked him from his horse. Through the slit of Richard's visor he could see—just as in his dream—Henry cowering behind a giant of a man Richard recognized as Sir John Cheyney. The man measured six-feet eight-inches and was astride a huge courser, but what did it matter? This day belonged to him, Richard knew, and he charged at Cheyney and dealt him such a blow with the spiked end of his war hammer that he pierced Cheyney's visor, drilled through his eye and into the brain. The giant fell like an English oak, brains spilling white and red onto the boggy ground, the war hammer still impaled in his skull.

As others of Henry's household realized what was happening, a few rode full tilt towards the scene while the rest barred Rob Percy's path and killed Richard's standard bearer. His was a thankless, vulnerable, but honorable duty, as those chosen could not hold both a flag and a sword while handling a destrier. Down went the royal standard just as Richard closed in on Sir William Brandon, Richmond's own standard bearer. Henry was screaming to his men to protect him when Richard now unsheathed his sword and slew Brandon, the green and white flag with its proud red dragon floating to the ground. His dream was almost a reality as he turned his attention to a hesitant Henry.

Close behind him Richard could hear fighting, and he thought he recognized Rob's voice, but just as he was attempting to take a run at Henry, White Syrie foundered. The right front hoof of the heavily armed destrier was sucked into the marsh and Richard heard the fearful crack of the animal's leg bone and knew he would be unhorsed. A random, unwanted thought struck him: where had he heard that sickening sound before? It was forgotten as he threw himself sideways to avoid the horse pinning him under its weight. He fully expected Henry to charge and finish him off, but the man was frozen—whether in shock or fear, Richard would never know, for he himself was now fighting for his life as Lancastrian men-at-arms had reached the scene.

Despite Signor Vicente's ability to create a lightweight harness, Richard's mailed feet were also mired in the soggy ground, and he desperately tried to free them. Defending himself from bills and halberds, he whirled his sword in a circle and caught one billman in the face, who screamed and fell back. Richard finally managed to stagger out of the quagmire but, as always when he fought on foot, his compromised lungs began to play him false, and he could hear his own panting magnified inside the helmet. *I can't breathe,* he thought panicked. *Lift the visor, you fool! Goddamn this vile body of mine to Hell.*

A sharp pain penetrated his jaw and he tasted blood. Someone jerked his helmet off, having cut through the chinstrap with a rondel dagger. At last he could breathe, but by then he felt blows to his protected back and one to his head. How many were there around him? He could not count, but his sword blade never stopped swooping and flashing.

He was not sure when he realized that he was going to die, but when he saw the blue and white badge of William Stanley on one of his assailants, he knew he was betrayed and the day was lost. With great effort he cried, "Traitor!" just as the same dagger was plunged through the top of his skull, and he could not help but scream in pain. He fell to his knees, blood streaming down his face, and turned his face to heaven.

"I am betrayed," he gasped, feeling yet another blow to his head and, now afraid, noticed the light was blurring and fading around him. "God has betrayed me!" he seethed. "He has taken everything from me," and when he heard White Syrie scream, he cried, "even my horse!" A weightlessness began to engulf him and he could no longer hold up his head; it felt full to bursting. *Is this the end?* he wondered, blood gushing from his ears, nose and mouth. *Take me, O God, take me now. I am the final sacrifice, and I can bear no more. Father, I pass the cup...*

Mercifully, Richard never saw the halberd raised behind him that sliced through the base of his skull, dealing the death blow. He fell forward onto the sacred soil of the kingdom he had tried so honorably to defend all his short life, and his noble heart stopped. He had been king of England for a mere two years.

Behind his lifeless corpse, his lifelong friends battled to reach him, but William Stanley's reinforcements blocked their efforts. It was as well Richard never saw John Kendall's arm struck from his shoulder by a sword on one side as a Stanley battle-ax cleaved his helmet like parchment on the other and his brains, like pink and white worms, spilled out onto the ground. Or saw Rob Percy speared through the gut, still clinging to his horse as men-at-arms surrounded him and dragged him to the ground, ripping his tabard and harness from him as he lay dying. They did not notice the little silver boar fall from the tabard to be buried in the mud for centuries.

"Long live King Henry!" was the last thing Rob heard, but with his final breath he managed to cry, "God save King Richard, the one true king." Thus Rob Percy died, ever the loyal friend.

A grisly battlefield tradition was taking place where Richard lay. Henry allowed the soldiers to strip Richard naked and take pieces of his harness as souvenirs. As one billman pulled off the padded gambeson under Richard's breastplate, a small pouch of green velvet fell unheeded to the mud, its auburn contents ground beneath the soldier's boot.

"Tie the usurper to the back of a horse!" Henry commanded, basking in his victory. "He deserves no better treatment. Take him to the Greyfriars to bury but instruct them to lay him out so the people see that the tyrant Richard is well and truly dead."

Three men easily lifted Richard's battered, bloodied body onto a pack horse brought forward for the task, and as they tied his hands and feet under the animal's belly, a sadistic, bloodthirsty Frenchman drew his dagger and viciously stabbed Richard between the buttocks, roaring: *"Va te faire foutre, salaud!"*

It was only then in his nakedness that Richard's cruel affliction was exposed and witnessed by a thousand men as York Herald was forced to ride the horse through the battlefield and onto the road for Leicester. As Richard's ignominious last journey began, and having learned of Richard's death, the royal army was already fleeing—Francis Lovell and Richard's son along with it.

"Christ's nails, he be but a runt!" Shouted a soldier sporting Oxford's streaming-stars badge, his leather jerkin black-stained with blood. Laughter, jeering and pointing now accompanied Richard between the columns of victorious troops, while the herald forced back tears of humiliation for Richard and dared look neither right nor left.

"Spawn of the devil!" shouted another. "Look at his 'ump. By God, 'tis monstrous," and many crossed themselves as the pale misshapen body jostled past.

"I'll say this for him," one stouthearted Englishman in Thomas Stanley's turncoat force called out. "He may have been crookbacked and a usurper, but for a runt he fought with courage and died like a king."

Two nights later, an auburn-haired woman knelt at the head of the crude bier on which Richard's body had been lain by the monks of Greyfriars. Kate had kept vigil all night, praying that Richard's tortured soul was now soothed in his wife's eternal embrace. But as dawn filtered through the leaded panes, one of the brothers touched her arm and motioned for her to leave.

It was time to bury the fallen king, he told her kindly.

Sadly, Kate turned her gaze away for the final time and slipped out of the side chapel. She could hear the chipping of a pickaxe on tile and earth somewhere in the nave near the altar, and the sound made her shiver.

"He is being buried in this church?" she asked. "Forgive me, Brother, but he should be buried alongside his wife in Westminster. He was the Lord's anointed, you remember? King Henry owes him decent burial."

"The new king has washed his hands of him, mistress. We must bury him swiftly here. But in recognition of his noble status, he will be buried with our founder in the nave. We dare not disobey."

Kate shook her head. "A king with no decency is no king of mine," she muttered and hurried away. She knew now what she must do. Feeling for the écu beneath her bodice, she returned to the Wygston house, a plan already in place in her mind. She must go to Kent and tell her son, Dickon, who his real parents were. She would finally claim him, entrust him with the talisman, and tell him the real story of Richard of Gloucester. Already she could hear the falsehoods that would be passed from mouth to mouth and from year to year and down the centuries. At least Richard's two sons would know the truth about their father.

At noon on the twenty-fifth day of August in the first year of King Henry the Seventh's reign, the abbot of the Grey Friars monastery stood at the hastily dug gravesite in the nave, his eyes lifted to the altar crucifix and his hands in prayer. He had chastised the grave diggers for not measuring the corpse properly, causing Richard's now-cleansed head to be unnaturally tilted over his left shoulder to fit his meagre grave. His arms were forcibly tied at the wrists, which fell to his right side, "to save room," the gravedigger said. At least a piece of russet had been laid modestly over his loins, but the wounds and bruises were still livid against his pallid skin. The abbot had also been disturbed by how shallow the hole was, barely deep enough to cover his body.

"At least he is buried in hallowed ground," the man had told his sacrist, before the short ceremony. "The poor man at least deserves that. But we cannot afford to delay or this new king may change his mind and throw him into the Soar. I did not dare commission a coffin or shroud for fear of reprisals. Henry wanted no expense and ordered me to simply dig a hole in some isolated spot within the grounds. I could not bring myself to obey that uncharitable command. King Richard gave a grant to this monastery on his progress, and he was a godly man, for all his faults."

Looking about him for eavesdroppers, the sacrist whispered: "I did hear the new king is so afeared his claim is weak, he has named the twenty-first day of August as the first of his reign." He looked sadly at the lifeless form being laid in the grave. "Had Richard lived but lost the battle, he would have been executed as a traitor. 'Tis as well the man died bravely in battle."

The abbot nodded. "Thanks be to God he did not live to see his own crown set upon Henry's head by the perfidious Lord Stanley. It had rolled under a bush, they say. Now, there was a traitor." He moved to the head of the grave and nodded to the brothers carrying spades. "It is time."

A soft chanting from the choir monks and the gentle sound of dirt falling rhythmically into the grave accompanied the abbot's prayer, his dulcet baritone intoning:

Te, Domine, sancte Pater, omnipotens aeterne Deus.... hear our prayers for your servant Richard, whom you have summoned out of this world. Forgive him his sins and failings and grant him a place of refreshment, light and peace....

And thus, while King Henry rode through the fickle, cheering Leicester crowds to give thanks in nearby St. Martin's Church, Richard Plantagenet's body disappeared clod by dusty clod into the Greyfriars earth to lie undisturbed and unclaimed for five hundred years.

EPILOGUE

I am not ashamed to say that I cried happy tears when I heard the news that DNA taken from bones found under a car park in September 2012 proved to be Richard's. It had taken ten years, a team of archeologists, a lot of money and a frisson of intuition from a determined Scotswoman to find Richard's grave at last. Now, with DNA technology, the identity of the bones could be verified.

I shivered at the words coming from a news conference at the University of Leicester in early 2013: "Beyond reasonable doubt, the individual exhumed at Grey Friars is indeed Richard III, last Plantagenet king of England," Richard Buckley, director of the University of Leicester Archeological Services, explained to a media-packed audience that DNA taken from the skeleton matched that of a 17th-generation descendant of Richard's sister, providing a positive identification. After 528 years of his grave being lost, Richard was finally found and exhumed for study.

Standing on Richard's grave in July 2017, the thick glass all that lay between me and the 500-year-old crude hole into which his mutilated body had been shoved, I was profoundly moved. Not a week before, I had finished describing Richard's leaving Leicester on his fateful march to Bosworth. Looking down on the eerie light projection of the skeleton in its original position, it was as though I, too, had dug through those layers of earth and medieval tiled floor to reveal the bones I have spent four years adding flesh to. Only then could I return to my manuscript and write Richard's ignominious end.

How well I understood Philippa Langley's emotions as she watched the painstaking uncovering of Richard's remains. It is a testimony to the world-wide interest the dig generated that the trench, in its humble car-park locale, has been respectfully preserved in a quiet room of its own, only the faint sound of monks chanting to accompany the experience. I was so lucky to be in the space alone on that mid-week rainy morning. Not one to believe much in psychic phenomena, I had goosebumps as I meditated on his shabby treatment at the hands of Henry VII, and I could almost feel Richard's restless spirit in that place.

Besides, after five decades of an obsession with this maligned man from history, and five books inspired by his fascinating life and family, why shouldn't I have rejoiced? Perhaps this astonishing archeological discovery might bring him peace and spark reparation of the black reputation that has shadowed his name since his death in 1485.

Who do we have to blame for Richard III's villainous notoriety? Mostly William Shakespeare, who wrote a damn fine play based on Tudor distortions of history, but he had so many facts wrong it is a wonder Richard didn't rise up from his paltry grave and sue the Bard for libel— or at least haunt his dreams! The real culprit wasn't Will, however. After all, he had simply resorted to standard sources of his day, such as the chronicles written by Raphael Holinshed, the court historian Polydore Vergil, and The Historie of King Richard III, a shameful piece of Tudor propaganda written by a pandering Sir Thomas More, councilor and Lord High Chancellor to King Henry VIII.

Two years passed after the discovery of the grave before a ceremony worthy of a king was envisioned. Even after being rescued from his paltry plot, Richard could not rest in peace. As it has had since Richard's death, controversy swirled about him as Leicester and York fought for the privilege of entombing him nobly. Months of media hype, letters to the editor, petitions from various groups, and even a lawsuit postponed the reburial of the last Plantagenet.

Most Ricardians favored York, a place where, as you have seen in the pages of this book, Richard felt most at home. The Minster and its governing body was ready to receive its "good king Richard." But so was Leicester's St. Martin's governance. It was often expedient to bury a nobleman in the abbey or church closest to his place of death, and who could blame Leicester City Council for protesting they had already kept Richard safe for 500 years (albeit, in ignorance).

As anyone who was able to be at or watch on TV the beautiful and respectful week of ceremonies that culminated in Richard's reburial in his own chapel inside St. Martin's, Leicester put on quite a show. The city was unprepared for how many interested or curious people lined up for hours to file past his bier: more than twenty-thousand of them from all over the world. How fitting it was that his simple, but beautifully wrought coffin was made by Michael Ibsen, the very descendant whose DNA had revealed the bones as Richard's. A comforting cocoon for Richard to lie in for eternity beneath the massive slab of Swalestone, with a deeply carved cross its only decoration.

I watched the funeral in my living room in U.S. at an ungodly early hour and marveled at the respect that Richard was finally accorded. His modern-day namesake, the duke of Gloucester—another Richard—read a prayer from Richard's own book of hours, on loan from the British Library. Then, at the evocative words of England's poet laureate, Carol Ann Duffy, spoken by Benedict Cumberbatch, I wept all over again. I knew then, this was the book I was meant to write.

My bones, scripted in light, upon cold soil,
a human braille. My skull, scarred by a crown,
emptied of history. Describe my soul
as incense, votive, vanishing; your own
the same. Grant me the carving of my name.

These relics, bless. Imagine you re-tie
a broken string and on it thread a cross,
the symbol severed from me when I died.
The end of time—an unknown, unfelt loss—
unless the Resurrection of the Dead ...

or I once dreamed of this, your future breath
in prayer for me, lost long, forever found;
or sensed you from the backstage of my death,
as kings glimpse shadows on a battleground.

If I have created a living, breathing protagonist out of the thousands of pages about Richard I have read during fifty years of trying to understand why this man, who only reigned for two years, has been one of the most divisive historical figures in English history, then I can perhaps now put this obsession to rest!

But first, I must acknowledge the liberties I took with my story before those readers who may be far better versed in the period than I jump up and down and point them out. As with all my books, I am painstaking in my research and only set a scene between characters in a certain time and place that might have been plausible. If there is nothing in the historical record to say it didn't take place, then I can take the plunge.

For example, one of the most fascinating mysteries of our history is what happened to the princes in the Tower. I have been consistent in my take throughout my six books, and I lay the blame on Buckingham because of a chronicled event in the summer of 1483. Buckingham did not go with Richard on his progress in July, despite being the king's BFF at the time. However, when Richard got to Gloucester, it is recorded that Buckingham arrived and a very short time later was seen riding fast out of town and onto the road to Wales, where his chief residence of Brecknock was located. He never reunited with Richard for the rest of the progress, and the next time we learn of him from the records is that he joined with the Lancastrians and rebelled against Richard. I, of course, invented the conversation/argument Richard and Buckingham had during the "very short time" in Gloucester, but I think it is very plausible that Harry eagerly gave Richard news of the princes' demise and was met with fury by their uncle. Richard did indeed write of him: "… the most untrue creature living."

So much more is known about Richard from his bones—mostly physical—and I have incorporated those findings in creating my character. It goes without saying the most crucial was the debilitating scoliosis. I am indebted to Dominic Smee for allowing me a glimpse into the psychological side of his own life given that the young man is living with the same degree of scoliosis as Richard's. Dominic is convinced that, like him, Richard tried to hide his affliction and thus trusted only a very few good friends after the onset in his late teens. The bones also revealed that Richard had consumed wine rather heavily in the last two years of his life. What a fascinating tidbit! And I take full advantage of the fact by allowing it to support my theory all along that Richard was a reluctant king and was in a spiral of depression from the Fall of 1483 when Buckingham turned traitor until he died at Bosworth. He drank to drown his dark, depressive thoughts.

The most fully realized fictional character in the book is my Kate Haute. Richard did have two, and possibly three illegitimate children. Katherine did marry Pembroke, and John of Gloucester was captain of Calais, and both were integrated into Richard's household during his marriage to Anne. Dickon, also known as Richard of Eastwell, is very much more conjecture than fact, but until someone proves otherwise, I think he was Richard's son (of a mistress, who could have been Kate!). No one knows who the mother of Richard's bastards was, but when I discovered from Rosemary Horrox's Study in Service that one Katherine Haute had received an annuity from Richard while he was still duke of Gloucester, I conjectured, as did Horrox, that she might have been his mistress.

April to July 1483 is one of the most complicated few months in English history, and as well as the fate of the darling little princes, no one quite knows why Richard turned on Will Hastings and so hastily executed him. Passionate about the law, Richard's denying poor Will a trial will always be fodder for Richard detractors. I have spent many an hour pondering what could have made Richard so angry, and my explanation is, I hope, plausible.

We do not know how Katherine Plantagenet died, but the records show the earl of Pembroke was a widower not long after Bosworth, and so I invented the manner of her death to coincide with the new "sweating sickness" that appeared in the summer of 1485. Losing his brother, his heir, his wife, and then Katherine in the space of two years seems to me to be more than one man could bear, given the enormous burden of kingship also thrust upon him unexpectedly. And no, I do not think Richard usurped the crown. That was Henry Tudor's road to the throne, not Richard's!

Some may question my depiction of the animosity between Richard and George, but from all I have read, the two brothers could not have been more different, and the angry in-fighting over the Warwick inheritance is well documented. George's denial of permission to wed Anne is fact, and George did hide her from Richard. It was the climax of Richard's antagonism towards George from childhood and served as the main source of conflict in this book. However, George's many treasonous actions toward Edward would certainly have turned the loyal Richard against his brother even without the Anne debacle. George was simply a bad lot.

Many of the scripted documents I include during Richard's time as protector and king are written verbatim, including his words after the royal oath—if a little 15th-century stilted.

Shakespeare, in his play Richard III, depicted Richard as culpable of several deaths, only one of which can in fact solely be attributed to him: Will Hastings'. The others are Tudor historians' and Shakespeare's conjectures. In my first draft, I had Richard present at the "execution" of Henry VI—at Edward's command. As I was rereading the scene, something made me decide to have Richard actually commit the murder, leading to the resulting darker side in this book. Richard was not a saint, as many Ricardians would have him be, and I believe he was a man of his violent time and cognizant of the dangers he faced being noble. The killing of the saintly Henry made Richard, for my purposes, a far more complex character, even though we still do not know exactly how Henry died.

I am choosing not to include a bibliography, because those readers who know me know that I am dedicated to as much truth as fiction allows. I love the details, like the fact the city of Gloucester did refuse the grateful gift Richard offered the citizens. New readers will find many of my resources cited in my other five books: A Rose for the Crown, Daughter of York, The King's Grace, Queen by Right, and Royal Mistress.

Anne Easter Smith, Newburyport MA

Acknowledgments

Over the twenty years that I have been writing my series of six novels, I have had incredible support from dozens of historians, archivists, curators, librarians, Ricardians, and a host of family and friends offering beds, chauffeuring and willing ears. Thank you all—you know who you are! And thank you to my beta readers: Margaret George, Rita Wright, Fontaine Dollas Dubus, Laura Stacey, Reniera Lupton, Christine Forsa, Maryann Long, Nancy Bilyeau, C.C. Humphreys, and my husband Scott Smith. This book would not have been ready to read by any of those kind people without the help and rigorous analysis of my first reader/editor Catherine Thibedeau.

To my daughters, who have encouraged me in this authoring endeavor, and especially to my husband and champion, Scott, my love and gratitude.

Heartfelt thanks to Dom Smee, who gave me hours of his time both on Skype and in person, and wasn't shy about sharing his experiences as a severe scoliosis sufferer. He happens to live in Leicester, happens to be a Wars of the Roses re-enactor, and just happened to be "on duty" in costume on the day they found Richard's skeleton. Such a coincidence. But then, truth has always been stranger than fiction, hasn't it?

I am so grateful to Philippa Langley for graciously allowing me to use her words from The King's Grave, which she co-wrote with historian Michael Jones, as a prelude to each section of this book. We are so fortunate she chose to follow her instincts when she stepped on what she thought was Richard's grave in the Leicester car park that day.

Although I am agent-less now, I must thank Sarah Warner of the now defunct Warner Literary Agency for her enthusiasm for this book at the outset of its writing. It was not her fault we could not find a traditional publisher for this sixth in the series about the York family in the Wars of the Roses. Thanks, too, to my first agent, Kirsten Manges, who took a chance on me all those years ago.

I would be remiss not to acknowledge the artistic talent of my friend Sanford Farrier and to thank him for the stunning cover design.

And finally, a grateful nod to fellow author Susanne Dunlap for the inside design and formatting and for introducing me to the savvy founder of Bellastoria Press, Linda Cardillo, who has been a delight to work with.

PARTIAL BIBLIOGRAPHY

Ashdown-Hill, John. *The Last Days of Richard III*. Stroud: The History Press, 2013

Clive, Mary. *This Sun of York*. New York: W.W.Norton & Co., 1962

Crawford, Anne. *The Yorkists*. London: Continuum UK, 2007

Gairdner, James, ed. *The Paston Letters*. Stroud: Sutton Publishing, 1986

Hammond, P.W. *Food and Feast in Medieval England*, Stroud: Sutton Publishing, 1993

Hicks, Michael. *Richard III*. London: Collins Brown Ltd., 1991

Horrox, Rosemary. *Richard III: Study in Service*. Cambridge University Press, 1989

Kendall, Paul Murray. *Richard III*. London: Unwin Hyman Ltd., 1955

Langley, Philippa and Jones, Michael. *The King's Grave*. New York: St. Martin's Press, 2013

Leyser, Henrietta. *Medieval Women*. London: Weidenfeld & Nicolson, 1995

Norris, Herbert. *Medieval Costume and Fashion*. London: J.M. Dent & Sons, 1927

Pitts, Mike. *Digging for Richard*. New York: Thames & Hudson Ltd., 2014

Pollard, A.J. *Richard III and The Princes in the Tower*. Stroud: Sutton Publishing, 1991

Ross, Charles. *Edward IV*. London: Eyre Methuen Ltd., 1974

____. Richard III. Berkeley: University of California Press, 1983

Scofield, Cora. *The Life and Reign of Edward IV, 2 vols*. London: Frank Cass & Co. Ltd., 1967

Thomas, A. ed. *The Great Chronicle of London*. London: Humanities Press Intl. Inc., 1983

CPSIA information can be obtained
at www.ICGtesting.com
Printed in the USA
LVHW041535101119
636871LV00001B/1